HOSHRUBA

THE LAND AND THE TILISM

Also by Musharraf Ali Farooqi

The Story of a Widow – A Novel

The Cobbler's Holiday Or Why Ants Don't Wear Shoes

The Adventures of Amir Hamza (translation)

Rococo and Other Worlds: Selected Poetry of Afzal Ahmed Syed
(forthcoming translation)

HOSHRUBA

THE LAND AND THE TILISM

TILISM-E HOSHRUBA: BOOK 1

Muhammad Husain Jah

With episodes and traditions contributed by

Mir Ahmed Ali, Amba Prasad Rasa, Ghulam Raza Raza,

Muhammad Amir Khan & Shaikh Tasadduq Husain

TRANSLATED FROM THE URDU BY MUSHARRAF ALI FAROOQI

RANDOM HOUSE INDIA

PENGUIN BOOKS

USA | Canada | UK | Ireland | Australia
New Zealand | India | South Africa | China | Singapore

Penguin Books is part of the Penguin Random House group of companies whose addresses can be found at global.penguinrandomhouse.com

Published by Penguin Random House India Pvt. Ltd
4th Floor, Capital Tower 1, MG Road,
Gurugram 122 002, Haryana, India

Penguin Random House India

Published by Random House India in 2009
This edition published in Penguin Books by Penguin Random House India 2021

10 9 8 7 6 5 4 3 2

ISBN 9788184000962

Typeset by Storykit and InoSoft Systems

Printed at Manipal Technologies Limited, India

www.penguin.co.in

FSC www.fsc.org MIX Paper | Supporting responsible forestry FSC® C043100

This is a legitimate digitally printed version of the book and therefore might not have certain extra finishing on the cover.

For my brother
ARIF
with whom I first read this tale

CONTENTS

Introduction

Musharraf Ali Farooqi

Imagine a tall mountain reaching into the skies; at the foot of it a large army of readers is gathered – you among them. You hear a loud, thunderous beat. It's me on kettledrums. From where you stand in the crowd you can barely see me. But you hear the beat loud and clear – what with all the mountain acoustics, and also because I strike the drums very loudly.

You and all the others are gathered for a long, perilous campaign. On the other side of the mountain lies the land of an all-powerful tale – the one you must conquer. It has consumed whole generations of readers before you. And like all great tales, it is still hungry – ravenous, in fact – for more. You may not return from this campaign, or you may come back so hardened you may never look at stories in quite the same way again. But these are not the only challenges.

The path leading to the heart of this tale is through a dark terrain laid with archaic language and craggy metaphors, strewn with ornate word puzzles that are a challenge to solve. Not many have gone across in the last hundred years. But the tale will not die or be forgotten. It only gets hungrier and hungrier for readers. In the night, when people open up their bedside books, it roars with a terrible challenge, "ARE THERE ANY WHO ARE MY MATCH?"

Should you now wish to listen, here's the story of this tale. It speaks of what this tale is, where it came from, and who created it. By telling you this story, I do not mean to delay you. By all means, advance and come back to me later, or never, if you like that better. I, for one, never read "introductions" first. I believe stories should be read without pompous fellows like me interrupting readers. I give this information by way of anecdote only because the account of this tale's origins is a fantasy in itself and, like you, I too am fond of a good story.

Know then, that from 1883–1893 in Lucknow, India, two rival storytellers, Muhammad Husain Jah and Ahmed Husain Qamar, wrote a fantasy in the Urdu language whose equal has not been heard before or since. It was called *Tilism-e Hoshruba* and it was over eight thousand pages long. This tale had been passed down to them – or so everyone thought – from storytellers going back hundreds of years.

But in truth, the *Tilism-e Hoshruba* was a monstrously elaborate literary hoax perpetrated by a small, tightly-knit group of storytellers from an earlier generation. How long it had been in preparation is not known. A story of such magnitude must have been in the making for many years. We know at least two generations of storytellers who were involved in the enterprise. The names of several men who propagated it most actively in their time have come down to us.

By the time *Tilism-e Hoshruba* appeared in print, everyone believed that it belonged to the cycle of tales of *The Adventures of Amir Hamza,* which could be traced back in India to the court of the Mughal Emperor Akbar (r. 1556–1605).

The Adventures of Amir Hamza originated in Arabia in the seventh century to commemorate the brave deeds of Prophet Muhammad's uncle, Amir Hamza. In the course of its travels in the Middle East and Central Asia, this story incorporated many local fictions and histories and became an entirely fictitious legend. Then, sometime between the eleventh and the fourteenth centuries, *The Adventures of Amir Hamza* found its way to India.

Emperor Akbar took a particular liking to this tale. He not only enjoyed its narration, but in 1562 he also commissioned an illustrated album of the legend. It took fifteen years to complete and is considered the most ambitious project ever undertaken by the royal Mughal studio. Each of its fourteen hundred, large-sized illustrations depicted one episode and was accompanied by mnemonic text in Persian – the court language – to aid the storyteller. Only ten per cent of these illustrations survived, but the royal patronage popularized the story and the Indian storytellers developed it into an oral tale franchise.

Oral tales had been told in India for thousands of years. Ultimately, every story tells of some event, but what storytellers choose to tell of the event and how they approach it is determined by the genre in which it is told. *The Adventures of Amir Hamza* was told in India in the *dastan* genre, which is of Persian origin. However, over hundreds of years, a distinctive Indo-Islamic *dastan* emerged in India that was informed by the cultural universe in which it developed.

In the nineteenth century, three hundred years after *The Adventures of Amir Hamza* found a foothold in the Mughal Empire, it was narrated in the Urdu language in two different *dastan* traditions. The first was a short legend, which recounted all the events preceding Amir Hamza's birth: the adventures that made him a hero, the details of his eighteen-year-long stay in the mythical land of Mount Qaf, and the events that followed his return to Earth, and his martyrdom.

The second *dastan* tradition was much longer, loosely arranged and of a more complex nature. It not only included Amir Hamza's adventures but also the exploits of his sons and grandsons. The martyrdom was postponed. Through telling and retelling, the storytellers enlarged the existing episodes and continuously added new details and adventures.

Meanwhile, a group of Lucknow storytellers had become disenchanted with the Amir Hamza legend and its regular fare of *jinns* (genies), giants, *devs* (demons), *peris* (fairies), and *gao-sars* (cow-headed creatures). Most of these elements were borrowed from Arabian and Persian folklore. The few token man-eaters and sorcerers thrown into the mix were found to be rather boring.

These storytellers strongly felt that the Amir Hamza story needed an injection of local talent – magic fauna and evil spirits, black magic, white magic, alpha sorcerers and sorceresses. All of them were in plentiful supply in India and would give the story the much needed boost. Moreover, some of these sorcerers had to be True Believers. Islamic history was chock-full of all kinds of occult arts and artists. A thousand camel loads of treatises had been written on the occult arts in Arabic, Persian and Urdu. Many renowned sorcerers were household names. It would be a shame to let that occult heritage go to waste.

But the storytellers were clear about one thing. The course had to be changed without rocking the boat. The proposed story had to remain a tale related to *The Adventures of Amir Hamza* – the brand that was their bread and butter. As long as the audience understood that the tale was a part of that famous cycle of tales, the storyteller would not lack an audience.

The godfather of this group of conspirators – and the likely mastermind of the planned hoax – was a Lucknow master storyteller, Mir Ahmed Ali. He sat down to prepare a fantasy tale that would have all of these ingredients, and more.

In the longer Amir Hamza cycle, every adventure began with a token mischief monger starting trouble in some place. Amir Hamza took it upon himself to fix it, and when he was finished, the mischief monger escaped elsewhere to create trouble anew. When one villain was defeated, another took his place. Amir Hamza dutifully followed and carried forward the storytellers' oral franchise. The audience only needed the most basic information about Amir Hamza, his companions and the past events to enjoy a new episode.

Mir Ahmed Ali was well acquainted with this structure and decided to exploit it. When he looked around for a mischief monger to start his tale, his eyes fell upon one of Amir Hamza's more celebrated enemies, Zamarrud Shah Bakhtari, alias Laqa. In fact, it would have been difficult to miss Laqa. He was a giant.

In the surviving leaves of Emperor Akbar's Amir Hamza illustrations we find some fine pictorial representations of Laqa. In one of my favorite illustrations, he is flying in the clouds astride a magic clay urn. He is accompanied by his cohorts, some of whom are playing bugles, cymbals, trumpets, and kettledrums. The fair-skinned Laqa with his long, flowing, pearl-strung beard, has a meditative look on his face. One day I measured him with my ballpoint pen, using his human cohorts as a rough scale. According to my calculations, Laqa came out of Emperor Akbar's studio some twenty feet tall. It is important to remember this figure because we will be referring to it again shortly.

At the end of one of Amir Hamza's pre-existing tales, Laqa was defeated and pursued by Amir Hamza's armies. Mir Ahmed Ali saw his opportunity and scooped it up: his story would begin right at the point where Amir Hamza was chasing the giant.

Next, Mir Ahmed Ali used occult arts of the Islamic world as his inspiration to create a magical world called a tilism, which is created by a sorcerer by infusing inanimate things with the spirit of planetary and cosmic forces. Once an inanimate thing becomes a tilism it appears in an illusory guise and performs supernatural functions assigned to it by the sorcerer. Tilisms can be small or large depending on their structure or the complexity of the formula used in creating them.

Now, tilisms had been present in *The Adventures of Amir Hamza* since Emperor Akbar's times. But they were shabby little things. Sometimes they were in the shape of a domed building atop which sat a bird of some kind. If someone shot down the bird, the tilism was conquered. Sometimes it was a visual illusion that had to be ignored, or a physical trap that must be avoided. At best, tilisms were small tracts of land that had some magical property assigned to them. This, and other such uninteresting stuff, had been sold in the name of tilism to this point.

But Mir Ahmed Ali thought up a tilism that would be a whole country and contain other tilisms within it. Its original founder sorcerers would be True Believers and the tilism would have an unalterable fate. The ruler of the tilism would be the powerful sorcerer Afrasiyab, titled the Master of the Tilism. With a sorceress empress, he would rule over a vast number of sorcerers and sorceresses. But having a wife would not keep the sorcerer emperor from lusting after other princesses and carrying on an affair with a beautiful boy. Because the emperor of sorcerers was a usurper, his empire would be filled with treachery and palace intrigues. And, most important of all, he would have an ongoing border feud with a neighboring tilism and its equally powerful sorcerer emperor.

Anything less complicated would have been an affront to Mir Ahmed Ali's imagination.

Such a dazzling, mind-and-socks-blowing tilism had to have an equally magnificent name. Mir Ahmed Ali decided on Hoshruba (*hosh* = senses, *ruba* = ravishing, stealing). And with that, he had the title for his story: *Tilism-e Hoshruba* or the Tilism of Hoshruba.

Mir Ahmed Ali parked the fleeing giant Laqa in a land neighboring Hoshruba. Amir Hamza and his army followed and landed nearby. But the story was not about Laqa or Amir Hamza. The main action was set in Hoshruba. One of Amir Hamza's sons was sent out hunting. He trespassed the boundaries of Hoshruba and killed one of the guardian sorcerers running on all fours in the shape of a fawn. The Emperor of Sorcerers decided to teach the prince a lesson. When Amir Hamza's camp raised noises, the emperor responded in kind. Amir Hamza sent for his diviners to figure out what to do next. They declared that the fate of Hoshruba was tied to Amir Hamza's grandson, Prince Asad, who would conquer the tilism with the help of five tricksters. With that, the scene was all set for action. And before we know it a campaign is launched to conquer Hoshruba.

Prince Asad enters Hoshruba with a large army and great preparations but in no time he is stripped of all that paraphernalia and left standing with only the clothes on his back. It turns out that he is completely useless in the tilism. The trickster Amar Ayyar, his four trickster companions and their newfound friend, the rebel sorceress Mahrukh Magic-Eye, must make war on the Emperor of Hoshruba, Afrasiyab. Amir Hamza watches from the sidelines and periodically indulges in cosmetic battles with Laqa and his minions lest the audience forget they are listening to a story from the Amir Hamza cycle of tales. But in a symbolic manner, the story has gotten rid of the Amir Hamza legend as soon as Prince Asad is rendered ineffective upon entering Hoshruba. He will remain a figurehead with only a ceremonial presence.

Mir Ahmed Ali wanted to make *Hoshruba* the most sharp-clawed, shiny-scaled tale in the whole of the Amir Hamza cycle so he liberally poured in vicious sorceresses, nubile trickster girls, powerful wizards and dreaded monsters and stirred the tale with non-stop action. In that process, Mir Ahmed Ali transcended the whole business of legend making and created a fantasy – the first, the longest, and the greatest fantasy of the *dastan* genre.

It also influenced the elements used in *Hoshruba* from the Amir Hamza legend. Some of the familiar characters appeared in it in a more fantastic idiom. We see this when we compare two characters common to Emperor Akbar's Amir Hamza illustrations and *Hoshruba*.

The first one is our giant friend Laqa. We remember his size and appearance from Emperor Akbar's illustrations. Now we read a description of Laqa in *Hoshruba*: "For some time now, Amir Hamza was engaged in warfare with the false god Laqa, an eighty-five-foot-tall, pitch-black giant. His head was full of vanity and resembled the ruins of a palace dome, and his limbs were the size of giant tree branches."

Mir Ahmed Ali knew better than anyone else in the world that in all matters giant, size mattered greatly. Anyone can see that the Laqa of the fantasy is a far handsomer giant than the Laqa of the legend. We salute the author for making him a pitch-black, false god besides, and for the whole palace-dome and giant-tree imagery.

The second character is Amir Hamza's master trickster, Amar Ayyar. We meet him as well in Emperor Akbar's illustrated story. In one illustration he is blithely kicking an enemy trickster. In another place he is setting fire to a dragon with naphtha. In both illustrations, Amar Ayyar is shown to be thin. Except for this relative slimness, he is indistinguishable from other soldiers in Amir Hamza's army.

Now we read Amar Ayyar's fantastic description in *Hoshruba*: "…a head like a dried gourd, eyes the size of cumin seeds, ears like apricots, cheeks resembling bread cake, a neck that was thread-like, and limbs akin to rope. His lower body measured six yards and upper body three."

Some of this marvellous detail could also be the natural result of hundreds of years of exaggeration through oral retelling, but it is equally likely that in the world of *Hoshruba,* exaggeration was employed, not only to create an enlarged picture of an event but also to provide one that was fantastic.

While the world of *Hoshruba* was fantastic, its details were not alien to its audience. Mir Ahmed Ali had modelled them on the world he knew best – the Lucknow of nineteenth century India. It was one of the centres of Indo-Islamic culture and civilization. The details of dress, food, etiquette and daily life in *Hoshruba* were borrowed from that living model. In a few places, the material and fantasy worlds overlap, as when we encounter Lucknow's iconic architectural landmarks in the tale.

Mir Ahmed Ali's story was ready but it could hardly be launched without an "original author." In the world of the Indian storytellers, glory came from association. It had always been fashionable for the storytellers to attribute their stories to the most prestigious past sources. Since Emperor Akbar's court had patronized it, Mir Ahmed Ali deemed the emperor's poet-laureate Faizi (1547-1595) the best candidate to be touted as the "original author" of *Hoshruba.*

The names of those who wrote the mnemonic text of Emperor Akbar's illustrations, as well as those who painted them, are recorded in history. Faizi is not one of them, but a small detail like that could hardly be allowed to stand in Mir Ahmed Ali's way. He brushed it aside royally and made Faizi the "original author" of *Hoshruba.* Mir Ahmed Ali would be the ghost-writer of a writer ghost.

It is possible that Mir Ahmed Ali chose Faizi precisely because neither Emperor Akbar's court chroniclers nor later historians ever mentioned his name in association with the illustrated Amir Hamza project. Perhaps Mir Ahmed Ali felt that one day someone would start digging for the truth and the trail of lies would lead straight to his grave. But, no matter what Mir Ahmed Ali's twisted motivation for choosing Faizi, all the formalities were now complete and the tale was ready to be unleashed.

I can imagine Mir Ahmed Ali narrating it for the first time for a select audience – entry by invitation only – gathered at a Lucknow nobleman's house. Mir Ahmed Ali, his host and some close friends sit at the head of the room resting against bolsters. The audience sits before them on a carpet. The host tells the group that Mir Ahmed Ali has discovered, purely by accident, a new tale of the Amir Hamza cycle, which his great-great-great-grandfather received directly from Faizi. It lay hidden in an old family heirloom in the form of notes. For the last three months, Mir Ahmed Ali has been busy arranging and decoding the notes and now he is done with his labors.

The audience demands that Mir Ahmed Ali share the tale with them without loss of time. Mir Ahmed Ali quickly excuses himself. He says there has been a misunderstanding. The tale, named *Tilism-e Hoshruba,* is not yet ready. Only one part of it is. Moreover, as he is allergic to dust, going through the old parchments gave him a sore throat. He cannot narrate that evening – a great shame because the tale is one the likes of which his audience has never heard.

Members of the audience look at each other with open mouths. Mir Ahmed Ali has never made such an atrocious claim.

"Such a tale! Such a tale!" Mir Ahmed Ali keeps repeating to himself.

A faint smile appears on the host's face. He whispers into a friend's ear, who also smiles and nods his head. The audience becomes increasingly impatient. Mir Ahmed Ali is absolutely quiet, the audience fully disposed to riot. The host calls for calm and orders another round of refreshments, which momentarily pacifies everyone.

Mir Ahmed Ali sits with closed eyes, softly intoning some verses from a *ghazal.*

After the round of refreshments is over, the host leans toward Mir Ahmed Ali and asks if he is feeling any better. Everyone waits in anticipation. "Not so much," says Mir Ahmed Ali.

Could he – asks the host – perhaps, maybe, possibly find the strength to narrate a little episode from the *Tilism-e Hoshruba*? Just a tiny little insignificant bit of a scene?

That he might do, Mir Ahmed Ali says after due reflection, his eyes half shut.

Members of the audience look at each other gleefully. They have never felt so lucky.

Mir Ahmed Ali clears his throat, glances around majestically, and begins in a clear, slowly rising voice: *The cupbearers of nocturnal revelries… the bibbers from the cup of inspiration…pour the vermilion wine of inscription… into the paper's goblet thus…*

God be praised, Mir Ahmed Ali has miraculously recovered. He holds forth with accompanying theatrics for a full three hours. The account of his sore throat was greatly exaggerated, but not his praise of *Hoshruba.* The audience sits entranced. When he stops, they clamor for more. Mir Ahmed Ali promises to tell them the rest the following night at the bazaar corner where he has an ongoing gig.

That night, many present at the narration have dreams of the scantily clad sorceress Sandal. Some dream of Prince Badiuz Zaman, "the moon of the constellation of excellence." We do not know if anyone dreamt of the fawn that "appeared near the river bank, cavorting and gambolling like a frolicsome beloved well-versed in coquetry."

Before he arrives in the bazaar the next evening, Mir Ahmed Ali sends out his disciple storytellers, Amba Prasad Rasa and Hakim Asghar Ali Khan, to bring him a report from the venue. They come back with the intelligence that a large crowd is gathered at the appointed place. They saw many new faces in the crowd.

That is just as Mir Ahmed Ali expected. He sets out with his disciples and arrives at the venue to loud, thankful murmurs from the throng. Everyone demands that Mir Ahmed Ali begin the tale from the beginning. And he does.

Only an infidel would doubt that it did not happen exactly in this manner.

From that day onward, the three storytellers narrate the *Hoshruba* in public and private gatherings. When they pass in the street, people look at them with terrible envy. They are the only ones who know what will happen next. People try all kinds of tricks on the storytellers to learn what they know of the next episode, but the affable storytellers become very taciturn whenever asked in the street, "What happened next?" Outside the storytelling sessions they speak not a word about *Hoshruba*.

In the coming days, the crowds steadily increase in number. Amba Prasad Rasa and Hakim Asghar Ali Khan arrive an hour before Mir Ahmed Ali and summarize the preceding events of the tale for the gathering before the maestro begins his narration. It will be several years before the tale will finally end. And even then, it does not end. In fact, people wait for the end so that they can revisit their favorite episodes.

Or perhaps it takes Mir Ahmed Ali many more years to end it because people keep demanding he narrate again some particular episodes they had previously enjoyed. He tries telling them to have patience, that an even better episode will soon follow, but nobody listens to him. Every day, Mir Ahmed Ali is assailed with requests – now this incident, now that passage. Like a beleaguered but indulgent parent, Mir Ahmed Ali feels obliged to give satisfaction. When he gets bored with reciting the same episode over and over again, he expresses his displeasure to the audience by narrating it breezily, without all its juicy details. People relent and let the storyteller have his own way for a few days, then return to their old ways. The drama continues.

As an oral, narrative genre, *dastan* draws heavily on improvisation, but once the story of *Hoshruba* was established it turned into an elaborate chess game. The result was predestined but not the individual moves that would always be improvised. As Mir Ahmed Ali added characters and scenes and improved on the earlier descriptions, he kept adding to the subplots that must flow toward the predestined end. He and his disciples had their own favorite episodes, which they embellished in this way during storytelling sessions.

The storytellers knew how many times a lie has to be repeated before it becomes accepted truth. They never forgot to attribute the tale to the Amir Hamza cycle of tales, and to Faizi. As far as audiences were concerned, they cared little where the tale came from as long as it was a good one and from the Amir Hamza cycle. And such an entertaining tale as *Hoshruba*! Why on earth wouldn't it be a part of *The Adventures of Amir Hamza* cycle – the grandmother of all fine tales?

All other stories of the Amir Hamza cycle paled in comparison with its popularity. The audience asked for *Hoshruba* and the storytellers complied. It was told in public and private gatherings, sometimes in long sessions that continued over many days.

In the period around the 1840s and 1850s, *Hoshruba* had taken Lucknow by storm. Travelers to Lucknow returned with the tales of *Hoshruba*. Attending Mir Ahmed Ali's narration was a sacred ritual for all Lucknow visitors.

The neighboring cities started feeling jealous. Before an all-out bidding war could break out between the princely states of India to steal the storytellers from Lucknow, a group of troopers astride fleet-footed Arabian mares, arrive in Lucknow early one evening covered in dust. Their leader remains cloistered with Mir Ahmed Ali and his two disciples for many hours and leaves early the next morning with his entourage.

The Prince of Rampur has made a pre-emptive strike. Mir Ahmed Ali has accepted the prince's invitation to become the court storyteller of Rampur. The terms of the offer and the perks are not disclosed.

When Mir Ahmed Ali packed his belongings, his two disciples, Rasa and Khan, also packed theirs. They would follow him. Along with their bed and bedding, Rasa and Khan also packed their families, including sons Zamin Ali and Ghulam Raza. Both boys would also become storytellers. One of them would write another version of *Hoshruba*.

When the caravan of storytellers sets out for Rampur in oxen-driven carriages, the citizens of Lucknow – men, women and children, young and old alike – accompany it on foot to the limits of the city. There is not a single dry eye in the crowd. Mir Ahmed Ali shamelessly cries loudest of all.

He would never have left Lucknow if he had not been convinced that he was leaving *Hoshruba* in safe hands. He had passed on his mantle to a young storyteller named Muhammad Amir Khan, who began narrating episodes from *Hoshruba* in Lucknow some time earlier, with Mir Ahmed Ali's blessings. He had a knack for creating the episodes about tricksters. Khan did not let Mir Ahmed Ali down. He continued spreading the tale among the Lucknow audience. He also wrote at least two volumes of the tale.

By the time the oxen-driven carriages arrive in Rampur, Mir Ahmed Ali has stopped crying. On the way, he has thought up a fine magic war involving a magic effigy that kills a sorcerer by casting a love spell over him. When he is led to his lodgings by the prince's attendants he tears open his bag, takes out his inkwell and paper, and starts scribbling. It was impossible to take notes during the jolting carriage ride.

Only an infidel would doubt that it did not happen exactly in this manner.

At the Rampur court, Mir Ahmed Ali continued his storytelling work. He also put on a lot of extra weight from eating all the good stuff from the royal kitchen. Life was kind to him. His cheeks were ruddy and he laughed easily. He composed two tales at this time, one in Persian, another in Urdu, but he did not write *Hoshruba*. Once he organized the different episodes of the story, he probably improvised the rest of the details just using notes.

It fell to his disciple, Amba Prasad Rasa, to transcribe his notes. We do not know how detailed these notes were, or whether Rasa added some details to them. That manuscript is now lost; until recently even its existence and provenance were unknown.

Later, Rasa's son, Ghulam Raza, who adopted the pen name Raza, was commissioned by the Rampur court to compose the tale of *Hoshruba*. He wrote it down in fourteen volumes between 1858 and 1880. His work remained in manuscript.

But *Hoshruba* began to acquire a life of its own. While Raza's work on his manuscript was coming to an end in Rampur, Mir Ahmed Ali's home town of Lucknow was again about to become the official headquarters of *Hoshruba*. Thanks to the work started by him and his disciples and carried on by Muhammad Amir Khan, *Hoshruba* was winning over the Lucknow audience in ever greater numbers.

By then it was commonly accepted as part of the Amir Hamza cycle of tales. In fact, it also had a specified place in the cycle as its fifth book. In the early 1880s, the erudite and enterprising Munshi Naval Kishore, owner of the Naval Kishore Press, decided to publish the entire, longer Amir Hamza cycle of tales. The Naval Kishore Press decided to start its publication project with *Hoshruba* because it was an independent story and already extremely popular in oral narration.

When Munshi Naval Kishore asked around for someone to compose the tale, he was given the name of Lucknow storyteller Muhammad Husain Jah. Kishore remembered him well. Some years previous, he had been commissioned to write a short *dastan, Tilism-e Fasahat*. The book was a testament to his mastery of prose. Kishore showed up at a *dastan* narration session and was impressed by Jah's masterful narration of *Hoshruba*. Jah was engaged to write the *Hoshruba* tale, and that was just as it should have been. Muhammad Husain Jah's father was a *rammal* or diviner, which means – why deny it – a sorcerer. The *Hoshruba* project was in excellent hands.

Jah knew his *Hoshruba* and, as a professional storyteller, he knew its real provenance. Now that he was commissioned to write it, he decided to compose a master version using all available written versions and oral traditions of his contemporary storytellers. Amba Prasad Rasa was still alive at the time. Jah obtained the version Rasa had prepared from Mir Ahmed Ali's notes. He also used the one written by Ghulam Raza in fourteen volumes, and the two volumes written by Muhammad Amir Khan. Besides those, he borrowed some episodes from a contemporary storyteller, Sheikh Tasadduq Husain. Then he sat down to compose his masterwork.

Jah must have had a delightful time comparing how the several storytellers differed in their accounts of each character and his or her peculiarities. The work would not be unlike making a composite literary sketch of each character. And he did, indeed, do a fine work of compilation. The result is a complex set of characters unparalleled in literature, and a highly subversive arrangement of roles.

That a woman, the sorceress Mahrukh Magic-Eye, should lead the camp of True Believers may seem curious now, but it was not so in the nineteenth century Indo-Islamic society where women had a vibrant social role. There are a few shy and retiring females as well; Mahjabeen Diamond-Robe and Almas Fairy-Face are two such examples. However, Queen Mahrukh Magic-Eye, trickster girl Sarsar Swordfighter, Empress Heyrat and sorceress Bahar of the Spring-Quarter are complex and powerful women entirely comfortable with their sexuality. They hold their own against male tricksters and sorcerers in intellect, physical prowess and magical powers. The strident personalities of these female characters did not emerge from the author's fancy but from the lives of the contemporary women. The *Hoshruba* sorceresses appear in the dresses of Lucknow princesses and noble women, speak in their idiom and follow their social etiquette.

The most complex and interesting character in all of *Hoshruba* is Emperor of Hoshruba, sorcerer Afrasiyab. In any heroic tale it is the hero who faces the greatest number of threats and challenges. In *Hoshruba,* it is not the Conqueror of the Tilism or the trickster Amar Ayyar who face the greatest number of odds. It is Afrasiyab. He must keep the increasingly demanding false god Laqa safe from Amir Hamza, take care of the menacing rebel sorcerers led by Mahrukh Magic-Eye, watch out for the rampaging tricksters and, finally, contend with the rival emperor of the neighboring tilism. In setting him up against all these challenges, Mir Ahmed Ali and succeeding storytellers probably wished to show Afrasiyab's power and resourcefulness. In the process, they also made him into a heroic character.

At a personal, human level too, Afrasiyab is very likable. Even his unbridled sexual appetite makes him a far more interesting character than the asexual Amar Ayyar and the frigid, battle-hardened Amir Hamza. Afrasiyab shows great sensitivity toward his beloved Princess Bahar, who has joined his enemies. He is magnanimous toward a couple whose only son has died in his cause. When he boastfully fulminates against the god of sorcerers to assert his grandeur, he sounds entirely believable. And the scene where he sacrifices his beautiful male lover to a vampire monster to save his empire is one of the most tragic and memorable in all his personal history.

The tale of *Hoshruba* is a contest between sorcerers and tricksters more than it is a war between sorcerers. Against the endlessly powerful sorcerers, the tricksters rely on their cunning, talent and wits. This is a fundamental departure in storytelling from *The Adventures of Amir Hamza* legend where holy figures of all stripes made frequent appearances to offer aid and counsel to Amir Hamza, and sometimes even did his work for him. In *Hoshruba,* it is hard to find a holy personage. When Amir Hamza and his camp are faced with dire situations, it is the tricksters who save the day.

The tricksters' mastery of the art of disguise plays a crucial role in their success. Sometimes their change of disguise from one person to another occurs so rapidly and in such complex mixes that it seems the creators of *Hoshruba* are playing a literary thimble-rig with the reader. Perhaps this was the contribution of the storyteller Muhammad Amir Khan, who was the trickster expert.

It is true that magic does not have any effect on Amar Ayyar's holy gifts – an inheritance from *The Adventures of Amir Hamza* legend – but equally, Amar Ayyar is also proscribed by a code of tricksters against using holy gifts to kill sorcerers. Even when Amar Ayyar uses his holy gifts, he employs them to aid his tricks or in self defense. This is another symbolic way in which *Hoshruba* neutralizes the influences from the *Adventures of Amir Hamza* legend where these devices were used directly. It can be said that throughout the fantasy, the focus has shifted from divine help to human resourcefulness.

Mir Ahmed Ali and other Indian storytellers had brought about a fundamental shift in the approach to storytelling. They made the Indo-Islamic *dastan* a completely new strain within the *dastan* genre. This dazzling uniqueness was one of the reasons for *Hoshruba*'s widespread appeal and popularity.

The second volume of *Hoshruba* came out in 1884. There was a delay of four years before the third volume was published in 1888–89. Considering the popularity of *Hoshruba,* the Naval Kishore Press hurried Jah, demanding that he finish the subsequent volumes speedily.

But Jah was in deep trouble. Merging the three accounts of the different storytellers and simultaneously composing his own version was difficult enough. At the same time, he was devastated by the deaths of his young son and daughter, which happened while he wrote the third volume. For a while he even stopped writing. He resumed at the encouragement of his publisher. He shares his trauma with his readers by duly incorporating the entire episode in verse in the *Hoshruba* narrative.

After he finished the fourth volume in 1890, or perhaps a little before that, the publisher informed Jah that he would be relieved of the responsibility of writing the three remaining volumes. Someone else had been hired to finish the project more quickly.

The fourth volume has no last words by the author, which was customary. Jah had surrendered the manuscript on an unhappy note, and it was little wonder. His replacement for the *Hoshruba* project was his rival storyteller, Ahmed Husain Qamar.

Here was a man with a nicely checkered past. According to his own account, his family participated in the 1857 Mutiny against the East India Company forces. Two of his brothers died in the fighting. Qamar survived and was cleared of the charge of mutineering but because he was not yet of age, he could not lay claim to his estate, which was confiscated by the government. He studied law and became an agent at one of the local courts but when he appeared for the confirmation examination, the old charge of participating in the mutiny was dug up and quoted as a reason for his disqualification. Around that time, Qamar became interested in storytelling and took it up as a profession.

Qamar took up the *Hoshruba* project where Jah had left off. After making a few self-important remarks about how he would have been the best choice to write the four earlier volumes as well, he got down to work. But just as he was getting started, and with great fanfare, a piece of news arrived that completely marred his happiness.

Apparently Jah's work on *Hoshruba* was close to his heart. He was not willing to give up without a fight. In the December of 1889, the same year *Hoshruba* was taken away from him, he played his hand by founding his own press and privately publishing the first part of the fifth volume of *Hoshruba,* with the promise of more – a lot more – to follow.

Qamar and the Naval Kishore Press sat up. They decided they were up to the challenge. That Qamar was extremely prolific also helped. Naval Kishore Press brought out the first part of the fifth volume in just a few months in 1891, followed shortly with the second part. The competition with Jah seems to have been the main reason for the haste: it is the only volume of *Hoshruba* that was published in two parts.

After publishing the first part of the fifth volume, Jah fell silent. Perhaps he was ill. He had mentioned a long period of illness in the third volume. Only one copy of this privately published, slim volume survived and was discovered recently by Urdu researcher Rifaqat Ali Shahid. Throughout the first four volumes, Jah had acknowledged the contribution of other storytellers. But it is in this privately published fifth volume that he methodically lists the three sources he had borrowed from. Its first four pages, in which he may have explained his reasons for leaving the Naval Kishore Press, are missing.

Qamar himself is uncharacteristically tight-lipped about the incident. In the notice printed in the fifth volume of *Hoshruba*, he cursorily mentions that "some chance events" ended Jah's association with the publisher.

Only fragmentary information is available about the professional relationship between Jah and Qamar. In his first published work, *Tilism-e Fasahat*, Jah acknowledges Ahmed Husain Qamar as his instructor. However, Urdu scholar Shamsur Rahman Faruqi has suggested that the uncharacteristic exaggeration and hyperbole he uses on the occasion suggests that Jah paid the compliment sarcastically. This theory is quite plausible because in a later edition, those words of hyperbole were removed. Qamar himself never made any claims to be Jah's teacher and we can be sure that had it been otherwise, Qamar would have proclaimed the fact daily from the roof of Naval Kishore Press while he lived, and had it engraved on his tombstone.

Qamar's head may not have been as large as the false god Laqa's, but it was as full of vanity. He loved himself with a powerful love that sometimes forced him to claim credit for deeds he had not done. He often experienced small episodes of jealousy during the writing of *Hoshruba*. In some weak moments, he declared himself to be the "original author" of *Hoshruba*. But then Qamar would have other weak moments in which, while deriding Mir Ahmed Ali or Jah, or calling their integrity into question, he would make statements that totally contradicted his earlier claim. All this abuse was hurled within the narrative itself, of course. The old mutineer in Qamar had not died. All his subversive talents were now channelled into the *dastan* genre.

Qamar also liked to make guest appearances in the narrative in the middle of scenes to give the characters a chance to praise him and his many talents. From magic slave girls to Laqa's devil designate, to the Emperor of Sorcerer Afrasiyab, everyone takes a turn praising Qamar's first-rate poetical mind, his skill in composing Persian verses, and his ability to decode knotty Arabic prose. Unlike Jah, who always acknowledged the least contribution to the narrative by his seniors and contemporaries, Qamar never credited anyone besides himself. But despite all these personality quirks and the licenses he took with the narrative, Qamar was as profoundly gifted as a storyteller as was Jah, although their talents lay in different areas.

Jah died between December, 1890, and October, 1893. According to Faruqi's research, he died at a relatively young age. The *Hoshruba* project was completed around the same time. The publication of the sixth volume in 1892 was quickly followed by the seventh and last volume in 1893.

Tilism-e Hoshruba became a bestseller. Between 1883 and 1930, eight editions were published from Lucknow alone. The tale acquired an iconic status in Urdu literature as the ultimate fantasy tale, and the word "Hoshruba" itself became proverbial for fantastic literature.

Faizi continued to be credited as its original author. His ghost must still be smiling from ear to ear. To have written the tale of Hoshruba with an unmoving finger would be a neat trick, even for a spirit. But the happiest ghost must be Mir Ahmed Ali's, his smile the broadest of all. Not only was his creation of *Hoshruba* accepted as a part of the Amir Hamza cycle, but it also became its defining, single most important tale, surpassing all others. No storyteller could ask for greater glory.

The *Hoshruba* tale later found other champions as well. A year before the world threw itself into the madness of the First World War, the Rampur storyteller Mirza Alimuddin (1854–1927) launched his personal campaign to write the *Hoshruba* tale. He campaigned longer, harder and more gloriously. From 1913–1919 he produced twelve volumes and two secondary legends associated with the *Hoshruba* tale.

Then there was Mir Baqir Ali (1850?–1928), the last renowned storyteller of India in the twentieth century. He was born into a family of royal storytellers at a time when *Hoshruba* was at the peak of its popularity. But in the 1920s, when he was in his last years, Mir Baqir Ali was unable to find an audience for his art. He privately published some stories for children to make a living, but failed. In the end, he gave up and made a living selling betel leaves. He breathed his last a year after Mirza Alimuddin's death. A sample of Mir Baqir Ali's storytelling method and glimpses of his last days were preserved in a literary sketch in *Dilli Ki Chand Ajib Hastiyan* by Ashraf Subuhi Dehlvi.

The *Hoshruba* history would be incomplete without the mention of the Pakistani painter Ustad Allah Bakhsh (1895–1978), who captured the magic and dense storytelling of *Hoshruba* in his glorious painting *Tilism-e Hoshruba.* This painting hangs in the Lahore Museum.

Without Jah and Qamar – two of Urdu's greatest prose writers – the hoax created by Mir Ahmed Ali and storytellers in his generation may not have received such wide acclaim. This tale, with its imaginative scope, poetic delicacy, ornate presentation, and metaphor-rich language, became the pride of Urdu literature because of these men. They will always be remembered as two of Urdu's greatest benefactors. Their ghosts, finally free of their professional rivalries, together might even be constructing a tilism of their own – on a much larger scale than Hoshruba. And we can be sure that Qamar's part of the tilism will be completed long before Jah ever reaches the halfway mark.

But these are not the only ghosts. Others have also made their presence known. In 2005, an Indian historian, Mahmood Farooqui, began studying the cultural history of the *dastans* and became interested in *dastan* narration. Farooqui and Himanshu Tyagi collaborated to start *dastan* narration from *Hoshruba.* Later, Danish Husain joined Farooqui as his partner. Their performances were held in both India and Pakistan and attracted a large following. Then, one day in 2006, the Indian historian Shahid Amin, told Farooqui of two short, crackling audio recordings of someone's voice, which he had recently discovered in the British Library. They belonged to the last famous *dastan* narrator, Mir Baqir Ali. These three-minute recordings were made in Delhi in 1920 as a part of the Linguistic Survey of India records. One recording was a rendering of the tale of the *Prodigal Son,* which all native speakers had to record for that project. Mir Baqir Ali was unable to finish the tale because his narration exceeded the short duration of the 78-rpm disk and had to be ended abruptly. The other recording was a short *dastan* of a foolish young nobleman who wishes to visit his in-laws and encounters countless obstacles on the way.

Mir Baqir Ali's ghost has resurfaced eight decades after his death, to say thank-you to someone who had renewed his tradition.

What if all the storytellers are also still with us "in spirit"? And what if one day this battalion of ghosts feels nostalgic, and enters a bookshop to check the latest edition of *Hoshruba* but doesn't find it on the shelves? Who will have the heart to tell them that because of our neglect and disregard of Indo-Islamic literature, the rich language of *Hoshruba* has become inaccessible, that our own indifference has now become the tall mountain, reaching into the skies beyond which this tale lies, out of reach for all but a few?

That situation must be avoided at all cost.

And this is why the army of readers is gathered here; why I beat the kettledrums.

Hear then that this translation of *Tilism-e Hoshruba*, the first in any language, is a secret passage through this mountain. You may now bypass the dark terrain of craggy metaphors where puzzles grow, and easily slip to the other side to engage this tale.

And once you are done, you must remember to take on the mountain of indifference. It would be a shame to disappoint all the kindly ghosts in the bookshop who brought you this most excellent tale.

– M.A.F. (December 5, 2008)

Translator's Note

Musharraf Ali Farooqi

Tilism-e Hoshruba was published in Urdu in eight large volumes totalling over eight thousand pages. If each of these volumes had been translated as a separate book, each English volume would have come to 1500 pages or more. I decided to divide each of the eight volumes into three, making twenty-four volumes in English.

This being the first book in a long series, I made several editorial choices that will be followed throughout the series. Some of these choices were imperative, others voluntary. I outline them here so that the reader is aware of them.

When *Hoshruba* was first published in 1883, it was already known to its readers and audiences through oral narration. The original Urdu text was meant both for reading and for use as an aid to storytellers. Muhammad Husain Jah had organized the tale with these considerations in mind. It is not surprising that a mere 26-line preface was deemed sufficient to detail the background of a tale spread over eight thousand, closely-written pages (See Original Preface to *Tilism-e Hoshruba* by Muhammad Husain Jah). After this briefest of introductions, Muhammad Husain Jah launched into the story and kept refreshing the reader's memory as needed with bits of information they already had.

One of my challenges was in presenting the text to a modern reader – for whom it is a first introduction to *Hoshruba* – without compromising the integrity of the original. I have attempted to meet the challenge by including two brief introductory chapters, titled "The Beginning of the History: Of Amir Hamza the Lord of the Auspicious Planetary Conjunction and the False God Laqa", and "Of the Tilism called Hoshruba and the Master of the Tilism, Emperor Afrasiyab". They provide the necessary background for a modern reader to fully enjoy the tale. Those who wish to read more about the history of the Amir Hamza legend may read *The Adventures of Amir Hamza.*

Like all classical Urdu texts, the entire *Tilism-e Hoshruba* text is unpunctuated. While this offers a translator greater flexibility in structuring a phrase, it also creates some difficulties in isolating individual sentences and presenting them in a flowing, continuous narrative. It is likely that two translators working from the same source text will come up with two very different phrasal structures. My translation is just one interpretation of the original.

There are no text breaks in the original except where a new chapter is marked. I have made subchapters with the names of characters who figure prominently in a particular passage to provide an easy reference to different characters in the narrative, and to allow visual relief to the reader of this voluminous work.

Poetry is an integral part of the *dastan* genre. The Urdu original of *Tilism-e Hoshruba* has several verse passages that are employed for a variety of uses: to describe events in verse; to present the *sarapa* (figure and beauty) of male or female characters; in letters and messages; as dialogue; as war cries; and as sayings. All these uses have a direct relevance to the events of the tale. Such poetry is retained in the translation, but while the Urdu original is in metric verse, mine is a free verse translation.

Poetry is also employed for other uses: as *chehra* (ornate preamble to the narrative); prefatory verses that are in the praise of wine and cupbearers and belong to the genre called *saqi-nama* (ode to the cupbearer); verses that randomly occur in the middle of a narrative but are not a bridge between the narrative that precedes or follows; and verses that are added to a prose description of natural scenery or a battlefield scene to reiterate its details. While such verses embellish the narrative, they do not contribute to the events of the story. Moreover, all this poetry can only truly be enjoyed in the original. Therefore, verses of this description were not included in this translation. Translating all of that would easily have added a year to the total translation project. I walked away from this labour with a degree of guilt but with the hope that this translation will ultimately generate interest in the Urdu text in which this poetry can be enjoyed in all its glory.

I worked from the unabridged lithographed text of the *Tilism-e Hoshruba* (Seventh edition) published in September, 1924, by the Naval Kishore Press, Lucknow, India. A facsimile edition was printed in 1984 by Sang-e Meel Publications, Lahore. I also consulted the unabridged lithographed text of the eighth edition, published by the Naval Kishore

Press in September, 1930. It was printed in facsimile by the Khuda Bakhsh Library, Patna, India, in 1988.

Finally, I must confess to the possible shortcomings of this translation. No scholarly, annotated version of the original *Tilism-e Hoshruba* text has been published in Urdu, which is sometimes an impediment to its accurate reading and translation. At times, I may have misread the author's intent or wrongly translated a word or phrase. I willingly take responsibility for all such inadvertent errors and will, upon discovery, correct them in subsequent editions.

A list titled "Magical and Marvellous Devices and Beings" which will be of immediate interest to the reader follows. The index of characters and the numerous legendary kings, warriors, sorcerers, historical figures, deities and mythical beings mentioned in the tale is provided at the end in the "List of Characters, Historic Figures, Deities, and Mythical Beings".

Magical and Marvellous Devices and Beings

Demon: Also called a *dev*. A gigantic being with horns and a tail, which also has a taste for fine clothes, jewelery and lavish palaces.

Doppelganger: An invisible being associated with every human being. Its existence is independent of its human counterpart's and unconstrained by considerations of time and space. When a doppelganger enters a corpse a dead person can revive and narrate the circumstances of his death.

Fairy: Also called a *peri* (female fairy) or *perizad* (male fairy). Winged male or female creatures that live on Mount Qaf.

Giant: A legendary, manlike being of huge stature. The false god Laqa is a giant.

Jinn: Creatures made of fire and invisible to the human eye. According to popular belief, jinns and fairies are the children of Jan, a being who once inhabited Earth and was banished for disobedience to the Supreme Being.

Lightning-bolt: One of seven sorceresses who exist in the form of lightning in a crimson cloud and strike as lightning bolts. They also appear in human form as beautiful, golden-skinned women.

Magic Bird: A bird made of magic by sorcerers to act as their eyes and ears and spy on enemy camps.

Magic Claw: A claw or hand made by magic that carries messages, objects or people. Sometimes magic slaves turn into magic claws to perform these functions.

MAGIC DOUBLE: A magical projection of Emperor Afrasiyab, which replaced him when he was away or when he had to disappear during imminent danger.

MAGIC EFFIGY: A magical being made by a sorcerer or sorceress that assumes human shape and can work the magic spells assigned to it by its master or mistress.

MAGIC FAIRY: Not to be confused with "FAIRY" above. A magic fairy is made by a sorcerer by magic. Magic fairies can be either male or female.

MAGIC SPIRIT: The spirit of a dead person, commanded by a sorcerer's spells. A magic spirit is set free at the death of the sorcerer who commands it. Unless captured by another sorcerer by reciting the capturing spells at the time of its master's dying, a magic spirit is released into the cosmos and becomes harmless.

MAGIC SLAVE: They are both male and female. Magic slaves and magic slave girls are magical beings that can fly in the air and travel under the earth. They can change into magic claws and carry away people and objects. Magic slaves are also employed by sorcerers to fight in the battlefield, and to guard sorcerers against dangers. They can be made of paper, lentil-flour, clay, wax, brass, or steel. They are made by the occult art of *nairanj* by which a sorcerer manipulates the properties of matter to create mechanisms.

MAGIC MIRROR: A magical mirror that projected Emperor Afrasiyab's presence into his court during his absence.

MAGIC TROOPER: A horseback warrior created by magic who fights at a sorcerer's command. It is impossible to kill magic troopers with weapons.

SORCERER: Someone who has a commanding knowledge of the occult powers of astral bodies, alchemy and magic, and can combine them to create a tilism or make spells.

TRICKSTER: Male or female warriors known for their cunning, quickness and mastery of disguise.

The Beginning of the History: Of Amir Hamza the Lord of the Auspicious Planetary Conjunction and the False God Laqa

The deft fingers of narrators weave this splendid legend with the golden thread of sorcery and spread it out thus, before marvelling eyes.

Emperor Naushervan of Persia dreamt one night that a crow coming from the East flew off with his crown, then a hawk flew in from the West, killed the crow and restored him his crown. In the morning he asked the interpretation of this dream from his minister, Buzurjmehr, who was singularly adept in all occult arts. Buzurjmehr made his calculations and replied that in the future a raider named Hashsham from the eastern city of Khaibar would defeat the emperor's army and capture his crown and throne. A warrior named Hamza from the western city of Mecca would then appear on the scene and would kill the raider and restore the regalia to the emperor.

Hearing the auspicious news, Naushervan sent Buzurjmehr to Mecca in anticipation of Hamza's birth to declare the boy the emperor's protégé.

On the day Hamza was born to the chieftain of a tribe, two other boys, named Amar and Muqbil, were also born in Mecca. Buzurjmehr predicted from occult foreknowledge that they would be Hamza's trusted companions. He foretold that Amar would become a devious trickster and Muqbil a matchless archer.

Meanwhile, in the far-away, enchanted land of Mount Qaf, a daughter was born to Emperor Shahpal, the lord of the jinns, fairies and demons. She was named Aasman Peri. Shahpal's minister and diviner made her horoscope and revealed that after eighteen years, the demons of Mount Qaf would rebel and overthrow Emperor Shahpal. Then a human being named Hamza would come from the world of men to defeat the demons and restore Shahpal to the throne. The horoscope also disclosed that Hamza would marry Aasman Peri. Upon learning of this,

Emperor Shahpal sent for Hamza's cradle from Mecca and kept him in Mount Qaf for seven days. Before he was sent back, Hamza was nursed on the milk of jinns, demons, fairies, ghouls and other beasts to expel the fear of those creatures from his heart.

As Hamza, Amar and Muqbil grew up they met with many adventures and received holy gifts and talents with whose help they triumphed over powerful enemies. Their fame and exploits won them friends and followers. Hamza was chosen as their *amir* or leader, and became renowned as Amir Hamza. Because he was born under a lucky astrological conjunction of Jupiter and Venus, he was titled the Lord of the Auspicious Planetary Conjunction.

As foretold by Buzurjmehr, Amir Hamza defeated the raider Hashsham who captured Naushervan's crown and throne and restored them to the emperor. While at Naushervan's court, Amir Hamza fell in love with the emperor's daughter, Princess Mehr-Nigar. Their love attracted the notice of Naushervan's evil minister, Bakhtak. He was no idle hand at mischief and, suspecting Hamza of carrying on secret trysts with Mehr-Nigar, Bakhtak began to stir trouble at court. Buzurjmehr did his best to protect Amir Hamza but Amir Hamza's amorous passion and reckless trysts with the princess made Buzurjmehr fear for his own reputation.

When the King of India rebelled against Emperor Naushervan, Buzurjmehr saw an opportunity to send Amir Hamza on a far-away campaign. He advised the emperor to promise Princess Mehr-Nigar's hand in marriage to the one who would subdue the rebel king. As Buzurjmehr expected, Amir Hamza accepted the challenge, was engaged to Mehr-Nigar, and sent off on the campaign to India.

In Amir Hamza's absence, Bakhtak hatched countless treacherous plots against him with the sanction of the fickle-minded emperor. But Amir Hamza foiled them with the help of his holy gifts, Amar Ayyar's cunning stratagems, and Buzurjmehr's assistance. When Amir Hamza returned victorious from his adventures, the palace intrigues continued against him. However, to the shame and chagrin of Naushervan and his court, Mehr-Nigar left to join Hamza.

Meanwhile, the foretold rebellion of demons was underway in the enchanted land of Mount Qaf. Emperor Shahpal sent for Hamza to subdue the rebellious demons. While Amir Hamza was away, Amar Ayyar countered the intrigues and plots hatched by Bakhtak and his son, Bakhtiarak. He defended his camp against Naushervan's armies and kept them from carrying away Mehr-Nigar. During his destined eighteen-year stay in Mount Qaf, Amir Hamza quelled the rebellion of the demons, married Aasman Peri and had a daughter with her.

After spending eighteen years in Mount Qaf Amir, Hamza finally returned and married Mehr-Nigar. He married several other women and fairies besides and had many sons and grandsons.

Amir Hamza appointed his grandson, Saad, King of the True Believers but retained command of the armies himself. Many sons were also born to the trickster Amar Ayyar and were appointed tricksters to Amir Hamza's sons.

Amir Hamza and his armies continued to battle tyrants, giants and sorcerers for the glory of the True Faith and encountered and destroyed many tilisms. Amir Hamza's knowledge of the Most Great Name[1] protected him against magic and sorcery. Many of these events are recounted in *The Adventures of Amir Hamza*.

For some time, Amir Hamza was engaged in warfare with the false God Laqa, an eighty-five-foot-tall, pitch-black giant. His head was full of vanity and resembled the ruins of a palace dome; his limbs were the size of giant tree branches. He proclaimed himself God and declared Bakhtiarak, son of Bakhtak, the devil-designate of his court. A great many infidels and sorcerers became Laqa's believers. However, the fates and fortunes decided by Laqa always turned out to be false. Calamity and misfortune marked his followers but Laqa had not yet run out of luck.

Of the Tilism Called Hoshruba and the Master of the Tilism, Emperor Afrasiyab

We are told that at the bottom of the untold past, a group of sorcerers met to create a tilism or magical world by using occult sciences[2] to infuse inanimate matter with the spirits of planetary and cosmic forces.

In the tilism, the sorcerers exercised powers that defied the laws of God and the physical world. They created illusions, transferred spirits between bodies, transmuted matter, made talismans, and configured and exploited Earth's inherent physical forces to create extraordinary marvels.

Once the tilism was created, the sorcerers named it Hoshruba. A sorcerer named Lachin ruled Hoshruba in its early years. Then one of his deputies, the cunning sorcerer Afrasiyab, deposed his master and usurped the throne. Afrasiyab became the Emperor of Hoshruba and Master of the Tilism.

Afrasiyab and his sorceress wife, Empress Heyrat, ruled over Hoshruba's three regions: Zahir the Manifest, Batin the Hidden, and Zulmat the Dark. These regions were also tilisms and contained countless dominions and smaller tilisms filled with thousands of buildings, enclosures, gardens and palaces governed by sorcerer princes and sorceress princesses.

Ordinary citizens of Hoshruba lived in the region of Zahir the Manifest. Empress Heyrat and the emperor's ministers, peers and confidants made their abode in Batin the Hidden. Zulmat the Dark was a secluded region of Hoshruba to which few had access. It was inhabited by two of Hoshruba's most powerful sorceresses.

An enchanted river called the River of Flowing Blood divided the regions of Zahir and Batin. A bridge that was made of smoke and guarded by two smoke lions stretched over it. It was called the Bridge of the Magic Fairies and from it a three-tiered tower rose to the skies.

On the lowest tier of this tower, magic fairies stood alert, holding trumpets and clarions to their lips. From the second tier, another group of magic fairies constantly tossed pearls into the river to the fish that swam, carrying them in their mouths. On the topmost tier, gigantic Abyssinians arrayed in double rows skirmished together with swords. The blood that flowed from their wounds poured into the water below and gave the River of Flowing Blood its name.

Emperor Afrasiyab moved freely between the three regions of Hoshruba. Whenever anyone called out his name in the tilism, Afrasiyab's magic alerted him to the call. The emperor's fortune revealed itself in the palms of his hands. His left hand warned him of inauspicious moments and the right hand revealed auspicious ones. He also possessed the *Book of Sameri,* which contained an account of every event inside and outside the tilism. And he had a magic mirror that projected his body into his court during his absence, and many magic doubles who replaced him when he was in imminent danger.

Besides sorcerers and sorceresses, Afrasiyab also commanded magic slaves and magic slave girls, who fought at his command and performed any and all tasks assigned them.

Emperor Afrasiyab was among the seven immortal sorcerers of Hoshruba who could not be killed while their doppelgangers lived.

But every tilism had a fixed lifespan and a tilism key that contained directions for its unravelling. The conqueror of a tilism was one who would use that key to unravel the tilism at the appointed time. Over the years, the whereabouts of Hoshruba's tilism key was forgotten. As Hoshruba's life neared its end, Emperor Afrasiyab resolved to defend his empire and tilism and foil the tilism's conqueror when he appeared.

Unbeknown to Emperor Afrasiyab the Master of the Tilism events were already unfolding outside Hoshruba that would soon test his resolve.

The false god Laqa was in flight after suffering fresh defeats at the hands of Amir Hamza the Lord of the Auspicious Planetary Conjunction, whose armies and spies hotly pursued him.

Each day brought Laqa and Amir Hamza a little nearer to Hoshruba.

Of the False God Laqa Seeking Refuge With King Suleiman Amber-Hair of Mount Agate, and of Amir Hamza's Armies Arriving There in Pursuit of Him

Sing O minstrel for my cup of life brims over
Under the nine vaults of heaven
From the revolutions of cosmos I intone like the pipe
At the fate of Jamshed and the fortunes of Kaikhusru

The master of discourse intricate and obscure
Has masterly adorned the lovely bride of the narrative

The cupbearers of nocturnal revelries and bibbers from the cup of inspiration pour the vermilion wine of inscription into the paper's goblet thus:

When Amir Hamza's armies drove away the false god Laqa from his previous abode, Bakhtiarak, the devil-designate of Laqa's court and the man of ill council, advised Laqa to head to the dominions of King Suleiman Amber-Hair of Mount Agate who was the master of innumerable armies and mighty warriors. The lands of Mount Agate were linked to Hoshruba, the tilism ruled by its master Emperor Afrasiyab.

He is the lord of throne, insignia and crown
Lord of the fish in the sea and moon in the heavens
His grandeur is complete without the aid of coronet
At his name the heavens tremble and present tribute

Laqa followed the iniquitous Bakhtiarak's advice and headed for the fortress city of Mount Agate. At the end of his long trek, when he arrived near its borders, the spies of King Suleiman Amber-Hair alerted him. The monarch decorated the city with lights, readied trays of gold and jewels for offerings, and marched out with his retinue to greet Laqa.

Suleiman Amber-Hair brought Laqa into the fortress city and conducted him into the royal palace with great fanfare. Nobles, ministers of state and privy councillors paid their respects to Laqa. The false god was seated on the royal throne encrusted with precious and rare jewels and gave audience within the cluster of dancers, silver-thighed cupbearers, and honey-tongued and jovial singers, whose sweet strains caused every eye and ear to become transfixed with wonder. Before long, the rounds of red wine made everyone forgetful of the fickle ways of time.

Next, the three commanders of King Suleiman Amber-Hair's armies presented themselves. They were:

> Manzur Crow-Eye – Nephew to King Suleiman and master of several hundred thousand warriors
> Nazir Crow-Eye – Nephew to King Suleiman and master of several hundred thousand warriors
> Lalan Red-Robe – Supreme Commander of King Suleiman's armies and unparalleled in the arts of war

These commanders prostrated themselves before Laqa and expressed their readiness to wager their heads and scatter their lives in his service. They reassured him that he could reside in Mount Agate without the least anxiety. Laqa took great comfort from their pledges and decided to make his home in Mount Agate. King Suleiman Amber-Hair threw a feast of celebration in Laqa's honor, and bowed his head in submission to his service.

Amir Hamza had dispatched four fleet-footed and zephyr-paced spies after Laqa the damned when he fled before his victorious armies:

> Namian Khaibari
> Tomian Khaibari
> Sarhang Makki
> Abu Tahir the Blood-Spiller

These spies were given instructions to discover where that bird of ill fortune had found a roost, and to gather particulars of the kingdom whose sovereign had offered him refuge. Amir Hamza's spies had disguised themselves and accompanied Laqa, and were present in the court of Suleiman Amber-Hair at that very moment. They listened to the presentations of Suleiman Amber-Hair's commanders and, after collecting all the particulars about the fortress city of Mount Agate and its military strength, hastened out of the fortress as quick as lightning and swift as wind to make their report.

Amir Hamza was seated with King Saad in the Pavilion of Suleiman. Its panels had been raised to allow them a view of the plains and their pleasant scenery. The spies arrived in great haste before King Saad, with their lips chapped and temples pulsating. They bowed their heads at the designated station, kissed the ground at his feet with lips of servitude and, raising their hands in visiting benedictions and prayers on the king, began:

"O Majestic and Just King,
May your excellence last as long as the sun in the heavens
May you keep goblets company as long as there's another morn
For as long as the crown of life remains on Khizr's head
May your fortunes remain as lofty as those of Alexander."

The messengers narrated with accuracy and detail all that they had witnessed: "The ill-fated foe Laqa that turned tail before your triumphant armies, that star-crossed, death-bound bear adrift in the desert of darkness, has arrived in Mount Agate and sought residence there. The king of that land has offered him refuge and words of support."

King Saad turned his gaze toward his commander-in-chief, Amir Hamza, who ordered the trickster, Amar Ayyar, to send for the camp commander, Aadi, and have the advance camp dispatched toward Mount Agate.

Upon the venerable commander's orders, the signal of departure was sounded in the triumph-bearing army. The braves decked themselves with arms and armor and prepared to march.

The cities of Greece and Syria shook to their foundations
With such preparations the advance camp was provisioned

Platoons, troopers mounted on Arabian horses and countless foot-soldiers began marching toward Mount Agate with majestic mien. The army's bazaars were also folded up and sent to the destination. Tents, pavilions and other court furniture were loaded up for transportation on camels and mules. The king, with his illustrious commanders, and Amir Hamza, with his peerless tricksters, headed out to lead the armies.

In the manner the spring gale issues out
To the desert the majestic entourage departed

After marching for one day and bivouacking for one night, Amir Hamza's illustrious army arrived in the vicinity of Mount Agate with splendor and set up camp. The king's pavilion was raised and the camp's bazaars opened up. Platoons began arriving and occupied the clear plains at strategic locations.

The foes' wits took flight like birds when they heard the timbals and kettledrums of Amir Hamza's army. King Suleiman Amber-Hair gave orders for his soldiers to assemble and shut the city gates. He deployed canons of brass and steel and fortified all the crenelations, ramparts, bulwarks and battlements.

The Disappearance of Prince Badiuz Zaman on a Hunting Expedition, and of Amar Ayyar Going in Search of Him

While the preparations for war were being made, and Amir Hamza was camped opposite the City of Mount Agate, the pleasant air and green plains enticed Amir Hamza's son,

Badiuz Zaman the brave, the router of armies
The moon of the constellation of excellence,

and filled him with a longing to go hunting. He sought Amir Hamza's permission but when he made no reply, Badiuz Zaman went to his mother, Gardiya Bano, and asked her to intercede for him. Gardiya Bano acquiesced and when Amir Hamza entered her chamber, she pleaded on the prince's behalf.

Amir Hamza reluctantly granted his permission, saying, "These plains are the abode of sorcerers. That was the reason why I had not granted my permission earlier, lest the prince should meet some calamity. At your interceding, I am granting him leave on condition that he return the next day and does not stay longer."

Badiuz Zaman accepted the condition. The whole night was spent making preparations for the hunt.

Before long, the Heavens' Hunter[3] emerged from his eastern abode carrying the net of rays on his shoulders and started hunting the planetary fixtures on the sky's fields. The world-illuminating sun of the high noon of the auspicious planetary conjunction, the star that lights up the six dimensions of the skies of triumph, to wit, Prince Badiuz Zaman the Magnificent, headed for the plains for hunting.

As the first crack of daylight appeared, the draughts of morning breeze stirred, the tapers flickered, the buds flowered, the love-struck nightingales made their outcries, the peacocks danced in the forests, the birds fluttered away from their nests in search of food and water. Every living being occupied itself with thoughts of the Creator, every heart was filled with the Progenitor's name, and like a veritable preacher the ringdove sang a sermon from the pulpit of the cypress in the name of the True God.

The eminent prince began hunting in the plains with his equipage and retinue, occupying his gaze with the pleasant air of the land and the mountains. Suddenly a fawn appeared near the river bank, cavorting and gambolling like a frolicsome beloved well-versed in coquetry.

Sporting a brocade sheet on his back
How beautiful and fairy-faced the fawn
His feistiness even a mistress could not attain
A veritable hunter in the meadow where hearts abound

When Badiuz Zaman beheld that beautiful and comely fawn, he became infatuated and besotted at the very sight and gave orders to his commanders: "Take him alive! Beware, do not let him get away!"

The prince's companions immediately encircled the animal and made a cordon. The fawn pricked his ears and bolted, breaking out of the cordon by leaping off the prince's head. Badiuz Zaman chased him on his horse at a gallop and followed him for many miles until he left behind all his companions and found himself alone. Near to losing the fawn, and unable to take him alive, he drew an arrow from his quiver; notching the arrow and drawing to his ear, he let fly.

The arrow pierced the fawn and it fell. The prince jumped down from his horse and slaughtered him. The moment that fawn died a most dreadful voice was heard that made even the heart of Taurus in the heavens shudder and sent tremors in the seven heavens and the seven seas. It proclaimed,

"*O son of Hamza! You committed a terrible deed by killing Sorcerer Ghazaal the Fawn. This is the land of Hoshruba and it is well nigh impossible to escape its bounds. Anything that may happen now would be too little*!"

The prince saw that the entire expanse had become dark with the billowing of sand and dust; a tempest of gales raged mightily. After a moment he lost consciousness and when he opened his eyes he found himself incarcerated in heavy chains. Resting his head on his knees, he became lost in reflection.

Be it known that the sons of Amar Ayyar are designated tricksters of the courts of Amir Hamza's sons. When a son was born to Hamza from a princess, a son was also born to Amar from the minister's daughter who attended to that princess. Thus Amar's son was deputed as the trickster of Amir Hamza's son.

A trickster named Umayya bin Amar, who was in the service of the prince of happy fortune, arrived on the scene where the fawn was killed and found the plains pitch dark and all the signs of doomsday's horrors manifested there. Umayya saw Badiuz Zaman's headless corpse on the ground, and the beauty that was the moon's envy lying before him all gored.

The trickster held up the corpse in his arms and broke into tears of grief. He rent the collar of his tunic in anguish and, throwing dust on his head, carried the prince's corpse on his horse to his camp. On the way he met the prince's entourage and when they saw that woeful sight, transports of sorrow assailed their hearts too. Weeping and wailing and throwing dust over their heads, all of them presented themselves before Amir Hamza. Witnessing that tragic misfortune, Amir Hamza and his companions gave themselves over to crying and making lamentations. The entire camp and the women's quarters rang alike with sounds of weeping and wailing. Badiuz Zaman's mother, Gardiya Bano, was inconsolable and presented a living picture of grief. She would recite:

> *"O solace of my heart and soul*
> *You departed leaving me alone.*
>
> *"You left without giving me news that you leave*
> *Caring not a whit for my loneliness."*

While the whole camp was occupied in mourning, Amir Hamza said to Amar Ayyar, "Harness my steed, Ashqar Demon-Born, and bring him to me so that I may depart in search of the murderer, kill him, and bring away his head." Amar Ayyar replied, "O Prince and Pride of Heavens, I have heard that nobody saw the prince's killer. The expanse had suddenly become pitch black, and when the darkness parted the prince's headless body was found there." Amir Hamza said, "By God there is some mystery in this matter, which the Heavens alone know. Send for the diviners!"

At Amir Hamza's order, the diviners Buzurg Ummid, Siyavush and Daryadil were sent for. They were the sons of Buzurjmehr, the minister of Emperor Naushervan of Persia. Their father had attached his sons to his camp to wait upon him with devotion. The tale of Buzurjmehr and Amir Hamza is recounted in *The Adventures of Amir Hamza*, and this much would suffice at present to acquaint the reader with their particulars. The diviners were masters in the arts of geomancy and astrology, and able disciples of their father. Amir Hamza seated them with great honor and asked them to find out what had passed with the prince.

The diviners drew the lots of perception on the board of introspection and drawing the horoscope, studied the manifestations of the year, the signs of the zodiac, and the lines of geomancy. After intense study and much contemplation and reflection they raised their heads and said, "O illustrious lord, Prince Badiuz Zaman is alive and safe. However, he is caught in the power of evil sorcerers and lies powerless and helpless in severe internment. The corpse that was brought before you was an effigy made of lentil flour.[4] If you recite the Most Great Name on water and sprinkle it on the corpse, the power of our Creator will be manifested."

As it happened, Prince Badiuz Zaman had strayed into Hoshruba, the tilism linked to Mount Agate. When the prince entered its frontiers, the Master of the Tilism and Emperor of Hoshruba, Afrasiyab, learned about it. He ordered one of the tilism's guardians, a sorceress named Sharara Flame-Spirit, to capture the prince. Sharara was ordered to leave the prince's effigy where he was captured so that it would serve as an example to other transgressors and deter them from entering the tilism.

As Amir Hamza recited the Most Great Name over the water and sprinkled it on the corpse, it returned to its origins – a flour effigy. Amir Hamza bowed his head in gratitude before God and gave thanks to Him who sent the news that his son was alive. He bestowed robes of honor on the diviners and had the effigy thrown away. All the lamentations and weeping in the camp ceased and everyone celebrated the news. Amir Hamza sent for Amar Ayyar and, after conferring much gold and jewels upon him, deputed him to find the whereabouts of the illustrious prince.

Amar Ayyar decorated himself with his occult contraptions and the holy gifts he had been bestowed on Mount Ceylone.

The transcriber states that when the armies of Amir Hamza had arrived to conquer India, Amar had made a pilgrimage to the shrines of the prophets (Peace be upon them) and there Amar fell asleep. In the realm of dreams he had the beatific and marvellous audience of several prophets and they told him that certain devices of trickery had been kept for Amar in the chamber of their shrine. Among them was the zambil, which was a bag within which existed a world comparable to the world on Earth. Upon command, it produced anything that Amar wished at any time, and accommodated anything that Amar kept in it.

Also among them, the cape of invisibility had such properties that when Amar wore it he could see everyone but none could see him. The Net of Ilyas had the miracle that it could carry a thing even if it weighed millions of tons, and make it feel as light as a small stone. Wherever Amar raised Daniyal's Tent and took shelter underneath, none was able to capture him, and anyone who entered it was caught and hung upside down. And when he wore the *dev-jama,* it changed seven colors from green to red to yellow et cetera.

Amar took possession of these items upon receiving the tidings. All this has been mentioned in *The Adventures of Amir Hamza.* Whenever the reader may hear about these objects, he may associate them with that legend. These were the same objects that Amar readied before setting out with great dispatch for the wilderness to search for Prince Badiuz Zaman.

Setting out in the expanse with such dispatch that birds of prey
Did not even catch the dust he stirred in his wake

The Meeting of Princess Tasveer and Prince Badiuz Zaman and Their Falling in Love

At the end of his journey, when that Pinnacle of Trickery and the Star of the Skies of Dagger Fighting arrived at the place where Prince Badiuz Zaman had been captured by sorcery, he saw a meadow even more delightful than the garden of paradise.

Admiring the air, Amar carried onwards on his mission. Suddenly, a group of girls appeared on the horizon and Amar hid himself in a bush.

Princess Tasveer

Coming his way was a party of coquettish girls as beautiful and lovely as the moon, and as stately as the sun in the heavens.

They were of ages between fifteen and sixteen years
Familiar to pangs of adolescence, and nights of desires

Between them was a princess whose beauty was the moon's envy. She was the gazelle of the desert of beauty and a prancing peacock of the forest of splendor. She walked with her hand placed on the shoulder of one of her attendants,

Like the rose in a cluster of nightingales, the supreme lord
Like the moon among stars, the lantern of heavens

and was outfitted in a fine costume and jewelery enchased with gems. Absorbed in the sights of the wilderness, she stepped with a graceful and haughty air.

Amar was regarding the whole scene from his hiding place when one of the princess's attendants felt the call of nature. She sat down to make water at some distance from Amar while her companions continued along their path. Amar reckoned that if he joined the princess's party he might find some clue that would help him locate the prince. He came out of the bush and threw his snare rope at the girl answering the call of nature. When she raised the alarm, Amar stuffed her mouth with a trickster's ball and drugged her unconscious. He tied her to a tree and, putting a mirror before his face, began putting on colored powder and trickster's lotions, changing his face to the girl's likeness. He took off her clothes and dressed himself in them. Leaving her tied there, Amar Ayyar rushed forward to join the party of attendants.

Taking Amar Ayyar for their companion, the girls said, "O Shagufa! You took your time. What else were you doing there besides answering the call of nature?" Amar realized that the girl whose disguise he had put on was called Shagufa. He answered, "Come now, I didn't take all that long!"

Talking together, they all approached a garden. Amar saw that its gates were open like the yearning eyes of a lover, and the cold wind that wafted there was like the Messiah's breath. The beauties entered that garden, whose splendor had no equal, and Amar beheld wondrous grounds that were the envy of the garden of paradise.

It was adorned with beautiful promenades and esplanades, paved with jewels instead of bricks. The trees were wrapped in gold cloth. The hedges of henna plants and grapevines decorated the silken grass bed. Like a drunken guest in a wine house, the breeze kept crashing into the ewers of trees. The goblets of flowers brimmed with the wine of freshness and beauty and exhaled a captivating redolence.

Sorceress Sharara Flame-Spirit

In the middle of the garden was a marble platform a hundred yards long and as wide on which a royal carpet was spread. A bejewelled, caparisoned regal throne was placed on it with a canopy made of strung pearls. A finely clad woman in her fifties was sitting on the throne, resting against the pillows with great pomp and majesty. The perfume box, betel box, dry-fruit box, and flowerpots were placed around her on the throne. She rose when the princess, whom Amar had accompanied, approached, and stepped forward with a smile to welcome her. The princess saluted her respectfully. Her attendants also curtsied to the older woman reverently and retreated respectfully in silence afterwards.

The older woman was none other than sorceress Sharara Flame-Spirit, who had put a spell on Prince Badiuz Zaman and imprisoned him. The visiting princess was her niece, Princess Tasveer, the daughter of Empress Heyrat of Hoshruba.

Sharara blessed and kissed Tasveer and seated her on the throne. She ordered accomplished dancers to present themselves and display their talents. A spectacular recital was soon in progress and cups of wine were served.

In the middle of these revelries, Sharara asked Tasveer, "My child, what brought you to these parts? Why did you inconvenience yourself by travelling on foot in the wilderness?" Tasveer answered, "Venerable aunt, reverent to me as my mother! I have heard that you captured one of Hamza's sons. I am most desirous of seeing a True Believer. Even though they are the creation of our Lord Laqa, they seem so powerful that even our Lord is completely helpless before them. They drive our Lord from land to land and pursue him relentlessly. I have also heard that these people laid hundreds of lands to ruin and destroyed and burned as many tilisms. I wish to see them to behold the might, power and majesty invested in them by Lord Laqa when he created them."

Sharara laughed and ordered the prisoner to be brought out so that his plight may be presented to the princess.

A party of sorceresses went away to carry out her orders. In the garden was an enchanted summerhouse where buildings stretched for miles on end. Badiuz Zaman was imprisoned in a chamber inside one building under the vigil of sorceresses. When they received Sharara's orders, the spell was taken off Badiuz Zaman. He was put in chains, fetters, handcuffs and leg-irons. Spiked iron balls were thrust in his armpits and his thighs were secured in steel clasps. Sorceresses led him out by a chain attached to his waist and presented him before Princess Tasveer.

The princess beheld the prince's comely face and his world-adorning beauty. She regarded a handsome and beautiful youth who was a world-illuminating sun of the sky of beauty and a lustrous pearl of the oyster of refinement.

The moment their eyes met, the bow of the prince's eyebrow released the arrow of love, which pierced through the princess's heart, making life a burden for her.

The princess laid her head on the throne and fell unconscious. After much to-do, Sharara restored her to her senses by sprinkling her face with rose-water, essence of musk, and restoratives.

Prince Badiuz Zaman beheld the ravishing beauty regain consciousness and regard him with a longing gaze. The Painter of Creation[5] had surpassed Himself in creating her dazzling beauty and the prince's heart became all aflutter. He felt it nearly break free from the oppressive imprisonment of his body to imprison itself in her locks. That beauty, who was the envy of the House of Mani, was called Tasveer,[6] but the sight of her unparalleled beauty was such that none could behold it without himself becoming transfixed with wonder like a mirror, and still like an image.

The inventive Transcriber of Nature had calligraphed with the pen of beauty the words "heart-ravishing" on the tablet of her face; one more beautiful did not exist in the whole gallery of Creation. The prince became enamoured of her with a thousand souls, and inconsolable in her love.

"Ah desire! Ah desire!" the heart cried
"I depart! I depart!" fortitude answered
The senses began to scatter and disperse
The heart held the standard of frenzy aloft
All sense of shame and dignity began to dissolve
And thus ensued a battle between the mind and heart

But he got hold of himself and became quiet, realizing that he was already a prisoner in the tilism and if his love were discovered, everyone there would become his enemy and his life worthless.

When Sharara saw Tasveer's suffering, she said to her attendants, "Take away the prisoner! My niece's virgin blood is unfamiliar with oppressive humours! She fainted because she has never seen anyone in such misery and distress before."

The sorceresses led Badiuz Zaman away, locked him up in his chamber, and left him. The prince forgot all the misery of his imprisonment in his new-found love and the memory of the princess began tormenting his grief-stricken heart.

He constantly recited couplets and said to himself, *O Badiuz Zaman! It is impossible that she would ever find you worthy of her attentions; her beauty has intoxicated her with vanity. If you ever found release from this prison, you would surely die a most wretched death in the prison of her love.*

While the prince was undergoing these pangs, Tasveer's longing eyes, too, searched for her flower of excellence. Unable to find what she most ardently desired, she drew an icy sigh from the depths of her pining heart. However, she became quiet as well upon reflection on the disastrous consequences of her passion.

Sharara asked her, "How are you feeling my dear child?" She answered, "Dear aunt, I don't know how to describe to you the sinking feeling in my heart and the dread that seized it at the thought of the prisoner's hardships and harsh imprisonment." Sharara answered, "My child! You are a princess and must not succumb to such anxieties. Felons and estimable folks appear daily before the royalty. Some are hanged or beheaded, while others conferred purses of gold and robes of honor from the royal bounty. Hamza's son is an enemy of sorcerers. He has been imprisoned at the orders of Emperor Afrasiyab, and it's a near impossibility that he will ever be freed. Had it been someone else, I would have gladly released him for your sake and conferred gold and riches on him besides. Now you have my leave to return to your garden. I see that your condition is not improving. Perspiration is covering your forehead still, and idle visions and horrors continue to torment you. If you stay here longer you will remain engrossed in such thoughts. It would suit you better to return to your house, distract your thoughts by conversing with your confidants, and occupy yourself no more with thoughts of the prisoner! Once you go away your spirits will revive like rosebuds breaking into bloom."

Tasveer rose from there and thought, *It was well that my aunt sent me away. Had I stayed here longer, a word of pining or a sigh of longing might have escaped my lips and disclosed my love. Once I am back in my garden, I will cry to my heart's content and unburden it of its sorrow.*

As she bowed from her waist to pay her respects to her aunt before leaving, the beauty, who was the envy of the full moon, became a picture of the crescent. Sharara blessed her and bid her adieu.

Tasveer's attendants, who were promenading in the garden, presented themselves when told of the princess's departure. Amar Ayyar, who was also among them in Shagufa's disguise, thought, *God knows where the princess will go from here. Prince Badiuz Zaman is imprisoned in this place. I must kill this strumpet Sharara and secure the release of my prince!*

The false Shagufa presented herself before Sharara and said humbly, "Your slave girl has become greatly enamoured of this place and this garden. I wish to remain at your feet awhile and not depart today. Besides, I have attained a degree of excellence in music, and now that I have found a connoisseur in you, I desire that you witness my accomplishments. You might find me worthy of your beneficence." Sharara answered, "O Shagufa! Tasveer's house and my house are as one. There is no separation between our households. You may stay here for as long as you wish."

Sharara turned toward Tasveer and said, "Tasveer, my child, leave Shagufa here with me!" Tasveer answered, "Very well, aunt!" She left shortly afterwards and the false Shagufa stayed behind.

Princess Tasveer went staggering and stumbling on her way, inconsolable with the pangs of love-induced grief. She kept saying to herself, *Ah, what a misfortune that I fell in love with the one who has sworn enmity to my life and my faith, as he is a slayer of sorcerers! His release from the prison is near impossible. Alas, alas, alas! He will lose his life for nothing!* She was occupied with these reflections when suddenly the real Shagufa arrived before her, all naked and in tears. Princess Tasveer wondered what had happened to her in the time that she had been left with Sharara, and who had stripped her of her clothes.

Shagufa threw herself at the princess's feet, and said, "My princess, I was accompanying you when I stopped along the way to answer the call of nature. A man appeared from the bushes all of a sudden and God knows what he did to me that I lost consciousness. He stripped me and left me tied to a tree. When I came to, I implored a passer-by to help me, and after freeing myself, I rushed before you. I consider myself fortunate that I again behold the face of Your Honor."

The princess marvelled at the story, and thought, *I should not breathe even a word of this to anyone. Perhaps one of Prince Badiuz Zaman's friends put on Shagufa's disguise and stayed behind to find some way for securing his release. If I talk about it, Sharara will hear of it and that poor soul will also be captured.*

In her love for the prince, Tasveer did not show any consideration even for her own aunt. She sent for her attendants, had a change of clothes brought for Shagufa, and said to everyone, "Look at this wanton girl! She did not want me to learn what she had in mind, so she took leave to stay behind at my aunt's house. Then she stole away God knows where so that even her clothes were stripped away." Shagufa protested and said, "Pray believe me, I speak the truth!" The princess replied, "Quiet, you liar! I will never believe a word you say! I swear by Lord Sameri that if you speak again I will have you punished most severely!" After threatening Shagufa against opening her mouth about the incident or spreading the news of what had passed with her, the princess diverted herself with the sights of her garden. She put her hopes in the Omnipotent Causer of Causes[7] to create a way for the prince's release.

When Tasveer stepped into her garden, she found it a veritable thorn in the absence of her nightingale-like beloved. She could find neither peace nor rest. Her heart was marked by the prince's love like the tulip; her gaze awaited the prince's sight like the narcissus; and, with longing in her heart, she waited for the noble prince, all delicate and fragile like the spikenard.[8]

Now we return to the account of Amar Ayyar, the Bearder of Infidels, the Beheader of Sorcerers, and the Dagger Fighter Par Excellence, who had stayed behind in Sharara's garden in Shagufa's disguise.

Until evening, the false Shagufa occupied herself with making pleasantries and repartees with other female attendants. Now she would pinch someone; now press her cheek against a girl; now slip the attendants' belongings into the zambil – a betel box here, a vanity box there. She carried on like this until evening and great excitement was caused by all her doings because nobody was able to find the thief.

Sharara had ordered food, wine and all manner of delicacies for dinner. After the meal, a carpet was spread on the crystal platform and the garden was lit up. The tent-pitchers decorated the summerhouse most beautifully by illuminating it with lamps, chandeliers, lotus-lights and other glass lights. Globes of light hung from every tree, making every branch drip with beads of light.

Gold and silver threads were cut into shreds, put in the fountainheads, and water released in the watercourses. When all the decorations were complete, singers, dancers and musicians were sent for and Sharara asked Shagufa to present herself.

The false Shagufa made her appearance dressed in a dancing girl's gown, wearing eighty-four ankle bells. She asked Sharara's female musicians and singers to sound their notes, then filled her mouth with pearls, produced a pair of reed pipes and put them to her lips.

Be it known that Angel Jibrail had taught Amar along with Amir Hamza. He had fed Amar three grapes. The first grape made Amar harmonious, with the harmony of Prophet Daud. The second grape allowed him to change into seventy-two different guises and, by the grace of God, assume the face that he turned his thought to. And the third grape gave Amar the power to fully understand and speak all languages of the world.

Tying one end of a brass wire to her big toe and pressing the other between her lips, the false Shagufa picked up a wine ewer and goblet in her hands and began dancing. She could make only a single ankle bell sound when she wished, or all together, or none. She strung pearls from her mouth onto the wire at every beat, and filled the goblet every so often to serve the assembly. Sounds of "Brava! Well done!" rose from all corners of the garden at her performance, which was full of dalliance and coquettish airs.

Sharara sat there, struck with wonder and marvelled whether what she saw before her was a human phenomenon, a spark, or a moving flame. It was an enchanting performance with the reed constantly playing the accompaniment, the pearls being strung continuously, and the wine circulating without end. Sharara showered the false Shagufa with praise and took off her necklace to give her as a reward. The false Shagufa made a salutation, went dancing to the sorceress and stuck out her head for Sharara to put the necklace around her neck. She then ended the tune and started singing with such fervor that everyone began to swoon from the song and the enchanting power of her melodious strains.

Sharara was enraptured and as she broke into tears from ecstasy, the false Shagufa stopped. The sorceress called out, "Do not stop the song now! You have brought me this far! Take me now to the end." The false Shagufa answered: "Allow me to tell you my situation in verse:

"The free spirits must drink wine
And my eyes are like the goblets
My clay was kneaded with the juice of grape
In the first sip of my life was a drop of wine
In the wine house of the world I am the wise head on whom
The clergyman passed the decree to remain continuously drunk."

When Sharara heard these verses, she realized the girl desired a drink but was too modest and well behaved to ask for it directly. She was pleased by her refined manners and the fact that she served wine to everyone without taking a sip herself. Sharara immediately ordered the wine service to be presented. The attendants rushed to obey her orders and brought everything, including trays of wine, goblets, decanters and ewers. Sharara said, "O Shagufa, I was most pleased with your performance today! I hereby appoint you my confidant and enroll you among my companions. Be the cupbearer in this company and give me some wine, too!"

The false Shagufa approached and made an offering of five gold pieces. Sharara conferred a robe of honor on her, which the false Shagufa put on, and began organizing the wine service. The false Shagufa arranged the decanters and ewers of wine like a bouquet under the chandelier, placing the green glasses next to the red, setting them in such a way that light would fall directly on them and it would seem as if flower bouquets were placed on the floor. She kept busy sorting the cups and ewers so that she could drug all the wine. She managed to do so without inviting notice then resumed dancing. Holding a wine ewer under her arm and filling up a goblet, she danced up to Sharara and offered the goblet to her, saying:

"Drink, for the days of sorrow will soon pass
They did not last before, and they shall now pass."

As Sharara extended her hand to take the cup, the false Shagufa tossed it into the air and caught it on her head without spilling a single drop. Then she extended her head before Sharara and submitted, "Nobles and royalty must be served wine on the platter of their servants' head, my lady!"

Sharara could not cease marvelling at the many refinements she witnessed in the attendant. She raised the cup to her lips and her breath came in contact with the wine. Immediately, the wine leapt to the sky in flame. Left holding the empty cup, Sharara came to her senses speedily. After imprisoning Badiuz Zaman, she had deputed magic spirits to alert her if some trickster arrived to seek the prince's release. It was a magic spirit that caused the wine to leap up in flame. Realizing that it was a trickster disguised as Shagufa, Sharara immediately recited an incantation and blew it on the attendant. Her face paint and makeup disappeared and Amar Ayyar appeared in his real form. Sharara ordered the sorceresses to arrest him and Amar was taken into custody without delay.

Sharara said, "You very nearly killed me, O rascal!" Amar answered, "O harridan! Do not think even for a moment that you are saved. Yours truly never returns unsuccessful from his mission. Rest assured that I will dispatch you to hell shortly!" Enraged by Amar's words, Sharara had him tied to a tree and put a magic cordon around the garden so that he could not escape from it.

Sharara wrote a letter to Emperor Afrasiyab, containing the particulars of Amar's capture. She informed him that she had arrested him and awaited the emperor's orders whether she should dispatch Amar's head to the court or send him there a prisoner. Sharara handed the letter to her attendant, Shola Rukhsar Flame-Cheek, with orders to take it to the court of the Emperor of Hoshruba.

Shola Rukhsar Flame-Cheek flew away by invoking her magic. She arrived at the banks of the River of Flowing Blood and called out, "O Emperor of Hoshruba! A messenger of Sharara seeks leave to be presented in your illuminated service!"

Afrasiyab was giving audience in the Apple Garden in the region of Batin when his magic alerted him to the call of Shola Rukhsar Flame-Cheek. He sent a magic claw, which picked up Shola Rukhsar Flame-Cheek from the riverbank and brought her before him.

Shola Rukhsar found herself in a summerhouse in the Apple Garden where Emperor Afrasiyab was giving audience with Empress Heyrat on a throne enchased with diamonds and gems and surrounded by thousands of nobles of Hoshruba and celebrated sorcerers. The sorcerers and sorceresses sat dressed in elegant costumes on ruby-sculpted seats whose feet were carved out in the shape of lion and elephant heads that spewed fire constantly. Among the many nobles present were:

Sorceress Princess Bahar of Spring-Quarter
Sorceress Princess Nafarman of the City of Purple Poppy
Sorceress Princess Zaafran
Sorceress Princess Taus
Sorceress Princess Mushkeen-Mu Wonder-Mane
Sorceress Princess Makhmur Crimson-Eye

The five trickster girls stood with deference before Empress Heyrat. They were:

Sarsar Swordfighter, Queen of the City of Portraits and the leader of trickster girls
Saba Raftar the Quick, Minister to Sarsar Swordfighter
Shamima Tunneler
Sunubar Snare-Roper
Tez Nigah Dagger-Fighter

The empress was attended by two sorceress aides:

Sorceress Yaqut
Sorceress Zamarrud

The emperor was attended by his four ministers:

Sanat Magic-Maker
Sarma Ice-Hurler
Baghban Magic-Gardener
Abriq Mount-Splitter

The emperor's ministers moved the fly-whisk of phoenix feathers above the emperor's head. All those present sat in quiet reverence before the grandeur and majesty of the royal court.

Shola Rukhsar curtsied before Afrasiyab and presented Sharara's letter. After reading it, Afrasiyab wrote in reply:

"Kill Amar without delay!"

Shola Rukhsar then took her leave. Afrasiyab sent for a magic claw, which carried her across the River of Flowing Blood. She started from there for Sharara's garden, which lay at a day's journey, and where Amar Ayyar the Nightingale of the Grove of Trickery was tied to a tree.

At some late hour in the night, Sharara retired to the summerhouse to sleep. Amar began cudgelling his brains to find some way of freeing himself and killing Sharara. He was occupied with these thoughts when one of Sharara's attendants, Saman Azar, happened to pass by. Amar gestured to her to approach him and said to her, "O faithful subject of Lord Laqa, I entreat you to hear me out!" When Saman Azar approached, Amar started crying. He said, "You know that I will be beheaded in the morning, and the executioner will deprive me of all my possessions. You know too, that I am a trickster in the employ of Amir Hamza and possess a great horde of jewels, pearls and gems. I will bestow my possessions upon you if you do me the kindness of witnessing my last wishes and acting in accordance with them."

Saman Azar was tempted by the talk of riches. She sat down by Amar's side and said, "Tell me what your last wishes are and how much gold and jewels you possess!" Amar answered, "Have no worries. There are riches enough to last you many lifetimes. Hear out my last wishes first! Once I am killed, you must purchase my corpse from Sharara and bury it after covering it in a winding-sheet. Next, go to my camp and distribute one half of my possessions among my children and my wife, and keep the other half for yourself." Saman Azar said, "Very well! Now tell me what those possessions are." Amar said, "Unfasten my one hand so that I may hand over all those possessions to you!" When Saman Azar unfastened Amar's hand, he took out his trickster's livery and put it on the ground. He said to Saman Azar, "My other hand is also tied. Unfasten it too, and take all that I ask you to take."

Once both his hands were free, Amar opened the trickster's livery and began putting out all items used in trickery – women's and men's costumes, sweetmeats, oils, and facial paints. Amar told her how he used them to disguise himself as a woman. He told her how he turned into a beggar, what he did to disguise himself as a king, and to what purpose the drugged sweetmeats and fruits were used, et cetera. Among other things, there was also a bag full of jewels and gold. Amar said, "This is yours!" Saman Azar felt she was in seventh heaven and put it to one side. As Amar resumed searching the livery, a small, most elegantly cut box of ruby, whose glitter illuminated the whole place, fell out of it and Amar quickly picked it up.

Saman Azar said, "What's in that?" Amar replied, "My very soul, that's what's in it! All that I have earned in my life I have kept in it!" Saman Azar said, "Give this to me as well now!" Amar answered, "It is my intention to be buried with it!" Saman Azar said, "At least tell me what is inside this box!" Amar replied, "Inside is a priceless jewel for which even the Empire of the Seven Climes[9] is too meagre a ransom!"

Saman Azar pleaded, "O Amar! In the end you will be killed. Give me this box as well and I will act most kindly toward your family and children!" Amar replied, "You would never have come across someone as liberal and generous in your life as me! Take it, it's yours, too! But do open the box for me and let me have one last look at its contents!"

Saman Azar took the box from Amar's hand and tried to open it but was unsuccessful. Amar said, "Hold it close to your chest and pull it by applying pressure with both hands!" Saman Azar did as she was told. The box opened and the drug powder in it flew into her face. She sneezed and fell unconscious. Amar then freed himself of his fetters and carried away Saman Azar to a secluded corner in the garden. He disguised himself as Saman Azar and changed her face and appearance into his own with tricksters' paints and oils. He applied an oil to her tongue that made it swell up and rendered her unable to speak. Then he carried Saman Azar to the tree where he had been tied and fastened her to it. Finally, putting all his tricksters' apparatus back into his livery, he went to sleep in Saman Azar's bed.

Amar slept on until the King of Stars[10] dismissed his court and Heavens' Prisoner[11] was led into the field of the skies by the chain of rays. Sharara and her attendants rose from their slumber at the break of dawn. After the morning rituals, Sharara went and sat on the carpet spread on the platform in the summerhouse. All her female attendants, including the false Saman Azar, appeared in her service. In the meantime, Shola Rukhsar Flame-Cheeks also returned with Emperor Afrasiyab's reply and presented it to Sharara. She ordered that Amar Ayyar be brought forth and deputed a Calmuck Tartar[12] woman to cut off his head.

The attendants unfastened the real Saman Azar disguised as Amar Ayyar while the Calmuck Tartar readied her dagger. Saman Azar was unable to protest because of her swollen tongue. She cried many tears and made signs but no one understood her. At Sharara's command, the Calmuck Tartar cut off Saman Azar's head with just one blow.

Because Saman Azar was a sorceress, a commotion arose at her death; her magic spirits clamoured, "*Alas Saman Azar was killed!*" and darkness enveloped everything. Amar took advantage of the darkness to hide in a nook.

Sharara of dark fortune was unnerved when she heard the noise and witnessed the darkness. She realized immediately that Amar Ayyar had pulled the wool over her eyes and escaped, and that the garden of Saman Azar's life was destroyed instead. She said to her attendants, "Go and check Saman Azar's quarters to see if that rebel is hiding there!" Her attendants flew like the zephyr to search for Amar but saw no one there and informed Sharara of it. She said, "Very well! Last night I put a magic cordon around the garden that would not allow anyone to escape from here. Fetch me the magic box that lies in the summerhouse on the center shelf! I am certain that thief is hiding among you disguised as an attendant. I will discover who it is with the help of the magic box."

The magic box was brought before Sharara. When she opened its lid everyone saw a bracelet-like device fixed to its center. Sharara told them it would clasp the wrist of the one who was in disguise, and ordered them to put their hands one by one into it. When no one's hand was caught in the clasp, Sharara said to them, "Put away the magic box. Amar is not among you. In the night I will invoke my magic and discover his whereabouts." The attendants took away the magic box.

Amar witnessed all of this from his hiding place. He looked around and saw a hut resembling the gardener's quarters. Amar approached it under cover of the trees and saw an old woman lying there. When he asked who she was, she told him she was the gardener's mother, Champa. Amar hit her in the face with an egg of oblivion, which exploded upon impact; the drug travelled down her nose and she fell unconscious. Amar put her in his zambil and, disguising himself as Champa, went before Sharara, walking with a cane.

The false Champa circled around Sharara's throne, offering herself as her mistress's sacrifice to protect her against calamities. Sharara said, "Tell me, Champa, why did you wish to see me?" The false Champa answered, "May I sacrifice my life to protect yours! I heard that a thief has escaped and you tested everyone in the garden. Your slave girl now submits herself for you to test her!" Sharara answered, "There is no need to test you! I will invoke my magic tonight. It will drive Amar out from wherever he is hiding and present him before me." The false Champa answered, "Tomorrow will be another day. I wish you to put me to the same test that others submitted to earlier today!" Sharara answered, "Very well then! Go and bring me the magic box!" The false Champa said, "I will bring it in no time. Tell me where it is kept." After receiving the directions, she hobbled off. Entering the summerhouse and finding it deserted, the false Champa opened the magic box and, taking care not to touch the clasp, filled up the box with drug mist. She put two cotton swabs steeped in an antidote in her nostrils so that the drug mist would not affect her. Closing the lid as before and walking slowly, she carried it before Sharara. The sorceress said to her attendants, "She is too old and frail to carry the magic box by herself. Take it from her hands." The attendants took it from Champa's hands and put it before Sharara while the false Champa positioned herself before her.

The moment Sharara opened the lid, a cloud of drug vapour rose like smoke and Sharara and all her attendants standing close to her sneezed and fell unconscious. The moment Sharara lost consciousness Amar cut off her head with one blow of his dagger. No sooner was Sharara killed than a great pandemonium broke loose. Stones and hail began to shower and her magic spirits began making deafening outcries.

Amar took advantage of the tumult to put on his cape of invisibility. He put the White Conch, whose call made even demons leap with fright, to his mouth. In the midst of that commotion everyone heard someone call out in a voice that struck terror in their hearts: "*Run or all of you will also die!*" The moment they heard it, Sharara's servants and attendants stampeded out of the garden. Amar cut off the head of every single attendant who lay unconscious with Sharara. The racket continued and everything remained enveloped in darkness for some time. Finally, everything subsided and Amar saw dead sorceresses lying all around him. All enchanted buildings and trees had disappeared from the garden. Only the real trees and buildings remained standing.

Amar beheld Prince Badiuz Zaman standing unfettered under a tree. Badiuz Zaman greeted Amar when the latter took off his cape. Amar asked him, "How were you freed?" Badiuz Zaman answered, "The chains and fetters were created by Sharara's spell. When she died they also disappeared. The door of the chamber where I was imprisoned fell open and I came out."

While Amar was conversing with Badiuz Zaman, a strong wind suddenly picked up. Whirlwinds rose from the ground and began twirling Sharara's corpse around and bore it away into the air. Amar said, "We must get out of here without an instant's delay! It seems the corpse of Sharara will be carried before Emperor Afrasiyab and some calamity will visit us before long."

Badiuz Zaman said, "If we had a conveyance, it would shorten our journey!" Amar answered, "I know a horse is on sale in these parts but it would cost you some little money!" Badiuz Zaman promised to pay Amar a hundred thousand rupees. Amar took out a pen and inkwell from the zambil and said, "Put it on paper! You are a young man. Later, if you refuse the payment, I will have some proof to take before a judge!" Badiuz Zaman laughed and wrote out a promissory note to the treasurer in Amar's favor for the money.

Amar put the note in his zambil and went outside the garden. He took out a horse and all its trappings from his zambil and brought him saddled before the prince. He said to the prince, "I have just bought it from a merchant outside the garden!" Badiuz Zaman answered, "And singularly fortunate it was, too, that he was standing right outside the garden door waiting for you in this upheaval!" Amar replied, "Have you learned anything in your life other than making speeches? Start moving before some other trouble claims us!" Badiuz Zaman mounted the horse and Amar accompanied him as they headed out of the garden.

On the way, Badiuz Zaman said to Amar, "It would be a disgrace for me to return straight to the camp without seeing Princess Tasveer. I have fallen in love with her. When she hears of my leaving, she will say that Hamza's son, who desired her, found it a better bargain to escape with his life and return to his camp."

Amar glared at Badiuz Zaman and said, "O worthless creature, what is this new song you have started singing before even returning to your camp! Keep moving or I swear by your father's honor that I will lash you until your skin has fallen off your back!" Badiuz Zaman said, "I would offer you my precious bracelet, which is worth hundreds of thousands of rupees, if you could find some way of uniting me with my beloved! I am in such a state that,

'Either I reach my beloved's side or my soul leaves my body
Between these choices I wager my life."

When Amar heard of the bracelet, he said in a gruff voice, "What do you take me for, a dealer in women? I wouldn't know how to procure girls for you! Tasveer, however, is a princess, and I will see what I can do! Come, hand me the bracelet now!" Badiuz Zaman gave the bracelet to Amar, who led him in the direction from which he had seen Tasveer come.

On the way, Amar showed him the spot where he had found Shagufa and narrated the whole story of his adventures. Badiuz Zaman laughed at Amar's account and they headed onwards.

ᘛᘚ

Ever since Princess Tasveer had returned from sorceress Sharara's garden she was in a state that,

The day passed in lamentations, the night in tears
My life passed in such a manner, with such agony and pain

Prince Badiuz Zaman's face had remained imprinted in her heart. It constantly called out his name.

When the princess's companions and confidants saw her state, they insisted on knowing what passed inside her heart. They said, "Tell us who he is to whom you have lost your heart. Give us the particulars of the despotic tyrant who has reduced you to such a condition that your eyes are constantly tearful, your senses are in disarray and your condition worsens from day to day. Confide in us so that we may find some way of bringing him to you." The princess said, "My malady has no cure. Even the Messiah cannot offer a remedy to my state!"

Her companions said, "May our lives be sacrificed to protect you! Whether it makes you happy or sad, there is no denying that Your Excellency has been in this state ever since she laid eyes on that prisoner." One of them interjected, "And so attractive and fine looking he was, too. I swear by my eyes that my own heart became all aflutter at his sight! It has remained imprisoned in his locks ever since I caught sight of him. The core of my heart has become all bloodied; my eyes have been robbed of all sleep; night and day I long to see his face."

When Tasveer heard these affectionate words from her friends and companions, she finally confessed her love for Prince Badiuz Zaman to them. She ordered her attendants to change into pigeons and ringdoves by magic and fly to Sharara's garden to keep watch and report whatever passed there.

Her attendants first returned with the news that Amar, who was disguised as Shagufa, had been caught. Tasveer became terribly despondent and was in the depths of the doldrums when they brought her the news of Sharara's death. That tulip-cheeked beauty blossomed, and said to her attendants, "Now the prince will be released and he will return to his camp. Go and bring him here and unite the seeker with the sought!" Her attendants departed immediately upon her orders.

ꙮ

Amar was leading Badiuz Zaman on his way when they saw five adolescent beauties coming toward them. The partings in their hair were lined with cinnabar and their bodies were covered with jewelery.

Comely, houri-faced and fairy-like, they cavorted together and stepped with fine comportment and lofty bearing.

They approached the prince's mount and after curtsying before him, said with folded arms, "Our mistress Princess Tasveer sends you her fond greetings and requests the honor of your visit, provided you do not consider it too much of an imposition. You may visit her garden and regale yourself there before carrying on your way."

Amar turned his face away with feigned anger and said, "We do not find sorceresses worthy of our notice and deem them unfit even to carry our chamber pot!" The girls turned a ferocious glance at him. They beheld a thin, wiry man making these remarks. Witty and full of humour as they were, one retorted, "Regard this midget jinn who came back from the dead!" The other said, "To me he seems like a peewee demon!" A third one said, "If you ask me, he is the great ape himself!" Amar replied, "I am a peewee demon who will teach you the lesson of your life!"

Badiuz Zaman said, "Surely, there can be no harm in a short visit and calling on the princess!" Amar said, "Whenever you hear a girl's invitation you fall head-over-heels in love with her. When we return to our camp I will have Hamza put you right once and for all!"

In short order, they accompanied Tasveer's attendants and approached the garden. One of the girls went forth and informed Tasveer of the prince's arrival. She ordered the garden to be decorated and all devices of pleasure to be provided. The carpet keepers quickly laid out carpets of ermine and gold tissue in the building and provided all royal comforts and the apparatus of revelry.

The princess had hardly reached the garden gates to wait for the prince when the sapling of the Lord of the Auspicious Planetary Conjunction's garden came into view riding his mount. As he approached, Badiuz Zaman dismounted and the attendants led away his horse.

Amar also accompanied Badiuz Zaman and, approaching the garden gates, found Tasveer looking their way, gazing like the narcissus. Clad in her embroidered satin dress and draped in gold jewelery, she presented a picture of majestic beauty.

With her one hand placed on the shoulder of her attendants, she came forward and smilingly put her hand in that of Prince Badiuz Zaman. She modestly said, "O Prince of auspicious fortune, you have honored this unworthy slave by deigning to pay her a visit. It is my privilege and pride to receive you!

"Had I notice of your arrival
I would have grown the path with jasmine and roses
I would not have allowed you to set foot on the ground
With the broom of my eyelashes I would have cleaned your soles."

The prince said, "I likewise suffer in your love, my princess,

"The dress I made from your alley's dust
My tears rent into a thousand shreds.

"All praise to the Gatherer of the Separated who brought us together!"

The two of them entered the garden conversing together like the rose and the nightingale.[13] The prince beheld the blossoming garden that was the envy of paradise. It was in full bloom and the foliage and the greenery of its trees mocked the Grove of the Virgin of the Heavens.[14] Its verdure was the envy of the down that grows on the faces of beloveds.

Next to every tree grown by nature, consummate artists had planted one made of jewels, injecting its flowers with the aroma of the original that the zephyr's movement dispersed to perfume the soul's garden.

Regarding the scenery, the two lovers entered the summerhouse where all comforts were provided. A wine tray was laid next to a seat. A bed enchased with gold and jewels, and a bedstead with tester and curtains was spread in the other corner. The place was decorated with mirror lights and carpets patterned with foliage.

After showing the summerhouse to the prince, Tasveer brought Badiuz Zaman to a house by the lake that was decorated like a bride and fully equipped and provided with all the paraphernalia of revelry. A lavish throne was provided there. The two lovers sat down beside each other on the royal carpet spread by the lakeside. Trays of wine were brought. Musicians and dancers were sent for and Venus-faced singers were summoned to entertain them.

Amar sat opposite the couple and began poking fun at them, saying, "Where did you find this ugly woman, O Prince? She has a sty on her eyelid and bald spots all over her head!"

Tasveer was greatly embarrassed to hear these words. Badiuz Zaman said, "My princess, this man is guided in all things by greed. If you were to make him a gift, he would begin singing your praises in no time!" Tasveer made the offering of a chest full of gold and jewels to Amar, who said, "To confer such regal gifts becomes her dignity for she is, after all, royalty. You are a lucky dog indeed Badiuz Zaman that you find yourself beside her, even though you are of humble birth – being the son of a keeper of the House of Kaaba!"[15] Badiuz Zaman said, "Regard O Princess, how he has turned against me!"

Everyone laughed at Amar's jests and the princess filled up a goblet of wine and offered it to Badiuz Zaman, saying, "It is the drink of love, O Prince! Please accept it!"

The prince answered, "O nightingale of the garden of excellence, you are a sorceress and I am a True Believer.

"See how great a difference there is between us.

"It would be difficult to establish friendship between us. If you renounce sorcery, however, I will join you in drinking and will spend my life in submission to your wishes." She answered, "I am not at all versed in sorcery for I am only an adolescent and have not yet learned magic. My time has been spent only in seeking comfort and luxury. Now I will convert to your faith. Mine is the case of the one,

"I am the infidel of love; I need not a truer faith
My every vein binds me to my oath of love."

With these words, Tasveer converted to the True Faith. They began drinking and quaffing cup after cup of roseate wine. Every moment they recited,

"O cupbearer pass the wine in rounds
And dispel all life's troubles from the mind."

As the dancers started performing, Amar began his capers. He took out a pair of scissors from his zambil and hid them between his fingers. Sneaking up behind the dancer, he cut off her gown so dextrously that no one saw it. In the middle of the dance, when the girl twirled, she became completely exposed from behind. Everyone started laughing and she became unnerved. Amar next cut off her gown from the front, and when she turned around she was completely disrobed. The princess called out, "You are a shameless wretch to be dancing like this!" When she looked down and found her gown torn, the dancer sat down from shame and everyone roared with laughter. Badiuz Zaman said, "It is all the doing of Amar!"

The princess could not stop laughing and the dancer cursed Amar Ayyar.

Badiuz Zaman was thus occupied in carousing with the princess when fickle providence became envious of their joy. The lake's waters, which had flowed quietly until now, became suddenly tumultuous. A great noise arose, which unnerved everyone. After a moment, everyone saw a fearsome demon come out of the water carrying a flint sheet. That abominable creature called out, "O Hamza's son, come what may, today you will not escape with your life from my hands!" Badiuz Zaman put himself between the demon and the princess and shouted, "Come face me, O wretch, for you are my prey!"

The demon swung the flint sheet and brought it down on the prince. He ducked and foiled the blow, dealing the demon a sword blow which cut him in two. Those two pieces hit the ground, thrashed about and fell into the water. After a few moments, the same demon again emerged whole of body from the lake and again attacked Badiuz Zaman. The prince again cut him in two and, as before, those parts fell into the lake, the demon became whole of body, and attacked the prince.

One of Tasveer's aides named Nairang, who was witnessing this, said to the princess, "This demon will emerge seven times from the lake in this manner and may be killed seven times. But when he emerges the eighth time, none will be able to kill him and he will overpower the prince." Tasveer said, "Tell me Nairang, if you know some way of killing this demon." She answered, "I only know that your aunt Sharara had deputed this demon to guard you. She had also made and put away a magic bow and three arrows in a chamber in this garden. If someone were to shoot one of those arrows at the demon from that bow he would be killed. But if none of those arrows reaches its mark, the demon will never be killed." Tasveer asked, "Where is the chamber?" Nairang replied, "Sharara had made that chamber invisible to the eye with a spell but now that she is dead, her spell will also be broken and we will see the chamber. If Your Highness were to step with me into the summerhouse, I will try to locate it."

Tasveer went into the summerhouse with Nairang and beheld a chamber she had never seen before. She opened it and saw lying there a bow and three arrows. She rushed with them to the prince, who had killed the demon a fifth time. She told him to shoot him with the arrow when he emerged next.

Badiuz Zaman waited by the lakeside with drawn bow. When the demon came out and rushed at him, Badiuz Zaman fired, aiming at his breast. By the Incomparable Creator's grace, the very first arrow met its mark, pierced the demon, and came out his back. The demon spun and fell to the ground. A blazing flame came out from the hole made by the arrow and burned him to cinder. A great pandemonium arose and after awhile a voice exclaimed, "*Sorcerer Muhafiz the Guard was killed*!"

Badiuz Zaman bowed his head in gratitude before the Judge of Mankind's Needs and comforted and consoled the princess.

Amar had put on the cape of invisibility the moment the demon appeared. He thought, *Now it is for Badiuz Zaman and the princess to decide on the course of action they wish to follow. The idiot has invited this calamity on himself. If it were for me he would have been comfortably home by now. I will now return to Hamza and tell him his son has been corrupted, and narrate his escapades.*

When the demon was killed, Amar showed himself again and said, "Beware O worthless boy! Leave this instant and hurry away, otherwise another misfortune will soon befall us!"

Badiuz Zaman said to Tasveer, "I will now take your leave!" She replied, "I will also come with you as I have nothing left to keep me here. When these tidings reach Afrasiyab, I will surely be put to death." Badiuz Zaman asked the attendants to bring his horse and, seating the princess by his side, said to the attendants, "You are merely the attendants. No one will take you to task for what happened here. Once we leave you may also depart to where you wish, or join us at our camp." Then Prince Badiuz Zaman headed for his camp with Amar.

Emperor Afrasiyab was waiting expectantly in the Apple Garden for Sharara to send him Amar's head when the whirlwinds brought Sharara's corpse there instead, and her magic spirits called out, "*O Emperor of Sorcerers, Sharara was killed!*" Afrasiyab became crimson with rage. He looked into the *Book of Sameri* to discover the whereabouts of Sharara's killer and of Badiuz Zaman, who had been in her prison. He discovered how Amar had killed Sharara, how both he and Badiuz

Zaman had arrived in Tasveer's garden, how Badiuz Zaman had killed the sorcerer Muhafiz, and how Amar and Badiuz Zaman were now headed for their camp with Princess Tasveer.

Sorcerer Azhdar Dragon-Mouth

Emperor Afrasiyab immediately recited an incantation and clapped. The sorcerer Azhdar Dragon-Mouth emerged from the ground spewing fire from his mouth, nose and ears, and made a salutation to Afrasiyab. Silver crescents covered his entire body and from elbow to shoulder idols were tied to his arms. Afrasiyab said, "Hasten O Azhdar, and detain Badiuz Zaman and Tasveer, who are headed with Amar toward the camp of the True Believers. Imprison them in the prison chamber of Hoshruba! But do not take Amar prisoner, instead allow him to return to Hamza and give him the news. That will terrify Hamza and he will desist from stepping into this land."

Azhdar Dragon-Mouth left immediately.

Badiuz Zaman had come many miles from Tasveer's garden when suddenly Azhdar Dragon-Mouth emerged from a bush in the shape of a dragon and blocked their path. Amar immediately put on the cape of invisibility but the prince rode ahead to confront the beast, and shot an arrow at him. The dragon spewed out a ball of fire and burned the arrow in flight. Badiuz Zaman shot many arrows, which the dragon burned likewise. Then the dragon opened his mouth and, drawing in air, swallowed Badiuz Zaman and Tasveer whole.

Amar Ayyar hurled many stones at Azhdar Dragon-Mouth with his sling, but none of them touched him. The dragon called out, "Go and narrate this event to Hamza, O Amar, and warn him that this is the wilderness of the tilism and he is forewarned against trespassing within its bounds. It is impossible for Badiuz Zaman to be released now. Hamza should reconcile himself to never again seeing his son, for anyone who comes here to rescue him will suffer a similar fate and be killed. I did not have orders to capture you, otherwise you would not have escaped me either!"

Azhdar Dragon-Mouth then disappeared and Amar headed for Hamza's camp, weeping and wailing, rending his tunic and throwing ashes on his head.

After traversing his journey, Amar arrived in the court where Amir Hamza was giving attendance. Amar made a salutation and sat on his Hoopoe Throne.[16] Amir Hamza and the king and all the chieftains asked him about his exploits. After offering the ritual salutations and blessings, Amar narrated the whole story of Badiuz Zaman and Princess Tasveer. Amir Hamza replied, "All praise to the Lord of Creation that my son still lives. We must find a way to conquer the tilism. For the present we have a battle on hand with Suleiman Amber-Hair. Once I have taken care of this matter, I will nominate someone to conquer Hoshruba." Amir Hamza then busied himself with preparations for the battle.

Of Suleiman Amber-Hair Sending a Missive to Emperor of Hoshruba Afrasiyab to Come to Laqa's Aid, and of Afrasiyab Dispatching Sorcerer Ijlal Against Amir Hamza with Forty Thousand Sorcerers, and of Amar Ayyar's Trickeries

The wonder workers of the book of eloquence and the composers of rarities of speech describe the court of rhetoric with a sorcerer's pen and paint it with these colorful words of the tale:

When Amir Hamza's armies (in whose footsteps victory follows) entered Mount Agate in pursuit of Laqa, Suleiman Amber-Hair beheld Amir Hamza's numerous forces, his equipage and retinue, and realized he would be unable to fight such a mighty army alone. He sent out missives with this message to the kings of the bordering lands:

> "Lord Laqa has sought refuge with me after suffering reverses at the hands of Hamza. You must needs rush to his aid, not out of any consideration for me but because he is your God. You must kill his foes and restore him to his divine throne. If you make delay after reading these words, the wrath of His Lordship will wipe you out of existence. His Lordship Laqa indulges these creatures who persecute him only out of mercy. He desists from killing them and maintains that these creatures were made in the reveries of his drunken sleep. As he was oblivious of himself in the ecstasies of his inebriation, his pen of destiny wrote them down as rebellious and vain. Now that destiny cannot be altered. It is for this reason that our Lord is unable to efface their existence and is so wroth with

> them that when these creatures beseech him with their contrite pleas, he scorns them and flies away from them. Seeing no hope of their redemption in Lord Laqa, these creatures have vowed wholesale rebellion against him. It is therefore incumbent upon you to arrive here post-haste to assist our Lord."

Having written this, Suleiman Amber-Hair sent it out to all the kings of the lands of Kohistan. He also wrote a letter to Afrasiyab, the Master of the Tilism, and dispatched it to the mountain situated between Mount Agate and Hoshruba. A wooden mallet and a magic drum were kept atop it for communication between the two lands. Whenever a message from Suleiman was received, the drum was struck and Afrasiyab sent a magic claw to fetch the message.

After Afrasiyab had sent for the letter and read it, he wrote the following reply and sent it to the mountaintop:

> "It is a great honor for me to come to the aid of Lord Laqa. He must wish to bestow honor on his slaves by not destroying his rebellious creatures himself, instead seeking one of his minions to distinguish himself in the campaign. Lord Laqa's will be done! Hamza and his armies are of absolutely no consequence. I hereby send a mighty sorcerer in Lord Laqa's service at the head of a forty-thousand-strong army of sorcerers. He will destroy the entire army of Hamza upon arrival in just one day."

Suleiman Amber-Hair's messenger awaited the reply. He brought it at once before his master, whom it pleased immensely, and Suleiman Amber-Hair began preparation for battle.

Sorcerer Ijlal

Leaving him busy with these arrangements, we return to Afrasiyab, who, after sending his reply, recited an incantation and clapped, whereupon a wisp of cloud materialized in the skies and descended to the ground. The sorcerer Ijlal, who was a king of one of the sixty thousand lands of Hoshruba and commanded an army of forty thousand sorcerers, dismounted that cloud, bowed to Afrasiyab, and asked, "Why has my master sent for me?" Afrasiyab said, "Lord Laqa has arrived in Mount Agate. He is being pestered by some creatures who have earned divine wrath and condemnation. Go forth and destroy them and rid Lord Laqa of their evil." Ijlal answered, "As you please!" He rode the cloud back to his abode and commanded his army to get ready to march. Then he prepared himself for the journey and warfare and mounted a magic dragon. All his sorcerers also sat on magic swans, demoiselle cranes, flamingos, peacocks and dragons made of paper and lentil flour. Wielding tridents and pentadents and carrying their apparatus of sorcery in sacks of gold cloth hanging from their necks, they departed toward Mount Agate with great pomp and ceremony, dripping wax over flaming, chaffing dishes and burning *gugal*[17] to cast spells.

Suleiman Amber-Hair and Laqa were seated in the royal palace in Mount Agate when suddenly a dark cloud filled the sky, a whirlwind began to blow and hailstones started falling. Familiar with these signs, Suleiman Amber-Hair realized they heralded the arrival of a sorcerer and immediately departed with the nobles of his court to receive him. Upon reaching the fort's gates, he beheld Ijlal arriving with his forty thousand sorcerers displaying their magic works. They were clad in saffron-colored waistcloths, and the leaves of sweet marjoram, thorn apples, and swallow wort were stuck in their belts.

Suleiman greeted them and conducted them into the fortress where Laqa sat on a throne. Ijlal and his companions prostrated themselves before him and made offerings. Ijlal sat to the right of Laqa's throne.

Suleiman lodged Ijlal's army in a scenic place and arranged a feast in his honor in the garden adjacent to the palace.

The garden was lavishly decorated for the occasion. Charming cupbearers, singers as musical as Venus, courtesans as beautiful as the moon, and jasmine-bosomed musicians presented themselves. Laqa adjourned the court and retired to that garden to indulge in pleasant diversions.

The spies carried all these tidings to Amir Hamza. He said, "Our protector is the One God who has no partners." Amar Ayyar, who was present in the court, said, "O Amir, ever since I arrived here, I have not set foot inside the fortress of Mount Agate. Now I desire to see its sights and witness the feast given for Ijlal." Hamza replied, "They are all sorcerers. Be warned! They might recognize and arrest you." Amar Ayyar answered, "Let what is destined come to pass! I wish to do a little commerce inside the fort." Hamza replied with a smile, "Then go in God's name. I, for one, would never bar you from conducting your business."

Sporting all his trickster's apparatus, Amar Ayyar headed for Mount Agate. Upon seeing some officers of Suleiman Amber-Hair's army deputed at the fortress gates, he disguised himself as a sorcerer. Then he went forth wearing clogs, a saffron waistcloth and a sack around his neck, and idols tied to his upper arm. Those who saw him did not accost him, taking him for one of the sorcerers from Ijlal's army.

Amar entered the city and found himself in a bustling marketplace with grand-looking shops on both sides of the stone-paved street. Leafy *maulsari*[18] trees lined the street on two sides and buyers, sellers, visitors, and all description of humanity thronged the place, which rang with the clinking of water-carriers' bowls and brokers' loud voices. Besides the crowds that thronged every quarter, Amar saw well-built buildings and a profusion of fine, stylish and captivating chambers. In the course of his perambulations, he arrived near the royal palace and observed the attendants heading to the garden where a feast had been arranged in Ijlal's honor. Amar accompanied them there and beheld the lavish scale of the festivities and the sumptuous arrangements that had been made for the occasion. He regarded a breezy and most wondrously refreshing garden nurtured by the True Gardener's bountiful hand. It rang with the carolling of birds and was redolent with myriad-colored blossoms.

The glow of lamps in the garden by the lake recalled to one's mind the radiance of lovers' hearts. A sumptuous carpet had been spread there, and Ijlal sat on a throne watching the dance. It was a carefree and happy picture with Suleiman Amber-Hair attending upon Ijlal, and wine being drunk.

Absorbed in these sights, Amar stationed himself behind Ijlal. He noticed a building in front of Ijlal's throne from where every so often a beauty gazed at Ijlal after parting the curtains hanging at the entrance. Amar saw that Ijlal's eyes were also fixed on her. With the assembly absorbed in the dance recital, nobody noticed that Ijlal's attention was elsewhere. Amar thought that perhaps that garden was adjacent to Suleiman Amber-Hair's harem and the women were watching the dance recital from its doors and rooftop. He reckoned that the one watching Ijlal's was perhaps one of Suleiman Amber-Hair's wives or daughters. Amar moved toward the house and stood by the curtain.

When one of the female attendants came out, Amar said to her, "My wife is in the queen's service. I would be indebted to you if you could send her out." The attendant replied, "It's the king's daughter, Princess Nasreen Amber-Hair, who is watching the dance from behind the curtain. The queen is in another room to which I don't have access. You may inquire about your wife in the room to your right." Amar answered, "Very well!" and moved away, having learned that it was the princess with whom Ijlal was exchanging glances.

Amar now thought of some trickery. He went to a deserted corner of the garden and disguised himself as a macebearer. He tied a turban and pinned it with a medal, put on a singlet of crinkled cloth and, sporting a flowing white beard and wielding a staff of vermiculated metalwork, he stationed himself near the door, resting his back against the wall with the curtain's folds caught behind him. When Princess Nasreen tried to lift the curtain, she found it stuck and tried to pull it out. Amar called out, "If that happens once more I will report to the king that the women behind this curtain make overtures to Ijlal."

The princess was stunned and mortified to hear that. She did not try to look out again, certain that if she did, the macebearer who witnessed her indiscretion would report her to her father.

When Ijlal noticed that the door from where the girl was gazing out at him was now blocked by an old macebearer, he became restless and wished to have him removed. However, he was unable to do anything about it because he realized that if King Suleiman found out, it would grieve him to learn that Ijlal showed designs on his harem by having the macebearer removed from his post of duty.

However, Ijlal grew more restless with every passing moment and he continued to look toward the door that Amar had blocked. Amar now made a sign to Ijlal indicating that he wished to speak to him privately. Reckoning that the macebearer must be the girl's confidant and carried a message from her, Ijlal got up from his seat. King Suleiman thought he had retired to answer the call of nature. Ijlal did not take any attendants along. Gesturing to Amar to follow him, he went to a flower garden and asked Amar why he had signalled to him.

Amar blessed Ijlal and replied, "O noble king, this slave has been Princess Nasreen Amber-Hair's attendant since her childhood and has raised her from an infant. She keeps no secrets from me. She has fallen in love with you and sends the message that if you truly love her you must ask her father to have a house reserved for you, to which only you and your most trusted and devoted sorcerers have access. You may order your sorcerers to fly her bed to your dwelling from the roof of her palace where she would be asleep at the appointed time. She will spend the night with you and in the morning the sorcerers may return her to her house. It was to convey this message that I sought a private moment with you. Now tell me when you will send for the princess so that I may tell her to sleep on the roof of her palace on that day."

Ijlal was in seventh heaven. He conferred his pearl necklace upon Amar and replied, "I would shower you with riches. Tell the princess that I too languish in separation from her. I shall have the house reserved today and the princess may go to sleep on the roof tomorrow evening when I will send for her."

After securing this promise Amar said to him, "Now you may go and make the preparations." Ijlal returned ecstatic to the assembly and began watching the dance recital as before.

Amar went back to the curtained door and entered the harem wearing his cape of invisibility. There he beheld Princess Nasreen Amber-Hair sitting with her attendants and watching the dance recital. Amar uncovered his head and limbs and approached the princess, proclaiming: "I am the Martyr No Torso and shall devour you all!" Seeing the spectre, the princess and her attendants fell on their faces in terror. Amar rubbed a drug-potion on their faces to render them unconscious. After hurriedly locking the chamber from the inside, he sat down to disguise himself as the princess. After putting on the princess's clothes he put her into the zambil. Once he was done with the disguise, he administered a restorative drug to the attendants, who came to their senses and found the princess beside them.

When the attendants were fully recovered, they said to the false princess, "O Princess of the World, in the name of Lord Laqa, let us leave this house; otherwise that monster will eat us up." She answered, "I proved of a stronger constitution than you crazy girls. I kept my senses when all of you had fainted." They said, "May our lives be sacrificed to protect yours. Come what may, we will not allow you to stay here a moment longer."

Without any suspicion, they conducted the false princess to the royal palace where she saw a most lavishly decorated house with numerous rooms and balconies, and a summerhouse replenished with all delights. Colorful drapes hung from every portico. The place was appointed with royal comforts and had a profusion of lattices and tapestries.

On arrival, the false princess ordered her bed to be made and a golden throne provided for her. Her slave girls began decorating Princess Nasreen's chamber. In this manner, the false princess learned the whereabouts of Princess Nasreen's bedroom. She retired there and lay down in great comfort.

Leaving the false Princess Nasreen reposing there, let us return to Ijlal. He requested King Suleiman to provide him a secluded house outside the city where he could prepare magic to deploy against Hamza. Suleiman gave orders that a house be provided for Ijlal and all furnishings and other comforts be arranged for him. The royal servants immediately furnished one in a royal garden outside the city.

Now Amar Ayyar's son, Chalak, had also entered Mount Agate, secretly following Amar in disguise so that in the event of his father's capture, he might secure his release. When Chalak witnessed the royal retainers hiring labourers to carry Ijlal's effects to the garden, he disguised himself as a laborer and offered his services. Pearl-strung canopies, tents, ceiling cloths and other such paraphernalia were being sent to the garden on laborers' shoulders and carts. Chalak was also given a carpet to carry there. He brought it to the garden and handed it to the servants. Afterwards, he asked, "Tell me if there's something else to do here so that I may consider my work done." They asked him to stay awhile and went and told Ijlal that the house had been furnished and they awaited his pleasure to set up the bed where he desired. Ijlal told them to send it to the roof.

The retainers accordingly ordered Chalak and other servants, who began moving the furniture to the roof. A lavish carpet was spread on the floor, the canopies were set up, the jewel-encrusted bedstead was placed and a gilded throne was arranged next to it on the carpet. The wine service was arranged opposite the water repository. When all these arrangements were complete, the laborers came down from the roof. Chalak however, hid himself under the bed and covered himself with a corner of the carpet.

When paying off the laborers, the retainers noticed that one laborer had not come to receive his wages. Confident that he would come to collect them by himself, they went and told Ijlal that everything was ready for him.

In the meanwhile, dawn had broken and the feast given by Suleiman Amber-Hair was at an end. After taking leave of his host, Ijlal retired to his house in the garden. He sent for the commanders of his army and told them he would be busy in creating new magic, and until sent for they must not disturb him. Ijlal took along his two companions, Intizam the Arranger and Munsarim the Organizer, and arrived in the garden. He saw it was the envy of paradise and blossomed as if it had been visited by a thousand springs. Every tree there was lushly blessed by the Gardener of Nature and every flower was rich with golden pollen.

Ijlal retired to the roof and, because he had remained up all night long, went to sleep on the bed while his companions occupied themselves in the garden. The day passed in this manner.

The false Princess Nasreen, on the other hand, remained busy all day dressing and beautifying herself with the princess's clothes and jewels. After four watches remained to nightfall, she ordered the attendants to take her bed to the roof as she desired to lie in the moonlight. The bed was set up on the roof. Screens of flowers were erected, carafes of rose-water and perfumes were unsealed, and bouquets were placed all around her. When every trapping of luxury was provided, the attendants said to the false princess, "May our lives be sacrificed to protect yours! Your bed is ready."

The false Nasreen headed for the roof in the company of beauties as lovely as the moon. She sat down on her throne and sent for some fruit.

As she sat offering the largesse of her beauty
Even the moon stood begging in the blue sky

The splendor of the false princess's beauty in the silver glow of the moonlight, her henna-tinged hands and feet, and the parting of her hair lined with strung pearls, which made even the Milky Way burn in envy, was a sight to behold. The false princess was like the resplendent moon of the sky of excellence around whom her attendants fluttered gracefully like Greek partridges.[19]

For one watch of the night they busied themselves in merriment and pleasantries. After some more time had passed, the false Nasreen lay down on the bed and, covering her face with a veil, feigned sleep. Her attendants lay down on the carpet around her but Amar, disguised as the false princess, was wide awake, wondering what would next transpire, and awaited God's marvels.

After a watch of the night had passed, Ijlal said to his companions, sorcerers Intizam the Arranger and Munsarim the Organizer, "I wish to confide a secret to you. If you could keep it to yourselves and carry out my wishes, I will richly reward you and appoint you the commanders of my army." They answered, "Just say the word; we will cut off our heads with our own hands and put them at your feet. Order what you will and your slaves will carry it out. As to secrecy, our own ears will not hear a word from our lips."

Ijlal said, "Bravo! I could not have asked for more! Hear then that I am enamored of Princess Nasreen Amber-Hair and she too pines away for love of me. We have made a pact that I will send for her tonight. You will find her sleeping on the roof of her palace. You should cast a spell on the other women you find there so that they do not awaken while the princess is gone, and the alarm is not raised."

Ijlal's deputies replied, "This task is hardly beyond our power. Your slaves shall carry out your orders this very instant."

Sorcerers Intizam the Arranger and Munsarim the Organizer recited an incantation, flew away, and presently arrived at Princess Nasreen's house.

They found the false princess lost in sweet sleep. One leg of her pants had slid up to her thigh, the other leg hung over the edge of the bed. Her body was covered in gold and jewels. The skirt of her chemise had been raised, revealing a stomach that shone like a silver tablet. Her hair had come loose and tendrils were stuck to her neck. In her youthful sleep she was wholly oblivious of where her hands were placed, how revealing was the angle of her legs, or what was covered and what lay open. From a distance, the sorcerers recited a spell that made the attendants sleeping beside the false princess's bed fall unconscious. A cold breeze began blowing and lulled to sleep all those who were still awake. The two sorcerers came down and lifted up the false princess's bed.

She was wide awake and realized that Ijlal had sent for her. She gave her fate into the hands of the Beneficent One and kept silent while the sorcerers conducted her bed speedily to Ijlal and placed it before him.

Ijlal had been counting every moment with great eagerness and was delighted to see them arrive with the false princess's bed. He said to them, "Now you may retire to take some rest and make sure nobody is allowed upstairs. You too must not come up without my first summoning you."

The sorcerers stepped downstairs, conferred and decided that one of them should take a nap while the other kept watch in case Ijlal sends for them for any reason.

In the meanwhile, Ijlal approached the false princess and removed the veil from her luminous face. He beheld a beauty so dazzling that even the eyes of old man heavens[20] never saw such in all his years, nor the ears of Creation ever heard. The brilliant bolt of her beauty blinded his eyes.

That moon-like beauty was the envy of Venus
She was the Beauty Fairy

Her luminous figure, beautifully cast
How to describe it? Call it a flame or the Light of Tur?[21]
The mole on her face was a garden of beauty
Her two cheeks two fields where moonbeams grew
Her lovely face surmounted with curls and locks
Was a sun that carried on its shoulders night
Her delicate ears, more fragile than petals
With their shapeliness made envious the oysters
Her neck was the door of the house of light
As luminous as if it were the house of sun
How to describe her bodice's tight and true fit
And how to describe how her breasts it embraced
She sported a lovely gold thread chemise
With perfect stateliness and grace
Her tightly wrapped, fitting dress
Seemed the vision of light in moon's garb
To describe her abdomen is to describe
The moon appearing from the constellation of Light
Finer than hair was her waist and delicate
To carry even the weight of hair she was averse
Let us now sing of her concealed beauty
To satisfy those whose pleasure such things are
The roundness of her hips as two crescents can't be described
To call them peerless and without compare is more just
The vision of her swelling thighs full of vigor
A thousand souls as sacrifice from lovers would claim
Her soles softer than rose petals were
A rosebed felt to them harsher than thorns
More than life itself anyone who beheld her loved
That marvel of delicate beauty that she was

Ijlal was near to fainting at the sight when he came to his senses and began massaging the false princess's legs. She turned over and got up and began calling out to her maids. Ijlal laid his head at the false princess's feet and submitted, "Your attendants are not present but this slave is at hand to carry out your wishes."

The false princess frowned at Ijlal and sat up, adjusting her dress. She tied up her loose hair in a bun with her face turned away from Ijlal, while swinging her dangling legs from the bed.

Seeing her coquettish ways, Ijlal became ever more enamoured of her. He began pacing around the false princess, who said, "What is this? Are you a jinn or a spectre? Who has brought me here? Whose house is this?" Ijlal answered, "O Life of the World and Comforter of Lovers' Hearts, this slave carried out all that your personal macebearer suggested."

Then Ijlal narrated to her his whole conversation with the old macebearer. The false princess smirked, got up smoothing her dress, and said, "O accursed sorcerer! O wily traitor! I shall return barefoot to my house now and suitably punish the old dotard who has accused me of such horrible lies and vilified me by branding me as your beloved. He will long rue his deed. Then I shall report this to my father and have him write Afrasiyab too, so that a cur like you may be expelled from Hoshruba. How dare you extend your hand to molest the honor of kings and corrupt daughters of good men?"

Ijlal was frightened out of his wits by her angry speech. He began importuning her, and said, "O Princess of the World! O my mistress! Do have a moment's rest in this place so that I may prove myself in your service and then have you conducted to your palace." The false princess replied, "You should go and prove yourself in the service of your mother or sisters. If you ever utter such words before me again you will live to regret them." Ijlal again entreated, "O Princess, do take a seat on the throne for a moment so that I may regale myself with your beauty's garden, and like a gardener feast my eyes on your unearthly charms. I have no other desire but to behold your splendor. O bliss of lovers' souls, O Empress of Beauties, I am your humble slave!"

Ijlal fell down at the false princess's feet. Noticing his entreaties and prostrations, she got up and jauntily walked up to the seat and sat down.

Ijlal meekly stood before her.

If the house is empty and you are with your beloved alone
You are pious indeed if you then restrain your desire

Every now and then Ijlal tried to extend a lustful hand toward her, but each time she either frowned at him or made an angry face. At other times she sighed to herself. Sometimes she beamed at him and hurled thunderbolts of calamity on the garden of Ijlal's soul, wounding him with the daggers of her smiles. In this manner they made overtures to each other, and lust on one hand and sham modesty on the other contended with each other.

When Ijlal's protestations increased, the false princess said to him, "You are nothing but a fatheaded fool given to empty talk. Where is the salt that would give savour to this love feast? You serve neither wine nor meat, and yet make all these love vows! Is this how you do your duty as a host by selfishly craving only your desires? Indeed, it is true that the essence of men is kneaded with selfishness. You specially have not the least trace of friendliness. Your only care is to achieve your purpose and show scant regard for me."

Embarrassed, Ijlal realized that she spoke truly because wine would dispel her inhibitions. After a few cups, she would cast off her modesty and he would then attain his desire. He sensed that his slumbering fortunes had now awoken and it was only a matter of time before he would find the beautiful princess in his arms. Ijlal immediately brought wine and platters of roast meat. He picked up an ewer and poured out the rose-colored wine in a crystalline goblet. Carrying the cup on his palm, he presented it to the false princess, saying, "Here is the elixir of love. Drink it and be merry and blissful!"

The false princess held the cup in her delicate hand and, turning her head sideways and sighing, put it to her lips. Immediately, she made a face and threw the wine on Ijlal's face. She said, "For shame! You call yourself a king but drink cheap wines. Indeed, the cheapest brew would be a hundred times better than what you served me. This wine is not fit for me." Ijlal answered, "O Princess, I am away from my homeland and do not have access to my possessions. What I offered you came from the wine service of your own father." The false Nasreen answered, "Royalty has recourse to all manner of comforts always. It wouldn't have caused you any great trouble to send for fine wine on the occasion of my visit. But why would you, with only your own selfish concerns at heart, ever consider such a thing? Now I have fallen into your clutches and shall serve out my fate's decree."

The false princess produced a flask of wine from her bosom. She filled a goblet with Ijlal's wine and put a few drops in it from her flask, which made the wine's color turn pink. Placing the goblet on her painted hand resplendent like the sun, she offered it to Ijlal, saying, "O uncaring man, I shall now be the cupbearer and you may drink this goblet of favour from my hands."

Seeing this munificence on the part of his beautiful cupbearer, Ijlal became ecstatic. He took the goblet from the hands of that beauty and emptied it.

Heaven's mercy! Those drops that the false princess had added from her wine flask were a most potent drug. Ijlal's head suddenly spun. He said, "O Princess, indeed you drink a heady wine. Just one sip made me lose my head." She answered, "Get up and walk around. It will refresh you. You will experience a new marvel with this wine."

Ijlal got up but he had hardly taken a few steps before he was taken unconscious and fell to the floor. The false princess drew a dagger from her bag and bore down upon Ijlal to behead him.

Amar's son Chalak had witnessed all these proceedings from under the bed and wondered about the true identity of the princess. When he saw that she had drugged Ijlal and meant to kill him, he realized it must be his father in disguise. While he marvelled at Amar's spectacular trickery, he realized that it would not do to kill Ijlal. He came out from under the bed and Amar, who was about to behead Ijlal, now sprang at him. Chalak foiled his blow and said, "I am your son, Chalak!"

Amar asked, "What are you doing here, O idiot? Why did you stop me from killing this sorcerer who is Amir Hamza's enemy?" Chalak replied, "My worthy father, when a sorcerer dies his magic spirits make heaven and Earth one with their cries. If you had beheaded him the commotion would have attracted the attention of his deputies, who are on duty downstairs and you would have been captured."

Amar replied, "What you say is true. What must I do now?" Chalak answered, "Change your disguise to Ijlal's while I disguise myself as Princess Nasreen and lie in her bed. Put Ijlal into your zambil and send for his deputies to return the princess to her palace. In this way we will depart without hazard and think of some new trickery for what may transpire next."

Amar found Chalak's plan to his liking. They both changed into their new disguises and the sorcerers Intizam the Arranger and Munsarim the Organizer were sent for, who conveyed the false princess's bed to her palace. Then they recited another spell to awaken the attendants who had fainted. Afterwards, they returned to the false Ijlal.

Princess Nasreen's attendants woke up to find it was close to daybreak. They busied themselves with their duties and after a while Chalak disguised as Nasreen also rose yawning and stretching. Amar had already told Chalak the location of the princess's chamber and the names of her attendants. The false Nasreen came down with them from the roof. She retired to her bedchamber and occupied herself with pleasant diversions.

In the morning the false Ijlal presented himself with his companions in Suleiman Amber-Hair's court where everyone received him with great honor. He took his seat and said, "O My Lord, lead your armies out of the fortress so that I may destroy Hamza's forces and return triumphant to Emperor Afrasiyab."

Laqa told Suleiman Amber-Hair to send the officers of the camp and the army commanders to prepare to march out of the fortress to fight Hamza. The tents, pavilions and tabernacles were packed and carted out and preparations for the battle with Hamza began.

Amir Hamza was giving audience in his court when the spies deputed in Suleiman's court presented themselves and, after visiting blessings on him, reported that Suleiman Amber-Hair was resolved on war and his forces were marching out of the fort. Accompanied by his commanders, Amir Hamza stood at the entrance of his pavilion to witness the foe's arrival.

Presently, the gates of the fortress of Mount Agate were thrown open and elephants carrying the banners of war poured out. Behind them marched a force of sixty thousand troopers wearing cuirasses and coats of mail. As they advanced shoulder to shoulder and row after row on tall steeds, the rattling of their arms and armor deafened even the ears of the heavens. Seventy thousand foot-soldiers walked behind them carrying fiery projectiles, swords and bows. Filled with arrows, their quivers looked like preening peacocks. The army of sorcerers wearing hoops and earrings followed, riding magic dragons and lions.

The false Ijlal led the army astride a magic dragon. He was dressed in a resplendent robe with a sorcerer's satchel hung around his neck and wore a *nau-ratan* bracelet[22] and a king's crown on his head. Using the ruse that he was saving up his magic for the battlefield, he had ordered sorcerers Intizam the Arranger and Munsarim the Organizer to make a magic dragon for him. They walked beside the magic dragon holding its saddle straps and showered flames and stones around them with their spells. Shouting the praises of gods Sameri and Jamshed and displaying the marvels of their magic, the sorcerers soon passed into the battlefield.

Behind their procession, forty elephants chained together brought forward Laqa's encrusted throne surmounted by its pearl canopy. Beside Laqa sat Naushervan's son, Faramurz. The bird of ill omen, the Lord Swine of Faith and the Prince of Infidels, to wit Bakhtiarak the Faithless, sat fanning Laqa with his kerchief. Laqa's throne was surrounded by many sanguinary commanders from different warrior tribes, who marched astride fairy-faced steeds.

They were followed by a several-hundred-thousand-strong force led by the commanders of Faramurz's army. Suleiman Amber-Hair's forces brought up the rear, led into the battlefield by his army commanders.

Amir Hamza beheld the foe's vast armies and, turning his heart to thoughts of God, said, "O Lord! The foe's army is like an army of ants and locusts, but You are Mighty and Unsurpassable still." Amir ordered his army to bivouac bordering the arena.

The war drums and timbals were sounded as he took command of his forces.

A very large, numerous army came out
The Earth started shaking, the sky filled with fear
The dust from Earth rose to the pinnacle of heavens
Column after column rolled out, warrior after warrior marched

Luxurious pavilions were set up. The pegs, poles and stakes were organized and screens were erected. Row after row of tents, canopies and enclosures filled the camp. The commanders were provided pavilions while the troopers were housed in tents. As the army was lodged, shopkeepers, traders, greengrocers, butchers and bakers spread out and set up shops. A magistrate was deputed for every section of the bazaar. The busy shops presented the picture of the bazaar of a metropolis.

Before long it was evening. Glass lights were lit in the camp along the passageways and lamps were kindled in shops. Everyone in the camp returned to their allotted stations and four commanders were deputed to keep vigil with several thousand troopers under their command. The magistrates began their rounds and culprits were taken to task. The horns trilled and cries of "Keep awake! Keep alert!" rang out.

Both armies remained on alert, camped by the battlefield for one day and one night. The next day in the evening, the false Ijlal ordered his sorcerers to beat the drums of war. Suleiman Amber-Hair, Laqa and all the kings present there ordered their armies to follow suit. Champions of the day of skirmishing and lions of the forest of carnage struck the kettledrums for battle. The field of carnage boomed and the vault of heaven reverberated with the sound.

The spies brought the news to Amir Hamza. After bowing to him, they proclaimed, "May you enjoy the wealth of longevity longer than Khizr and your treasury be richer than Kaikhusrau's. May the foe of dark fortune waver and be routed before your might. Today the drums of war have been struck in the impure camp of the infidels, and their whole army of eunuchs is bent on waging war. It is certain that tomorrow they will descend in the arena to fan the fires of strife and mischief. As to the rest, all is in a good way."

Amir Hamza looked toward King Saad who said, "O Amir, order by the Almighty's consent, grace and succor that drums of war should answer from our camp, too, and the Timbal of Sikander be struck. May what the Scribe of Fortune and the Writer of Destiny has engraved on our brows come to pass."[23]

The tricksters headed where the Timbal of Sikander and the Music Band of Suleiman were kept. The cover of the Timbal of Sikander had been removed and the masters of the kettledrums stood ready. They had awaited the king's orders ever since the enemy's kettledrums had been heard. When the tricksters delivered the word, they struck the timbal. The Earth and the heavens trembled at its sound, the Eagle of the Heavens[24] fluttered its wings in terror at the blast, the Bull of the Earth[25] felt its heart sink. The whole world was shaken from mountains to the deserts.

Amir Hamza's camp heard the call to battle. Young and old, the brave and renowned alike were alerted that come the dawn, the Angel of Death would ply his trade in men's lives: that heads would fly off necks and garlands of wounds would be distributed. The king adjourned his court early and every commander returned to his designated pavilion. The final preparations for skirmishing and battle were made. The swords were polished and furbished and the bows heated and straightened over the fire.

While the courageous occupied their minds with maneuvers for the battlefield, the cowardly scratched their faces with despair. The valiant observed enemy positions with joyous interest and lily-livered ones racked their minds to find some avenue of escape. While the faces of the gallant were ruddy with valor as they surveyed their coats of mail, helm and armor, the craven stared blankly with blanched faces.

In the enemy camp, the clapper-drums were beaten; chillies and fragrant gum-resin smouldered in fires. Sorcerers wrought their magic and outlined magic circles with blood on the ground. The pitch-faced magic spirit Kalva was being summoned in every corner. Two watches into the night, criers circulated in both camps to raise the warriors' spirits. The camps rang with these sounds throughout the night. Finally it was time for the Emperor of the Russet Throne of the East[26] to make his appearance with all its magnificence and grandeur. The darkness of the night fled in disarray before the advance guard of dawn.

At sunrise, fully armed troopers and warriors from both camps began pouring into the battlefield in strings, arrays and groups. Amir Hamza said his morning prayers in his Roving Prayer Tent and solicited the Lord Almighty's help. Raising his hands in prayer, he asked for victory in the court of God and entreated that the Unsurpassable and Mighty One return him triumphant against the army of villains.

"You who are eternal in Your kingdom
You who represent the morn in night's darkness
Humble me, I have before me a huge task
Solve it for You are the only aid of mine."

As Amir was engrossed in his prayers, Muqbil Vafadar, commander of the archers and noble Amir Hamza's slave, presented himself and said, "Amen!" When Amir inquired about his army's readiness, Muqbil replied,

"The two armies descended in the arena
Together assembled are in vastness a Mount Qaf.

"They await the august arrival of Your Lordship." Amir said, "Bring my chest of weapons." Muqbil produced the chest in which Amir Hamza's arms and armor were kept. Amir Hamza decorated his august and distinguished self with the holy accoutrements, sporting the helm of Hud, the mail of Daud, the bow of Saleh, the spear of Sam, and foot-guards, thigh guards and cuirass, and stepped out.

He found his groom waiting for him, holding the reins of his steed, Ashqar Demon-Born, which was fully caparisoned and saddled. The groom saluted Amir and presented the horse. Ashqar neighed with pleasure at the sight of his master. Amir Hamza traced with his finger the letters 'Help O Ali!'[27] on his steed's neck and put his distinction-bestowing foot in the stirrup that eagerly awaited it. He raised himself into the saddle holding the horse's mane. The rein holder adjusted the folds of Amir Hamza's robe and all the onlookers loudly exclaimed, "In the name of Allah!"

Holding his dragon-like, two-pronged spear in his right hand, and catching in his left the reins of his steed that was Zephyr's envy, Amir recited the *naad-e Ali*[28] and spurred Ashqar Demon-Born.

After sending their respective forces into the battlefield, Amir Hamza's five hundred and fifty-five commanders and progeny presented themselves before him with great majesty. Among his commanders were:

Karit Shield-Whirler
Noman bin Munzir Shah Yemeni
Aamir Rodbari

Saif the Ambidextrous
Abul-Adan the Warrior
Tauq bin Heyran the Warrior
Jamhur World-Conflagrer
Tartus Hatchet-Thrower
Faraz Aad Maghrebi

Among Amir Hamza's progeny were:

Alam Shah
Malik Qasim
Isfandiar Shah Gilani
Darab World-Conqueror
Iraj bin Qasim
Khurshid bin Hashim
Hashim Swordfighter
Karib the Courageous
Asad bin Karib

Besides them, Amir Hamza's two deputies were also in attendance:

Landhoor bin Saadan
Malik Azhdar

With his army commanders as his riding companions, Amir Hamza arrived at the august entrance of the private pavilion of the Shadow of God, the Master of Suleiman's Throne, the Refuge of the World, Master of the Most Esteemed Seat, King Saad, and awaited his arrival in the place of audience.

Suddenly, the royal chamber's panels parted with a loud whirring noise and the signs of the king's approach manifested themselves.

Twelve thousand children, beautiful as the moon, marched out from the entrance wearing lavish golden costumes, sporting gold bracelets, carrying pots of aromatic unguents, and sprinkling powdered aloe-wood and ambergris. They were followed by thousands of candelabra holders in crimson uniforms holding gold and silver candelabra. Behind them walked others holding enchased crystalline goblets with lit candles. Thousands of palace guards and eunuchs followed them, overseeing the various arrangements. Surrounded by the royal servants, the king's throne was brought forward on the shoulders of female palanquin bearers dressed in costly and precious skirts, wearing bracelets with crocodile-head finials, sporting fish-shaped earrings, medals and jewelery. Each and every one of them was uniquely charming, and their bodies were ripe with the bloom and vigour of youth.

The royal attendants shouted, "In the name of Allah, the Most Beneficent and Merciful!" Amir Hamza, along with his commanders, stood at their designated stations to salute the king. The moment he appeared, all bowed their heads in submission. A macebearer shouted, "O Powerful King and Lord of the World, Amir Hamza, the Lord of the Auspicious Planetary Conjunction, stands before you!" As the king raised his eyes, Amir made a bow. The king placed his hand on his heart to express his love for him. Amir made a salute. All the other commanders presented themselves, offered salutes and kissed the foot of the throne. The king ordered everyone to mount their steeds. The commanders surrounded the royal throne and escorted it to the battlefield. The drums were struck and the criers shouted war chants.

The stars in the heaven flickered at the break of dawn and the wafting morning breeze was as fragrant as the ambergris. Fanned by a spring gale, the king headed with great pomp and circumstance toward the battlefield.

Suleiman Amber-Hair's armies were positioned on the opposite side of the arena with Laqa and Faramurz's forces. The heavy-set warriors and majestic and mighty champions sat astride rhinoceroses, regarding their enemy with fierce frowns. Broad-swords hung from their necks. They carried maces on their shoulders and spears in their hands.

The battlefield seemed ready to explode into hostilities when the sky became overcast with lowering, pitch-black clouds, lightning began dancing above the arena and the sorcerers' army poured into the arena led by the false Ijlal atop his magic dragon. Hurling lightning bolts, showering stones, blowing bugles and horns, and ringing bells and gongs the sorcerers took their positions.

The thunderous approach of both armies cleft the heart of the Bull of the Earth, made the birds forget the direction to their nests, and sent shivers down the spines of combatants. The billowing dust changed the sphere of air into a sphere of dust. The mirror of sky was clouded and the fountain of sun was blocked.

The billowing dust from the hooves of the steeds
Made the layers of Earth six, and eight the skies[29]

Finally, the groundsmen came forward and began dextrously levelling the battlefield with mattocks and tidying the trenches and ambuscades. They carried away the pebbles, stones, twigs and thorns in piles, and cleaned the ground of the shrubbery and bushes until it shone like a mirror. Then it was the water-carriers' turn to sprinkle the ground, every one of them a veritable Khizr. Wearing their uniforms of gold tissue and red cotton waistcloths, with water bowls belted to their waists and waterskins mounted with sprinklers slung over their shoulders, they went about their business and, with their labours, put to shame the showers of August.

Soon all the dirt and dust was settled and the warriors were able to see their adversaries' faces. They beheld the warriors dressed in mail and armor, and every soldier covered in metal from the spire of their helmets to the toe of their foot guards. Everywhere one looked one saw warriors clad in iron.

The armies arranged themselves in combat formations, including the vanguard and the rearguard, the center and the flanks, the ambuscade and the exit guards; all fourteen positions were drawn and reinforced like the Rampart of Sikander.[30] The pugnacious foot-soldiers of the vanguard stood like the bulwark. Troopers surged like waves in a sea of warriors. Horses stood muzzle to muzzle, flank to flank, tail to tail, and hoof to hoof. They pushed back any criers from the enemy camp that advanced and pushed forward criers from their camp. The music of war filled the air and the horses neighed and reared.

Suddenly, the musical voices of minstrel boys floated on the air. Wearing colorful dresses and sporting turbans tied on their heads at an angle, they melodiously sang the transient world's denunciation to the accompaniment of *sarod,*[31] and proclaimed: "O warriors, neither the mighty Sam nor Nariman remain. The sanguinary champions have left no mark on the face of Earth and sleep in death. The iron-bodied warriors no longer remain among the high and the low of the land. In the flash of an eye, old man heavens has interred many rank-destroying warriors and formidable youths as renowned as Rustam. Only their valour is spoken of still; the account of their courage alone keeps them alive. Battles are a wonderful test.

"Everyone is allotted a five-day life
Majnun is gone, it is now my time.

"In the darkness of the battle, sword is the only flame that guides. The head and the neck long for separation. Indeed, a terrible conflict consuming warriors is the true life. Earn renown O warriors! Skirmish and win laurels! The one whose foot retreats today will never again walk with his head held high."

The criers then left the arena but their speech acted like heady Portuguese wine on the valiant warriors – the lions of the forest of courage. They became intoxicated with valor and their eyes became bloodshot. They kissed the hilts of their swords and stirred restlessly in their saddles.

The false Ijlal ordered sorcerers Intizam the Arranger and Munsarim the Organizer to fly his dragon by magic into the arena. They clapped their hands after reciting a spell and the magic dragon flew to the center of the arena. The false Ijlal exclaimed, "O Hamza, you are in the presence of Lord Laqa. Prostrate yourself before him without delay or else I shall pulp your head. Come into the arena now and fulfill all your heart's desires." Amir Hamza turned Ashqar Demon-Born's head toward the royal throne and his standard-bearer unfurled the dragon-shaped standard.

It was announced that no one but Amir Hamza may answer the sorcerer's challenge. All the commanders and captains of the army dismounted. The army's colors were displayed. Amir Hamza arrived before King Saad's throne, dismounted and requested permission for combat. The king offered Amir a decoction of sugar and herbs in the goblet of demon Ifrit's skull.[32] Amir drank it and handed the empty cup to the king's royal guard. After imbibing the cup of royal favor, receiving a robe of honor and permission for combat, Amir again climbed into the saddle like the bright sun climbs up into the sky.

The commanders bid goodbye to Hamza, who spurred his horse toward the field. Ashqar Demon-Born charged like a lion into the arena.

The horse that was like lightning and wind
A demon of a fairy born
More delicate than the flow of water its stride
Faster than speed itself its gait
The softness of his ears and mane recalled
The spikenard, the musk willow, a spikenard bouquet

Ashqar Demon-Born reached the false Ijlal in just a few strides.

After exchanging challenges with Amir Hamza for some time, the false Ijlal produced a crested coconut from his sack and began reciting incantations. But what others took for his invocation was, in fact, a message to Amir Hamza in the Jinni language. He said, "I am not a sorcerer but your trusted servant, Amar Ayyar. You may now recite the Most Great Name and capture me, but do so in a way that I receive neither injury nor break any limbs. You are a portly fellow whereas I am bony and thin." Amir Hamza looked closely at him. Seeing the telltale mole on the white of Amar's left eye, he was astonished at Amar's trickery.

The false Ijlal now blew on the coconut and hurled it at Amir Hamza, who recited the Most Great Name to counteract it and everyone saw the coconut fall to the ground without inflicting any harm on him. Giving rein to his horse, Amir Hamza recited the Most Great Name again and blew it on the false Ijlal, which caused the magic dragon to return to its essence and become a lump of lentil flour. The false Ijlal dismounted and the onlookers saw him attack Amir Hamza with his trident. Amir Hamza dismounted too and, foiling the false sorcerer's blow, lifted him up by his waistband. Amir Hamza exclaimed, "O horde of sorcerers, regard that I have captured your commander!"

At these words, the army of sorcerers attacked Amir Hamza from all sides.

He gave the false Ijlal into the custody of a trickster who had accompanied Hamza into the arena. While the trickster retired to his encampment with his captive, Amir Hamza recited the Most Great Name and attacked the enemy. At that moment, Prince Faramurz and Suleiman Amber-Hair also ordered their commanders to go to the aid of the sorcerers.

The King of True Believers also sounded his war cry. The two armies collided and dark clouds inundated the arena from all sides in which swords danced like lightning.

The two armies merged and one army became
The world the floor of the Judgment Day became

In the heat of the battle, Ijlal's deputies summoned the commanders of their army and advised them that it would be improper for them to continue fighting since their leader had been taken prisoner, and it remained to be seen whether or not he would submit allegiance to Hamza. They advised them to pull out and submit to their leader's choice once the conflict was decided. All the sorcerers pulled out from the conflict while Laqa and Suleiman Amber-Hair's forces gave fight. Many vain heads rolled down off their necks. The camp of the True Believers rang with their champions' war cries.

Amir Hamza cried,

"The Commander of the Arabs, the lion-hearted Hamza
Whose mighty hand puts Sohrab and Rustam to shame!"

From another corner Landhoor shouted,

"O fugitives, I am Hamza's deputy, the supreme master of lance,
Emperor of India, the Champion of the Times, Landhoor!"

Malik Azhdar, the master of the two-pronged spear, the slave of the holy prophet and Ali, proclaimed from another corner,

"I am Malik Azhdar the wrathful
Commander of the armies of the faithful!"

The blades of the warriors on both sides clashed mightily, and for some time nothing could be heard except their cling-clang. The injured found neither quarter nor water. Swords flashed like lightning bolts and arrows fell like rain. Heads came down like hailstones, separated from their torsos they littered the ground, and a river of blood surged in waves on the battlefield. Garlands of wounds were distributed. Manly warriors sought congress with the pansies as a bridegroom seeks congress with the bride. As the poet has described,

Blood flowed from every armor chink
The warriors washed their hands of life's hopes
They shot their bows with mighty effort
And hearts broke into bloodied smiles, pierced with arrows
The curved sword blades bartered with life's blood
And a rainbow of gore spread into the sky
As a strong wind scatters about dry leaves
The horde of infidels in the field were strewn
The braves now reached for and drew their daggers
And vigorously pursued the evil-hearted foe
Of blood a brave tiger can never have enough
A lion on his hunt none can dare stop
How to describe the fate of the enemy horde
Written on the swords of the rank-destroying braves
They made screams aplenty, the evil foe
And their hearts and senses speedily lost

The armies of the True Believers fought bravely and Laqa and Suleiman Amber-Hair's forces were routed. Unable to bear the intensity of the battle, the enemy retreated. Bakhtiarak realized that once again they had been denied hope of victory and might be forced to find another refuge. Taking that into consideration, he ordered that the drums of retreat be beaten. The trumpet's blast declared cessation of hostilities and the combatants separated.

While Amir Hamza's champions returned to their camp flying on the wings of victory, the ill-fated enemy crawled back to its camp in ignominy and shame. Amir ordered the dead to be carried away. Three thousand men from Amir Hamza's camp had tasted martyrdom while three hundred thousand foes had been dispatched to hell. The martyred received burials while the infidels were interred like dogs. The wounds of the injured were sutured and their cuts and lesions bandaged.

Amir Hamza did not hold court that day. The next day he sent for the false Ijlal and asked him, "Tell me whether or not you recognize the True Master of Both Worlds!"[33] The false Ijlal answered, "For as long as I live I shall be His slave!" Amir Hamza then rewarded him with a robe of honor. The false Ijlal rode back to his army and sent for his commanders and announced, "I have yielded to Hamza and you too must follow suit and not defy my wishes." Some sorcerers, whose evil hearts were cast with darkness, returned to Afrasiyab after hearing their commander's resolve, but most of them offered their continued allegiance. They returned with the false Ijlal to be inducted into Amir Hamza's service and receive robes of honor.

Then Amar Ayyar produced the real Ijlal from his zambil and tied him to a column of the Pavilion of Hashsham in the court. He pulled out his tongue and stuck a needle in it so that he could not cast spells, and gave him restorative salts to smell. When Ijlal opened his eyes he found himself a captive and was terrified to see before him another man who looked like his exact copy. Amar said, "O Ijlal, open your eyes and regard your circumstances. I am the chief of the commanders, the lord of the kings of Arabs and non-Arabs, a fearless runner who gives pause to manly sprinters and leaves the unmanly limping behind in a cloud of dust. I am the Sun of the Sky of Trickery, the Moon of the Sky of Dagger Fighting, the Prince of Tricksters, and the accomplished disguiser, Amar Ayyar the worthy. Did you witness how easily I caught you by the Almighty's grace? It was not Suleiman Amber-Hair's daughter but this abject slave of God whom you sent for from the palace roof and who took you captive. Your entire army has submitted and joined Amir Hamza's ranks. I also hold your beloved princess prisoner. If you were to submit allegiance, you would be united with her and find reprieve. And if you are concerned about the loss of your kingdom, Amir Hamza would give you one which is four time vaster than your own."

Witnessing the circumstances and hearing Amar Ayyar's speech, Ijlal became convinced that Laqa was indeed a false God. He reasoned that, had it been otherwise, Laqa would not have fared so ill, and his well wishers would not have come to harm at Amar's hands. Ijlal signalled that he was willing to submit. Amar removed the needle from his tongue and untied him. Ijlal came forward and threw himself at the feet of Amir Hamza who blessed him and conferred a robe of honor on him.

Amir Hamza said to Ijlal, "Take a seat where you wish. In this court the commanders are free to choose their station." Ijlal felt a desire to sit with the warriors of the left flank and made his request. The commander of the left flank warriors, Malik Azhdar, welcomed him with honor and affection.

Amir Hamza said to Ijlal, "You must renounce sorcery because it is not our custom to indulge in magic. All of us here are men of the sword." In deference to Amir Hamza's wishes, Ijlal renounced sorcery and Laqa worship and converted to the True Faith.

Amir Hamza ordered celebrations and an assembly of revelry was organized. Coquettish cupbearers carrying goblets of sense-ravishing wine arrived. The roseate wine was drunk and the cheerful cries of 'Drink and be merry!' rose from all corners.

Amir Hamza drank alongside his men. A dance recital had begun, and everyone occupied themselves with merrymaking. Suddenly, the pavilion's screens rose and a comely maiden, whose beauty recalled the moon's allure and whose charming airs could be likened to Venus, arrived in the assembly dressed in a lavish costume and curtsied before Amir Hamza. Ijlal recognized his beloved, Princess Nasreen Amber-Hair, and was embarrassed by her immodesty at entering a congregation of men. Amir Hamza, too, was surprised to see the princess before him.

The princess said, "O Amir, I am Amar Ayyar's son, Chalak!" Ijlal marvelled at how the trickster had deceived everyone in the princess's guise. Chalak narrated how he learned that the false Ijlal had been taken captive by Amir Hamza's camp, and Suleiman Amber-Hair had returned to the camp after the cessation of hostilities. He rode out of the city in a palanquin on the excuse of visiting Suleiman Amber-Hair. Once his conveyance came out of the fort, however, the false princess tore out of the palanquin and scurried toward Amir Hamza's camp. The princess's attendants, servants and palanquin bearers were caught by surprise. They gave chase but the false Nasreen ran at great speed and soon disappeared from sight.

Amir Hamza asked Amar to produce the real Princess Nasreen from the zambil and take her into the women's quarters. Amar replied, "I will produce her from the zambil only if my palm is greased. As you know well, the zambil's function is to gorge, not disgorge. What goes inside the zambil becomes part of it; just like whatever falls inside a salt mine becomes salt." Amir Hamza laughed at Amar's speech and awarded him several hundred thousand rupees.

Amar first collected the amount from the treasurer then took Princess Nasreen out of his zambil. He provided her with a pavilion and Amir Hamza sent a royal dress for her.

The bewildered princess wondered how she had got there and sat puzzling when Amir Hamza presented himself. He told her about Amar Ayyar and the circumstances of her arrival, and said, "Your lover, Ijlal, is present in my court. Now you are free to decide whether to marry him and reside in this camp or not. If you decide against it, I shall have you conducted back to your father in safety." Witnessing such munificence on Amir Hamza's part, the princess replied, "I wish to convert to your faith."

Amir Hamza presided over the wedding of Ijlal and his willing princess and conferred riches and estates on them.

When Suleiman Amber-Hair's servants brought news that his daughter had eloped, he drew his sword and vowed to follow her to Hamza's camp to kill her. But Bakhtiarak held him back, saying, "You are not alone in this misfortune. Two of Lord Laqa's own daughters have eloped with Hamza's sons."[34]

Suleiman Amber-Hair finally relented, but Laqa said to Bakhtiarak, "O bastard and devil, why did you have to mention what passed with my daughters?" Bakhtiarak answered, "My Lord, there is no cause for you to become vexed. I mentioned them only to illustrate the wondrous ways of your providence." Amidst such banter the subject was dismissed.

Before long, the king's spies returned and gave an account of what had passed in Amir Hamza's court. Everybody learned the true identities of Princess Nasreen and Ijlal. Bakhtiarak roared with laughter and said to Suleiman Amber-Hair, "His Excellency Ijlal had arrived from Hoshruba with great fanfare. All praise to my lord and master Amar Ayyar, who carried him away before he even had a chance to do battle. Bravo! You, O Suleiman, have no control over events in your own household. How can you be trusted with the command of an army and the administration of a kingdom? How could you fight a courageous and alert man like Hamza?" Suleiman answered, "I shall write another note to Afrasiyab and ask for assistance again. This time I will conduct myself with greater caution."

Suleiman wrote another note to Afrasiyab giving a complete account of Ijlal and requesting him to send some mighty sorcerer to Laqa's aid. He sent the message to the mountaintop according to custom.

Sorceress Hasina Magic-Beauty

When Afrasiyab heard the gong he sent the magic claw to fetch the letter. Afrasiyab became livid upon reading it and said to his courtiers, "You have now learned that Ijlal has turned traitor. He has renounced Lord Laqa's religion and joined the True Believers. I would that a sorcerer or sorceress among you should go to Lord Laqa's aid and bring that ingrate Ijlal captive to me."

As Afrasiyab ended his speech, sorceress Princess Hasina Magic-Beauty rose and said, "Your slave girl shall undertake this mission." Afrasiyab bestowed a robe of honor on her and said, "I place you in the protection of lords Sameri and Jamshed. Go forth and be wary of the tricksters!"

Princess Hasina retired to her land and ordered the twenty thousand sorceresses under her command to get ready for war and prepare to depart for Mount Agate. While the sorceresses began their preparations, Afrasiyab dispatched a reply to Suleiman's letter. Suleiman Amber-Hair was greatly pleased by the favorable reply and the news of Princess Hasina's impending arrival.

The Conqueror of the Tilism

Amir Hamza's spies brought news that Afrasiyab had responded to Suleiman's request and a sorceress was on her way to aid Laqa.

Amir Hamza said, "Until the tilism is conquered, there will be no end to sorcerers. My son, Badiuz Zaman, will also remain incarcerated." Amir then sent for the diviners. He received them with honor and said, "I would that you determine the name of the Conqueror of Hoshruba[35] by your calculations, and find out whose hand will strike down Afrasiyab."

In obedience to Amir Hamza's wishes, the diviners made their calculations, drew the horoscope and considered the auspicious and inauspicious points on the table of geomancy. After much reflection and pause, they said, "O Lord of the Auspicious Planetary Conjunction! Nobody except God knows what lies in the future. We can only determine according to the calculations of geomancy that your maternal grandson, Prince Asad, should depart to conquer the tilism. He should be accompanied by five tricksters: Qiran the Ethiope, Burq the Frank, Jansoz, Zargham the Lion-Hearted, and a fifth one whose name we cannot reveal, but it starts with the letter A. Amar Ayyar immediately understood that they aluded to him. He called out, "The tricksters alone would not suffice. A diviner must also make the entourage."

The diviners protested to Amir Hamza that they had not wished to identify Amar because they knew he would make objections. They told Amir Hamza that it was their duty to tell him the result of their calculations, and now he may deal with the matter as he saw fit. Amir Hamza said to Amar, "You must go since your name is revealed by the calculations of geomancy." Amar answered, "I will do no such thing!"

Amir Hamza rewarded the diviners and dismissed them after presenting them with robes of honor. He then said to Prince Asad, "My dear child, prepare for the campaign and depart to conquer Hoshruba!" Prince Asad rose from his seat, saluted Amir Hamza, and returned to his pavilion to prepare for the journey.

Amir Hamza sent for a million rupees and, dividing it into two halves, distributed one half for travelling expenses among the four tricksters named by the diviners, and offered the other half to Amar Ayyar for the campaign's expenses. When Amar saw such largesse, he said, "O Lord of the Auspicious Planetary Conjunction, I have no appetite for money and riches. I would never have consented to step foot into the tilism, but I find I have no choice since your son is being held prisoner and I must secure his release. However, you did wrong in corrupting my disciples with money."

Amar said to the four tricksters, "O worthless creatures, you will foolishly squander this half million rupees in no time. It will be safer with me and would be available to you in time of need. Indeed, how can you claim to be a trickster if you need to spend your own money to journey to the tilism? Instead of *taking* money to the tilism you ought to *bring* money from Hoshruba. If I accept money it is because I have numerous other expenses besides." The tricksters realized that Amar had caught sight of the money and would not rest without grabbing all of it. In the end, they could do little else but present their own share to Amar, who stuffed it into his zambil and returned to his pavilion to make arrangements for the journey.

Once Amar's back was turned, however, Amir Hamza gave more money to the four tricksters who busied themselves with preparations for departure.

Of the Departure of the Lion of the Forest of Valor Prince Asad to Conquer Hoshruba Along With Amar Ayyar and His Disciples, and of Their Taking Separate Routes into the Tilism

The travellers to the path of meaning, the conquerors of the tilism of eloquence, the explorers of marvellous lands and scribes of singular discourse, conquer the wonders of the tilism of inventions with the tablet and pen and set foot into the realm of imagination with wondering minds thus:

After arriving in his pavilion, Prince Asad ordered forty thousand intrepid troopers to prepare to depart for the campaign to conquer Hoshruba. At the command of the prince, who was equal to the heavens in dignity, the tents and pavilions were loaded onto carts and the brave commanders armed and readied themselves for departure. Prince Asad visited his kind mother and Hamza's daughter, Zubaida Sher, in the women's quarters. He placed his head at her esteemed feet and kissed them with reverence. He said, "My venerable mother, your slave is ready to depart for the tilism to secure the release of his uncle, Prince Badiuz Zaman. Grant me leave with a happy heart and forgive all my voluntary and involuntary misdemeanors."

Princess Zubaida Sher was already suffering pangs of grief over the loss of her brother Badiuz Zaman. When she heard of her son's departure, her eyes welled up with tears. She embraced Asad and kissed his forehead.

The news spread in the women's quarters that Prince Asad was going away to secure Prince Badiuz Zaman's release. Princess Gardiya Bano, his maternal grandmother, broke into tears upon hearing the news of his planned departure. All the wives of Amir Hamza blessed Prince Asad by tying gold pieces pledged to Imam Zamin[36] to his arm. They sent him away with their good wishes, reciting the prayer to ward off the evil eye.

From there, Asad went to the armory and decorated himself with arms and armor. Forty thousand turquoise-encrusted suits of armor and sharp and shining swords were handed out to the warriors from the armory. Several thousand pairs of gold and silver kettledrums were loaded on elephants and camels. Cartloads of gold and silver pieces were procured for the journey. The prince spent a day in the camp taking his leave of the commanders. All the nobles and chiefs of Amir Hamza's court visited his pavilion to embrace him and wish him Godspeed. He remained busy with these engagements for one day and one night.

When the Westbound Traveler[37] appeared from the mansion of the east, resolved to trek the stages of the heavens, the clarion of departure was sounded in Prince Asad's camp. The drums were struck, the trumpets and the kettledrums sounded and Prince Asad set out after saying his morning prayers.

When Amir Hamza finished praying in the Roving Prayer Tent, he inquired, "Why are the trumpets sounding?" His companions answered, "They announce the departure of Prince Asad." Amir Hamza said, "I wish to witness his departure and behold his dear face once again." He came out and stood with all his nobles at a vantage point along the way.

Presently, elephants fitted with steel mirrors and draped with sheets of gold-brocade came into view. Atop them sat the standard-bearers with unfurled banners inscribed with the praises of the Eternal God. Every flag was the augur of the line, "Verily, we have conferred clear victory upon you."[38] Behind them came the cannons mounted on camels and elephants, and the gold and silver kettledrums. Clad in shining gold cloth, brocade short-coats, red turbans and gold-embroidered belts, the kettledrummers marched past, striking and thunderously beating the drums mounted on elephants and camels. They were followed by rocket bearers on camelback, sitting on jewel-encrusted seats. The gold-draped, spirited camels wearing woven necklaces of gold and silver thread advanced with lofty air and elegant gait. Thousands of foot-soldiers walked alongside, ready for battle. Wearing dark red turbans, attired in long tunics and *khurdnok* shoes,[39] holding lion-headed muskets on their shoulders sheathed in gold cloth, they marched in groups and clusters and, although only five thousand in number, appeared a force twenty times as many.

Four thousand display horses strutted past next, bobbing their heads, caparisoned in gold cloth, wearing chains and sporting double aigrettes on their heads. Each horse was covered with steel armor and rump-guards. Their grooms walked beside them moving fly-whisks. Several thousand water-carriers wearing waistcloths of coarse red cotton and dressed in uniforms of gold brocade walked past behind them, sprinkling rosewater, *keora*-water,[40] and essence of orange blossoms to settle the dust. The weeders accompanied them, cleaning the ground and picking up the stones and pebbles.

Then followed a group of children, whose cheeks had the radiance of flame, and whose foreheads were bright as the moon. Bearing gold and silver chaffing dishes over which they sprinkled powdered aloe-wood[41] by the fistful, they made the wilderness the envy of the beauties of Tartary and the perfumer's perfumery. They passed by with great elegance, showing their razzle-dazzle, clad in colorful costumes and wearing jewel-encrusted bracelets. The macebearers walked behind them, carrying their gold and silver vermiculated staffs and making proclamations before the prince's conveyance.

Riding under a lion-headed standard, Prince Asad the mighty, rank-destroying, Valiant Lord of the Battlefield, finally appeared in the din of a thousand kettledrums adorned with enchanted armor and a turquoise coat of mail. Gold and silver pieces were showered over his head by the onlookers as sacrifice to ward off the evil eye from him. Forty thousand intrepid troopers brought up the rear of this magnificent retinue clad in body armor fitted with cuirasses, with swords stuck in their sword belts and heavy maces resting on their shoulders. Drunk on the wine of courage, they rode in twos, holding the reins high, with the short spears balanced between the horse's ears.

Catching sight of Amir Hamza, Prince Asad saluted him, dismounted and presented himself before his grandfather. Amir Hamza embraced him. As he prayed for his grandson's triumph and victory, Amir Hamza found himself overwhelmed by emotion. Prince Asad said to him, "Grandfather, I leave you in the care and protection of God Almighty." All the commanders in Amir Hamza's entourage warmly embraced the young prince. Before leaving, he asked his grandfather,

> *"O my venerable lord and master,*
> *What are your injunctions for the journey?"*

Amir Hamza answered,

> *"May you have an auspicious trek*
> *And return in safety from your travels.*

"May the Almighty God soon restore you to us. May you triumph over your foe in the tilism. Go forth now. I invoke the protection of the Almighty and Insuperable Lord of Both Worlds."

Prince Asad kissed Amir Hamza's feet. He mounted his steed and the army marched forth with great pomp and show and the ease and facility of a spring gale. As Amir Hamza turned back, his commanders wiped tears from the corners of their eyes. The women's quarters already rang with cries. The prince's attendants loaded and carted away tents, pavilions, luggage, furniture of the court, and the apparatus of hunt and chase. The musicians packed their lutes and rebecks.

Amir Hamza had not yet reached his pavilion when he heard the jingling of bells. As he looked up he saw the Prince of Tricksters, the worthy Amar Ayyar coming forward, wearing his commander's cap, in the company of his four trickster disciples. Dressed in tricksters' livery, short-coats of gold brocade and broadcloth shoes, they cut smart and alert figures. With snare ropes tied around their heads, slings wrapped around their arms, and a sack of sling stones hanging from their necks, the tricksters prostrated themselves and kissed Amir Hamza's feet. As he embraced them, they shed copious tears at the prospect of separation from him.

Amar Ayyar said, "O renowned lord and just appreciator, do not forget this childhood companion of yours. Remember me in your prayers in consideration of my long service to you. The outcome of this campaign is unknown. We are headed to encounter the Emperor of Hoshruba, Afrasiyab. As I head for the tilism and put my life in the hands of destiny, I appoint my son Chalak as the head of the tricksters. You may assign him any service that you would have assigned me. I hope he will not fail you."

Amir Hamza consented and gave the news to Chalak and other tricksters who had come to see Amar Ayyar off on his campaign. All of them sincerely and readily accepted the arrangement and Chalak was deputed as their commander. Then Amar Ayyar, too, left with Prince Asad's army.

ജ്ജ

After travelling some distance, Amar said to his four disciples, "My brothers, we must all act on our individual impulses and follow our own counsel. We must separately cross the distance and enter the tilism from different points. This has the advantage that if one of us runs into the hazardous or is captured, the others can help and rescue him. If we were to travel together, we might all be captured together and left helpless."

The tricksters separated at Amar's orders. Qiran the Ethiope took one direction, Burq the Frank another, Zargham headed along one path and Jansoz took a different one. Amar Ayyar did not follow the route taken by the prince's procession but proceeded forward, leaping and bounding on a separate track.

Of Prince Asad Entering the Tilism and Arriving in the City of Disregard

The prince of auspicious fortune crossed the borders of Mount Agate with his grand equipage and retinue and arrived at the mountain between the fortress kingdom of Mount Agate and Hoshruba. He saw the high mountain rise for leagues into the skies and disappear into the heavens. Neither the lasso of imagination could snare its summit, nor the bird of thought fly above its peak.

The noble prince stopped by the mountain and his truth-discerning eyes regarded that wonder of God's creation. From the top of the mountain to its foot, *koriyala*[42] flowers grew in abundance. Their black petals were the envy of black tulips, and their white spots the dreams in the eyes of stars. The scene recalled to his mind a bouquet of spring blossoms. Waterfalls cascaded down the mountain. The cock pheasants laughed and the pining nightingale trilled its notes.

Atop the mountain stood the magic gong used by Suleiman Amber-Hair and Afrasiyab for communication. Beside it sat a hundred-year-old man.

As Prince Asad was about to enter the mountain pass, the old man cried out, "O youth, desist from your disastrous ambition. Do not step into a dragon's mouth with open eyes. The tilism lies beyond this mountain. It is a land full of perils. Those who enter never leave. They find no exit but the door of doom. Take pity on your young years. Turn back or you will part with your sweet life!"

The prince retorted, "Hear O foolish dotard that braves don't fear death. They do not retreat once they have stepped forward with courage. I am Prince Asad, Conqueror of the Tilisms of this planet of marvels, and the grandson of Amir Hamza. I have wagered my life on this campaign. Your words of warning will not make me turn back."

When the old man heard the name of the noble prince, he called out, "If it is your intention and resolve to destroy the tilism, go forward in the name of Allah! Who will dare stop you! Sally forth and fulfil your purpose!"

The prince rode on. As he entered the mountain pass with his army, magic birds rose, flying from the mountain, and the gong sounded. The birds took news to Afrasiyab that the Conqueror of the Tilism, Prince Asad, had entered Hoshruba with a large army.

Afrasiyab immediately dispatched messages to the border guards to arrest Prince Asad on sight. Every sorcerer learned of Prince Asad's entry into the tilism and resolved to stop him and take him prisoner.

After Prince Asad came out of the mountain pass, he arrived in a lush field of captivating air where green pastures stretched for miles on end, redolent with the perfume of wild flowers. The dense and lush bushes were the envy of the locks of mistresses. A river ran through the pasture. The undulation of the waves smote the heart as it recalled to mind the gait of beloveds. The greenery was like the Virgin of the Ethereal Sphere.[43]

Accompanied by his virtuous companions, the prince of lofty attributes went onward admiring the landscape. They came upon a garden and Prince Asad's companions said to him, "Your Honor should enter this garden and admire its flowers and fragrant herbs." Asad headed toward it and saw that the entrance of the garden was carved out of porphyry, black stone and minerals and shone like a mirror. The portals of the entrance hung open like the longing arms of a lover. The garden had neither guard nor warden; spring was its only keeper. The prince and his entourage entered and beheld all manner of flowers in bloom, lakes criss-crossing its expanse, and burbling fountains. They saw bejewelled columns, balustrades made of inlaid gold and sacks of gold tissue covering the clusters of fruit that hung from grapevines. Trees swayed in the breeze like creatures overtaken by frenzy. The fruits exchanged kisses as they brushed together. The branches of the trees were neatly balanced and trimmed into wondrous shapes. Crystal walkways surrounded the lake, and next to them, dazzling grassy patches put the brightness of emeralds to shame. The melodious gurgling of fountains in the lakes would have made even a nightingale's heart cry with envy. The clarity of the water was enticing. The garden was a paradise where every flower and bud lived contented and fulfilled by the bounty of the gentle breeze laden with the fragrance of ambergris.

And yet the prince and his companions found the garden completely deserted. Neither man nor beast could be seen there. From the center of the garden rose a canopied platform a hundred yards long, surrounded on all sides by tulip gardens. The prince settled down on the platform while his army bivouacked around him.

Hardly a few moments had passed when a loud cackle was heard. The tulips in the flowerbeds suddenly blossomed and dragon heads darted out from each flower. Before anyone could take stock of the marvel, the dragons spewed fire and inhaled. The entire camp of Prince Asad, along with the men, tents and equipage went flying into the dragons' mouths. Prince Asad alone remained on the platform. As he stepped down and rushed after his companions, he heard a thunderous crack behind him. He turned and saw his horse grow wings and fly away.

As the prince stood confounded by these marvels, the garden and the tulip beds returned to their original form.

Prince Asad shed tears in the memory of his companions and cried out, "O fickle heavens! O capricious universe! You could not bear to see me in the company of friends! You marked me to endure the hardships of this wilderness alone!" He grabbed his sword's hilt in anger many times, and rose to smite someone to vent his rage. But there was no one there.

The sight of that garden now appeared to him like that of a thorn. There was not a single friendly face to be seen. Feeling powerless, he sat down on that platform and thought, *O Asad, this is a tilism. Many such adventures and trials lie before you still. The sorcerers of the tilism will test you in many encounters. One must not become flustered at the very first ordeal. Go forward with courage and seek the way to your destination by yourself.*

The prince looked around the garden and found another gate from which he exited and headed onwards. He walked for three days and three nights but saw not a single place to rest or lodge. Even the flowers growing in that tilism's wilderness presented him with unkindly faces. His feet broke into blisters and his tongue into lamentations. The prince carried on his way reciting this couplet:

"Help O Khizr, this wilderness is a calamity
I find it impossible to ford this catastrophe"

Finally, on the third day, Prince Asad saw the precincts of a city and with great difficulty arrived there. The glowing city walls were made of crystal and adorned with intricate patterns and portraits of kings and sovereigns. The artistic depiction of hunting grounds, forests, mountains and rivers seemed all but real.

The gate of the city stood open and the portal swayed on its hinges like a rutting elephant. Thousands of fearsome sorcerers stood wielding steel magic balls. Their foreheads were marked with *tilaks*[44] and their bodies were adorned with skulls carved of sandalwood. They had changed form by magic into animals with human heads, and humans with elephant, dragon and lion heads. They busied themselves making oblations of lard in the crackling bonfires to prepare spells. The citadel stood close to the city gate. It had thousands of towers guarded by brazen-bodied and elephant-bodied sorcerers. Bells and gongs rang loudly and salutations to sorcerer gods Sameri and Jamshed were chanted.

Nobody stopped Prince Asad as he entered the gate witnessing these marvels. He found the city bustling with life. The alleys and quarters shone like the hearts of lovers. The spotless shops and markets sparkled. The nobility and the laity both occupied themselves in commerce. People milled about and money and goods exchanged hands. Every shop in the market was decorated and well organized. The goldsmiths were established in one quarter with cowries, coins, dirhams and dinars[45] lying in piles on cloth sheets spread before them. The drapers and mercers had their own area where they sat displaying open rolls of silk and satin. The sweetmeat vendors sold all kinds of choice and delicious sweets on salvers of gold and silver. Bakers, greengrocers, butchers and peddlers each had a section marked for them where they were congregated. The florists' shops presented a picture of spring, and the coquettish wine-sellers and elegant courtesans delighted the onlookers with their flirtations and airs.

Young women wore gold brocade skirts wrapped in the manner of waistcloths, some were clad in saris of which they used one half as mantles, yet others were covered in mantles decorated with gold-brocade borders which dazzled brighter than the sun. They sported tight and true fitting tops adorned with gold-lace which framed the knobs of their breasts, wore jewel-encrusted bracelets, three-tiered anklets, and showed their coquettish ways that enchanted the hearts of lovers. As greengrocers they weighed out the fruits in scales made of vermiculated gold and silver, and refreshed the eyes of those of an amorous bent with the pomegranates of their breasts and the apples of their chins.

The prince walked around the city seeing these sights. Because he was hungry he stopped at a sweetmeat vendor and gave him a fistful of gold pieces for a salver of sweets. The vendor threw back the gold pieces he was given by Asad, saying, "Save your gold, O stranger! I do not accept it." Asad took it back and asked, "What fault do you find with it?" He replied, "I have heaps and heaps of these gold pieces. Children play with them like pebbles."

The vendor addressed one of his employees, who brought out a mass of gold and jewels in the skirts of his robe to show Asad.

When Asad inquired who exercised writ over the land, the vendor answered, "Emperor Afrasiyab." Asad next asked the name of the city and money used for trade. The vendor replied, "This is the City of Disregard. We use paper money for trade."

He took out a rupee from his money box to show Asad, and said, "This is our currency." The piece of paper was impressed with the portrait of a king on one side and florid patterns on the other.

The sweetmeat vendor said to him, "If you pay me in this money you may have what you like. If not, you can try your luck elsewhere."

Asad walked away and stopped at another shop where he tried to buy some food but received the same answer. Asad became angry and said to himself, *After all, this place is called the City of Disregard. I, too, should plunder the whole marketplace and revolt against them.*

Asad grabbed a salver of sweets from a vendor who raised cries of "Thief! Thief!" People quickly gathered from all corners. When they approached, Asad caught them by their necks and bashed their heads together, dispatching a few men to hell. A hue and cry arose and the magistrate rushed to the scene. Asad drew his sword and wounded a few men. Then he took a sweetmeat vendor's bench, placed it in the middle of the thoroughfare and, placing the salver of sweets in his lap, sat down to eat. He soundly thrashed anyone who dared approach.

Empress Heyrat

The shopkeepers went as a body to complain before the ruler of the city, sorceress Empress Heyrat.

Emperor Afrasiyab had populated the City of Disregard in the region of Zahir for his empress so that she could have access to all amenities and services when she visited Zahir. A three-tiered, domed tower called the Dome of Light stood in the region of Zahir and gave one a view of the tilism. The first tier was inhabited by twelve thousand sorcerers. Several thousand bells and gongs were installed in the second tier. If struck by the gong-ringers the denizens of the tilism fell unconscious. The third tier was reserved for Empress Heyrat, who was at that moment seated there viewing the sights of the tilism. A dance recital was underway at the Dome of Light and seventeen hundred slave girls adorned with jewels stood humbly before her.

Suddenly, cries of "Help! Redress!" broke out in the assembly. Heyrat asked her sorceress-aide, Zamarrud, to inquire who had been wronged and to bring her the details of the matter. Zamarrud spoke to the plaintiffs and led them under the Dome of Light for an audience with the empress. At the inquiring of the empress, the citizens complained of Asad's high handedness. Empress Heyrat dispatched her female attendant, Gulshan, to arrest the thief so that he could be suitably chastised.

Gulshan left with the plaintiffs and upon reaching the bazaar beheld a comely youth sitting on a bench in the middle of the thoroughfare. His beauty was the envy of the Moon of Canaan.[46] He wielded a sword in one hand and ate sweets with the other. The whole marketplace dazzled with the resplendence of his luminous beauty. From its light every nook and corner of the place had become the envy of the Valley of Ayman.[47] No one had ever seen or heard of such beauty.

The moment Gulshan set eyes on Prince Asad she fell head-over-heels in love with him. She called out, "Who are you, O stranger, who inflicts tyranny on the subjects of our empress and steals from them to feed yourself?" Prince Asad looked up and saw a sorceress dressed in a sari coming toward him. She carried a sorcerer's sack around her neck and her forehead was marked with a cinnabar *tilak*. The prince thought, *It is certain that she would take me captive by using a magic spell. Then all my show and might will come to nought. It would be best to use deception to chastise this strumpet.*

Prince Asad called out to her, "Come closer so that I can give you my particulars and accompany you to your empress." As Gulshan approached, Asad made sheep's eyes at her. Gulshan believed he had become enamored of her. She decided she would ask the empress to confer him upon her as a reward, then bring him home and ravish him. She immediately put her hand in Asad's hand, saying, "Come, let me take you to the empress." Asad gave her a violent tug and as Gulshan fell, he caught her by the neck. He tore off a strip of cloth from his clothing and stuffed it into her mouth so that she could not cast a spell on him. He pinioned Gulshan and tied her to a column of the shop with her mantle. Asad gave her a few strokes of the lash for good measure which made Gulshan wince with pain. He then returned to eating sweets.

The vendors protested and threatened but no one dared approach Asad. They returned to report to Empress Heyrat, who laughed when she heard of Asad's cunning, and said to her sorceress-aide Zamarrud, "Go and take him prisoner and secure Gulshan's release." Zamarrud recited incantations and flew away.

Immediately upon arrival, Zamarrud cast a spell on Prince Asad that made him lose power over his limbs. She released Gulshan and put a magic claw around Asad's neck. Accompanied by Gulshan, she flew away with the prince, arrived in the Dome of Light and threw Prince Asad before Empress Heyrat.

The prince saw a beautiful woman clad in gold finery sitting on a throne and seventeen hundred slave girls standing before her with bowed heads. Asad turned his face away. Stunned by Asad's beauty, Empress Heyrat said to him, "O captive of grief and sorrow, of which garden are you a blossom? What chance brought you to these parts?" Prince Asad answered, "I am the grandson of Amir Hamza, the Lord of the Auspicious Planetary Conjunction. I have come here to conquer the tilism."

Heyrat was confounded to hear Amir Hamza's name. Bewildered, she ordered her attendants to bring her a box. When they returned with it, Heyrat opened it and took out a portrait. Comparing it with the face of the prince, she found not the least difference between the two. She asked the prince, "Is your name Asad?" He answered, "Yes, this lowly slave of the Sublime Lord is indeed called Asad."

Heyrat said to her attendants, "Doubtless he is the Conqueror of the Tilism, since his name and particulars match the description given in the portrait. Throw him in the wilderness of the tilism. If he is indeed the Conqueror of the Tilism he will find his way out of it. Otherwise he will become lost and perish there." The sorceresses recited incantations that made the prince lose consciousness. They carried him into the wilderness of the tilism and left him there.

After a moment, the prince opened his eyes. Finding himself in a pasture, he rose and headed onwards. He witnessed a delightful garden, like the image of paradise. The ringdove sang of its love for the cypress, the dove of its love of the box tree, and the nightingale made plaints for its beloved rose.[48] There were wells of sweet water at every few steps whose depth sang of the dance of the buckets. The beautifully marbled promenades made the grapevine envious. The place was fragrant with the smell of the jasmine, eglantine, night-flowering jasmine, double-flowered jasmine, tuberose and narcissus. In one place the red poppy flowered like bowls carved of rubies. The periwinkle bloomed in another corner. The sweet redolence of the orange, citron and lime trees inundated the senses. The spikenard sat enchantingly with its wind-swept curls and the lily sang the praises of the Gardener of Nature with a hundred tongues. The spring gale floated drunkenly above every flowerbed, full of conceit at their bloom.

Streams and rivulets bounded by flowerbeds criss-crossed the garden. Trees enveloped in redolence and laden with flowers and fruits dotted the expanse. The surface of the lake undulated like a beloved's gait. Lush, green and refreshing grasslands stretched for miles on end, abounding in deer, spotted antelopes and axis deer. The black cuckoo, the Indian bee-eater, parrots and maynahs sang on their perches and swung from tree branches. In the lake, the birds broke the surface of the water with their beaks. They wet and cleaned their feathers, flapped, and juddered.

Regarding these sights, Asad arrived at a flower garden where a number of men were busy tending the grounds. Asad inquired about the name of the place and asked why they tended the garden. They replied, "This is the Tilism of the Garden. All of us are princes of different lands. We set out on hunting expeditions and ended up in this place. Despite many attempts we could not find a way out of here and had no choice but to make it our abode. A princess lives here who is fond of flowers. We pick flowers and thread garlands for her. Her attendants come in the evening to take them to their mistress and bring us food in exchange. We forever keep our eyes on the bounty of God and live on that food. You, too, should now make garlands with us and eat and live here, since you will be unable to escape this garden. You will pass your life and receive food in the manner we describe."

Asad answered, "I seek God's protection from this idea! May you prosper with your work; I will have nothing to do with gardening." They answered, "You have freshly arrived, your stomach is full and you are all fat and plump. Once you have stayed here a few days and starved, and your fat has begun to dissolve, you will readily join us."

Asad moved away without responding to those comments. He decided to pick some fruit from the trees and drink from the stream. But when he reached for fruit hanging from the branches, it suddenly rose beyond his grasp. The fruit that had fallen on the ground also disappeared when he tried to pick it up. He attempted to climb the trees but found it impossible. He tried to drink from the stream but couldn't. When he put his hand in the stream, water became sand at his touch. Helpless, he sat down in one corner. Toward the end of the day, slave girls beautiful as the full moon arrived in the garden leading female laborers carrying salvers of food. They called out, "O prisoners of the tilism, bring the garlands and get your food." All the gardeners ran and exchanged the garlands they had made for food. The slave girls departed and the gardeners sat down to eat. Poor Asad could only watch them from a distance as they finished every last bit without offering him a morsel. That night Asad slept on an empty stomach.

The moment the heavens' Gold-Feathered Bird[49] arrived in the sky's pasture from its eastern nest, the prince rose and said his morning prayers. The prisoners occupied themselves as usual with the task of picking and threading flowers. After some time, they approached the prince and said to him, "O freshly bloomed flower of the orchard of youth! O pride and adornment of the garden of felicity! Why are you bent on eclipsing the spring of your life with the autumn of anguish? You have a face like a flower, but it is beginning to wilt. Come with us, make garlands, and have your fill of food in the evening. Or else you will die from hunger and thirst in the wilderness of the tilism and neither a morsel of food nor a drop of water will you find." The prince answered, "Return to your work and stop trying to persuade me." The gardeners went back to picking flowers.

Finally that day also ended, and the slave girls arrived with salvers of food.

The prince got up menacingly and ordered the slave girls to put all the food on the ground and leave. At his threats they called out to the prisoners, "Come quick! This fellow is stealing your food." All the prisoners gathered there and accosted him. Asad broke the heads of a few of them with the hilt of his sword, slapped the slave girls and kicked the female laborers. He snatched all the food and stripped the slave girls of their clothes. He sat down within sight of the prisoners and started eating with great relish for their benefit. The slave girls returned naked to their mistress, crying and wailing loudly.

Princess Mahjabeen Diamond-Robe

Their mistress was none other than Princess Mahjabeen Diamond-Robe, Emperor Afrasiyab's niece and a princess of the tilism. On the first day of every New Year, Afrasiyab enthroned Princess Mahjabeen Diamond-Robe on the throne of the tilism and held festivities in her honor, in which eighteen thousand princesses and kings of the lands of Zahir the Manifest, Batin the Hidden, and Zulmat the Dark paid her their allegiance and made her offerings.

Because of Mahjabeen Diamond-Robe's fondness for that meadow, Afrasiyab had constructed a house there for her. Mahjabeen Diamond-Robe lived in it with her aunt and Afrasiyab's sister, sorceress Sandal the Crone.

Sandal was away at Afrasiyab's court when the slave girls arrived before Princess Mahjabeen Diamond-Robe crying. When the princess asked the reason for their distress, they replied that a new prisoner, who refused to make garlands and displayed the arrogance of might, had arrived in the tilism. He beat them as well as the other prisoners and snatched all the food.

The princess said to them, "Send the palace guard to take the food to the prisoners." The palace guard headed to the garden and the palanquin bearers walked behind her carrying salvers of food. Upon arrival, the palace guard called out, "O accursed prisoner, you have invited severe chastisement by raising your hand against royal officials and stealing food. How you bolt it down as if it was ordered for you! Indeed, your death flutters above your head."

Asad was incensed at these words and thought, *I should make them suffer as much as I did in this horrible place.* He rose and beat up the palace guard, took off her mantle and snatched her staff and bracelets. The palanquin bearers ran for safety, dropping the slavers of food. The prisoners of the Tilism of the Garden hid themselves in the first nook that offered a refuge.

The great pandemonium created as Asad chased the palanquin bearers brought Princess Mahjabeen Diamond-Robe out from her house. She saw a beautiful youth chasing her servants.

His two eyes were like two fawns who hunt beloveds
His two eyebrows like two calamities were
Whenever he opened his lips to laugh
Salt on the hearts of lovers he sprinkled

His face was resplendent as the sun and was set with a pair of coal black eyes. He was a latter day Yusuf in beauty. Even the dead in their graves opened their eyes to admire his bursting youth and winsome gait. The moment Princess Mahjabeen Diamond-Robe beheld him, she fell violently in love and called out, "There, there, O youth! What are you doing?"

When the prince looked up he saw a fairy-like beloved who made his heart the prey of flying arrows of her gaze. He saw a luminous sun of the sky of excellence and an inestimable pearl of the oyster of love. Her jet black locks made light of the subterranean darkness. The luminous and neat parting of her hair was the envy of the Milky Way. Her forehead was bright and high like the aspirations of the lofty minded. Her brows were shaped like bows. Her breasts were swollen like pomegranates. Her perfect chin looked like a delicious apple. In her delicacy and charm she was like an elegantly cut ruby. Her gait was like the gait of the partridge dove, her speech sweet as a parrot's, her height akin to a box tree, her cheeks as beautiful as the moon. Her shapeliness robbed the beauties of the world of all their conceit and they hid from her. She was the sun of the sky of elegance and beauty.

The moment Prince Asad saw the light-incarnate beauty of Princess Mahjabeen Diamond-Robe he lost his heart and soul to her. The princess smiled and accosted Asad, saying, "O youth, the acts of stealing and thieving are most unbecoming. Tell me what you desire." Regaled by her pearl-scattering speech, the prince replied, "O gracious friend! O essence of elegance! I was culpable of stealing food because I despaired for my life. I snatched food only after I had gone without several meals." The princess said, "That you had been starving is obvious. But how can I help it? You must find yourself a shelter and a source of food."

The prince replied, "O Princess, I am thirsty for your comely sight and beg you the alms of your beauty." The princess said, "Shamelessness is alive and well, I see. I ask you one thing and you reply about something else. I say one thing and you hear another. Go away! Leave now!" Asad answered, "O Princess, how can I leave now? Before the dictates of love we are all helpless. I would not raise my head from your doorstep now."

As they were having this conversation in the wilderness, the slave girls said to the princess, "It would be unwise to stay out in the open. Someone may accuse you of impropriety and cause you grief by pointing the finger of blame at you. It would be best to return home and bring him with you." The princess said to Asad, "If you are really so starved, accompany me to my humble house. There you may have your meal and rest awhile." Smiling and exultant, Prince Asad followed the princess to her house.

Princess Mahjabeen Diamond-Robe left Asad behind and climbed the stairs to her room. She gave orders to her slave girls to set up a golden throne.

In his eagerness, Prince Asad tried to follow the princess. After he had climbed a few steps he was suddenly lifted up by invisible hands and thrown down. The prince made another attempt and the same thing happened. He was thrown down similarly each time he tried to climb after the princess.

In the meanwhile, the princess came out. She laughed at Prince Asad's state, and said, "Did you think it would be child's play to enter my chamber?" Then she said to her sorceress-aide, Dil Aaram, "Aunt Sandal put a magic cordon around my chamber so that no stranger could enter it. Work some spell so that a path is made through it, and I can take Asad inside." Reciting an incantation, Dil Aaram struck her hands together and a path was immediately created through the magic cordon.

Princess Mahjabeen took Prince Asad upstairs and seated him on the throne. At her orders, the slave girls laid out all manner of fine foods and tasty and colorful dishes. The princess said to Asad, "Help yourself and once you have eaten you may leave." Asad replied, "O my life and soul, ever since I saw the apple of your chin my hunger and thirst have been satisfied. Now I am destined to feed on the flesh of my heart and drink my life blood. All I want now is to have you before my eyes. If you wish us to share food, step into the garden of True Faith, renouncing both sorcery and infidelity's thorn-filled darkness."

The princess was stunned to hear these words. She thought awhile, then said, "I have not yet learned sorcery but I feel reservations about renouncing Lord Laqa and giving up the faith of Sameri. These names and persons are venerable and mighty." Asad answered, "O Princess, if Laqa was indeed a true god, my grandfather Amir Hamza would not have been able to drive him from place to place."

Princess Mahjabeen was delighted when she heard Amir Hamza's name and realized Asad was the scion of a noble and distinguished house. Enlightened by Asad's words, she renounced Laqa worship. The prince and the princess then shared a meal while making love talk.

Sorceress Sandal the Crone

Suddenly, a whirlwind began to blow, they were enveloped in darkness and flaming bolts of lightning danced around them. Alarmed, the prince sought God's protection from evil as he saw the hideous sorceress Sandal the Crone, arrive riding a dragon. She was wrapped in a black mantle and wore a blue kerchief on her head. Her hair was tangled and matted, her face was covered with clay, and necklaces of bones and skulls hung around her neck.

Seeing Princess Mahjabeen cavorting with Asad, she called out, "O brazen girl! O destroyer of family honor! Who are you consorting with?" The princess hurriedly rose from Asad's side and replied, "Aunt, this hungry and thirsty prisoner of the tilism has wandered here. I took pity on him, called him over and gave him food. Now I will send him away."

Sandal the Crone kept her silence but decided to change the princess's residence thinking that if she continued to live there, she might become corrupted. Sandal knew that Afrasiyab's prisoner was destined to die but she was captivated by Prince Asad's comely looks, and said to herself, *I am old and no one ever gives me a second look. I should ask Afrasiyab to spare this prisoner's life and give him to me. This prisoner would be only too happy to have his life spared. I will take him with me and ravish him to my heart's content. Indeed I must ravish him even now, and take him to my bed.*

Sandal the Crone made herself into a fifteen-year-old damsel by magic so that anyone who saw her was struck by her charm and beauty. She accosted Prince Asad and said, "O youth, it is improper to thieve and steal." Then she said to Princess Mahjabeen Diamond-Robe, "I am going to my room. Send him inside after persuading him to lie with me. I will then forgive your trespasses; otherwise you will be punished for cavorting with him."

After Sandal the Crone retired to her room, the princess said to Asad, "Congratulations! My aunt has fallen in love with you. What wonderful good luck that God bestowed on you a shapely and graceful beloved a mere seven-hundred-years old! Why indeed would you pay me any attention now! Go take your pleasure with her."

Asad rose without responding to the princess and headed toward Sandal's room. Princess Mahjabeen Diamond-Robe's eyes welled up with tears. She took Asad's hand and said, "Have you already forgotten your professions of love? Or did you never mean what you said to me?" Prince Asad embraced the princess, wiped away her tears and consoled her, saying, "My love, I remain your slave. You will witness what I shall do when I am with this harridan Sandal." The princess kept shedding tears but Asad tore himself away from her and entered Sandal's room.

Prince Asad saw Sandal sitting undressed on a throne with great coquetry. A tray of wine lay next to her. A couch with jewelled legs lay close by. Asad went and sat next to her. At first Sandal pretended coyness and ignored him, then gave Asad a cup of wine. Asad took it from her hand and said, "O love of my life, give me a sip from your cup so that I may drink what has touched your lips and bring solace to my heart. I am thirsty for the pure cup of union with you." Prince Asad then picked Sandal up in his arms. While she cried, "No! No!" coquettishly, he laid her on the couch, put one hand on her neck, and entwined his legs with hers. Sandal reckoned that Prince Asad's desire was awake, and her own would be now fulfilled.

Instead, Asad started strangling her. She thrashed about violently but was caught in the talons of the lion and could not find release. As she choked to death, she could not even utter a spell. She did not draw another breath and the bird of her soul flew away from her body's cage. At that moment, a terrifying sound was heard as if the sky had burst asunder, and Prince Asad jumped off to one side.

Princess Mahjabeen Diamond-Robe had been watching the scene from the gap in the door. Earlier, she had burned with jealousy seeing Asad cavorting with Sandal, and said to herself, *He told me one thing and now see him become enamoured of this crone and make love talk.*

But in just a moment, the thunderous sound broke upon them, darkness enveloped the world, whirlwinds began to blow and stones and fire showered. A great clamour was heard and after a moment a voice proclaimed, "*Alas, I was killed by deceit. Sandal was my name. I had yet to pick desire's flower from the garden of youth when the winds of death wilted the flower of my life in its seven hundredth year.*"

Unnerved, Princess Mahjabeen Diamond-Robe said to her aide Dil Aaram, "What a terrible calamity that he has killed my aunt." Dil Aaram replied, "My princess, he killed her for love of you and showed no consideration for his own life. Go and see how he fares and what has happened to him."

The princess stepped into the room with Dil Aaram. By that time the darkness had parted. They saw Sandal's corpse lying naked and Prince Asad standing on one side, smiling. The princess came up to him crying, and said, "What did you do; you killed my aunt!" Asad replied, "And what say you about the skill with which I dispatched her to hell?" Mahjabeen Diamond-Robe replied, "Praise the Lord! What is to be said about courage such as yours, which shows no mercy even to someone who shows you love. After killing my aunt you expect me to praise your act?" Asad put his arms around the princess's neck and kissed her, but she pushed him away, saying, "Do you now want to choke me to death, too?" Asad replied, "O my soul, I offer my life in sacrifice to protect yours. Do you think I would survive for a single moment if I harmed you in the least?"

While they were having this exchange, suddenly Sandal's skull cracked open, a colorful bird came out of it and flew away crying, "*Alas! Alas!*"

Dil Aaram said, "Princess, it was not a bird you saw but the magic that has inhabited Sandal's vile body all these years. Now it will fly directly to Afrasiyab and give him a complete account of what happened here. The two of you will be taken captive like Princess Tasveer and Prince Badiuz Zaman."

Petrified with fear, Princess Mahjabeen said, "What must I do now?" Dil Aaram replied, "Take Asad along and escape from the tilism." Asad interjected, "I have come to conquer the tilism and will not leave without killing Afrasiyab."

Mahjabeen Diamond-Robe implored Dil Aaram, saying, "O Dil Aaram, I do not know sorcery. If you can, take us with you out of here." Dil Aaram answered, "My magic is not powerful enough to confront any sorcerer sent by Afrasiyab or to help you escape from the tilism. But I shall step down now and transform myself into a hill by magic. You may come with Asad and hide in one of its caverns. In that manner I will help you get away."

The princess acquiesced. Dil Aaram stepped down, rolled on the ground and became a hill. Princess Mahjabeen Diamond-Robe and Asad hid themselves in it. The hill uprooted itself and headed out. All the slave girls and attendants of the princess began shedding tears at the sight. Dil Aaram paid them no heed and went away carrying the prince and the princess.

ജര

In the meanwhile, the bird that had emerged from Sandal's skull reached Afrasiyab in the Apple Garden. The emperor was seated on the imperial throne, the nobles and ministers were gathered and dancers were entertaining the assembly when the bird fell before Afrasiyab's throne and cried out, "*O Emperor of Hoshruba, Sorceress Sandal was killed by Asad's hand.*" A flame darted from the bird's mouth, its feathers caught fire, and it burned to cinder.

Afrasiyab wept when he heard the news and ordered the whole court to dress in mourning. He sent for Empress Heyrat from the City of Disregard and apprised her of the news. Empress Heyrat, too, broke into tears upon hearing of it. Accompanied by all the nobles of his court and grandees of the tilism, Afrasiyab arrived where Sandal's body lay. Princess Mahjabeen Diamond-Robe's attendants fell down at Afrasiyab's feet professing their innocence. When Afrasiyab inquired about Mahjabeen Diamond-Robe, they gave him all the details of Asad's meeting with the princess and what had come about.

Afrasiyab said, "It is impossible for them to escape the tilism. Let me first attend to Sandal's last rites and burial. Then I shall punish that shameless wretch Mahjabeen."

Afrasiyab ordered the imperial procession of the tilism to be assembled. The ringers of bells and gongs and the believers of gods Sameri and Jamshed presented themselves. Magic slaves of steel made by the founders of the tilism arrived on horseback to accompany the procession. All the nobles of the tilism gathered and carried the corpse of Sandal with great pomp and ceremony according to the letter of Jamshed's faith.

After Afrasiyab had disposed of these matters, he retired with a heavy heart to the Apple Garden and penned an irrevocable order to the kings of the domains of Hoshruba, alerting them to Mahjabeen Diamond-Robe and Dil Aaram's escape with Amir Hamza's grandson Asad. He ordered that the criminals be captured on sight and sent to his court as prisoners.

Of Sorceress Princess Mahrukh Magic-Eye Changing Her Loyalties

Afrasiyab addressed the first of these letters to Princess Mahrukh Magic-Eye. She was the grandmother of Princess Mahjabeen Diamond-Robe, and related to Afrasiyab.

Mahrukh Magic-Eye was a wise and accomplished sorceress and astrologer, and an augur without match who ruled over twelve thousand sorcerers. She had moved her quarters from the region of Batin to the City of Manycolors in Zahir after an inauspicious event involving Emperor Afrasiyab and her son Shakeel, who was enamoured of Empress Heyrat's daughter, Khubsurat. The prospect of their union displeased Afrasiyab. The emperor spared Shakeel because Mahrukh Magic-Eye was one of the nobles of Hoshruba and acquainted with its secrets, but Afrasiyab separated Khubsurat from Shakeel by imprisoning her in a magic Ferris-wheel in a garden in Batin.

Afrasiyab showed Mahrukh much favor for appearances' sake but kept a wary and watchful eye on her always. He realized that if he were to arrest her granddaughter, Princess Mahjabeen, like he had Princess Tasveer, Mahrukh Magic-Eye might take offence, rebel, and join the Conqueror of the Tilism. In his letter to Mahrukh Magic-Eye, Afrasiyab wrote:

> "O Princess Mahrukh Magic-Eye! Your granddaughter has eloped with Prince Asad. Despite my elevating her to the status of a sovereign of the tilism and augmenting her rank, she showed scant regard for me and washed her hands of her honor and repute. Upon the receipt of this letter you must find Mahjabeen and produce her in my presence so that I may let her off with only a reprimand for your sake, and kill the Conqueror of the Tilism. If you show the least hesitation in carrying out

> these orders, however, your land and property will be confiscated and you will be beheaded for rebellion."

After penning this furious message, Afrasiyab gave it to his respected servant, sorcerer Zunnar, to take to Mahrukh Magic-Eye and bring back an affirmative response.

Zunnar set off on his journey and arrived in the City of Manycolors. Mahrukh Magic-Eye was informed of his arrival and received Zunnar with great respect. He was brought into the royal palace where a feast was arranged and song and dance recitals and revels were held in his honor. After fulfilling her duties as a hostess, Mahrukh Magic-Eye asked Zunnar, "What is the occasion for which you have honored this slave's humble abode?" Zunnar handed her the letter sent by Emperor Afrasiyab.

After she studied its contents, the prudent Mahrukh Magic-Eye said in a gentle voice, "O Zunnar, please wait a few moments. I will write my answer after I have reflected on the contents of this letter and sought my councillors' advice." Zunnar waited there and Mahrukh Magic-Eye retired to a separate house.

Well-versed in the art of augury, she made a horoscope to determine the fortunes of Afrasiyab and Asad. Her calculations confirmed that Afrasiyab would die at the hands of Prince Asad, who would be the Conqueror of Hoshruba. Those who would stand with him would save their lives, win honor, and rise in esteem while those who stood against him would be killed, have their houses ravaged, and be denied refuge.

When all this was revealed to Mahjabeen Diamond-Robe by celestial knowledge, she thought, *I should join Princess Mahjabeen Diamond-Robe, who is the light of my eyes. Afrasiyab is a faithless traitor and it would be best to shun him for he imprisoned Lachin, who was the real Emperor of Hoshruba. He also holds a grudge against my son because of Shakeel's love for Khubsurat and tortures his beloved in a thousand ways. It would be little wonder if my son gave up his life in grief for his beloved and passed away from this world. I should save the lives of my son and granddaughter. I must fight Afrasiyab and quench the fire of anger in my heart. There will be no better time than this. The moment is auspicious and the Conqueror of the Tilism has also appeared.*

With this in mind, Mahrukh Magic-Eye wrote the following reply to Afrasiyab's letter:

> "O Emperor of Hoshruba and King of Wizards, the royal order obeyed by all the world arrived before this feeble creature. Your humble servant's honor was redoubled and rose to the pinnacle of heavens. The reproaches expressed against my granddaughter have caused great astonishment and wonder among

> your devoted servants. Your humble subject has ever remained the target of censure and reproof in your court. Some blame or other has always found a way to attach itself to her name. You have not turned your gaze of kindness and glance of compassion toward her for ages, and she resides far away from the abode of your felicity and luxury. In this particular case, however, she must not at all be held to blame. Before the dictates of love we are all helpless. No one should be expected to surrender the light of his life to the executioner's blade. One would save the other even at the cost of his own life. In short, this lowly servant finds herself unable to search for Mahjabeen, arrest her, and submit her neck to the relentless blade. You are my lord and master and may reward or punish me as you see fit. You must do what you must and exercise your power and judgment to the fullest. I shall have nothing more to do with you now and shall not agree to Mahjabeen Diamond-Robe's humiliation. I dare not write more lest it be considered insolence."

When the reply was ready, she handed it to Zunnar, who set out for Afrasiyab's court.

Mahrukh Magic-Eye ordered her twelve thousand sorcerers to prepare to march. After getting dressed and armed, they presented themselves before her. The army folded up its camp and loaded the tents and pavilions. Mahrukh Magic-Eye also took her mother, sorceress Mah, along and sent a note to her son Shakeel, who had renounced household comforts in his love for Khubsurat and passed his days and nights in the mountainous wilderness of Kohistan. After the feud with Afrasiyab, Mahrukh Magic-Eye had deputed twelve thousand sorcerers to live with Shakeel in the wilderness and guard him. In her message Mahrukh wrote:

> "My son, I have had a falling out with Afrasiyab. You must return to me and bring your army along."

Shakeel was only too pleased to receive the note from his mother and decided that he would now either die fighting Afrasiyab or become united with his beloved. He immediately returned with his twelve thousand warriors. Thus Mahrukh Magic-Eye set out with a force of twenty-four thousand men in search of Princess Mahjabeen Diamond-Robe.

Of Afrasiyab Sending the Sorcerers Zulmat Pitch-Face, Dukhan the Steam and Shola the Blaze to Arrest Prince Asad and Princess Mahjabeen Diamond-Robe

When Zunnar presented Mahrukh Magic-Eye's reply to Afrasiyab, the emperor burnt in a blaze of rage. Realizing it would be undignified for him as the emperor to be seen marching against a mere female, he ordered three sorcerers, Zulmat Pitch-Face, Dukhan the Steam, and Shola the Blaze, to take Mahjabeen Diamond-Robe prisoner. He told the sorcerers that the three of them together would suffice for Mahrukh Magic-Eye's whole army and ordered them to arrest the sorceress's supporters as well. After receiving their orders, the sorcerers left.

Now hear of Prince Asad and Princess Mahjabeen Diamond-Robe, whose love and infatuation with each other increased every moment. Dil Aaram carried them as a hill for a thousand miles but could not get out of the tilism boundaries. She saw Mount Quartz, Mount Azure and many wonders and marvels of the tilism. She saw gardens grown with thorns and ones grown with flowers. She traversed the Kohistan wilderness and then passed by the River of Flowing Blood. When she realized she had come a long way, she stopped and asked Princess Mahjabeen Diamond-Robe and Asad to come down from the hill. Once they descended, Dil Aaram returned to human form and led the two of them along deserted paths.

After travelling some distance, they came upon a green pasture where flowers blossomed in profusion and leafy trees stood at every few steps by flowing springs and streams. The princess said, "O Dil Aaram, while I find some comfort in this wilderness, I feel I am dying from hunger and thirst. Let us rest awhile so that we may recover from the fatigue of the journey. I would like it very much if I could find something to eat."

Dil Aaram's heart filled with sorrow at the princess's plight. She said to herself, *Alas! There was a time when seventy thousand princesses bowed their heads of obedience before her and held the foot of her throne while this noble princess went out to promenade. Today she struggles through the wilderness without help or aid. There are neither criers nor throne nor the shade of a royal parasol. It is indeed true that both kings and beggars are equal in the august court of the Emperor of Love. Whether or not we will even escape with our lives and find refuge remains in question. Both Earth and heavens have sworn enmity to us and a thousand sorrows and afflictions lie in wait with bared fangs. Afrasiyab will be searching for us now and must have dispatched any number of sorcerers to arrest us. Calamity may strike us at any moment. The face of the Bride of Death fills the mirror of thought. The princess is tired. Let us rest awhile and see what transpires and what fate holds.*

Dil Aaram finally stopped by a hill in that pleasant expanse. As Princess Mahjabeen began lamenting her fate in love, Prince Asad consoled his sweet beloved. The princess said, "O faithless man, see what troubles have visited me after professing love for you. I do not protest because fate has decreed this, but do get me some food if possible so that my pangs of hunger may subside." Asad replied, "Wait here for me O Princess, while I go to hunt a deer and roast it for you."

Asad picked up his bow and quiver and set out, leaving the princess in Dil Aaram's care. He found some quarry a long distance from the hill; and chasing it led him even farther away from the princess.

After waiting a long time for the prince, Dil Aaram said to the princess, "I should go and call the prince back lest he encounters a sorcerer and is taken captive."

Dil Aaram also went away, leaving Princess Mahjabeen Diamond-Robe by herself. She cried ceaselessly at her separation from the prince and the sorry state she was in and said to herself, *I wonder how long the fickle heavens will drive me from place to place.*

The sorcerer Zulmat Pitch-Face dispatched by Afrasiyab to arrest her arrived there as the princess was engrossed in these thoughts.

When he saw Mahjabeen Diamond-Robe sitting alone he thought, *She is lovely and covered with gold and jewels. The emperor has ordered her to be put to death. I should use deception to take her to my house and ask her to satisfy my desire. If she agrees I will bide my life in great comfort and luxury as she is both rich and beautiful. At her disappearance everyone would think she escaped with Asad. Nobody would suspect me of keeping her.*

With this in mind, Zulmat approached the princess and saluted her. Frightened by the rascal's appearance, the princess guessed he had come to arrest her.

Zulmat said, "O Princess, I am your friend. Why did Prince Asad and Dil Aaram leave you?" She replied, "They have gone in search of food and water." Zulmat who had asked that question just to apprise himself of her circumstances, now slyly said, "Prince Asad came to my garden and I have entered into his service. He sent me here to bring you along and awaits you in my garden." The princess replied, "I will accompany you once Dil Aaram has returned." He answered, "Once I take you to my garden I will return to fetch Dil Aaram as well."

The princess accompanied him to the garden and saw a luxuriant expanse. Trees stood laden with flowers and a redolent breeze blew over the flowerbeds. The princess sat down in the summerhouse on a jewel-encrusted chair and asked, "Where is Asad? Please send for him."

Zulmat answered, "O Mahjabeen, you must never utter Asad's name again. Know now that I am besotted with you and have brought you here by deceit. If you agree now to lie with me, your life will be spared. You will find a safe haven with me and when Asad is killed and Emperor Afrasiyab's anger has subsided, you may return to your home."

Mahjabeen Diamond-Robe was terrified by these words and said, "O Zulmat, understand well that if you dishonor me I shall immediately swallow the ruby of my ring and kill myself." Zulmat began importuning her and laid his head at the princess's feet. When the princess did not soften, he reverted to intimidation and threats. The princess solicited the court of heavens, saying, "O Creator of Both Worlds and the Defender of the Oppressed, save my honor from this tyrant's hands!"

God so willed that the second sorcerer, named Dukhan the Steam, sent by Afrasiyab with Zulmat to arrest Mahjabeen, arrived thereupon. The princess's voice led him to the garden and when he saw Zulmat harassing her, he rebuked him, saying, "O shameless cur, what are you doing?"

Seeing Dukhan there, Zulmat realized that his secret had been exposed. He knew that Dukhan would make his report to Afrasiyab, who would punish him for his devious act. Deciding that he must kill the intruder and ravish the princess afterwards by force, Zulmat recited an incantation on a steel magic ball and hurled it at Dukhan. The ball exploded in smoke, which enveloped the whole garden in darkness.

Dukhan pulled a waterskin from his sack, poured out some water and recited a spell over it before throwing it upwards into the darkness. That darkness condensed into smoke and gathered in one corner of the garden. Dukhan splashed water on Zulmat and its drops turned into fire sparks, setting fire to Zulmat's body. Engulfed in flames, he burned to a cinder. The garden boomed with horrible sounds and great pandemonium broke out. The calamity was dispelled after some time and a voice proclaimed, "*I was killed. Zulmat Pitch-Face was my name.*"

After killing Zulmat, Dukhan approached the princess. He found her very presence lit up with the flame of her beauty. Infatuated with the princess's charm, Dukhan, too, fell prey to evil temptation and humbly said to her, "O Princess of beauties, if you agree to lie with me, my head will forever remain bowed in obedience to your pleasure. I will intercede with the emperor and have your offence forgiven. I am, after all, one of the emperor's confidants, not some ordinary sorcerer."

When the princess heard the wretch speak these words she said, "O Dukhan, you remind me of the man who rescued a lamb from the wolf only to slaughter and eat it himself. Drive any idle thoughts from your mind. If you try to molest me I will kill myself."

Dukhan realized that the princess was enamored of Prince Asad and would not grant his wish. He recited a spell that made Princess Mahjabeen Diamond-Robe fall in love with him.

Immediately Princess Mahjabeen declared, "I have no objection to what you propose."

The sorcerer realized that he must leave the house where he had entered and murdered the owner. If one of Zulmat's heirs or Afrasiyab's officials arrived, it would cause him endless trouble. He would lose the princess as well as his life. Dukhan walked out of the garden. The princess, caught in his spell, followed him. They left the garden and headed for Dukhan's house in the wilderness.

In the meanwhile, Prince Asad returned after hunting the deer and did not find the princess where he had left her. He went in search of her and saw Dukhan with the princess, who followed the sorcerer at a quick pace, as if spellbound.

Prince Asad shot an arrow at Dukhan, which took him unawares. The arrow pierced the sorcerer's chest and broke his back. Dukhan rolled down dead. A great din and clamour arose. Asad approached the princess, who had returned to her senses upon the sorcerer's death. With tears coursing from her eyes, she embraced Asad and told him all that had happened.

Asad took the princess to a mountain pass, untied his mantle and spread it on the ground. He gathered wood from the wilderness floor and lit a bonfire by striking his sword against a stone. He roasted and ate the deer with the princess, fetched water from the nearby spring, which they drank, and offered thanks to God.

They had hardly settled down when a lightning bolt flashed, a blast of thunder sounded, and the third sorcerer whom Afrasiyab had dispatched, the pitch-faced and black-hearted Shola the Blaze arrived. He challenged Asad and Mahjabeen Diamond-Robe with the cry, "I am Shola the Blaze. Now you have no means of escape!" Prince Asad grabbed the hilt of his sword and rushed forward to answer the challenge.

Shola read an incantation and struck his hands together and Asad sank waist deep into the ground. In the meanwhile, Dil Aaram returned from her search for Prince Asad. Witnessing the sorcerer, she hurled a brass-plated magic coconut at the sorcerer. Shola the Blaze uttered an incantation that counteracted Dil Aaram's magic. He turned into a flame that wrapped itself around Asad, Mahjabeen Diamond-Robe and Dil Aaram, and flew away with them.

But on the way to Afrasiyab's court, it occurred to Shola the Blaze that an aider of Asad or Mahjabeen Diamond-Robe might intercept him and snatch away his prisoners. He decided it would be best to kill them instantly and take their heads to Afrasiyab to receive land and riches in reward. With that in mind, he descended and prepared to execute his plan.

Princess Mahjabeen Diamond-Robe cried out, "O shameless tyrant, first behead me so that I am saved the sight of my lover lying covered in blood and dust."

As Shola stepped forward to behead the princess, Prince Asad called out to him, "O eunuch, kill me first. No man must see his woman killed before his eyes and be breathing still."

As Shola now turned back toward the prince, Dil Aaram cried out, "O founder of tyranny, how is it possible that a slave should live while his masters are murdered? Put an end to my life before you kill either of them!"

Confused by their protestations, Shola wondered whom to kill first. In the meanwhile, Asad turned his heart to thoughts of God and, with great fervor, importuned the Aider of the Weak, praying, "O my Lord, save us from the evil of this despot and cause this infidel to be dispatched to hell."

No sooner had the prince finished praying than the fathomless sea of God's mercy began to swell and surge and the hand of fate sent a demon against that tyrant.

It so happened that Amir Hamza's wife and the empress of Mount Qaf, Aasman Peri, had dispatched a demon to bring her the news of Amir Hamza's welfare, as was her custom. The demon was headed toward Amir Hamza's camp when his ear was attracted by grief-stricken voices rising from the ground. Looking down, he recognized Asad and regarded a sorcerer on the verge of killing the prince.

The demon immediately caught Shola the Blaze in his grasp. Twisting and breaking Shola's body and limbs, he made a morsel of the sorcerer and swallowed him whole. But the moment he ate the sorcerer, the demon felt his breath being driven out of him. He began running around in panic and wondered what had he eaten that created such tumult in his belly. He found peace only when the clamour rising after Shola's death had subsided.

Prince Asad was released from captivity. The demon saluted him and inquired about his welfare. When Asad asked who he was, the demon replied, "Your grandmother Aasman Peri dispatched me to inquire about Amir Hamza's welfare. I am now headed to his camp." Asad said to him, "Pay my respects to grandfather Hamza and also convey my regards to all the commanders of the camp." Asad then gave the demon an account of all that had passed with him and asked him to report it to Amir Hamza as well.

Prince Asad then said, "You did wrong in killing that sorcerer. Had we desired, we could have set the demons of Qaf to eliminate the entire nation of sorcerers. But it is against the code of chivalry to set demons against men. What humans can achieve with their power must not be delegated to other creatures. It is cowardice to seek the help of jinns and demons in the battlefield. If God had willed me to live, he would have created some other cause to save my life. If the sorcerers have recourse to magic, we have recourse to tricksters who can kill by deceit. It is justified to pay out the wages of sorcery in the coin of deception since warfare is based on subterfuge, and neither God nor his prophet prohibited using artifice on the battlefield. You may depart now, but never again commit such an error."

The demon saluted the prince and flew away. Asad led princess and Dil Aaram into a mountain pass where they hid.

In the meanwhile, both Afrasiyab and Princess Mahrukh Magic-Eye continued their search and dispatched sorcerers in every direction to find some trace of them.

Of the Entrance of Amar Ayyar into Hoshruba Along with his Four Notorious Tricksters, Of their Killing Sorcerers and Finding Prince Asad and Mahjabeen Diamond-Robe, And of their Meeting with Mahrukh Magic-Eye

Those who are steeped in speech untainted by deception and ruse and create enticing discourses and conquer the secret tilisms with their magical narration and miraculous solutions, wager their heads without forethought in this manner in its treacherous paths. The matchless Amar Ayyar of brilliant tricks and marvellous devices and his four tricksters headed for Hoshruba from different directions. They entered it at different points and took separate paths through the wilderness to cross the tilism's frontiers. But they kept abreast of each other's situation. Disguised as sorcerers, they travelled its lands and saw lush forests, the River of Flowing Blood, mountaintops, and many other marvels of the tilism. They saw magicians' houses everywhere. The sorcerers manning check posts played with their magic and caused showers of fire and stones to fall around. The tricksters witnessed these wonders and spectacles and kept moving onwards.

Sorcerer Muqarnas Silver-Body

Amar Ayyar arrived in a forest made of silver where, for miles on end, silver grew instead of grass. Amar said to himself, *I wish I could stuff this whole forest into my zambil. Alas, I cannot. There is nothing I can do about it, and no way for me to uproot this whole jungle.* Then it occurred to Amar to cut all the grass he could and carry it away in his zambil. He took out a scythe from the zambil and started cutting grass hurriedly. He kept looking around lest someone should catch him in the act.

After he had gathered a little grass, someone called out, "Here, O cunning thief! I was lying in wait for you and now I have caught you!"

Saying to himself, *What an accursed fate is mine!* Amar looked up to see who addressed him. Coming toward him shouting curses, he saw Muqarnas Silver-Body, a sorcerer whose body and hair were made of silver. Black snakes coiled around his head and he carried a sorcerer's contraptions.

Amar Ayyar ran at the sight of the sorcerer but Muqarnas recited a spell and struck his hands together. Amar's feet suddenly became stuck to the ground and he was unable to move a single step. Muqarnas approached with a drawn sword and asked Amar, "Are you the trickster Amar whom Emperor Afrasiyab seeks? I had created this silver forest by magic to entrap you. Now that I have found you I will present your head at Afrasiyab's court and receive my reward." Amar answered, "I am only a poor, unfortunate grass-cutter, not the Amar you seek." Muqarnas answered, "It's futile to use your cunning on me. I know the truth about you. Emperor Afrasiyab forewarned me."

While they were having this conversation, Qiran the Ethiope witnessed the whole scene from a lookout point and thought of a trick. Muqarnas was about to behead Amar when he heard someone call out, "Wait a moment, my brother!" Muqarnas turned and saw a sorcerer coming toward him wearing hoops in his ears, snakes around his neck, and wielding a trident. Muqarnas waited for him to approach. When the sorcerer came near, he said to Muqarnas, "Do not kill this thief until he has revealed where he hid my property. He took all my possessions and stole one of my two inestimable pearls."

Qiran, who was disguised as the sorcerer, showed Muqarnas a pearl the size of an egg. Muqarnas immediately took a fancy to it and said, "O brother, you have a unique treasure here. Let me have a good look at it. And do tell me where you found it." The false sorcerer answered, "I live on Mount Pearl where these pearls grow from the ground by the miracle of Lord Sameri. I selected two pearls from among them. I carry this with me now and the other this thief took." The sorcerer then handed the pearl to Muqarnas, who inspected it well from all angles and praised it a great deal. The false sorcerer said, "My brother, you must blow on it in order to witness its true radiance and see how it glows and shines."

Muqarnas Silver-Body brought that egg close to his mouth and blew a warm breath onto it. Immediately the pearl opened and smoke shot out in puffs. It travelled into Muqarnas's head by way of his open mouth and nose. Muqarnas swooned and fell to the ground. The false sorcerer, who had given him the pearl, shouted the war cry,

"I am swift as the gale of spring
The consummate master of dagger-throwing

A fire-breathing dragon in the battlefield
A ferocious lion, Qiran the Ethiope of name,"

and struck Muqarnas with his cleaver, smashing his skull.

A great commotion took place. The whole forest was wiped out of existence and a landscape of horrible desolation materialized in its place. Amar Ayyar found himself released from captivity. He embraced Qiran and praised his trickery. Qiran said, "What you saw is only the result of your training. Now tell me what you propose to do and where you plan to head." Amar answered, "We will be well-advised to travel separately. Go your way while I go mine. May God protect you."

Qiran saluted Amar Ayyar and left.

Sorcerer Mahtab Moon-Maker

The magic birds carried the news of Muqarnas's death to Afrasiyab. The emperor immediately struck his hands together and a magic slave of steel sprang from the ground. Afrasiyab said to the magic slave, "Take my note to the sorcerer Mahtab Moon-Maker, who lives in the Flashing Wilderness."

The magic slave departed and Afrasiyab ordered the sorcerers of Muqarnas's family to perform his last rites and search for the murderers. After disposing of Muqarnas's corpse, they too started searching for the tricksters.

Meanwhile, the magic slave brought Afrasiyab's note to the Flashing Wilderness and gave it to Mahtab Moon-Maker. He read Afrasiyab's note in which the emperor had written:

> "O Mahtab, Amar and four other tricksters have entered your forest after killing Muqarnas. Arrest them and do not be neglectful."

The magic slave departed after delivering the message.

Mahtab Moon-Maker conjured a house by magic in the middle of the forest and decorated it most lavishly with no convenience or luxury left wanting. A golden bed was laid out and a luxurious carpet spread on the floor. After deputing a few magicians on guard duty outside the house, Mahtab Moon-Maker cut the shape of the moon out of paper and pasted that paper moon on the door of his house. He recited a spell and it became bright and luminous like the full moon. Afterwards, Mahtab Moon-Maker sat drinking wine inside the house.

Suddenly, it occurred to Mahtab that he would have difficulty identifying the tricksters because they always struck in disguise. He decided to create a spell by which the tricksters would be recognized no matter what disguise they wore. Mahtab Moon-Maker cut out the shapes of sparrows from paper and recited a spell that made them come alive. They flew away and perched on the ledge of the roof. Mahtab implanted them with magic so that whenever Amar or any other trickster entered the house, one of the sparrows would fly to the ground, call out his name and burn up. After making these arrangements Mahtab Moon-Maker settled down, his mind finally at peace.

In the meanwhile, Amar Ayyar and the other tricksters crossed the desolation where Muqarnas lived and entered the Flashing Wilderness. From far away Amar Ayyar beheld a house in the middle of the forest lit up by a bright object that resembled the real moon, except it appeared even brighter and more luminous. He saw magicians sitting outside the door, fires burning under cauldrons and food being cooked. The magicians chanted and played tambourines in Sameri's honor. Regarding this sight, Amar said to himself, *These strumpets' sons are enjoying themselves. I must kill them and clean the forest of their vile presence.*

Amar disguised himself as a sorcerer and headed toward them. When he arrived at the house he praised the chanting of the magicians. They asked his name and where he lived. Amar answered, "I am called Nay Navaz the Flutist and I reside on Mount Calmuck." The magicians invited him to join their company and sing for them. The false sorcerer sat down and started singing in a captivating voice, which reached Mahtab Moon-Maker's ears and made him restless. He stuck his head out of the door of his room and asked the magicians to bring the man inside. The magicians led Amar indoors.

The moment Amar set foot inside the house a sparrow flew down from the ledge, called out "*Amar comes!*" and burned up.

When Amar heard the sparrow announce his name, he immediately put on his cape of invisibility. When Mahtab saw the singer disappear, he said to the magicians, "He was not a singer but Amar Ayyar. He hid himself when the sparrow revealed his identity. Go back to your duties now and stay very alert."

The magicians marvelled at these events. They went outside to confer and decided that they would now arrest any stranger who arrived there.

Amar Ayyar learned all the particulars of their arrangements and while the sorcerers returned to their duties, he went deep into the wilderness and blew his trickster's whistle. Trickster Burq the Frank heard his whistle and presented himself.

Burq said, "What is the matter, O master!" Amar said to him, "Dear boy, it is my wish that you disguise yourself as me, and head for that house where the magicians are gathered and magic sparrows announce people's names. The magicians will arrest you thinking that you are Amar, and feel satisfied on that account. Then I will arrive, perform my trickery and secure your release."

Burq said, "Very well." He immediately disguised himself as Amar and headed for Mahtab's house.

As the false Amar approached the magicians, they set upon him the moment they saw him. As he was being taken prisoner, the noise reached Mahtab Moon-Maker. He asked the magicians whom they had captured. They replied, "It is up to you to identify him now. We are certain for our part that it is Amar Ayyar." Mahtab Moon-Maker said, "Bring him here so that I may identify him." The magicians brought the false Amar forward. When he set foot inside, the magic sparrow flew down from the ledge, called out, "*Burq comes!*" and was burned up.

Mahtab Moon-Maker said to him, "Tell me O trickster if your name is Burq." The false Amar answered, "No, my name is Amar." Mahtab Moon-Maker said, "My magic sparrow does not lie." The false Amar replied, "If my name was Burq why would I have called trouble down on my head by claiming I was Amar? Do I not know that Hoshruba is full of Amar's enemies? However, if you do not wish to believe me I am not in the least troubled." Mahtab Moon-Maker said to himself, *He must be speaking the truth because if a criminal like him had a chance to hide his identity he would have certainly availed himself of it, and not invited trouble by making a false claim.* Mahtab Moon-Maker asked the false Amar, "I believe you, O Amar, but why did you not conceal your identity from me? Why didn't you claim you were Burq?" The false Amar replied, "My claim would have been futile. You could have easily discovered the truth as you have recourse to all kinds of magic." Mahtab Moon-Maker said, "You speak true but since the magic sparrow announced you as Burq, is it possible that you are known by that name, too?" The false Amar answered, "My real name is indeed Burq, but everyone calls me Amar." Mahtab Moon-Maker said, "Didn't I tell you that my magic does not lie! Now I know that both you and my magic were right. However, I must put you through another test and see if your face corresponds to the portrait the emperor sent to help me identify Amar."

Mahtab Moon-Maker took out a portrait of Amar Ayyar from the chest. When he saw not the least difference between it and the prisoner's face, Mahtab felt certain that it was the real Amar. He tied him up in a corner of the room and felt most pleased with himself.

Now hear of the real Amar Ayyar, who watched these events from far away. After Burq was captured, Amar disguised himself as a beautiful girl whose world-adorning beauty would make even the full moon shrink to a crescent from embarrassment and shame. She resembled a brilliant flame of light, a marvel of God's handiwork. To compare her to a houri or a fairy would have been an injustice to her beauty. No one had ever seen or heard of such splendor. Her coquettish manner and airs and graces were pleasant and becoming.

Her forehead was like the full moon but outshone the moon in the sky in brightness. Her gazelle-like eyes lined with collyrium darted like the fearful deer of China. Her carmine lips were like a box of ruby, her luminous cheeks like the Mirror of Sikander,[50] and her teeth like a string of pearls. Her delicate arms looked crystalline, and when her wrist appeared out of her sleeve, it was as if a burning taper was disclosed from under the glass tube of the chandelier. Her bosom was the incarnation of light, her abdomen was like a crystal slab, and her breasts were entirely inestimable. In short, her body from head to waist seemed made of light. So luminous was her leg that even if her seekers had forever remained engrossed in thought, they could never have reached its proximity.[51] It seemed that her thighs were kneaded with powdered stars. The delicacy of her feet was such that if the toes seemed carved of sandalwood, the heels would be fashioned from fragrant aloe-wood. Such was the comely shape and appearance Amar took on.

From head to toe her allure
Attracts my heart, and claims it for its own

Then the false damsel adorned herself with a red dress, put on gold jewelery, a bracelet, and tore the skirts of her robe to shreds. She screened her luminous aspect by covering it with dark ringlets, and it looked as if the bright moon had been eclipsed by black clouds. With these preparations, she headed out from there crying bitterly like a spring cloud. She hid herself in the bushes in front of the room where Mahtab Moon-Maker was engrossed in admiring the beauty of the forest and set up crying and wailing.

The false damsel made loud plaints and protested the fickle ways of the heavens. She denounced the ephemeral world, saying, "O wretched sky! O heavens that revolve askew! Tell me my crime for which you punished me thus? Alas! Alas!" Amar worked his persona into such a frenzy of tears that even the hearts of stones would have turned to water. When her wailing and lamentations reached Mahtab Moon-Maker's ears, he looked into the bushes. There he saw a bride of the first night and a bright moon of the sky of beauty sitting, eclipsed by grief and sorrow. With her dress in shreds, her hair in tangles, and her chest lacerated by the dagger of grief, she sat alone, crying and lamenting her state.

Mahtab Moon-Maker desired to learn her story and ordered his magicians to call the woman over with great kindness. The magicians walked over to her but that delicate creature ran away at the sight of them, stumbling and falling. The magicians importuned and solicited her on their master's behalf that he only wished to hear her story, but she made no answer. They returned to Mahtab and told him that she refused to hear them.

Mahtab was smitten by her beauty which made the resplendent sun envious. He went himself, and when that rose-like beauty tried to run away from him too, he caught her hand. The rays of her radiant beauty blinded Mahtab's eyes as he regarded her comely face and shapely body. He lost power over his limbs and his heart pulsated violently. Mahtab almost fell into a swoon and neared losing consciousness but regained his senses and said to the false damsel, "O envy of the sculpted beauties, I plead with you in the name of lord Sameri to share your tragic tale with me. Tell me which sea of beauty produced this lustrous pearl and which precious shell held this inestimable gem. Why do you look so wan and anguished? What affliction do you suffer, tell me?"

The Venus-faced, false beauty now heaved a cold sigh from the bottom of her sorrowful heart and cried so inconsolably that Mahtab Moon-Maker found it difficult to hold back his own tears. When he implored her again to tell him of her sorrows, the false bride replied, "What should I tell you of my sorry plight? How could I enumerate my many afflictions? The one whose comely face I wish to behold I will now only see in the Future State. Alas, he left me and become one with clay. I had not yet cooled my eyes by his sight before he left this world. Surely the narcissus will sprout from my grave to mark one who died for love![52] Know O dear friend, that I am the daughter of an illustrious sorcerer who was a merchant by profession. I fell in love with my cousin, a mere boy in the prime of youth. The down of adolescence had yet to grace his face when my father learned of our love. We were affianced, and my father prepared to hold the nuptials. A Zanzibarian had long been infatuated with me, although I never returned his advances. Upon hearing of my impending marriage, the tyrant raided our house with scores of marauders on the day planned for my wedding procession. Before my husband could drink the sherbet of union, he was served the bitter cup of death. My parents and my uncle were killed while I escaped into the wilderness from that calamitous terror. Now you know my whole story. I will be a guest briefly in this ephemeral world, for my sorrows will soon carry me away to the Future State."

Mahtab Moon-Maker's eyes welled up with tears listening to this heart-wrenching account. He tried to console the false damsel whose narrow mouth resembled an unopened bud, and said, "O charming beloved, one must not forever grieve for the departed! You must accompany me to my humble abode and bring it to life with your joy-bestowing feet. Spend the rest of your life in the company of this true lover and happily bide your time. I have the honor of being one of Afrasiyab's counsellors. I am the master of a tilism myself, and have all kinds of powers at my command. I shall forever remain your slave and look after your happiness." That dainty false beauty replied, "A crazy-minded and accursed person such as myself is unfit to take up residence with anyone."

Mahtab Moon-Maker made vows, prostrated himself before her, and entreated her ceaselessly. Then that charming beloved said, "What is your name O friend, and what is your occupation and trade?" He replied, "I am the sorcerer Mahtab Moon-Maker. My dominions extend from here to the frontiers of Mount Azure."

She touched her earlobes and said, "A sorcerer! Heaven's mercy! I am afraid of their very name. The trappings and working of magic scare me to death. The sorcerers are thousands of years old and change their form from man to woman and woman to man in a trice."

When Mahtab Moon-Maker heard her reply, he said to himself, *Why did I have to declare myself a sorcerer! I have now ruined all my chances.* He said to her, "O beloved, may I sacrifice my life to protect yours. I shall never perform magic in your presence. Moreover, I am young – a mere stripling of three hundred and twenty-five years." That false beauty, the destroyer of faith, declared, "Make a vow that you will never perform sorcery." Mahtab Moon-Maker immediately swore in Jamshed's name and promised he would not revert from his word.

Finally, the false damsel accompanied Mahtab Moon-Maker to his house.

The moment that rose-like creature stepped inside, a magic sparrow flew down from the ledge and cried, "*Amar comes!*" and burned up. Mahtab Moon-Maker said to himself, *I have captured Amar once already. I also verified his face with his portrait and that, too, confirmed it. This magic sparrow must be lying.* While Mahtab Moon-Maker was engrossed in these thoughts, the false damsel said, "It was for this reason that I did not wish to accompany you. Now I shall leave. I told you that magical devices will be the death of me."

Smitten with her beauty, Mahtab Moon-Maker replied, "O darling, the tricksters keep attacking, and I made these magic sparrows for my protection to alert me of their presence." She replied, "I cannot bear it. This magic sparrow just called me a trickster. Now I suppose you ought to avoid me because I am a trickster and could kill you!"

As she headed out, Mahtab Moon-Maker stopped her by holding her in his embrace and, after much flattery and praise, persuaded her to return. As she stepped inside another magic sparrow flew down from the ledge, cried, "*Amar comes!*" and burned up. That false beauty asked Mahtab Moon-Maker, "Now tell me, who did the magic sparrow alert you against?" Mahtab Moon-Maker replied, "It seems that some fault has occurred in my magic. And since it also frightens you, I shall eliminate it altogether."

Mahtab Moon-Maker recited an incantation and struck his hands together, which caused all the sparrows to fall to the ground and burn up. Mahtab Moon-Maker said, "Now you may settle down here in comfort." The false damsel sat down on the golden couch and noticed Burq lying tied up in a corner. Their eyes met and Burq realized it was Amar Ayyar in disguise.

In the meanwhile, Mahtab Moon-Maker sent for food and said to the false damsel, "You are hungry. Eat something. Thereafter we will seek pleasure from each other and rest." The mouth of that rosebud opened to say, "I haven't had a sip of wine in many days. My senses are in disarray. Now I feel neither hunger nor thirst. I long only for wine. Before you lay this sumptuous feast for us, give me a cup of wine." Mahtab Moon-Maker immediately brought a tray of wine. He put it before her and said, "Here! Drink to your heart's content." This rose-like false creature filled a goblet with roseate wine and offered it to Mahtab Moon-Maker, who said, "You haven't had wine for some time. I would that you have a sip first." She answered, "I will have it in my turn. This cup is for you."

While they were having this exchange, Afrasiyab remembered he had not heard from Mahtab Moon-Maker since he sent the note. Wondering why he had not captured Amar Ayyar yet, Afrasiyab decided to look into the *Book of Sameri* to see what passed with him. He learned that Amar sat beside Mahtab Moon-Maker disguised as a woman and was about to kill him.

The emperor recited a spell and a magic slave sprang up from the ground. Afrasiyab said, "Rush to Mahtab Moon-Maker and tell him that the woman sitting beside him is Amar Ayyar, and the one lying tied up in a corner is Burq the Frank. Tell him to arrest both of them and bring them here." The magic slave left immediately with the emperor's message.

The false damsel had filled her mouth with drug powder and also mixed it in the wine she gave to Mahtab Moon-Maker. The sorcerer had not yet taken a sip when the ground trembled and the false damsel reckoned that some calamity had arrived. The next instant the magic slave dispatched by Afrasiyab sprang up from the ground. With a frightened cry, the false damsel threw herself into Mahtab Moon-Maker's arms, and he said to her, "Don't be afraid!" She pressed her cheek against Mahtab's and blew the powdered drug from her mouth into the sorcerer's nostrils. He sneezed and fell unconscious.

The magic slave cried, "*O Mahtab, this is Amar Ayyar. The emperor has ordered you to arrest him.*" But by then Mahtab Moon-Maker lay comatose and deaf to his cries. The magic slave stepped forward to deliver the emperor's message into Mahtab Moon-Maker's ears. Seeing him approach, the false damsel threw the Net of Ilyas and caught him. Then leaving him in a corner tangled in the net, she released Burq and killed Mahtab Moon-Maker. A commotion of thunderous noise broke out and darkness fell over everything.

When the magicians appointed by Mahtab Moon-Maker rushed into his room, Amar and Burq beheaded them with dagger blows. A blaze arose, killing many a sorcerer. The few who survived were too terrified to set foot indoors and ran away to escape the calamity that had struck inside.

After some time, when things returned to normal, Amar released the magic slave from the net and said to him, "Go tell that clown Afrasiyab that I shall soon behead him by the grace of my majesty and glory."

The magic slave took off immediately. Amar looted all the goods and riches of Mahtab Moon-Maker and stuffed them into his zambil. Then Amar and Burq headed for the forest.

Burq said, "Tell me O master, what your plan is." Amar answered, "I will go my way dear boy and you should go yours, but do come to me in my hour of need." Burq made a salute and went leaping and bounding in one direction while Amar Ayyar took another.

Sorcerer Azar of the Portrait Tablet

The magic slave reported Mahtab Moon-Maker's death to Afrasiyab and the news of Amar Ayyar catching him in the net. The emperor was seized with rage and fury.

As he prepared to capture Amar himself, his courtiers humbly said, "O Emperor of Hoshruba, it does not become your dignity to go to capture one of Hamza's tricksters. Among your slaves are many who are capable of bringing even Hamza captive. A common trickster like Amar Ayyar is of absolutely no consequence. You are the Master of the Tilism. To arrest Amar you should dispatch one of your servants after teaching him magic that helps him recognize the tricksters no matter what disguise they put on."

Afrasiyab realized they offered wise counsel.

The Emperor of Hoshruba now cast a fiery look toward a flowerbed in the garden that started to burn from the heat of his gaze. Afrasiyab himself became a flame and disappeared inside that blazing flowerbed. A moment later he emerged carrying a gemstone tablet in his hands, painted with the portrait of a beautiful maiden.

Afrasiyab struck his hands together and the earth cleft asunder to disgorge a sorcerer of hideous aspect and form, who was named Azar.

Afrasiyab handed the tablet to him and said, "O Azar, go and bring me Amar Ayyar prisoner. He lurks in the Flashing Wilderness after killing Mahtab Moon-Maker. I give you this tablet to help you recognize him. You must look at it whenever you come upon anyone along the way. Although it currently displays the portrait of a woman, if a trickster appears before you the picture will change to the true face of that trickster. You will be able to recognize him in any disguise. If the person is not a trickster, the portrait will remain unchanged."

Azar left and began searching for Amar in the Flashing Wilderness.

In the wilderness, Amar Ayyar was saying to himself, *O Amar, who knows what fate holds in store in this adventure. It is an enchanted land, hundreds of thousands of sorcerers abound in this tilism, and it is impossible to kill all of them. Who knows where the tablet of tilism is hidden, or what passed with Prince Asad. God alone knows whether he is still alive or dead!*

Amar sat engrossed in these thoughts when he sighted a sorcerer searching for someone in all directions. Amar said to himself, *I must kill this wretch so that the number of sorcerers is reduced at least by one.* Amar put on a sorcerer's disguise himself and approached the sorcerer who was none other than Azar.

Azar saw a sorcerer of terrifying aspect coming toward him spewing flames from his mouth, nose and ears.

Azar accosted him and said, "Who are you?" The false sorcerer answered, "You must give me your name first." Azar introduced himself and described his search for Amar Ayyar. The false sorcerer said to him, "I am on the same mission. I have been searching for Amar since

I heard of my relative Mahtab Moon-Maker's death." Azar said, "Let us then search for Amar together."

The false sorcerer readily accompanied Azar and remained on the lookout for an opportunity to overpower and kill him.

Azar suddenly remembered that the emperor had instructed him to look at the tablet with the portrait whenever he met someone on the way. When Azar looked at the portrait, it had changed into Amar's real face – someone with a head like a dried gourd, eyes the size of cumin seeds, ears like apricots, cheeks resembling bread cake, a neck that was thread-like, and limbs akin to rope. His lower body measured six yards and upper body three. Azar's senses took flight when this marvellous vision unfolded before his eyes. He realized that in the sorcerer's disguise was a trickster whose real shape and form were depicted in the portrait.

Azar recited a spell by which Amar lost the use of his limbs. Azar produced a chain from his sorcerer's bag and tied Amar with it. When Amar protested, saying, "Why do you torment me in this manner, brother?" Azar replied, "O wily man, don't try your tricks on me. You are the one known as Amar Ayyar, and I know that for a fact."

Enraged, Amar said, "I would not bet on your living too long. You'll be dispatched hellward in no time. One hundred and eighty-four thousand tricksters have entered the tilism and soon one of them will put an end to your life." Azar replied, "I will kill all of them and not be frightened by your words." Then Azar led Amar away.

Zargham saw from far away that a sorcerer had taken Amar prisoner. He tried to find some way of securing his release. He overtook Azar by two miles, where he saw a cowherd grazing his animals. Zargham went before the cowherd in the disguise of a local man and said to him, "A wolf is creeping up on one of your cows in the bushes." As the cowherd turned and ran toward the bushes, Zargham threw his snare rope and tightened it around the cowherd's neck so that he could not make the slightest noise. Zargham then pulled him down to the ground and drugged him unconscious.

Zargham disguised himself as the cowherd by putting on his garb, tying the kerchief on his head and wearing a waistcloth and doublet. After hiding the real cowherd in the bushes, he began grazing the herd.

Presently, Azar arrived, leading Amar. Because it was sunny and he had travelled a long distance, he said to the false cowherd, "If you have a rope and a bowl, fetch me some drinking water from a well." The false cowherd answered, "You have come from far it seems. If you wish I can bring you some fresh milk. You may drink that instead of water." Azar replied, "Very well, bring it!" The false cowherd whistled to a cow and milked her in a brass pot, drugged the milk and handed it to the sorcerer.

Azar was about to drink the milk when he recalled that Mahtab Moon-Maker was killed by two tricksters. Suspecting that the cowherd might be one, Azar looked at the portrait. It depicted Zargham's face.

After reciting a spell, Azar captured him, too. Zargham cried and protested, saying, "I am a cowherd, why do you torture me? Is this how you return a good deed?" Azar answered, "O crafty wretch, I recognize you all too well." He chained Zargham to Amar and went forth.

Amar said to Azar, "Didn't I tell you that thousands of tricksters have arrived in the tilism. Arresting the two of us will not save you. You will die soon. It would be best for you to submit your allegiance to us." Azar thought, *Indeed he speaks the truth. The tricksters are scattered all over the tilism. I wonder how I will reach the emperor's court in the region of Batin. I must not speak to anyone on the way without first consulting the portrait.*

After making this resolve, Azar continued on his way.

While the tricksters were dispersed in the tilism, they remained abreast of each other's affairs by climbing up high points along the way and following each other's movements. Burq had seen Azar leading away two tricksters as prisoners. He sat down in a mountain pass and, using tricksters' paints and lotions, made himself into a beauty as radiant as the moon. He painted his hands and feet with lac dye[53] and put rings on every digit of his hands. He dressed himself in a *lahgam*[54] skirt and mantle, combed the hair over his temples and filled the parting with cinnabar. Lining his eyes with collyrium and sporting a *tika*[55] on his forehead, Burq put on hoops and earrings, bangles and anklets, and wore toe-rings on every toe. The heart-ravishing false damsel then headed toward Azar in a wine seller's disguise, stepping with a coy and flirtatious air, carrying a bottle of drugged wine in her hands.

Azar saw a woman striding alluringly toward him whose beauty was the envy of houris and fairies and whose very essence was fermented with playfulness and coquetry. She caused the hearts of the lovers to throb in step with her. Azar fell in love with her at first sight, and called out, "O wine seller, come here and pour me a little wine." That false beauty lifted a corner of her veil, smiled and answered, "This wine is not for sale."

Azar lost his senses and reason upon seeing her beautiful face. He approached her and said, "Where are you headed?" Her mouth opened like a flower bud in answer, and she said, "I go where I please. Who are you to ask me questions? Do you imagine yourself the city magistrate?"

Azar caught her hand when he saw her answer with a coy smile, for he reckoned that she could be easily persuaded to satisfy his desire.

The false wine seller protested half-heartedly and then said, "Someone might surprise us here. While you have nothing to lose, I have to be mindful of my name and reputation." Azar said to her, "Let us go and sit under a leafy tree and drink a cup or two of wine. Let us converse a little; afterwards you may go where you please. What is the hurry? It would give us the chance to make each other's acquaintance. If you would accept my love, I will always remain obedient to you. Whatever I earn I will bring home to you."

The false beauty broke into a peal of laughter. She said, "Go and make your acquaintance with your sisters! Do you think I have no husband? I don't stop to make small talk with strangers met along the way." Azar began imploring. He prostrated himself before her, declaring, "I am no stranger! I am a citizen of Hoshruba and the emperor's servant."

That false beauty replied, "No matter who you are, I am not one to be taken in by men's words." Azar realized now that she spoke like a coquette. He tied the chain with which he had imprisoned Amar and Zargham around his waist and carried the wine seller away in his arms despite her protests, and put her down under a tree.

Azar tied Amar and Zargham to the tree trunk, spread a sheet and, seating the false wine seller, said to her, "My soul violently longs for your love. Come sit beside me and bring cheer to my heavy heart." That moon-like beauty heaved a cold sigh in answer, and recited,

"I have long imbibed of love's pains and pleasures
You can only deceive the one new to this game."

Azar took her in his arms and attempted to kiss her but she pushed his face away with her hand saying, "Enough of these lies and deceptions. Yours is a momentary infatuation, I know well. Unfaithfulness lies in the essence of men. Still, if you wish to be my lover, swear to me in the name of Lord Sameri that you will never speak to another woman."

Azar immediately swore an oath. Then the false wine seller poured him a cup of wine. As he took the cup in his hands, Azar realized that he had not yet consulted the tablet given him by Afrasiyab. Before indulging in pleasure-seeking with the wine seller he decided to look at the tablet for the sake of caution. When he looked, the portrait revealed Burq's face. Azar recited a spell and blew it on the wine seller, which made her makeup evaporate and Burq appear before him without disguise. Azar tied him up with the chain as well and said to himself, *I have to contend with a string of tricksters who lay traps for me at every step!*

Amar Ayyar said to him, "O son of a whore, think not that you will escape alive. You'll be killed in the blink of an eye."

Azar felt greatly frightened by Amar's words but kept moving onward with his prisoners.

The trickster Jansoz sighted Azar from afar and followed him furtively. Azar arrived at a beautiful garden full of flowers that was lavishly constructed by some sorcerer in the middle of the wilderness. Azar entered the garden and, tired from his journey, rested by a flowerbed. Noticing that, Jansoz disguised himself as a gardener, stuck shears in his belt, filled the skirts of his robe with flowers and, carrying a mattock on his shoulder, entered the garden dragging a tree he had dug up in the forest.

Azar thought the gardener had returned with a tree he had gone to fetch from the forest. He approached the false gardener and asked, "Whose garden is this?" The false gardener replied, "It belongs to Princess Banafsha." Azar thought she must be one of the thousands of sorceresses who inhabited Hoshruba and did not ask him any further questions.

The false gardener made a few bouquets and sprays of flowers and arranged them in a basket with fruits in the middle. He put it before Azar, who gave him some money and picked up a fruit. Before tasting it Azar remembered he must take a look at the portrait. When he did, it had turned into a portrait of Jansoz. Azar cried out, "O wretch, you thought you could trick me! I know you are a trickster." Jansoz tried to escape but Azar arrested him by reciting a spell, and tied him up with the same chain.

Azar was now terrified of the tricksters and hurriedly left the garden. As he led his captives onwards, it occurred to him that he should lie in hiding and send a note to the emperor informing him that he had caught some tricksters but many more were still at large and on his track. He decided to ask the emperor to send some sorcerers who could produce the captive tricksters before him, since he himself could not fly with the prisoners tied to him. Thus decided, Azar headed onwards looking for some hiding place.

This time, Azar was sighted by Qiran the Ethiope, who saw a sorcerer leading away his master Amar Ayyar and three other tricksters as prisoners.

Qiran wondered why four tricksters, who had successively attempted to kill the sorcerer, had failed in their mission. His mind dove into the sea of trickery and presently emerged with a pearl of thought. He realized the sorcerer must possess a magic that revealed the identity of the person before him. Qiran tried to think of some ruse by which to kill Azar without going near him or letting him hear his voice.

The trickster's mind now went to promenade in the garden of trickery and presently returned with the flower of ingenuity. He calculated the path through which Azar must pass, overtook him, and quickly cut wood from the wilderness to make four poles. He laid a roof of leaves on top and covered it with a creeper from the forest to give it the appearance of a fakir's hut. Then, disguised as an Azad fakir[56] wearing cord necklaces, Qiran put cotton plugs soaked in faint-repellent drugs into his nostrils. He placed a burning clay-brazier before him and burning logs around him. He tossed handfuls of drugs onto the fire. The smoke that rose filled the hut and its surroundings.

After some time, Azar arrived leading the prisoners and saw a hut beside which a holy basil plant grew. A fakir sat inside swaying in deep meditation, oblivious to the world. A deerskin lay spread beside him and a bowl for smoking hemp was placed in a corner. A fire burned in front of the fakir, with fire tongs stuck in a clay-brazier. To all appearances, he looked the perfect image of an ascetic.

Azar stepped forward and touched the false fakir's feet with veneration. He humbly stood before him and requested, "Sir, bless me that I may reach Afrasiyab's court safely for the tricksters are on my scent and are baying for my blood." The false fakir turned a fiery look at Azar, who collapsed, frightened by his gaze.

After Azar had inhaled a sufficient quantity of smoke from the drug, the false fakir said to him, "O fool, know that I am also a trickster and lie in wait here to murder you." Terrified, Azar tried to rise to his feet and apprehend the false fakir but the drug had worked its effect. No sooner did he rise than he fell down.

Qiran stood up and struck with his cleaver, shattering Azar's head into a thousand pieces.

Hail and stones began falling, and terrifying cries filled the wilderness. After a pause, a voice proclaimed, "*I was killed! Azar was my name.*" A bird of brilliant plumage came out of his skull and flew away toward Afrasiyab's court crying "*Alas! Alas!*"

Azar's death brought release to Amar Ayyar and the three tricksters. Qiran saluted Amar Ayyar, who praised him. Amar and the other tricksters again returned to the wilderness and proceeded in different directions.

Amar headed onwards furtively. The shades of night had fallen. The Traveller of Heavens[57] had retired to dwell in its Western Lodge. The Trekker of the Desert of Space[58] joined the company of astral companions. The beasts of the wilderness retired to their dens and lairs, and the birds of the air returned to their tree perches.

Each trickster found shelter in the mountain passes; they took out bread from their bags and ate. They drank from the springs and offered thanks to the Nourisher of the World before going to sleep. Amar, however, remained hungry. He said to himself, *I will not take out bread from my zambil. This is the great disadvantage of being in Hamza's service! One has to eat from one's own pocket. Now it is night and I cannot even go anywhere to find food. That accursed sorcerer Azar also kept me tied up the whole day. There's nothing to do now but to exercise patience and sleep on an empty stomach.* Amar Ayyar lay down to sleep on a rock but when he felt unbearably hungry, he picked fruit from the tree and ate. Then he reluctantly took some dry bread from his zambil, quelled his hunger, and finally went to sleep.

The bird that had come out of Azar's skull arrived in the Apple Garden before Afrasiyab and cried out loudly, "*O Emperor of the Tilism, Azar has been killed*!" Afrasiyab shook with rage and bit his lips in anger. He ordered a sorcerer to go to the wilderness where Azar's corpse lay and bury his body and bring back the tablet he had given Azar to recognize the tricksters. Afrasiyab instructed the sorcerer not to spend the night in the wilderness. His orders were to obtain the tablet, bury the corpse, and return as soon as he was finished.

Afterwards, Afrasiyab retired for leisure and pursuit of pleasure. The sorcerer carried out his mission in the wilderness, returned, and handed the tablet to Afrasiyab.

The night ended and the Sorcerer of the East,[59] sporting the sack woven with golden rays, appeared on the doorstep of the miracle-working heavens. At the crack of dawn the notorious tricksters each bowed their heads before God and then carried on their way, alert and with lofty ambitions.

Sorcerers Rahdar and Faulad

Emperor Afrasiyab also awoke from his sweet dreams. He headed for the Apple Garden to give audience where the courtiers presented themselves. Dancers began entertaining the assembly and wine was drunk. When Afrasiyab's mind had been warmed by the wine, he turned to two sorcerers, Rahdar and Faulad, and said to them, "Amar and four tricksters have entered the tilism and arrived at the River of Flowing Blood after killing sorcerers. Meanwhile, Mahrukh Magic-Eye is headed for Forest of Narcissi in search of Prince Asad and Mahjabeen Diamond-Robe, who are hiding in a mountain pass. Do not concern yourself with the tricksters at present; proceed to where Asad is hiding as both Mahrukh Magic-Eye and the tricksters will arrive there in due time; you could capture all of them together."

Afrasiyab gave them some soil and said, "This is from the graves of Sameri and Jamshed. Any sorcerer, no matter how powerful, will fall unconscious if you hurled some on him." Rahdar and Faulad left on their mission after receiving the soil from Afrasiyab.

Now hear of what passed with the tricksters. Alert, quick of step, and racing with their shadows in the mountains and deserts of the tilism, each of them continued on their separate paths in search of Prince Asad.

Amar Ayyar, still hungry from the previous night, looked for some town or village where he could ply his tricks and have a meal at others' expense. He had gone some distance when he saw a city's precincts. Amar quickly bridged the distance and arrived near its walls. He saw the city walls were made of marble decorated with colorful patterns. The steel door of the entrance stayed open like the eyes of the lover seeking his beloved. But Amar saw no human being there, let alone a guard.

Amar found the shops in the city well stocked and piles of a variety of fine and select goods at every step. But no shopkeepers minded those goods. The shops of mercers and jewellers were open but devoid of any human presence. Tall buildings, pleasant squares and fine houses all lay empty with no one to inhabit them. Amar explored every corner of the city and arrived in a field where he saw a strong and secure castle whose walls reached to the vault of the heavens.

Amar found the door of the castle open with nobody to bar his way. He stepped inside and saw a royal court with seats and chairs laid around a jewel-encrusted throne. Four paper magic slave girls sat on four chairs beside the throne.

As Amar stepped forward, the magic slave girls said, "*O wretch, you found your way here as well!*" Surprised to hear them speak, Amar reminded himself that he was in a tilism. He decided not to pay too much attention to these marvels and quickly left the place. After leaving the castle, Amar returned to the city market and picked up some goods from the empty shops. He was about to put them in his zambil when suddenly the earth cleft asunder and one of the four magic slave girls Amar had encountered in the castle emerged from the ground and caught hold of his hand. She cried, "*O thief deserving of beheading, put back whatever you have stolen from the shops or you will pay dearly for it.*" Amar Ayyar quickly replaced everything. The magic slave girl released his hand and returned into the earth. Amar headed onwards but, with all these goods lying there free for the taking, he could not resist the temptation and again picked up some goods. Immediately, the ground opened up again and, realizing that the magic slave girl was about to emerge, Amar ran with his loot. He ran long and hard but when he finally stopped in an alley to rest, the ground cleft again and the magic slave girl emerged. She caught Amar's hand and dragged him back to the scene of the crime.

Amar again had to put back all that he had taken. The magic slave girl disappeared and Amar headed onward, helplessly saying to himself, *O miserable me! Between yesterday and today I have not earned even two cowries. What a wretched fate is mine!*

Finding no other recourse left to him, Amar made his way back into the wilderness.

Sorceress Khumar

After a long journey, Amar Ayyar arrived at the shores of the River of Flowing Blood. He beheld a full and swelling sea stirring with turbulent waves. Every so often the blood-thirsty crocodiles that swam in it raised their heads, snapped their jaws, and dove back into the water.

Amar saw the Bridge of the Magic Fairies with its three-tiered tower from which the blood of the Abyssinians fell in a cascade into the river. Amar tried to ford the river in vain. The abode of renowned sorcerers, Batin, lay on the other side of the river and no one could enter it without Afrasiyab's permission.

After failing in his attempt to enter Batin, Amar Ayyar sat down in a secluded nook with his trickster's paints and lotions and made himself into the likeness of a sixteen-year-old boy. He masked his moustache and whiskers with a cloth and painted over it to give his face the look of a simple, innocent youth. He lined his eyes to their edges with collyrium and tinged his hands with henna. He dressed in a yellow shirt and silken pyjamas, sported a bracelet on his wrist and wore tasselled slippers sewn with gold and silver threads strung with pearls. Amar took a bowl and string out of his zambil, threw the fishhook into the river, and held the line waiting by the riverside.

It so happened that the powerful sorceress Khumar, with whom Afrasiyab was secretly in love, was returning along that very path astride a dragon to her home in the region of Batin. When she reached the riverside, she saw the youth standing there. She noticed the down of adolescence had not yet graced his face; he was of good height and a matchless pearl of the sea of beauty and grace. His eyebrows were like crescents and his body glowed like the silvery full moon. Seeing him standing there holding his fishing line, Khumar was surprised at his ingenuousness; he did not seem to know that no fish could be caught from this magic river. Deciding to advise and counsel the youth to save himself the fruitless labour, Khumar dismounted, approached the youth and said, "Dear boy, what idle fancy has entered your mind that you hope to catch fish in a magic river?"

Hearing her voice, the false youth looked up and saw a young sorceress whose beauty was the envy of the resplendent sun and the moon. Her hair was strung with pearls, she wore a lavish costume and gold ornaments and pearl necklaces hung from her neck. Amar noticed her riches and salivated with greed. He thought, *At last God sent me a fat prey after starving me for two days. I must murder this sorceress and steal her dress and gold. I will finally be able to pay off some of my creditors.*

He looked at Khumar with a smile and said, "What did you say? I didn't quite hear you." Khumar replied, "I only wish to tell you that this river is not real. It is made of magic, and it is useless to fish in it. Desist from your fruitless labour and go home." He answered, "What lies! I have already caught several fish and made their kebabs. After I catch a few more I would bring their kebabs to my wife to make up with her." Khumar drowned in the sea of amazement when she heard that he had caught fish in the magic river. She said, "Where do you live my dear, and who is your wife?" He answered, "We were married yesterday. When I tried to lie with my wife she told me she wanted to eat kebabs of fish caught from the River of Flowing Blood. Until I brought them for her she would neither talk, nor open her mouth, nor say a word. I fish here for this reason."

Khumar broke into laughter at his words and said, "O silly, silly boy! Your wife is a whore. She planned your destruction by sending you here, hoping you would be killed for impudently fishing in the River of Flowing Blood. She could then enjoy herself with other men. Beware! Do not fish here again, ever! Come with me and I will find you a wife who is like the moon in her beauty. Get rid of that whore of a wife of yours."

The false youth answered, "You yourself are a strumpet and whore! Go away! I will sacrifice my life for my wife in the blink of an eye." Khumar said to herself, *He is completely naive and an artless, youthful boy. No one has snared him in love yet. He is completely unfamiliar with the nectar of union and the thorn of separation. It is for this reason that he is so committed to his wife. If possible, I should take this youthful boy with me and drink from the spring of his comely beauty and please myself by his looks. I should not speak to him harshly at all but in honeyed tones.*

Khumar approached him and said, "O envy of the moon, where do you live?" He answered, "In the vault of your heart." Khumar smiled and caught his hand, saying, "Come, give me a taste of the kebabs you have made of your catch." He replied, "What cheek! What would I take my wife if I gave you the kebabs?"

Khumar embraced him and said, "I would become your wife." He asked, "Would you really become my wife? Tell me the truth." Khumar answered, "I speak the truth." He embraced her, kissed her profusely, and said, "All I want is a wife. What matters whether it's you or someone else? Come, let's retire to a corner and I will give you kebabs to eat." Khumar chose a tree by the riverside where the false youth spread a sheet and seated her. Then he produced fish kebabs from his pocket and set them before her. Khumar said, "The pleasure of eating will have been redoubled if we had wine." He answered, "My house is not far from here. I cannot take you there because my wife would make an uproar if she saw you. I will fetch the wine and return speedily by invoking my magic." Then he rose and disappeared from sight by putting on his cape of invisibility. Seeing him vanish suddenly, Khumar thought he must be an accomplished sorcerer.

Amar took out a flask of wine from his zambil and, after drugging it, took off his cape and reappeared before Khumar. He placed the wine before her. She poured a cup and offered it to him. The false youth put the cup to her lips and said, "O life of the world, you must drink it first." Khumar was very pleased with his frolicsome ways and opened her lips whereupon he emptied the entire contents of the cup into her mouth. The moment the wine travelled down, Khumar sneezed, fell to the ground in a swoon, and lost consciousness. Amar immediately took off her clothes and jewelery. Deciding that it would take too long to individually remove the pearls strung in her hair, he shaved off her head with a razor.

But when Amar drew his dagger and bore down upon Khumar to slit her throat, the water in the river began buffeting and dashing about. The custodians of the River of Flowing Blood rushed toward him. Amar speedily put on his cape of invisibility and disappeared.

The custodians carried Khumar away to Afrasiyab, who lamented the pitiful state of his beloved and had her dressed. He restored her to consciousness and asked her what had passed with her. Khumar replied, "I saw a youth fishing in the River of Flowing Blood. When I stopped him he told me he had already made kebabs of the fish he had caught. I was surprised to hear that and when he offered me some I ate them. Then I fell unconscious." Khumar did not disclose her infatuation with the youth.

Afrasiyab replied, "O Princess, he must be a trickster. They have entered the tilism and now you must remain alert to such traps wherever you go or the tricksters will overpower and kill you. They are great fraudsters and deceivers. I have sent two sorcerers to arrest them. Once they return I will dispatch Empress Heyrat with an army of sorcerers to battle Mahrukh Magic-Eye and kill Asad."

Afrasiyab then struck his hands together, and resplendent magic birds flew down from the trees of Apple Garden to the emperor. He said to them, "Go and perch yourself on the trees where Asad and Mahrukh Magic-Eye are gathered, listen to their council and bring me a report." The magic birds flew away after receiving the command.

Amar Ayyar kept walking along the banks of the River of Flowing Blood but could find no way to cross over to the other side. After some time, he arrived near a majestic mountain adorned like a bride with jewel-like flowers. The foot of the mountain shone like the hearts of the pure, and fields of saffron stretched on for miles on end. The whole forest looked yellow from the spring flowers. A waterfall cascaded down the mountaintop from where the sound of music floated down. Amar climbed over the mountain pass and reached its peak. When he raised his head he saw a marvellous sight: Some twenty moon-like beauties dressed in saffron and crimson costumes sat on a splendid carpet watching a dance recital.

Some women sat on swings hanging from the trees while others pushed them, sending the swings so high into the air it seemed those infidel beauties wished to touch the heavens. Every one of them was as full of pride as a preening peacock, and their conceit at their own beauty made them flighty and vain.

Amar thought of retiring to a corner to put on a girl's disguise and join them, but the moment his feet touched the peak, they started crying, "*Amar comes! Amar comes!*"

Unable to do anything else, Amar quickly put on the cape of invisibility, saying to himself, *These are the stages of the tilism. They will not be surmounted except by the Conqueror of the Tilism. It is pointless to join these women who must be magic slave girls created by the founders of the tilism.*

Amar climbed down from the mountain and headed onwards.

He finally arrived at a mountain pass where he saw Prince Asad sitting beside a houri-like beauty, while a sorceress stood close by. The sight resembled the conjunction of the sun and the moon in the constellation of Aries. Amar called out, "Well done, my boy! Go ahead and waste your time with women while on the mission to conquer the tilism."

Asad rose to greet Amar, who embraced the prince and prayed for his longevity. Then Amar looked darkly at Mahjabeen Diamond-Robe and said, "May God protect us against the devil, O Asad. What a remarkable appetite you have shown by choosing this ugly, ungainly woman for your companion!"

Seeing that Amar's words mortified and embarrassed the princess, Prince Asad whispered to her, "O Princess, do not take offence at his words. He is notoriously avaricious. If you conferred a little something on him he would immediately start singing your praises." When the princess took off her bejewelled bracelets and made an offering of them to Amar, he said, "O Princess, what made you think that this lowly person, grandson of Hamza the Arab, was your match? Even great and mighty kings would be unfit companions for a majestic princess like you." Asad, Mahjabeen and Dil Aaram all began laughing at Amar's words.

Amar said, "May God keep you smiling and happy always."

Prince Asad said, "O Princess, now the tilism is sure to be conquered. While I kill the enemy warriors, Amar Ayyar will dispatch the enemy sorcerers to hell." The princess felt pleased to hear these words.

Now hear of Mahrukh Magic-Eye, who had set out with an army of twenty-four thousand sorcerers. Leaving her son Shakeel to follow her with the army, she went forward in search of Prince Asad. As she arrived near the mountain pass where Asad and Mahjabeen were assembled, Dil Aaram, who was on the lookout, announced her arrival to the princess.

Fearful that her grandmother was coming to apprehend them, the princess said to Asad, "This is a great calamity."

Asad said, "I shall go and kill her." While he went toward Mahjabeen Diamond-Robe with a drawn sword, Amar put on the cape of invisibility, realizing that he would be powerless to help others if he were captured.

When Princess Mahrukh Magic-Eye saw Prince Asad coming toward her with hostile intent, she said to him, "O venerable prince! Why do you advance toward me with sword unsheathed? I am your friend and have come to give my allegiance to you. I am Princess Mahjabeen Diamond-Robe's grandmother. Let me see my granddaughter."

Princess Mahjabeen Diamond-Robe rushed forward and fell at the feet of Mahrukh, who pressed the head of her granddaughter to her bosom and said, "My child, we will see what fate befalls us as Afrasiyab is all-powerful. While I have broken with him, I am no match for his might. He can destroy us in the blink of an eye."

Asad retorted, "That wretch has no wherewithal to destroy us as long as God is our Aid and Protector. You may rest here in comfort; we are ready to wager our lives and heads to protect you. You have joined us and must rely on God's beneficence and mercy."

Mahrukh Magic-Eye answered, "What you say is true, but one must also reckon with the facts." Asad answered, "The Shaver of Infidels' Beards and the Slasher of Sorcerers' Necks, Amar Ayyar, is present among us and he will one day kill Afrasiyab like the unclean dog that he is." Mahrukh Magic-Eye answered, "I have tested many who made such boasts. None could hold against Afrasiyab's power. However, since I have joined you, I will not turn back now. I shall live and die with you."

Dil Aaram spread a sheet on the ground and all of them sat down. Amar Ayyar, however, did not reveal himself out of apprehension that perhaps Mahrukh Magic-Eye spoke with deceit, waiting for everyone to gather there before arresting them.

Mahrukh Magic-Eye said to Prince Asad, "I have learned from astrological divination that you are the slayer of the Emperor of the Tilism. What I said in praise of Afrasiyab's grandeur and might was meant only to test your courage. God be praised you have a steely heart. Indeed, you are a man among men and the lion of the forest of valor."

While they were engaged in talk, Afrasiyab's minion sorcerer, Rahdar, arrived on the scene and, seeing Mahrukh Magic-Eye with Prince Asad, called out, "Beware O ingrate! You can't antagonise the crocodile and hope to live in peace in the river. You will find no refuge from the emperor's wrath."

Seeing him upon them, Mahrukh Magic-Eye took out a steel magic ball from her sack, recited a spell over it, and threw it at Rahdar.

The ball exploded into thousands of fiery bolts, which shot toward Rahdar. The sorcerer took out the soil that Afrasiyab gave him from the grave of Jamshed. He threw it up into the air and it dispelled the fiery bolts. Rahdar now stepped forward and sprinkled a pinch of the soil on Mahrukh Magic-Eye and Dil Aaram, making them unconscious. Asad charged next and struck out with his sword but Rahdar recited an incantation that made the prince immobile. The sorcerer captured everyone, including the princess, and headed for Afrasiyab's court.

Amar took off his cape of invisibility, loaded a large sculpted octagonal crystal in his sling and called out, "O Rahdar, wait a moment." As Rahdar stopped, Amar was able to take aim. He fired and Rahdar's head flew off his neck and dropped far away. Horrible noises of his magic spirits were heard and Mahrukh Magic-Eye regained consciousness. She saw whirlwinds blowing and voices loudly calling out, "*Catch them! Arrest them*!"

Mahrukh Magic-Eye invoked magic that dispelled the noise. She saw Rahdar's headless corpse lying on the ground and a strange creature standing nearby. As Mahrukh did not recognize Amar, she decided to capture him. Amar read her intention and hit her in the face with an egg of oblivion. Mahrukh Magic-Eye fell unconscious and Amar again put on his cape of invisibility.

Dil Aaram and Asad awoke from the spell. When they restored Mahrukh Magic-Eye to consciousness, she asked what had happened to her. Asad answered, "Amar Ayyar killed Rahdar and released us, but when you tried to capture him he rendered you unconscious and disappeared." Mahrukh Magic-Eye said, "Please call him back." Prince Asad answered, "You can ask him yourself."

Mahrukh Magic-Eye called out, "O Prince of Tricksters, I am very eager to meet you. Please show yourself. Am I so unworthy of beholding your august face that you hide yourself from me." Amar's voice came, "You must make an offering before I give audience. If you are willing to do so, I will happily show my face."

Prince Asad and all others laughed at Amar's answer but Mahrukh Magic-Eye took off her gold and jewels and said, "The offering is ready." Seeing his prize, Amar promptly presented himself and stuffed the gold and jewels into his zambil.

Mahrukh Magic-Eye found Amar's appearance extremely ungainly and vulgar. She said to herself, *How is it possible that someone like him would be able to confront a great threat like Afrasiyab?* Amar realized that Mahrukh Magic-Eye looked upon him with disapproval, and said, "You are thinking that this lean and thin creature will be of no help and won't be able to encounter challenges." Mahrukh Magic-Eye answered, "You must be extremely wise to decipher what passed in my heart." Amar replied, "I can read even the frowns on people's brows like a sentence and tell whatever passes in their hearts."

While they were having this discussion, the sorcerer named Faulad dispatched by Afrasiyab arrived on the scene and shouted from far away, "Beware O rebels! Now I am here. You cannot hide from me."

Amar turned to Mahrukh Magic-Eye and said, "I would like to see how a mighty sorceress like you fights him." Mahrukh Magic-Eye replied, "I was unconscious when you killed the first sorcerer and could not see how you did it. I would like to witness you kill him." Amar answered, "I will do so presently and kill him like a filthy cur."

Amar stood up and encountered Faulad, saying, "O shameless wretch, why do you boast and bark so? Come here, I have marked you for my prey." Faulad took out a magic coconut from his sack and began reciting a spell whereupon Amar produced an orange and began mumbling something over it. Faulad thought that Amar was also a distinguished sorcerer.

Amar said to him, "You are indeed a shameless wretch who fights with the help of others. Who is this sorcerer behind you who comes to your aid?" As Faulad turned to look, Amar leaped and reached beside him. As Faulad turned back realizing the deception played on him by Amar, an egg of oblivion hit his face. Faulad sneezed, swooned, and as he began sinking unconscious to the ground, Amar struck with his dagger. Faulad's head flew off his shoulders and fell many steps away. Noises akin to the uproar of doomsday rose and darkness fell upon them.

Mahrukh Magic-Eye read a spell and struck her hands together, making the darkness disappear. She saw Amar standing aside with his prayer beads in hand, reciting "O Lord my Protector! O Lord my Aid! Save me by Your grace!" Mahrukh Magic-Eye approached him and said, "O Emperor of Tricksters! Bravo! Well done! The speed with which you dispatched that sorcerer to hell was most impressive. I pronounce myself your handmaiden. Please join our company."

While they were thus engaged, a dust cloud rose on the horizon, drumbeats sounded and men dressed in gold cloth and costumes woven with gold and silver thread appeared. The report of kettledrums mounted on camels and elephants shook the expanse of mountains and deserts. They were followed by sorcerers of frightful aspects wielding the paraphernalia of sorcery and mounted on magic dragons spewing fire.

Suddenly, fireballs and stones rained from the sky and they saw Mahrukh Magic-Eye's son Shakeel come forward mounted on a swan whose body glowed like fire. Twenty-four thousand sorcerers surrounded him, marching in ranks astride magic peacocks, elephants and other fiery magic beasts and birds.

Finally, accompanying Prince Shakeel's army, dragons brought forward the throne of Mahrukh Magic-Eye's mother, sorceress Mah, and the tents and pavilions with the apparatus of war.

Prince Asad remarked, "It resembles the entourages of Amir Hamza's commanders in its magnificence." Mahrukh Magic-Eye said, "O Prince, it is the army of your slave, my son Shakeel. I hope you will put the hand of mercy and favor on his head and provide comfort to his heart."

Seeing his mother standing with Prince Asad, Shakeel dismounted. He approached and saluted the prince and Amar. Asad embraced Shakeel and Amar offered him words of encouragement.

Mahrukh Magic-Eye ordered that the army should bivouac. The groundsmen immediately set about it with their mattocks and began clearing the ground of shrubbery and bushes. They made the surface of the wilderness clean and clear like a mirror. Trenches were made, wide in some places, narrow in others. They dug a ditch in one place and a tunnel in another. The war apparatus was readied. The pavilions of the commanders were pitched. The camp was established. Pavilions, poleless tents, winding tents and quadrangular tents were installed, and the army finally took rest.

The female quarters were set up separately. Tall and majestic, the royal pavilion was set up in the middle of the encampment near a water source. The boundaries of the royal encampment were marked around it. The stations of the court were placed. The audience chambers of the commanders and kings were set up in an area in the middle of the encampment, their chairs surrounding the peacock throne. The services were installed next, and the kitchens, the water repository and the wine services. A bazaar was established along a crossway and traders and chandlers marked their shops with their flags; no sooner did the bazaar open than it was thronged.

Mahrukh Magic-Eye presented herself before Prince Asad and said, "You may now give audience as the throne is ready to receive you." The prince answered, "I have no desire for kingship. As the grandson of the commander-in-chief of the armies of True Believers, I have a claim only to soldiering. Princess Mahjabeen Diamond-Robe should be given this trust. She must answer to the King of the True Believers and send a yearly tribute of gold to King Saad's court."

Prince Asad asked Amar, "Since you are a distinguished astrologer, tell us when it would be auspicious for the princess to ascend the throne."

Both Amar Ayyar and Mahrukh Magic-Eye, who were peerless in their knowledge of divining arts, conducted Mahjabeen Diamond-Robe by her hand to the throne and coronated her at a moment of felicitous conjunction of stars and an instant of blessed union of astral bodies. Everyone, including Prince Asad and Mahrukh Magic-Eye made offerings to her.

The cries of "Congratulations! Felicitations!" rose from all corners. Dancers of Venusian charm and beauties as resplendent as the Sun presented themselves. Musicians struck their tablas and the dance recital began. Houri-like cupbearers arrived carrying goblets and ewers filled with roseate wine. The carousing began and from all corners voices called out "Imbibe! Drink!" The drinkers praised the cupbearers constantly, saying to them, "O amiable friends, may you happily keep passing drinks forever and may revels and celebrations such as these never cease."

Queen Mahjabeen Diamond-Robe next distributed the robes of office. She conferred ministership on Mahrukh Magic-Eye and appointed Dil Aaram as Queen's special cohort. Asad chose the post of the army's commander for himself. Amar Ayyar was given the rank of the imperial counsellor, and it was stipulated that the sovereign must follow Amar's council or be dismissed. An audience of the ministers was then held by Mahrukh, who deposited with the keeper of the treasury all the riches she had brought.

Mahrukh Magic-Eye ordered the induction of recruits for the ranks of sorceress and nonsorcerers. Drums were beaten as battle preparations began. Criers, sent out to all neighboring towns and villages, announced that anyone desiring employment should report at Queen Mahjabeen's camp. Soon, recruits began arriving in their camp. They made offerings to Mahrukh Magic-Eye, and she chose the deserving and worthy amongst them to become commanders and deputy commanders of troopers.

Meanwhile, the tricksters Zargham, Qiran the Ethiope and Jansoz arrived from their separate ways and entered the camp disguised as sorcerers. They found Amar Ayyar and Mahrukh Magic-Eye enlisting soldiers for war. They took offerings before Mahrukh Magic-Eye, who asked them, "Who are you?" The false sorcerers replied, "We are the residents of the City of Wonders. We have come to enter your service as magicians." Mahrukh Magic-Eye asked, "What compensation do you require for your services?" They answered, "A thousand rupees each." Mahrukh Magic-Eye said, "Let me first test your magic."

The tricksters answered, "Very well!" Qiran the Ethiope took out a coconut from his bag and, after reciting incantations over it, threw it at Mahrukh Magic-Eye. She struck her hands together to dispel it but the coconut hit her in the face and exploded, releasing smoke and Mahrukh Magic-Eye fell down unconscious.

The sorcerers gathered in the court tried to dispel the magic and revive her with incantations but none succeeded. Everyone assembled acknowledged the false sorcerers as great magicians and requested they remove the spell from Mahrukh Magic-Eye. Qiran sent for some water. After making a show of reciting a spell over it, he sprinkled some on Mahrukh Magic-Eye's face, which revived her immediately.

The false sorcerers asked, "Did you find our magic satisfactory?" Mahrukh answered, "Indeed, yours is a most potent magic. It is now settled. You will receive a thousand rupees each." The false sorcerers said, "We require a month's salary in advance and a seat next to Amar Ayyar." Mahrukh Magic-Eye ordered a month's advance salary each to be paid then said, "Let me procure Amar's permission for seating you next to him."

Mahrukh Magic-Eye brought the false sorcerers into Queen Mahjabeen's court. The false sorcerers saw a royal throne whose four corners were mounted with bejewelled peacocks of emerald feathers. Their tails rose upwards and joined together to make a canopy over Mahjabeen Diamond-Robe, who sat with great majesty and grandeur, wearing a crown of garnets and rubies and a priceless necklace. She wore a robe stitched with gold and jewels and sported a waistcoat sewn with gold thread and a resplendent cummerbund. Dil Aaram was standing behind her moving a fly-whisk made of phoenix feathers while thousands of sorcerers stood humbly before her. Prince Asad sat near the throne and Amar Ayyar was perched on a jewel-encrusted throne. The false sorcerers made Amar Ayyar an offering of the purses received from Mahrukh Magic-Eye. The moment their eyes met, Amar Ayyar recognized his disciples and rose to embrace them.

Surprised, Mahrukh Magic-Eye asked Amar if he knew them. Amar answered, "O Queen, they are the tricksters of the armies of the True Believers and their names are Zargham, Qiran the Ethiope and Jansoz. Another one, whose name is Burq, has also entered the tilism. I am not aware of his whereabouts but I hope to meet him soon."

Mahrukh Magic-Eye met the tricksters and was pleased by their arrival. She ordered four tents furnished with beds, carpets, tables, chairs and all comforts and conveniences, set up for them near the royal pavilion. Then she said to the tricksters, "You may go and rest yourselves." Qiran answered, "I never reside in encampments. The mountain passes and caves serve me for tents as I am the favored one of the Lion of God." He leapt over the walls of the royal pavilion and disappeared into the wilderness.

Amar said to the others, "Make these tents your abode and guard the camp. Live inside the tents but make sure that if someone searches for you there, they're unable to find you." The tricksters said, "Very well!" They retired to the tents to wash and refresh themselves. After eating, they returned to the court and watched with rapt attention a dance recital that was in progress there.

Now hear of what passed with Burq the Frank. He too had been traveling in the wilderness and keeping a watchful eye on the tricksters. From a high station he saw a large army camped in the wilderness. Burq entered the camp in the guise of a sorcerer and upon making inquiries found out that it was the encampment of Amar Ayyar and Mahrukh Magic-Eye and received a complete account of the events. Burq said to himself, *My master and his companions are now happily settled. I should perform some glorious deed before joining them.*

Burq retired to the wilderness and began searching for the prey of his choice. On a thoroughfare he saw a well with a brick ledge. Burq said to himself, *It is situated in a central location. The residents of the tilism must pass this way to quench their thirst.* Burq changed his appearance to that of a Brahmin.[60] He wore a rosary around his neck, drew a line on his forehead, dressed himself in a waistcloth, and sat on the ledge of the well with a bucket tied to a string.

After some time, a group of fifty sorcerers belonging to one of Hoshruba's lands stopped by the well. They carried the sum of one hundred thousand rupees to submit in tribute to Emperor Afrasiyab. When they saw the false Brahmin sitting on the well, they said to him, "Give us some water to quench our thirst." The false Brahmin gave them water and said, "I have some parched grains. If you wish you may have some for a very good price." They asked him, "What is the price?" He answered, "Four paisas per *ser*."[61] Tempted by the reasonable rate, the sorcerers bought the grains from him, dissolved them in salt water, and drank it up.

The moment they swallowed it they fell unconscious to the ground. Burq quickly beheaded all of them. A thunderous uproar rose at their killing and after some time, when the noise had died down, Burq dug a hole in the ground under a tree with his dagger and buried the money. Then he headed back to the camp in a sorcerer's guise. He approached the court and said to the attendants, "Go and tell the Emperor of Tricksters that the sorcerer named Jan Nisar the Life-Sacrificing has arrived." When they brought him the message, Amar wondered who he might be and ordered that the man be sent in. The attendants conducted the false sorcerer inside. He looked around and was pleased upon noticing the glory of the court. He saluted Asad, Mahjabeen Diamond-Robe and Amar Ayyar, and humbly made the offering of a note to Amar.

Upon opening and reading the note, Amar learned that one hundred thousand rupees lay buried for him at a marked location in the wilderness. All he needed to do was to go and dig it up to receive it as an offering. When Amar looked closely at the false sorcerer, he recognized Burq. Amar embraced him and said to Mahrukh Magic-Eye, "This is the trickster Burq the Frank about whom I told you."

A comfortable tent and all amenities were provided for Burq as well. He retired there to bathe and divest himself of the fatigue of his journey. Then he had his meal and fell asleep.

Amar Ayyar went to the place in the wilderness marked by Burq and arrived near the well. He dug out the money and stuffed it in his zambil. He said to himself, *I have only one dutiful pupil who paid consideration to redressing my worries; the rest of them are all rank idiots.* He returned to the camp engrossed in these thoughts and retired for a rest.

ꕥ

The magic birds Afrasiyab had ordered to monitor the doings of Prince Asad and Mahrukh Magic-Eye witnessed everything from their perches in the forest trees. They had seen Mahrukh Magic-Eye's arrival, the killing of sorcerers Rahdar and Faulad, the gathering of the armies and their reception, and the announcement for recruitments for war. They now returned to Afrasiyab and gave him a detailed report of the events.

Enraged, Afrasiyab sent a note by a magic slave to Empress Heyrat in the City of Disregard to return urgently for consultations.

Heyrat arrived on a magic throne with her slave girls, attendants and companions. Afrasiyab said to her, "O Empress, regard the ingrate Mahrukh Magic-Eye, who plans to fight me. She is enlisting an army and has joined hands with the Conqueror of the Tilism. If I ordered a single magic fairy of the Bridge of the Magic Fairies to blow its trumpet, the entire creation would fall unconscious from its blast. I find the very notion of Mahrukh Magic-Eye planning to do battle with me laughable." Heyrat answered, "Emperor, I shall send for Mahrukh Magic-Eye and persuade her to see sense. I will ensure that she never dares even think of fighting Your Excellency."

Afrasiyab answered, "Very well. Send for her and try to reason with her. I exercised restraint due to the fact that she is your relative, but I also held back since I am the master and she the subject. The founders of the tilism have written that a time would come when the subjects and slaves of the Emperor of the Tilism would rebel against him and resolve on war and carnage. It is mentioned that at that juncture it would bode well for the emperor to show leniency and indulgence and avoid armed conflicts, for he stands to suffer most from them. O Heyrat, I swear these considerations alone kept me from combat and conflict, otherwise I would have effaced the existence of these rebels in a trice."

Heyrat answered, "There's no doubting the reasons for your restraint."

She sent a note to Mahrukh Magic-Eye which read:

> "O Princess, it would bode well for you not to engage in conflicts and war with someone whose salt you have eaten and under whose nurturing shadow you have spent your life. As a token of munificent protection and lordly indulgence toward you, you are hereby ordered to present yourself upon the receipt of this august edict to submit your allegiance as a slave of the emperor so that I may have your trespasses forgiven by him. In the event of your continued defiance and aggression, even I, a worthless slave of the all-powerful emperor, will crush you like an insignificant ant. You will take heed from this warning if you wish your continued well-being, and submit your immediate compliance. End of message and kind regards."

Heyrat gave the letter to a magic bird to take to Mahrukh Magic-Eye. The magic bird arrived in Mahrukh's court carrying the letter in its beak and sat in her lap. Mahrukh took the letter from its beak and asked the bird, "Who has sent you?" The magic bird answered, "*Empress Heyrat.*" As Mahrukh Magic-Eye read the letter her face was drained of blood and she trembled with fear. When Amar Ayyar saw her in this state he took the letter from her hand and read it, then angrily tore it up and wrote a reply in these words:

> "All praise is due only to God and His Prophet.[62] Hear and be informed, O Heyrat and Afrasiyab, that I am the

Bearder of Sorcerers and the Beheader of Magicians. Mine was the dagger that slit the throat of renowned sorcerers and took their lives even when they took refuge in the depths of seas. There's no accounting of the number of sorcerers I have killed nor of the grand and mighty kings renowned to the highest heavens carried away on coffin planks from their thrones by my agency.

"I am that King of Tricksters
Who exacts tribute from kings
Believe me when I say my notoriety
Shines brightly like the sun in the praises sung by men
When I decide to sprint on a day
I burn the world with my fiery pace
Never would the Zephyr keep pace with me
I could touch West and return in half the time
Those who heard my deceitful song
Soon bid adieu to their lives
I am the one to pull out shoes from dead asses
From death itself I have often taken a loan
Do not let my ungainly looks deceive you
Into thinking I am not adept in my art
The one whom I marked for my own
Surely relinquished all hopes for his life
I am a calamity for women and men
I am the Angel of Death of my time.

"It is incumbent upon you to present yourselves at the august door of Queen Mahjabeen Diamond-Robe along with Princess Tasveer and Prince Badiuz Zaman. Queen Mahjabeen Diamond-Robe, who is the sovereign of the tilism, will have your transgression forgiven by Amir Hamza, the Lord of the Auspicious Planetary Conjunction. In the event of you contravening the commands expressed in this edict, I promise that I will have your noses cut at the tip, your faces blackened, and have both of you mounted on an ass and paraded in these dominions as sure as my name is Amar."

Amar Ayyar handed this note to the magic bird and said to him, "Tell that whore and strumpet Heyrat that I will soon shave off her hair. That harridan should feel free to do as she likes and exert herself to the best of her ability. God shall protect us."

The magic bird returned to Heyrat. After delivering Amar's letter and conveying his message word for word, the bird said, "*Mahrukh Magic-Eye started trembling upon reading the letter but a thin, gangling man sitting by her tore up your letter and wrote a reply in the form of this abusive message.*"

Heyrat carried the letter before Afrasiyab and said to him, "You spoke the truth when you said these rebels would not desist from mischief mongering unless they were punished. Regard how disrespectfully they answered my letter. That common trickster and thief has addressed many an inauspicious word to both you and me."

When Afrasiyab took the letter from her hand and read it, his face turned crimson with rage. He bit his lips in anger and said, "An ant only grows wings when her death is near. That whore Mahrukh Magic-Eye has invited great trouble on her head."

Leaving Afrasiyab making preparations for battle, we return to Mahrukh Magic-Eye and Amar Ayyar.

After the magic bird had flown away, Mahrukh Magic-Eye said to Amar Ayyar, "You made a blunder by cursing Heyrat. You may rest assured that calamity will soon strike us and all of us will be killed." Amar answered, "O Princess, don't become so low spirited. Even after having clearly determined by astrological divination that Prince Asad will finally triumph, you still have these anxieties. I noticed you became disconcerted upon reading the letter. It would have insulted the brave commanders present in our court. They would have lost their hearts if they had seen dread on their leader's face. I uttered those harsh words so that all of them might hear and take heart that we cannot be powerless if we address Afrasiyab in that manner. You must steel your heart. Do not become distressed at the least sign of disturbance. We'll see how the All-Powerful God acts because He is the Protector and Aid of the helpless."

Mahrukh Magic-Eye acquiesced to Amar's advice. We leave them now amidst their hopes and fears and give an account of Emperor Afrasiyab.

Of Afrasiyab Sending Three Sorcerers with an Army of Sixty Thousand Against Mahrukh and Amar Ayyar; Of the Tricksters Going into Action Against Sorcerers; And of the Fierce Battle Between the Two Camps

The warriors of the battleground of rhetoric, valiant lords of the expanse of speech, the bearers of victorious standards of the chroniclers' armies, and the ensign-bearers of the narrators' triumphant forces, thus spur the fleet-footed steed of tongue in the arena of speech, and in this manner show the eloquent essence of their discourse in the domain of narrative.

When Afrasiyab and Heyrat realized that the beautiful heart of Mahrukh Magic-Eye of excellent speech, which once shone like the sun, was now clouded and misted with grief and vexation, they were left with no recourse but to declare war against her.

Sorcerers Jamosh, Shahbaz, and Kohan

Empress Heyrat decided to march against Mahrukh Magic-Eye herself but Afrasiyab intervened and said, "As long as a single slave remains, it is beneath the dignity of the empress and the wife of the Master of the Tilism to march against a worthless subject."

Afrasiyab recited a spell and struck his hands together. Suddenly, clouds rose from every direction and covered the sky. Thousands of golden, colorful lightning bolts flashed. The clouds showered sparks and rained stones. Then the canopy of clouds parted and revealed three hideous, ungainly and evil sorcerers named Jamosh, Shahbaz and Kohan sitting upon three thrones, which descended from the sky.

They curtsied before Afrasiyab, kissed the leg of his throne and asked, "Why has the emperor summoned his slaves?" Afrasiyab informed them of Prince Asad and the feud with Mahrukh Magic-Eye and said, "You should march together against the rebels with a force of sixty thousand sorcerers and bring them to me as prisoners."

The sorcerers departed for their camps and summoned their commanders. They informed them of Afrasiyab's orders and the drums of departure were beaten and tents and pavilions loaded onto magic dragons. Sorcerers mounted magic beasts and flew away displaying magic works. They crossed the River of Flowing Blood and arrived near Mahrukh Magic-Eye's camp.

Queen Mahjabeen Diamond-Robe and Prince Asad were holding court when they heard a thunderous noise outdoors. Mahrukh Magic-Eye said to Amar Ayyar, "The enemy forces are approaching."

The moment the tricksters heard these words, they left the court and scurried into the wilderness.

Presently, the conveyances of the sorcerers came into view. Mahrukh Magic-Eye and the sorcerers in her court recited counterspells to forestall any harm from the rain of fire and stones that heralded the approach of sorcerers. The armies of the foe arrived with great show and ceremony and bivouacked opposite Mahrukh Magic-Eye's camp.

The tents were raised, the pavilions set up, and the bazaars opened up. Sorcerer Jamosh and his companions held court, made magic birds and sent them to gather intelligence. Other sorcerers made oblations of lard into fires to work their spells.

Jamosh ordered that the drums of war be struck. His slaves rushed to carry out his commands. The trumpets were blown, the magic drums were beaten, and their report deafened even the ears of heavens. In short, everyone witnessed a commotion like the Day of Judgment.

The magic birds deputed by Mahrukh Magic-Eye returned to the court bearing news. After singing praises of Mahrukh with their humble tongues and visiting blessings on their mistress, they announced, "*The war drums have been struck and everyone in the enemy camp is ready for battle.*" The magic birds then flew away to gather further intelligence.

Queen Mahjabeen Diamond-Robe glanced at Prince Asad. The prince said to Mahrukh Magic-Eye, "In the name of God the Avenger, the trumpet and the drums of war should answer from our camp as well."

The attendants rushed to carry out the command and sounded the call to war. Mahrukh Magic-Eye and Shakeel blew the magic trumpet, whose blast shook the Earth and echoed in the vault of the heavens. Everyone was put on notice of the impending battle and the brisk trade in death that would ensue the following day.

The day passed in these preparations and vigil squads from both camps started making their rounds. The braves checked and readied their arms and armor in anticipation of the slaughter and carnage of the battle. Sorcerers from both camps prepared their magic. Jamosh smeared the ground with swine blood and started beating a clapper-drum. He made steel magic balls, magic slaves of lentil flour, and recited spells on magic arrows made of twigs. He burned fragrant gum resin and offered blood sacrifices to invoke the magic spirits in his possession.

On her part, Mahrukh Magic-Eye lit lamps before idols, lighted a bonfire, made oblations of incense and seeds, and emptied wine bottles into the fire. She made a waxen magic effigy of a beautiful woman and adorned her with ornaments made of twigs. She threw her into the bonfire, recited a spell, and struck her hands together, saying, "Go now O magic effigy and return when it's time." The effigy melted in the fire and Mahrukh retired to her pavilion for rest.

Tricksters Burq and Zargham, who had left the court, now set out to work their trickeries.

Burq whitened his hair, eyebrows and eyelashes and made himself into an old woman. Dressed in wide-bottomed pants, wrapped in a mantle and carrying a box under one arm, he headed for Kohan's pavilion. He progressed slowly with the help of a cane and kept shaking his head like a frail old woman.

Zargham tied a turban on his head, a cummerbund around his waist, and threw a folded woollen kerchief over his shoulder to disguise himself as an attendant. He started doing rounds of the encampment. By chance, one of Kohan's servants arrived in the bazaar on an errand. The false attendant approached and greeted Kohan's servant, who asked, "How are you my brother?" The false attendant replied, "I am well but I must have a word with you urgently or else a terrible misfortune will strike you." Kohan's servant felt frightened at these words. He thought the false attendant must be a noble's servant who had heard some inauspicious news concerning him.

He asked, "Tell me, what is the matter my brother." Insisting on the need for privacy, the false attendant led him by the hand to a deserted corner, then said, "There's someone behind you." As the man turned to look, the false attendant threw his snare rope, which tightened around the neck of Kohan's servant so that he could not make a sound. Zargham drugged him and, making himself into his likeness and putting on his dress, entered the tent where Kohan's servants were lodged. He waited for his orders to learn the duties of the person he pretended to be. As he sat engrossed in these thoughts, someone said to him, "O cupbearer, make the wine service ready. His lordship may send for the wine now." Zargham realized that he was supposed to be Kohan's cupbearer and immediately got busy arranging the wine bottles.

In the meanwhile, Burq arrived outside Kohan's pavilion in the old woman's disguise and started crying loudly for help and redress. Kohan came out of his pavilion and asked, "Who are you and why do you cry?" She replied, "My son, I don't know where to begin the tale of my misfortunes. I live in a nearby town but since their arrival Mahrukh Magic-Eye's armies have robbed me of my possessions. I have come to seek redress since the hand of fate struck me so unjustly." Kohan said to her, "Come and rest in my pavilion. In the morning I will slay all the rebels and you will receive twofold all your lost goods."

Blessing Kohan with every breath, she accompanied him to his pavilion. Seeing a box under her arm, Kohan asked, "What is in that box?" She replied, "I have nothing to hide from you, but it would be best if you opened it in private." Kohan dismissed all his attendants and servants from the pavilion. She handed him the box, saying, "Here, look for yourself. You'll soon learn what's inside." As Kohan lifted the lid, a puff of drug powder hit his face. He sneezed and fell unconscious. Burq threw off his disguise, drew his dagger and bore down to slit his throat.

But Kohan had deputed a magic slave girl of clay in a corner of the pavilion to guard him in times of peril. The moment Burq sat on Kohan's chest, the magic slave girl ran and caught the trickster, threw him on the floor and tied him up. Then she sprinkled water on Kohan's face to bring him to consciousness and said, "*It was not an old woman but a trickster who nearly killed you.*" Kohan said to Burq, "O wretch, I almost died at your hands. Let me capture your aiders and abettors in the morning. Then I will behead the whole lot of you together."

Kohan tied Burq to a column and said to his attendant, "Ask the cupbearer to bring the wine service. I'll have a cup or two of wine before going to bed. Tomorrow I have to face combat." The attendant alerted the false cupbearer, trickster Zargham, to produce the wine service. He brought the bottles of drugged wine and cups and offered them to Kohan, who drank and immediately fell unconscious. When Zargham attempted to kill Kohan, the same magic slave girl again ran out from the corner and caught him too, and took him captive. Then she sprinkled water on Kohan and said, "*He is another trickster who attempted to kill you.*" Kohan tied Zargham as well to a column.

Meanwhile, signs of dawn manifested themselves and the arrival of Emperor Sun was proclaimed in the golden court of the heavens.

Kohan rode out with his army of sorcerers at dawn. Sorcerers Jamosh and Shahbaz also prepared for battle and their armies entered the battlefield with great splendor and fanfare. Counting on the aid of the Majestic Lord, Mahrukh Magic-Eye and Shakeel led out their army of forty thousand sorcerers and new recruits.

Prince Asad rose from his sleep, made ablutions, and prostrated himself in prayers to God. Then he presented himself fully dressed and armed at the door of Queen Mahjabeen Diamond-Robe. The drums and trumpets announced her arrival and the female throne bearers brought out Mahjabeen Diamond-Robe's throne. The macebearers and attendants led the way calling out, "Show deference! Clear the path!" All the commanders offered her salutes. The palms imprinted on the banners fluttered in the wind as if offering salutes to the sovereign. Queen Mahjabeen Diamond-Robe's army encircled her throne. Dil Aaram rode beside her on a magic peacock and, with great ceremony and magnificence, they entered the arena.

Sorcerers from both camps readied the battlefield. One recited a spell that invoked thunderbolts to strike and burn the bushes and trees littering the arena. Another brought about rain clouds and showers to rid the arena of all dust and dirt. Finally, the battlefield was all clean and clear and arrays were formed. Sorcerers tossed magic citrons and magic limes in the air and flashed brass salvers. The slogans, "Long Live Sameri!" and "Long Live Jamshed!" and the terrible drone of the magic spirits filled the air.

The left and right flanks of the armies were organized and ranks were established. Criers from both camps marched out and shouted, "Today, neither Sameri nor Jamshed nor Zardhasht remain. After performing their magical miracles they have hidden themselves and now drink at the Inn of the Hereafter. O illustrious sorcerers, today is the day of battle. It is now your chance to wager your lives for everlasting renown."

As the criers made their proclamations and retired, the valiant warriors became intoxicated on the heady wine of courage and the surge of valor. Sorcerer Shahbaz flew into the arena on his magic dragon, showed a display of his magic, and called out, "O ingrate Mahrukh Magic-Eye, come forward and face me!"

As Mahrukh Magic-Eye flew her throne forward, every soldier in her army solicited victory from the heavens. When Mahrukh faced Shahbaz, he fired a magic arrow at her. She recited a counterspell and struck her hands together, turning the arrow in mid flight toward Shahbaz. Next he recited a spell over a steel magic ball and threw it at her. Seeing it approach, Mahrukh Magic-Eye read an incantation and flew away from her throne.

Even as Shahbaz's magic ball hit the throne and shattered it to pieces, Mahrukh Magic-Eye fell from the heavens in the shape of a sword and cleft Shahbaz in two, along with his dragon.

Stones and fire rained from the skies and a horrible boom was heard announcing the death of sorcerer Shahbaz. His slaves charged upon Mahrukh. The enemy sorcerers threw cotton seeds and white and black mustard seeds into burning braziers, tore off their chilli necklaces and flung them at Mahrukh. The necklaces turned into dragons and advanced upon Mahrukh Magic-Eye.

Mahrukh's son Shakeel signalled to his magicians, who recited incantations and clapped their hands. A quake shook the Earth and the sky became overcast. Thunderbolts and rain fell. The soldiers in the enemy camp fell unconscious whenever a drop fell on their heads.

Witnessing this, sorcerer Jamosh entered the arena. He cut out the shape of the sun from paper and, placing it on his palm, recited a spell. The paper sun flew shining to the skies and spread its light. The magic clouds that had filled the sky parted and soldiers in Mahrukh Magic-Eye's army turned to stone when the light of the magic sun fell on them.

Wielding their tridents, Kohan and Jamosh now attacked Mahrukh's army and killed thousands of sorcerers. Both sides hurled magic citrons, magic limes and coconuts at each other.

Prince Asad could not hold himself back any longer. He said to Queen Mahjabeen Diamond-Robe, "I must also draw my sword now." She feigned to encourage him, saying, "Very well!" But as soon as Prince Asad took the reins of his steed and charged, Mahjabeen Diamond-Robe said to Dil Aaram, "The prince does not know sorcery. He will fight uselessly and be taken prisoner."

The prince's steed had not yet reached the enemy ranks when Dil Aaram struck her hands together. Prince Asad's horse grew wings and took flight. He tried to control it and used the whip but the horse only stopped once it was high in the air, suspended between the Earth and the sky. Prince Asad bit the back of his hand in frustration as he helplessly watched the battle underway on the ground. Dil Aaram kept watch to make sure the prince remained safe from calamities and that no sorcerer took him captive.

While Mahrukh Magic-Eye's camp was in this state of commotion, the sorcerer Jamosh fought his way toward Mahrukh Magic-Eye and threw a cluster of needles at her after reciting a spell. Mahrukh Magic-Eye dove into the ground and, breaking the surface of the earth, emerged at Jamosh's back. She shouted her war cry and shot an arrow, which flew through Jamosh's back and he fell dead to the ground.

Thousands of frightful noises rose. The sun made by his magic turned to paper and floated down to the ground. Its light dimmed and extinguished and the sorcerers of Mahrukh Magic-Eye, who had turned to stone, returned to life and started fighting.

When Kohan saw events take this turn, he immediately slashed his thigh open. He drew his own blood and sprinkled it on a fistful of gravel. Then he recited a spell and threw it in four directions. Suddenly a dark whirlwind engulfed them and everyone closed their eyes. When they opened them a moment later, they saw huge mountains ready to fall on Mahrukh Magic-Eye's army. Seeing this sight, Shakeel's army hastily retreated.

At that moment, Mahrukh Magic-Eye recited an incantation, struck her hands together, and called out to the waxen magic effigy she had made and cast into the fire, "O magic effigy, it is time!"

Immediately upon her call, a lightning bolt flashed and the jingling of ankle bells was heard. A beautiful woman covered with ornaments, sporting a fine costume and riding a flying throne came into view. To compare her exceeding beauty even to a houri's would have been an insult to reason. The spring of her youthfulness and her swelling bosom were a sight to behold.

She took up position on the battlefield and when Kohan came fighting toward her, that moon-like beauty called out to him, "*O Kohan, I came here for your sake but you neither address me nor show me the least attention. now I will leave.*" When Kohan heard these words and beheld the glowing aspect of that fairy-like creature, he was wounded by the dagger of her charm. As he approached her, she asked, "*Tell me what are your intentions?*" He answered, "I am in love and besotted with you. Both my heart and soul are smitten to their very cores and possessed with thoughts of you." The fairy-like creature answered, "*It would be difficult for you to have me.*" As she spoke these words she fanned Jamosh with her jewel-enchased hand fan. Feeling its wafts of air, Jamosh started reciting love couplets. As the beauty moved away on her flying throne Kohan called out to her, "Don't leave me in this state between life and death."

When she returned at Kohan's importuning and solicitations, he put his head at her feet. In her presence he became completely unmindful of himself and forgot he was on a battlefield. The magic effigy said, "*What kind of love do you profess toward me when you fight Princess Mahrukh Magic-Eye, for whom I am a humble slave? Call back your soldiers and dispel your magic.*" Kohan recited a spell and the very mountains he had raised with his magic became gravel and fell down. Kohan also ordered his army to stop combat. When they stopped, they too became engrossed in the beautiful vision of the magic effigy and lost power over their senses and reason.

Kohan solicited the magic effigy to grant him the nectar of her love.

She replied, "*I have heard that you have captured the tricksters. Send for them.*"

Kohan immediately produced the tricksters before her.

Princess Mahrukh Magic-Eye conferred robes of honor and gold upon them. Zargham and Burq were set free and returned to their camp. After giving the news of their well-being to their commanders, they again disappeared into the wilderness.

After the tricksters were freed the magic effigy said, "*O Kohan, if you are indeed a true lover, sever your head with your own hands.*"

Kohan drew his dagger and placed it on his neck, reciting,

"It is a great honor for me that my head
Should fall at my beloved's feet."

As he prepared to sever his neck, the magic effigy stayed his hand and said, "*If you were to kill yourself, who would enjoy the splendorous spring of my beauty? I shall fulfill your desires on condition that you make Princess Mahrukh the offering of Heyrat's head. only then may you drink the sherbet of our union.*"

After Kohan made the pledge, the magic effigy said to his army, "*O my steely resolved lovers, drag that strumpet Heyrat by her hair before me, or else bring me her head.*" At these words, Kohan and his entire army tore off their collars in their amorous passion. Leaving their tents and equipage behind, they headed toward the region of Batin making cries of, "Catch that strumpet Heyrat! Don't let her escape!"

They crossed over the River of Flowing Blood and arrived near the Apple Garden where thousand of sorcerers in Afrasiyab's service were deputed. When they challenged Kohan and his army, Kohan's men attacked and started slaughter and carnage. Bodies fell down in piles and a great commotion arose.

Hearing the noise, Afrasiyab and Heyrat stepped outside the Apple Garden and beheld Kohan heading toward them, fighting like a man possessed. When Afrasiyab consulted the *Book of Sameri* it revealed that Mahrukh Magic-Eye had made a waxen magic effigy and the army of sorcerers were under a spell that could not be broken.

Reckoning the situation, Afrasiyab recited a spell on a steel magic ball and hurled it at Kohan's breast. It shattered his spinal column and shot out of his back. Afrasiyab rained thousands upon thousands of thunderbolts on Kohan's army and all of them burned to death as well.

As the sorcerers died, the magic effigy that had enchanted them also burned away. Witnessing that, Mahrukh Magic-Eye said to her companions, "It seems that Afrasiyab killed Kohan and his companions. Since I created the magic effigy to enchant them, when they died, she too burned up."

The drums of victory were beaten and the camp of the enemy was plundered. Mahrukh's army moved forward and bivouacked where Kohan's pavilion once stood. The camp of Queen Mahjabeen Diamond-Robe was set up many miles ahead of its previous site.

Prince Asad was brought down from the sky and joined the court. All the commanders adorned their stations and thrones and a dance recital began. The cupbearers circulated goblets of wine. Prince Asad asked Princess Mahrukh Magic-Eye, "Why did my horse fly away with me?" She answered, "O venerable prince, you do not know magic. Out of consideration for your safety, Dil Aaram recited a spell and made your horse fly away lest some sorcerer should harm you." Prince Asad retorted, "Do you take me for a coward? I swear upon my honor that if anyone attempts such a thing in the future he will answer with his life. Know O Princess, that regardless of the circumstances, we are always in the forefront in combat. To run to save our lives on the day of battle is a thing of great shame for us." Mahrukh Magic-Eye replied, "Very well. Your wishes will be respected." All of them then occupied themselves with carousing and pleasure-seeking.

Of the tricksters who had retired into the wilderness, four returned to the encampment, but Qiran the Ethiope did not join them.

Sorcerer Bubran Lion-Rider

While Mahrukh Magic-Eye's camp was thus occupied, Afrasiyab conferred with Heyrat, saying to her, "It was an evil hour when I was forced to kill my slaves and subjects by my own hand. An army of sixty thousand sorcerers and three renowned commanders died in the blink of an eye. The founders of the tilism spoke true when they wrote that a time would come when common slaves would confront the Emperor of the Tilism, and it would bode ill for him if he did not indulge them. Indeed, that time has come and we are living in that period. But certain it is, O Empress, that whether the tilism remains or is destroyed, and whether we live or die, I shall not allow this recalcitrant faction, these disloyal ingrates, to escape chastisement. Should one place on the head what must remain underfoot?"

Afrasiyab was making this speech when fire and water rained together from the sky. Realizing this signified the arrival of an eminent sorcerer, Afrasiyab ordered his high-ranking courtiers to go forth to welcome him. They departed and after some time the sound of drums and trumpets filled the expanse between the Earth and heavens.

A sorcerer riding a lion arrived at the gates of the Apple Garden leading an army of twelve thousand sorcerers. His face was cast in a horrible mien by magic and he wore a necklace of Sameri and Jamshed's portraits. Leaving his army at the gate, he entered the garden and saluted Afrasiyab and Heyrat.

Heyrat recognized her nephew Bubran Lion-Rider. She embraced and blessed him and seated him next to her. Heyrat asked, "What has brought you to these parts, my dear?" Bubran Lion-Rider answered, "I have heard that some of my uncle's servants have rebelled against him and are bent on sowing mischief. I have come to crush their heads. I ask you to send me on the campaign against them to deliver the punishment they deserve." Heyrat answered, "My dear, your uncle has many commanders on hand to punish them. These rebels are wholly worthless; it is beneath your dignity to engage them in battle. They are still at large because of a few tricksters from Hamza's camp who entered the tilism and killed sorcerers by deceit. Were it not for them, the rebels would have been destroyed a long time ago."

Bubran insisted on marching against the rebels and vowed to kill the tricksters and the leaders of their camp. At long last he received permission from Afrasiyab and, with a large army of sorcerers to accompany him, he made ready to depart.

The region of Batin rang out with the news that Empress Heyrat's nephew was marching against the rebels. Many an eminent sorcerer came to see Bubran Lion-Rider off on his campaign.

Heyrat said to Bubran, "You must camp near the River of Flowing Blood because Mahrukh Magic-Eye is camped a day's journey from there and the City of Manycolors is also nearby." Bubran submitted to these commands and ordered his army to march.

Heyrat said to Afrasiyab, "O Emperor, Your Lordship should take a seat in the Dome of Light from where you can see the entire tilism and witness the battle."

Bubran Lion-Rider crossed the River of Flowing Blood with his army and arrived near the City of Manycolors. There he ordered his army to set up camp and they pitched their pavilions. Hearing the sounds and clatter, Mahrukh Magic-Eye dispatched magic birds to learn why the drums and timbals sounded. They flew toward Bubran Lion-Rider's camp to gather news.

Queen Mahjabeen Diamond-Robe, Prince Asad and others were giving audience when the magic birds returned and announced, "*The army of the conceited enemy has camped by the riverside. It seeks to ford the river of life and reach death. All the rest bodes well.*"

Upon receiving this news, the tricksters left the court and disappeared into the wilderness.

Princess Mahrukh Magic-Eye said, "Our army should also advance and move the camp forward." The army marched, carrying the paraphernalia of war as ordered. Queen Mahjabeen Diamond-Robe's throne was brought forward with great ceremony by sorceresses who made a ring around it.

Before long, the two armies faced each other with only the battlefield separating them. Bubran avoided combat that day. He deputed a guard of twelve hundred sorcerers around his camp and put another hundred sorcerers around his own pavilion with orders that they must allow neither friend nor foe to enter because the tricksters struck and killed under disguise. After assuring him that his orders would be strictly adhered to, the guards took their positions at the entrance of his pavilion.

In the meanwhile, the day came to a close and the army of stars poured into the arena of the heavens. Armed with the dagger of its rays, the bright-faced moon began its vigil in the sky.

In the evening, the soldiers retired to take rest and sleep. Burq, who had retired into the wilderness with other tricksters, went into a mountain pass where he disguised himself as an ascetic. He tied on a knee-length waistcloth and smeared dust on his body. Adding extensions to his hair that reached down to his knees, he stuck false finger nails a hand span long to his fingers. He tied one arm as if it were withered and, holding a pitcher of drugged wine under the other, passed in front of Bubran Lion-Rider's pavilion. Upon sighting the sorcerers on duty outside, he circumvented them. Considering him a venerable ascetic, the sorcerers made him a respectful bow but instead of answering, the false ascetic ran from them.

The sorcerers conferred and decided that he must be a holy man. They resolved to follow him and accost him if possible in order to query him about their future prospects. A large number of them got up and pursued the man. When the false ascetic noticed them following, he sat down and drew lines on the ground. As they approached, he again ran away and stopped only after he had put a long distance between them. Then he tossed a handful of dust toward the sky and started mumbling. When the sorcerers approached, the false ascetic escaped again. Once out of their reach, he started to whirl in a spot. The sorcerers stood watching him while he spun. The false ascetic then sprinted away and the sorcerers resumed the chase. The false ascetic brought them far away from their camp and, placing a pitcher of drugged wine on the ground, ran and hid in the bushes.

The sorcerers were convinced that the ascetic was an intimate friend of God and did not associate with worldly folks, and left the pitcher behind for them when they followed him. They said to each other, "Let us see what's in it." They saw the mouth of the pitcher covered by a bowl and, upon lifting it, found it full of wine. One sorcerer said, "Drinking the wine of an ascetic – who is surely an intimate friend of God – will bring benefits both in this world and the next." Another said, "Surely if we imbibe it no disease would ever touch us." Another added, "Not only would it ward off disease, it would even introduce longevity!" In short, all of them sat down and each drank a cup of wine.

Then they got up and headed to Bubran Lion-Rider's pavilion, expressing regret at losing the holy man from sight. They had gone a little distance and breathed the cold forest air when the drug showed its effects. Their heads went down and legs went up. They fell on their faces and lost consciousness. Burq, who was hiding in the bushes in the ascetic's disguise, came out with drawn dagger and began beheading them. He quickly relieved some fifty sorcerers of their heads.

A great pandemonium broke lose. Hail fell, lightning bolts flashed, stone slabs rained, and magic spirits screamed. The decapitated corpses of the sorcerers flew away toward Bubran Lion-Rider's pavilion.

Bubran was drinking wine in his pavilion when the corpses arrived and he rushed out in panic. The sorcerers ran to the scene of carnage and saw whirlwinds rising and a great commotion afoot. They saw a man wielding a dagger beheading sorcerers lying unconscious.

In the meanwhile, Bubran also arrived on the scene. He recited a spell and clapped whereupon Burq's feet stuck to the ground. After a moment, when the noise and din died out and the darkness parted, Bubran brought Burq as a prisoner into his pavilion and said to him, "O wretch, tell me truly who you are?"

Burq answered, "I am the Angel of Death of sorcerers and have come to kill you. Had I known that beheading these sorcerers would make such a racket and the corpses would fly away to your pavilion, I would have dug a hole and thrown them into it, burying them alive. Still, nothing is lost. I shall soon dispatch you to hell. Things do not remain the same forever. I was free a moment ago, am captive now, and shall be free again shortly. I will then kill you and return in safety to Mahrukh Magic-Eye's camp."

Bubran's heart sank when he heard Burq's speech. He praised the trickster's courage and daring in his heart and realized that Heyrat had spoken the truth when she told him that the tricksters were the devil's own mothers.

Bubran steeled his heart and replied, "Make all the threats you like, O Burq, but I will kill you in the morning all the same. I will not kill you right now in the hope that I might capture another trickster who attempts to secure your release." Burq answered, "This is most excellent. The next trickster to arrive here will surely send you to hell."

With Burq tied up and his feet stuck to the ground, Bubran put a magic cordon around the pavilion so that anyone entering it could not leave. He then went to bed.

Earlier, the commotion of Burq's killing the sorcerers had attracted the ear of the trickster Qiran the Ethiope. He regarded the scene from far away. After Burq was arrested, Qiran disguised himself as a sorcerer and entered Bubran's camp. He thought of entering Bubran's pavilion but decided against it, thinking he would be unable to escape if there was a magic cordon around it. Qiran made his rounds around the camp in search of some way to attain his end but was unsuccessful.

Meanwhile, the dawn rent her collar in grief at Burq's imprisonment and the Shining Executioner of the Heavens[63] entered the execution chamber of the sky wielding the sharp sword of its rays. After rising from his sleep, Bubran drank a few cups of red wine and came out of his pavilion. He ordered the sorcerers to bring his conveyance and told them that upon his return from the morning excursion he would kill the insolent trickster captured the previous night. The sorcerers brought Bubran's lion. He mounted it and rode out into the wilderness.

Seeing Bubran leave, Qiran also headed for the forest. He searched inside a lion's den and found a beast. Since Qiran was the favored one of Caliph Ali, the Lion of God, he fearlessly went forth and challenged the lion. The lion struck but Qiran foiled his attack and, catching the beast's paws with one hand, landed a powerful blow with the other. Overwhelmed, the lion sank to the ground.

From his trickster's bag, Qiran took out a saddle and trappings similar to the ones he had seen on Bubran Lion-Rider's mount and fitted the lion with them. Then he disguised himself as Bubran and rode the lion to the sorcerer's pavilion. As Qiran approached, Bubran's attendants presented themselves, taking him for their master. The false Bubran said to them, "Go into my pavilion, remove my magic and bring out the trickster so that I may kill him in full view of Mahrukh's army. I will dismount only after settling this affair."

The sorcerers removed the spell from Burq and brought him out. The false Bubran led him out of view of the attendants. Once they had come a safe distance, Qiran revealed his identity to Burq and said, "Go now and be cautious in performing your trickeries." Burq marvelled at seeing Qiran on the lion's back and said, "You alone were endowed by God with the strength to overpower a wild lion."

Both of them retired into the wilderness where Qiran removed the saddle and all trappings from the lion and set him free, saying, "Go now! Your work is done here." The lion ran away into the wilderness the moment it was released. Burq returned to Bubran's camp in disguise and remained in search of an opportunity to kill the sorcerer.

When the real Bubran returned from his excursion and his sorcerer attendants saw him they believed he had returned after killing Burq. When Bubran dismounted and entered his pavilion he found his captive gone. He asked his attendants, "Where did that trickster go?" They replied, "Your Honor himself took him away a moment ago." Bubran said, "I have only just returned from my excursion. How could I have taken him away in the interim? Have you lost your senses?" All of them swore to the veracity of their account and narrated it to him in its entirety. Stunned, Bubran thought, *Indeed these tricksters are very resourceful to have carried out their mission in such a short time, disguised as me. How they fetched the lion is the devil's own business. It now looks difficult to escape from their hands.*

Bubran sent for his sorcerer attendants and said to them, "Now, even if you see Afrasiyab or Heyrat arrive do not let them into my pavilion without my express permission; arrest them immediately." After issuing these orders to his sorcerers, Bubran sent for wine and started drinking. He decided that he would strike the drums of war that evening to combat Mahrukh and her army the next day and return triumphant after killing the rebels.

Leaving him busy in these calculations, we return to Afrasiyab and Heyrat.

In the Dome of Light, while making love prattle, Heyrat said to Afrasiyab, "Emperor, it has been two days since my nephew left on the campaign against the rebels. We haven't learned what passed with him. My heart is restive. Look into the *Book of Sameri* and inform me of his welfare."

Afrasiyab looked into the book and told her of the trickeries performed by Burq and Qiran. Heyrat was unnerved and said, "I fear those tricksters will kill him. When those sons of strumpets can catch a wild lion from the forest, they are capable of anything." Deciding that she must call her nephew back and send someone else to replace him, Heyrat wrote a note to Bubran:

> "Return to the court as I have something of an urgent nature to discuss with you. You must come alone, leaving the army behind."

Heyrat gave the note to her sorceress-aide, Zamarrud, and said, "Take my message to Bubran and tell him that I send for him."

Sorceress Zamarrud was a beauty whose face was bright like a luminous moon. Her dark locks were long as lovers' nights of separation, her swelling bosom presented a pair of magnificent breasts, her whole body seemed cast of light, her carmine lips tinged with *missi*[64] recalled to mind a glowing sunset, her teeth rolled the honor of pearl strings into dust, and thousands of hearts of lovers floundered in the dimple of her chin. This moon-like beauty invoked her magic and flew away with Heyrat's note, arriving in Bubran's camp with demure and coy airs.

As she tried to enter Bubran's pavilion, the sorcerers surrounded Zamarrud and took her captive. They went and told Bubran, "Sorceress Zamarrud has arrived but we took her prisoner and did not allow her to enter." Bubran replied, "I am now on the alert. Send her inside. She might not be a trickster after all." The sorcerers allowed Zamarrud to enter Bubran's pavilion.

Bubran took off his ring and after reciting a spell over it threw it on the ground. He said, "O Zamarrud, pick up this ring and be seated. If you are the real Zamarrud, you will be able to pick it up, otherwise it will burn your hand and you won't be able to touch it." Zamarrud answered, "Upon my arrival I was first dishonored by being imprisoned; now you make me perform stunts!"

She recited a spell, picked up the ring and, with knitted brow, sat down on a chair.

When Bubran offered her a drink she said, "Get away from me. I have nothing to do with cowardly and feeble men like you. If you were so frightened of the tricksters, why did you come here to fight them in the first place?"

Witnessing Zamarrud's beauty and hearing her angry words, Bubran was smitten with love and thought of seeking congress with her. He put his hand on her cheek and said, "O my princess, don't be so cross.

Since you say so, I readily admit to being cowardly and feeble. Have some wine with me now." Zamarrud lowered her head with modesty as she recognized Bubran's intentions and said, "I wish you wouldn't say such things to me. If you are not careful, I will report you to your aunt, the empress!"

Bubran did not say more when he heard those words, and Zamarrud gave him the note from Heyrat. After reading it, Bubran said, "I will depart from here in the afternoon and arrive at the Dome of Light by evening."

Zamarrud flew away with the reply but kept looking back to gaze at Bubran. The malady of love had claimed Bubran as its own, and he rolled on the bed of anguish in desire.

Burq, who was present in Bubran's camp looking for an opportunity to work his trickery, sighted Zamarrud. He accompanied her to the end of the camp but felt helpless when she flew away by magic.

Before long, however, Burq thought of a trick. He went to a mountain pass and disguised himself as Zamarrud. This false Zamarrud put on a light green dress that made her look ravishing, and adorned herself with emerald jewelery so elegantly that her verdant beauty rankled like a thorn in the eyes of the garden of the world. Her kohl-lined, gazelle-like eyes became the wine service for those intoxicated with love and led them to the land of self forgetfulness. Her glowing cheeks were the envy of the sun; her mouth, the perfection of narrowness, ridiculed the claims of flower buds and made them die of envy. Her fragile neck was cast as gracefully as a wine ewer's, and it seemed her delicate lips were made for granting bliss.

Carrying a decanter of drugged red wine, the false Zamarrud sat down in a meadow and recited love couplets with great coquetry and dalliance. She thought, *Now any sorcerer who comes this way will fall my prey and I will kill him.*

Because it was noon, Bubran postponed the battle till the next day. He ordered his sorcerers to guard the camp, flew off toward Heyrat's court, and passed over that pleasant garden where the false Zamarrud was seated. Seeing Bubran Lion-Rider flying by, she loudly recited,

> *"I once died for your least notice*
> *Say a prayer at my grave now, O beloved."*

When Bubran looked down he saw the false Zamarrud sitting in the meadow. He called out to her, "O Zamarrud, I see you haven't yet returned to my aunt. Tell me if anything is the matter?" The false

Zamarrud heaved a cold sigh and said, "What is it to you? There's no accounting for those lost in the desert of love. They sit where they fancy to bring the day of separation to a close."

Bubran reckoned that Zamarrud had not agreed to a tryst with him earlier and repulsed his advances because his whole camp was observing them. But because she had fallen in love, she waited in his path, looking his way because he had mentioned he would return to court in the evening. Bubran descended and approached her. Seeing Bubran come near, the false Zamarrud recited the couplet,

"I would snare the bird of auspicious omen
If you were to pass by my abode."

Bubran smiled in reply and, reciting,

"God made my plaints reach their mark
I saw my beloved's disregard turn to longing,"

he tried to pull the false Zamarrud next to him and kiss her sweet lips.

She said, "No! Never! Do not touch me. Faithlessness such as yours remains unsurpassed in the world. I spent my whole day pining away in your love and striking my head in anguish against mountains and deserts. You come only now to make protestations of your love? O Bubran, since the day I saw you in the court my heart has been smitten with the curse of love. I know not what has possessed it."

Bubran replied, "O my life and soul, I too find life a burden without you. How may I explain that I felt utterly helpless and powerless before you? I was struck dumb by the grandeur of your beauty and my lips could not open to reveal what was in my heart. I suffered great anguish and became intoxicated on sorrow. But now the two of us can derive pleasure from each other's company and forget the past days of our suffering."

The false Zamarrud recited,

"I have given you myself with my word
You are become mine and I am now yours."

Pressing her cheek against Bubran's, the false Zamarrud put her arms around his neck. Seeing this display of her love, Bubran was near to dying from ecstasies of joy. Overwhelmed by passion, his unrequited desires stirred within him and Bubran could no longer hold himself back. He pressed the false Zamarrud to his breast and sought union with her. She said, "Let us first drink some wine, then we will enjoy ourselves."

She poured the wine into the cup and offered it to Bubran, saying, "Here, drink this nectar of love." He extended his hand to receive it.

꧁꧂

Now hear of Heyrat. The real Zamarrud returned to court and told the empress that Bubran promised to visit her in the evening. When it was evening and Bubran did not come, Heyrat said to Afrasiyab, "O Emperor, look into the *Book of Sameri* and find out why my nephew hasn't yet returned." When Afrasiyab looked into the book, he beat his head in distress and said, "He is about to be killed by the trickster Burq! The two of them are sitting in a wilderness under a mountain."

Heyrat turned to the real Zamarrud and said to her, "O Zamarrud, hurry and alert Bubran. I am sending magic spirits to accompany you and give you the clay of Jamshed's grave to render Bubran unconscious and bring him here." Zamarrud departed carrying the clay from Jamshed's grave.

She arrived in the wilderness and called out, "O Bubran, desist! Do not invite your death upon your head. Make not the least delay and arrest the one sitting next to you for he is the trickster Burq the Frank."

The false Zamarrud became troubled upon seeing the real Zamarrud and, hearing her words, said to Bubran, "O Bubran, the heavens could not see us cheerful even for a single moment and conspired against our happiness. See, a trickster now arrives in my disguise to deceive you."

Blinded by his lust, Bubran was sorely annoyed to see a Zamarrud look-alike approaching. He became convinced that it was indeed a trickster. He told the false Zamarrud sitting beside him to hide herself so that he might apprehend the one approaching. While the false Zamarrud hid herself in the bushes, Bubran rose to his feet and waited.

The real Zamarrud came near Bubran and said, "What became of the trickster sitting next to you?" Bubran answered, "He ran away upon seeing you." Saying this, Bubran caught Zamarrud's arm, and said, "O evil man, I understand all your snares and deceptions!" At this, the false Zamarrud also came out of the bushes and shouted, "Do not let this wretch escape, O Bubran!"

Bubran recited a spell and hit Zamarrud with a magic slap. It would have sent the head of any ordinary sorceress flying off her shoulders but since Zamarrud was Empress Heyrat's aide and an accomplished sorceress herself, she turned her face to stone by reciting a spell.

Incensed, she sprinkled the clay of Jamshed's grave on Bubran, who fell down unconsciousness. Burq was pondering his next move when Zamarrud recited a spell and called out, "Hold!" The ground caught Burq's feet and he was unable to move.

Zamarrud cut the shape of palms out of paper and recited a spell that turned them into magic claws. She ordered, "O magic claws, carry away these two to the Dome of Light." The magic claws flashed like lightning bolts and carried away Bubran and Burq.

Zamarrud also followed the magic claws to the Dome of Light.

Upon arrival, Zamarrud said to Heyrat, "My Lady! Your nephew cannot differentiate between his friends and his foes. He was so possessed by lust and such blindness had come over him that he hit me with a magic slap. Any other sorceress in my place would certainly have died. Here is your nephew now, and here's the trickster who was sitting in his lap. I shall now quit your service as I am not used to being treated ill and rough."

Heyrat offered words of consolation to Zamarrud and brought Bubran to consciousness. When he opened his eyes and saw Heyrat and Afrasiyab before him, he rose to his feet and saluted them. Heyrat said to him, "You sit with your arms around a trickster and when Zamarrud comes to your rescue, you slap her in complete disregard of the honor due me. You have not the sense to tell friends apart from foes."

Bubran answered, "I indeed committed that error, for which I seek forgiveness." Heyrat now looked at Burq and said, "And see what a perfect likeness this wretch has produced. It's small wonder that Bubran was deceived. Tell me Zamarrud if you see the least difference between your face and the face of this devil deserving of beheading and nipping in the bud. No, Zamarrud, you must not take offense because in matters of desire even great ascetics and warriors lose self-restraint."

Heyrat recited a spell that made Burq's makeup disappear and revealed his real face.

The empress said, "Listen, O Burq, I am letting you go free. Go and tell Mahrukh Magic-Eye to help ward off the death from her head by presenting herself into my service along with Mahjabeen. I promise to have their offenses forgiven by the emperor." Burq answered, "Make all these glib speeches like a whore and ignore the fact that your days are numbered. You would do well to enjoy the life that is left you for soon the crows and kites will feast on your corpse. Do you take Mahrukh for your father's slave girl that she should come running to you at your bidding?"

Enraged at his insolence, Heyrat ordered a sorcerer to behead Burq. Seeing this, Burq turned his heart to God and solicited the court of heavens for aid. The arrow of his petition met the target of approval and Bubran said to Heyrat, "Dear aunt, this trickster has gravely diminished my standing. Give him into my power to kill him in full view of Mahrukh's camp so that all of them may receive instruction from his terrible end."

Heyrat said, "Nephew, I won't let you return now." Bubran replied, "I've been publicly humiliated. If you do not allow me to return I will slit my throat with my own hands." With those words, Bubran drew his dagger and pressed it against his neck.

Heyrat took Bubran's hand into her own. She gently censured Bubran and tried to persuade him against returning. Bubran did not listen and in the end Heyrat allowed him to depart with Burq. She said to Bubran, "Go, and kill this trickster without loss of time, then settle the score with the enemy and wipe them from the face of the world. I shall send renowned sorcerers to your aid."

Bubran cut out the shape of a lion from paper and recited a spell that brought it to life. He put Burq on the lion's back, sat down behind him, and rode back to his camp.

Now hear of the trickster Qiran the Ethiope, who had sought some news of Burq the Frank. He spent the whole day searching for him until the Beautifier of Life adorned the damsel of night with the jewelery of stars, implanted the spangle of the moon on the sky's brow, and illuminated a world that lay enveloped in darkness.

Qiran happened by that wilderness where Burq was taken prisoner by Zamarrud. Hardly a few moments had passed before he saw Bubran coming with Burq on the lion's back. Qiran realized that Burq had been taken prisoner. He filled drug powder in the folds of a paper and stuck the paper inside an envelope that he stamped with Heyrat's forged seal.

Disguising himself as a sorcerer, he ran after Bubran calling his name. Bubran heard him and stopped. When Qiran approached, Bubran asked that he identify himself. Qiran replied, "I am Empress Heyrat's messenger." Bubran said, "I have just returned from her court. I did not see you there. Why would she dispatch a messenger so soon after I left?"

Qiran, who did not know the details of Bubran's court visit, replied with knitted brow, "I don't know all that. All you are required to do is to read this letter and give your reply to what is asked. And do tell me, O Bubran, since you maintain that you did not see me at the court, if servants must always cling to their masters? I was at my station when the empress sent for me and gave me this letter to deliver to you. Why do you split hairs with me over a trifle?"

Bubran took the letter from his hand and said, "It's dark, come with me to my camp so that I may read it and give you my reply." Qiran answered, "Then I must leave. You may send your reply by some other means. You are a sorcerer and can easily read it here by lighting up a magic torch. If you wish, I can light one for you." Qiran's words pricked Bubran's pride. Bubran picked a twig up from the ground and recited a spell that immediately lit it up like a torch.

Bubran handed it to Qiran to hold up so that he could read the letter in its light. As Bubran tried to remove the letter stuck in the envelope, Qiran threw a drug on the torch flame and pushed it in Bubran's face. Bubran turned his head away quickly but not fast enough to avoid inhaling the smoke. His face was burned by the torch and he inhaled the drug. As he swooned and fell, Qiran struck out with his cleaver and smashed his head. Bubran thrashed about and died. A calamity was immediately set loose. Terrifying sounds boomed.

Freed from captivity, Burq ran to his camp and Qiran the Ethiope retreated into the wilderness. Burq went and told Mahrukh and Shakeel to ready their army because Bubran had been killed. Shakeel immediately blew the magic trumpet. His army prepared for combat and the sorcerers mounted their magic dragons and peacocks. Mahrukh and Shakeel attacked the enemy camp with their forty thousand renowned sorcerers. Steel magic balls, garlands of red chillies, clusters of darts and magic needles rained on the foe. Bubran's army was caught off guard. They paid for their slowness with the lives of thousands of their men. Whirlwinds rose, lightning bolts flashed, magic citrons, magic limes and coconuts were exchanged between the two camps and a river of blood issued forth.

Amar Ayyar was in the wilderness when he heard the sounds of "Catch!" and "Kill!" and ran toward them. When he saw Bubran's army being slaughtered, he too drew his dagger and joined the fray, keeping the cape of invisibility ready in case sorcerers surrounded him. He rolled on the ground and with every sweeping blow severed up to three pairs of legs. He leaped and jumped from the shoulders of one sorcerer to another. When they tried to catch his legs he beheaded them. As the sorcerers died, Amar cut off and secured their money pouches. He entered Bubran's pavilion and carried away its entire contents with the Net of Ilyas.

Prince Asad also rode out upon hearing the commotion. Dil Aaram brought Mahjabeen's throne. The drums were struck and the royal throne advanced. Queen Mahjabeen deputed fifty magicians to guard Prince Asad clandestinely so that enemy sorcerers could not capture him by putting him under their spell. These magicians accompanied Asad, furtively reciting counterspells. Prince Asad drew his sword and fell upon the army of sorcerers. He made heaps of the slain and piles of the dead. With every charge, Prince Asad made his war cry,

"I am Asad the accomplished horseman who, on the day of battle
Rips out the heart of lions and tears apart the hide of tigers
I am the emperor who returns victorious
I am Asad the Lion-Hearted, progeny of Hamza."

As swords flashed and clashed mightily, Dil Aaram advanced with Mahjabeen's throne raining fire and water on the enemy forces. The enemy camp was gripped by confusion. Only the brave stood fearlessly and without the least trepidation, their chests thrust out. Prince Asad stirred the battlefield with his sword and killed thousands.

Finally, Bubran's retreating army crossed over the Bridge of the Magic Fairies and arrived weeping and howling at the Dome of Light. Afrasiyab and Heyrat learned that Bubran's army had returned in defeat.

Heyrat cried out, "Someone tell me quickly whether my nephew is alive and well." Bubran's men answered, "He was killed by the tricksters long ago and must now be in Lord Sameri's company in the hereafter." Heyrat beat her head in anguish and cried, "Alas for my dear boy! These tricksters deserving of beheading took his life in the end."

The Dome of Light rang with lamentations and mourning.

Afrasiyab recited a spell and clapped. Whirlwinds and storms materialized and bore away the corpse of Bubran from where it lay and brought it to the Dome of Light. All the renowned sorcerers clad themselves in black and made arrangements for his last rites.

Mahrukh Magic-Eye and her armies pillaged the tents and pavilions of the enemy, the drums of victory were beaten, and clarions sounded in victory from her camp.

Their army advanced and set up camp where Bubran's army had previously bivouacked, within sight of the River of Flowing Blood and a short distance from the City of Manycolors. Once the army had camped, the tricksters arrived, made offerings to Mahjabeen Diamond-Robe, and received robes of honor. Singers and dancers presented themselves and a dance recital got underway.

Sorcerer Faulad Drug-Glutton

Before long it was morning and the Emperor of the Armies of Stars[65] retreated from the arena of the sky. The golden standard of Emperor Sun fluttered in the zephyr on the morn of victory. The conveyance of the King of Planets[66] entered the desert with great majesty.

After Bubran Lion-Rider's last rites had been performed with royal fanfare, Heyrat said to Afrasiyab, "Pray give me leave to march against the traitors and kill them." Afrasiyab replied, "This time I will send someone to take care of the tricksters first, a sorcerer who will not be incapacitated by weapons or drugs."

He then recited a spell and called out, "O Faulad Drug-Glutton, present yourself!" No sooner had he issued the command than a towering and hideous sorcerer on a fiery rhinoceros descended from the sky and saluted Afrasiyab.

The emperor said, "Depart hastily with twelve thousand sorcerers as Hamza's tricksters have entered and caused mayhem in the tilism. Bubran Lion-Rider has been killed. Until now I showed indulgence toward the rebels, thinking they might see the light and return to the path of obedience and deference. But it seems that death has marked them for its own. I am sending twelve steel magic slaves to accompany you. They can be neither drugged nor killed. They will help you capture the enemies."

Afrasiyab clapped again and twelve steel magic slaves wielding swords sprang out of the ground and he said to them, "Accompany Faulad and obey his commands."

Faulad said, "Your Highness, there is no need for them. I alone can overpower the rebels. I would have to drink many doses of drug in my wine before feeling even the slightest intoxication. Weapons have no effect on me. Neither can the tricksters prevail against me, nor sorcerers or mighty warriors fight me." Afrasiyab said, "There is no harm in taking the magic slaves along as a precaution. Go and fulfill your mission."

Faulad saluted Afrasiyab and departed. A twelve-thousand-strong army of sorcerers with their tents and equipage accompanied him. The twelve magic slaves rode beside Faulad. The criers of the camp called out, "Clear the way! Show deference! Keep your distance!"

They sped on their path and, after crossing the River of Flowing Blood, arrived near Mahrukh Magic-Eye's camp.

The sound of their drums reached the ears of the righteous warriors and Mahrukh dispatched magic birds to gather intelligence.

The magic birds flew away and returned after gathering particulars about the arriving army. With their gracious tongues they sang the praise of Queen Mahjabeen. "*May the queen have a long life. May her enemies always remain indisposed and ill. A wretched sorcerer named Faulad Drug-Glutton has arrived with his army and the intention of waging war against the servants of your illuminated Highness.*"

After making their speeches, the magic birds flew off to gather more intelligence about the foe.

Mahrukh said to Amar Ayyar, "We come from God and to God we must return! Faulad Drug-Glutton is a bloody scourge against whom all weapons are useless. He can drink up great loads of drugs without batting an eye, and his body is proof against warriors' weapons and sorcerers' spells."

Amar replied, "O Princess, the assistance of the Creator of the Universe alone suffices against all challenges. Shaddad the Vile, the great infidel of the past had similarly safeguarded himself against his death. He had set all manner of conditions to God: that the moment of his death should be neither morning nor night; that he should not die either standing, lying or seated. All of these conditions the All-Powerful God accepted just to show him His supremacy and omnipotence. When Shaddad satisfied himself that he would escape death, he went to inspect the paradise he had constructed to rival God's own. It was the break of dawn. He arrived at the threshold of his paradise and was about to enter it. His one foot was in the stirrup and the other not yet on the ground when the Angel of Death arrived to extract his soul. He was carried away by death and dispatched hellward, full of unrequited hopes and unfulfilled desires. Faulad Drug-Glutton is nothing more than a clown and neither Afrasiyab nor that despicable Laqa are of any consequence at all. O Princess, whoever shuns the True God and tries to assume His divine seat remains a loser in this world and the next. Do you not see how Hamza constantly drives Laqa from place to place, with the false god's head covered with the dust of ignominy? Put your trust in God's beneficence. Even if you fall into dire trouble, do not let your faith waver in the least. I will now depart to kill the ignoble Faulad."

With these words, Amar headed out of the court. Other tricksters had already left after receiving news of the enemy's arrival and were busy planning their strategies.

Let us now give an account of the tricksters Amar, Zargham and Jansoz. They infiltrated Faulad Drug-Glutton's camp in the disguise of sorcerers. Amar headed for the place of audience and said to the attendants, "Go and inform your master that sorcerer Maut the Death has come to see him." When the message was conveyed to Faulad he ordered Maut to be presented.

False sorcerer Maut entered the court and saw Faulad Drug-Glutton sitting on a throne from which a thousand tongues of flame continuously darted out. Faulad wore a crown that glowed like the heart of fire and his waist was encircled by a chain of flames. Hundreds of sorcerers in hideous guises were seated around him while the twelve magic slaves of steel marched up and down wielding swords. Sparks fell from their mouths when they conversed. The criers and attendants stood at their stations.

The false sorcerer saluted Faulad. When the attendant called out, "Your Honor, before your eyes!" Faulad Drug-Glutton raised his eyes and accepted the greetings with a nod. He saw black snakes with darting tongues were tied around false sorcerer Maut's head. He wore pearl necklaces, a gold chain around his waist, and carried a sorcerer's gold cloth bag. Faulad Drug-Glutton thought him a mighty and patrician sorcerer. He asked Maut to approach and respectfully offered him a seat. After the false Maut sat down, Faulad asked his name and particulars and inquired about the reason for his visit.

The false sorcerer, Maut, replied, "I live in the City of Manycolors. Mahrukh Magic-Eye confiscated all my goods and chattels and for the longest time I prayed for her destruction. However, I was powerless to confront her on my own. The news of your arrival brought me untold joy and I thought of presenting myself to pay my respects." Faulad Drug-Glutton said, "You did well in coming here. Consider this place your home. I will soon kill these ingrates and solicit the emperor to confer their belongings on you." Faulad Drug-Glutton sent for a robe of honor and conferred it on the false Maut, who made an offering in return and became a close confidant of Faulad.

Zargham and Jansoz continued to make rounds of the enemy camp, trying to gain entry into Faulad's pavilion. They saw two attendants come out of his pavilion and followed them. Seeing a deserted spot, they called out, "Please hear us, friends!" When the attendants stopped, the tricksters approached them and said, "We brought some perfume to sell to your master but were unable to gain admittance. Perhaps you could sell it on our behalf."

The attendants replied, "Let us see what perfume you are selling." The tricksters pulled two glass carafes from their belts and offered them to the attendants, who smelled them and fell unconscious. The tricksters took off their clothes and threw the attendants in a nearby ditch.

Putting on their clothes, they disguised themselves as the attendants. After entering Faulad Drug-Glutton's pavilion they took their positions behind the sorcerer.

In the meanwhile, Amar Ayyar offered Faulad a goblet of wine mixed with a large dose of a powerful drug. Faulad took the goblet from his hands and drank it up without the least caution. The drug had no effect on him. However, from tasting the wine, Faulad recognized the presence of a drug and realized that sorcerer Maut must be a trickster. He quietly recited a spell and blew it on Maut, who suddenly became stuck to his seat. Faulad Drug-Glutton said, "O trickster, I know you have come to kill me. Come now, give me all the drug you have."

Hearing these words, Zargham and Jansoz, standing in disguise behind Faulad Drug-Glutton, said to each other, "Since he could not be drugged, let us kill him with daggers. The worst that can happen is that we will be arrested. God the Ultimate Master will protect us."

They drew their daggers and attacked Faulad Drug-Glutton from both sides but the daggers broke into shards when they hit Faulad's body. The tricksters tried to run but Faulad cast a spell and they fell down on their faces. Sorcerers overpowered them and presented them, along with Amar Ayyar, before Faulad Drug-Glutton. He put them under an incarceration spell and said to his sorcerers, "Set up a pavilion next to mine and imprison them inside." The pavilion was set up and the tricksters imprisoned. Faulad Drug-Glutton recited a spell and put a fire cordon around the pavilion.

Faulad said, "As planned, I was able to catch the tricksters by the grace of the Emperor's rising fortunes. Strike the drums of battle so that I may speedily kill Mahrukh as well."

At Faulad's orders, his soldiers blew the magic trumpet and tooted the bugle of war. The whole camp was alerted to the news of the impending battle. The magic birds returned to Queen Mahjabeen's court. After visiting blessings and singing praises of the queen they narrated the capture of the tricksters and Faulad's blowing the magic trumpet. Then they flew away to spy on the foe once again.

Frightened by the news, Mahrukh said to Queen Mahjabeen Diamond-Robe, "Did you hear that the tricksters have been captured? None of us is powerful enough to confront Faulad. If you agree, we will all run away under cover of night and hide ourselves in some refuge. I know the path out of the tilism. I will take all of you to Amir Hamza. He will be able to confront the Emperor of Hoshruba."

Prince Asad replied, "O Princess, Amar Ayyar has been captured a thousand times and broken free as many times. Worry not the least in this regard and order your men to answer the call for battle. It would be very shameful for the servants of Amir Hamza to retreat. If we went before him as escapees, he would drive us away from his presence saying, 'Why did you retreat? Did you hold your miserable lives too dear? I now have no business with you.' Still, you may go if you desire. Since you are a woman, Amir Hamza will not deny you refuge. I, however, could never consent to this proposition."

Mahrukh replied, "We are with you. If such is your resolve, pray order the call to war answered from our camp with full force." Prince Asad told the sorcerers and commanders of his army to strike the drums of war with the grace of the Munificent God and the sanction of the Almighty Lord. The servants of the prince carried out his commands. The timbal was struck and the army prepared to fight to its last man.

In the meanwhile, the Luminescent Emperor lowered its standard of light rays from the heavens to retreat and the dark night prevailed. The braves readied their battle gear. Every single soul prepared itself to face doom and keep its tryst with mistress death. Mahrukh Magic-Eye and Shakeel sent for four hundred mighty sorcerers, who chanted spells and threw offerings of lard into flames. Clapper-drums were beaten around bonfires. The sorcerers threw waxen dragons into the blazing fires and bound them with oaths to present themselves when called. Magic spirits were summoned and sacrifices offered to them for their assistance. Every sorcerer of the army invoked his magic and made sacrifices of king crows and kites.[67] Chillies and gum resin were burned and the cling-clang of metal rose from every corner of the camp.

Prince Asad also armed and readied his men for battle. Those who did not know magic polished their swords and daggers. For four watches of the night the two armies made preparations. The vigils made their rounds and the martial music played continuously until life's dawn prayers washed away the darkness of night's heart. The blessed tongue of morning recited the Chapter of Light[68] and took an oath in the name of the illuminating sun, which ascended its throne to give brilliant audience.

Armed and clad in armor, Prince Asad presented himself at the doorstep of Queen Mahjabeen Diamond-Robe. Mahrukh Magic-Eye and Shakeel presented themselves in the royal chamber of audience after sending their men to the arena in platoons and detachments under the leadership of army commanders. Queen Mahjabeen Diamond-Robe arrived with great fanfare and received salutes from everyone gathered there.

Dil Aaram made the royal throne airborne and Prince Asad, along with all the nobles of the camp, accompanied it to the battlefield. At regular intervals, the criers and the attendants called out, "Clear the

Path! Show deference! Keep your distance!" Amidst this hubbub, all of them entered the arena.

Faulad Drug-Glutton had spent the entire night preparing his magic. He strode out on his fiery rhinoceros in the morning and took command of his twelve thousand sorcerers. The twelve magic slaves accompanied him with drawn swords. Bugles tooted, gongs and bells sounded, and Faulad's rhinoceros started galloping,

A rhinoceros whose hoof splits stones
And bores into the iron heart of Mount Qaf

The enemy descended into the battlefield with great preparations. Sorcerers rained thunderbolts and water to clear the arena for battle and settle the dust. Masters of columns and flanks arranged the army into fighting formations. Criers made their proclamations:

"Wipe out Rustam's name from the register of the valiant with your example!
Today, smell the flower of the shield, partake of the fruit of the sword!"[69]

"O braves, struggle! Sit not like pansies all dressed!"

"Today is the day of battle. Skirmish!
Defend your name and repute. Clash!"

After the criers withdrew from the field, Faulad Drug-Glutton spurred his rhinoceros into the arena and called out, "O tribe of rebels, be ready to be dispatched to the plains of death. Come out and face the battle before you."

Hearing his tall claims, Shakeel took permission from Mahjabeen Diamond-Robe to answer Faulad's challenge and confronted him. Faulad said to him, "Deal me your best blow. Show me what weapon you possess." Shakeel recited a spell and struck his hands, and darkness engulfed Faulad. Magic claws materialized in that darkness and attacked Faulad with lances, arrows and swords.

Faulad spurred his rhinoceros, picked up a fistful of clay and, after reciting a spell on it, hurled it toward the sky. Immediately, the darkness was cast away and the magic claws disappeared. Faulad recited a spell on a magic coconut and threw it at Shakeel. It exploded and surrounded him with its smoke. Shakeel fell to the ground in a faint. Faulad ordered a magic slave, "Fetch him!" The magic slave pinioned Shakeel and brought him to Faulad.

Seeing this sight, other sorcerers sought Mahjabeen Diamond-Robe's permission to confront Faulad. One after another, Faulad overpowered each of them by making them unconscious with exploding magic coconuts. Then the magic slaves took them prisoner.

Finally, Princess Mahrukh herself entered the arena to confront Faulad Drug-Glutton. She invoked a spell that made dust storms rise from all four directions and disperse the smoke created by Faulad's magic. Mahrukh Magic-Eye then hit the ground with a magic citron that broke and a magic dragon materialized. It spewed fire with its mouth and inhaled mightily, pulling Faulad Drug-Glutton into its open jaws.

As Faulad was being pulled into the dragon's mouth, he called out, "O magic slaves, come to my rescue. The whore Mahrukh has employed powerful magic against me."

The magic slaves attacked the dragon as a body and tore and destroyed it to shreds in no time. Then they attacked Mahrukh herself. She tried many spells and struck them with magic slaps but nothing repulsed the magic slaves.

Mahjabeen Diamond-Robe now ordered her army to save Mahrukh Magic-Eye. It charged from all directions with cries of "Stop them! Capture them!" The sorcerers cast spells, lightning bolts fell, and infernal sounds rose.

Seeing this turn of events, Faulad Drug-Glutton threw four magic coconuts toward the four corners of the arena. They sank into the ground and immediately afterward flames rose from the ground and a wall of fire surrounded Mahrukh Magic-Eye's army on four sides. The smoke produced by this fire rose and settled down like a lid above the walls of fire. Whenever anyone from Mahrukh Magic-Eye's army tried to escape the fiery confines, the fire burnt them, and if they tried to fly out, the smoke made them unconscious.

While Mahrukh's army was thus imprisoned, the magic slaves who had attacked Mahrukh finally overpowered and bound her and led her before Faulad. He put magic handcuffs and fiery shackles on both Mahrukh and Shakeel and put them on a cart. Then he ordered his army to march. The tents and pavilions were dismantled and packed on the conveyances. The drum beat announced the start of the return journey and the army headed on its way. Amar Ayyar, Jansoz and Zargham were also led away as prisoners.

Faulad Drug-Glutton now recited a spell and clapped and the fiery wall imprisoning Mahrukh's army moved by itself behind him. With the wall of flames advancing on them, the prisoners had no choice but to move with it. In this manner, Mahrukh's whole army marched inside a fiery ring behind Faulad, weeping and wailing and calling out to Almighty God for succor.

Laughing uproariously at the plight of his prisoners, Faulad ambitiously led his men forward. Qiran the Ethiope and Burq the Frank regarded this terrible sight from afar. Except for them, the whole army, including its tricksters and commanders – even the dogs who followed the camp – were now prisoners of that fiery cordon. Burq started crying at the sight and said to Qiran, "Master, I shall now attack this whore's son Faulad and either cut him to bits with my dagger or give my life in the attempt."

Qiran answered, "No purpose will be served by your trying to kill him as neither weapons nor drugs have any effect on him. All your trickeries will fail. We must put our trust in God and follow them. When they halt to rest we will try to come up with some useful strategy."

After making this decision, both Qiran and Burq, from separate paths, clandestinely followed Faulad Drug-Glutton's army.

Meanwhile, in the Dome of Light, Afrasiyab looked into the *Book of Sameri* to see what had transpired with Faulad. The book revealed that Faulad had taken prisoner the entire army of the rebels and was bringing it, captive in a cordon of fire.

Afrasiyab vainly set his crown on his head at an angle and said, "O Heyrat, regard the terrible fruits of rebellion. All the rebels have been miserably incarcerated." Heyrat replied, "Your Excellency must ensure that every single one of them is strung up."

Afrasiyab sent an inestimable robe of honor for Faulad with a message, which read:

> "O my illustrious commander! Bravo! Well done! A thousand accolades on your securing a quick victory in battle. I send you a robe of honor. Rest assured that greater honors and distinctions will be bestowed upon you. You will only rise in rank and distinction with every passing day. Bring all these rebels to the Pleasure Garden located in the region of Zahir near the City of Purple Poppy. There is no need to inconvenience yourself by crossing over the bridge. I will come to Zahir myself to mete out punishment to the rebels."

After dispatching the sorcerers, Afrasiyab, along with Empress Heyrat and renowned sorcerers, headed for the Pleasure Garden and arrived there with great majesty.

Overlooking the garden was a field where Afrasiyab ordered scaffolds to be raised, and sent for the executioners.

Thousands of executioners clad in waistcloths and wearing garlands of human ears and noses presented themselves. Broad swords were stuck in their belts. The rags on their shoulders for wiping the blades stank of fresh blood. They called out, "Whose cup of life has filled to its brim? Who is the culprit whose thread of life the emperor wants severed?" Afrasiyab ordered them to be ready when his commander brought the sinners the following morning or the morning after. The executioners made their beds under the scaffolds and were soon engrossed in dreams of the rewards they would receive from the emperor for their labors.

Afrasiyab gave audience inside the Pleasure Garden. The trees in the garden were wrapped in gold cloth, water was released in the watercourses and the fountains spouted. A dance recital began. The dulcimer, flute, lute and rebeck played, and the revels were soon underway.

The sorcerers dispatched by Afrasiyab arrived in Faulad's camp. They dressed him in the robe of honor and presented the emperor's missive to him. Faulad was in seventh heaven after reading the letter. He changed his course to head for the Pleasure Garden as Afrasiyab had ordered. He marched continuously with the prisoners until he arrived at the City of Purple Poppy.

Sorceress Nafarman

Faulad saw the golden walls of the City of Purple Poppy. Thousands of sorcerers in magical guises were assembled before the fortress at the gates of the city. Bonfires were lit and smoke rose from all corners from lard offerings made to prepare spells. Beds of tulips and poppies stretched for miles from the foot of the fortified city.

Princess Nafarman, a noble and accomplished sorceress, was the governor of the City of Purple Poppy. She was wealthy and affluent, and a great beauty besides. When her magic birds brought news that Faulad Drug-Glutton had entered the precincts of her city on his way to the Pleasure Garden, she mounted a magic peacock and headed out to greet him bearing gifts and offerings.

As she rode out of the city, she beheld a ring of fire that stretched for miles and heard the weeping and wailing of prisoners from within.

She beheld Faulad Drug-Glutton marching with his twelve magic slaves and the army of sorcerers. Princess Nafarman brought her magic peacock forward and called out, "Bravo, O warrior! A most excellent accomplishment! Pray stop a moment to have a word with me!"

At her greeting, Faulad stopped. His army halted and he cast a spell to halt the ring of fire as well. Princess Nafarman approached Faulad and said, "I would like to invite you to my fortress. Sup with me before you continue on your journey."

Faulad decided that he could take a break as he had marched continuously without rest and the fortress offered a luxurious and safe stop. He answered, "I have rebels in my custody and must continue onwards. But as I cannot disregard your wishes, I will present myself before you shortly." After securing his promise, Princess Nafarman returned to her city and gave orders that the city be decorated in Faulad's honor.

The whole city was bedecked like a bride. The shops were adorned and the shopkeepers put on fine golden dresses for the occasion. Princess Nafarman made preparations for Faulad's stay in a spring-blooming garden and allocated a heart-charming chamber and joy-bestowing hall for his entourage. A luxurious carpet was spread out in Faulad's honor. Arrangements for a feast were made and after all the preparations were complete, Princess Nafarman came out of the city with her nobles and courtiers to welcome her guest.

Faulad left his army to guard the ring of fire and headed for the metropolis with his commanders and the twelve magic slaves. Princess Nafarman and Faulad met on the way and entered the city together.

Upon entering the City of Purple Poppy, Faulad witnessed a prosperous city populated with happy people. Taking in the sights, he finally arrived at the spring blooming garden that had been allocated for him. Praise the Lord! The loveliness of that garden surpassed any sight Faulad had ever seen. Golden spires rose from the gates surrounding the garden. They were surmounted with sunflowers carved from garnets that outshone the sun, and jewel-carved, emerald-feathered peacocks that carried pearl ornaments in their beaks. He entered through a pair of doors carved out of ivory. Inside, the walls of the garden were made of brass, decorated with red gold and exquisitely studded with jewels.

Faulad found the garden in full bloom. He saw the tastefully laid flowerbeds, the fine pathways, and the beautiful watercourses. The promenades were inlaid with rubies. The trees were laden with flowers. Vines heavy with fruit clusters and hedges of henna plants decorated the expanse. Water gurgled through the tiled watercourses, each spring shone as clear as the heart of the pure, and the courtyards were clean and spotless. Flocks of birds perched in every tree and the songs of the nightingales and the ringdoves proclaimed the arrival of spring with great fervour. Full of manycolored flowers, the sight of the garden put the House of Mani to shame.

There was a luxurious summerhouse in the heart of the garden lavishly appointed with a richly woven carpet, seats and thrones. All the accoutrements of luxury and comfort were provided and the place was brightly lit up with glass lights. Faulad entered and sat down as the twelve magic slaves and his commanders took their positions around him deferentially. At Princess Nafarman's orders, the dance recital began. Beautiful cupbearers poured roseate Portuguese wine in bejewelled goblets. The wine worshippers importuned the cupbearers to fill desire's cup.

Princess Nafarman presided over the arrangements and made sure all necessities for the revelry were provided. It was soon dark. The moonlit night, the breezy garden, and the noise of the singers together produced a most auspicious ambience for the evening. The revels were at their height and the garden was filled with an audience engrossed in singing and dancing. At every melodious strain of the singers, they felt shivers of ecstasy.

Now hear of the tricksters Qiran the Ethiope and Burq the Frank. They followed Faulad Drug-Glutton's camp crying and wailing, hoping to find their chance and thinking of some way to free Mahrukh Magic-Eye's army.

When they saw that Faulad's army was about to stop and camp, they infiltrated it disguised as sorcerers and learned all the details of Princess Nafarman's invitation and the feast she had arranged in Faulad's honor. After gathering this information they followed Faulad to the gates of the city. While Faulad headed for the spring blooming garden and occupied himself there in carousing, the two tricksters stopped outside the city gates.

Qiran asked Burq to disguise himself as a laborer. Burq immediately put on a waistcloth and stood barefoot with a cloth-ring for carrying loads placed on his head. Qiran disguised himself as a cook and put on dirty clothes stained with turmeric and oil spots. He stuck vegetable knives in his waist, threw on his shoulder a cloth used for straining butter and sifting spices, and headed with Burq toward Faulad's camp where he purchased a large quantity of greens, potatoes and yams.

With Burq carrying the vegetables on his head in a basket, the two of them headed for the city and soon arrived at its gates. The guards and sentinels barred their way and told them they would not let them pass without permission.

Qiran said to them, "We are the designated cooks for the feast. We are taking vegetables from Faulad's camp at Princess Nafarman's orders." The guards said, "Wait here until we receive clearance for you to enter." The false cook replied, "I am going back. You may yourself deliver these vegetables for the kitchen and when the meal is late you can answer for that, as well." He threw the entire contents of the vegetable basket on the ground and turned to go.

The guards conferred and realized that if there was a delay in cooking and the supper was late Faulad would rise from the table hungry. The cook would be queried and he would blame the guards for not letting him pass. As a consequence, they would not only lose their jobs but their necks as well. They decided to let the cook pass and called out to him, "Master Cook, come back! You may enter. Nobody is stopping you."

The false cook answered, "I have no such desire. I won't turn back now."

The guards ran after him and held his arm, saying, "Don't be cross. You may freely enter." The false cook replied, "Even should I return now I won't be able to prepare the food in time. I was delayed because of you and you must answer for it. No, I am decided. I won't return."

The guards importuned the false cook but he remained adamant. Finally, all the guards made a collection and offered it to him, saying, "Master Cook, don't be cross with us. We are also bound by orders like you. You can freely enter now. We made a mistake in recognizing you. Buy some sweets with this money."

In the end, Qiran the false cook accepted the money. He put the vegetables back in the basket, which he gave to Burq to carry on his head. They both entered the city and saw the marketplace filled with all manner of goods and the citizens busy trading.

Qiran approached a greengrocer and said to him, "We are selling these leftover vegetables from the kitchen, given to us as our share. If you wish you may buy them at a discount." The greengrocer offered Qiran two rupees, which he accepted and went forward.

Qiran and Burq now disguised themselves as attendants. They entered the garden where the feast in Faulad's honor was being held and found the garden and its buildings a sight to behold. Bedding for the singers and dancers was laid out by the flowerbeds. Faulad was seated on a throne. The apparatus of revelry, the water and the wine services were placed around his throne. The saplings of the garden of beauty were gathered around him and he was completely engrossed with their singing and dancing.

Qiran said to Burq, "We must find a way to kill Faulad before the night's over. If the sun rises with Mahrukh's army still imprisoned, our camp will meet its end and be slaughtered. Faulad will march straight to Afrasiyab and we will be helpless there." Burq replied, "Master, I am unable to think of any device. Even if by some trick I were to approach him, I wouldn't be able to kill him or make him unconscious."

Qiran said, "Take a good look at the sorcerer sitting beside Faulad and memorize his face. I can think of a device to achieve our end if you disguise yourself as him and capture Princess Nafarman."

Burq immediately went into a deserted corner of the garden and disguised himself as Faulad's companion. Once he was ready, Qiran lit up a taper and led the way with the false sorcerer following him. They came out of the garden and arrived at the royal palace and inquired about Princess Nafarman. The servants told them she was overseeing the arrangements for the feast. Qiran asked them to inform her that someone had come with a message from Faulad.

When Princess Nafarman came out, she met Burq disguised as Faulad's companion.

Nafarman said, "Why did you inconvenience yourself? You should have sent for me." The false sorcerer said to her, "If you could spare a few moments to speak to me in private, I will fulfill the mission entrusted to me by Faulad." Princess Nafarman assented and, leaving her servants behind, followed the false sorcerer, who led her into a deserted blind alley with Qiran following. As he was walking beside Nafarman, he made her unconscious by hitting her in the face with an egg of oblivion. The false sorcerer administered another dose of drug potion, then pulled out her tongue and stuck a needle in it so that she could not cast a spell even if she regained consciousness. He then took off Nafarman's clothes. Qiran chose a spot and carried Nafarman into a tree where he tied her to a branch covered with thick foliage. In the meanwhile, Burq had changed his disguise to Princess Nafarman's. Qiran now said to him, "Go to the gate of the garden and wait for me."

The two tricksters separated and Burq headed for the garden door in Princess Nafarman's disguise.

At the sight of their sovereign, the attendants and nobles of her court presented themselves in false Nafarman's service. As they stood respectfully before her, a man in ragged clothes came and saluted the false princess. From the sparklers and fireworks he carried in his hands, he appeared to be a pyrotechnist.

The false Nafarman recognized Qiran in the pyrotechnist's disguise. To learn what Qiran had in mind, she asked, "O pyrotechnist, do you have any fireworks ready, or can you prepare some?" The false pyrotechnist replied, "Your Honor, I can prepare some for you." The false Princess asked, "How much would it cost us?" He answered, "One hundred thousand rupees." The false Nafarman said, "This is a princely sum." He replied, "Don't give me the money. Just provide me with the gunpowder I require for the display. Whatever is spent will be accounted for. You may only compensate me for my labor." She said, "How much gunpowder do you need?" He answered, "I need twenty-five drums."

The false Nafarman ordered the captain of the armory to grant twenty-five drums of gunpowder to the pyrotechnist. Before long, the carts laden with drums of gunpowder arrived and the pyrotechnist said to the false Nafarman, "Order this gunpowder to be sent behind the garden wall and have the area cordoned off with a tent. I will prepare the fireworks myself with a secret recipe that will use up all this gunpowder in a single magnificent discharge."

The false Nafarman now understood what the pyrotechnist intended.

As requested, a large tent was put up at the back of the garden where the gunpowder was stored and everybody was forbidden entry there.

Once he was left alone, Qiran the false pyrotechnist took a pair of daggers and tunnelled from there all the way to the summerhouse where Faulad Drug-Glutton was seated with the magic slaves and his commanders. Because Qiran the Ethiope was a puissant youth, he tunnelled from the north boundary of the garden to the south, and from the east boundary to the west before one watch had passed. He made two fuses by plaiting his mantle and filled up the tunnel by pouring all twenty-five drums of gunpowder into it. He put the fuses in the mouth of the tunnel and came out of the tent.

The false Nafarman awaited the false pyrotechnist at the garden's door. He presented himself and said, "Your Honor, the fireworks are ready. If you accompany me, I will show how masterfully I have prepared them. But I request that you accompany me alone." The false princess said to the nobles and attendants, "Stay here. I will send for you later." Then she accompanied the false pyrotechnist to the back of the garden.

Qiran said to Burq, "I have made a tunnel and filled it with gunpowder. Go and untie Nafarman from the tree and make her conscious. I will light the fuses and this whole garden will blow up to the skies. Let Nafarman witness Faulad's dreadful end and shed tears at her helplessness. As a needle is stuck in her tongue, she won't be able to cause us any harm."

Burq climbed the tree, untied Nafarman and restored her to consciousness. When Nafarman opened her eyes she found herself perched high in the tree in a frightful state. In the meanwhile, Qiran lit the fuses and ran away. Heaven's mercy! When the burning fuses reached the tunnel, such a powerful explosion was heard that it seemed the heavens had burst asunder. Faulad, along with his commanders and magic slaves, was blown to bits with the summerhouse. Darkness fell over everything. Gunpowder, stones, walls and pieces of the summerhouse rained from the sky over the whole city. The shock of the explosion unlatched doors, caused fetuses to abort, and a panic-stricken populace to pour out into the streets. A great din like the Day of Judgment broke loose.

All of Princess Nafarman's attendants ran toward the garden to find out what calamity had hit them. A rampage started. Suddenly terrible cries rent the air as the magic spirits proclaimed the sorcerers' deaths. Above all of them rose the cry, "*I was killed. Faulad Drug-Glutton was my name!*" Fire and stones rained more heavily than before.

Finding the field to himself in that turmoil, Qiran lit up fire bombs and targeted the city buildings. Conflagrations started in many parts of the city. Many people were burned to death. Before those blazes could be put out, Qiran started more fires. The whole city rang out with the cries of "Help O Jamshed! Help O Sameri!" The fires engulfed the whole city and the citizens streamed out of the city gates.

Now hear of what passed outside the city walls. At the death of Faulad Drug-Glutton, his fiery cordon around Queen Mahjabeen's army disappeared at once. Mahrukh, Shakeel, Amar and other tricksters imprisoned in magic chains and fetters were released.

When Amar heard the terrible explosion, he said to Mahrukh, "There! It's done!" Mahrukh said, "What do you mean?" Amar answered, "I tell you the truth. The sound we just heard was that of Faulad dying. I reckon that either Qiran or Burq dispatched him to hell. Let us get out of this prison chamber. Our armies will not be far behind. We must now kill Faulad's twelve thousand sorcerers."

Mahrukh, Shakeel and others came out of the prison chambers, made their war cries, recited spells, and clapped. A dark dust storm rose and arrows that sent the prison guards running for cover rained from the skies.

Dil Aaram said to Queen Mahjabeen, "My lady, your grandmother, Princess Mahrukh Magic-Eye has declared war. Your army is standing as ready for battle as it was the moment the fiery cordon surrounded it. You too, must now attack Faulad's camp." Mahjabeen ordered her throne to be carried forward and fell upon Faulad's army with her entire force.

Sorcerers from both sides recited spells and exchanged magic citrons and limes, magic steel balls, clusters of arrows and needles, and garlands of chillies. Lightning bolts flashed. Tridents and pentadents flew.

Prince Asad sounded his war cry and rode into the thick of the battle. Amar Ayyar attacked with Princess Mahrukh from another front. He too, shouted his war cry and, drawing his dagger, flung himself into the fray singing,

"I am a star among tricksters
In the world of cunning unique
With my arts, subterfuge and ruses
I bring calamities on entire tribes
From my sharp sword even the lions retreat
And seek refuge in the wilderness
My name is Amar, King of Tricksters
Angel of Death of the infidels!"

Each time he did a somersault and dove, he severed the legs of ten men. With every leap he beheaded ten infidels. As they fell dead to the ground, Amar cut off and secured their money pouches.

Prince Asad and others showed such resolute and excellent swordsmanship that not a single soul survived in the army of Faulad Drug-Glutton. The brave warriors encircled the enemy sorcerers and put each to the sword. Then they advanced on the City of Purple Poppy.

The night had ended in the meanwhile. The King of the Stars[70] beat a retreat after receiving a wound from the malevolent ray dagger of the King of Noon.[71] The Emperor of Planets[72] now showed his might. He conquered the cities of Earth and sky and deputed his agents in every nook and corner of the heavens.

It was reported that the populace and army of the City of Purple Poppy had gathered outside the city walls. Mahrukh Magic-Eye fell upon them with her entire force. Tired after a whole night of commotion and dispirited in the absence of Princess Nafarman, the army of the infidels put up a brief fight before turning tail. The citizens asked for mercy. Mahrukh Magic-Eye ordered that general clemency be awarded and it was declared by the blaring of trumpets. Then she led the citizens back into the city.

Qiran approached Burq and said to him, "Our army has taken the city. Let us now take Nafarman before Princess Mahrukh." They drugged Nafarman, bundled her up, and headed on their way.

Mahrukh Magic-Eye had already conducted Mahjabeen Diamond-Robe into the Hall of Audience. The criers proclaimed throughout the city that those who would disobey the new ruler would be severely punished.

A dance recital was underway at the Hall of Audience and the nobles of the city were making offerings to Mahjabeen when Qiran and Burq arrived with Princess Nafarman. Mahrukh embraced both tricksters and seated them on golden thrones. When she asked them about their adventure, Qiran told them how he had dug the tunnel and blown it up with gunpowder. The whole court laughed upon hearing of his ingenious trick.

Mahjabeen conferred sumptuous robes of honor on both Qiran and Burq. They presented their rewards to Amar Ayyar, who stowed them away in his zambil and then took out a kerchief made of a coarse, thick cloth and put it on Qiran's shoulder like a robe of honor. Qiran said, "Oh my! Today my honor is redoubled. No one before me was conferred such a reward by my lord and master." Burq said to Amar, "Master, I participated equally in this mission with Qiran. Please confer a similar reward on me, too." Amar answered, "You are not worthy of such rewards as yet. Qiran saved my life. You must not compare yourself with him. It is indeed his privilege alone to receive this honor." Burq replied, "You will not have long to wait. I shall perform such a marvellous piece of trickery that you will be forced to confer a like reward on me."

Then Qiran the Ethiope and Burq the Frank tied Princess Nafarman to a column in the Hall of Audience and restored her to consciousness. The last time Nafarman had opened her eyes she had witnessed the tunnel exploding and her city burning. Now, when she opened them she saw another marvel: Queen Mahjabeen sitting on her throne with Prince Asad.

Imagining that she was having a nightmare, Princess Nafarman closed her eyes. Amar Ayyar called out to her, "O Princess Nafarman, this is not the realm of dreams but of consciousness. The one for whom you threw a feast was blown to bits and killed. Your lands have fallen to the servants of Queen Mahjabeen Diamond-Robe. You will be forgiven if you submit your allegiance; otherwise you must die."

As Nafarman was a wise and powerful sorceress, she realized the unravelling of the tilism had begun and that Prince Asad was, indeed, the Conqueror of the Tilism. She signalled that she was willing to submit allegiance. Amar now got up and removed the needle from her tongue and unfastened her.

Princess Nafarman kissed the throne of Queen Mahjabeen, who conferred a robe of honor on her and said, "When the tilism is finally conquered you will receive the lordship of many other kingdoms besides your own." It was announced in the city that any of Princess Nafarman's army commanders who wished to remain faithful to her should present themselves.

The dispersed army of the City of Purple Poppy started arriving from the desert and mountain passes. All of them were asked for their allegiance and, upon submitting it, were restored to their previous ranks. An additional army of twenty-five thousand sorcerers was thus gathered. After these victories, Amar said to Princess Mahrukh, "We must no longer remain in this fortress. It is a short journey from here to Afrasiyab's court; if he attacks we will not be able to put up much resistance. His armies will surround us and we will be caught here like mice in a trap. We must return to our old camping grounds. If some powerful sorcerer takes us prisoner there our tricksters will kill him when he camps on the return journey."

Mahrukh immediately acted on Amar's advice and ordered the army to march. Princess Nafarman said to her, "I will accompany you now. When Afrasiyab hears of my conversion he will not spare my life."

In short order, the camp prepared for marching and the tricksters and commanders, along with Princess Nafarman, set out on the journey riding magical birds and beasts.

They returned and camped near the City of Manycolors where they had first fought Faulad Drug-Glutton. The stately royal pavilion – as majestic as the firmament – was raised and Mahjabeen sat on the throne. Dancers performed and the imbibing of wine started. With the camp happily settled and occupied with these amusements, Qiran the Ethiope returned to his station in the wilderness.

Emperor Afrasiyab awaited Faulad Drug-Glutton's arrival in the Pleasure Garden and whiled away his time in pleasure-seeking. The scaffolds were ready and the executioners were on hand.

The following day, some refugees from the City of Purple Poppy arrived near the Pleasure Garden crying for redress. Afrasiyab ordered them to be produced in his court. When the plaintiffs were conducted inside, Afrasiyab asked them to relate their woes. They cried out that the Fortress of the City of Purple Poppy was destroyed and gave a detailed account of Faulad Drug-Glutton's death. Afrasiyab slapped his thigh in amazement and Heyrat broke into tears.

Sorcerer Arzhang of the Stone Figurine

Afrasiyab comforted Heyrat on the news of Faulad Drug-Glutton's death and the fall of the City of Purple Poppy, saying, "O Heyrat, had I but wished I could have ordered a monster from the Grotto of the Seven Monsters to gobble up Mahrukh's entire camp. But I indulge these rebels still because I have fostered and nurtured them for so many years. How can I kill them all of a sudden? I wish to chastise them in a manner that will convince them to give up their rebellion and bring me Asad and others as prisoners."

Heyrat said, "Your Excellency, a person must act himself to guard his own interests. Pray give me leave to advance on them and accompany the army of the tilism with me. I will confront the foe and bring all of them prisoner before you." Afrasiyab answered, "O Heyrat, did you not see how the tricksters killed Faulad by blowing up the tunnel? How can I send you with an easy mind against such bloodthirsty insurgents? Now, I too, shall remain hidden in the region of Zulmat and will not appear in Zahir."

Heyrat asked, "Your Excellency, how would I receive orders from you?" Afrasiyab replied, "You may come to Zulmat yourself. I will appear to you but remain enclosed in the Magic Mirror. You will see and hear me but it will be my magic double. The sorcerer who is dispatched next against Mahrukh must take every precaution. He must turn his camp grounds to stone by magic so that the tricksters cannot tunnel underneath it."

Sorcerer Arzhang was present in the court, fanning the emperor with a kerchief. He was Afrasiyab's disciple in sorcery and a grand sorcerer himself. As Afrasiyab spoke these words, he came forward and humbly said, "Your Excellency, it was for such a day that you enlisted me in your service. Order me to go and put an end to their mischief and bring the rebels before you as prisoners. The tricksters would neither be able to approach me nor blow me up with a tunnel."

Afrasiyab asked, "What magic would you employ?" Arzhang answered, "Whenever anyone approaches me I will recite a spell. If he is a trickster the spell will remove his disguise and I will arrest him. Nobody will be able to tunnel under my tent because I will turn the ground to stone." Afrasiyab said, "Very well, then! Mahrukh must still be in the environs of the City of Purple Poppy. Arrest her, but be extra cautious when dealing with the tricksters."

Arzhang immediately headed out of the Pleasure Garden and sounded the magic bugle. Renowned sorcerers gathered at his call and Arzhang said to them, "Ten thousand sorcerers must accompany me to destroy the enemy." The sorcerers readied themselves and, mounting magic lions, tigers and dragons, set out with Arzhang.

After completing the journey, Arzhang and his armies arrived with great fanfare near the City of Purple Poppy. They saw the city lying in ruin and destruction with its buildings burned, its army absconded, and its citizens in panic as refugees in their own city. Arzhang camped there and wrote a letter to Mahrukh, which read:

> "All praise is due lords Jamshed, Sameri and Laqa. O band of rebels, learn that I am Arzhang. There is no repelling my magic. None in the entire tilism has ever dared to challenge my might. None who has confronted me has prevailed. I will wipe out all traces of your existence in a trice. I will send all of you to your graves. O Mahrukh, you will come to a bad end if you do not present yourself immediately upon receiving this letter. End of Message. Compliments!"

After writing the letter, Arzhang took out a stone figurine from his sorcerer's bag and said, "O magic slave girl, take this letter to Mahrukh." That magic slave girl took the letter and dove into the ground.

Mahrukh was watching a dance performance in her court amidst all the paraphernalia of revelry when the magic slave girl emerged from the ground and jumped into her lap. She delivered the letter and demanded a reply. Mahrukh became anxious after reading the message.

Noticing the look of distress on her face, Amar asked, "Is anything the matter?" Mahrukh replied, "One of Afrasiyab's disciples, Arzhang, has come to fight us. He was trained by the emperor himself and brought up as his own son. Now there's nothing left for us but to die, since we do not have the wherewithal to fight him." Amar said, "Put your trust in God as you answer his challenge. All those who came to fight us before were as vainglorious as the pharaoh. But you must remember that for every pharaoh there's a Moses. You saw how the tricksters killed all of them. The eyes of bitter longing and pining shed tears at their sad and terrible fate; crows and kites dined on their corpses; even a grave was denied them."

At Amar's advice, Mahrukh wrote out a reply to Arzhang's letter.

First she wrote the name of God
For with His name it is obligatory to begin
Then she wrote the praise of the Prophet
The one worthy of all devotion
Then she wrote the following reply:
"I wait for you like a sword.
The commander of my valiant army
Is the stalwart warrior, Prince Asad of happy fortune.
Do you not regard the telltale signs of your downfall,
Have you not paused to consider, O sinner,
How the mighty sorcerers were dispatched hellward
In just a trice, by the hand of Amar Ayyar
You too are marked for destruction by the heavens
Unless you repent and give up all thoughts of battle
We have every desire to spare your life. But if not,
No quarter would be asked or given, you must remember."

After writing this sharp reply, Mahrukh handed it to the magic slave girl, who dove into the ground, returned to Arzhang, and handed him the letter.

After reading it, Arzhang prepared to march to the battlefield. Mahrukh also ordered her army to be ready for battle.

Princess Nafarman said to her, "Your Excellency, I beg leave to return to my city and to write to Arzhang that I found it expedient to falsely swear allegiance to you and Amar because I had been captured by the tricksters and your armies had overrun my lands. I would invite him to my city for a feast and tell him that I will join forces with him to exact my long-planned revenge on your camp and avenge myself by killing the rebels. When he arrives I will kill or overpower him and take him prisoner."

Mahrukh replied, "I will not let you face all these risks alone. What if he took you captive first?"

Burq interjected and said to Mahrukh, "Let Princess Nafarman depart with her army. In the process of receiving her message and replying to it, Arzhang will halt his march. I will find the opportunity to put him to death. Do not inconvenience yourself by leading your army into battle just yet."

In the end, Mahrukh gave Princess Nafarman leave to return to her city. However, she secretly dispatched her son Shakeel with fifteen thousand sorcerers to lie in wait near Arzhang's camp. Shakeel departed and the tricksters Burq, Zargham and Jansoz accompanied him. After arriving near their destination, they positioned themselves near the enemy and bided their time for an opportune moment.

After Princess Nafarman returned to her fortress, she penned a letter to Arzhang importuning him and offering excuses for her inaction. She wrote:

> "O protégé of Emperor Afrasiyab, this slave girl was overtaken by calamities. I had no friend or aid in the evil hour that befell me. There were no options left for me and no way out but to submit my allegiance to Mahrukh Magic-Eye. It is my good fortune that you have arrived in these parts. Please increase my honor by visiting my humble abode. I will avenge myself on these recalcitrant rebels and join hands with you in making war on them."

A high-ranking sorcerer brought Nafarman's letter before Arzhang, who read it and decided to check the truth of its contents. He recited a spell and struck his hands together whereupon a magic slave emerged from the ground carrying a piece of paper and presented it to Arzhang. It read:

> *"Nafarman has written this note to trap you by deception. She has joined Amar Ayyar and plans to kill you by deceit after inviting you to her palace. Beware, do not be fooled by her tricks."*

Arzhang returned the paper to the magic slave who sank into the ground. Then Arzhang wrote a reply to Princess Nafarman's letter, which read:

> "O ungrateful wretch, I am well aware of your devices. Do you think you can fool me with your words? I am the mighty Arzhang, not some ordinary sorcerer. I will capture you and your accomplices in a moment and put you to a painful death. Now you must count your days. After arresting Mahrukh Magic-Eye I will capture you,

too. There is nowhere in this tilism you can run to or
hide where my hand cannot reach. Before long, you will
receive due punishment for your devious conduct."

Arzhang gave the reply to a messenger who departed to deliver it.

Now hear of the tricksters. After Shakeel's army camped they went out in disguises and started making rounds of Arzhang's pavilion. Zargham made himself into an attendant and positioned himself inside the pavilion while Jansoz waited at the entrance in a sorcerer's disguise. After a while, when Arzhang looked up and saw the false attendant, he felt uneasy. He immediately recited a spell that made all the paint and lotion evaporate and Zargham's real face appeared. Arzhang gave him a paper and said, "Take this letter to Princess Nafarman!" Unaware of the loss of his disguise, Zargham came forward and extended his hand to take the paper. Arzhang caught his hand and said, "How dare you think you could trick me, O wretch?" Zargham tried to draw his dagger but Arzhang recited a spell that made him lose the use of his limbs.

Arzhang called out, "Is there anyone on duty?" The false sorcerer, who was Jansoz, rushed in answer to his call. Arzhang said to him, "The tricksters have begun to attack. I have arrested one. Take him to the prison." The false sorcerer answered, "Release him from your spell so that I may imprison him in mine." Arzhang did as he requested and the false attendant led Zargham away. Suddenly, Arzhang grew suspicious, and he recited a spell. The two tricksters had not yet reached the entrance of the tent when the real face of Jansoz was revealed. Realizing that he too, was a trickster, Arzhang captured him. Then he recited another spell, which sank both Zargham and Jansoz up to their waists in the ground.

The day ended in the meanwhile, and the Painter of Nature painted the shapes of planets and stars on the page of the sky and the Artist of Creation lifted the curtain on the beautiful and shapely moon.

In the evening, Burq secretly went to Princess Nafarman and said, "O Princess, whenever a trickster goes near Arzhang his disguise is revealed. I have decided not to go near him and I request that you provide me with a pavilion, a jewel-encrusted bed and a luxurious carpet." Nafarman answered, "They are at your disposal. They will be provided for you when you want them." Burq loaded all those things onto a cart and headed out of the city. He chose a flower-lined pasture near Arzhang's pavilion that was abundant with springs and pools.

Burq sent the cart back to the fortress and set up his pavilion in that scenic and pleasant spot. He encircled it with flowers to give it the appearance of a large bouquet. Then he covered it with garlands steeped in a perfume drug and, after proofing his own senses with an antidote, sprinkled the perfume drug in large quantities both inside and outside the pavilion.

Burq set the bed, covered it with a sheet, arranged cushions and pillows, and rubbed the perfume drug all over the furniture. He put a seat under the bed and pulled up the panels of the pavilion that opened onto a verdant grassland that refreshed the soul.

A carpet of moonbeams spread over the whole expanse. The grains of sand sparkled like the stars in the heavens. Springs burbled all around on their banks; deer, buffalo, hog deer and axis deer frolicked in the moonlight.

Burq disguised himself as a fakir by smearing his face with ash and plaiting and coating his hair with clay. He put hoops and earrings in his ears, wore bead necklaces and bracelets of crystal beads and placed a gold cloth-ring on his head. He spread a deerskin at the entrance of his pavilion and sat there playing a tambourine and singing a devotional song in Sameri's praise.

Meanwhile, Arzhang secured the boundaries of his pavilion after imprisoning both tricksters inside so that neither friend nor foe could enter. He also sent away his attendants and cast a spell that turned the ground to adamantine so that no one could tunnel in from underneath.

Arzhang settled down after making all these preparations and heard the captivating notes of someone singing Sameri's adulation. He discovered the music originated from the forest at the back of his pavilion. He headed out and arrived near Burq's tent. Moonlight bathed the entire grassland. Seeing Arzhang approach, Burq got up and ran and hid himself in the bushes beside a spring. When Arzhang reached the pavilion, he noticed the deerskin spread there and beheld a fully appointed pavilion lying empty. The place was now all quiet.

When he entered the pavilion, Arzhang found it a most lavish abode, redolent with a fragrance that perfumed the very core of his soul. As he sat down on the bed, he suddenly wondered if it might be a trickster's dwelling. He recited a spell whereupon a magic slave girl of stone emerged from the ground carrying a piece of paper. Arzhang took the paper from her hands and read the following written on it:

> *"This is the pavilion of the trickster Burq the Frank. He has already killed you. Now you are dead."*

Even as Arzhang was reading it, the perfume drug had worked on his senses and overpowered him. He sneezed and fell unconscious. Burq, who had stealthily come out of the bushes where he was hiding and closed on Arzhang, entered the pavilion and instantly beheaded him.

A thunderous commotion and a din like doomsday broke out and stone slabs rained from the sky. A cry rent the night, "*I was killed! Arzhang was my name.*" Burq hurried to where Shakeel was lying in wait with his army and told him it was time for them to attack.

Hearing Arzhang's death cry, the sorcerers of his camp ran to investigate. Zargham and Jansoz were released because Arzhang's spell was broken and they ran to inform Princess Nafarman in the City of Purple Poppy that the sorcerer had been killed and that she must charge without delay and conduct a night raid on Arzhang's camp.

Nafarman quickly mustered her army and attacked Arzhang's camp while Shakeel charged it from another side. The foe faced a night raid on two fronts. Swords flashed and sorcerers deployed their magic. The battle raged the whole night and the mettle of the swordsmen was tested. In the morning, when the golden standard of Emperor Sun rose between the mountains and the Fair-faced Turk of Morn dispatched the Milky Way into the land of dreams, Arzhang's army retreated in defeat toward the Pleasure Garden.

Princess Nafarman pillaged the tents, equipage and goods of the retreating enemy. Burq also ransacked the fields to collect an offering for Amar Ayyar. He said to Nafarman, "You must not stay here but return and join Mahrukh." As Nafarman's army was ready at her call, they started cheerfully toward Mahrukh Magic-Eye's camp playing festive music. Before long they arrived at their destination and joined Mahrukh's triumph incarnate camp.

Mahrukh embraced all of them and the sound of congratulations and felicitations filled the air. Queen Mahjabeen conferred a precious robe of honor on Burq and rewarded the other tricksters as well.

In the meanwhile, Arzhang's defeated army arrived near the Pleasure Garden beating their chests in lamentations and tearing their collars into shreds.

Emperor Afrasiyab was busy carousing. A dancer was performing, wine was being drunk, and seventeen thousand renowned sorcerers were sitting around him respectfully. Suddenly, the noise of wailing and lamentations reached his ears. When Afrasiyab inquired, he learned that Arzhang had been killed and the army that had accompanied him had fled in defeat.

Afrasiyab sent for the commanders of the army and sought details of Arzhang's death. After he learned all the facts and particulars, Afrasiyab bit the back of his hand with teeth of distress.

Heyrat said to him, "Your Excellency, I can no longer remain a silent witness. I ask for leave to punish the mutineers myself." Afrasiyab replied, "Your departure would still be unsuitable. You should, instead, go to the Apple Garden with the nobles. I am headed for the region of Zulmat. We will decide on a suitable course of action upon my return."

Then Afrasiyab mounted his throne and sixty-four thousand drums from the skies announced his departure. Magic fairies played musical instruments and danced on boreal thrones. They carried vermiculated pitchers filled with rose water, *keora* water, and essence of orange blossoms on their hips. They squirted each other with loaded sprays of these fragrances and juggled balls of light. Afrasiyab's four ministers took their positions on the four corners of his throne and fanned him with fly-whisks of phoenix feathers. A crimson cloud materialized to shadow the emperor's throne and rained pearl droplets. Afrasiyab's throne floated away like the wind. As it whizzed past, magic trees, birds and humans cried out in veneration, "*All glory to Afrasiyab! All praise to Afrasiyab!*"

Soon Afrasiyab was lost from sight as he disappeared into Zulmat the Dark. No one saw how or from where the Emperor of Hoshruba entered that mysterious region.

Sorceress Bahar of Spring-Quarter

After Afrasiyab's departure Empress Heyrat mounted her magic peacock and went to the Apple Garden with her nobles and ministers in train. She ascended the throne and all her courtiers and sorcerers took their allocated stations. A dance recital started and cupbearers as beautiful as the moon began passing around cups of red wine.

They were thus occupied when, suddenly, a cool and pleasant breeze picked up. The sky became overcast. The trees swayed, intoxicated with the fervor of spring, and every flower bud in the Apple Garden broke into full bloom. The magic birds flew into the garden and chirped before Heyrat, "*O Empress of the World, your younger sister, Princess Bahar, is approaching.*" Heyrat said, "Now I know why it suddenly seemed as if the spring quarter was upon us. A welcoming party should go out and conduct her here with great honor."

High-ranking sorcerers went in a procession to greet Princess Bahar.

The garden of Princess Bahar's beauty was nurtured by the munificent showers of Nature's Gardener. She was a virgin and her figure was like a beautiful cypress in the pasture of life. She resided in the City of Mount Solace and seldom attended the court. Emperor Afrasiyab, who was smitten and besotted with her, had sought union with her on several occasions. However, Bahar always resisted the emperor's advances out of respect for her sister. Many renowned sorcerers pined equally for Bahar's love but their knowing of Afrasiyab's fondness for her kept them from asking for her hand in marriage. Heyrat also knew of Afrasiyab's feelings and she ardently wished to drive Bahar from Hoshruba. However, to her sister's face and in public, Heyrat kept up the pretence of great fondness for Bahar.

When Princess Bahar entered the Apple Garden everyone rose in her honor. Heyrat embraced her, asked about her welfare, and seated Bahar beside her on the throne. At a sign from Heyrat the cupbearer offered goblets of wine and they started drinking.

Bahar had come to discuss the deaths of the sorcerers and the recent turmoil in the tilism. After the wine warmed and relaxed her, she asked Heyrat, "Tell me sister, what is this commotion that has broken the peace of our tilism?" Heyrat replied, "I don't know where to begin! All I know is that whore Mahrukh Magic-Eye has invited a great calamity on her head. She has joined the rebels, is stirring a revolt, and has killed many of the emperor's servants. Now I will march against Mahrukh, arrest her, and visit her with retribution worse than anyone has suffered in the history of the tilism."

Princess Bahar took offense at these words because Princess Mahrukh was related to them. She said, "Sister, what you say is most unjust. We have blood ties to Mahrukh Magic-Eye and Mahjabeen Diamond-Robe that cannot be disregarded. You cannot strike a body of water with a stick and divide it! How dare you claim that you will publicly humiliate and kill her! Mahrukh is no less powerful than you or I. Of course, she is no match for the emperor, the immortal sorcerers, the Seven Monsters of the Grotto, or the dwellers of the River of Seven Colors and the Blue River. However, in all respects she is on a par with each of the emperor's four ministers and with the two of us. I have heard that Mahrukh's magic dragon very nearly swallowed Faulad Drug-Glutton. If the magic slaves had not rescued him, it would have been impossible for Faulad to return alive from the arena. How could you speak about a grand sorceress of the tilism like Mahrukh in such terms?"

Heyrat turned crimson with rage at Bahar's speech and said, "O strumpet, you sing adulations of Mahrukh before my courtiers and attempt to frighten them? You must also be in cahoots with the rebels. That is why you take their side."

Heyrat now addressed her courtiers, saying, "When my own sister is colluding against me how can I expect others to remain loyal! Does water flow thicker than blood? Hear her praising Mahrukh Magic-Eye to my face! Regardless of any blood ties between us, Mahrukh Magic-Eye is now my enemy. Should I seat her above my head when justice demands that she should be humiliated and crushed underfoot?"

Hearing these harsh words, Princess Bahar said, "I've had enough of this! You will hold your tongue! Loyalty and disloyalty will be proven in good time. I don't wish to hear your drivel. I swear by my honor that if I hear your poisonous tongue wag against me ever again, I will teach you a lesson you will never forget. It will put an end to all your royal and imperious airs."

While they were having this altercation, Afrasiyab's conveyance arrived from the region of Zulmat. His magnificent entourage and conveyance came to a stop and Afrasiyab dismounted, playing with a perfumed golden ball and making pleasantries with the courtiers who rose in his honor, bowed their heads, and offered salutations.

When the emperor ascended the throne he noticed Princess Bahar stringing a garland of tears that issued ceaselessly from her eyes, like an oyster burbling forth shiny pearls. It seemed that the hands of beauty had decked the lovely face of this bride of spring with a veil of pearls. The rosy hue of her face revealed that her delicate emotions were in turmoil. Afrasiyab was upset upon seeing Bahar in this state and asked, "O envy of Zephyr's garden, may no sorrow ever torment you. Tell me what grief has caused the flower of your heart to wilt?"

Bahar answered, "I have been called disloyal to the emperor! It is now my desire to visit Mahrukh Magic-Eye's camp and unleash the winds of autumn on the blossoming garden of her fortunes. Her aiders and abettors may plead like nightingales but I will show them no mercy. The tree of every rebel's soul will be cut down or lie uprooted in the Garden of Life. But, O Gardener of the Empire's Garden, I will no longer have a seat at your feet. Like a flower's perfume finally exits the garden, I too, must depart now from Hoshruba."

When Afrasiyab heard these heartbreaking words from the mouth whose narrowness recalled the embouchement of flower buds, saw Bahar's narcissus-like eyes fill up with dew drops of tears, regarded her lips, delicate as rose petals, quivering from passion and acrimonious speech, and noticed her loss of composure as she uttered these words, Afrasiyab chastised Heyrat, saying, "If you brand a person like Princess Bahar as disloyal can you escape a like charge yourself?" Heyrat replied, "I know all too well what lies behind your words. Your fake and hollow righteousness won't deceive me even for a moment. I can recognize a man's intentions in his eyes. Of course you would come to her defense."

These cutting remarks were not lost on Bahar and discomfited her further but they silenced Afrasiyab because they addressed his guilt.

Bahar resolved in her heart to battle Mahrukh Magic-Eye and destroy her army, then go into exile. She humbly said these words, which fell in the garden of speech like a shower of rose petals: "Your Excellency will appoint one of your loyal commanders to fight the foe. I request that I should be granted this campaign."

Afrasiyab realized that if he stopped Bahar now Heyrat would get a chance to say that he was protecting his beloved. He gave Bahar leave, saying, "Very well, you may take charge of the mission but you must not directly engage with the foe. Ask one of your commanders to destroy Mahrukh Magic-Eye's camp. I will send you further assistance as well."

Bahar replied, "To this day I have never sought anyone's aid. Even if Your Excellency himself came to my assistance I would be mortified with shame and sever my neck with my own hands. Pray do not send anyone to help me."

Afrasiyab answered, "Indeed, it would be unnecessary. You are brave and stalwart yourself." He conferred a robe of departure on Princess Bahar, who mounted her conveyance and returned to Mount Solace with frowning and angry mien.

Afrasiyab was deeply grieved by Princess Bahar's departure on that unhappy note. A day after her leaving, he also left in rancor and departed for Mount Quartz by himself.

After her arrival in Mount Solace, Bahar ordered the commander-in-chief of her army, Maykhar Rhino-Head, to muster her army. Bahar's yellow pavilion was loaded onto a magic dragon and sixty thousand sorceresses and sorcerers decked with their magic equipment prepared to march.

The next morning, when the Sovereign of the Heavens appeared on the throne of sky with his parasol of golden rays, the magic bugle was sounded for the march and the army started on its journey.

Princess Bahar ascended her throne, bouquets of flowers were placed before her, a cloud shadowed the throne and a light, pleasant drizzle followed her conveyance. As her throne passed by, flowerbeds sprang up and the flowers bloomed in greeting. Her attendants held a golden canopy above her head. Magic fairies appeared in the air and squirted each other with paints while singing the songs of Holi.[73] The sorceresses and sorcerers accompanying Bahar made sacrificial offerings of flowers of gold and silver to protect her from evil and displayed their magic works.

Sorcerer Maykhar Rhino-Head

Maykhar Rhino-Head marched at the head of the forces riding a magic dragon; an army of sixty thousand sorcerers followed behind him. The army traveled in stretches of ten miles with great majesty. When they stopped to rest after completing a day's journey from Mount Solace, Maykhar Rhino-Head said to Bahar, "If Your Excellency will give me leave I will advance with twelve thousand sorcerers and arrest Mahrukh's soldiers. That way, when Your Honor arrives on the scene you will not be burdened with having to make arrangements for war and need only supervise the beheading of rebels and sending their heads to the emperor." Bahar answered, "Very well! Go forth and defeat the enemy with the spell I have taught you."

Maykhar Rhino-Head sped on his mission taking along twelve thousand sorcerers from his own personal force. He traveled with dispatch and arrived near the august camp of Mahrukh Magic-Eye where he set up his pavilion and struck the drums ordering his soldiers to bivouac.

As his men set up camp, Maykhar erected another pavilion adjacent to his own and sat down with his sorcery apparatus to invoke his magic. He made a ring with swine blood, stood on a sandalwood bench, and started reciting a spell. Then he bathed in swine blood himself and burned thorn apples, swallow wort, mustard and cotton seeds on flaming braziers to cast the spell.

The magic birds flew into the court after noticing Rhino-Head's men set up camp. They eloquently sang the queen's adulations and said, "*Princess Bahar's stalwart commander, Maykhar Rhino-Head, has arrived bent on mischief.*"

Mahrukh said to Amar Ayyar, "Only God can protect us now. It is a disaster that Princess Bahar has been sent on the campaign against us. Let alone fight her, we are not even her commander's equal!" Amar Ayyar replied, "God is the Protector. You must not fret about it." While Mahrukh and Amar Ayyar were occupied in this conversation, the tricksters left the camp and headed for the wilderness.

Despite Amar's words of comfort, the whole camp was thrown into a state of great agitation and turmoil at the news of Maykhar Rhino-Head's arrival. While cowards deserted the ranks from lack of self-confidence, those who were brave and loyal became convinced that they would now meet their deaths.

Sorceress Surkh Mu Wonder-Mane

Amar was ready to head to the wilderness after comforting everyone when a cloud suddenly appeared in the sky and showered down thousands of stars. Princess Nafarman said to Mahrukh, "Your Excellency, it seems Princess Surkh Mu Wonder-Mane, the governor of the City of Scarlet Locks, is approaching."

Mahrukh sent Nafarman and others with a welcoming party to conduct Princess Surkh Mu Wonder-Mane into the court. Amar delayed his departure to learn more about the new arrival.

A powerful sorceress and a great beauty, Princess Surkh Mu Wonder-Mane was held in high regard by Emperor Afrasiyab. She was both rich and powerful and had thirty thousand sorcerers under her command. She had come on the mission to convince Nafarman, her soul sister, to break with Amar Ayyar so that she might intercede for her with Afrasiyab and have her offense forgiven.

Nafarman went with the welcoming party and greeted and embraced Princess Surkh Mu. When Surkh Mu entered the court Mahrukh rose to greet her and offered her a golden throne. Surkh Mu saw Mahjabeen Diamond-Robe giving audience, the court in session, and Amar Ayyar sitting on a jewel-encrusted chair. Because Afrasiyab had already made known Amar Ayyar's description within Hoshruba she recognized him without difficulty.

Surkh Mu laughed upon regarding Amar's strange form and said to Nafarman, "My sister, it's a pity that you revolted against the emperor and invited misfortune down on yourself." Nafarman answered, "My sister, the star of Amar Ayyar's glory is ascending. Afrasiyab will be killed and the tilism conquered. Those who side with Amar will survive and others will be destroyed. You too must join hands with us."

Princess Surkh Mu laughed at Nafarman's words and said, "What droll things you say! Where is the comparison between Emperor Afrasiyab and Amar Ayyar? How can you contrast the heavens with the Earth ? Talk some sense! Tell me, what could Amar Ayyar do even if he killed sorcerers in the thousands? The armies of the Emperor of Hoshruba are without count and number. Imagine a city with hundreds of wells and each well filled with swarms of mosquitoes. Now imagine those swarms to be the armies of sorcerers at Emperor Afrasiyab's command. If he were to release even a single swarm from a well, his armies would inundate the entire lands of the tilism. Who can fight the Emperor of Hoshruba? Even if I forced myself to believe that Amar Ayyar could surmount these impossible odds, how would he acquire the tilism key? Without the tilism key there's no conquering the tilism.

Afrasiyab himself does not know where the tilism key is hidden. Tell me, how would Amar ever find it?"

Nafarman answered, "The Almighty God, the Creator of Causes, will find a way for the tilism key to be found and for Hoshruba to be conquered. Are you not familiar with the saying:

"If the enemy is strong
The Protector is stronger still."

Princess Surkh Mu replied, "Alas sister, it seems that you and I must now part ways. I shall never offer my allegiance to a lowly person like Amar Ayyar."

While they were exchanging these words, Maykhar Rhino-Head completed the spell and made his offering to the magic spirits. Drenched in swine blood, he stood at the entrance of his pavilion, recited an incantation and blew it in the direction of Mahrukh Magic-Eye's camp. Suddenly a cloud covered Mahrukh's camp and a cold breeze picked up. Surkh Mu said to Nafarman, "Beware, this is a sign of approaching trouble." She tried to fly away to escape the calamity but the cloud enveloped Mahrukh's whole camp. A waft of cold air hit Surkh Mu's face and she fell unconscious. When she came to after a few moments, she said to Nafarman, "Now I too, have been engulfed in this trouble because of my love for you."

Everyone in the camp, including Nafarman, Mahrukh, Shakeel and their other commanders were taken unawares. They had imagined that Maykhar would sound the drums of war and face them in the arena. They recited counterspells but they proved ineffective. Gusts of cold air hit them and they too, fell senseless.

They opened their eyes after a moment and asked for wine, recited verses in its praise, and swayed drunkenly. They picked up ewers and goblets and drank and indulged in horseplay, slapping each other and pulling each other's whiskers. In their inebriation, some thought that the floor was a swelling sea and, holding their noses, attempted to dive headlong into it. After awhile, the whole camp gathered together and sang Holi songs to the accompaniment of drums, fifes and stringed instruments. The air filled with music, the loud voices of the drunkards, and the gurgle of ewers. The entire camp remained thus occupied. If someone tried to escape, a waft of cold air issued from the clouds and made him unconscious.

The three tricksters who had left the camp regarded the state of their companions from far away. They signalled with their whistles and Qiran the Ethiope joined them. They gave him a complete account of the event and Qiran retired to think of some solution. The other three tricksters went away in different directions.

After Maykhar Rhino-Head completed his spell, he ordered water-carriers to fetch him bath water to wash his blood drenched body. Qiran happened to pass by the riverside where water-carriers were filling their waterskins. He asked where they would take the water and, upon learning that it was meant for Maykhar, Qiran said to one of the water-carriers, "I have brought a message for you. I have something a friend of yours entrusted me to give you." The water-carrier was tempted by these words and thought, *Even though I do not know this man, perhaps someone sent me a gift. I should collect it from him.*

Qiran took the water-carrier to a deserted place and hit him in the face with an egg of oblivion. The water-carrier fell unconscious and Qiran tied him to a tree. He put on a coarse waistcloth and slung the waterskin on his shoulders. Qiran fastened his belt and took his tools and, concealing his cleaver inside, returned to the riverside disguised as the water-carrier. There he filled up the waterskin and headed for Maykhar Rhino-Head's camp. Seeing the water-carriers streaming into the sorcerer's tent, the false water-carrier followed them inside.

He saw Maykhar sitting on a bench. The water-carriers came forward, poured water over him and went out to refill the waterskins. The false water-carrier stepped up behind Maykhar. He opened the mouth of the waterskin with one hand and took out his cleaver with the other. After pouring out the contents of the waterskin, he pulled it over Maykhar's head. Bewildered, the sorcerer tried to turn around but Qiran struck, breaking Maykhar's head with his cleaver. As Maykhar fell to the ground unconscious, Qiran speedily cut off his head.

A terrible clamour broke out. Darkness covered everything. The sorcerers ran toward Maykhar's tent. The false water-carrier leaped out of the tent and escaped. As the sorcerers poured into their commander's tent, they heard a terrible cry exclaiming, "*I was killed. Maykhar Rhino-Head was my name!*"

The sorcerers carried away his corpse amidst weeping and wailing.

The cloud that covered Mahrukh's camp parted and dispersed. Everyone came out of their drunken trance and returned to their senses.

Princess Surkh Mu said to Nafarman, "I will leave now. I don't know what happened here and what dispelled it." Nafarman replied, "All of us were under Maykhar's spell. Some trickster has killed him and the spell has been removed."

Surkh Mu Wonder-Mane trembled with fear when she learned how quickly the tricksters had dispatched Maykhar hellward. She said, "Sister, this event has convinced me of what you stated about the tilism. What alacrity on the tricksters' part! Bravo!" Nafarman said to her, "Don't go anywhere. Stay and see what happens next." Surkh Mu stayed on to witness what other marvels would unfold.

ꟷ

In the meanwhile, Qiran returned to the wilderness and signalled with his trickster's whistle. Burq hurried to him and asked, "Master, why did I see flames and hear noises rising from Maykhar's camp?" Qiran replied, "I dispatched Maykhar to hell. Hurry and bring Mahrukh Magic-Eye's army to slay the enemy."

Burq sped to Mahrukh's camp and said to her, "Maykhar has been killed. Attack his army without loss of time." Mahrukh ordered magic bugles to be sounded and the army quickly prepared. In no time, sixty thousand sorcerers fell upon Maykhar's twelve thousand men.

Both sides deployed the use of magic. Slabs of ice dropped from the sky. A sorcerer created a river, another produced a rain of fire, yet another caused a shower of stones. Magic arrows and barbs fell in a hailstorm on the warriors. It was as if the end of the world had been proclaimed by the heavens.

Mahjabeen ordered her throne to be carried into the battlefield. Dil Aaram showered lightning bolts on the foe with her spells. As usual, Amar Ayyar went jumping and leaping around to rob, pillage and kill. He remained occupied beheading sorcerers and cutting off their legs.

Prince Asad now made his war declaration,

"Asad the renowned, the mighty lion
The favored one of the Lion of God
When I descend into the battlefield with drawn sword
From all corners rise cries of 'Mercy' and 'Quarter'."

Dark clouds had risen from all directions. Swords flashed like lightning. Heads fell like raindrops. Shakeel fought alongside Prince Asad, routing the enemy while safeguarding the prince from their magic.

Within a short time, Maykhar's twelve thousand sorcerers were destroyed. The servants and shopkeepers accompanying them escaped toward Princess Bahar's camp. Mahrukh and her army pillaged and ransacked the enemy's encampment and returned to their camp. The commanders retired to their pavilions to rest. Celebrations began and offerings were made to Queen Mahjabeen on the occasion of her victory and triumph.

Princess Surkh Mu Wonder-Mane also rose from her seat and made an offering to Mahjabeen and said, "Your Excellency, if I were to return to my lands Afrasiyab would not spare my life since I was here with you when the battle started. Now, consider me one of your slave girls. I will live and die with you." Mahrukh embraced Surkh Mu Wonder-Mane and conferred a robe of honor on her.

Surkh Mu dispatched a message to the commander of her armies, Shamshad Elephant-Body, to join her with his entire army and the treasury. She gave the letter to a sorcerer who flew away toward the City of Scarlet Locks by invoking his magic.

Now hear of Princess Bahar. She continued to advance and awaited the communiqué from Maykhar Rhino-Head that would inform her of the rebels' arrest so that she could behead them and send their heads to Afrasiyab's court.

Princess Bahar set up camp in a verdant forest when one day a group of sorcerers arrived crying and wailing. Hearing their cries for redress, Bahar sent for them and inquired about the reason for their distress. They told her about the destruction of their camp and how the garden of Maykhar Rhino-Head's life was visited by a calamitous autumn. Heaven's mercy! Bahar's face was drained of all blood. She bit the back of her hands with fury and rage. Without loss of time, she mounted her magic peacock, a huge and towering bird comparable in size to a simurgh.

His wings and feathers were like tree branches
His legs like the legs of a throne
His beak as long as a column
And a great cavern of a mouth

Bahar left behind her entourage and headed alone for Mahrukh's camp. When her army commanders saw Bahar marching in by herself, they quickly mounted their conveyances and beat the drums to order the army to march with her. Bahar said to them, "I will go alone, take on the enemy, and destroy them by myself. I do not wish to take the army with me because enemy tricksters mix among soldiers to stir up mischief and will be difficult to identify in a crowd. You may follow me but stop within ten miles of Mahrukh Magic-Eye's camp. It will not take me long to capture all of them and I will return soon." Bahar took along a few companions and attendants and headed onwards.

In the meanwhile, a festive mood reigned in Mahrukh's pavilion. Everyone was occupied in making merry, except Mahrukh Magic-Eye, who knew that upon learning of Maykhar's death, Bahar would attack and cause mayhem.

Amar also learned that Maykhar Rhino-Head had preceded Bahar and now that he was dead it was only a matter of time before some calamity would visit them. He said to Mahrukh, "God will be your Protector. You must not despair and instead remain steadfast in the face of misfortune. I hear that Bahar is on her way and it will not bode well for us if I remain in the camp." Amar left the pavilion and other tricksters also headed for the wilderness.

As Mahrukh busied herself with plans to ward off Bahar's magic, a cold breeze like the breath of the Messiah wafted in. Mahrukh's entire camp broke into shouts of "Spring is here! Spring has come!" Mahrukh and the commanders of her army involuntarily came out of their pavilions. They saw Bahar's magic peacock with emerald feathers preening outside the camp and the sorceress princess in the saddle.

All the soldiers and commanders of Mahrukh's camp came out of their tents and pavilions and gathered in one place to gaze on Princess Bahar's resplendent face and her world-adorning beauty. Bahar recited a spell and clapped, causing clouds to rise from every direction. Mahrukh and her sorcerers recited counterspells and clapped to ward off the magic but to no avail. In the next moment, a yellow dust blew up from the ground and everyone in Mahrukh's camp closed their eyes. When they opened them, they saw expansive, luxurious orchards wherever they looked in which the breeze wafted intoxicatingly. They beheld a yard-high crystal wall that stretched for miles on end.

After Mahrukh's army had closed its eyes, Princess Bahar took out a paper, pen and inkwell from her sorcerer's sack and wrote a tilism to create a garden with properties that would enchant anyone who stepped into its bounds. Since the garden was a tilism, tricksters could not enter it to rescue their companions once they stepped in it and became its prisoners.

When Mahrukh's camp saw Princess Bahar fly on her peacock into the garden, all of them followed her inside. They beheld a luminous crystal platform that seemed to be made of light. A canopy of strung pearls rose over the platform. An ermine carpet was spread on the floor. Beautiful, moon-like cupbearers were gathered with goblets and ewers. They regarded Princess Bahar seated on a jewel-encrusted throne with lamps and bouquets placed before her. She wore a luxurious dress covered with jewels and held a jewel-enchased stick in her hand. If the rosy-cheeked beauties of the Garden of Life had beheld Bahar's beauty they would have sacrificed their lives a thousand times for her. Even the beautiful Zulaikha had never seen such grace in her dreams. Bahar's beauty was so astonishing that even charming fairies were fit only to be her slave girls. Her hair was a net for the birds of lovers' souls; it entrapped the hearts of her admirers helplessly in its locks.

Her tongue was the keeper of celestial secrets
Her mouth the custodian of mysteries divine
The bright lobe of her ear made the morn of doomsday shy away
Its dark mole the dark mark on the heart[74]
The swelling of her double chin was luminous like the sun
And the crease underneath an image of the crescent
The jasmine bushes bearing their bouquets
Expressed the fervour felt by the flower garden
Her soft jasmine bosom and her dainty walk
Disclosed a bold shyness, a timid audacity
Such were her shoulders, arms, wrists and hands that
The worshippers of beloveds would swear to them their life's allegiance
Had the connoisseurs of beauty regarded the fine sheen,
Of her breasts, and the dark knobs of her nipples
"Because her bosom is clear as the mirror
It reflects the pupils of her eyes" they'd have exclaimed
When she dewed it smelled of rose essence
Before the refulgence of her stomach the moon hid its face
The shining navel of that inestimable pearl
Was like the face of Venus on the face of Earth
Like the line of sight is hidden in the eyes
Her waist existed and yet it did not
So remarkably cast were her thighs
Even the glance of imagination could find on them no purchase
Why her shank should not rival the Light of Tur
The soles of her feet rivalled the cheeks of houris

Witnessing the garden's bloom and Bahar's lovely aspect, everyone, including Mahrukh Magic-Eye and all the companions and commanders of her army, cried out, "O Princess Bahar, we are your admirers and followers; we're ready to sacrifice ourselves like moths on the burning taper of your resplendent aspect. Show us favor in our miserable condition. Admit us into your slavery, O Princess! Augment our honor by allowing us to wait upon you."

Princess Bahar showed them not the least favor and picked a bouquet and flung it toward them. Again, all of them closed their eyes. That bouquet dispersed and every single flower petal was transformed into a garland. When Mahrukh's companions opened their eyes they found these garlands around their wrists.

Under Bahar's spell they all importuned her and cried, "Forgive us, O Princess, for we were led astray by Amar Ayyar the sly thief and trickster. Now pardon our trespasses and lead us before Emperor Afrasiyab." Bahar said, "Very well, follow me. I will take you to the emperor." With a leap, she mounted her magic peacock and headed out of the garden. Her prisoners followed her like a frenzied crowd, passionately reciting love couplets. The tilism garden disappeared after Bahar stepped out of its bounds.

The tricksters witnessed from their stations their camp marching frantically behind Princess Bahar. They signalled with their whistles and gathered together. Burq said to Amar, "Master, I ask leave to work my trickery." Amar Ayyar said, "Bahar is a powerful sorceress and you will not prevail against her. And even if you did you would have to kill her to secure the release of our companions. I wish to capture Bahar alive and persuade her to join our cause. However, you are free to act as you please if you can achieve your end without killing her." Burq and the other tricksters told Amar they could not secure their purpose without murdering Bahar. Amar then asked them to desist from taking any action and instead wait for him to find a solution.

Amar Ayyar put his hand on his zambil and asked Prophet Aadam for a miracle, saying, "O Aadam, change my appearance to that of a fourteen-year-old boy." After praying, Amar took out the goblet of Prophet Ishaq and sprinkled himself with its pure and untainted heavenly water.

Immediately, a change came over him.[75] He became a beautiful fourteen-year-old boy dressed in a red tunic, satin pants and richly embroidered shoes. A three-fold belt was tied around his waist and he sported an embroidered cap sewn with pearls and jewels. The thirteen charms he wore around his neck signified he had not yet reached his fourteenth year. His moon-like beauty showed innocence, yet the look in his eyes revealed a romantic disposition. His cheeks were soft as roses and he was matchless in beauty and coquettish airs.

After attaining this appearance, Amar Ayyar entered a scenic forest that lay four miles from the path taken by Princess Bahar. He stationed himself in a luxuriant grove reminiscent of the garden of paradise. Amar unfastened his tunic and took off his cap. With his eyes closed and his hands on his ears, he tearfully intoned love couplets and *ghazals*[76] that sang of separation between lovers.

As Bahar advanced forward with her prisoners, a captivating voice reached her from a mile away and affected her profoundly. Princess Bahar was not only an expert in creating tilisms but was also equally gifted in musical arts and had a taste for the pleasures of life. Entranced by the voice, she flew on her magic peacock toward it.

When she arrived at the spot Bahar saw a charming adolescent boy singing with his eyes closed and holding a tree branch. He sported earrings, a necklace and armlets studded with jewels. His hands were painted with henna and his luminous aspect shone brighter than the full moon. From his luxurious clothes he appeared to be the darling of his family. He sang so exquisitely that even the birds and beasts were entranced. A bird was perched on that beloved youth's arm, another sat atop his head, and a third had climbed onto his hand. But he sang completely oblivious to what went on around him.

Bahar approached the rosy-cheeked, false beauty and asked him, "O elegant cypress of beauty's garden, of which happy garden are you a sapling? Indeed, your parents must have hearts of stone to let you stand here on this road that is full of peril."

Hearing her voice, the false youth opened his eyes and turned a frightened face toward Bahar. Then he saluted her humbly and said, "I will leave. I did not know that this garden belonged to you." His cheeks flushed with blood and Bahar realized she had frightened the innocent boy. She dismounted and came toward him. The false youth began to retreat, asking for her forgiveness with clasped hands and saying tearfully, "I made a mistake! You will never see me here again!"

Bahar thought, *How terrible! He is so very innocent. God knows how he happened by here.* She spoke softly to the boy, saying, "Don't be afraid, child. I'll be kind to you. Tell me the name of your parents." Hearing Bahar's words, the false youth stopped, and said affectedly, "Promise me you will not punish me. It was because my sister beat me that I ran away and came here." Bahar was saddened to hear that fear had driven the boy from his home into the wilderness. She felt sorry for his parents and realized they must be searching for him. She said, "Have no fear. I will not punish you." The false youth said, "Do you promise in Lord Sameri's name?" Bahar said, "I promise in Lord Sameri's name that I will not punish you."

The false youth took a few hesitant steps toward Bahar but quickly retreated and his frightened look returned.

Bahar thought, *How cruelly he must have been punished that his fear does not leave him!* She took out a colorful bouquet from her sack and offered it to the false youth, saying, "Do you want this?" Now the false youth realized that if Bahar cast a spell over him it would foil his plan. He smiled at the sight of the flowers and said, "Yes, I do." Bahar hid it and opened her arms wide, saying, "Come into my arms then and you can have the bouquet."

The false youth ran and embraced her, saying, "Now sister, give me the flowers. Give me the flowers you showed me." Bahar kissed his cheeks and said, "Think of yourself now as my son." He asked, "Will you continue to be my kind sister?" Bahar answered, "Yes, I will." He said, "Then give me the flowers." Bahar asked him, "Where is your home?" He replied, "It is far from here. You can see my house by that tree, far away." Bahar said, "Liar, it is not so close that you can see it."

While they were engaged in this conversation, Bahar's companions and attendants also arrived on the scene. The false youth tore out of Bahar's embrace at the sight of them and said, "I will go now."

Bahar said to her attendants, "The child is shy and frightened. Head to the camp. I will join you there."

After her attendants departed, Bahar asked the boy, "You were ready to leave your sister?" He replied, "Do you want me to accompany you to your home instead?" When Bahar said yes, he asked, "Will you catch me a deer?" Bahar said, "What will you do with a deer?" The youth answered, "I remember my sister saying that she would cook venison for me on the day I got married. Now that I am in the forest I want to catch a deer and take it with me. It will please my mother and she will find me a wife." Bahar laughed at his childish speech and said, "See how happy you become at the thought of a wife, foolish boy! If you become my son I will find a princess to be your bride. Give me the name of your father. I will send for him and ask his permission to adopt you." He answered, "My father is the sorcerer Umayya, and my mother's name is Gulrang. Come sister, I will take you with me to my house." Bahar answered, "I think you have gotten lost. Come with me and I will send my attendants to locate your house and send for your father." The false youth answered, "Very well! But I want to sit with you."

Seating him in front of her on her peacock, Bahar headed toward her camp, located ten miles from Mahrukh's garrison. A few moments later, she arrived and sent for her commanders, saying, "Mahrukh's army is following me under my spell. As long as the magic garlands remain on their wrists they cannot break free of it. You must remain cautious and place vigils to ward off any unforeseen threats."

Bahar said to her attendants, "Provide all the apparatus of revelry in my pavilion and remain alert. But as I can guard myself, do not stand outside my pavilion nor step inside for tricksters might enter in your disguise. My heart is racing. I am tired and weary and exhausted by the journey. I won't be able to behead the rebels tonight. I will kill them tomorrow."

While Bahar's army went and cordoned off Mahrukh's camp and deputed vigils, her attendants got busy. They provided a golden throne and jewel-encrusted bed in Bahar's pavilion. They laid out choice foods on colorful platters and arranged the wine service and trays of kebabs. They served delicacies and, after stocking bread platters, betel boxes, perfume boxes and snack boxes, all the attendants left her pavilion.

Princess Bahar entered with the false youth, ordered the carpet keepers to raise the panels of her pavilion, and said to them, "The shades of evening are now falling. Light the pavilion, then go and rest." The carpet keepers lit up the glass lights and went away, leaving Bahar and the false youth alone in the pavilion.

In the meanwhile, the day came to a close. The Dancing Girl of the Heavens[77] donned her star-studded skirt and presented herself to perform before the King of the Stars.[78] The Bright-Faced Turk of the Sky[79] armed himself with a dagger and mounted a vigil at the entrance of the heavens' pavilion.

Bahar offered some fruit and sweetmeats to her guest and laid out delicacies and choice foods before him. He ate the fruit but did not share the food with Bahar. After having her meal, Bahar sat on the throne and said, "My dear child, sing a little for me." The false youth produced a fife and began playing, and sang songs of love and separation. Enraptured by his voice, the beasts of the forest gathered outside Bahar's pavilion. Even the breeze became still. A complete trance was cast over the surroundings. His singing moved Bahar so powerfully that she cried without cease like a cloud of spring quarter and stared wonderstruck at his divine talent.

After one watch of the night had passed, he put down the fife. Bahar could not bear it and entreated him to carry on playing. She said, "Dear child, do not abandon me to die of anguish after lacerating my heart. Play on so that my wounded heart may find solace." He replied, "I feel a headache coming on." Bahar thought that perhaps he felt shy and if she gave him a glass of wine he would lose his inhibitions and sing with greater pathos. She filled a goblet and offered it to him, saying, "Drink this sherbet, my child!" He said, "Do you think I do not know this is wine? We drink it at our home. Put the whole wine service before me." Bahar set the wine service before the false youth and he began arranging it according to his way. Placing red cups near green ewers, he organized the bottles like flowers in a bouquet. Bahar was most pleased to see these refinements and reckoned he must be the scion of an illustrious family.

In the process of arranging the wine service the false youth used sleight of hand to drug the wine. He said to Bahar, "You must drink first, O Princess, for you have the pride of place in this assembly. I will drink a cup after you." Bahar marvelled at his delicacy and drank up the wine when he offered her the cup. Then he offered her a second glass, saying, "It is against the conventions of drinking to drink a single cup or refuse the cupbearer." After offering Bahar a few more cups, he poured a few for himself and cunningly emptied them down his collar, tricking Bahar into believing he too, was drinking.

Afterwards, he took up the fife again and started playing. By now Bahar was fully intoxicated. She kissed the mouth of the wine bottle every few moments and broke into songs. She became oblivious to all concerns and continued drinking while the singer sang. The rest of the evening passed in this manner and by its end, Bahar was completely unmindful of her body and soul.

Finally, the Beloved of the Sky[80] looked out from her eastern bed to show the creatures of night her resplendent face, and the World-Illuminating Lamp[81] dismissed the assembly of stars.

The false youth saw Bahar lying unconscious on her throne. Her pants had climbed to her thighs and her bosom lay uncovered as her mantle had slipped, leaving it exposed. Amar pulled out Bahar's tongue and pierced it with a needle, then tied her to a column of the pavilion and made her smell restorative salts.

Bahar sneezed and regained consciousness. Amar greeted her and said, "Sister, you still haven't found me the deer." The memories of the previous night were still impressed on Bahar's mind. When she tried to answer, she realized she could not speak because her tongue had been pulled out and pierced. She immediately returned to her senses, and gestured to Amar to know what had happened to her.

Amar produced a whip from his zambil and shouted furiously, "I am the King of the Tricksters, the Bearder of Non Believers and Beheader of Sorcerers.

'I am the master trickster
The embodiment of wisdom and cunning
A calamity for infidels everywhere
Amar Ayyar, of all tricksters the prince.

"Regard the handiwork of the True God, O Bahar, how I captured you and rendered you helpless. You would live if you submit your allegiance; otherwise you must be speedily dispatched to the Future State."

Because Bahar had had an altercation with Heyrat, she signalled to Amar that she was prepared to submit her allegiance and asked to be freed. Amar immediately removed the needle from her tongue.

After her release, Bahar felt tempted to deceive Amar in the same manner he had fooled her. She was also angry that a lowly trickster should demand the allegiance of a powerful sorceress like herself. She considered too, that Heyrat was, after all, her own sister and she must not join a revolt against her.

As Bahar turned a fiery gaze toward Amar, he said to her, "Know O Bahar that I released you on your word that you wished to offer allegiance. Do not imagine even for a moment that I have no power over you now that you are free. I swear by my faith that I will kill you with as little compunction as I kill a mosquito or common ant. You can do now all that you have in your power, and exert yourself to the best of your ability. You may send for all your sorcerers and helpers too." With these words, Amar headed out of the pavilion. Bahar cried out, "Someone catch this thief!"

Sorcerers came running at Bahar's call.

Amar Ayyar opened up Daniyal's Tent like a canopy and sat down under it while Bahar and her sorcerers surrounded him.

Bahar said to Amar, "O rascal, now you have nowhere to run." She threw a bouquet of flowers at Amar that made beds of tulips and poppies spring up all around Daniyal's Tent. The bloom of the flowers made it appear like a spring day. However, as magic had no effect on the miraculous Daniyal's Tent, Amar remained safe from Bahar's spell inside it.

Witnessing that, Bahar said to her sorcerers, "Do not break the cordon around him. I shall now enter the tent and catch him myself." The moment Bahar set foot in Daniyal's Tent her head went down and her feet went up and she found herself hanging upside down from the entrance, all her magic forgotten. Amar gave her two lashes with his whip, which made that delicate beauty wince with pain.

Amar next reached into his zambil and took out four fairies and a bed with jewel-encrusted legs. He ordered Daniyal's Tent to show its miraclous powers and expand. The tent enlarged and became a pavilion surmounted by ruby-studded spires, its screens and curtains sewn with jewels. The fairies arranged the furniture on the carpet. Amar laid himself on the bed while the fairies busied themselves massaging his limbs. Amar said to them, "Your lord and master has not slept a wink the whole night. You will wake me up at your own peril." Then he closed his eyes.

When the sorcerers saw Bahar hanging inside the tent they cast spells and attempted to rescue her. But the moment they set foot inside they too, were suspended like Bahar and forgot all their magic.

A fairy woke Amar up and said, "You have visitors." Amar angrily said to her, "I told you not to wake me, but you never listen." Amar took out his whip and began lashing the sorcerers. They started howling and crying for help. The sorcerers outside began invoking their magic. One of them created a river of fire that engulfed Daniyal's Tent; the flames surged like torrents but could do no harm to Amar or the tent.

The sorcerers outside dispelled the magic river of fire to see if Amar had been killed, but they saw him thrashing the sorcerers as before. Upon witnessing that sight, the sorcerers began reciting spells anew. They showered stones on Daniyal's Tent, drowned it in a magic flood, even attempted to cut it down with swords. But none of that had any effect on it, and anyone who stepped inside was suspended upside down like others before him.

Amar Ayyar now addressed Bahar, saying, "Had I wished I could have captured and killed you long ago without seeking recourse to these tricks. But I have been proscribed the use of holy gifts for killing people. We tricksters employ tricks and deception only against sorcerers. If you fought in the tradition of chivalry, we would not enter the fight. Prince Asad and our soldiers would answer your challenge. I ask you again to submit your allegiance or else, I swear, in the name of Almighty God that I will kill you and nobody would be able to harm a single hair on my body." Bahar said, "Release me. I will submit my allegiance."

Amar ordered Daniyal's Tent to release Bahar. After she was freed, Bahar again questioned whether she must give her allegiance to Amar or embrace death.

Amar read her face and realized that she still hesitated in making her decision. He said, "O Bahar, it ill becomes your dignity as a wise and astute sorceress and a beautiful woman to thoughtlessly prostrate yourself before Laqa. Indeed, I find it a marvel. If Laqa had any power or means, how could Hamza drive him from place to place? It proves that Almighty God is the True Creator of both worlds. Why must you renounce the authority of the Lord and True Creator and worship one of His creatures? Tear yourself away from this thorny path and enter the garden lit by the light of truth. It is a matter of time before both Laqa and Afrasiyab are killed. You must not think that Laqa can save him."

Amar made many powerful arguments about the True God's omniscience. He had already implanted fear of him in Bahar's heart with his tricks. Now, revealing his grandeur by the miracle of Daniyal's Tent, he finally prevailed over Bahar and her heart was cleansed of all pollution. She felt light at heart and peaceful. Since Bahar was already taken with Amar's singing, she readily put her head at his feet and said, "I am now your humble slave girl."

Amar embraced Bahar and said, "O Princess, I may have called you my sister from deceit in the beginning, but I consider you now my sister in earnest. God willing, you will attain a high rank in this tilism." Bahar replied, "And I promise that I will be at the forefront when any sacrifice is needed."

After making this pact with Amar, Princess Bahar stepped out of Daniyal's Tent and said to her army commanders, "I have submitted allegiance to Amar. It would be best for you to follow suit. If not, you may go where you please." The sorcerers gave her their pledge of obedience without protest.

Bahar now recited a spell and clapped. It dispelled the frenzied state that had gripped Mahrukh Magic-Eye's camp. The flower bracelets around their arms wilted and fell off and everyone regained command of their faculties. The remainder of Princess Bahar's fifty thousand sorcerers also submitted their allegiance to the True Faith. Amar Ayyar rolled up Daniyal's Tent and accompanied Princess Bahar, who wished to present herself before Mahjabeen and make an offering.

After Bahar made her offering to Queen Mahjabeen, Prince Asad and Mahrukh Magic-Eye embraced her and said, "Your arrival has raised our spirits and strengthened our morale."

Afterwards, Queen Mahjabeen brought everyone back to their camp. The armies of Mahrukh Magic-Eye and Princess Bahar merged and Mahrukh found herself in command of well over a hundred thousand sorcerers.

All the commanders returned to their stations and occupied themselves with celebrations and carousing. Bahar was given a jewel-studded seat in Queen Mahjabeen's court. Singers and dancers presented themselves and roseate wine was drunk. The tricksters also returned to the camp and joined the festive assembly.

While they were thus occupied, the magic birds flew in and announced that Princess Surkh Mu Wonder-Mane's commander-in-chief, Shamshad Elephant-Body, was approaching. Mahrukh Magic-Eye sent a welcoming party to receive him and ordered that his men should be lodged in her camp.

Upon arrival, Shamshad Elephant-Body presented the goods and treasures he had brought at Surkh Mu Wonder-Mane's orders. Soon the revels and carousing resumed in the camp.

Sorcerers Shadeed, Qahhar, and Azaab

Now hear of Emperor Afrasiyab, who had retired to Mount Quartz after Princess Bahar left on the campaign against Amar and Mahrukh.

Afrasiyab sought diversion in the sights and sounds of the scenic expanse. Mount Quartz resembled a bouquet of vibrant colors from the many flowers that covered its face, and from the goldcloth-draped trees that stood laden with blossoms. The warbling of birds echoed in the air. But instead of consoling him, the sight reminded Afrasiyab all the more of Princess Bahar. He tried to recite a few love couplets to quieten his pining heart but when it remained restive he penned a letter of apology to Princess Bahar that was full of excuses about the incident involving Heyrat. He wrote:

> "O Empress of the Land of Beauty, Sovereign of the Kingdom of Graciousness, Princess of the Clime of Charm and Allure, Mistress of all Moon-like Beauties, Sweet Tongued Beloved, Light of Fairies' Bright Aspects, Illuminator of Love's Face, Spring of Lovers' Souls, and Rosy-Cheeked Princess Bahar, may the garden of your hopes remain always abloom with desire's flowers! May every branch of hope's tree bear fruit as luscious as your lips! May the grove of your peace and comfort always remain lit up like the morn's smile! May the eve of sorrow and grief forever hide its face from you like a grief-stricken soul! My dear beloved, I melt away in sorrow ever since you left my court with an unhappy heart. Do not take offense at Heyrat's words. I remain your true lover as always. Pray return from this dangerous campaign and confer on your lover the cup of your audience. Another servant of the empire will replace you on this mission and put paid to the rebels. The throne of beauty is the only throne that befits your person, your lover's breast the only bed where you may repose. You must exert yourself in your lover's bed, not on battlefields."

After he finished writing, Afrasiyab recited a spell whereupon a magic slave emerged from the ground. Afrasiyab handed him the letter and ordered him to take it to Bahar wherever she might be found. The magic slave departed and arrived in Mahjabeen's court where Bahar was seated, and delivered her the message. After reading it, Bahar wrote in reply:

> "Salutations, Emperor Afrasiyab, the illustrious master whose armies are like the armies of stars, who is like the Jupiter in nature and Venus-like in charms, who is wise like Mercury,[82] and the most excellent commander of the sorcerers. May you remain free always of the sorrows of love, and remain forever the beloved in the eyes of the beauties of the world. Your epistle arrived redolent with the perfume of love. It was a bouquet from the garden of desire and the freshest fruit of love's orchard. The love that you speak of, however, is but a dream. I would that you remain ever engrossed in the mirror of Heyrat's beauty. I would that you renounce love for me. But if you insist on professing it still, I desire that you present yourself with Prince Badiuz Zaman and Princess Tasveer, whom you have imprisoned, and submit your allegiance to Amar Ayyar. I have sincerely pledged my allegiance to him and vowed to give my life in his service. End of Letter. My regards!"

Bahar handed her reply to the magic slave, who took it to Afrasiyab on Mount Quartz. Upon reading Bahar's letter, a fiery "Aah!" rose from Afrasiyab's breast and scalded his senses and reason. He struck his hands together in anguish and a bank of clouds rose in the skies from which a single cloud swam to Mount Quartz. Riding that cloud were three sorcerers, named Shadeed, Qahhar and Azaab, who were the rulers of the lands adjacent to Mount Quartz. They saluted Afrasiyab and noticed his downcast face and distressed look. They stood humbly before him awaiting their orders.

Finally, Afrasiyab said, "O Shadeed, Qahhar and Azaab, you must immediately depart with a large army and bring back Princess Bahar, whose resentment toward me has driven her to join the enemy. You must first use persuasion but if she refuses to accompany you peacefully, you must fight and take her prisoner. However, Princess Bahar is a powerful sorceress and will not be easily captured. I am now headed for Lord Jamshed's mausoleum from where I will send you the lord's mantle. It is a powerful gift of the tilism. You may depart now and wait for it to arrive."

❧

The three sorcerers returned to their lands. They mustered armies of seventy thousand sorcerers each and departed on their mission. After marching and bivouacking, and after a night and a day they arrived near Mahrukh Magic-Eye's camp and set up tents and pavilions. The camp was organized, the army bivouacked, and the sorcerer commanders Shadeed, Qahhar and Azaab stationed in their pavilions.

The magic birds brought the news to Queen Mahjabeen and Mahrukh, who sent for the commanders of the army and enjoined them to remain on alert. The camp was alerted and the commanders and sorcerers began invoking their magic lest Shadeed should attack upon seeing them off guard. The bugles began trilling in platoons and regiments and weapons were polished and burnished.

❧

Emperor Afrasiyab returned to the Apple Garden where everyone paid him respects. The emperor sat down despondently on his throne with knitted brow. Heyrat asked, "How are your humors, Your Excellency?" Afrasiyab answered testily, "Your feuding with Bahar has caused her to join hands with the rebels."

Heyrat replied, "That chit of a girl has become too proud; she no longer considers others her equals. Her evil heart was already set on making mischief and she praised Mahrukh Magic-Eye to my face. Your Honor must not bemoan her leaving us. You have countless faithful servants who would arrest Bahar in a trice at your command and produce her before you."

Afrasiyab replied, "This is all talk and empty words. I spent hundreds of thousand of rupees in nurturing and training Mahrukh, Nafarman and Bahar, and instructing them in magic. How could I kill them all of a sudden? I still nurse a hope that they will return to my allegiance. Therefore, I am headed for Lord Jamshed's mausoleum to bring his mantle. I would that you return to the Dome of Light as I don't require your presence here. It bodes ill for rulers when they antagonize their army commanders instead of winning their hearts and offering them encouragement."

Afrasiyab then left for Jamshed's mausoleum while Heyrat returned disconsolate and dejected to the Dome of Light.

❧

After the sorcerers Shadeed, Qahhar and Azaab camped they sent a string of missives to Bahar full of admonitions and injunctions. They asked her to return to the folds of Afrasiyab's obedience and told her that all was not yet lost. They warned her against siding with the rebels and destroying the faith of their gods Sameri and Jamshed, but each time Bahar offered them a terse reply. The sorcerers wasted a whole day trying to convince her, but to no avail.

Finally, the day came to an end. The sorcerer Night took out stars from its sack of darkness to make its offering and the inauspicious Saturn[83] squatted in the heavens to invoke its magic. Thus they conspired together against the morning sun.

Shadeed and the other sorcerers conferred and decided that if they waited until Afrasiyab sent them Jamshed's mantle they would be called cowards and pansies throughout the length and breadth of the tilism. They convinced themselves that Bahar was an insignificant threat and, rather than waiting for Jamshed's mantle, they must declare hostilities and arrest her speedily to earn renown on their own. They ordered the drums of war in their camp to be beaten at once.

Mahrukh's magic birds brought her the news and her camp also answered the call to battle. The drums were beaten and the magic bugle trilled. The battle preparations remained underway for four full watches of the night. Bengalese horns trilled, evil spirits were tamed by songs to wreack havoc, and magic spirits were invoked with blood sacrifices. Then spirits were summoned and tempted to offer their help with sweetmeats. The sorcerers targeted their rivals by composing magic spells with their names and lighting lamps with the blood of wagtails and crows. The wicks of the lamps were trimmed. Soil and rocks from cremation grounds, ashes of oil sellers' corpses, and bones of the dead were gathered. The spells were readied and the properties of the magical citrons, limes and oranges were assigned to them. Adulations of gods Sameri and Jamshed were sung. The bonfires were stoked to burn the whole night. Then the sorcerers retired to catch a wink of sleep.

The warriors sharpened their shining daggers and ground them on stone to make their edges even keener. Swords were made serrated and broad swords were sharpened to give them deep edges. They became sharp and keen to the degree that one could not safely slide one's finger along the blade. Every sword became a mirror that reflected the face of death's bride.[84] The iron shone so brightly that men were tricked into marching to the arena believing it was already the morn of battle. The warriors made claims of their bravery the whole night and talked of nothing else but the battle.

Finally, the Conjuror of the Skies produced a golden orb from its eastern pocket and entered, juggling it in the ring of heavens. The Turk of Sun sharpened his luminous dagger on the whetstone of the firmament.

Prince Asad said his morning prayers at the crack of dawn. The sorcerers who had submitted allegiance to him were sworn to the faith of sorcery until the enemy's destruction, and yet they turned their hearts to thoughts of God to solicit His aid.[85]

Presently, the morning gong rang in the camp, the bugle sounded, and everyone started preparations for the march to the battlefield. The officers mounted their steeds and the foot-soldiers and troopers made vows of valor.

Dil Aaram came into view bearing aloft Queen Mahjabeen's throne by magic. Mahrukh Magic-Eye, Shakeel, Nafarman, Surkh Mu Wonder-Mane, and Princess Bahar arrived before Queen Mahjabeen with great majesty, riding magic thrones and peacocks. They made low bows to her and escorted Queen Mahjabeen's throne. Renowned sorcerers riding magic geese and magic dragons poured into the arena row after row, column after column, rank after rank, file after file. They were joined by Prince Asad with his army of warriors. Displaying his equestrian skills, the prince sat astride a giant steed of enormous rump.

When Prince Asad took position at the head of the army as the commander-in-chief, lightning bolts danced in the arena and terrible, thunderous noises were heard. Dark clouds rose from the direction of the wilderness and, leading their armies, the sorcerers Shadeed, Qahhar and Azaab arrived with great fanfare. They flooded the arena like a tidal wave. They hurled thunderbolts that burned down the shrubbery and removed obstructions between the rival camps, then settled down the dust with magic showers.

The army commanders arranged their men. Warriors on both sides formed fourteen rows as impregnable as the Rampart of Sikander. The criers recited the valorous deeds of past kings to stir thoughts of brave deeds in the hearts of their men, and the minstrels sang martial songs. Their cries and songs turned the warriors' hearts to thoughts of martyrdom and earning glory on the battlefield.

Sorcerer Qahhar rode to the center of the arena atop his magic dragon and displayed his might by causing showers of fire and stones. He cried out, "O rebels, come out and face me to be chastised as you deserve."

Nafarman flew her magic peacock to Mahjabeen and sought leave to answer Qahhar's challenge. Mahjabeen conferred a robe of honor on her and gave her into God's protection. Nafarman now encountered Qahhar the lost soul.

Both deployed their magic against each other. Qahhar threw a magic coconut at Nafarman, which exploded upon hitting Nafarman's leg and broke her thigh bone. As Nafarman fell down wounded, Surkh Mu Wonder-Mane came forward on her magic throne and, after obtaining leave for combat, faced Qahhar.

Qahhar threw another magic coconut at Surkh Mu, who foiled his attack. She took out a box carved out of ruby after untying her hair, opened its lid, and tapped out sparkles from it onto the palm of her hand. She blew on them and they flew to the sky, shining brightly like stars. Suddenly, those stars shot down like meteors. They fell on Qahhar and pierced the ground after breaking his spine. A noise like the Day of Judgment was heard. Mahrukh's sorcerers quickly recited spells and overpowered Qahhar's magic spirits by slitting open their thighs and making blood sacrifices. At length the clamour subsided.

Sorcerer Azaab came into the arena next. Shakeel rode out to fight him astride his magic dragon. Azaab repeatedly attacked Shakeel with his trident but Shakeel foiled his attacks. Then Shakeel recited a spell and dealt a sword's blow to Azaab. The magic sword fell on Azaab like a lightning bolt and burned down the garden of his soul; the second enemy commander was also dispatched to hell.

Sorcerer Shadeed entered the arena in high dudgeon. He put his hand in his sorcerer's sack and threw a magic snake into the arena, which bit Shakeel. The latter tried to recite counterspells but they proved ineffective. When Shakeel fell down unconscious Mahrukh dispatched attendants to bring him back to the camp. Sorcerer exorcists were deputed to watch over the wound so that the magic venom did not kill him.

Surkh Mu Wonder-Mane now entered the arena and Shadeed deployed the same magic snake against her. Surkh Mu cut a peacock shape out of paper and recited a spell that made it come alive. As the magic snake darted toward Surkh Mu, her magic peacock swooped down and carried it away in its beak.

As both friends and foe alike praised Surkh Mu's magic, Shadeed went into a mad rage. He notched an arrow and let fly after reciting a spell. Surkh Mu struck her hands together and forty magic shields barred the arrow's flight. Shadeed's magic arrow, however, pierced through all of them and struck Surkh Mu's shoulder; injured, she retired from the arena.

Shadeed called out, "O Bahar, I have come to arrest you. Come out and face me! How long will you hide in corners and nooks?"

Bahar sat on her throne with great allure and magnificence, with bouquets placed around her. Several hundred attendants clad in gold finery, wearing pearls in their ears and carrying flower baskets, stood humbly before her. When Shadeed issued his challenge she flew on her throne, picked up a bouquet and threw it toward the jungle. A black cloud that was darker than the pitch black night rose from the mountains and darkness fell over the entire expanse. Bahar now opened her vanity box and applied silver dust and *tilak* to her forehead. Suddenly, everyone saw a moon and stars light up the darkness that engulfed them. The day became a moonlit night.

As Shadeed recited counterspells and clapped, Bahar threw a second bouquet and called out, "O spring, appear!" Suddenly a cool breeze picked up and the sorcerers in Shadeed's army began clapping wildly with joy. Bahar threw a third bouquet and thousands of comely moon-like women materialized carrying musical instruments. Some of them were of the Turkic race, others Frankish, yet others Indian. They represented every race and tribe and their beauty was the envy of the sun and the moon. They played their instruments so alluringly that the enemy army became enamored of their Venusian charms.

Bahar now threw a fourth bouquet. Everyone in the enemy camp shut their eyes and upon opening them, saw spring appear in all its glory. The redolence of the flowers spread with the moonlight. For miles on end, the eye saw only gardens and orchards. The flower buds yawned and blossomed. Drunk on its own perfume, the fragrant breeze circulated and like a tipsy guest in a wine house, crashed against the ewers of trees.

Bahar dismounted and entered the flower garden followed by her female musicians. When Shadeed and his men marched after them they saw Bahar approaching. Her beauty was so dazzling and complete that even if a houri had beheld it she would have given herself in slavery to Bahar.

A violent passion for Bahar suddenly overcame Shadeed.

Bahar signalled to one of her attendants, who brought a knife and a basin and called out, "O admirers of Princess Bahar's incomparable beauty, which resembles the brilliant sun, your merciless mistress needs a blood sacrifice from her admirers. Here is the blade and the basin. Come and prove your passion."

The sorcerers in Shadeed's camp ran and competed with each other to be the first to make the sacrifice. They hurried before Bahar's attendant, who slit open their arms and collected the blood in the basin. When one lost consciousness another replaced him and died in the same manner. An amazing spectacle unfolded as blood sacrifices claimed man after man and the living vied with each other to make the fatal offering.

Bahar signalled another attendant to summon Shadeed. The attendant loudly called, "O Shadeed! Hasten before Princess Bahar, who summons you to her presence!" Shadeed walked toward Bahar upon hearing her call.

Bahar called to and led Shadeed deeper into her magic garden. He followed her voice spellbound, importuning and begging her to show him favor. When he approached he saw Bahar promenading in the garden carrying a flower cane. She wore a garland on her arm. Her hair was tied in a bun to one side of her head, the skirt of her mantle had slipped down to uncover her bosom, and the bottoms of her trousers were as tight as skin and gathered in folds at the knees.

Shadeed felt a frenzy of passion take hold of him a hundred times more powerfully than before. As he stood humbly before her, Bahar hit him with her flower cane and said, "Is this how you fulfill your lover's duties? Heyrat cursed and abused me before the whole court but you never sought recompense from her!"

Shadeed answered, "O solace of my soul, indeed, I never learned of the incident." Bahar hit him a few more times with her flower cane and said, "O bastard, now that you have learned of the incident what laurels have you won in defending my honor?" Shadeed answered, "At a word from you I will thrash Heyrat with my shoe and drag her before you." Bahar lashed him even more severely with the cane and said, "O clown, would you only act if I ordered you? Do you not feel any violent compulsion yourself to avenge my disgrace?"

After being hit with Bahar's magic cane, Shadeed became oblivious to every consideration. His senses were completely lost to Bahar's spell and he said, "O beloved, I will drag that harridan Heyrat before you by her hair this very instant." Bahar said, "I have no trust in your word. Send for the commanders of your army." Shadeed sent for them and Bahar stopped her attendant from blood-letting them further.

When Shadeed's commanders streamed before Bahar, she said to them, "I swear to the truth of what I state upon my honor and wish to inform you that Heyrat cursed and abused me. The one who kills her like a dog I will reward by sharing my bed with him."

Bahar now ordered her attendant to put magic garlands on the arms of all commanders and tied one on Shadeed's arm with her own hands.

Shadeed and his entire army headed for the Dome of Light feverishly reciting love couplets while thousands of others lay dead from the blood-letting. Except for its tents and equipages, their whole camp was emptied.

After they were gone, Bahar removed the silver dust from her forehead and recited a spell and clapped, causing the magic spring to disappear. The moonlit night was dispelled and the sun reappeared.

Kettledrums were beaten in celebration and Mahrukh Magic-Eye's camp trussed up all the loot from Shadeed's camp. Mahjabeen scattered gold pieces over Bahar as a sacrifice to protect her from evil and sang her praises. A resplendent robe of honor was conferred on Bahar by Queen Mahjabeen. Their armies took rest and festivities began in celebration of the day's events. The tabla began playing and a dance recital started.

While Mahrukh's camp was occupied in these revels, Shadeed crossed the River of Flowing Blood in great disarray and distress, arriving near the Dome of Light spellbound by Bahar's beauty and full of the violent fervor induced by his desire.

He began hurling abuse at Heyrat and shouting, "Catch that whore Heyrat! Bring me that harridan and strumpet! How dare that wretch abuse my beloved Bahar!" Shadeed and his army began ravaging the City of Disregard. They killed any sorcerer who resisted them. A great tumult arose and the citizens shouted for redress and succor.

Heyrat, who was present in the Dome of Light, heard these noises and sent sorcerers to investigate the matter. They soon returned and apprised the empress of the situation.

Heyrat ordered the gong-ringers who inhabited the ground tier of the Dome of Light to stop Shadeed and his men. They immediately confronted Shadeed and skirmished with the marauding army. Magic was deployed by sorcerers on both sides. The gong-ringers were mighty sorcerers and they killed Shadeed's men in the thousands. Shadeed himself, however, fought his way to the Dome of Light but because it was protected by a tilism he was unable to climb it and fell down each time he tried.

Leaving Shadeed trying to climb the dome and his army fighting with the gong-ringers, we return to give an account of what passed with Emperor Afrasiyab when he left Heyrat and entered the dark, secret region of Zulmat.

Afrasiyab crossed the Desert of Being and forded the River of Fire to arrive near the mausoleum of Jamshed. Hundreds of thousands of sorcerers were stationed there in gruesome and dreadful magical guises.

A palace entirely made of jewels was suspended in the air. Thousands of bells hung from the palace of as many domes. The palace was appointed with seven swings where Jamshed's seven handmaidens sat.

As Emperor Afrasiyab approached flying, the bells began ringing and created a din. The handmaidens of Jamshed jumped off the swings and came toward him. Afrasiyab stood on one leg while he prayed to Jamshed and cut a piece of flesh from his other leg to place as an offering on the palace dome.

Upon receiving admittance, when Afrasiyab stepped inside the palace, the seven handmaidens saluted him and asked, "O Emperor of Hoshruba, what brings you here this day?" He answered, "I am headed for the mausoleum of Lord Jamshed." The handmaidens answered, "The mausoleum of Lord Jamshed still lies a long distance away but its boundaries start here. You can receive the gifts of the tilism even at this place. Tell us the purpose of your visit."

Afrasiyab answered, "I seek Lord Jamshed's mantle in my fight against a plague of opponents. Amar Ayyar, who is denounced by the gods in the *Book of Sameri,* has entered the tilism. Thousands of sorcerer disciples of Lord Jamshed have been killed and mutinies brew in Hoshruba."

Jamshed's handmaidens replied, "Lord Jamshed's mantle is yours for the taking: since you are the Emperor of Hoshruba and may do as you please. But you will not find here his ring, necklace and other souvenirs for they lie in the neighboring tilism, Nur Afshan of dazzling light. Alas, you caused the destruction of your lands and now you are eyeing the souvenirs of the tilism. Lord Jamshed had foretold that the last emperor of Hoshruba would be an incompetent bungler; he would lose his writ over the tilism and cause the destruction of all its souvenirs and marvels. It appears, indeed, that you are the one described. It seems our end is near too, for you would one day also order us to fight at your side. the chest in which you will find Lord Jamshed's mantle lies before you. you may take it for all we care!"

With these words, one of the handmaidens flung the key to the chest toward Afrasiyab.

Tears welled up in Afrasiyab's eyes at this speech and he said to them, "I will not take Lord Jamshed's mantle if it displeases you. I made every possible effort not to battle Mahrukh. That was the reason I indulged her even when she committed unforgivable offenses. It is still my desire that the rebels should return to my allegiance. I seek the mantle only to overpower and arrest them and restore them to honor after a quick reprimand."

The handmaidens answered, "When you made all these preparations, why did you not send the trickster girl Sarsar Swordfighter and her companions against Amar Ayyar? She would have guarded the sorcerers you sent and Amar and his tricksters would not have had the field to themselves." Afrasiyab answered, "You speak true. Upon my return I will dispatch the trickster girls against the enemy tricksters."

Afrasiyab then picked up the key to the chest in which Jamshed's mantle lay. When he opened its lid a flame leaped out of it and scorched Afrasiyab. He cut open a vein and made an offering of his blood that extinguished the flame.

Afrasiyab saw Jamshed's jewel-embroidered, silken mantle lying inside, filled with the soil from his grave. The mantle was proof against all magic and rendered useless even powerful magic of mighty sorcerers like Afrasiyab. When it was snapped into the wind against a rival army they fell unconscious, no matter how powerful the sorcerers or how numerous their horde.

Sorcerer Rutas

Afrasiyab flew away after securing Jamshed's mantle and arrived in the Apple Garden in the region of Batin. He recited an incantation and clapped. A mighty sorcerer named Rutas, whose body glowed like fire, emerged from the ground and bowed before the Emperor of Hoshruba.

Afrasiyab said to him, "You are a distinguished sorcerer of the tilism. I confer Lord Jamshed's mantle on you because I can think of no worthier recipient. Take it with you and bring me Mahrukh Magic-Eye and Bahar as prisoners." Rutas answered, "Your Excellency has bestowed too great an honor upon me. I am nothing but a humble slave of Lord Sameri, and a loyal subject and vassal of Your Highness."

Rutas received Jamshed's mantle proudly and put it away with great care. Then he asked Afrasiyab, "Should I depart alone or take an army with me?" Afrasiyab answered, "I already sent an army with Shadeed and others, but do take along twelve thousand sorcerers as a precaution. Depart immediately and bring all prisoners to the Dome of Light where I am now headed. It is within easy reach from all corners of Hoshruba and from its vantage point I will be able to watch over the battle."

While Afrasiyab mounted his throne and departed, Rutas returned to his abode and mustered a twelve-thousand-strong army of sorcerers. The marching drums were beaten and his army set out with its tents and equipage. Rutas rode at the head of the army astride a magic flamingo.

ꕥ

Now we return to Afrasiyab, who arrived near the Dome of Light to see the City of Disregard in turmoil, a great commotion brewing, and the air rent by cries of "Redress! Succor!" Afrasiyab saw sorcerer Shadeed making attempts to climb the Dome of Light and understood immediately that Bahar had cast a spell on him. In his wrath, Afrasiyab wanted to reverse Bahar's magic so that Shadeed's senses would be restored and the same frenzy would overtake Bahar. But one consideration stopped him: that such an action would likely kill Bahar, and even if she survived she would forever hold a grudge against him. He knew it would not do to antagonize or harm his beloved for then his desire would remain unrequited.

Afrasiyab picked a magic citron and hurled it at Shadeed. It shot through his chest and a great din arose as Shadeed died. Afrasiyab then pointed his fingers and ten lightning bolts fell on Shadeed's companions and burned to cinder their gardens of life as well.

The noise and commotion caused by their deaths took a long time to subside. When Afrasiyab finally entered the Dome of Light and Heyrat saluted him, he said, "This was all the doing of your sister Bahar, who put Shadeed under such a powerful spell that he became entirely forgetful of himself. But, ultimately, you must shoulder the blame for her causing the death and destruction of such a large number of my men."

Heyrat answered, "Your Excellency should grant me leave to go and chastise that strumpet." Afrasiyab answered, "I will find a way to arrest and punish Mahrukh since she rebelled against me and my authority. You may have a free hand in the matter of your sister, however. Deal with her as you see fit. I have already sent Rutas with Jamshed's mantle to arrest both Mahrukh and Bahar. If he is unsuccessful, you may advance against them."

Trickster Girls Sarsar Swordfighter, Saba Raftar the Quick, Shamima Tunneler, Sunubar Snare-Roper, and Tez Nigah Dagger-Fighter

Afrasiyab then entered a chamber of the Dome of Light, which looked out over the River of Flowing Blood and a view of the regions of Zahir and Batin. He sat down on a throne and his four ministers and the nobles of the court took their stations. A dance recital began and Heyrat poured wine for the Emperor and passed him the cup.

Afrasiyab ordered a sorcerer to send for his trickster girls. The sorcerer departed for the City of Portraits to deliver the emperor's message.

Afrasiyab had conferred the governorship of the City of Portraits on his chief trickster girl, Sarsar Swordfighter. Saba Raftar the Quick was her minister while Shamima Tunneler, Sunubar Snare-Roper, and Tez Nigah Dagger-Fighter were her deputies and confidants.

The five beautiful, adolescent trickster girls were childhood companions. They were matchless in trickery and despised magic and sorcery. When they received Afrasiyab's message they put on their trickster's livery, armed themselves, and headed for Afrasiyab's court. In due time, they arrived, saluted the emperor and stood humbly awaiting his orders.

Afrasiyab said, "O Sarsar, Amar Ayyar and his trickster companions have entered the tilism and killed hundreds of sorcerers. I thought that sorcery would prevail over trickery just as tyranny is repelled by might. But the tricksters continue to wreak havoc in the land. Because only a trickster knows how to fight another, I am sending you on the campaign against them. Confront them and bring them to me as prisoners. While you do not know magic and sorcery, you will have unimpeded access to all three regions of the tilism. No one will obstruct your way in the regions of Zahir, Batin or Zulmat."

After receiving her orders, Sarsar and the other trickster girls curtsied before Afrasiyab, received robes of departure, and left. They sped like the wind and reached the wilderness near Mahrukh's camp before the arrival of Rutas and his force and busied themselves planning their strategy.

Amar Ayyar and the tricksters were training in the wilderness when they heard the sound of tricksters' bells and pricked up their ears. When they investigated the source they saw five adolescent beauties armed with tricksters' contraptions and weapons, springing forward in giant leaps and strides, suspicious even of their own shadows.

Their hair was tied in buns to one side of their heads, their mantles were knotted in front bracing their shoulders, the bottoms of their pants were tightly fastened and they wore warriors' socks and shoes. Slings were tied to their arms, snare ropes to their heads, and sacks of sling stones hung around their necks. Besides wielding scimitars, daggers, bows, arrows and shields, they were also richly caparisoned with ornaments and jewels.

At their head was Sarsar Swordfighter, sporting the crown of charm and allure, speeding forward with great pomp and splendor. The swellings of her bosom were themselves like two veiled warriors – headstrong and vain. Her gait crushed the hearts of lovers for whom her beauty was like the elephants of calamity and the troopers of catastrophe. Coquetry and dalliance walked in her wake, carrying the skirts of her robe of vanity. She was followed by her minister, Saba Raftar the Quick, whose essence was kneaded with capriciousness, and who had an equal claim on beauty with her dark complexion and conjoined eyebrows.

Beside them were the other three trickster girls, all sprightly and spirited and destroyers of lovers' lives, names and honor. Before their gait, the elegant cypress hid its face in shame; they even taught the rose the vain airs of a beloved.

Upon sighting them, Amar blew his trickster's whistle. Qiran heard it and speedily joined Amar and the other tricksters. The trickster girls drew their daggers upon hearing the whistle, made their war cries and charged Amar Ayyar and his companions.

After deciding on secret codes for combat, the tricksters also shouted their war cries. As Amar charged, Sarsar confronted him. Saba Raftar accosted Qiran, Shamima challenged Burq the Frank, Sunubar encountered Jansoz, and Tez Nigah locked her gaze with Zargham's.

The tricksters were felled by the arrows of love upon beholding their beauty. They were wounded by the darts of their eyelashes and lacerated by the daggers of their eyebrows. Love couplets broke out from their lips.

Amar Ayyar addressed Sarsar, singing,

> *"As a dispersed army takes to marauding*
> *Your loosened black locks destroyed my faith."*

Sarsar attacked with her dagger, saying,

> *"Who die not in the fetters of my locks*
> *They die without faith, I proclaim."*

Qiran said to Saba Raftar, "O charming beloved,

> *"You make my heart your dagger's target*
> *Injure not yourself, it is but your own home."*

Saba Raftar struck with her dagger like lightning, and replied,

> *"There's no remedy for the ill fated ones*
> *None may revoke with a plan what is destined."*

Burq intoned as he confronted Shamima,

> *"A thousand years later when you return*
> *'O Beloved! Greetings!' My grave will call."*

Shamima replied with a smile and a blow of her scimitar,

> *"I wish my enemy to suffer the fate of a tent peg, ever*
> *Hammered, buried in earth with a noose around his neck."*

In the middle of the skirmish, Jansoz addressed Sunubar thus:

> *"The world lies undone but your alluring eyes still dart around*
> *A hundred doomsdays have passed but your beauty has yet begun."*

Sunubar frowned and declaimed with great coquetry and vanity as she came near,

> *"For my tribe a hundred calamities, for my harvest a thousands lightning bolts you are*
> *And yet so plainly still I call you the solace of my heart."*

As Zargham fought with Tez Nigah, he proclaimed,

> *"Are the rules of friendship to be now rewritten*
> *And friends not inquire after friends in love's prison?"*

Tez Nigah laughed at his longing and said,

> *"Don't sing to me the song of your suffering*
> *From hearing this tale alone I burn, Ah! Ah!"*

In short, after exchanging these innuendos and hints, the tricksters and the trickster girls continued fighting with daggers and shields. The trickster girls threw the snare ropes at the tricksters and they coiled around their necks and waists but the tricksters leaped into the air as swiftly – like sight passes through the frame of spectacles. The nooses slid down their feet and fell to the ground. Even as the tricksters landed, they struck with their scimitars and the trickster girls leaped back ten feet in retreat.

They soon spread out in a four mile wide expanse. They ran and chased each other, leaped and gambolled, rolled on the ground locked in combat, attacked each other with eggs of oblivion, ducked and dodged, parried with scimitars and struck with, and blocked daggers. The tricksters locked their swords with the trickster girls, jumped into their laps and tried to steal kisses. The trickster girls would let them come close then bite them.

They fiercely fought each other for two hours until the trickster girls escaped, shouting, "O wretches, you will see how mercilessly we will kill you!"

The tricksters retired to a mountain pass where Amar said to them, "My brothers, I wish to declare in your presence that I have chosen Sarsar as my charming beloved. If any of you kill her, he will have to answer to me." Qiran said, "Yours truly is besotted with Saba Raftar and all tricksters are likewise duty bound to protect her." Then Burq the Frank spoke of his love for Shamima, Jansoz of his passion for Sunubar, and Zargham exacted from the other tricksters a vow of protection for Tez Nigah. Thus, all five of them learned of each other's beloveds.

Amar said, "When Hoshruba is conquered and the trickster girls are arrested, Amir Hamza will have the power to send them to their deaths if they refuse to embrace the True Faith. But in the meanwhile, it would be improper for us to seriously harm them."

Thus the tricksters made a pact that in the battle with the trickster girls they would not harm each other's beloveds. After this council they returned to guard their camp.

The trickster girls also retired to a nook in the wilderness. Sarsar said to Saba Raftar the Quick, "I notice that you look preoccupied. You moisten your lips constantly, have a wan look on your face, walk with an uneven gait, and seem frenetic with your hair all dishevelled. Confess to me what all these signs signify!"

Saba Raftar replied, "Your Honor asks *me* to confess? I did not open my mouth earlier for fear of sounding presumptuous. But now that Your Honor herself teases me, I must allow truth to trump deference: Pray regard your lovely face in the mirror and you will see how plainly love shines from your aspect. With your eyes all moist from desire and your senses in disarray it is little wonder that you search for your symptoms in others." Sarsar answered, "God forbid! It's you who has the habit of falling in love at the very sight of a man. You are indeed mad to suspect *me* of being in love. And even supposing I were in love, my lover is the Emperor of the Tricksters, the first minister of Hamza, his councillor and mind of reason. I can be excused. What are your reasons for falling in love? What makes you think your love compares at all to mine?"

Saba Raftar replied with a little laugh, "Pray do not take offense if I say that the man attracted to me is none other than the favored one of the Conqueror of Conquerors, Ali. He is the Prince of Ethiopes besides, and the one whose labors have often granted Amar a new lease on life. I too, have my reasons as you can see. But I wonder why Shamima, Sunubar and Tez Nigah look love stricken."

Shamima replied, "How wonderful, Saba Raftar! Since you could not reprimand Princess Sarsar, you try to hide your embarrassment by attacking us. I understand why you feel that way. I can see why you make this prattle. You really are a sly one! Well, to each her own! But what fault do you find with my lover? He is a prince from the land of the Franks and a worthy disciple of Amar Ayyar! If you must needs point finger at anyone, point it at Sunubar and Tez Nigah."

Sunubar took exception to this and retorted, "You have the bad habit, Shamima, of using others to say what's in your heart. It is you who are lustful. Although my lover is far superior to yours, I think little of him. If Saba Raftar says Qiran is the favored one of Ali and the Prince of Ethiopes, let me tell you that my lover is Jansoz, his son. Yet, he may pine away for love of me all he wants; I will remain deaf to his entreaties. What of that, fourteen thousand men like him sigh and suffer for love of me! The charge you lay on me would stick only on Tez Nigah."

Tez Nigah answered, "For shame! You try to stick all kinds of blame on me. Everyone likes to speak well of their own. I have nothing to do with Zargham but if someone claims that he loves me, I would only say that he is better than all those whom you have just praised. First of all, like Qiran, he is also a favored one. Moreover, he is the personal trickster of the Conqueror of the Tilism, who will one day rule Hoshruba. If you ask me, anyone who resides in the tilism may be deemed his subject already."

Sarsar laughed uproariously at that and said, "Congratulations! May Your Honor live long! From today we must salute you since we are your lover's humble subjects. With him as our lord and master, we need not fear a thing!"

Tez Nigah broke into a sweat from embarrassment as everyone began teasing her. She replied, "Why do you think of me as the crazy one? All of you praised your swains but the moment I opened my mouth you started making fun of me. I am not good at dissimulation whereas all of you are loquacious and shameless. How you keep at it! And when I retort you make fun of me all over again!"

Saba Raftar answered, "Listen girl, don't get so prickly and tetchy. There's no reason to feel embarrassed. The only thing our princess ever said was that we have now become your subjects. After your preposterous comment, that was all she could say. Don't make such ridiculous claims again if you don't wish to sound silly."

The five of them carried on the friendly feud for some time as an excuse to identify their lovers to their companions. An unspoken arrangement was reached that, for the sake of appearances, they would continue to battle the tricksters but protect them in secret. Then they dispersed.

In the meanwhile, Rutas, with his twelve thousand sorcerers, arrived and bivouacked near Mahrukh Magic-Eye's camp. When Mahrukh received the news she too, alerted and warned her camp. The tricksters and trickster girls also witnessed the arrival of Rutas's forces and began planning their respective strategies.

Rutas rested for a day. The next evening, when King Sun retired to his western post after making his round of the sky, and the torch of the moon was lit in the heavens, the heavens' old farmer, carrying the mattock of the Milky Way, arrived in the field of sky to water the crop of stars.

The beating of the drums of war and trilling of the magic bugles was heard from Rutas's camp and the air was rent by the cries of "Slay! Slaughter!"

Magic birds flew into Queen Mahjabeen's court and proclaimed with great decorum, "*The enemy has struck the drums of war and harbours impious intentions.*" Mahrukh Magic-Eye said, "Order the drums of war to answer from our camp. God is our Protector." Immediately, her officers struck the drums of war and martial music from the Turkic flutes began floating on the air.

Every warrior became alert and busied himself in preparation for battle. For four watches of the night the air was filled with the noises of sorcerers preparing their spells and the din of the braves readying their weapons. Finally it was time, when the Beautifier of the World[86] held up the mirror of sun before the lovely face of the beloved morn[87] and, filling the parting of the coiffure of World's Bride with dawn's sandal dust, displayed its luminous face to the world.

At the break of dawn, Mahrukh, Bahar and Nafarman began marching toward the arena with their armed contingents. Queen Mahjabeen arrived in the battlefield with great fanfare in the company of Prince Asad. At that moment, the enemy forces also entered the arena. The sorcerers arrayed themselves. The warriors made ranks. The battlefield was readied and the criers proclaimed, "O braves, this world is the abode of grief and admonition. This field of carnage is the domain of honor and distinction. You must barter your valor to take away riches from this field. None has remained and none shall remain but the name of the brave and valiant alone."

After the criers became silent, Rutas himself came forward and displayed his magic by creating a shower of stones. He then called out, "O ingrate rebels, is there anyone among you who dares to face me and withstand my magic?"

While the sorcerers loyal to Mahrukh stirred to answer his challenge, Rutas recited a spell and clapped. Suddenly, thousands upon thousands of magic birds came flying from the direction of the wilderness and began perching on the heads of Mahrukh's soldiers. Whenever a magic bird landed on someone's head he immediately turned into a tree, shoots sprouted from his body, green leafs covered him, branches protruded swaying from his trunk, and birds made their nests in them.

Mahrukh, Shakeel and other renowned sorcerers recited counterspells to ward off Rutas's magic.

The charming Bahar gave audience with utmost glory on a peacock throne. She surmised that by displaying his magic and turning her soldiers into trees, Rutas indirectly challenged her.

She descended from her throne and, adjusting her mantle, arrived before Rutas. She undid her hair, took out a small box and opened its lid. Inside it was a small, beautifully carved ivory figurine. Bahar cut her finger and let fall a few drops of blood onto the ivory figurine and said, "O magic slave girl of Sameri, regard the magic birds that perch on my men and turn them into trees. Is this how you recompense me for bestowing you the honor of placing you on my head?"

The magic slave girl laughed, leapt out of the box, and disappeared.

A few moments later everyone noticed a colossal net spread over the length and breadth of the sky. They saw flocks of Rutas's magic birds struggling inside the net. The magic slave girl, with a knife in her hand, brought the birds out from the net and slaughtered them. Their blood splashed on the trees and returned them to human form.

When Rutas witnessed this scene and saw Bahar standing before him he realized that she would, momentarily, cast a spell over him too; he would be unable to break it and it would bring an inglorious end to his mission.

Rutas took out Jamshed's mantle, flew up by magic and snapped it in the air above Mahrukh's army, releasing the soil of Jamshed's grave. Including Bahar, Mahrukh, and Queen Mahjabeen, all the commanders of Prince Asad's camp fell unconscious. Finding their commanders incapacitated, panic took hold of the army. A stampede began and Rutas's sorcerers took thousands of prisoners. Rutas put them in magic handcuffs and fetters and again snapped Jamshed's mantle, saying, "O mantle, I ask you in the name of Lord Jamshed to revive those who are unconscious so that they may witness their sorry plight and take admonition." Bahar, Mahrukh and others at once regained consciousness. Finding themselves prisoners and helpless, they kept silent.

Rutas told his army that he was tired from the battle and would take the prisoners to Afrasiyab's court the following day. He ordered his men to rest. His army bivouacked and the captives were incarcerated and vigils deputed.

Rutas retired to his pavilion and sat on his throne. He ordered his menials and attendants to remain outside and sat inside with his mistress. Fearing that the tricksters would make him their target, he recited a spell that would cause anyone entering his pavilion, other than his mistress, to immediately fall unconscious. Finally, he felt at peace and occupied himself with pleasure-seeking.

The tricksters saw from a distance how Rutas had imprisoned their companions. They held a council and entered Rutas's camp in disguise. Zargham called one of Rutas's attendants over and said, "I have something important to tell you." When the attendant came with him to a secluded spot, Zargham hit him in the face with an egg of oblivion. Then, taking off his clothes and disguising himself as the attendant, Zargham returned. When he headed for Rutas's pavilion, the servants said to him, "Don't go in. It is forbidden." Zargham said, "I have good reason for entering the pavilion." But the moment Zargham stepped in, he fell unconscious. Rutas caught him and blew a spell that made the makeup evaporate and Zargham's real face appear. The sorcerer imprisoned him in his pavilion with a spell and resumed cavorting with his mistress.

Next, Jansoz neared his pavilion disguised as a dazzling, beautiful cupbearer and said to the attendants, "I am looking for employment. If your master can spare a moment I would like to solicit his attention." The servants replied, "We have orders to keep everyone away. Still, if you wish to go in we will not stop you, but you must bear the blame for his displeasure." Jansoz said, "I will return momentarily, after a quick word with him." He took a few steps into the pavilion and fell unconscious. Rutas arrested him as well, and also made Jansoz's makeup disappear with a spell. As Rutas returned to his mistress, he realized that the tricksters had begun their attacks.

Burq saw from far how the two tricksters had entered Rutas's pavilion but failed in their mission. He made exploratory rounds in the vicinity and reached the personal pavilion of Rutas's mistress where he saw one of her servant boys preparing her hookah. Burq said to him, "O evil boy, why did you beat my dog yesterday?" The servant boy was confounded and wondered what dog he was being questioned about. He said to Burq, "I think you are mistaken." Burq dragged him away by his ear, shouting, "So now you deny everything! Let me take you to the witness. Let him narrate your deeds before you. Then you'll see what a fine thrashing you'll receive at my hands." Burq took him to a deserted corner, rendered him unconscious, and disguised himself as the boy. Then he returned to the camp and started preparing the hookah.

An attendant arrived in the meanwhile and said, "The lady wants her hookah and you still drag your feet and laze around." Burq replied, "It's ready. It only has to be lit." He quickly mixed a drug with the tobacco, readied the hookah, and handed it to the attendant. The attendant said, "Take it inside yourself; we are not allowed to enter the pavilion." When Burq entered the pavilion, he too fell unconscious and Rutas arrested him like the other tricksters. He recited a spell that removed Burq's disguise and revealed his real appearance.

Rutas thought, *Lords Sameri and Jamshed must be looking upon me with favor since I have arrested the tricksters without any great effort.* He put a spell on the tricksters that incapacitated their limbs then resumed love play with his mistress.

Amar Ayyar now entered Rutas's camp in the disguise of the trickster girl Saba Raftar the Quick, carrying a forged order from Afrasiyab that was carefully layered with fine drug powder and sealed. The false Saba Raftar arrived at Rutas's pavilion and said to the attendants, "Inform your master that Saba Raftar has arrived with a message from the emperor." The attendants replied, "We are not allowed entry but you may enter the pavilion."

The false Saba Raftar realized that there was some reason why they refused to enter. She called out from the entrance, "O Rutas, I am Saba Raftar. I have brought you the emperor's letter." Rutas said, "Come inside!" She answered, "Is this how you greet your emperor's missive? You aren't bothered even to come to the pavilion's entrance? You must be on very familiar terms with the Emperor of Hoshruba to act in this manner!" Rutas felt embarrassed at these words and stepped out.

The false Saba Raftar greeted Rutas, handed him the letter, and asked for a reply. Rutas said to her, "Please come inside and have a drink while I write a reply." She said, "You freely invite anyone who calls on you into your pavilion? Have you no fear of the tricksters?" Rutas answered, "The pavilion is enclosed in a spell. Any trickster who enters it will be rendered unconscious." She said, "I am a trickster girl and don't know any magic. Why would you call me inside only to render me unconscious? I had a feeling you had taken some precautions against the tricksters and wasn't going to enter and break my limbs by falling."

Rutas praised her cunning highly and removed the spell from the pavilion. Then he led her inside by the hand. The false Saba Raftar saw the three tricksters lying motionless in a corner. A beautiful and charming courtesan was sitting on a throne, clad in finery and adorned with gold. The false Saba Raftar sat to one side. As Rutas pulled out the paper the drug powder flew out and he got a whiff of its perfume. Curious about the strange scent, he sniffed the letter and immediately fell unconscious. The false Saba Raftar threw an egg of oblivion at the courtesan's face and made her unconscious too. Then, without loss of time, she drew her dagger and beheaded Rutas. The magic spirits cried out and fire and stones rained from the sky.

The three tricksters imprisoned by Rutas's spell were freed upon his death. While Amar Ayyar took off the courtesan's jewelery, the rest of his tricksters ransacked the pavilion. Burq reached for and secured Jamshed's mantle, jumped over the wall of the pavilion, and escaped. Hearing the commotion, sorcerers from Rutas's camp came running to the scene. Amar and the other tricksters escaped by jumping over the pavilion walls.

When Rutas was killed, Mahrukh and her companion sorcerers also found themselves free of his spell. Bahar and Mahrukh flew by invoking their magic and hurled pepper garlands, needle clusters, and steel magic balls at the enemy from above. Magic clouds billowed into the sky, thunderous noises were heard, lightning flashed and thunderbolts fell. A flaming shower of fire rained down. Bahar hurled a bouquet that made spring appear. Thousands of enemy sorcerers headed into the wilderness in a frenzied state. Mahrukh and Shakeel slew thousands of them. Nafarman and Surkh Mu Wonder-Mane fired arrows and caused a rain of stars.

Then fire and stones fell from the skies
The smoke from the magic fires rose
Flames arose now from one direction, now from another
The sorcerers' magic spirits made plaints
Thousands laid down their lives in great misery
Many turned tail to escape alive

In the end, Rutas's army was routed and destroyed. Mahrukh and Mahjabeen returned to their camp victorious and covered in glory. The criers announced the end of hostilities. Mahrukh's army, which had dispersed in the mountainside, began to return. The camp was populated as before, and celebrations began.

ꟗ

After he escaped from the pavilion of Rutas, Amar looked for the trickster who had taken Jamshed's mantle to confiscate it from him. He went into the wilderness and blew his whistle. Zargham and Jansoz presented themselves but Burq did not show his face, fearful that Amar would snatch the mantle.

Amar asked Zargham and Jansoz, "Who among you took Jamshed's mantle?" They answered, "We swear by our loyalty to the Lord of the Auspicious Planetary Conjunction that we did not take it." Amar said, "Burq did not come at my whistle. It would seem that he took it."

Whip in his hand, Amar started out in search of Burq.

After Burq escaped from Rutas's pavilion it occurred to him that Amar would certainly snatch the mantle from him if he stayed in the region of Zahir. He thought, *Master has his zambil and his cape of invisibility. I have nothing to protect me against sorcery. I should not surrender Jamshed's mantle to him.* Thus decided, Burq headed toward the region of Batin.

Now hear of the trickster girls. They were planning their strategy to foil and arrest the tricksters when Rutas was killed and the ensuing clamor rose from his camp. Sarsar said to Saba Raftar, "O Saba Raftar, Amar Ayyar's killing Rutas does not bode well for us. The emperor will blame us and claim that we were unable to protect him. We must arrest the tricksters without loss of time."

All of them dispersed to hunt for the tricksters. While Saba Raftar went toward the Dome of Light, Sarsar headed for Mahrukh's camp.

On her way, Sarsar saw Amar standing at a vantage point searching for Burq, whip in hand, dispatching the couriers of thought in all directions. Sarsar disguised herself as Burq in a nook, then ran out within sight of Amar Ayyar. He rushed after the false Burq and said to him, "O Burq, tell me truthfully if it was you who took Jamshed's mantle; if so, you must surrender it to me immediately." The false Burq clasped his hands together in supplication, prostrated himself at Amar's feet and said, "Master, please bestow the mantle on me!" Amar cracked the whip, saying, "Have you taken leave of your senses? Surrender it this instant!" The false Burq pulled Amar's feet and as he fell, hit him in the face with an egg of oblivion. Amar was rendered unconscious. Sarsar spread out the trickster's cloak, secured Amar's arms, legs, waist and neck with the loops of the snare rope and bundled him up. She then slung Amar over her shoulder, tied a trickster's knot in front, and sped like an arrow for the Dome of Light.

The real Burq was headed toward the Dome of Light and saw Saba Raftar speeding away in the same direction. He quickly disguised himself as Sarsar and appeared within sight of Saba Raftar, who called out, "Your Honor, where are you headed?" The false Sarsar answered, "We must not stop here. Come with me to a safe spot." When Saba Raftar approached, the false Sarsar caught her hand and said, "These tricksters are the devil's own progeny. I just had an encounter with Amar Ayyar, who is now hiding here in the bushes. We must surround him, you from one side, I from another."

As they advanced toward the bushes the false Sarsar suddenly exclaimed, "Who is following us?" When Saba Raftar turned to look, the false Sarsar hit her in the face with an egg of oblivion and made her unconscious.

The false Sarsar changed her own disguise to Saba Raftar's and put Amar Ayyar's disguise on her. Then the false Saba Raftar made a bundle of the false Amar Ayyar and, throwing him over her shoulder, headed toward the Dome of Light.

Because Burq possessed Jamshed's mantle, he was able to cross the River of Flowing Blood in Saba Raftar's disguise and arrive at the Dome of Light without incident. A few sorcerers he met along the way asked him, "Whom have you captured Saba Raftar?" The false Saba Raftar always gave the same reply: "I have caught Amar Ayyar!"

Thousands of sorcerers stood before Afrasiyab at the Dome of Light. A dance recital was in progress with the emperor giving audience when the false Saba Raftar arrived, saluted the emperor, and threw the bundle in front of him. Afrasiyab asked her, "Who is inside the bundle?" She replied, "It is none other than Amar Ayyar!" Then she opened the bundle and tied the real Saba Raftar disguised as Amar Ayyar to a column.

In the meanwhile, Sarsar also arrived at the Dome of Light carrying Amar Ayyar. A great commotion rose when it was heard that Sarsar also brought Amar Ayyar in a bundle.

The false Saba Raftar said to Afrasiyab, "Your Honor, it seems that after I captured Amar Ayyar some enemy trickster disguised himself as Sarsar to gain entrance here. I will hide and then you can arrest the one who claims to be Sarsar." The false Saba Raftar then crept out of sight under Afrasiyab's throne.

In the meanwhile, Sarsar entered and placed Amar Ayyar's bundle before Afrasiyab. A sorcerer arrested Sarsar at a sign from the emperor and opened the bundle she had brought. The false Saba Raftar crept out from under Afrasiyab's throne. Seeing Amar Ayyar trussed up in the bundle, she began crying loudly and said, "Your Excellency, this enemy trickster has disguised himself as Sarsar and made the real Sarsar into the likeness of Amar Ayyar." Afrasiyab now released the real Amar Ayyar and ordered the real Sarsar to be tied to a column.

The false Saba Raftar planned to drug the wine. In the meanwhile, Sarsar cried out, "Your Excellency, you have been deceived. I am the real Sarsar." But despite her crying and making protestations, nobody paid her any heed.

The false Saba Raftar said to Sarsar in a whisper, "I am Burq, my dear mistress. Not only did you take my master captive but you also run about in full view of strangers without a veil. What would you say if I clipped the tip of your nose as a reprimand?" Sarsar began crying and asking for help. The false Saba Raftar said, "Give a good thrashing to this enemy trickster."

When Sarsar was beaten black and blue she cried out to Afrasiyab, "Your Excellency, why do you not consult the *Book of Sameri*. It will reveal my true identity."

Afrasiyab liked her counsel and sent for the *Book of Sameri*. At that moment the false Saba Raftar said, "Your Excellency, I would like to share a confidence with you. But I must whisper it in your ear." As Afrasiyab leaned toward her, she plucked Afrasiyab's crown with one hand, and smacked him with the other. Then she cried out, "I am Burq the Frank!" and ran to escape.

Afrasiyab ordered, "Don't let him get away!"

Reciting their spells, the sorcerers ran to catch Burq. In the ensuing chaos, Amar Ayyar, who was now free, began looting the place. He took out the Net of Ilyas and with one sweep carried away Heyrat's betel box, golden vanity box, and jewel-encrusted chair, stowing it all in his zambil.

In panic, Afrasiyab stood on his throne and recited a spell that sent thousands of magic slaves running to his assistance. Amar put on the cape of invisibility and climbed down the Dome of Light. Burq also rushed downstairs. Sorcerers targeted him with their spells but, because Burq possessed Jamshed's mantle, the spells had no effect on him. Those who drew near to arrest him found their bodies breaking out in flames and catching fire from the power of Jamshed's mantle. Thus, all the sorcerers returned unsuccessful.

Afrasiyab ordered the real Sarsar and Saba Raftar to be released and offered them words of consolation and comfort.

Amar and Burq now began looting the City of Disregard. Amar flung the Net of Ilyas on shops and swept away their entire contents to the very last carpet on the floor. When the hue and cry rose in the marketplace shops started shutting down in panic.

A passer by asked a shopkeeper, "Why all the commotion?" The shopkeeper answered, "Amar Ayyar has entered the city and is ransacking the bazaar." The passerby thought it unlikely that Amar alone could ransack the whole city, reckoning that he must have brought his whole army to help him. He went on his way and said to all he met, "Run for your lives! The enemy armies have invaded. Blood is flowing in the streets."

A man who heard that account ran in terror. Seeing him run, others also ran. Soon they began stampeding in all directions. Everyone kept repeating, "The enemy army has invaded."

People ran down the streets holding the hands of their children. Some inquired after safe conduits to escape with their families. One man began crying loudly that all of them were trapped and doomed.

The braves armed themselves and sat with great aplomb outside their homes, ready to give their lives to defend their honor. Their acquaintances brought them news constantly, reporting, "Sirs, you must not stay here. Why give your life for nothing? The jewelers' market was put to the sword. The square is being looted. We are leaving. You must join us." But the braves answered them, "We will first challenge the intruders and if that does not deter them we will fight to our last breath. Our swordplay will teach a fine lesson to the invaders."

Amar Ayyar and Burq the Frank continued their ravages in the disorder that prevailed. The money traders lost their money bags and the jewellers their jewel boxes. The haberdashery was looted, the clothiers' bundles disappeared, pots and pans vanished before people's eyes. People dropped all their belongings and ran to save their lives. Others jumped into their neighbors' empty houses to pillage and steal. Some thought it best to throw their arms, armor and belongings into empty wells for safekeeping. Some took refuge in cellars. One man called others claiming that his brother was employed in Amar Ayyar's army and he possessed a note guaranteeing reprieve to all who took refuge with him.

When Afrasiyab was apprised of this upheaval in the city and told that the populace was running to seek refuge from Prince Asad's forces, he ordered that sorcerers should set out and destroy the army of the foe. As the sorcerers departed on their mission Afrasiyab and Heyrat also came down from the Dome of Light.

The empress recited a spell and immediately hundreds of thousands of dragons materialized and charged toward the city.

Amar Ayyar took refuge under Daniyal's Tent and Burq the Frank put on Jamshed's mantle. They hid themselves as the dragons swallowed people in the streets. The sight confirmed the rumors that the enemy army had attacked the city. It resulted in even greater chaos and pandemonium. When the dragons returned to Empress Heyrat after swallowing the citizens of the City of Disregard, she said to Afrasiyab, "My dragons swallowed up the entire enemy army!"

While she was making this claim, a sorcerer carrying a bundle on his back arrived in Afrasiyab's court and saluted the emperor. Afrasiyab asked him what he had brought. The sorcerer replied, "I have brought you Amar Ayyar!" and started untying the bundle. As everyone leaned forward to see, the sorcerer jumped up and smacked Afrasiyab and took away his second crown too. Then he called out, "I am Burq the Frank," and ran away.

Afrasiyab's minister, Sanat Magic-Maker, recited a powerful spell that caused the loss of consciousness in everyone except Afrasiyab and Heyrat. However, it had no effect on Burq because of Jamshed's mantle. Everyone regained consciousness after Sanat Magic-Maker recited a counterspell.

In the meanwhile, the trickster girl, Shamima Tunneler, arrived and stood in a corner after saluting Afrasiyab. The emperor said to her, "Go and bring me Amar Ayyar." Shamima replied, "If Your Excellency does not take offense, I can suggest a method to capture Amar Ayyar." Afrasiyab bid her speak but Shamima requested privacy. Afrasiyab granted her request and met her in seclusion. The trickster girl jumped up and whacked Afrasiyab and took off the emperor's third crown, declaring, "I am Burq the Frank!" Again the trickster ran and escaped.

This time, Afrasiyab's second ranking minister, Sarma Ice-Hurler, cast a spell and slabs of ice began falling from the sky. It became freezing cold and the teeth chattered in people's mouths. These calamities killed hundreds of sorcerers in the city. Sarma Ice-Hurler finally revoked his spell and said, "By now Amar Ayyar and Burq the Frank must have been killed."

Just then a sorcerer came running into the court and exclaimed, "Your Excellency, I seek redress. I am being looted." As Afrasiyab clapped to see what passed with Amar Ayyar, the sorcerer suddenly cried, "Burq the Frank stands behind you ready to steal your crown!" When Afrasiyab turned around, the sorcerer jumped up, clouted Afrasiyab, snatched his fourth crown and made away with it, crying, "I am Burq the Frank!"

Afrasiyab's third ranking minister, Baghban Magic-Gardener, tore off and flung one of the garlands from around his neck. Immediately, thousands of beds of roses sprang up all over. The flowers soon bloomed and red birds[88] flew out of them and began searching everywhere for Amar and Burq. But Amar lay in the safety of Daniyal's Tent and Burq could not be located because of the power of Jamshed's mantle.

Unable to find the tricksters, the red birds began landing on the citizenry. The moment a bird landed on anyone's head he lost his mind and, roaring with passion and reciting love couplets, headed for the jungle. The whole city was overtaken by a strange madness and people embraced and kissed each other. Seeing that his spell had failed to capture any trickster, Baghban Magic-Gardener revoked it.

Suddenly, Burq appeared before them without a disguise. Afrasiyab recited a spell and everyone saw the floating, life-sized Magic Mirror materialize, which displayed his image at its center. From a distance, Burq threw a stone at it but it was deflected by the mirror.

Afrasiyab's fourth minister, Abriq Mount-Splitter, recited a spell over some magic stones and hurled them at Burq. Those stones became giant hills and flew toward Burq. But because he was in possession of Jamshed's mantle they seemed to him only the size of pebbles. However, when they fell on the city – heaven's mercy – they buried and killed thousands of inhabitants, causing great upheaval in the city. The powerful sorcerers managed to emerge from under them by reciting counterspells but many ordinary sorcerers died upon impact. Abriq Mount-Splitter finally revoked his magic upon hearing the furore.

Amar emerged from Daniyal's Tent and, wearing his cape of invisibility, continued to loot the city. He then moved Daniyal's Tent to where Afrasiyab stood. The courtiers saw Amar lying on a jewel-enchased bed inside the tent while two fairies pressed his legs. Afrasiyab declared to his courtiers, "Amar seems a most powerful sorcerer. Are there any among you who can overcome and arrest him?" A sorcerer named Tamtaraq stepped forward at the emperor's call and, reciting a spell, stepped into Daniyal's Tent. Immediately, his legs went up and his head went down and he was suspended upside down, all his magic forgotten.

Amar got up from the bed and made a coal fire. Then he cut off a piece of Tamtaraq's flesh. When he howled with pain, Amar said to him, "O bastard, I will now roast you as I am partial to sorcerer flesh!" Hearing this speech, the sorcerers were terrified. Tamtaraq's brother, Waqwaq, came running and said to Amar, "Don't eat my brother! I will pay you a thousand gold pieces." Amar answered, "I would not settle for less than five thousand." Waqwaq replied, "Very well! You will have your five thousand gold pieces but you must release my brother." He brought five thousand gold pieces and piled them near Daniyal's Tent.

Amar first made Tamtaraq unconscious and cut off the tip of his tongue. Then with a sweep of the Net of Ilyas, he collected the gold pieces and threw Tamtaraq out.

Waqwaq carried away his brother. Seeing that Tamtaraq was unable to speak and discovering that the tip of his tongue had been severed, Waqwaq was enraged. He targeted Amar with all kinds of magic, raining stones on Daniyal's Tent and lighting an inferno around it. But he was unable to inflict any harm on Amar or the tent.

Amar now pulled out the four columns of Daniyal's Tent and raised it over his head like a parasol. Both Amar and Burq headed out of the court.

When Afrasiyab consulted the *Book of Sameri* he saw it had become blank. He said, "I will also leave now!" and departed.

At that moment, a dark dust cloud rose and thousands of gongs and bells rang out in the skies. The conveyance of another Afrasiyab arrived with great pomp and ceremony and everyone paid him their respects.

It so happened that after Burq deceived Afrasiyab in Saba Raftar's disguise, Afrasiyab looked in the palm of his left hand to read his fortune and learned that for him the next two watches of the day would be inauspicious; it would be best for him to depart and save himself the disgrace he would expose himself to by remaining there longer. Afrasiyab clapped and softly called out, "Come, O my magic double!" It immediately materialized and replaced Afrasiyab, and the emperor disappeared. The sorcerers present in the court were too occupied with the tricksters' antics to notice the change.

Afrasiyab now addressed his magic double in the Magic Mirror, "You may leave now! I regret the indignities you suffered at the hands of the tricksters!" At these words, Afrasiyab's magic double dissolved away in the mirror.

Now, when Afrasiyab consulted the *Book of Sameri* he saw written there:

> "Magic had no effect on Burq because he was in possession of Jamshed's mantle. What pressing need had you to acquire a piece of Lord Jamshed's clothing and a gift of the tilism? It was on account of this contumely that your double was buffeted and disgraced by Burq. Had you stayed in the court, you'd have suffered the same fate."

Seeing the resourcefulness and reach of the tricksters, Afrasiyab was enraged and said to his trickster girls, "Fools! Did I depute you so that the tricksters could wreak havoc in my city?" Sarsar replied, "O mighty emperor! I had arrested Amar Ayyar at your august orders even though he is the Prince of Tricksters and it was no easy task to capture him. But Your Excellency did not deem my protestations worthy of your attention. However, I will fulfill your wishes again."

Afrasiyab said, "Burq can cross over the River of Flowing Blood because he is in possession of Jamshed's mantle. But Amar does not have any tilism gifts and will not be able to cross. If he took the route from where Prince Asad entered the tilism, he would not have to cross the river. However, the distance to his camp would grow longer. The path would stretch to become equal to the length Prince Asad has traveled into the tilism. You must follow Amar and arrest him regardless of the route he chooses. Once you have accomplished your mission, send me the news and remain stationed across the River of Flowing Blood. I will kill Amar in full view of Mahrukh Magic-Eye and her camp."

Sarsar left after receiving her orders.

Be it known that the City of Disregard had forty doors, each of which opened onto a different path. Some doors led out of Hoshruba. Other doors led out of the region of Batin to the banks of the River of Flowing Blood. Yet other doors led from Batin directly into Zahir, bypassing the river.

Sarsar thought that Amar must have taken the latter route. To search for him she followed the path that bypassed the river and entered Zahir.

Sorcerer Namrud

After Sarsar left, Afrasiyab addressed his court, saying, "I find myself in a bind. Whenever I dispatch someone to capture Bahar, he is promptly killed. Is there no one among you who can go and bring me Bahar as a prisoner?"

A sorcerer named Namrud rose from his seat and said, "The servants of the Emperor are not helpless before rebels like Bahar. I ask leave to depart on the campaign. In the flash of an eye, I will bring her to you as a captive." Afrasiyab answered, "Very well! You have my permission. Take the army along."

Namrud replied, "It would be unworthy of me to fight Bahar with an army's help. Moreover, it is difficult to identify tricksters when they infiltrate a large army to work their mischief. I shall not take any attendants along either. I will barge directly into Mahrukh Magic-Eye's camp and arrest Bahar. I'll see how they stop me!"

Namrud invoked his magic, grew wings, and flew away.

Now hear of Burq the Frank. He was able to cross over the River of Flowing Blood by virtue of Jamshed's mantle. But when he arrived in the region of Zahir he was seen by the trickster girls Shamima, Sunubar and Tez Nigah. They challenged him and both parties drew swords.

Although Burq was all alone, he acquitted himself with great distinction. Soon Jansoz also happened by and joined Burq in the fight. The two of them fought their way out of the trickster girls' cordon. Burq, who was fearful of someone snatching Jamshed's mantle from him, separated from Jansoz and headed out on his own.

The trickster girls pursued them. Finding Jansoz alone, they surrounded him. Sunubar threw her snare rope at him from behind. As Jansoz jumped out of its loops Shamima threw another that entangled him. Jansoz fell down and Tez Nigah quickly made him unconscious with an egg of oblivion. With Shamima's help she made a bundle of him and gave it to Sunubar, saying, "Take him to the emperor. The two of us will now look for the other tricksters."

As Sunubar carried the bundle to Afrasiyab's court she was sighted by the trickster Zargham. He ran two miles ahead of Sunubar and spread out the loops of his snare rope along her path and covered them with grass. Holding the other end of the snare rope in his hands, Zargham hid himself in the bushes and waited.

When Sunubar approached the trap her heartbeat quickened with a sense of foreboding. As a precautionary measure, she called out, "O trickster, I recognize you!" Zargham thought that Sunubar had indeed recognized him and decided to come out of the bushes, but then paused and wondered if Sunubar only pretended to have seen him. He decided to remain hidden a little longer. While he made these calculations, Sunubar loaded and fired her slingshot. The stone fell close to Zargham. Now he was convinced that Sunubar had indeed seen him. He was about to emerge from his hiding place when Sunubar shot her sling in another direction. Zargham concluded that Sunubar had made those claims in pretence to deceive her enemies. He remained hidden and on the alert.

After satisfying herself that nobody lay in ambush for her and the dread she felt was only on account of her solitude, Sunubar leapt to continue on her way and landed right in the middle of Zargham's trap. She was about to make a second leap and clear it when Zargham roared like a lion. As Sunubar momentarily hesitated, he pulled the end of the snare rope; its loops closed on Sunubar and she fell down. In one leap Zargham reached her side and made her unconscious with an egg of oblivion. Then he untied Jansoz and restored him to consciousness.

Zargham was tying Sunubar to a tree when Sarsar arrived there in her search of Amar. Seeing that the tricksters had taken Sunubar prisoner, Sarsar drew her short sword and charged them, shouting, "O wretches, now you won't escape from my hands!"

Zargham and Jansoz drew daggers and confronted her, saying, "Our lady, the day master Amar conquers you he will make you sift grain and turn the hand mill. He provides his wives neither food nor clothes and makes them press his legs all night besides." Sarsar said, "May I inter your master in a deep grave! May his life end in the prime of youth! I will show you whose lady I am! I will teach you wretches a fine lesson!"

Sarsar showered them with abuse and started fighting. Her short sword and their daggers flashed liked lightning. Sarsar fought her way to where Sunubar lay and hit her in the face with an egg of awareness. Sunubar sneezed and regained consciousness. She also joined the fray and the tricksters no longer had the upper hand against Sarsar. However, Sarsar did not wish to be deterred from her mission to catch Amar and sped away in the middle of the fight. Seeing her escape, Sunubar too, ran away after dodging the tricksters.

When Sarsar arrived at the banks of the River of Flowing Blood she saw Amar wandering on the other side, searching for a way to cross again into Zahir. Sarsar crossed over into Batin and threw a muslin kerchief steeped in perfume drug along Amar's path. When Amar passed along he noticed an expensive kerchief lying on the ground with its corners knotted up. Amar picked it up and found fifty gold pieces tied from one corner, some rupees and coins from another, and sweet betel nuts and cardamoms from a third. He thought it must have been dropped there by one of Batin's noble sorcerers.

As he put away the gold pieces and the rupees into his zambil the smell of the perfume drug filled his mind. He swooned and dropped unconscious to the ground. Sarsar made her war cry and came out from her hiding place. While making a bundle of Amar she decided to summon a trickster girl and dispatch her to Afrasiyab's court to apprise the emperor of these developments.

Burq saw Sarsar from far away and crossed over into Batin disguised as the trickster girl Tez Nigah. He made his hairdo like the trickster girl's, wore a greenish yellow mantle and colored his lips with *missi* and betel juice. He made the cast of a severed head from pasteboard and also made arms and legs covered with false skin. Then he took out a bottle of blood from his trickster's bag and, covering his own head with the pasteboard cast, poured blood all over it and on its exposed veins. Attaching the pasteboard neck to the head with a strap of false skin, he scattered the pasteboard limbs around to give it the appearance of a dismembered corpse. Then he lay down on the path he reckoned Sarsar would take and hid his limbs under his clothes.

In due time, Sarsar passed that way and saw a dismembered corpse. Fresh blood flowed from the neck attached to the head with a shred of skin. Sarsar's heart sank when she approached and recognized Tez Nigah's face. Her eyes welled up with tears. Sarsar dropped Amar's bundle and embraced the corpse crying and loudly wailing, "Alas, those wretched tricksters killed my sister. Alas my sister Tez Nigah! You were separated from me!"

As she was crying, a jet of blood shot out from the slit throat of the corpse and sprayed Sarsar's face. She sneezed and fell unconscious. Burq the Frank made his war cry and got up. Spreading his trickster's mantle, he laid Sarsar on it and placed Amar beside her. Then he applied plugs of restorative salts to their nostrils and both Amar and Sarsar regained consciousness.

Burq now approached Sarsar, greeted her and said, "Pray accept my salutations, O my lady! Look at you lying shamelessly here in broad daylight beside my master. If you could not find a garden nook for pleasure-seeking at least you should have taken the trouble to retire into a pavilion. You must not forsake the minimum requisites of decency."

As Burq said these words, Amar Ayyar opened his eyes and, finding himself lying next to Sarsar, amorously embraced her, crying, "Come to me, O Life of the World! O Solace of the Hearts of Lovers!"

Finding herself in that predicament, Sarsar answered, "You bastards deserving of beheading! You sucked on the teats of a bitch as infants." With that she kicked Amar as he amorously called out,

"O to hear the jingle of your ankle bells
When your feet drum my chest on the night of union."

Sarsar blushed crimson at these words. She leapt away and escaped.

Amar now caught Burq's hand and said, "Son, I will not ask for Jamshed's mantle from you. But do come along with me to the court." Amar led him to the court where Burq presented Afrasiyab's four crowns to Asad and Mahjabeen, who made an offering of them to Amar. Queen Mahjabeen conferred several hundred thousand gold pieces on Burq in reward and Bahar too, presented him with fifty thousand gold pieces. The renowned commanders of the court sang Burq's praises continuously and calls of "Bravo! Well done!" rose from all corners.

Moon-like cupbearers carrying goblets of wine circulated in that paradisiacal congregation and songsters sang captivating songs in mellow and harmonious notes to delight the assembly.

Amar now said to Burq, "My dear, I must ask you to hand over Jamshed's mantle now. Amir Hamza had ordered that such marvellous devices and the mementoes of the prophets must be employed against the enemy only as a last resort. And look at you! The moment you found yourself in possession of Jamshed's mantle you headed straight for the City of Disregard and challenged Afrasiyab. Had I wished, I could have donned the cape of invisibility, beheaded all enemies and conquered the tilism. But we must remain an aid and assistant to the Conqueror of the Tilism merely in the capacity of tricksters. Now, do surrender Jamshed's mantle to me."

Burq answered, "I do not depend on Jamshed's mantle for my trickeries. God willing, even without it I will kill thousands of sorcerers." He handed Jamshed's mantle to Amar Ayyar.

While they were engaged in this conversation a horrible sound suddenly broke upon them. A magic claw swooped down with a flash of light and carried away Bahar and a thunderous voice proclaimed, "*I am Sorcerer Namrud!*" The courtiers and Princess Mahrukh Magic-Eye rose from their stations in agitation. Thousands of magic coconuts and citrons targeted the magic claw. But none of them had any effect because it was the magic claw of a mighty sorcerer.

Amar Ayyar and the tricksters followed the flight of the magic claw, which landed with Bahar on a mountaintop. The sorcerer Namrud proclaimed by magic in a dreadful, booming voice, "*O tribe of ingrates, know that I am stationed on this mountaintop so that none may say that I carried off Bahar furtively. I challenge the courageous ones among you to snatch her from me.*"

Namrud deputed a magic slave on the peak of the mountain to alert him if anyone approached. Then he spread a magic carpet and sat down. He sat Bahar, who had fallen unconscious after catching Namrud's powerful gaze, down on one side of him.

Amar Ayyar climbed the mountaintop in the guise of a sorcerer carrying a bowl full of brightly shining pomegranate seeds the size of chicken eggs. The magic slave deputed on the peak warned Amar not to proceed further. When Amar did not desist, it called out to Namrud, "*Be alert, Amar Ayyar is approaching!*" Namrud replied, "Let him come!"

Amar arrived before Namrud, greeted him, and said, "O Namrud, your magic slave lies! I am, in fact, a servant of Emperor Afrasiyab, who sent these pomegranate seeds for you from the Apple Garden." Namrud laughed and said, "O Amar, you have no equal in slyness. I won't fall for your tricks but do let me see what kind of pomegranate seeds you brought me."

Namrud took the bowl from Amar's hands and saw pomegranate seeds of a marvellous variety. When he took out a few for closer inspection, steam rose from them and a wisp of the vapor traveled up Namrud's nostrils. He sneezed and fell unconscious. Amar Ayyar cut off his head without loss of time.

Clamour and noises arose, darkness fell, and after a few moments, a plaintive cry was heard, "*I was killed! Namrud was my name.*" A bird of bright plumage emerged from his skull and flew off toward Afrasiyab's court.

Princess Bahar was freed from Namrud's spell at his death. She returned with Amar Ayyar to Mahjabeen's court where everyone celebrated her release and revels began.

The shiny-colored bird that came out of Namrud's skull arrived in Afrasiyab's court. It informed him of Namrud's end and burned up.

When Emperor Heyrat again insisted on leading the campaign against the enemy with an entourage of renowned sorcerers, Afrasiyab finally gave her permission. Heyrat busied herself planning the campaign and marshalling the army.

Sorcerer Sarmast

Now hear of Laqa. Earlier we had learned of Suleiman Amber-Hair sending a missive to Afrasiyab requesting him to send someone to aid Laqa. The Emperor of Hoshruba had dispatched sorceress Hasina on the campaign. However, when Hasina reached her city to make preparations, she fell ill and could not proceed to Laqa's aid. After some time, Suleiman Amber-Hair sent a second letter to Afrasiyab with the same message.

The magic claw carrying the letter for Afrasiyab arrived as Empress Heyrat was busy preparing for her own campaign. After reading Amber-Hair's letter, Afrasiyab turned to one of the commanders of his army, sorcerer Sarmast, and said to him, "O Sarmast, you must go to Lord Laqa's aid." Sarmast retired to his abode upon receiving his orders. He gathered an army of twelve thousand sorcerers and marched toward Mount Agate with great majesty and glory.

Of Sorcerer Sarmast Fighting Amir Hamza; Of the Trickery Performed by Chalak; Of Empress Heyrat Marching with a Sanguinary Army and Waging a Long War Against Mahrukh; And of the Trickeries Performed by the Tricksters and Trickster Girls

The face-adorners of the bride of valor and the bedeckers of the glorious damsel who has a taste for carnage, draw the comb of speech through the locks of their darling narrative and dot the letters on the mirror-like bright face of the page as if drawing dark moles on her comely face to ward off the evil eye.

When Empress Heyrat prepared to march against Mahrukh, some seven million sorcerers, including many renowned magicians of the tilism, prepared to accompany her on the campaign. Afrasiyab also sent two of his ministers, Abriq Mount-Splitter and Sarma Ice-Hurler to escort Heyrat. The empress mounted the throne and her sorceress-aides, Yaqut and Zamarrud, began fanning her with fly-whisks of phoenix feathers.

Thousands of magic drums sounded as her throne rose into the air and climbed into the clouds. The throne took on the shape of an enamelled building in which her jewel-encrusted throne lay surrounded by thousands of ruby-inlaid chairs. Bright and blazing like a flame, Heyrat's body hovered over the throne. Magic bugles and bells sounded along the course and chants of "*Long live Sameri!*" were heard as her procession flew along its path.

At Heyrat's signal, a sorcerer threw magic citrons into the air that burst with thunderous sounds like the simultaneous discharge of tens of hundreds of canons and caused thousands of stars to fall from the heavens and disappear above Empress Heyrat's head as a sacrifice for her life and to ward off harm.

Skirmishers of the battlefield flew alongside Empress Heyrat astride magical beasts, making the Earth and the heavens cry for reprieve from the deafening cling-clang of their arms and armor. The ranked and conceited sorcerers and sorceresses progressed forth mightily and with great splendor and arrived like a swelling tide in the precincts of the City of Manycolors.

Mahjabeen Diamond-Robe and Mahrukh Magic-Eye were seated on their thrones when they heard the tolling of magical bells and the thunder of drums that shook the Earth. All the commanders of their camp headed out of the court and witnessed the arrival of Empress Heyrat and the sorceress's army.

Everyone who saw the sight of that swelling horde called out, "O Protector! We seek Your protection!" Mahrukh and others were unnerved by the sight of Heyrat's procession and their camp was thrown into commotion.

Heyrat's army bivouacked on the other side of the arena. A hundred ruby-encrusted spires shone above their camp and for miles across the horizon the tents of sorcerers were pitched. The bazaars opened up in Heyrat's camp and brisk trade began in all parts of the market.

The royal camp overlooking the Hall of Assembly was a sight to behold. Heyrat dismounted her throne, entered the court and ascended her station, which was ringed by the seats and thrones of throat-slitting warriors and sorcerers as mighty as Sameri. The forest of valor became crowded with lions. The trickster girls came out from their wilderness stations, presented themselves, and got busy making preparations for the impending battle.

Leaving all of them busy in their preparations,

Forget for a moment this tale
And hear in its place another story

Let us digress here to narrate the account of the sorcerer Sarmast, who had departed with great pomp and magnificence and twelve thousand sorcerers toward Mount Agate in Laqa's aid. After traversing many stages, his army emerged from the boundaries of the tilism and arrived in the neighbourhood of Mount Agate.

Finding himself in the vicinity of a thick and enchanting forest, Sarmast desired to go hunting. He set up his camp at the foot of the mountain and, leaving his army camped there, started the hunt. After he had hunted many birds, wild asses and wild cows, a deer pierced by his arrow escaped and Sarmast gave it chase on his horse.

Amir Hamza's son, Darab the World Conqueror, was already hunting in that part of the forest. As the deer ran past him he notched and shot an arrow that brought down the deer. As it collapsed the prince slaughtered it. In the meanwhile, Sarmast reached the scene and, noticing Darab standing over his prey, challenged him, saying, "How dare you slaughter my prey?" Darab replied, "O brave, I would never have targeted this vulnerable animal had I known that it was your prey. Please accept this deer, as well as all the animals I have hunted today, as a gift, and forgive my error."

Sarmast, who was intoxicated with the heady wine of vanity, did not accept the Prince's excuse. He rebuked Darab, saying, "O unworthy fool, do you tempt me with meat because you think I covet it? I am the sorcerer Sarmast and shall now hunt you down for your contumely."

The prince answered, "You sorcerers pride yourselves on magic; if you faced me in sword combat I would show you your true worth in no time." Sarmast answered, "I give you my word that in our combat I shall not recourse to magic. Let us see what you are capable of, give me your best blow!" The prince answered,

"You should fulfill your desire first
For I let my enemy always deliver the first blow."

Sarmast drew his sword. Rising in his stirrups and summoning the entire strength of his body into his arms, he unleashed the blow on Darab's head. The prince brought his steed up to Sarmast's and, contracting himself like a flower bud, covered his entire body with his shield. The shield received the full impact of Sarmast's blow but only the hilt and the shank of Sarmast's sword struck it. The angle from which the sword fell did not land a useful blow and was foiled by the prince.

Sarmast had not yet pulled himself together when Darab drew his sword and called out, "Be warned and beware lest someone should say that I attacked you without warning,

"You dealt me a blow now receive one from my hand
That will erase all happy thoughts from your heart."

Darab now dealt the blow. Seeing the sharp blade come down with Darab's mighty arm, Sarmast emptied his saddle and jumped onto the horse's crupper to block with his shield. The lightning-like sword of the prince of lofty fortunes cut through the shield like a thunder bolt passes through dark clouds. It cut Sarmast's helm and armor, his turban and under-cap[89] and sank two digits deep into his skull.

Sarmast quickly stopped the progress of the blade with his hand armor and, with a twang, the sword came out of his skull, but a screen of blood covered Sarmast's face and he fell down from the injury unconscious.

Darab's first impulse was to behead him but he thought better of it; the consideration that slaying the injured and helpless was beneath the dignity of valiant men stayed his hand. He was engrossed in these thoughts when, suddenly, a dark storm began blowing and Sarmast's foster mother, the pitch-black, cruel-faced, ugly sorceress Nagan, materialized before Darab.

Enraged from witnessing the condition of her foster son, she cast a spell. A fiery tower rose around Darab and imprisoned him, allowing no avenue of escape. Then she carried Sarmast in her arms to safety. In the meanwhile, Zardam, who was one of Sarmast's retainers, arrived on the scene with the army at the same time that Prince Darab's forces also landed there.

A battle broke out between the camps. The sorcerers employed magic and the armies of Prince Darab were defeated in no time. They were routed and retreated into the mountains while Sarmast's army returned to its camp.

Prince Darab's trickster, Fattah Kishori, who accompanied his army, infiltrated Sarmast's camp in a woodcutter's disguise. He carried his sandals dangling from the end of a stick on his shoulders and logs of wood on his back.

In the meanwhile, some of Darab's men returned to their camp and reported the events to Amir Hamza, who prepared to march to the prince's rescue. An advance party of his companions and nobles immediately left to aid Darab.

In the enemy camp, sorceress Nagan treated Sarmast's wounds with a magic salve that healed them at once. She instructed Sarmast in the delicate strategies of battle, advised him to leave for Laqa's court, then departed. Sarmast started for Laqa's court carrying Darab on a cart as his prisoner. Trickster Fattah and his army followed.

Laqa was seated on his throne when a dust storm arose. It became so dark that nothing could be made out and fire and stones rained down from the sky. Frightened out of his wits by these marvels, Laqa crept under his throne to hide.

A few moments later, Sarmast, whose arrival was heralded by these events, entered the court and, noticing the vacant throne, asked, "Where is Lord Laqa?"

Bakhtiarak welcomed him with all the tokens of honor and said, "Please be seated. Our Lord will join us momentarily." Bakhtiarak screened off the area around the throne and tried to persuade Laqa to come out from under it. Bakhtiarak said, "If Your Lordship makes a habit of hiding there in fear, it would weaken the faith of your believers." Laqa finally came out and was restored to his dignity and majesty. Once he resumed his seat on the throne, the screens were removed.

Sarmast prostrated himself before Laqa and told him that the Emperor of Hoshruba had sent him to help fight Hamza. Laqa conferred a robe of distinction on Sarmast and King Suleiman and Bakhtiarak provided a pleasant station for his army to set up camp.

Clapper-drums began beating and gongs were rung. The sorcerers rested and meat and wine were served in the court. A dance recital started and a musical assembly got underway.

❧

Amir Hamza's spies, who were present in Laqa's court, returned to their camp and arrived in the Pavilion of Suleiman at the station of audience. They prayed with humility and devotion,

> *"You, whose courage matches Faridun's, and magnificence equals Dara's*
> *You, whose person dispelled all tyranny from the world,*
> *May your kingdom, riches, magnificence, and knowledge*
> *Last forever and prosper till the end of time.*

"A sorcerer named Sarmast has arrived with an army of twelve thousand sorcerers of dark fortune to aid Laqa. He plans to fight your servants and your evil-hunting forces. He has also brought Prince Darab as a prisoner with him."

Amir Hamza cancelled his departure to secure Darab's release; now that Sarmast was there, he would face him on the battlefield.

❧

At Laqa's court, a feast was held in Sarmast's honor. Laqa sent Sarmast's deputy, sorcerer Zardam, the leftovers from his plate. As the macebearer came out carrying the food tray and looked around in search of a laborer, the trickster Fattah Kishori stepped out disguised as a laborer and offered to carry it. On the way, the false laborer purposely stumbled and dropped the food. Cursing him, the macebearer started putting the bowls back onto the tray. The false laborer also helped and, without the macebearer catching him, used the opportunity to drug the food. They soon resumed their errand and arrived at Zardam's pavilion.

Zardam was mightily pleased when he learned that Laqa had sent him his leftovers as a special favor. In the meanwhile, the false laborer hid himself behind Zardam's pavilion. After Zardam and his companions ate the food and fell unconscious, he entered the pavilion by slitting open the panel, and beheaded all of them.

Immediately, the terrible cry and uproar of the magic spirits rose. People ran toward Zardam's pavilion screaming, "Catch him! Don't let the murderer escape!" Fattah raised the pavilion panel, made his war cry and escaped, adding his voice to the chorus of those running to catch him.

When informed of these events, Sarmast said to Bakhtiarak, "I will not rest a moment longer! Order the drums of war be struck. I will destroy the rebels one and all." Bakhtiarak answered, "As you please!"

In the time that remained before the close of day, last rites were performed for Zardam and his companions.

Finally, the world-illuminating sun was imprisoned; the billowing forces of the Abyssinian of the Night unfurled their dark flag of mourning in the world's inn; the Daughters of the Corpse[90] entered the cemetery of the skies and the shower of dew fell on all creation like tears of grief. At Sarmast's orders, the drums of war were beaten and the clarions sounded.

The spies of the King of True Believers presented themselves before him. After singing his praises, they informed him of the news. Trickster Chalak headed for the Music Assembly of Solomon and struck the Timbals of Sikander and Hashsham. The Earth and the heavens reverberated with the report. The Turkic flutes, the pipe of Kayumars, and the fife of the ancient king Afrasiyab sounded.[91] For four full watches of the night, arms and armor were readied. The criers exhorted the braves and champions to remain alert with their proclamations. Valiant warriors prepared to lay down their lives in the battlefield when the night ended and it was time. When the Night's Watchman,[92] along with its army of stars, finished his vigil, the arrival of the Emperor of the Fourth Heaven[93] was proclaimed from his eastern chamber to the four corners of the world.

At the break of dawn, the two armies came forward and streamed into the arena in platoons and groups.

Amir Hamza was occupied in prayer in the Roving Prayer Tent when the trickster Chalak arrived with the news that his great army had filled the arena and awaited his arrival. Amir came out decorated with arms. His worthy and noble commanders congregated around him, and Amir rode Ashqar Demon-Born to the threshold of the king's private pavilion. King Saad, the Shadow of God, the Refuge of the World, emerged from the pavilion on the throne of Solomon. The criers called out, "In the Name Of Allah!" and all the commanders bowed to their sovereign. The drums were struck, kettledrums were beaten and attendants called out, "Make way for the king's procession! Show deference and keep your distance!" Ringed by his commanders, the king's conveyance headed toward the arena as Laqa arrived with sorcerer Sarmast.

The warriors arranged themselves in ranks and columns. The groundsmen levelled the uneven areas of the arena. The water-carriers sprinkled the arena and settled the dust, leaving the whole battlefield clean of all shrubbery and debris. The criers from both camps came forward and recited challenges to the enemy to rouse their warriors.

After securing Laqa's permission, Sarmast flew into the arena astride his magic dragon and challenged Amir Hamza's camp, saying, "O accursed creatures of Lord Laqa, who among you dares to come forward and face me?"

King Saad gave Mandvail Isfahani leave to fight and he confronted Sarmast.

The sorcerer recited a spell and, presently, a dust cloud arose from the direction of the wilderness and a fully armed magic trooper materialized and said to Mandvail, "Give me your best blow!" As they parried with lances, the magic trooper was able to disarm Mandvail with a strike of his lance. When Mandvail drew his sword, the magic trooper wrested it from his hand by securing hold of his glove, lifted him from his saddle by his cummerbund, and slammed him to the ground. He took Mandvail prisoner and gave him into the custody of Sarmast's army.

The magic trooper called out to the True Believers, "Those among you who covet death must come out and face me." One after another, Amir Hamza's commanders faced the magic trooper and were taken prisoner by him. Several hundred commanders of Amir Hamza's camp were captured in this manner.

Finally, the day came to an end. As the twilight caught the skirts of Sun's robe and pleaded with him not to hide his face, the Virgin of the Heavens retired to mourn her beloved day in the chamber of darkness.

Sarmast ordered that cessation of hostilities should be announced by the beating of drums. He returned to his camp and the two armies returned to rest for the night.

The trickster Chalak now headed out to discover the origins of the magic trooper.

In Laqa's camp, Bakhtiarak said to Sarmast, "Hamza is the master of the Most Great Name. No spell will work on him when he enters the arena, and the Name will render void all your magic."

Sarmast recited a spell to summon his foster mother, sorceress Nagan, and said to her, "We must capture Hamza, who is the master of the Most Great Name – the revoker of spells."

Nagan said, "I will prepare some magic to capture the Most Great Name. Once I have done so, Hamza will be unable to recall it. I will now go into hiding to escape the tricksters' attacks."

Bakhtiarak said, "I fear the tricksters will strike tonight to free their commanders. It would be preferable if you stayed." Nagan gave Bakhtiarak an amulet and said, "When you are in need, place this amulet in fire and I will come immediately to your aid." Then Nagan flew away.

Chalak tried to find a trace of the magic trooper but was unsuccessful. He then disguised himself as an attendant and entered the pavilion of Bakhtiarak, who recognized Chalak at once.

Be it known that Amar Ayyar had killed Bakhtiarak's father, Bakhtak, and cooked and fed his pottage to Bakhtiarak. Ever since, Bakhtiarak had acted with great humility and deference toward the tricksters and did not meddle in their business, knowing they could kill him as easily and without the least compunction.

Bakhtiarak now greeted Chalak, showed him every sign of honor and seated him at a high station. Bakhtiarak asked, "What brought my venerable master's son here today? I also wish to know whether or not my life will be spared." Chalak answered, "As a matter of fact, your death hovers above your head. I came here to ask you something and am resolved in the event of your not answering truthfully to relieve you forever from the burden of life." Bakhtiarak covered himself in a white shroud and lay down at Chalak's feet as if already dead.

Chalak said, "Get up. You must not die so quickly. First eat some dates from my hand." Bakhtiarak whined, "Your Honor may ask me what you wish, or kill me should it please you more, but why must you make me unconscious with drugged dates?" Chalak drew his dagger and snarled, "O wittol! How dare you make objections! Quick, eat these dates!" Bakhtiarak replied, "Very well! I will comply."

Bakhtiarak ate the dates and fell unconscious. Chalak bundled him up, leaped out of the pavilion and sped toward the wilderness where he climbed up a hill from where he could keep an eye on anyone who might follow him. After satisfying himself that he was not pursued, Chalak restored Bakhtiarak to consciousness and asked him, "Tell me truthfully the origins of the magic trooper." Bakhtiarak replied, "If I tell the truth will you spare my life?" Chalak replied, "Why do you ask for my word? Should it be my pleasure, I will reprieve your life, and should I feel like it, I will behead you."

Bakhtiarak answered, "All I know is that sorceress Nagan has gone into hiding to capture the Most Great Name; she gave me an amulet to call her in time of need by placing it in fire. Should you wish, I could summon her." Bakhtiarak had planned to secure his release and have Nagan capture Chalak. However, Chalak too, had thought of a trick. He said to Bakhtiarak, "Very well, you may summon Nagan."

Bakhtiarak started a fire and put the amulet into it. Immediately, a whirring sound was heard and Nagan arrived. She asked Bakhtiarak, "Why did you call me?" Bakhtiarak did not dare say a word about Chalak; he only pointed in the direction where Chalak stood, signalling her to arrest him. But Nagan did not understand him because Chalak had hidden himself a moment before she arrived. As she looked in all directions uncomprehendingly, Chalak, who was ready with his slingshot, fired a well-aimed shot at Nagan. Her head flew off her shoulders and fell far away from the impact. She dropped to the ground dead and was dispatched hellward, even before the commotion caused by her death had subsided.

Bakhtiarak too, dropped to the ground and closed his eyes but Chalak dragged him to a tree and tied him to it. Now disguised as Nagan, Chalak headed toward Sarmast's camp. Seeing his nanny, Sarmast greeted her respectfully and asked, "Have you already captured the Most Great Name?" The false Nagan caught Sarmast by the hand and said, "I learned that these three days will be inauspicious for you. It would be almost impossible for you to escape the tricksters. If you accompany me I will show you how to ward them off."

The false Nagan took Sarmast into a wilderness where she gave him an apple from her sack and said, "Eat this apple. It is from the garden of Lord Sameri. It will lengthen your life and nobody will be able to kill you." Sarmast ate the apple and dropped to the ground, unconscious. Chalak immediately beheaded him. A great noise and pandemonium engulfed them and fire and stones rained from the sky.

Prince Darab and other commanders of Amir Hamza's army captured by Sarmast were released from his magic. They decided to put an end to Laqa's menace once and for all. They drew their swords and fell upon Laqa's army. The sorcerers' camp was taken by surprise. They reckoned there were powerful sorcerers among the True Believers, who had killed their leader, Sarmast. Convinced of this, they turned tail. The valiant True Believers killed infidels for many hours.

When the bloodshot eyes of the Darling of the Night[94] hid her face in a veil of crimson tears, and the skirts of the day were painted red by dusk, the commanders of the army of True Believers returned to their camp. Laqa retired to the fortress of Mount Agate in grief and defeat, and the sorcerers retreated into the tilism.

King Suleiman Amber-Hair sent another message to Emperor Afrasiyab soliciting his aid.

Emperor Afrasiyab was seated in the Dome of Light while Heyrat was arrayed out against Mahrukh. The sorcerers from Sarmast's defeated army presented themselves before Afrasiyab and the magic claw brought him King Suleiman Amber-Hair's note. These events thoroughly incensed and nettled Afrasiyab and he grasped the tricksters' capacity to cause damage. He considered how difficult a time he had had trying to capture their leader, who had entered his tilism with just a handful of his companions. And he realized what a terror they must have been for Lord Laqa, who had had to contend with thousands of tricksters in Amir Hamza's camp.

Afrasiyab first sent a message to Empress Heyrat. He wrote:

> "Empress, you must not beat the drums of war as yet. If you battle the rebels now, the tricksters will interfere with your campaign and sabotage it. You must first send the trickster girl Sarsar to capture the tricksters. Afterwards, confronting and defeating Mahrukh and her rebellious horde will be a small matter."

He sent the note to Empress Heyrat with a magic slave and then wrote one to sorceress Princess Hasina Magic-Beauty. It read:

> "O Princess, you had left with the promise to go to Lord Laqa's aid but I learned that you fell ill afterwards and could not fulfill the undertaking. If you're still indisposed, please inform me so that another sorcerer can be nominated for the campaign. If, however, you

> are now restored to health, you may proceed and complete your mission."

Afrasiyab dispatched that letter too, with a magic slave who brought it to Princess Hasina. She wrote in reply:

> "I am fully recovered now by the Grace of Lord Jamshed. I will depart shortly on the mission assigned to me and Your Honor may put your mind at ease on that account."

The magic slave returned to Afrasiyab. The emperor was satisfied by Hasina's reply.

When Afrasiyab's note reached Heyrat, she said to the trickster girl Sarsar, "The emperor orders that you go and take Amar Ayyar captive." Sarsar answered, "Very well!" Putting on a trickster's dress and weapons, she set out on her mission.

Now hear of the tricksters. They were busy making revels in Mahrukh Magic-Eye's camp when the news of Empress Heyrat's arrival was received. They retreated into the wilderness to plan some trickery to ransack her camp.

Engrossed in these thoughts, Amar Ayyar came upon a wedding party in the environs of the Dome of Light. He saw a group of sorcerers drinking wine and watching a dance recital under a canopy while the groom sat on a throne attired in a luxurious golden dress. Amar was delighted by the sight and thought, *A destitute fellow like me will never come across a better opportunity. I must rob them and provide for myself.*

Amar went to a nearby cave where he disguised himself as a minstrel, fixed a beard on his face that reached down to his waist, and rubbed lotions on his face to acquire a ruddy complexion. Disguised as an old man with a wrinkled face and bent back, he put on a chemise and turban; then he returned to the assembly carrying a tambourine in his hand and a pair of flutes stuck in his belt.

The false minstrel sang a congratulatory song with such pathos that he captivated everyone.

A sorcerer named Taseer, who was the father of the groom, reckoned the false minstrel was a master of musical arts. He showed him much reverence, seated him by his side, and said, "Have a drink or two. Consider this your own house. I will also make you an offering according to my status." The false minstrel said, "May you rise in dignity! May you attain a higher rank. May your lordship prosper forever." Then he sat down to sing and play the flute.

Sarsar, who was searching for Amar Ayyar in the wilderness, heard the sound of singing. She went to investigate and saw a minstrel regaling the wedding party. She recognized Amar Ayyar at first sight. She listened to Amar's singing for some time and thought, *Praise the Lord! My lover is not only a renowned man but also a consummate master of all arts*!

However, Sarsar was there on Afrasiyab's orders to capture Amar. She entered the assembly and whispered to sorcerer Taseer, "This man is Amar Ayyar. You must arrest him immediately." Seeing Sarsar's lips move, the false minstrel realized that she had recognized him and counselled Taseer to capture him. He walked straight up to Taseer and said, "Look who comes behind you." As Taseer turned, Amar knocked him on the head and made away with Taseer's pearl-embroidered headgear.

As the sorcerers ran to catch Amar, Sarsar stopped them, saying, "Wait here, I will go and catch him myself." Sarsar drew her dagger and went in pursuit of Amar. As he stopped in the wilderness for a moment's rest, Sarsar arrived and challenged him, saying, "Here you are O wretch. Now you won't be able to escape me." Hearing her challenge, Amar also drew his dagger and they started fighting.

Burq the Frank arrived on the scene in the meanwhile and said to Sarsar, "I offer my salutes to my lady!" Sarsar answered, "O Burq, your master styles himself the Emperor of Tricksters. Why is he unable to fight me on his own? If he is indeed so powerful and great why does he need the crutch of your assistance? If his claim is just, you should go away and leave me and your master alone to sort out this matter between us."

Burq replied, "Indeed, I have no business intruding here. Everyone must allow a lover and his beloved privacy. I know you wish to be rid of me so that you can make love to him." With these words, Burq left them.

As Burq walked away, he saw Saba Raftar coming from the opposite direction. He realized that if she joined Sarsar it would spell trouble for Amar. Burq challenged Saba Raftar, who drew her sword and fell upon Burq.

A sorcerer named Sayyah happened to pass where Amar Ayyar and Sarsar fought. He was on his way to attend the wedding of sorcerer Taseer's son. Seeing the two fighting in the wilderness, he captured them by magic.

Sarsar said to him, "Why have you arrested me? I am a servant of the emperor." Amar interjected, "She lies. I am a minstrel and she's my wife. Because I am old and infirm she runs after other men. When I catch her red-handed and attempt to kill her lovers she comes in my way and fights with me. Today I am resolved to put an end to her mischief. Release me now so that I may slice off the tip of this strumpet's nose."

Sayyah said, "I heard that Afrasiyab sent Sarsar to fight the tricksters. But I do not recognize her since common folks like me have no opportunity to set foot in the emperor's court. I cannot say which one of you is telling the truth."

Amar said, "You may learn the truth at the wedding ceremony of sorcerer Taseer's son." Sayyah said, "Very well. I was headed there myself."

With the help of a magic claw, he carried Amar and Sarsar to the wedding gathering and asked sorcerer Taseer about them. He answered, "All I can tell you is that the minstrel arrived here and was followed by this woman. The minstrel ran away after snatching my headgear, which is a sure sign that he is a trickster. As I have never seen a trickster or trickster girl before, I cannot verify that this woman is Sarsar. However, having captured them presents a wonderful opportunity for us to gain admission to the royal court. You should take both of them to Empress Heyrat, who has arrived in the region of Zahir." Sayyah answered, "I can invoke my magic and discover their true identities. But as you state, they are our passports to the royal court. I will leave for Empress Heyrat's court after participating in your ceremony."

Sayyah tied up Amar and Sarsar, and sat down to watch the dance recital.

Now hear of Burq the Frank. In the midst of fighting Saba Raftar, he jumped into a cave. Saba Raftar jumped in after him, dagger drawn, and shouted, "There's nowhere you can run to now."

Burq had fixed the snare rope to the mouth of the cave. When Saba Raftar jumped in, Burq pulled the rope and Saba Raftar fell into his lap entangled in the snare rope. Burq made her unconscious with a drug then disguised himself as Saba Raftar. The real Saba Raftar he dressed up and disguised as Amar Ayyar. Then he tied the false Amar Ayyar into a bundle and headed to where the wedding party was assembled.

Noticing the false Saba Raftar carrying a bundle, everyone gathered to see whom she had caught. The false Saba Raftar approached and saw Amar and Sarsar sitting tied up.

The false Saba Raftar blessed Sayyah the Traveler, then said, "Why are you holding my sister prisoner?" Sayyah replied, "I could not tell the difference. Now I will take both of them before Empress Heyrat."

The false Saba Raftar said, "How could you not tell the difference between a woman and a man? I am Sarsar's vizier girl. The one you have tied up is Princess Sarsar, but the minstrel is one of Amar Ayyar's companions. I caught the real Amar Ayyar!"

Sayyah wished to establish the truth of her account. One of the attendees said to him, "I have the portraits of the tricksters and trickster girls with which you can verify their faces."

Once their identity was verified, Sayyah released the real Sarsar and tied up the false Amar, who was really Saba Raftar in disguise.

After she was released, Sarsar recognized Burq but she said to herself, *These idiots and clowns assembled here are all blind to sense and reason. They would meet the punishment they deserve at the tricksters' hands. Let them reap their rewards since they humiliated and disgraced me. I should leave them to their just deserts.*

When Sarsar left, the false Saba Raftar said to Taseer, "I made a pledge that after I captured Amar Ayyar I would hold a celebratory feast and be a cupbearer for the sorcerers. All praise to Lord Sameri that after I caught Amar I came upon an assembly of sorcerers. It is my desire to serve wine to everyone in this gathering. I will compensate you for the wine used today from your cellar. All I ask is that you let me be the host." Taseer answered, "Think of it as your own home. Drink and serve to your heart's content without thought of expense."

The false Saba Raftar smiled and took charge of the wine service. She drugged the wine while arranging the cups and goblets, and then served the assembly. After they fell unconscious, she released Amar Ayyar, who was in the minstrel's disguise. Immediately, Amar began looting the assembly while the false Saba Raftar beheaded the sorcerers.

In the meanwhile, Afrasiyab opened the *Book of Sameri.* Since Empress Heyrat's departure on the campaign he had consulted it often to make sure that his wife did not suffer humiliation at the hands of the tricksters. The false Saba Raftar had beheaded only a few sorcerers when the *Book of Sameri* alerted Afrasiyab to her doings, and the emperor learned that Amar and Burq sowed strife in the environs of the Dome of Light. Afrasiyab thought, *How long must I endure these tricksters' depredations? Today I must capture and kill Amar!*

The emperor sent for sorceress Khumar, who was already wroth with Amar after their earlier encounter when Amar had duped her and shaved her head on the banks of the River of Flowing Blood. Afrasiyab ordered Khumar to produce Amar and Burq before him as prisoners and release the real Saba Raftar.

Khumar grew magic wings and flew away. She soon arrived at the scene and called out to the tricksters, "Stop, O wretches!" Burq quickly escaped the moment he heard her challenge. Amar hid himself in a nook too, but Khumar came down from the sky in the form of lightning and carried away Amar Ayyar in her magic claw. She recited a spell that set Saba Raftar loose, who ran away once freed from her bonds. Next, Khumar pointed her finger toward the sky and a puff of cloud materialized above the wedding guests who lay drugged. It rained and restored everyone to consciousness. Finding the sorcerers lying murdered around them, they said, "Witness what the tricksters have reduced us to with their evil deeds!" Then they went about their business.

Khumar arrived at the Dome of Light, saluted the emperor and produced Amar before him. Amar had fallen unconscious, buffeted by the powerful gusts of wind as he was being carried by the magic claw. When he opened his eyes he found himself in Afrasiyab's court and saluted him.

Afrasiyab said, "Tell me O Amar if you ever believed that you would see this day?" Amar replied, "I did indeed; I will now rob your court and shave your beard. I came here today for this very purpose."

Enraged by this reply, Afrasiyab sent a note to Empress Heyrat in which he wrote:

> "O Empress of the World, we have captured Amar Ayyar. You should hand over the command of your camp to your deputies and return so that I may kill him in your presence to pleasure your heart and comfort your eyes."

Afrasiyab dispatched the note with a magic claw and imprisoned Amar in a steel cage.

When the magic claw delivered Afrasiyab's note to Heyrat, she broke into joyous laughter and looked more pleased than she ever had. She summoned her army commanders and gave them the news. She instructed them to take care of the camp in her absence and ordered the music assembly to play festive music in anticipation of Amar Ayyar's death.

As the drums began playing celebratory notes, Heyrat clad herself in a red dress, covered herself with ruby jewelery, and departed for the Dome of Light mounted on a magic peacock.

In the meanwhile, the magic birds brought news of Amar's capture to Mahrukh Magic-Eye and Mahjabeen Diamond-Robe and informed them of the celebrations in the enemy camp, and of Empress Heyrat's departure to preside over Amar's killing.

Princesses Bahar, Nafarman and Queen Mahjabeen ordered their armies to get ready to march to Amar's rescue or die fighting in the effort. Mahrukh Magic-Eye said, "It's nearly impossibile to reach the Dome of Light." Prince Asad said, "No mortal has the power to kill Amar. He is the Beheader of Sorcerers and the favored one of seven prophets. He will only die after he himself asks for his death three times. Afrasiyab has no power to harm even a hair on his body. We must all pray to the True Savior for Amar's well being and safety."

All of them called out in prayer, "O Supreme Creator and Kind and Merciful Lord, all of us converted to the True Faith and became enlightened on account of Amar Ayyar. Because of his efforts we put our belief in You – the One God without partners. We pray You to take Amar into Your care and protection."

While they prayed, a joyous and happy Empress Heyrat arrived in the Dome of Light. The courtiers paid her their respects and she took her seat beside Afrasiyab. The attendants of the empress put bowls of dry fruit, perfume boxes and flower vases before her. Heyrat opened a gold betel box, prepared a *gilauri*,[95] and put it into Afrasiyab's mouth with her own hands. Then she put her arms around the emperor's neck coquettishly and said proudly, "You must not allow any delay in sending that tyrant to his doom."

Afrasiyab issued his orders and the crier announced to all citizens of the City of Disregard to gather in the field opposite the Dome of Light to witness Amar Ayyar's sorry state. Only a short time remained in his life before he would be meted out a humiliating and painful death, receiving the deserts of his evil life.

The citizens of the City of Disregard started gathering in the field. They said to each other, "Regard the results of rebellion; one washes his hands of his life." The wise and sagacious took instruction from Amar's example and said, "O brave men, witness that it is the same Amar who brought even Lord Laqa to grief and who is the deputy of the Lord of the Auspicious Planetary Conjunction. The skewed revolutions of the fickle heavens can see no man of pride and majesty prosper for long. It tyrannically killed many renowned men and the earth covered them with a veil of dust."

Amidst these cries and hubbub, the Turk of the Heavens[96] was led away to his westerly prison. Mourning was proclaimed in the world's inn for Amar. Presently, the eve of sorrows descended, all clad in black.

Afrasiyab recited a spell, which determined that as long as he was alive no one would be able to open the lock of Amar's cage. Then Afrasiyab removed the spell from Amar's body. When it was removed Amar felt he could move inside the cage.

As the evening progressed, everyone in Afrasiyab's court busied themselves in revelry, their minds finally at peace that Amar could not break out of his prison.

Since nobody was deputed to keep watch on Amar, after some time had passed, he took out a pasteboard effigy from his zambil and disguised it with his likeness. He then put on the cape of invisibility and left the effigy in his place. He retired to a corner of the cage where he was invisible to everyone but the All Seeing God.

All night long people kept arriving in the field overlooking the Dome of Light and tablas played continuously.

Eager to take revenge on Amar for stealing from them, every sorcerer decided to strike Amar at least once when he was dragged out of the cage. One promised to pierce his heart with his trident and short spear. Another proclaimed that he would pull out Amar's tongue from its root. Yet another sorcerer planned to extract Amar's eyes from their sockets.

Amidst such talk, the dawn broke and the Luminous Bird[97] fluttered out of its cage from the eastern sky in preparation for its flight across the sky. It illuminated the assembly of creation by its lustrous feathers. Dams of darkness broke and the world was flooded with light.

When it was morning, Afrasiyab recited a spell to unlock Amar's cage and ordered the sorcerers to bring him out. They caught Amar's effigy by its collar and pulled it out. Clad in the cape of invisibility, Amar too, came out of the cage. While the sorcerers belabored his effigy, Amar started looting the possessions of the beautiful and lovely sorceresses and the moon-faced slave girls with the Net of Ilyas. He stuffed betel boxes, dressing boxes, glasses, perfume boxes, water utensils, platters and makeup boxes into his zambil.

Finally, Amar said to one slave girl, "Now I am going away!" She turned to the one standing next to her and said, "Someone just said to me that he is leaving."

Amar called out loudly, "O clown Afrasiyab, I am now going away!"

The sorcerers were frightened when these words rang out in the court. All the seats, thrones, tables, carpets, curtains and screens in the court disappeared all of a sudden. At that moment, Amar's effigy also broke into pieces and the sorcerers realized to their great chagrin that the one they thought was Amar was, in fact, a pasteboard effigy.

Afrasiyab turned to sorceress Khumar and said, "O wretch! To impress me with your resourcefulness you brought me a pasteboard effigy of Amar! Confess the truth of the matter to me at once!" Khumar answered, "O Emperor, when I produced the captive you yourself conversed with him. If it were a pasteboard effigy I had brought you, how did it speak? And if you suggest that I had made a magic slave to deceive you, consult the *Book of Sameri* and you will learn the truth. Any mischief on my part will be revealed."

When Afrasiyab looked into the *Book of Sameri* he learned that Khumar told the truth and discovered that Amar had escaped after tricking him.

Now Afrasiyab ordered his minister, Baghban Nature-Gardener, to catch Amar and produce him without delay.

Baghban recited a spell that caused a column of smoke to rise, billowing from the Earth to the Ninth Heaven.[98] Baghban commanded that column, "Bring me Amar Ayyar wherever you find him. Do not release him even for a moment after his capture."

The column of smoke disappeared in search of Amar.

Now hear of Amar Ayyar. After he emerged from the Dome of Light, he robbed all those who had assembled to witness his execution. Their caps, headgear, turbans and cummerbunds began to disappear as Amar swept the crowds with the Net of Ilyas. The commotion caused by these events was followed by a stampede as people ran crying, "We see ourselves being robbed but do not see the hand that robs us. Run before some calamity strikes us."

The field was soon deserted. People locked the doors of their houses. The bazaars shut down. Amar headed for his camp from one of the gates of the City of Disregard, looting and stealing all he could along the way, and took off his cape of invisibility. He was on his way when the smoke column surrounded him and carried him away like a cyclone. It brought Amar to Baghban Nature-Gardener, who caught Amar by the hand and led him to Afrasiyab and said, "My Lord, I present this troublesome creature before you as ordered."

Afrasiyab regarded Amar with a fiery glance and said, "Tell me how you would like to be put to death." Amar replied, "I see nobody under the skies who can cast even an evil glance at me." Afrasiyab said, "Do you not realize that you are now in my power to punish as I please?"

Amar retorted, "It still remains a question whether I am in your power or you are in mine. Only this is certain, that I can punish you speedily and so rigorously that you would not recognize your own face."

Afrasiyab was incensed by Amar's words but he kept his calm and said to his courtiers, "He is like the man who unburdened his heart by cursing and abusing his captor once he knew he had forfeited his life."

Afrasiyab asked Amar, "Tell us why you believe nobody can harm you." Amar said, "O Emperor of Hoshruba, first you must tell me who you reckon Laqa to be?" Afrasiyab replied, "We consider him our God." Amar asked, "Tell me then whether or not it is true that life and death are in God's hands?" All the sorcerers present declared, "Indeed, Lord Laqa has absolute power in all matters. He may kill or bring to life at will."

Amar said, "I want you to know then that I kill sorcerers by the will of Lord Laqa. Otherwise, an ordinary mortal like myself would have no power to kill mighty sorcerers and retainers of the Emperor of the Tilism. As the saying goes,

> *'Even should both heaven and Earth conspire*
> *The one whom the Lord guards none may harm.*

"Lord Laqa sent me into Hoshruba to destroy those creatures of his who become unmindful of their lord. Learn that I am Lord Laqa's Angel of Death and kill and destroy all those heedless, rebellious creatures against whom he deputes me. I have Lord Laqa's ear and am privy to his confidences."

Afrasiyab and all the sorcerers said, "Indeed, it is as he describes. Not a blade of grass moves without the will of Lord Laqa. Amar speaks the very truth."

Some sorcerers declared, "It is also true that we are often guilty of trespasses against our Lord."

Others intoned,

> *'Neither a mote increases or decreases*
> *Nor a grain moves without God's consent."*

Afrasiyab rose from his throne and reverentially kissed Amar's hand. He removed the spell from Amar and said respectfully, "O Lord Laqa's Angel of Death, please increase our honor by seating yourself in my court, and reveal who among us have you marked for your own."

Amar sat down on a bejewelled chair and said, "O Emperor, I cannot reveal Lord Laqa's secrets but if you wish I can show you the other marvellous gifts conferred on me by my Lord. I can confound you by my mastery of seventy-two different disguises, or entertain you with my gift of song. The will of Lord Laqa, however, is a secret of which I am unaware myself. There's nothing I can tell you of it."

Afrasiyab said, "It's true that no one but Lord Laqa himself knows his will. Please display for us the talents and gifts that you described."

Immediately, Amar became invisible where he was sitting. Everyone in the court cried out, "Indeed he was the Angel of Death sent by Lord Laqa."

Amar retired to a secluded corner where he took off his cape of invisibility and disguised himself as a beautiful damsel. The false damsel put on a luxurious dress, adorned herself with gold and jewels, and came before Afrasiyab. She gracefully greeted the Emperor of Hoshruba, who was stunned by her ravishing beauty and allure. Finally, Afrasiyab asked, "O rosebud of the garden of elegance, who are you and what has brought you here today?" The false damsel answered coquettishly, "O Emperor, your slave girl is in love with you and her heart finds no solace." Afrasiyab took her by the hand and seated her beside him.

Empress Heyrat was cut to the quick by Afrasiyab's actions and her heart conflagrated in a blaze of jealous rage. That houri-cheeked false beauty then turned to Heyrat and said, "O Empress, I am not a woman but the Lion of the Forest of Trickery, Amar Ayyar."

Afrasiyab was stunned and thought, *Indeed, he must be the favored one of Lord Laqa.* Afrasiyab lavishly rewarded Amar for his mastery in disguise and said with great deference,

"Indeed you are the one privy to the Lord's secrets
All his hidden mysteries you clearly see.

"Please regale us now with your gift of song and intone your honeyed notes within this assembly of friends."

At Afrasiyab's request Amar danced and afterwards played the pipe. Then he sang so melodiously that all those present in the assembly were entranced and swayed rapturously in time with his singing.

With everyone ecstatic and in transports of joy, Amar took control of the wine service and drugged the wine. He poured a cup and brought it to Afrasiyab, then threw it into the air and caught it on the palm of his hand.

Afrasiyab's heart overflowed with love and kindness and he drank the drugged wine. All the sorcerers in the court also had their fill of wine from the hand of their cruel, tyrannical cupbearer – Amar the notorious. He drugged them one and all.

As Afrasiyab felt a gust of cold breeze against his face he shouted, "O Amar, every one of our one hundred and seventy-five gods has arrived to hear you sing. Lords Sameri and Jamshed too, offer their praise." Amar replied, "You must not allow any of them to leave the assembly."

Heavily drugged, Afrasiyab rose and dancing from his throne holding Heyrat's hand, but they soon fell unconscious onto their faces. The sorcerers in the court cuffed and buffeted each other and dropped senseless in the midst of altercation. Some spoke inanities, pulled moustaches and slapped each other's faces. Yet others delivered a detailed account of their family and kin to those around them. In the end, everyone lost consciousness.

Amar drew his dagger and beheaded some twenty sorcerers and swept the assembly with the Net of Ilyas. A great din and racket rose as the sorcerers were killed. Clouds gathered in dark clusters, lightning flashed and magic spirits cried.

Amar stepped toward Afrasiyab and Heyrat to kill them. But the moment he approached the throne, the ground cleft and magic fairies clad in gold cloth and wearing pearl earrings emerged. They carried sprays and bowls filled with the essence of rose and musk. They put Afrasiyab's head in their lap, sprayed his face, and said to him, "*O Emperor, regain consciousness.*"

As Afrasiyab opened his eyes, the magic fairies sank back into the earth. Amar hid himself among the sorcerers' corpses disguised as a corpse, placing pieces of flesh dripping with blood on his face and neck.

When Afrasiyab looked around, he saw the whole assembly looted bare, all his courtiers fallen unconscious, and many sorcerers lying dead.

Afrasiyab looked up to the sky and made a sign, whereupon a rain cloud immediately materialized. It started raining and the raindrops restored the unconscious to their senses.

Heyrat said, "Emperor, witness how Amar has tricked us again."

Afrasiyab replied, "There is no place where he can run and hide from me. I will have him captured in an instant."

Afrasiyab exclaimed, "May all that is stolen reappear!" At these words, the thrones, chairs, cups, ewers, flowerpots and carpets reappeared as before. The assembly resumed and the sorcerers removed the corpses from the court.

Afrasiyab ascended the throne and consulted the *Book of Sameri*. He discovered that Amar lay disguised as a corpse among the slain sorcerers. The *Book of Sameri* advised Afrasiyab not to try to capture Amar himself; that he must return to the region of Batin because the next few hours were inauspicious for him. Once Afrasiyab learned this, he said to the sorcerers, "Do not carry away the corpses yet; Amar is hiding among the dead."

In the meanwhile, Sarsar arrived there after hearing the news of Amar Ayyar's capture. Afrasiyab said to her, "Go and look for Amar among the dead and take him prisoner. He lies among them disguised as a corpse."

The sorcerers were engrossed by Sarsar's doings as she started searching for Amar among the dead. Afrasiyab seated his magic double on the throne and disappeared without anyone noticing his absence or when the change occurred.

Sarsar finally found Amar. She jumped on his chest and tried to pinion him but Amar caught Sarsar's neck with his legs in a scissors hold and executed a lock that toppled her over and brought him on top. He blew a powdered drug into Sarsar's nose that made her unconscious. Carrying Sarsar in his arms Amar ran away.

As the sorcerers stood watching and marvelling at the scene, Heyrat cried, "Don't stand idly and gawk! Catch him before he carries Sarsar away."

The sorcerers ran at her orders but Amar managed to escape the Dome of Light. He sped like the wind and arrived in the City of Disregard.

Realizing that the city was full of sorcerers and they could easily capture him, Amar headed for the wilderness at the back of the Dome of Light and escaped toward the area used by Empress Heyrat as her private grounds. Seeing the trickster girls Saba Raftar and Shamima coming, Amar threw Sarsar into a cavern and, drawing his dagger, started fighting the trickster girls.

That part of the City of Disregard was a thoroughfare. One of Afrasiyab's retainers, a sorcerer named Hoshiar the Cunning, who was on his way to the emperor's court, passed there on his magic bird with his servants and attendants. Seeing the trickster girls fighting a stranger, he reckoned it must be Amar. As Hoshiar recited a spell to catch Amar, the trickster girls stopped him saying, "O Hoshiar, do not interfere in a fight between tricksters. Tricksters never seek a sorcerer's help to catch an opponent." Hoshiar said, "Talk some sense. One must destroy the enemy by any means." As he began reciting an incantation, Amar put on the cape of invisibility and disappeared.

In the meanwhile, the sorcerers who had followed Amar from Afrasiyab's court also arrived there. The trickster girls said to them, "Amar threw Sarsar in a cavern before our eyes." The sorcerers headed there to rescue her.

Amar, who had not left the scene, jumped into the cavern. He produced a pasteboard dragon from his zambil and raised its head from the cavern's mouth. The approaching sorcerers saw a dragon spewing fire and ran from it. They stopped at a safe distance and did not dare advance. From afar they recited spells to capture snakes, clapped, and made protective magic circles – none of which had any effect on the pasteboard dragon.

The sorcerers said to each other, "It's a mighty and powerful dragon that will not be dispelled. What a pity that Sarsar should lose her life in this manner."

To retrieve Sarsar from the cavern, they offered much gold and jewels to a companion of Hoshiar. His name was Hamnasheen and he was as peerless a sorcerer as he was impossibly old. As he advanced reciting an incantation, Amar pulled the dragon inside. Witnessing this, Hamnasheen thought the dragon had been dispelled by his spell. He boldly jumped into the cavern where Amar had laid a trap with his snare rope. Hamnasheen fell down entangled in it and Amar immediately drugged him with an egg of oblivion.

Amar again raised the dragon's head at the mouth of the cavern. The sorcerers standing far away thought the dragon had killed Hamnasheen too. They started reciting incantations and spells again. In the meanwhile, Amar stripped Hamnasheen, threw him into the zambil, and put on his clothes. Disguised as Hamnasheen, he came out of the cavern pulling the dragon with a rope a few steps behind him. He called out to the sorcerers, "I found no trace of Sarsar or the dragon in the cavern."

When the sorcerers saw the dragon creeping up on the false Hamnasheen, they cried, "The beast is upon you! Run for your life." Hearing their cries, the false Hamnasheen left the dragon and ran toward his companions. He fell down unconscious beside Hoshiar. His teeth were clenched and his skin began turning blue. Hoshiar said to the trickster girls, "We cannot rescue Sarsar."

The trickster girls got busy trying to rescue Sarsar themselves. Hoshiar took the false Hamnasheen on a conveyance to Afrasiyab's court.

Hoshiar saluted Afrasiyab and approached the throne to give an account of Hamnasheen and their encounter with the dragon. Afrasiyab's magic double, who had replaced the emperor, ordered that a physician be sent from the City of Disregard. Upon arrival, he gave the false Hamnasheen an antidote and put him on a bed in the courtyard for further treatment.

ஐ

In the meanwhile, Sarsar returned to her senses inside the cavern and came out. On her way, she passed the false dragon and the sight of it shocked and terrified her. She ran for her life, never once looking back.

On the way to Afrasiyab's court she met Saba Raftar and Shamima. When she asked them about Amar's whereabouts they replied, "After throwing you into the cavern he put on his cape of invisibility and disappeared. We are sure he escaped." Sarsar said, "It would be pointless to present ourselves in the emperor's court now. It would earn us nothing but shame. Everyone would point a finger at us and say we were unable to capture Amar. Let us search for him in the wilderness." With those words, the three trickster girls parted.

ஐ

In the court of the Emperor of Hoshruba, the real Afrasiyab's returned with his majestic entourage. He ascended his throne and everyone paid their respects. Afrasiyab said, "O my magic double, you may now leave!" The emperor's magic double disappeared.

The sorcerers mistakenly imagined that they had been humiliated and drugged by Amar Ayyar earlier only because the real Afrasiyab had not been present in the court. Some said that it would have been impossible to drug the Emperor of Hoshruba. Others said nobody could claim to have seen the emperor, whose rank and station were secret; after serving him all their lives they had yet to differentiate between his many appearances and were unsure if they had ever set eyes on the real Afrasiyab.

Once the court was in session, the dancers presented themselves and revels started. Sorcerer Hoshiar gave an account of his companion Hamnasheen to Afrasiyab. The emperor said, "Congratulations on his deliverance. How is he now?" Hoshiar answered, "By the grace of Lord Sameri, he is well." At that juncture, the false Hamnasheen, who pretended to have recovered his senses, rose from his bed, presented himself, and greeted the emperor.

When Afrasiyab asked him how he felt, the false Hamnasheen replied, "By the grace of Lord Sameri and Your Excellency's honor, I am now fully recovered."

Afrasiyab offered him a seat in the court where he sat down to watch the dance recital. But before long he found fault with the singer and began criticising her art, commenting, "She is not on the beat! There, her voice trembled! There, she gasped for breath! There, her voice quivered! See how she sings against the accompaniment! Now she lisps; she is completely unharmonious."

Hearing this, Afrasiyab said, "O Hamnasheen, you seem to know a great deal about singing!" The false Hamnasheen replied, "By Your Majesty's grace, I have witnessed many celebrated recitals. I am an authority on many arts – not only the art of the song – all because I live in the time of an august emperor like Your Excellency."

Afrasiyab said, "Very well, sing something for us."

The false Hamnasheen saluted the emperor humbly, sat down and started singing a *ghazal*.

Afrasiyab was greatly pleased by the false Hamnasheen's singing and conferred a robe of honor on him. The false Hamnasheen said, "I know a spell to illuminate a candle in whose light one can see the court of Indra in all its glory and watch fairies dancing. I discovered this spell in my grandfather's book; he had learned it in Bengal." Afrasiyab enthusiastically said, "O Hamnasheen, light that candle without delay so that we can witness this marvellous magic." He answered, "Please send for five *sers* of lard and equal amounts of pitch and butter."

At Afrasiyab's order, the requisite materials were produced. The false Hamnasheen screened himself off from others and made a large torch with the material provided and added large amounts of drug into it. Then he lit up the candle in the center of the court and its smoke started filling the palace. The false Hamnasheen said, "All of you must stare at the flame, and shortly you will witness the fairies dancing." Then he sat aside and began mumbling, pretending to recite a spell.

Everyone in the court, including Afrasiyab and Heyrat, stared at the flame. In the crowded assembly people leaned over each other to watch the spectacle and see what marvel would transpire. After a while, the smoke from the drug filled their nostrils and addled their brains. They started calling out, "It's true, fairies are dancing in the flame." Others said, "Regard Indra giving audience." Some others started dancing themselves. Finally, everyone, including Afrasiyab and Heyrat, fell unconscious to the floor.

The false Hamnasheen beheaded another twenty sorcerers and swept through the palace with the Net of Ilyas, stealing all the furniture with which the court had been refurnished.

Loud noises rose again and pandemonium broke out. The magic spirits of the murdered sorcerers called out their names one last time, dust storms rose and whirlwinds circled around.

Amar drew his dagger and stepped toward Afrasiyab intenting to behead him. The ground cleft suddenly as before and magic fairies emerged. Amar quickly put on his cape of invisibility and left the Dome of Light. The magic fairies restored Afrasiyab to consciousness by spraying his face with the essence of rose and *keora* then returned to the earth and the ground closed upon them.

Seeing his court in disarray, Afrasiyab summoned a magic rain cloud whose shower restored everyone to their senses and extinguished the drug candle Amar had lit. At the emperor's command, the whole palace was again appointed with furniture.

Everyone sat on their thrones and stations and continued to marvel at Amar's audacity and cunning.

Afrasiyab said disingenuously, "There's no doubt that Amar is the favored one of Lord Laqa. He cannot be killed by any means. He spoke the truth when he said he would kill all against whom Lord Laqa sent him. I am certain he will carry out his mission."

Then Afrasiyab turned to Heyrat and said, "However, I am myself under Lord Laqa's orders to kill Amar. Therefore, I request my empress to go forth and battle Mahrukh Magic-Eye while I contemplate some further strategy. It would be unwise to send for Amar Ayyar to be brought here."

Empress Heyrat mounted a magic peacock and returned to her camp in the region of Zahir, with her moon-faced attendants.

After Amar escaped from the Dome of Light it occurred to him that once before when he had tried to escape he ended up wandering on the banks of the River of Flowing Blood; if he tried again he would not find a way from there to his camp.

Amar disguised himself as a sorcerer and walked around the City of Disregard. In one place he heard some sorcerers talking. One said, "Amar is a veritable scourge. He fooled the emperor a second time and escaped." Another said, "He won't be able to escape because the River of Flowing Blood will bar his way." A third sorcerer said, "This land has forty doors. He will reach the region of Zahir only if he takes the eastern door." Finally, yet another sorcerer said, "You speak as if an accomplished trickster like Amar would not know the exit."

Amar Ayyar then headed for the eastern door of the city. He arrived at the outer limits and saw a magnificent gate guarded by thousands of sorcerers. As he was already in a sorcerer's disguise, he sprinted through the gate. When the gatekeepers asked his destination, Amar replied, "I am in Empress Heyrat's service and go in pursuit of Amar Ayyar. I cannot delay my errand to reply to your questions and invite the royal ire."

Amar cleared the gate and headed onwards. After traveling some distance, he saw the River of Flowing Blood and Empress Heyrat's encampment. Amar continued on and traveled a little distance before he finally saw Mahrukh Magic-Eye's camp and entered it.

Everyone who saw Amar ran to embrace him. A warm and noisy welcome followed the cries of "Amar has arrived!" All the commanders of the army, who had prayed for his safety and well being, came out of the royal court. Bahar, Mahrukh, Mahjabeen and Nafarman all embraced Amar and made gold offerings as a sacrifice to ward off any harm from befalling him. All of them proceeded to the royal pavilion and drums were struck in celebration. Amar sat on his station and recounted his adventures in Afrasiyab's court. The whole court laughed uproariously at his exploits.

In the meanwhile, Empress Heyrat also joined her forces as drumbeats announced her arrival. Her commanders received her and she ascended her throne. Before long, she was occupied with planning for battle.

Sorceress Hasina Magic-Beauty

Now hear of sorceress Princess Hasina, who departed in aid of Laqa toward Mount Agate. Leading an army of sorcerers and flying on her magic throne, she arrived at her destination after a few days' journey and entered the fortress of Mount Agate.

Laqa was giving audience and watching a dance recital when red clouds appeared in the sky, heralding the approach of sorcerers. Bakhtiarak and King Suleiman Amber-Hair rose to welcome the arriving party. Soon Hasina's army of sorcerers descended, along with their beautiful commander. She had augmented her beauty and comely face with magic and everyone who saw her was greatly impressed by her charming looks. Laqa's commanders welcomed her and conducted her into the court. Bakhtiarak arranged for the army of sorcerers to be camped opposite Amir Hamza's camp.

Upon entering the court, Princess Hasina prostrated herself before Laqa, who said, "Since you bowed your head you will receive the bounty of my grace."

Hasina rose and sat on a throne while Laqa conferred a robe of honor on her. Hasina asked, "O my lord, who are these accursed creatures who have the temerity to consider themselves your equals?" Laqa said, "That is a very long tale that the devil designate of my court could tell for he knows it well."

As Hasina turned to Bakhtiarak, he gave her the whole account, from Amir Hamza's advent to the present. At the end, Bakhtiarak said, "O Hasina, you can witness an example of Amir Hamza's ravages even in the tilism itself. Amar Ayyar and Prince Asad are still at large; even the Emperor of Hoshruba has been unable to capture them."

Princess Hasina said, "Order the drums of war to be struck in my name. In no time I will wipe the entire camp of rebels out of existence."

Bakhtiarak sniggered at her words and said, "You have just arrived. I suggest you see the sights of this world awhile. Death will soon find you and nothing will remain." Hasina replied, "You see spears and lances even in a carafe of urine."[99] Bakhtiarak answered, "I spoke thus because one trickster alone caused such mayhem upon entering the tilism; here you will have to contend with one hundred and eighty thousand tricksters. While only Prince Asad went into the tilism, his father and grandfather have been putting up an unremitting fight. These recalcitrant creatures of Lord Laqa cheat death at every opportunity." Hasina replied, "I will succeed by the grace of Lord Laqa. At my hands, you will soon see the rebels come to a bad end."

Hasina rested a few days to recover from the travails of her journey and was given a feast by King Suleiman Amber-Hair. Dance recitals and revels continued. Finally, during an afternoon audience, Hasina said to Laqa, "Tonight the battle drums should be beaten in my name. Tomorrow morning I will destroy the enemy."

When the Emperor of Heavens retired from the russet court of afternoon to rest in his western palace, when the black pavilion of the Prince of Darkness[100] was pitched and the dark tent ropes stretched out to the four corners of the world, drums of war were beaten in Laqa's camp as per Hasina's wishes.

The messengers brought the news to the court of the King of the True Believers and gave an account of Princess Hasina's arrival to the courtiers of the mighty king with these words: "The sorceress Princess Hasina has arrived from the tilism and plans on doing battle tomorrow morning. The war drums are being beaten in the enemy camp." The King of True Believers said, "Battle drums should be struck in our camp, too."

Amar's son, Chalak, headed for the Music Gallery of Sikander and struck the Timbal of Sikander. The trumpets blared the call of impending strife and evil. Every brave became alert and made preparations for battle. The noise of drums and clarions rose from all corners.

All night long the warriors remained busy in battle preparations. When the Sultan of the Golden-Headgear[101] ascended the throne of light and the World Conquering Emperor[102] entered to rule the field of heavens, Laqa rode out with great pomp and majesty, surrounded by an entourage of evil sorcerers. Princess Hasina rode her magic throne into the battlefield and arrayed her forces.

Amir Hamza also finished his morning prayers and, along with all the commanders of the army, presented himself at the Hall of Audience. After a moment, King Saad's entourage appeared from the private pavilion. All the commanders bowed, made a ring around his throne and conducted him onto the battlefield.

The masters of the column and ranks arranged their men for battle and the groundsmen levelled the arena. The water-carriers sprinkled the ground to settle the dust. The criers sang of the futility of life and proclaimed the denunciation of the world to the warriors with these words: "Yes, O braves! Here's the ball and here's the field. The battlefield provides an opportunity to earn renown. Redeem your lives by scattering them in your noble cause. Those who do not cover themselves with glory in battle are not long remembered. Nobody recalls the mighty kings that lived nor sees a trace of their graves. Shine in the arena of battle and earn everlasting fame."

After the criers withdrew, a warrior named Bubran Lion of Battle came forward from Laqa's army after receiving permission for combat and made a display of his martial dexterity. He cried, "Come out and fight!" and challenged the commanders of Amir Hamza's camp with these words: "Is there anyone among you who can confront me? If there is such a one, let him prepare to be made dust."

From Amir Hamza's camp, the warrior Bahram sought King Saad's leave to answer Bubran's challenge and rode into the arena to fight him. During lance combat, Bahram relieved Bubran of his weapon but Princess Hasina cast a spell and Bahram felt his power drain out of his body. Bubran lifted Bahram out of his saddle by his metal cummerbund and slammed him to the ground. He sat on Bahram's chest and pinioned him. Thereafter, he signalled to a trickster in King Suleiman Amber-Hair's service, who made Bahram unconscious with an egg of oblivion and carried him away a prisoner to his camp.

Bubran Lion of Battle again called out, "Those who wish to meet their deaths should come out and face me." Mandvail Isfahani faced him next but Hasina's spell rendered him powerless too, and he was also taken captive.

Next, Muhleel Jang Iraqi came out and was likewise captured. In this manner, seventy commanders of Amir Hamza's forces, including Aala Gurd, Mala Gurd, Kapi Arzal and Kapi Zalzal became prisoners.

At that moment, the standards of the left flank were unfurled and the kettledrums mounted on elephants and camels were struck. The rank-splitting, column-destroying champion, Prince Hashim Swordfighter, son of Amir Hamza, brought his horse forward and sought King Saad's permission for battle. The king conferred a robe of honor on the prince and said, "Go forth in the protection of God!" When Prince Hashim sought Amir Hamza's forgiveness for any sins of omission or commission, he embraced his son and put a protective necklace around his neck to ward off magic. He recited Prophet Ibrahim's prayer on Prince Hashim and gave him leave.

Hashim raced his mount toward the battlefield,

Hashim the warrior headed for the arena
Astride a fairy-faced mount, a battle charger

Hashim crossed the expanse between him and the adversary in just three strides and clashed powerfully with Bubran, disarraying the senses of his foe. Bubran unsheathed his shining sword and brought it down on the head of the worthy prince, who used excellent skill to foil the blow. The prince then drew his own sword; he feigned to deal Bubran a side blow but landed one on his head instead. Princess Hasina cast spells to stay his hand but none of her spells worked because the prince wore the protective necklace. The prince's sword finally cleft Bubran in two. Drums and clarions sounded in the camp of True Believers and the valiant prince challenged the enemy warriors again.

This time, sorceress Hasina came out to answer his challenge. Everyone thought it was the sorceress who confronted the prince but unbeknown to all, she had concealed herself and sent a magic effigy in her exact likeness to fight the prince. The magic effigy dealt the prince a sword blow. The prince dodged it and struck one himself that cut the magic effigy in two. Both pieces of her body flew skywards and, after a moment, ankle-bells chimed and anklets tinkled.

The prince saw sorceress Hasina arrive. Her lovely hairdo, her charming stature and her life-breathing lips gave cheer to those sunk in hopelessness and sorrow. Her lips wounded and lacerated hundreds with the sword of smile and the Turks of her eyes, armed with the daggers of eyebrows, killed hundreds of thousands.

When Prince Hashim Swordfighter beheld the stunning beauty of that destroyer of patience and composure, he called out,

"Plant the tree of friendship that may bring hearts cheer
Uproot the plant of enmity that only bears untold grief

God entwined the thread of my life with your locks
Command your ruby lips now to grant me life."

That beauty, whose cheeks were resplendent as the moon, said, "O august prince, O life-sacrificing lover, you swear love to me and yet fight your beloved. Come, surrender your weapons to me."

Prince Hashim handed over all his weapons, including his sword, shield and dagger. The beauty said, "A necklace is more becoming around the neck of the beloved. Why do you wear it? Put it around my neck." Hashim replied, "O charming friend, O incarnate beauty,

"If you asked I would surrender you my life
And submit as readily something dearer still."

With these words, he put the protective necklace around the neck of sorceress Hasina, who turned and started toward Laqa's camp. Prince Hashim followed her, reciting,

"I would not turn from my purpose till I achieve my end
Either I will seek union with my beloved or lay down my life in the attempt
If my grave were opened the rising smoke
Would tell the world of my smouldering heart within
Show your face O beloved that the world may fall at your feet
Say a word that they may release their suppressed sighs
I do not chase beauties in the manner of those unfaithful
I will lie at your door until I give up my soul."

As Prince Hashim reached Laqa's camp, one of King Suleiman Amber-Hair's tricksters made the prince unconscious with an egg of oblivion and took him to the prison where he was incarcerated with Amir Hamza's other commanders. Laqa ordered the drums to announce the cessation of hostilities and his army returned to its camp and rested.

Amir Hamza also returned to his pavilion and, after taking his bath, arrived at the court. He saluted the king and took his seat. In view of the capture of his army commanders, King Saad had called off all dancing and festivities and an oppressive silence reigned in the court.

Meanwhile, Laqa returned to his camp to the sound of festive music. Revels were held and wine flowed. His soldiers found respite from their hardships and relaxed. Laqa rested the following morning.

Finally, in the world's private pavilion, the evening that burns lovers like tapers threw a dark veil on morning's beautiful face and that time approached when the night envelops and conceals all.

Laqa again ordered the drums of war to be struck. The messengers brought the news to the King of True Believers and the call to war was answered from his camp by a blast of the Timbal of Sikander. The whole night the armies remained busy in preparations. When morning's beloved saw her face in the sun's mirror, and the day was fully lit and emerged from the night's belly, lords of the arena led their men into the battlefield and rank-destroying champions arrayed themselves in files. Amir Hamza, with the King of True Believers, and Laqa with the iniquitous Hasina, took positions on opposite sides of the arena. The sorcerers too, formed ranks while playing musical instruments, singing chants, wielding tridents, and pentadents, and displaying their apparatuses of warfare. Once the battle arrays were drawn, it was time for carnage to begin.

Sorceress Hasina rode out on a magic peacock and challenged the camp of True Believers, saying, "I seek combat, O disloyal subjects of Lord Laqa. Today you will receive your reward and the sword will make you its prey."

Upon hearing her challenge,

The righteous son of the noble Hamza
Alam Shah of name, titled the Rustam

who was famed as the Rustam Elephant-body, the pride of the Pavilion of Suleiman and destroyer of warriors of elephant-might, took his father's leave for combat and entered the arena to face Princess Hasina.

Hasina further augmented her beauty by reciting a spell. Her forehead was radiant like Venus. Her ruby lips were more crimson than Badakhshan rubies,[103] and her sparkling teeth outshone pearls and put them to shame. Her smile was like a shower of salt on the lacerated soul of lovers, and with her coquetry, her manner and her airs, she slew her lovers without the help of a knife.

The moment Prince Alam Shah beheld her, the spell of her love was cast. Even though Amir Hamza's sons and commanders never fall victim to the beauty of a sorceress – no matter how charming – Alam Shah was captivated by Hasina because of her magical beauty. He became completely oblivious to all considerations and could see nothing except his beloved's face. He forgot all deference due Amir Hamza and the King of True Believers. His senses all in disarray, he recited love verses. Tears of blood welled up in his eyes and sighs and lamentations issued from his lips, disclosing the secrets of his passion.

After declarations of love were exchanged between Hasina and Alam Shah, she turned toward her camp and the prince followed her. Bakhtiarak ordered the cessation of hostilities for the day. Amir Hamza returned to his camp from the tragic events of the day with a heavy and afflicted heart.

In Laqa's camp, Bakhtiarak sent the commanders to welcome Alam Shah, who conducted him inside. Laqa was giving audience when Prince Alam Shah entered. All the courtiers rose to pay him their respects.

Alam Shah sat down beside Hasina infatuated, and kept reciting love couplets.

Bakhtiarak asked Alam Shah, "Why has Your Excellency honored us with a visit?" Alam Shah answered, "O Bakhtiarak, I would become your sworn slave if you could persuade Hasina to lie with me." Bakhtiarak replied, "I will explore every possibility and do my very best to achieve your end. Your luck will have to do the rest. I will now talk to Hasina." Bakhtiarak advised the prince to allow him privacy with the princess. Prince Alam Shah sat at a distance on a golden chair while Bakhtiarak sat beside Hasina to talk to her.

Bakhtiarak said, "O Princess, this son of Amir Hamza had once fallen in love with a sorceress who told him she would marry him only if he gave her his father's head in marriage money. The prince confronted and fought his father to fulfill her wishes. I advise that you also put some conditions on your union with the prince. Ask him to bring you Hamza's head; tell him that he must present the Pavilion of Suleiman as well, for you will marry him inside it. And order him to prostrate himself before Lord Laqa. I would advise you to remain cold and distant toward him and not let his youthful beauty tempt you to lie with him. There are two advantages to creating a conflict between him and his father: Nothing would be better than Hamza's dying at his son's hands, or Alam Shah himself dying in the attempt. Fatherly grief would not allow Hamza to survive long afterwards. Moreover, when he attacks his camp in the name of your love, no one will harm him. He would kill thousands of his own men."

Hasina said, "O Bakhtiarak, you have come upon a most marvellous scheme that would cause the True Believers to kill themselves in an internecine war. Regarding your request that I desist from granting the prince his desire, know that lascivious thoughts cannot weaken me in such situations. Although I am four-hundred-years-old and fond of ravishing youthful men, I would not jeopardise an important mission on account of lust. Go now and do what you must, but do send the prince to me at night so that I may cool my eyes with his beauty and enjoy myself by kissing and fondling him without allowing him to satisfy his desire."

Having come to this agreement with Princess Hasina, Bakhtiarak went before Prince Alam Shah and said, "O august prince, I did my very best in your service. At first Princess Hasina would not consent, but she gave in after much persuasion. However, she is adamant that you must bow your head before Lord Laqa, bring her your father's head, and present to her also the Pavilion of Suleiman before she grants your wishes."

Alam Shah said, "I shall bow my head before Lord Laqa without delay." That very instant the prince prostrated himself before Laqa, who was greatly pleased and conferred a robe of honor on Alam Shah. Laqa exclaimed, "I will that my creature Hasina should marry this man."

Alam Shah said to Bakhtiarak, "Have the drums of war struck in my name so that I may battle the camp of the True Believers and bring back Hamza's head and the Pavilion of Suleiman for Princess Hasina." Bakhtiarak answered, "I shall take the news to Princess Hasina that her lover has agreed to all her conditions and prostrated himself before Lord Laqa. I will then bring you her message. I cannot order the drums of war to be struck in your name as yet because she may accuse me of sending her lover into battle without her permission. I would have nothing to offer in defense of my actions."

Bakhtiarak returned to Hasina and said, "O Princess, my plan is working just as I expected. Alam Shah is restless to go and fight his father. However, another concern now weighs on my heart. Hamza is the master of the Most Great Name – the dispeller of magic. When Alam Shah confronts him, Hamza will be able to remove your magic from him and the prince will come out of the spell. He will return to his senses and all my hard work would go to waste."

Hasina answered, "I too, endeavour to erase the Most Great Name from the tablet of Hamza's heart by sorcery and cast a spell that will make him unable to recall it. But the powerful magic needed to bring this about cannot be prepared overnight. It will be a few days before it is ready."

Bakhtiarak said, "I would advise you to retire with Alam Shah to some pleasant garden. You may kiss and fondle him and share meat and wine with him. Have your pleasure with him in every manner except the ultimate act. I will think of more plans in the meanwhile."

Bakhtiarak now returned to Prince Alam Shah and said, "O Prince, I communicated your situation to Princess Hasina. She expressed a wish to spend some private moments with you and forbade me from striking the drum of war in your name as yet. You may leave on your mission only after both parties have fulfilled their desires. It seems to me that by setting these conditions, she only wishes to test your fidelity. She is a great warrior herself and it was not on account of any weakness that she set those conditions for you. Now you may go and enjoy yourself with her."

Alam Shah replied, "I am ready to fulfill her wishes. I will do as she commands."

Bakhtiarak spoke to Suleiman Amber-Hair and a garden blooming with flowers was reserved for Princess Hasina and Prince Alam Shah. Cups and ewers, musk-perfumed goblets, royal carpets, an array of fine foods, and all instruments of luxury and leisure were provided, along with moon-faced cupbearers and elegant and worthy slave girls. Hasina entered the garden holding Alam Shah's hand and beheld the pretty garden where spring reigned. There was a profusion of watercourses beside which cypress and leafy trees grew. Fruit hung from the trees in clusters and every tree was covered with flowers. The garden and its fauna seemed entirely free of the fear of autumn or the hand of the hunter or the pruner.

In the middle of the garden was a fully appointed summerhouse provided with all comforts. A throne was set up in the corner and a carpet and a royal bed were laid out. Melodious singers and moon-bodied dancers were in attendance. The two lovers sat down on the throne and made love talk. They sipped the crimson wine and kissed and embraced each other.

When Prince Alam Shah attempted to satisfy his desire, Hasina stopped him on one pretext or another. Sometimes she glared angrily at him with knitted brow. When Alam Shah expressed annoyance and anger at her coquettish refusals, she smiled, put her arms around the prince's neck, and said, "O jasmine-bodied prince, while I am willing to scatter and sacrifice a thousand lives at your feet, I am bound by Lord Laqa's decree. By his grace, I will allow you to drink the nectar of union with me very soon. Just wait two days longer."

When the prince still would not desist, she brought him to the bed on the pretence of lying with him but when the prince was at the peak of his passion, she recited a spell that put him to sleep.

It also left Hasina burning with desire and she thought, *If I lie with him and Lord Laqa's mission is hindered, I will earn universal condemnation in the tilism and Afrasiyab will send me into exile. As Bakhtiarak suggested, it would be prudent to remain the master of my passion for the next few days. After Hamza is killed, I will carry this beautiful youth to my home in the tilism and ravish him to my heart's content. But I must not let him be killed, even if I let him encounter*

Hamza for the pleasure of Lord Laqa. Bakhtiarak spoke like a pimp when he said it would be equally beneficial whether the prince killed Hamza or Hamza killed the prince.

Princess Hasina remained occupied with these thoughts. Sometimes she thought, *There is no knowing what the fickle heavens hold for us. I should lie with him before some calamity overtakes us.* Soon fear of Laqa would overcome her; the thought filled her with dread that upon learning the truth, Laqa might destroy both her and her lover.

Thus, Princess Hasina and Alam Shah remained occupied with each other with all the previous restraints. Whenever Hasina attended the court, Alam Shah accompanied her.

All these events were reported to Amir Hamza by his messengers and spies. The army commanders grieved at the news of the prodigious warrior, Alam Shah, renouncing the True Faith. King Saad said to them, "Prince Alam Shah is under a spell and not the master of his senses. If he attacks us, no one must injure or kill him."

Everyone was greatly perturbed by this command. It made any encounter with Alam Shah perilous, allowing the attacker all the advantages and privileges and the defenders none. The whole camp was disturbed, and Amir Hamza continuously mourned his son.

Witnessing this sorry state of affairs in his camp, Amar Ayyar's son, Chalak, decided he should put an end to them by killing Princess Hasina. In the meanwhile, Bakhtiarak also sent one of his tricksters, Tarar the Speedster, to capture Hamza so that Alam Shah could destroy the camp of the True Believers without hindrance.

Trickster Tarar the Speedster

Tarar the Speedster decorated himself with trickster's devices and left. When he arrived near the camp of True Believers he disguised himself as an attendant and entered the camp with other retainers and officers of the camp. He positioned himself in a nook and when the king adjourned the court at a late hour and everyone rose, Tarar the Speedster hid himself under a throne.

When the king and all the commanders and officers returned to their resting places, Amir Hamza remained in the Pavilion of Suleiman. The vigil made rounds of the camp and the horn trilled at regular intervals. Muqbil Vafadar sat on night duty outside Amir Hamza's pavilion armed with his bow and quiver. When Amir Hamza's snores floated on the air, Tarar the Speedster threw moths made of a drug at the candles and tapers. They fell on the flames and the smoke from the drug spread in the pavilion. The attendants who pressed Amir Hamza's legs fell unconscious. Tarar the Speedster now rolled out from under the throne and reached Amir Hamza's bedside. He removed the sleep veil from Amir Hamza's face with the help of a rod and, filling a tubular device with a drug, put one end into Amir Hamza's nostrils. As he inhaled, Tarar blew from the other end to send the drug into Amir Hamza's nostril. It overpowered his senses, he sneezed and fell unconscious.

Next, Tarar approached the entrance of the pavilion and called out to Muqbil in Amir Hamza's voice.

Muqbil replied, "I am at your service," and entered.

The moment he stepped in, with an egg of oblivion Tarar made him unconscious as well. He dragged Amir Hamza's attendants by their feet onto the floor and spread his trickster's mantle on the bed. After tying Amir Hamza with his snare rope and wrapping him in the trickster's mantle, Tarar bundled him up and came out of the pavilion carrying him on his shoulders.

He made his way out of the camp under the cover of the tents. He ducked at any sign of danger and proceeded when it cleared. When he saw the soldiers of the vigil he flattened himself like a lizard against the ground; when they passed he moved forward, mimicking the walk of cats and dogs. In this manner, he made his way to the end of the camp from where he sped leaping and bounding to his destination.

On the way, it occurred to Tarar the Speedster that if he carried Amir Hamza to his camp the tricksters would secure his release. He arrived in a mountain pass and wondered if he should behead Amir Hamza and take his head to Laqa's court instead. Then he thought, *A trickster of the caliber of Amar Ayyar is still alive, who would surely avenge Hamza's death on me. Hamza's progeny and commanders as well would wreak havoc upon hearing the news. Moreover, Alam Shah is also present in the camp. His filial love might awaken at the sight of his father's head and he might ask why I killed his father and demand vengeance. Then I would pay with my life.*

In view of these considerations, Tarar put the bundled up form of Amir Hamza in a dark and narrow cave in the mountain pass and blocked the entrance with a stone.

He returned and gave Bakhtiarak a complete account of how he had imprisoned Hamza in a place where he would die from hunger and starvation. Bakhtiarak said, "You did well in not bringing Hamza here. The tricksters would have freed him in no time."

In the morning, the news of Amir Hamza's kidnapping caused a great uproar in the camp of the True Believers. King Saad dispatched the tricksters Abul Fatah and Samak to search for Amir Hamza and bring news of him.

Bakhtiarak now visited Hasina and said to her, "Now you will be able to achieve your end. You may go ahead and pit Alam Shah against Hamza's camp to slay them with his hand. Hamza has been kidnapped at my orders." Hasina said, "Very well, order the drums of war to be struck." Next, Hasina said to Alam Shah, "If you wish to lie with me you must now fulfil your promise and bring me your father's head."

Alam Shah replied, "Blow the bugles of war. I will cut Hamza to pieces."

Having secured Alam Shah's pledge in this matter, Bakhtiarak headed for Laqa's court, where he gave him a complete account and asked for the drums to be struck in Alam Shah's name. Upon his orders, Laqa's minions left to issue the call to war.

Sorcerer Hoshiar the Cunning

While these preparations are underway, let us hear of Amar Ayyar.

As Empress Heyrat made her plans to battle Mahrukh Magic-Eye, Afrasiyab dispatched the sorcerer Hoshiar the Cunning to arrest Mahrukh and all her supporters and give them into Empress Heyrat's custody.

Afrasiyab gave Hoshiar two carafes filled with magic water, one of which caused loss of consciousness while the other dispelled it. Afrasiyab said to him, "Mix the water that causes loss of consciousness with a large quantity of regular water and sprinkle it around your camp to create a protective ring. Any trickster who crosses it will fall unconscious. When you go into combat, splash the water on your adversary and it will make him lose his senses too. In this manner, you will capture the rebels' entire camp. When the tricksters attack, you must arrest them similarly."

Hoshiar returned to his house with the magic water and ordered the sorcerers under his command to prepare to march. When the powerful sorceress Mugheela, who was Hoshiar's mother, learned that her son was leaving on a campaign, she made preparations to secretly accompany him. After completing his arrangements, Hoshiar returned to Afrasiyab. The emperor gave him the robe of departure. Hoshiar mounted a magic dragon and left with his twelve thousand sorcerers riding magical birds and beasts, ringing gongs and blowing bugles.

The sorceress Mugheela grew magic wings and followed them but remained hidden from all.

When Hoshiar arrived near Heyrat's camp she sent a welcoming party to receive him. Her commanders conducted Hoshiar into her presence while his army bivouacked and set up pavilions and tents beside Heyrat's camp.

Hoshiar gave Empress Heyrat a detailed account of his mission and said, "Please order the drums of war to be beaten. Tomorrow I will destroy the rebels' whole army." Heyrat acquiesced to his request and her commanders struck the clarion.

The magic birds flew into Queen Mahjabeen Diamond-Robe's court. With raised beaks they sang her adulations and praises in chaste words and eloquent terms and announced, "*The Sorcerer Hoshiar has arrived at Afrasiyab's order. Heyrat has issued the call to war with the intention of combat and carnage. Now you may decide what you please.*" After communicating these words the magic birds flew away.

Mahjabeen said to Mahrukh Magic-Eye, "You too, must answer her call to battle and start preparation this evening." Mahrukh replied, "Very well." She sent for the commanders of the army, issued orders to give the call to war, and before long the whole camp received the news.

In the evening, when the throne of dusk was laid on the blue skies and the Emperor of Afternoon[104] hid his face and escaped into the dominions of the west, the clarion was sounded from Mahrukh Magic-Eye's camp and the drums of war were beaten as thunderously and terribly as the blast of the Last Trumpet. The arena rang with a call to the True Believers to prepare for war.

The illustrious sorcerers, the Jamsheds of the times, the equals of Sameri, all began to invoke their magic. The warriors inspected the readiness of their arms. Queen Mahjabeen Diamond-Robe adjourned the court and entered her private pavilion. All the tricksters, including Amar Ayyar, departed for the wilderness and hid themselves in hilly passes.

Prince Asad inspected the preparedness of his men. Mahrukh Magic-Eye, Surkh Mu, Nafarman, Shakeel and Bahar each invoked rare and powerful spells, knowing they would have to face Empress Heyrat on the battlefield. They made magic slave girls and gold-feathered magic peacocks, readied ancient spells from the times of Sameri, promised sacrifices of the foe to magic spirits and secured pledges from them to come to their aid when summoned. The whole night was spent in these preparations.

The carpet-keeper of fate threw an azure spread on the golden throne of heaven and the Lord of the Day[105] entered the World's Hall of Audience.[106] The lions of the forest of valor, the valiant lords of fields of carnage, renowned sorcerers and noble commanders started for the arena. The sorcerer commanders rode magic thrones and beasts. A special suit of armor and choice weapons adorned Prince Asad's strong and powerful body for the impending combat with Heyrat's army.

Ringed by her army, Mahjabeen Diamond-Robe rode her throne to the battlefield with great majesty.

From the station of audience to the battlefield, there was an unending display of Mahjabeen's paraphernalia of grandeur and luxury. Row after row of war elephants and camels stood covered with golden saddles, with the champion warriors and standard-bearers of the army in seat. The star-studded sheets that covered the elephants made the starry skies envious. Several thousand Arabs scattered gold and silver coins in an offering to ward off the evil eye from their sovereign. They were followed by the kettledrums mounted on elephants and camels. The drummers clad in gold and silver brocade dresses sang the tunes of *lalit*, *bherveen*, and *bhibhas*.[107] The criers marched alongside, inciting and stirring warriors to combat with their exhortations.

All of a sudden, Empress Heyrat's procession materialized on the horizon. Those assembled saw thousands of enamelled palaces come flying in the air while sixty-four thousand magic bugles heralded their approach. Sorcerers and sorceresses clad in fine clothes flew beside them and began pouring into the arena. They sported bracelets of pearl and coral and wore hoops and earrings. Mounted on gold-feathered magic peacocks, the sorceresses were clad in saris worked with precious jewels. Carpets of gold cloth were spread in the enamel palace in which Empress Heyrat sat, and hundreds of thousands of sorcerers stood alert behind her. Clapper-drums and bugles played in the assembly, and a dance recital was in progress.

All the pomp and grandeur of Mahjabeen Diamond-Robe's procession waned before Empress Heyrat's splendorous entourage.

At sorcerer Hoshiar's order, the sorcerers dropped lightning bolts on the arena to burn up the shrubbery and trees. A magic cloud rained and settled all the dust and dirt. The proclaimers of war made announcements and the criers shouted their declarations. They sang the denunciation of the ephemeral world and reminded the warriors that only the brave were remembered for their deeds after they were gone.

After they withdrew, the left and the right flanks and the advance guard and the center of the army were formed.

The sorcerer Hoshiar entered the arena with Empress Heyrat's leave and sought combat after displaying the marvels of his magic. Princess Surkh Mu Wonder-Mane flew her magic dragon into the arena to answer his challenge.

Hoshiar shot an arrow at Surkh Mu Wonder-Mane. She recited a counterspell and a magic claw carrying a dagger appeared in the arrow's path and cut it in two in mid flight. Surkh Mu now untied her hair. Thousands of stars rolled out of her hair and flew to the sky from where they fell like a comet shower on Hoshiar's forces, killing thousands. Enraged, Hoshiar took out the flask of the magic water that caused loss of consciousness and mixed it with the water in a waterskin. He poured the entire contents of the waterskin onto a bale of cotton and recited a spell.

The bale of cotton flew up into the sky like a cloud. It covered Mahjabeen Diamond-Robe's camp and rained down. Anyone on whom even a single raindrop fell lost consciousness. Surkh Mu Wonder-Mane, who stood in the arena, was the first victim of the magic raindrops that now rained in a cascade. Bahar, Mahrukh Magic-Eye and some other illustrious sorcerers raised magic canopies over their heads but the magic raindrops pierced these canopies and they all fell unconscious. The camp was thrown into disarray and Mahrukh's army took to its heels.

Prince Asad took the reins of his horse with the intention of laying down his life in battle but he too, lost his senses when a raindrop fell on him. His army escaped and took refuge in the mountains, the deserts, and the wilderness. The renowned sorcerers who commandeered the armies and did not flee were rendered unconscious. They were pinioned at Hoshiar's orders, who then instructed his men to announce the end of the battle.

Empress Heyrat returned to her court scattering gold pieces as a sacrifice to ward off the evil eye from Hoshiar. She ordered celebrations and her army unbuckled itself and rested.

Heyrat wrote the entire account of the battle to Afrasiyab and ordered the prisoners to be brought before her. They were all unconscious. Hoshiar put them under magic incarceration, stuck needles in their tongues, and sprinkled them with the magic water that restored them to consciousness. The prisoners opened their eyes and found themselves in that sorry state. They lowered their heads and did not speak.

Empress Heyrat said to Mahrukh Magic-Eye, "Did you forget this day would come?"

Mahrukh, whose tongue was pierced, could only answer by pointing heavenward with a gesture that God was her Lord and Master. She and her companions similarly offered terse replies to Heyrat's comments in a manner that enraged the empress.

Heyrat thundered, "Raise the scaffolds! The Angel of Death will soon ply his trade; the life of not a single rebel shall be spared." At her orders, executioners who excelled at skinning and sawing bodies presented themselves, the scaffolds rose, and the news was proclaimed in all parts of the tilism.

Heyrat ordered the sorcerer Hoshiar to incarcerate the rebels and set up a protective magic ring around the camp to keep the tricksters at bay.

Hoshiar led all rebel commanders to his pavilion and tied them to the posts. He said to his attendants, "Tell the water-carriers to fill their waterskins and bring them to me so that I may mix magic water with their contents. They may then sprinkle the water to make a protective ring around the camp. Go now, but leave one person on duty inside the pavilion."

The attendants executed his orders and the water-carriers arrived at Hoshiar's pavilion carrying waterskins. One after the other, they went before Hoshiar. He asked them to rub their bodies with a few drops of the restorative magic water as protection and mix the other kind that induced unconsciousness into their waterskins. The carriers then left to create the protective magic ring.

Now hear of the tricksters. After they witnessed the rout of their camp and the capture of their army commanders, they went into action to rescue them.

Qiran the Ethiope headed for Hoshiar's camp dressed as an attendant and from afar noticed the water-carriers sprinkling liquid around the camp. Qiran felt some unease on seeing them at work at that unusual hour. He decided some evil was in the water, which must be avoided. He took another path into Hoshiar's camp and saw a water-carrier coming his way. Qiran asked him, "Did you finish the work?" He answered, "It will be days before a protective magic ring can be made around such a large camp as Heyrat's. It's not something that can be done overnight." Qiran now realized that he was right to avoid the water-carriers and that any who crossed it would fall under its spell.

Qiran waited outside Hoshiar's pavilion for an opportunity.

In the meanwhile, the attendant deputed inside the pavilion finished his two-hour shift and called out, "I have finished my shift. Another should replace me." Qiran spoke up, "I waited to relieve you. You may go now as I am on duty." After the attendant left, Qiran stepped inside and stood behind Hoshiar, fanning him with a kerchief.

In the meanwhile, Zargham and Jansoz also disguised themselves and headed for Hoshiar's camp. However, they did not pay much attention to the water-carriers sprinkling the camp at that unusual hour. As a result, the moment they entered the ground marked by the magic water they fell unconscious.

Hoshiar had secretly deputed sorcerers inside the ring to alert him if they saw anyone fall unconscious. They carried Zargham and Jansoz before him. Hoshiar recited a spell and blew on the tricksters, which made their disguises evaporate. Seeing their changed faces, he realized they were tricksters. He said to himself, *By the grace of Lord Sameri, I have two tricksters in my clutches.* He tied them to the pavilion posts and resumed drinking, all the while he continued giving the magic water to the water-carriers.

By now, Amar also arrived near Hoshiar's camp. Noticing the water-carriers, he turned and went in another direction. He came upon a water-carrier who sat eating in his small tent. Amar changed his disguise to a water-carrier's and tied a waistcloth made of coarse red cotton, hung the water-carrier's belt around his neck and tied a turban, one end of which he wrapped around his neck. Amar tied water bowls and fastened the belt, slung the waterskin over his shoulder and, holding it in the manner of an old hand, went and greeted the water-carrier.

He asked Amar, "Where do you work?" The false water-carrier replied, "These days I have no employment. I request you as a fellow water-carrier to find me work with your master." He said, "Water-carriers are needed to sprinkle water around the camp. I will be able to find you work." Amar asked, "Why do you eat at this late hour?" The water-carrier replied, "My brother, it's because I find no time to eat between carrying and sprinkling water." Amar commented, "Sometimes commanders have strange notions. What could be accomplished by sprinkling water around the camp?" The water-carrier told him everything about the two kinds of magic water and their properties.

After obtaining this information, Amar made some small talk then took out some sweetmeats from his pocket and offered them to the water-carrier, saying, "Have some."

The water-carrier ate the sweets that were drug-laced and fell unconscious. Amar hid him in a corner of the tent and after disguising himself as the man and wearing his clothes, he went before Hoshiar and said, "Your Honor, all the water was used up. I now need some more for my waterskin."

Hoshiar gave Amar the magic water to make people unconscious. Amar said, "Also, give me some of the other kind." Hoshiar asked, "Didn't you receive some earlier?" Amar answered, "It was my brother who received it. Now he is exhausted and I do his work."

Hoshiar gave him some of the restorative magic water, which Amar rubbed on his body. He then poured some magic water into his hand. Hoshiar shouted, "What are you doing, O dolt? You must mix it in the waterskin." Amar answered, "Regard what I do now! You will soon realize who is a dolt."

Amar splashed the water from his hand into Hoshiar's face. He fell down unconscious without a word and Amar speedily cut off his head. Hoshiar's magic spirits screamed and a tumult ensued. Amar immediately took hold of Hoshiar's water carafes. From all corners a chorus of voices shouted "*Catch them! Slay them!*" Amar released Zargham and Jansoz, who pulled out the needles stuck in the tongues of Princess Mahrukh and Bahar. Once released, they helped their companions become free while Amar looted the pavilion with the Net of Ilyas.

The noises made by Hoshiar's magic spirits sent Hoshiar's attendants running to his pavilion, along with Hoshiar's mother, sorceress Mugheela. She charged into his pavilion, recited a spell, and hammered the ground with clenched fists, which made Amar sink up to his waist into the earth. As Mugheela rushed forward to carry Amar away, Qiran, who still stood at his post as Hoshiar's attendant, called out, "Here!" As Mugheela turned to look, Qiran hit out with his cleaver. Mugheela's brains flew all over the place and her skull was smashed into a thousand pieces. As she rolled in agony and died, the terrible noises of her magic spirits filled the air. Amar was released from the ground and resumed looting the pavilion. In the meanwhile, all the commanders of Queen Mahjabeen's camp were set free and started fighting Hoshiar's companions.

Prince Bahar now invoked her magic and created a veritable picture of spring. Gardens filled with flowers and aromatic herbs manifested themselves. The entranced enemy sorcerers waxed poetic in praise of spring.

Bahar ordered them to charge and put Heyrat's camp to the sword. Hoshiar's army immediately attacked Heyrat's forces.

Unmindful and oblivious to the revolutions of the fickle heavens, Empress Heyrat was giving audience surrounded by her sorcerer ministers when Hoshiar's forces targeted them. Thousands were killed in Heyrat's camp in the first charge. Chilli necklaces, needle clusters, and magic arrows were exchanged on both sides and steel magic balls were hurled at each other by the sorcerers of the two armies. Thunderous noises of magic spirits rose, lightning bolts struck, ice slabs fell from the skies, black clouds billowed up and clustered over as a terrible darkness in which not even a hand could distinguish its pair spread over the combatants.

Heyrat stood on her throne in a panic and shouted, "Light the magic torches!" As her sorcerers and sorceresses recited spells to light the magic torches, Mahrukh invoked powerful magic that extinguished all of them. A wholesale carnage of Heyrat's forces now began and blood flowed onto the ground in such quantities that – except for the tulip or the *calamus draco*[108] – no grass would ever sprout there again.

Heaven's mercy! A day like doomsday was unleashed on Heyrat's camp. Hoshiar's forces, specially trained for combat duty by the Emperor of Hoshruba, killed thousands of Heyrat's men. Prince Asad the valiant also slew hundreds with his relentless sword.

From her throne, Empress Heyrat dove into the ground. Presently, the whole world juddered and the mountains collided with each other as if something had shaken the Earth from its foundations. Princesses Mahrukh and Bahar sought counsel together, concluding that they must satisfy themselves with the God-gifted victory obtained over Hoshiar's forces and declare the cessation of hostilities, since they could not combat Heyrat's magic.

The magic fife from Mahjabeen's camp announced the end of combat. Mahrukh and her commanders separated themselves from their adversaries and returned triumphant and victorious. The tricksters, who had escaped after killing the sorcerers, also reported back to their camp. When Mahjabeen's dispersed forces, which had retreated into the forests and mountains, heard of their commanders' return, they too, began returning to the camp. Before long, the camp's bazaars opened up, the pavilions were filled, and Mahjabeen sat on her throne watching a dance recital.

In the enemy camp, Empress Heyrat emerged from the ground and was received by her army commanders, who stood at the ready to lay down their lives in her service. A part of Heyrat's surviving forces had absconded, others had dispersed. She gathered all of them in the Hall of Assembly while her army pitched their tents and bivouacked once more.

Heyrat sat in her court awhile with knitted brow. Then she handed the charge of her forces to her deputies and flew back to Afrasiyab astride her magic peacock.

Afrasiyab had recently returned from the Dome of Light to the Apple Garden when Empress Heyrat's conveyance arrived. The courtiers rose to pay their respects. Heyrat sat beside Afrasiyab and gave him the entire account, from the slaughter of the sorcerers' army to the circumstances in which Hoshiar had met his death. When Afrasiyab consulted the *Book of Sameri*, he saw it written there:

> "It was your magic water that was employed by Amar Ayyar to kill Hoshiar and Mugheela."

Afrasiyab trembled with rage when he learned this and said, "O Empress, you may return to the camp. This time I will send terrible calamity upon the despicable rebels. They will die a horrible death."

As directed by Afrasiyab, Heyrat returned to the camp. Her servants and attendants received her with great deference and she resumed her seat on the throne.

Sorceress Khatif Lightning-Bolt

It is recounted that Hoshruba had seven sorceresses who lived in the form of lightning bolts. They struck as noisily as claps of thunder and burned the enemy alive on the battlefield with powerful bolts. After Heyrat left, Afrasiyab sent for them. No sooner did the Emperor of Hoshruba issue his orders than a crimson cloud containing the seven flashing lightning bolts materialized in the sky. As it approached the cloud descended and the seven lightning bolts rolled onto the ground and acquired the forms of gold-skinned females. The names of these sorceresses were Mehshar, Lamae, Khatif, Shola Bar, Chashmak Zan, Satial Nur and Saiqa Bar. They were richly dressed and covered with gold and jewels. They greeted the emperor and asked, "Why has Your Excellency sent for his slave girls?"

Afrasiyab said, "One of you must depart to help Empress Heyrat in her campaign, and the rest will await orders at your stations."

Sorceress Khatif Lightning-Bolt answered, "This slave girl will march against the rebels and punish them." Afrasiyab conferred a robe of departure on Khatif and the seven sorceresses returned to their lands.

Sorceress Khatif Lightning-Bolt mustered a hundred-thousand-strong army of sorcerers and, with all the tents and pavilions loaded on conveyances, she advanced thunderously and with great razzle dazzle to join Empress Heyrat. The sorcerers cast spells to transform their faces into monstrous shapes and forms and the entire army rose into the sky riding clouds and carrying fiery weapons. The loud and frightening cracks of thunder flying past turned the gall of men to water.

Ugly of face and uglier of nature
Hideous of mien, unsightly, evil-spirited
Tyrannical, ruthless, drunken louts
Foul-mouthed and bursting with vanity
Wicked-hearted, pitiless warriors
The sorcerers departed to battle their foe

Meanwhile, in the court of the Emperor of Hoshruba, the trickster girls Sarsar and Saba Raftar presented themselves after sorceress Khatif Lightning-Bolt had departed. To express his displeasure, Afrasiyab turned his face away from them. The trickster girls said, "What is our crime, Your Excellency?" Afrasiyab replied, "You were retained and received sustenance to serve the empire and obtained your salaries without moving a finger. Regard Amar and his companions! They killed several of my renowned sorcerers after entering the tilism. You, however, never killed any rebel commanders or brought even a single one of them a prisoner to me."

Sarsar was chagrined by the emperor's angry words of censure. She bowed her head in shame and replied, "I shall depart and do all I can to capture Prince Asad, who styles himself the Conqueror of the Tilism, as well as Mahjabeen Diamond-Robe, who is the queen of the rebels. It would break the spirits of the rebels and rob them of their figurehead and driving force. May the emperor forgive my mistakes and cleanse his pure heart of any rancour toward his slave girl."

Afrasiyab was pleased by Sarsar's speech. He conferred robes of departure on the trickster girls and sent them on their mission. Then he occupied himself with pleasant diversions.

Of the Capture of the Lion of the Forest of Valor, Prince Asad and Queen Mahjabeen by the Foxiness of the Trickster Girls; Of Mahrukh Magic-Eye Becoming the Queen by Amar's Counsel and of their Encounter with Sorceress Khatif Lightning-Bolt; Of the Defeat of Mahrukh Magic-Eye's Army and of the Tricksters Targetting the Sorceresses

Those held captive by the chain of narrative and bound in the discourse that augments the pleasure of the assembly capture this episode in these words, and imprison it thus in the writing of a fable:

The trickster girls Sarsar and Saba Raftar sped on their mission to capture Prince Asad. They crossed the River of Flowing Blood and arrived near Mahrukh's camp.

Sarsar disguised herself as a macebearer. She carried a golden mace, wore a short-coat, and sported a turban pinned with a medallion worn with one end hanging loose. She made rounds of the camp looking for an opportunity to perform her trickery.

Saba Raftar dressed like a farm owner. She wore a knee-length waistcloth and a quilted coat, with a towel wrapped around her head.

The trickster girls found the camp a model of organization and discipline. The camp magistrate was busy making his rounds and the shops carried on their business in an orderly fashion. A brisk trade took place between smartly attired buyers and well dressed sellers. There was a bazaar before every pavilion and a constant traffic of commanders and sorcerers flowed in the passageways.

The trickster girls roamed in the camp in disguise until the World-Illuminating Wanderer[109] finished his trek to settle in the land of the west, and the planetary fixtures opened and bedecked their shops in the field of sky.

Queen Mahjabeen Diamond-Robe adjourned her court after a long session and the commanders returned to their pavilions. Asad and Mahjabeen returned to the bedchamber in their private pavilion and sat on a luxurious couch. The trickster girls took up positions at the entrance of their pavilion and observed the Turkic, Calmuck Tartar and Nubian slave girls going about their daily tasks in and out of the pavilion.

Saba Raftar followed a Nubian slave girl and greeted her, saying, "I am a farm owner. The queen has raised my taxes and reverted the title for the land given me for my services to her. My case has been sent to the tribunal for Princess Mahrukh Magic-Eye's decision. I would be forever grateful if you could put in a good word for me with the princess." Then Saba Raftar offered a platter laden with fruit and several hundred gold pieces to the slave girl. She was most pleased by the false farm owner's generosity and promised him she would intercede with Princess Mahrukh to have the case decided in his favor. She filled her pockets with the gold pieces and started eating the fruit. But the fruit was laced with drugs and in no time she dropped unconscious.

Saba Raftar carried the Nubian slave girl to a deserted corner, stripped her and put on her clothes and disguised herself in her likeness. She hid the slave girl there and entered Mahjabeen's bedchamber.

In the meanwhile, Sarsar had marked another slave girl for her target. She approached the girl in the macebearer's disguise and said, "Why did you curse and abuse the macebearers yesterday?" The slave girl answered, "You don't know me, O pimp and wittol! Watch your tongue if you don't want me to snatch your mace and have you severely rebuked by the queen." The false macebearer caught the girl's hand, saying, "I must take you to my officer." As the slave girl cursed loudly, the false macebearer slapped her with a drug-filled hand. The slave girl fell unconscious.

She was carried by Sarsar to a deserted place. There, the trickster girl made herself into the girl's exact likeness. She removed the unconscious girl's clothes and put them on herself. After hiding the girl there, Sarsar also entered Mahjabeen's bedchamber.

She saw Asad and Mahjabeen sitting beside each other on a luxurious couch, taking pleasure from the ambrosial assembly and each other's company. The wine tray lay close at hand and they drank together. Melodious songsters of Venusian charm sang, and a jewel-studded bed was ready with all luxuries and comforts. Sarsar now disguised herself as a slave girl and joined the attendants and diligently performed any task given her. While Sarsar drugged the wine as she brought it from the cellar, Saba Raftar drugged the food she served in the Nubian slave girl's disguise. Prince Asad and Mahjabeen were finally drugged. They struggled to rise and walked unsteadily to the bed where they dropped unconscious. Their companions and attendants, who had had the same drugged food and wine, also lost consciousness. Next Saba Raftar drugged the retainers and guards as well.

Sarsar picked Prince Asad up from the bed and tied him up in her trickster's mantle while Saba Raftar rolled up Mahjabeen into a similar bundle. They left the others lying unconscious and headed out of the bedchamber. With a trickster's usual cunning and concealment, they hid themselves from the eyes of the vigil squads and reached the outer limits of Mahjabeen's camp. From there they sped like the wind and passed over the River of Flowing Blood, arriving quick as lightning in the Apple Garden, where they spent the remaining hours of the night.

Finally, the sun's flare lit the bedchamber of the juggling heavens to remove the dizziness cast over the sleepers; the caravan of night passed, the bright day showed its face, and the oblivion of sleep was dispelled from the sleeping.

The magic trumpets blew. Afrasiyab's courtiers assembled and the Emperor of Hoshruba gave audience. The two trickster girls presented themselves and placed the bundles they had brought at the emperor's feet. They said, "The sinners Mahjabeen and Asad are presented before Your Excellency as ordered."

Afrasiyab was jubilant and said to his courtiers, "Put a spell on the rebels so that they cannot rise. Then restore them to consciousness."

The sorcerers carried out the emperor's orders.

Prince Asad opened his eyes and found himself in Afrasiyab's court where a throng of renowned sorcerers was assembled. The Emperor of Hoshruba gave audience surrounded by his ministers, who sat on fire-spewing thrones. Prince Asad called out, "I offer peace and greetings to those in this assembly who consider God to be One and without partner, and believe Muhammad to be His prophet and humble servant."

The sorcerers stuffed their fingers into their ears at Asad's praising the unseen god.

Angered by Asad's greeting, Afrasiyab sent for an executioner to behead him. Then Afrasiyab advised Mahjabeen to renounce her love for Asad. But Mahjabeen would not hear of it and said, "Even if I had a thousand lives, I would sacrifice them all for Prince Asad."

She recited,

"I announce this to the whole world
He is the envy of the rose and I his nightingale

He is the cypress and I his ringdove
I sing of a grieving heart
I pledged my troth to the prince
I wouldn't hear of another's name
I wouldn't let even the angels and houris
Come near me in his absence."

Afrasiyab ordered the executioner to take Mahjabeen into his custody as well.

Their hair dishevelled, their eyes welling up with tears, Asad and Mahjabeen, the lover and the beloved, gazed mournfully at each other. Each asked the other's forgiveness for any grief unintentionally caused. Mahjabeen then turned her heart to thoughts of the Almighty God and prayed with great humility and meekness, seeking His protection and soliciting His aid in releasing them from their calamity.

The arrow of prayer flew from the bow of her lips and sank into the target of divine acceptance.

The ministers and nobles approached Afrasiyab before he could give the final order to the executioner. The emperor asked, "What is it that you desire?" They replied, "If Your Excellency would grant us leave to speak, we would like to express our thoughts." Afrasiyab said, "You may speak without fear of harm. Say what you wish that is cordial and affable and the emperor will grant your wishes."

In view of the emperor's munificence, the courtiers said, "The founders of the tilism did not write that the Conqueror of the Tilism would be immediately executed. May your Excellency consult the *Book of Sameri* and act as it guides."

Their wise counsel found favor with Afrasiyab. He praised their sagacity and consulted the *Book of Sameri,* wherein he saw written:

> "It is not preferable to kill Asad because Amar would avenge his death. He will wear the cape of invisibility and behead everyone; there will be no stopping him. You must keep the Conqueror of the Tilism under detention and capture Amar and the other tricksters as well. Then you can put all of them to death simultaneously."

After reading these words, Afrasiyab called out to his courtiers, "You spoke true when you said that the *Book of Sameri* does not counsel Asad's execution. Take both Asad and Mahjabeen and imprison them in the Dome of Light. With a spell I will conceal from the eyes of men the doors of the City of Disregard that open into Zahir. Nobody will be able to counter my spell and neither any trickster nor helper from the rebels' camp will be able to come to their aid."

No sooner did Afrasiyab give his order than hundreds of thousands of tyrannical, wicked, brazen, misanthropic sorcerers put magic fetters on Asad and Mahjabeen. Carrying red and black magic snakes in their hands and coiled around their arms and legs, they led the prisoners to the City of Disregard.

When they arrived in the city, its entire populace, men and women alike, came out to see the sight, and proclaimed, "How the rebels who caused all the mayhem in the tilism have fallen!" Asad and Mahjabeen – the luminous candles of the assembly of excellence – were imprisoned in a small, dark cell and thousands of sorcerers were deputed to guard them.

Afrasiyab recited a spell that concealed the doors of the City of Disregard that opened into the region of Zahir, and the surging waves of the River of Flowing Blood covered them.

While Afrasiyab made these arrangements, Mahjabeen's army commanders, including Princesses Bahar and Nafarman, went to the queen's private pavilion in the morning to escort her into the court. The slave girls, drugged unconscious by Sarsar and Saba Raftar, also came to and returned to their duties. On the way, they met Mahjabeen's attendants as they came rushing out crying and wailing from her private pavilion. Princesses Bahar and Nafarman asked, "What is the matter?" They replied, "Someone kidnapped the Queen of the World and the valiant prince in their sleep." The commanders wailed when they heard the terrible news and the entire camp was thrown into turmoil.

Their cries and laments reached Amar in the wilderness, who returned to the camp where he received the awful news. He went into Mahjabeen's private pavilion and recognized the marks left by Sarsar and Saba Raftar's feet. He said to Mahrukh, "It was Sarsar who kidnapped them." Mahrukh wept copiously when she heard this and cried, "Now Afrasiyab will never spare their lives!"

These words turned the whole camp into a churning sea of grief and Mahrukh mourned Asad and Mahjabeen without cease.

At that moment, Princess Nafarman parted the veil from Mahrukh's face and said, "O Princess, such are the ways of the fickle heavens – a providence that never dispensed happiness. These events happen daily on its watch. But while you may complain of it, you must not allow your perseverance to weaken or your resolve to waver. You must not let go of your equanimity and composure."

Princess Bahar also wept and rent her collar to shreds. Like the cloud of spring quarter, she cried non-stop, exclaiming, "O capricious fate, see how you inflicted this sorrow upon me. Now I will wander aimlessly forever. Neither will anybody have me nor will I have anyone to sustain and support me in my loneliness."

Amar dried everyone's tears and said to Mahrukh, "You had ascertained for yourself from occult foreknowledge that Prince Asad will conquer the tilism and kill Afrasiyab. It is unbecoming for you to abandon yourself to grief. You should replace Queen Mahjabeen on the throne and take charge of the camp. God willing, Asad will be freed soon and the Gatherer of the Separated will bring us all together again. The sons of Amir Hamza are visited often by calamitous and inauspicious moments. Do not let that make you anxious. This difficult time will pass and the prince will be freed. If Afrasiyab harms the prince, I swear on my name and honor that I will put on the cape of invisibility and behead every single sorcerer. You must put your trust in God alone and close your heart to grief."

In short, when the mourning ended, Amar declared to the camp that during Mahjabeen's absence Mahrukh would be their queen. Mahrukh accepted the trust with a heavy heart.

Then the court was held as before and the commanders and courtiers made offerings to Queen Mahrukh. The tabla played again in the court as a musical assembly began, and Amar left to work his trickery.

ꕥ

In the meanwhile, sorceress Khatif Lightning-Bolt arrived, flashing in a crimson cloud with her one-hundred-thousand-strong army, and entered Empress Heyrat's camp with great ceremony and fanfare. Heyrat also received Afrasiyab's missive containing an account of the capture of Asad and Mahjabeen. The empress sent a welcoming party to conduct sorceress Khatif into the court, set up a high pavilion for her accommodation, and furnished it with all comforts.

Sorceress Khatif was given a throne in the court but for fear of the tricksters, she retained the form of a lightning bolt; all anyone could see was a lightning bolt that flashed above her throne.

The magic birds brought Queen Mahrukh a report of these events and she took measures to safeguard her camp.

Sorceress Khatif Lightning-Bolt wrote a letter to Queen Mahrukh that read:

> "If you present yourself before me I will have your trespasses forgiven by the emperor and he will confer lands and riches upon you. Renounce your rebellious ways and submit your neck in obedience before the Emperor of Hoshruba."

Khatif deputed a magic slave to deliver the message to Mahrukh, who wrote in reply:

> "O Khatif Lightning-Bolt, you should know that Amar Ayyar is called the Beheader of Sorcerers. The very mention of the tricksters' names turns the gall of sorcerers to water. You must submit your allegiance or you will speedily be meted out your just deserts."

Incensed upon reading this, Khatif advanced on Mahrukh's camp by herself like a blazing flame. Her deputies blew magic fifes and trumpets and hurriedly mounted magic birds to accompany their commander.

Hearing the news of the imminent attack, Mahrukh organized her forces. They too, mounted their magic conveyances and arrayed out against sorceress Khatif.

Khatif struck Mahrukh's camp in the form of thunderbolts. Renowned sorcerers of Queen Mahrukh's camp invoked their magic and forty magic shields provided them cover. The whole battlefield became overcast and thunderbolts continuously dropped and burned up a harvest of lives in Mahrukh's camp.

Terrible cries rose from the two camps as magicians on both sides received and delivered strikes. Bodies piled up on each other. The fields of carnage bore the fruit of death. The links of the chains of breath continuously snapped. By sunset, thousands of celebrated sorcerers in Mahrukh's camp were dispatched to the land of doom.

Then Khatif Lightning-Bolt called out, "O Mahrukh, what you saw today was a small taste of my wrath. I now retire for the day. Come tomorrow I will efface all traces of your existence from the world. You will die without a grave or a winding-sheet and be made dust."

The drums for the cessation of hostilities were beaten in Khatif's camp. She retreated and Mahrukh returned dispirited and grieving to her camp. Her army followed Mahrukh, marked and burdened by the terror of the coming day. The cowards absconded under cover of night and the brave prayed and solicited their Lord's help.

ഌഌ

Amar Ayyar arrived near Khatif's camp by the banks of a river adjacent to Empress Heyrat's encampment. He disguised himself as a young man and dove into the water. One of Khatif's attendants noticed him and asked, "What do you dive for, young man?" He answered, "Whatever fate yields: I retrieve *cowries*, paisas, rupees, whatever is offered me." The attendant said, "If I threw paisas would you retrieve them?" Amar said, "Yes!" The attendant threw some paisas into the river. Amar retrieved them for him and received them as his reward. Finally, the attendant said, "Now it's time to attend to my duty. I have to prepare the hookah for sorceress Khatif, who will be looking my way. Meet me here again tomorrow."

Amar accompanied the attendant. On the way, he gave him some tobacco and said, "You should fill this tobacco in the hookah-snake today. It is a rare variety. If sorceress Khatif likes it I will give you the seller's name." The attendant took the tobacco.

Amar said, "Do smell it! See what a nice aroma it has." The attendant smelled the tobacco and immediately fell unconscious because it was laced with a perfumed drug.

Amar disguised himself as the attendant, put on his clothes and, after preparing the hookah, entered Khatif's pavilion where he witnessed a lightning bolt flashing above the throne.

Amar called out, "The hookah is ready, Your Honor!" At these words, the lightning bolt stopped flashing; it drew together on the throne and materialized into a golden-skinned woman resplendent as the sun. As Amar presented the hookah, sorceress Khatif Lightning-Bolt glared at him. Amar took out the carafe of magic water he had stolen from the sorcerer Hoshiar, poured some water into his hand, and splashed it on Khatif's face. She immediately fell unconscious, but before Amar could kill her the throne flew off to the sky, along with the unconscious Khatif. Amar was confounded by this marvel and ran to report what had transpired to Queen Mahrukh.

The moment Mahrukh received the news she sounded the magic bugles in her camp. Her army quickly readied itself and Mahrukh charged Khatif's camp. Caught unprepared and by surprise, thousands of Khatif's sorcerers died in the assault. The remainder readied themselves and fought back. Magic was deployed and detachments of enemy sorcerers charged and skirmished with the attackers. The cries of "Catch them! Imprison them!" rose in Khatif's camp.

Sorcerers from both sides hurled thousands of magic citrons and magic coconuts. As they burst, fire-breathing dragons emerged and began swallowing enemy warriors. Hundreds of blazing arrows fell like a comet shower from the sky onto the combatants.

When Heyrat received these tidings she rushed to the battlefield and tried to repulse Mahrukh's assault.

> *When the warriors raised their sword-wielding arms*
> *Every earthly calamity "Bravo!" said*
> *The majestic warriors then mightily charged*
> *Disarraying from the shock even the sun in the heavens*
> *The points of lances with every clash*
> *Like so many sparklers, showered flames*
> *The hearts of stones turned to water from the flash of swords*
> *Like mercury, the mountains quivered from trumpet blasts*
> *The arrows on their tail feathers so swiftly did fly*
> *That even winged angels could not match their flight*
> *So copiously did the mace and sword spark flames*
> *Their abundance to a cinder burned entire forests*
> *The waves of flowing blood dyed the saddles*
> *The waves of blood dyed the whole forest crimson*

As thousands of Khatif's sorcerers had been killed, the rest could not stand their ground too long. They turned tail and retreated. Despite Heyrat's efforts to stem the tide, she was helpless to keep her own army from losing ground as large swaths of Khatif's retreating army swept them in waves.

Empress Heyrat struck the timbals to announce the cessation of hostilities. Mahrukh, who wished to avoid confronting Heyrat's directly, readily turned back and the two armies finally retired to their camps to rest.

A musical assembly was soon underway in Mahrukh's court, where everyone praised Amar Ayyar's trickery.

Sorceress Mehshar Lightning-Bolt and Raad Thunder-Clap

In the meanwhile, the throne of sorceress Khatif arrived before Emperor Afrasiyab in the Apple Garden. He looked into the *Book of Sameri,* wherein he read the following:

> "It was your own magic water with which Amar Ayyar humiliated her and rendered her unconscious. Amar would have killed her but because she is a powerful sorceress her magic spirits bore her away on the throne."

Afrasiyab recited a counterspell to remove the magic from Khatif and she came to. Because she had been splashed with the powerful magic water, however, she became ill and the Emperor of Hoshruba gave her leave to return to her land.

Afrasiyab now sent a magic slave to summon sorceress Mehshar Lightning-Bolt. When Mehshar received the call she started out with great preparations, along with her sorcerer son, Raad Thunder-Clap, and arrived in the emperor's court.

Afrasiyab said to her, "O Mehshar, I order you to assist the empress and fight the rebels."

Sorceress Mehshar Lightning-Bolt took a hundred thousand sorcerers with her. Flying on the throne with lofty ambitions, flashing, raining flames, she and her son disappeared into the clouds, followed by their entire army and its tents and pavilions.

The marching army behind its commander
Was like the stars following the moon
The page of the field was scribbled
By the dark scrawling lines of riders and troopers
The myriad colors of their standards
Made the desert floor a colorful bouquet
Throwing the world into unearthly commotion
They caused a turmoil greater than a tempest
The gall of the Cow of the Earth they turned to water
Let alone the Earth, they made the heavens tremble
Countless like the grains of sand
The armies filled the horizon from end to end

Be it known that the Emperor of Hoshruba had constructed many sight-seeing stations and pleasant gardens for his excursions throughout the tilism. When sorceress Mehshar's army was at two days' distance from Mahrukh's camp it halted in one such garden, situated in a lush, green forest.

A sorceress named Baran was the ruler of a nearby majestic mountain. She was unmatched in beauty and comeliness; many a sorcerer pined away for love of her. Mehshar's son, Raad Thunder-Clap, was among those marked by the love of her calamitous beauty. When the army landed, Raad decided to soothe his eyes with the sight of his fairy-like beloved, and set out for her abode.

Upon arrival, he bribed one of Baran's sorceress attendants with gold and jewels to inveigle her mistress to come out on the palace balcony so that her listless lover could derive some comfort in admiring her beauty.

The attendant brought Baran out on the balcony on some pretext. Enthralled by her beauty, Raad Thunder-Clap was lost in admiration.

In the meanwhile, Baran's other lovers also arrived on the scene. Seeing Raad before the palace of their beloved, a blaze of jealousy lit up in their hearts. They cast a spell to render Raad deaf and mute and arrested and pinioned him. Then they led Raad into the wilderness to kill him, keeping far away from his mother's camp.

At the same time, Amar arrived in the wilderness, thinking to himself, *Sorceress Khatif escaped but it is certain that before long Afrasiyab will send another scourge on us.*

Absorbed by these thoughts, Amar saw three sorcerers leading a young man into the wilderness as prisoner. From the youth's noble physiognomy, Amar reckoned him to be a renowned sorcerer. Amar thought, *If I deliver him from their clutches he might feel indebted to me and join our cause.* Amar put on the *dev jama* that changed into seven different colors, adopting a new hue every moment. He covered his face with ten pasteboard masks that had several mouths from which snakelike tongues darted out. He stuck pasteboard arms onto his body and smeared it with a lotion that made every pore of his skin appear to spew flames. Then Amar blew the White Conch that struck terror even into the hearts of demons.

The sorcerers leading Raad into the wilderness froze in their tracks upon hearing the blast of the White Conch and felt their feet turn to sand. As they looked around with frightened eyes, Amar appeared. They beheld, advancing toward them, a ten-headed creature of horrible mien, whose body was covered with flames and whose attire changed colors from red to blue to black to green to yellow every moment.

Frightened out of their wits by this sight, the sorcerers prostrated themselves before the creature. Amar called out, "I am the Angel of Death of Lord Laqa!" The sorcerers trembled with fear and asked, "What is the reason for your visit?" Amar answered, "I come to extract the soul of the sinner you lead to death. But your lives too, have reached their end and I must claim them too."

The sorcerers entreated him, "O Angel of Death of Lord Laqa, tell us some way to defer our doom that we may taste of life's pleasure awhile longer." Amar answered, "If you offer alms, that may move Lord Laqa to show mercy on you." The sorcerers bestowed on Amar all the gold and jewels they carried on their persons.

Amar took out an apple from his zambil and offered it to them, saying, "Each of you should eat a slice of this. It will extend your lives." The three sorcerers had a piece each. After a moment, when the drug-laced apple's effects were felt, they shouted, "O Angel of Death, we feel our hearts palpitating!" Amar answered, "It is because the blood vessels lengthen as one receives longevity." The sorcerers soon fell unconscious and Amar unsheathed his dagger and beheaded all of them. The slain sorcerers' magic spirits made a hue and cry and a racket rose.

Having been rendered deaf and mute by magic spells, Raad Thunder-Clap now regained the faculties of hearing and speech. Once the commotion subsided, he glared suspiciously at Amar, who said, "You glower at me now even though I saved your life?" Raad asked, "What is your name?" Amar answered, "I am an angel of Lord Laqa."

Raad Thunder-Clap said, "O angel of our Lord, I was taken unawares by these sorcerers. I am the son of sorceress Mehshar Lightning-Bolt. With my magic I can dive into the ground to emerge beside the foe and roar like the sound of a thunder clap. The sound bursts the skulls of the enemies and even if mighty sorcerers should escape death, the impact of my thunder clap yet makes them fall unconscious. My mother strikes them in the form of a lightning bolt and can cleave them in two. Afrasiyab sent us to battle Mahrukh Magic-Eye and we are headed to decimate her camp."

Amar said to himself, *It was most fortunate that I ran into him. Otherwise they would have proved a terrible scourge. Now I must find a way to kill him too.* While Amar made these calculations, a puff of cloud materialized and sorceress Mehshar Lightning-Bolt arrived on the scene. After she had found Raad missing from the camp, she searched for him frantically, anxious that no enemy trickster should kill her son.

When Amar saw her coming he put on the cape of invisibility. Witnessing Amar's sudden disappearance, Raad was convinced that Amar was, indeed, the angel of Laqa. Sorceress Mehshar recognized her son and descended. She changed into the form of a woman and embraced her son. Seeing the dead sorcerers lying around, she asked Raad who had killed them.

He told her how he had been captured and how the angel of Laqa had brought him freedom. Mehshar said, "It is most unfortunate that he left. Had I seen him I would have filled the skirts of his hopes with riches of desire." Raad said, "The angel of Lord Laqa disappeared all of a sudden. Perhaps he is still present but invisible. Let me call to him."

Raad called, "Show us favor if you are present O angel of Lord Laqa. My mother wishes to see you."

Amar took off the cape of invisibility and appeared. Sorceress Mehshar bowed her head reverently before Amar and said, "You are our benefactor. Because of you Lord Sameri again conferred the robe of life on my son. I wish you would accompany us to our camp as an honored guest and visit our quarters. I will do all I can to recompense your act of kindness." Amar answered, "I have no objection."

Sorceress Mehshar recited a spell that summoned a jewel-encrusted flying throne. She seated Amar and Raad Thunder-Clap on the throne and accompanied them to her camp, flying in the form of a lightning bolt. They arrived above her camp and descended into a vast garden in full bloom. Amar saw the garden was lined with fruit-laden trees and clustered with flowers. A majestic palace furnished with the rarities of the world rose in the nave of the garden.

Sorceress Mehshar seated Amar on a couch and presented salvers laden with gold and jewels as offerings. She said, "While these offerings may not be worthy of Your Lordship, I hope you will accept them. And do tell me your real name." Amar answered, "I already told you that I am an angel of Lord Laqa. You repeat yourself to no purpose."

The sorceress sent for her box and took out the *Folios of Jamshed* to ascertain whether or not Amar told the truth. The *Folios of Jamshed* read:

> "The man before you is Amar Ayyar, the supporter of Mahrukh Magic-Eye, who disguised himself to save Raad's life. Before he creates any trouble, you must make him an offering and send him away. You are further advised to kill him should an opportunity offer itself, for Amar is a great menace."

Mehshar turned fiercely toward Amar upon learning this.

Amar said, "What harm have I done you? Have you taken leave of your senses that you look fiercely at me? It reminds me of the saying that no good deed goes unpunished." Mehshar replied, "You fooled me with your talk before but you can do so no more. I know your name is Amar. Now tell me, O enemy of my emperor, what should I mete out for your punishment?" Amar replied, "It was on account of your humility that I spared your life earlier. Now do your worst and show me not the least compassion." Mehshar said, "I am indebted to you. How can I return your kindness with evil? Take these offerings of gold and jewels and depart." Amar answered, "Rest assured, I have no plans of taking up residence with you."

While they had this conversation, Afrasiyab consulted the *Book of Sameri* to learn what had passed with sorceress Mehshar. He saw written there:

> "The sorceress Mehshar has brought Amar into her camp and seated him on a couch. She converses with Amar and makes him offerings of gold and jewels."

Afrasiyab raged marvellously when he learned of this.

Sorceresses Khumar and Makhmur Crimson-Eye

Be it known that at that moment two powerful sorceress sisters, Makhmur Crimson-Eye and Khumar were present in the court.

Makhmur Crimson-Eye was loved by Afrasiyab just like her sister Khumar and Princess Bahar. And like them, Makhmur Crimson-Eye did not respond to Afrasiyab's advances because of her fear of Empress Heyrat's vengeance. She was sitting elegantly beside her sister when Afrasiyab angrily ordered her, "Go at once to the garden near Mahrukh's camp where Mehshar Lightning-Bolt sits with Amar Ayyar. Bring Amar to me as a prisoner and punish Mehshar if she intervenes."

Makhmur invoked her magic and flew off. She soon arrived in the camp of Mehshar, who gave her a seat beside herself. Makhmur censured Mehshar, saying, "You have angered the emperor by receiving his enemy, Amar, with honor. You would do well to end the matter here and let me take him to the court as a prisoner, or else you will invite the emperor's wrath and forfeit your life."

Mehshar answered, "My sister, it is against my faith and principles to allow any harm to come to Amar after he saved my son's life." Makhmur said, "Abandon such thoughts. Drop all your scruples and fear only Afrasiyab. You will lose your life if you show intransigence in this matter. You may wish to lay down your life for Amar but I will not disobey the emperor. I will take this wretch as a prisoner with me."

While they argued, Amar found his chance. He splashed some magic water from the carafe on Makhmur Crimson-Eye's face. She immediately fell unconscious. As Amar drew his dagger and ran toward her, a magic claw swooped down and carried Makhmur away.

Mehshar said to Amar, "You must leave immediately. I too, must go and hide somewhere in the tilism. Afrasiyab has now become my enemy. He will kill me upon sight. You made a terrible mistake by trying to harm Makhmur."

Amar answered, "O Mehshar, remember,

> *"If the enemy be strong,*
> *The Protector is stronger still.*

"Why must you go and hide in some nook in the tilism? Come with me to Mahrukh's camp and bide your time there in peace. Regard that all who have joined our ranks are still alive with their honor intact. It's a matter of time before, God willing, the tilism is conquered. Then you will witness that those who joined us will receive higher ranks and greater honor in Amir Hamza's court. Even if we are overwhelmed by Afrasiyab – as you fear – you would fare no better or worse than the rest of us. Sharing a calamity reduces its severity. The choice is up to you. I have given you my best counsel."

Mehshar said, "You speak true. Come, we are with you. I will not escape and hide, I will join you and die fighting. Let us start in the name of God."

Sorceress Mehshar Lightning-Bolt rose and ordered the drums of departure to announce the march. Her orders were carried out and the tents and pavilions were packed and loaded onto the magic conveyances. Mehshar ascended the flying throne and seated Amar beside her. Then she departed for Mahrukh's camp with great majesty.

Sorceress Lamae Lightning-Bolt

When sorceress Makhmur regained her senses she found herself in Afrasiyab's court. She said to the emperor, "As I argued and quarrelled with Mehshar, Amar splashed magic water on my face and I fell unconscious."

When Afrasiyab looked into the *Book of Sameri*, he saw this written there:

> "Amar made Makhmur Crimson-Eye unconscious with the magic water. Now Mehshar Lightning-Bolt has joined ranks with Amar and departed for Mahrukh's camp."

Afrasiyab immediately clapped and a magic slave materialized. The emperor ordered, "Summon sorceress Lamae Lightning-Bolt!"

The magic slave delivered the message without loss of time.

When sorceress Lamae presented herself, Afrasiyab said, "Go and arrest sorceress Mehshar Lightning-Bolt, who is headed for Mahrukh Magic-Eye's camp."

Sorceress Lamae took along a one-hundred-thousand-strong sorcerer army and flew away on her mission, flashing majestically in the form of lightning.

On the way, it occurred to her that instead of intercepting Mehshar on the way to Mahrukh's camp, she should arrest her there along with other rebels. It would not only save her two separate campaigns but also earn her greater renown too. She proceeded with dispatch to Empress Heyrat's camp. The empress welcomed her upon arrival and Lamae Lightning-Bolt's army set up camp and bivouacked.

Sorceress Lamae remained in the form of a lightning bolt all day long for fear of the tricksters' attacking her. When one watch of the day remained, the torch of the sun slowly burned up in the assembly of heaven and the moon's candle lit up and spread its light in the cosmic congregation. Only then did the sorceress show herself in her court in human form. She ordered the war drums to be beaten. The call to war was given and the whole camp was thrown into turmoil as they made preparations for battle.

The magic birds brought these tidings to Queen Mahrukh. At her orders, bugles trilled to answer the enemy's call to war. The preparations for battle and carnage started and remained underway for the next four watches of the night.

When the Lord of Darkness[110] retreated and the King of Golden-Headgear came out of his eastern palace and gave audience on the throne of sky, sorceress Lamae and Empress Heyrat entered the arena; one flashing brilliantly in a magic cloud, leading her one-hundred-thousand-strong army of sorcerers, the other in her enamelled palace accompanied by her numerous force.

Queen Mahrukh and Princess Bahar rode in on magic thrones at the head of their army. The blaring magic bugles deafened the ears of heaven and a great turmoil shook the earth as the sorcerers' hordes marched. The sorcerer groundsmen dropped thunderbolts to clear the arena of shrubbery. Magic clouds cast by their spells rained and settled the ashes and dust.

Criers from both sides came out to enthuse the warriors, and called out, "You must return triumphant to your camp and earn renown for your noble and valiant ancestors."

After the criers emptied the field, sorceress Lamae flickered in the arena in the form of lightning. With a flashing bolt, she cleft all her challengers from Mahrukh's camp into two. Then she flashed with a blinding light that filled the sky. When no challenger came out from Queen Mahrukh's camp sorceress Lamae struck Mahrukh's army columns, killing and burning thousands.

Mahrukh's army ranks were thrown into upheaval and her celebrated sorcerers recited counterspells to avert sorceress Lamae's magic.

Mahrukh took off her crown and supplicated in the court of God Almighty in the name of Fatima.

> *"Send aid O Fatima, daughter of Muhammad*
> *Send aid O light of the Majestic Prophet's house*
> *This feline army has come to kill me*
> *Send aid O Lioness of God."*

The arrow of Mahrukh's prayer reached the mark of acceptance. Everyone on the battlefield saw a magic cloud arise from the wilderness with the standard of Mahrukh's camp fluttering above it. Next, thousands of sorcerers riding magic dragons came into view, led by sorceress Mehshar, who sat with great magnificence beside Amar Ayyar on a flying throne.

Mehshar's army took position on one side of the arena while she made her war cry and struck sorceress Lamae's army in the form of a thunderbolt, killing thousands. When she regarded this sight, sorceress Lamae stopped attacking Mahrukh's army and charged at Mehshar. The two became entwined. The spectators saw two entangled, quivering, flashing lightning bolts in the sky and flashing bolts filled the arena. Whenever the lightning bolts struck, sorcerers in Heyrat's camp shouted, "O Sameri! O Jamshed!" They tooted their bugles, struck drums and raised and unfurled their colors. The racket resembled the din of doomsday.

In the meanwhile, Raad Thunder-Clap dismounted his throne and dove into the ground by invoking his magic. As Mehshar and Lamae fell entangled to the ground and rolled across the arena in combat, the earth suddenly cleft and Raad raised his head beside sorceress Lamae. He made a booming roar like thousands of thunderclaps striking simultaneously.

Because Lamae was a powerful sorceress, the impact did not shatter her skull. Instead, she fell unconscious. As sorceress Mehshar rose, rumbling into the sky and flashed, ready to strike down Lamae, a magic claw swooped down and carried sorceress Lamae away.

Raad Thunder-Clap now tore out of the ground in the midst of Lamae's ranks and roared, shattering the skulls of countless sorcerers. Many fell unconscious. Sorceress Mehshar flashed and fell, cleaving bodies in two wherever she struck. Lamae's army started to retreat even as Heyrat ordered Lamae's commanders to defend their positions.

Meanwhile, Mahrukh advanced and her army clashed with Heyrat's forces. Magic was deployed on both sides; Raad continuously emerged from the ground and roared; Mehshar continuously struck. A great pandemonium and uproar was witnessed in both camps as magic citrons and magic limes were hurled by sorcerers at their opponents.

With her spell, Princess Bahar summoned a magic spring that captivated the enemy sorcerers. Surkh Mu Wonder-Mane unfurled her hair and shooting stars showered on the foe, killing them in great numbers, Princess Nafarman wreaked havoc on the enemy with the magic she cast. Sorcerer Shakeel piled up the enemy sorcerers on the field.

Wherever the flaming lightning bolts fell
They cleared the expanse of enemy's existence
The army submerged in the waves of blood
Where blood-splashing swords in every surge struck
The warriors ready with their swords unsheathed
The archers shot at targets that came into view
Necks fell under the curved blade as if it were the prayer hall arch
Every headstrong infidel was a humbled soul
The shining blade of the dagger swam in life blood
The skulls of the foe as dagger handles were already marked

When Heyrat beheld this picture of her army's defeat, she struck the drums to announce the cessation of hostilities. She flew to the sky where she invoked magic to cause a surging river of fire to pour down into the arena and it began raining flames. Mahrukh also struck the drums to call her army back to camp. Heyrat extinguished the river of fire and returned to her court.

Mahrukh entered her encampment and held an assembly of her commanders.

Sorceress Mehshar and Raad Thunder-Clap made offerings and submitted their allegiance. They were welcomed by all the commanders in the camp and Mahrukh conferred robes of honor on them. She took off her precious necklace to present to Raad Thunder-Clap and gave him the rank of commander. Soon, preparations began for the celebrations. Mahrukh feted Mehshar and Raad and goblets of wine were passed around.

Leaving Queen Mahrukh's camp busy in these revels,

Let us wheel around the steed of pen
And write of sorceress Hasina's adventures

Hasina had put Prince Alam Shah under her beauty spell and issued the call to war at Bakhtiarak's advice. One day, when the world-illuminating greater star[111] retired to its westerly abode and its luminous minister, the lesser star,[112] took over the reign of the land, war drums were struck in Laqa's camp in the name of Prince Alam Shah.

The messengers of Amir Hamza's camp delivered this news to the auspicious ears of their just king. King Saad ordered that war drums be beaten in answer from their camp. The valiant champions and warriors began their preparations for battle. The armory distributed arms and armor to soldiers, who decorated themselves with weapons of their choice. The steeds were fitted with reins and saddles. For four watches of the night, everyone remained busy in these measures.

When the eastern mint issued the coin of the sun and it became currency in the bazaar of the heavens in lieu of the moon's dinar,[113] the King of True Believers emerged from his private pavilion and received the salutations and blessings of his commanders. His Excellency led his army to the arena astride his battle charger, Siyah Qitas. The ceremonial royal horse trotted beside him.

From the other side, Laqa, in the company of Prince Alam Shah and sorceress Hasina, descended like a scourge. Alam Shah sat astride a fairy-faced horse beside Laqa's throne. All the commanders and officers of Laqa's army were arrayed out behind him. Hasina had magically augmented her beauty and anyone who laid eyes on her was captivated by her charm.

The grounds keepers of the two armies dug up and levelled the elevated patches and filled up depressed areas of the arena to make it smooth and level for battle.

Next, the battle arrays were formed, and after they were established, Alam Shah sought Laqa's leave for combat and took the reins of his steed. He raced his horse into the arena and challenged the valiant True Believers thus: "Any of you who considers himself my match should come out and face me." Everyone in the army of True Believers wept at his words and said, "We would never raise our hands in combat to harm our prince."

At that moment, the steadfast pillar of the army of True Believers, the heart and soul and second in command of Amir Hamza the Lord of the Auspicious Planetary Conjunction, and the Lord of the lands of

India, to wit, King Landhoor bin Saadan came forward astride his battle elephant. He sought and received his king's leave to go and counsel the prince.

When Landhoor confronted him, Alam Shah said, "O *pheni*-eating,[114] worthless Indian, you think you are my equal? Very well then! Give me the best blow from your repertoire of knocks." Landhoor said, "O Prince of lofty station, I dare not fight with you as I am your slave and you my master. But it is most lamentable that you not only rebelled against your king but also challenged your noble father against all considerations of duty and honor in the quest of a shameless harridan, whore, and prostitute." Alam Shah fiercely answered, "O Indian, how dare you utter these vile words against your mistress and owner, and my honored and pledged wife. I shall make an example of you!"

He brought down his sword on Landhoor's head but Landhoor deflected the blade with a strike of his hand, foiling the prince's blow and catching his wrist. Alam Shah took hold of Landhoor's collar. As they struggled, their mounts collapsed under them. The two combatants emptied their saddles. They tied up the skirts of their coats, rolled up their sleeves, grappled with each other, and exerted themselves against the other's might. It seemed as if two rutting elephants or two demons were locked in combat and clashed their heads together.

Sorceress Hasina cast a spell that drained Landhoor's power and might; he felt his limbs become lifeless. Alam Shah pinned Landhoor to the ground and gave him prisoner to Laqa's soldiers, who incarcerated Landhoor with other commanders of Amir Hamza's camp. As the trickster, Tarar the Speedster, had already captured and imprisoned Amir Hamza in a cave, there was nobody who could challenge Alam Shah. The prince now drew his sword and attacked the army of True Believers.

Amir Hamza's surviving army commanders saw no choice but to fight back. The King of the True Believers charged into the arena and Laqa's armies also attacked. King Saad made his war declaration,

> *"I am the king of kings, majestic as Faridun the Great*
> *I am the spring to the splendorous garden of Kaikaus*
> *and Jamshed*
> *My arm is as strong as Bahman's arm*
> *I am brazen-bodied like Isfandiar!"*

The two surging armies clashed with a roar and merged in sword combat. The cling-clang of arms and war slogans of champions mixed with the cries of the injured and dying.

The commanders of the True Believers' army showed consideration to Alam Shah and avoided harming him. The prince, however, injured and maimed many and martyred several of them.

When Alam Shah injured King Saad too, the royal attendants carried their king away on a movable throne. The tricksters valiantly transported the women of Amir Hamza's camp on their backs to the safety of the hills. The army commanders emptied out their camp and pavilions and, along with King Saad and their men, took refuge in a mountain pass.

Alam Shah charged into the empty camp and secured the Pavilion of Suleiman. Finding that he had no challengers, Alam Shah ordered his attendants to carry away the pavilion. Later, he ordered that drums be struck in Laqa's camp to call the warriors to camp.

Alam Shah declared, "Tomorrow I will attack the mountain hideout where the True Believers have taken refuge and kill every single one of them." Laqa returned to the fortress showering gold on Alam Shah's head as a holy offering to ward off any harm that might befall him. The warriors rested and celebrations began in the fortress of Mount Agate.

Alam Shah said in the court, "Now I should be married to Princess Hasina. I have obtained the Pavilion of Suleiman. Soon I will bring back Hamza's head too."

Hasina, who was only too eager to lie with the prince, said to Bakhtiarak, "Do not make further delays. Marry me now to the prince." Bakhtiarak answered, "You will spoil my plan with your impatience, but I will do as you wish. Prepare yourself to be married so that you can take your pleasure with the prince."

Sorceress Hasina returned to her abode and ordered her attendants to decorate the garden and adorn her quarters. They released water in the watercourses, pruned the trees, and festooned the summerhouse where all the instruments of musical assembly were provided. Revels were organized in the Pavilion of Suleiman too, for the pleasure of Prince Alam Shah. Musicians, singers and dancers regaled the assembly. Goblets of roseate wine were passed. The revels continued and Alam Shah sat bedecked as a bridegroom on the throne.

Leaving Laqa's camp occupied in merrymaking, let us hear an account of Amir Hamza's camp. King Saad lay bleeding and unconscious in the mountain pass and his champions and nobles were also injured. When the king regained his senses, he said, "Raise me onto my steed's saddle, fasten me to it and send me into the battlefield. To lay down my life fighting is far preferable to me than an ignoble existence such as this!" At these words, the women gathered there wept and wailed. When the dizzincss subsided and the king again opened his eyes, he said, "Our camp encountered all these troubles because Amar Ayyar was not with us. We have many tricksters but they are tricksters in name alone. There are none that are capable of getting us out of this trouble."

The trickster Chalak was cut to the quick by these words. He said to himself, *I should kill that whore Hasina or lay down my life in the endeavor.* He put on his trickster's livery and set out for the Fortress of Mount Agate.

When Chalak arrived in Laqa's court he witnessed wedding arrangements underway. He disguised himself as an attendant and asked a passerby, "Whose wedding is taking place here?" The man gave Chalak all the details regarding sorceress Hasina's nuptials with Prince Alam Shah and told him that Hasina would be wed from her garden. Chalak obtained the directions to Hasina's garden and headed there.

Chalak disguised himself as a sorcerer, marked his body with sandalwood powder, plaited his hair and smeared it with dust. He tied the portraits of Sameri and Jamshed to his arms, put on a saffron-colored waistcloth and affixed a diamond tablet on his forehead; it was carved with the words, "Special Aide to Emperor Afrasiyab." It made his forehead look like it was carved out of diamond. Carrying a trident and chaffing dish, the false sorcerer entered Hasina's garden. To any who asked his particulars, Chalak replied, "I am sent by Emperor Afrasiyab."

When the news was conveyed to sorceress Hasina she came out of her bridal chamber to welcome the false sorcerer, who introduced himself as Makkar the Cunning. Hasina took him into the summerhouse and asked him to make himself comfortable. Makkar gave her a letter and said, "I don't have orders to sit down. The emperor has sent you this message and awaits an answer."

Hasina read the letter given her. It read:

> "Well done, O Hasina! You accomplished a great deed by destroying Hamza's camp. I brought back some fruit from my visit to the Garden of Sameri, which I distributed among my faithful servants. I offer you your share by the hand of the sorcerer Makkar. By eating this fruit you will receive the gift of longevity, since the Garden of Sameri is full of marvels. I bind you by an oath on my life that you eat this fruit when you receive it. Allow only your close confidantes to remain in your

> presence when you eat it lest the shadow of an impure person is cast on the fruit and defiles it. Then you must speedily put an end to the battle and return to court to receive lands and riches as your reward. End of the letter. Regards."

Hasina was overjoyed upon reading the letter and sent all her slave girls to await her outside the garden. She allowed only a handful of close confidantes, who were most immaculately clean, to remain by her side. After making these arrangements, she said to Makkar, "Please present the fruit sent by the emperor."

The false sorcerer sent for trays, then took out many brightly colored, shining and fresh fruit from his pocket and arranged them on the trays. He made a respectful bow before the fruit then offered it to Hasina. The sorceress put the tray on her head as a sign of respect and said, "There is no end to the emperor's kindnesses. He never fails to remember or show favor to his slave girls. As the emperor has bound me by an oath on his life to eat the fruit, I wish to eat it in your presence, O Makkar, so that you can bear witness to my actions before the emperor."

Then Hasina ate the fruit and also offered some to her confidantes. As soon as they ate the drug-laced fruit, Hasina and her companions fell unconscious. Chalak slaughtered Hasina and beheaded her attendants. Immediately, their magic spirits caused an uproar and sorcerers and sorceresses ran into the garden.

Chalak took advantage of the spreading darkness to remove Amir Hamza's protective necklace from Hasina's neck and escape after jumping over the garden wall.

In the meanwhile, the turmoil continued and sorcerers ran in all directions in the ensuing confusion.

Now hear of what passed in the Pavilion of Suleiman, where Alam Shah sat dressed as a bridegroom. When Hasina was killed the spell she had cast on him was removed. The prince fell unconscious as the spell was broken. When he came to he found himself sitting in Laqa's court dressed like a Laqa worshipper.

He asked the courtiers, "What are my circumstances?" They replied, "You prostrated yourself before Lord Laqa and today is the day of your wedding." Then they gave Alam Shah a complete account of how he fell in Hasina's love and fought and routed the camp of the True Believers.

Alam Shah rose in a blazing rage and cried, "Alas, that infidel made a staunch True Believer like me prostrate myself before him and murder my companions by my own hand!" Alam Shah drew his sword and made his war declaration,

> *"Alam Shah, the Prince of Elephant Might*
> *My might made the throne of Marzuq tremble*
> *I am the one whose name in every assembly*
> *Will be now proclaimed Rustam Elephant-Body!"*

A sword fight broke out in Laqa's court. Amir Hamza's army commanders Landhoor, Hashim Swordfighter and others, who had been imprisoned together in a tent, were also freed of sorceress Hasina's spells upon her death. When they heard Alam Shah's war cry and the rising racket reached them, they broke their fetters and rushed out swinging the chains that had imprisoned them. They killed the guards, snatched their weapons and charged into Laqa's court.

In the meanwhile, Alam Shah fought his way out of the court and fell upon Laqa's camp. Taken unawares, Laqa's soldiers defended themselves as best they could but by that time Alam Shah had already killed thousands, throwing Laqa's camp into upheaval.

Chalak rushed to the mountain pass to apprise his army of the news. The commanders who were not too badly injured quickly marshalled their men and charged Laqa's forces.

It is recounted that Amir Hamza, who was thrown into a cave by the trickster Tarar the Speedster, regained consciousness after a day. He broke his bonds, removed the stone that blocked the cave entrance and came out.

However, he lost his way in the mountains and wandered for two days. Then he came upon a woodcutter and hired him as a guide to find his way back to his camp. Amir Hamza arrived at his camp when Alam Shah charged Laqa's camp. Amir Hamza recited the Most Great Name and rendered useless the magic spells cast by sorceress Hasina's companions. A pitched sword battle now raged between the two camps. Heads flew off shoulders and were kicked around like beggars' bowls.

Finally, Laqa's army was defeated. The false god took refuge in the fortress of Mount Agate while the sorcerers retreated into Hoshruba.

Amir Hamza's army captured the war booty and brought back the Pavilion of Suleiman. It was set up at the same spot in Hamza's camp where it had stood earlier. The wounds of the injured were sutured. The army bivouacked, the bazaars opened up, and the women of Amir Hamza's camp returned from their mountain refuge. The trickster

Chalak presented the protective necklace to Amir Hamza, who rewarded him with a robe of honor.

In the meanwhile, at Bakhtiarak's behest, King Suleiman Amber-Hair again sent a message to Afrasiyab. It read:

> "O Afrasiyab, I request you in Lord Laqa's name to send someone else to aid our lord. Sorceress Hasina crossed Lord Laqa by falling in love with Hamza's son, therefore our lord destroyed her. Now he again awaits your help. It is hoped you will presently carry out his wishes."

The message was sent to the mountain, the gong was rung, and the magic claw materialized and carried off the letter.

Sorcerer Aafat and Princess Hilal Magic-Wringer

Now hear of what passed in the tilism. Afrasiyab sat in the Apple Garden when the magic claw that had carried off sorceress Lamae Lightning-Bolt brought her before him. The emperor removed the spell that held her and returned her to consciousness. After hearing sorceress Lamae's account, Afrasiyab beat his head in shame and chagrin. He sent off sorceress Lamae to her land and thought of assigning sorceress Chashmak Zan Lightning-Bolt to the campaign against Mahrukh.

At that moment, a sorcerer named Aafat, who was one of the emperor's close confidants and illustrious commanders, laughed at Afrasiyab.

Afrasiyab, who grieved at his recent reversals, was enraged by Aafat's ill-timed laughter. The emperor said, "O insolent man, how dare you laugh instead of consoling your master and weeping at his circumstances?" Aafat replied, "O Emperor, I laugh when I consider the rising fortunes of Amar Ayyar and Mahrukh Magic-Eye and how they humiliate your devotees, the renowned sorcerers of the tilism, who are the equals of Sameri and Jamshed. Amar trounced them and all of them turned tail. Verily, it's a near impossibility to triumph over Amar." Afrasiyab was incensed by these inauspicious words and said, "O ill-natured, worthless man, go away and never come back! How dare you dispirit and dishearten my courtiers by impertinently praising the enemy before them?"

Being of a noble nature, Aafat could not hold back after hearing Afrasiyab's harsh words. Aafat said, "O Afrasiyab, it is such displays of vanity that brought Lord Sameri's wrath down on you. As we know,

"Any who raised the head of vanity was condemned
To this day the Tutor of Angels[115] walks in ignominy."

"You have not renounced your arrogance despite repeated humiliations. I speak true. You will never be able to kill Amar Ayyar. Everyday I feel more inclined to believe that his faith is indeed the true faith."

Afrasiyab said, "It appears to me that you have joined Amar, which is why you sing his praises and take his side. I'll teach you a lesson for your insolence. I would like to see how Amar saves you now."

Afrasiyab ordered the sorcerers present in his court to arrest Aafat. When the sorcerers rose to arrest him Aafat tried to counter their spells but was overwhelmed by their greater number and was pinioned by them.

Afrasiyab ordered, "Take him across the River of Flowing Blood into Zahir and burn him alive in the open field that stretches from the Dome of Light and overlooks Mahrukh's camp so that she too, may witness his terrible end and take admonition from it. That area is also accessible to the tricksters. I would like to see who dares to release him. Tonight this man of ill fortune should remain imprisoned in the execution grounds. Come morning, I will arrive at the Dome of Light and sit in the window that overlooks Mahrukh's camp to witness the burning of Aafat on the pyre, and the helplessness of his sympathisers."

Several thousand sorcerers led Aafat away. The entire region of Batin rang with the news and sorceress Aafat's wife, Princess Hilal Magic-Wringer, also received the tidings. She headed out with several hundred beautiful slave girls to see her husband for the last time. Aafat's friends and attendants wept and wailed and accompanied the princess, their hair dishevelled and collars rent. But they followed her at a distance because of their fear of the Emperor of Hoshruba.

When the party of sorcerers leading Aafat as prisoner arrived in Zahir a great hue and cry arose in that region.

Empress Heyrat's magic birds brought her the news and she rode out on her throne to witness the sight. All the officers of her camp accompanied her. Magic bugles tooted and the criers made proclamations that anyone who rebelled against the Emperor of Hoshruba would be likewise punished and experience a similar plight.

In due time, the news also reached Queen Mahrukh's camp that Aafat was condemned to be burned alive for the words he spoke in favor of Amar and Mahrukh. Everyone, including Amar Ayyar, received the news and became restive. Mahrukh ordered that the magic trumpet should be sounded and readied her army to attack and snatch Aafat from Afrasiyab's clutches. Then Amar said to her, "O queen, if you were able to triumph over the armies of the Emperor of Hoshruba, we, the tricksters, would have speedily killed the emperor instead of undergoing any hardships. It is impossible for you to snatch Aafat from them. I advise instead that some of your sorcerers should fly into the sky by magic and hide there, and some more should invoke magic to sink into the ground. A part of our army should lie in wait here and another part should prepare to ambush. When they hear my war cry and witness Afrasiyab lying unconscious, they should attack the enemy camp and start the carnage. However, you must make these arrangements under cover of night. Let the remainder of the day pass without these preparations or your intentions will be revealed to the enemy. I must, however, start now and plan some trickery."

Amar Ayyar went on his way. He arrived in the wilderness and blew his whistle to summon his trickster companions. When they gathered, Amar informed them about their mission. Each trickster described the trickery he would perform to achieve his end. Amar approved of the trickery they described, which will be revealed in due time. Afterwards, the tricksters left on their respective missions and Amar went his own way.

On the other side, villainous sorcerers led Aafat into the field. Empress Heyrat's entourage also arrived and was stationed on one side of the field. Afrasiyab had ordered that a pyre be built and Aafat kept incarcerated during the night.

When the bride of the day arrived in the house of lamentations dressed in black, and the evening of sorrows displayed her mourning face, a guard and vigil was deputed on sorcerer Aafat. Empress Heyrat's entourage bivouacked in their place. The vigil squads remained on the alert and constantly made rounds of the camp. A sorcerer named Tadbir, appointed to supervise the building of the pyre, ordered that the forest be cut down to obtain wood.

As advised by Amar, Queen Mahrukh and half of her army slipped away under cover of darkness. Once they arrived near their marks, they invoked magic, flew to the sky, and sank into the ground as planned, to lie in ambush.

The trickster Burq the Frank reached the open field and saw sorcerer Tadbir supervising the arrangements for the pyre. Burq disguised himself as a woodcutter and, carrying an axe on his shoulder, went before him.

He said to Tadbir, "As I was cutting a tree, a flame leapt out of its trunk and turned into a fairy and started dancing. I ran away in fright and came to report it so that you may also witness this marvel." Tadbir was greatly surprised. He accompanied the false woodcutter, who led him to a deserted place where he made Tadbir unconscious with an egg of oblivion, put on his clothes, and assumed his disguise. He bound the real Tadbir and threw him into a cave, then returned to the field and resumed work.

When building the pyre, Burq left a cavity in the middle that could accommodate up to three persons. While Burq made these arrangements, Qiran the Ethiope dug a tunnel from the forest leading up to the cavity in the pyre. Disguised as sorcerers, the tricksters Zargham and Jansoz helped prepare the pyre and threw large amounts of drugs onto the logs.

While the tricksters made these preparations, Amar Ayyar headed along the bank of the River of Flowing Blood and arrived at a colorful garden that was the envy of paradise. Tall and soaring trees lined the garden. Every plant was bestowed richly by the bounty of the Eternal Gardener. And yet the garden was draped in sorrow and every flower sat on its branch with a rent collar, robbed of its beauty and charm.

Amar entered the garden and witnessed a woman dressed in black, who sat surrounded by several hundred slave girls wailing and lamenting. The woman was none other than the wife of sorceress Aafat, Princess Hilal Magic-Wringer. In the past, she had used that garden in Zahir for her pleasure jaunts; now she stopped there to spend the night in mourning before joining her husband to burn alongside him. That luminous moon of beauty sat marked by the eclipse of dread in the midst of her attendants, remembering her husband and suffering violent pangs of grief.

When Amar heard her lamentations, he realized she was sorcerer Aafat's wife. Amar hid in a garden nook and disguised himself as an old woman. White-haired, with bent back and walking with the help of a stick, the false old woman arrived before Princess Hilal crying, "Ah, my son!" She introduced herself as Aafat's nanny, vowed her life's sacrifice to keep the princess from harm, and cried copiously in her embrace. Then she said to Princess Hilal, "O Princess, accompany me to the gate of the garden. Come alone as I am going to attempt your husband's rescue and want you to hear the details." Princess Hilal left her slave girls behind and followed the false old woman, who led her to a deserted spot and made her unconscious with an egg of oblivion. Amar now disguised himself as Princess Hilal, put on her clothes and put the real princess into his zambil.

The false Princess Hilal returned to her companions. After a few moments, she declared, "Lord! Lord!"[116] Her companions and slaves fell down at her feet and cried, "O delicate flower of beauty's garden, consider your youth and desist from the thoughts of dying with your husband. For the sake of lords Sameri and Jamshed, keep the fire of separation from burning your heart away." The false Hilal answered,

"The one struck by fatal love's arrow
Finds life a veritable burden to pass.

"I would not feed my body to the fire of disunion. I find it far preferable to die united with my lover and escape separation's blaze." The false princess cried bitterly after calling out,

"No one should witness the flame of searing love rising
Lovers burn and turn to ash without giving out smoke."

Then the false princess sang,

"If my lips utter a sigh it would burn up the world, set aflame the forest
But this wicked heart remains unburned though my sighs fill it."

Then she ordered her attendants, "Bring my bridal dress and costume. I will decorate myself for my last journey on the path to eternal union when I enter the assembly of spirits in the company of my husband."

The attendants brought out the dress and jewelery and carried them on trays to the false Princess Hilal, who decorated her locks, strung pearls in her hair, and left it loose. As she adorned herself, the layer of *missi* and lac dye on her lips was so captivating it robbed the lovers of all their sensory possessions and bled their souls. She decked herself in a red dress to further ignite the flame of love in the hearts of lovers; her attire showed her breasts to advantage with their high angle, further robbing the lovers of their peace of mind.

In short, after she was all dressed, fragrant as the jasmine and adorned as a *sati*,[117] her lovely slave girls worshipped her and placed garlands and sweetmeat offerings around that delicate beauty. The false Princess Hilal sat on her throne and laughed joyously, for

Happy and cheerful she headed for her lover's court

The false Hilal tossed and played with a magic coconut as the carriers led her throne to the pyre.

As she was carried along the paths of the tilism, sorcerers, citizens of the tilism and other creatures followed her. All of them promised offerings in her name if she answered their prayers. They worshipped her and asked for her blessings. When the false Princess Hilal saw throngs crowding the way, she stopped the procession and sang the denunciations of the worthless world. She enjoined everyone to engross themselves in thoughts of God. She said, "Hear that the one who loves his Lord, in whose soul the Lord resides, whose heart the Lord fills with Himself, the one who gives up his body and soul in His name, for such a one it is easy to give up life too. Without the oppressive garb of bodily existence, he discovers true happiness. The perfect act in this world is to love the Lord, for it leads to being in His presence every moment and becoming one with Him in the end."

Pipes and cymbals played before the *sati*'s throne. She offered some the flowers torn from her garlands; to others she gave the ashes from the ceremonial worship fire. She went along her path offering injunctions to all who would listen.

Finally, the bright and luminous star emerged from the dome of the east, burning in the fire of separation of the Night Sky's Beauty,[118] and rode out on the throne of heaven to show the world the burn marks of his lover's heart.

By the time it was daylight, the *sati*'s procession arrived in the field where the pyre had been built. Afrasiyab came out of his bedchamber and took his seat in the Dome of Light.

The calamity-struck Aafat, with his grieving heart, prayed continuously to God. He importuned the Lord and prayed to Him in the name of His favored ones, saying, "O my Lord, like Mahrukh, I too have converted to the True Faith. Ward off this calamity from my head."

Sorcerer Aafat had not finished praying when a commotion suddenly rose and the false Princess Hilal's procession arrived there. All those assembled rushed to see her. They thronged around her throne and inquired of her about their prospects. Some were curious to know when a child would be born to them. One who was destitute inquired when he would come into riches and estate. The false Princess Hilal answered their queries and her procession kept moving onward.

Witnessing the hubbub, Afrasiyab asked the sorcerers in his court, "What is the reason for this disturbance?" One of them answered, "The wife of sorcerer Aafat has arrived to burn with her husband as a *sati*."

When Afrasiyab sent for the false *sati* and she arrived before him, the emperor nearly lost consciousness, overwhelmed by her great beauty.

Afrasiyab endlessly reasoned with her, saying, "O charming beloved, give up the thought of dying a *sati* and ask me for land and riches and take me for your slave in love." That false, moon-faced beauty answered, "O Emperor, my spirit would attain peace only when the fire of separation is quenched in my heart. Without it, gold and riches and estate are all as dirt to me."

The sorcerers had already seated Aafat atop the pyre as instructed by the emperor. The false princess jumped down from the throne, joined Aafat and seated him in her lap.

The sorcerers approached and burned a lamp under her palm to collect lamp black and test whether or not her love was true and whether or not the fire of love had already consumed her body and soul. Everyone bore witness to the truth of her love: the flame did not burn her hand, the false princess Hilal kept smiling as lamp black collected on her palm.

By now the field was fully crowded. Empress Heyrat and her sorcerers stood around the pyre. Zargham and Jansoz, who were busy making arrangements in sorcerers' disguises, brought canisters of oil and butter they had mixed with drugs and poured them on the logs of the pyre. Burq the Frank, disguised as sorcerer Tadbir, lit up a bunch of dried grass and threw it on the logs. Immediately, a flame blazed and sheets of fire rose up from the pyre. Amar – still disguised as the false Hilal – wrapped Aafat in the Net of Ilyas, stuffed him into the zambil and jumped into the cavity at the center of the pyre. Qiran already awaited him at the tunnel's mouth and led Amar out the other end.

In the meanwhile, the whole pyre caught flame and smoke rose from the drugs sprinkled on the logs. The drug potions mixed in the oil and butter that Zargham and Jansoz had poured on the pyre spread for miles. One after the other, the sorcerers who were gathered around the pyre, including Empress Heyrat, sneezed, and fell unconscious.

With faint repellent plugs in their noses, Amar and Qiran made their war cries, drew their daggers and began beheading enemy sorcerers. Soon Burq the Frank, Zargham and Jansoz also joined the killing spree.

Hearing the war cries of the tricksters, Queen Mahrukh, Princesses Bahar, Nafarman, Surkh Mu and others appeared in the sky and emerged from the ground to wreak havoc with their spells. They hurled steel magic balls, magic citrons and magic limes that shattered the spines of enemy sorcerers. As they died, the flames conflagrated higher and whirlwinds swept the field. The smoke rose so densely and in such abundance that it filled the chamber of the Dome of Light from where Afrasiyab surveyed the scene. All his courtiers were drugged senseless upon inhaling it. The Emperor of Hoshruba, who leaned out of the window, became unconscious himself and fell tumbling down the Dome of Light. Suddenly, the earth cleft and magic slaves emerged from the ground and caught him to break his fall.

Mahrukh Magic-Eye's army came out of their hiding place and ambushed Afrasiyab's sorcerers, who were killed, not in the thousands but in the hundreds of thousands. A wave of carnage surged and covered the foe. A river of blood began to flow.

When Mahrukh unsheathed the magic sword
Sparks flew in the thousands
Lightning and thunderbolts everywhere struck
The enemy corpses piled up in the battlefield
Such a terrible din rose from the arena
The old man heavens trembled with fear
The foe disappeared into fires of hell
Where Mehshar Lightning-Bolt fell
Like death, come to separate the body from soul
Like a thunderbolt it hovered on the head of the foe
The Cow of the Earth averted its eyes
From the blinding flash in the heavens
Even the bright star of the skies trembled with fear
When it recalled its flash and glare
From the sword's dazzling flash
All vegetation burned up all of a sudden
The flames of the sword burned brighter
And like clouds heads began to shower blood

Amar looted the enemy's goods and belongings and stripped the dead of their clothes. During the ensuing commotion, magic slaves carried Empress Heyrat to safety. They also restored Afrasiyab to consciousness. When he opened his eyes, Afrasiyab beheld the field in a doomsday like ferment, with his men swimming in blood and gore. Too ashamed by the sight, he awakened Heyrat from her faint and, by growing magic wings with a spell, flew away toward the region of Zulmat.

After Heyrat regained her senses, she invoked a magic cloud that rained and brought everyone to consciousness. As Heyrat prepared to repulse the attackers, Queen Mahrukh and Princess Bahar realized that they would be unable to capture the Dome of Light, and if Heyrat ordered the River of Flowing Blood to do so, it would surround them and they would become its prisoners. They immediately sounded the clarion to call their armies back to camp. The tricksters retreated into the wilderness. Thus, after the bloodshed and slaughter of the foe, Queen Mahrukh's triumphant force returned to the safety of their encampment where large scale celebrations and revels were planned.

In the meanwhile, Amar and his trickster companions also presented themselves. Amar took sorcerer Aafat and Princess Hilal Magic-Wringer out of the zambil. Finding themselves rescued from the jaws of death and in the safety of the royal pavilion, they looked around in surprise.

Amar gave them all the details and said, "O Aafat, it was I who rescued you from the pyre in the disguise of the *sati*." Aafat prostrated himself before Amar, who raised him into his embrace. Aafat made an offering to Queen Mahrukh and was awarded a robe of honor. Aafat and his wife Hilal were assigned their own pavilion, where they retired to rest and celebrate.

The bodies of Empress Heyrat's slain sorcerers were carried away on her orders and her army returned crying and wailing to its camp. Heyrat thought of avenging herself on Mahrukh's camp but decided to wait for Afrasiyab's instructions in the matter.

By this time, a downcast Afrasiyab returned from Zulmat to the Apple Garden. He angrily ordered his first minister, Baghban Magic-Gardener, "Bring Amar a prisoner from Mahrukh's court and punish anyone who interferes."

Baghban sank into the ground by magic to travel subterraneously to avoid the danger of encountering tricksters.

In Mahrukh's court, Amar Ayyar suddenly felt disquieted and became apprehensive. He realized that after suffering that terrible humiliation at his hands, the Emperor of Hoshruba would not let the matter pass but would try to take revenge. Amar said to himself, *Afrasiyab will certainly dispatch someone to arrest me. It would be best for me to go into hiding.*

Amar brought out a Kashmiri warrior from his zambil.

Be it known that Amar keeps many infidel sorcerers and warriors as prisoners in his zambil. They are fed by their jinn guards and the confines of the zambil appear to be a city to these prisoners. Furthermore, there are seven cities within the zambil. This zambil, which appears to the human eye in the shape of a small purse, was gifted to Amar by Prophet Aadam the Friend of God.

Amar made the Kashmiri unconscious, disguised the man as himself, put him into a bed in the front yard of the royal pavilion, and then disappeared by putting on the cape of invisibility.

In the meantime, Afrasiyab's minister tore out of the earth in Mahrukh's court and shouted, "Baghban Magic-Gardener is my name!" Mahjabeen's sorcerer commanders hurled steel magic balls and magic citrons at him. Baghban foiled them and recited a spell that started a cold breeze that put Mahrukh's entire court to sleep. When Baghban did not find Amar in the court, he decided to search outside before looking for Amar in the wilderness. He searched for Amar in the yards and inside the tents until he found him asleep in the yard and carried him off, putting a magic claw around Amar's waist.

Before flying away, Baghban removed his spell from Mahrukh's court. As they returned to consciousness, he shouted from the sky, "O rebels, the emperor only gave me orders to arrest Amar or else I would have beheaded all of you. I am taking Amar away. Is there any among you powerful enough to snatch him from me?"

The sorcerers in Mahrukh's court readied their magic coconuts and magic devices to fight him again but Amar, who was present there in his cape of invisibility, whispered into Mahrukh's ear, "I am hidden under the cape of invisibility. Stop your sorcerers from challenging him."

Mahrukh intervened and said to her courtiers, "Do not confront him. God will protect Amar. Let Baghban take him away." The sorcerers did not challenge Baghban, who flew away and in a short time arrived in the Apple Garden and threw the false Amar before Afrasiyab.

The emperor summoned the headman and ordered that the prisoner be brought to consciousness and executed. The sorcerers restored the false Amar to his senses. When the Kashmiri warrior opened his eyes he was confounded to find himself in the court of the majestic emperor. When he saluted Afrasiyab, the emperor said, "Regard O wretched trickster how quickly I apprehended you. Now you will die a most painful death!" The warrior said, "O Emperor, I am your humble servant, not a trickster. I am of your own faith – a Laqa worshipper." Afrasiyab replied, "I will never be deceived by your false words again." He ordered the executioner, "Kill him!"

The warrior again beseeched Afrasiyab, "O Emperor, satisfy yourself by every means but do me justice. I am from Kashmir. The True Believers defeated me and wished to convert me to their faith but I did not accept. Then Amar imprisoned me in his zambil. I am still perplexed by the way I was released and brought here." Afrasiyab became doubtful when he heard his imploring and pleading and looked into the *Book of Sameri*. It read:

> "The warrior tells the truth. Amar disguised him in his likeness. Then Baghban carried him away."

Afrasiyab ordered that the face of the warrior should be washed. The paints and lotions washed away and the warrior's real face was revealed. Afrasiyab released him and conferred a robe of honor on him, and the warrior entered the emperor's service.

Afrasiyab now said to Baghban, "It was not Amar whom you produced before me." Baghban answered, "I brought him here thinking he was Amar. I should not be faulted since I am not adept in the art of tricksters; I truly thought it was Amar."

Afrasiyab accepted Baghban's excuse. The emperor now sent a magic claw to fetch the trickster girl Sarsar from Heyrat's camp. The magic claw produced Sarsar in no time. When Sarsar saluted the emperor, Afrasiyab said, "You are a trickster. Search for Amar Ayyar and bring him to me a prisoner. If you fail me I swear upon my faith that I will kill you with my own hands. Do you not see the daring deeds performed by the enemy tricksters? What is the purpose of my having you as a trickster girl?"

Sarsar went away trembling in fear of the emperor's wrath. She armed herself and departed on her mission. When she crossed the River of Flowing Blood, she met up with the other trickster girls and gave them the news. While they left to perform their trickeries, Sarsar disguised herself as an attendant and arrived in Mahrukh Magic-Eye's camp.

As Sarsar made her rounds, she saw one of Mahrukh's slave girls leave her pavilion on an errand. Sarsar approached her and said, "I request that you find me employment with the queen." The attendant answered, "Go and submit your request in the court. I have no say in these matters." Sarsar accompanied her and they went conversing together until they reached a deserted spot. There, Sarsar made her unconscious with an egg of oblivion and assumed her appearance, putting on the attendant's costume and making herself into her likeness.

Then Sarsar returned to Mahrukh's court. When she appeared before the queen, Mahrukh said, "Go and put a water bowl by the chair in the privy chamber. I have to attend to the call of nature." Sarsar filled the water bowl and carried it there. In the meanwhile, Mahrukh also made her way there. Sarsar found her chance to make Mahrukh unconscious with an egg of oblivion. She then sat down to make herself into Mahrukh's likeness and put on her clothes. Sarsar tied Mahrukh into a bundle and carried it dangling from one hand, heading for the storage area. She asked the attendants of the storage to step out as she wished to put something away in privacy. After they left, the false Mahrukh locked the real Mahrukh in a chest. Then she sent for the attendants, showed them the chest and said, "You are warned on pain of death not to open this chest!" The attendants put the royal seal on the chest.

The false Mahrukh now returned to the court and sat on the throne.

After some time, she said, "Lay out the food in the front yard. I wish to have my meal." As ordered, the cook laid out the food and the false Mahrukh sat down to eat.

Amar Ayyar removed his cape of invisibility and returned to the royal pavilion. When he came in and did not see Mahrukh on the throne, he asked for her. The courtiers told him she was having her meal in the front yard. When Amar came out, the false Mahrukh said, "Please have some food with me." At first Amar declined but when the false queen insisted that he eat a little, Amar joined her.

After they had eaten, the slave girls brought the bowls to wash their hands. The false Mahrukh offered Amar her hand towel, pushed her betel box toward him, and dismissed her attendants, saying, "You may wait for me in the court. I now wish to consult with Amar privately." After they left, Amar wiped his mouth with the hand towel, which was steeped in a drug. Amar sneezed and immediately fell unconscious. Sarsar made a bundle of him, slit open the tent, and made her way speedily toward the River of Flowing Blood.

The guards and soldiers saw her carrying a bundle but as she was disguised as their queen, they did not dare challenge her. However, Burq the Frank, who came from the direction of the wilderness, sighted the false Mahrukh flying out of the camp and recognized her as a trickster girl. He immediately drew his short sword and attacked her. Sarsar too, unsheathed hers and fought back. She approached Burq fighting and targeted him with her snare rope. Burq jumped up to clear its coils and upon landing hit Sarsar with an egg of oblivion, which made her sneeze and fall unconscious.

As Burq reached for the bundled up Amar, he heard Saba Raftar's war cry from the wilderness. She challenged Burq and fell upon him with her dagger drawn. As Burq fought her, Saba Raftar reached over to Sarsar and hit her in the face with an egg of awareness, which brought Sarsar to consciousness. Seeing Burq and Saba Raftar busy fighting, Sarsar saw her chance and ran away carrying Amar. As Burq tried to follow her, Saba Raftar blocked his path. Burq blew his trickster whistle so that another trickster would hear his call and stop Sarsar.

Sarsar realized that if other tricksters came to Burq's aid she would be cornered. She headed for the path that passed through the second tier of the Bridge of Magic Fairies. Sarsar called out, "O Bridge, give me way in the name of Emperor Afrasiyab!" The smoke parted immediately at her words, a path was revealed and Sarsar disappeared into it while

Burq watched helplessly. Saba Raftar also dodged Burq and escaped, and the trickster returned to his camp.

Upon arrival, Burq heard cries that Amar and Mahrukh had disappeared while having their meal. When Burq learned the details he said, "It appears to me that Sarsar carried away Amar and the real Mahrukh is lying unconscious somewhere in our camp."

The storekeeper said, "The queen had put something away in a chest. We should check its contents." When Burq opened the chest he found Mahrukh locked within. He restored her to consciousness and seated her on the throne. The slave girl who had been rendered unconscious by Sarsar also returned to the court. Mahrukh was greatly distressed to hear of Amar's capture and the whole camp continuously discussed the sad and tragic event.

Now hear of the trickster girl Sarsar. As she escaped from Burq and passed over the Bridge of Magic Fairies, Amar regained consciousness. He opened his eyes and found himself tied in a bundle and carried on Sarsar's back through a narrow, dark, and dreadful passageway that would turn the gall of braves to water. Amar regarded all this and kept silent.

Sarsar now reached the Desert of Flames and called out, "O Desert of Flames, give me way in the name of Emperor Afrasiyab!" The flames made way too, and Sarsar crossed the Desert of Flames and came to stop when her path was blocked by a wall of darkness so intense that it could not be ascertained where the world ended and the heavens began.

Suddenly, a sorcerer whose body glowed like a flame, materialized and caught Sarsar around her waist with a magic claw. He swung her over his head and hurled her into the air. Amar closed his eyes in fear and when he opened them after a moment he saw that a fiery magic slave was carrying them away. It arrived at a river of fire and dove into it where there was nothing but utter darkness. Amar was frightened out of his wits and kept silently reciting "Help, O Merciful God!" The fiery magic slave swam across the river and came out on the other bank. There, a magic trooper materialized and flew away, holding Sarsar by the hand.

Finally, Amar saw a mountain appear in the distance. The magic trooper landed there and threw Sarsar down the mountain. Amar closed his eyes as Sarsar fell tumbling down. When he opened his eyes he saw Sarsar had landed in Afrasiyab's Apple Garden.

It was a garden that was created as a tilism. Protected from the hands of autumn, and the revolutions of time and chance, trees laden with flowers in eternal bloom lined the garden. Verdure and bright shrubbery refreshed the sight wherever one turned his gaze. The song birds and creatures made of magic sang and warbled in their honeyed tones, *"O Afrasiyab! O Afrasiyab!"* The garden's entire landscape and buildings were a tilism. Every chamber and house was as charming as a fairy, with the columns and roof fitted with intricate fixtures and the summerhouse clustered with jewels.

An array of aromatic herbs and flowers grew there
An array of tilisms populated that expanse
The walls and doors were made with magic
On a different scheme than all doors and houses
Neither fire could burn nor rain soak them
Neither summer nor winter within were felt
If one desired a thing within its walls
That object presently appeared on a shelf therein
The birds and beasts there of jewels were carved
They ambled and flew far within its walls
Roamed in the shape of animals all day
And worked in the form of humans all night long
Lustrous night lamp rubies embedded in walls
In the day shone as rubies, in the night glowed as lamps
Every flower, every thorn in that garden was of magic made
Its roses and rose buds had no equal in creation
The hours of clocks chimed and invisible, rang
With the sound of dancing and clapping
When left open the garden chambers
Rang with the music of a myriad instruments
And once closed the chambers gave off
A thousand pleasant strains organ like
Velvet carpets laid out and spread on its floors
With the runes from Suleiman's time on it inscribed
The drapes and curtains in that garden's tilism
Drew at one's desire and closed at one's wish

Afrasiyab sat on a throne in the center of the summerhouse and gave audience. Thousands of sorcerers stood humbly before him with their arms folded on their breasts.

Upon arrival, Sarsar saluted the emperor and put the bundle of Amar before him. She said, "I present the emperor's enemy. Your Honor's slave girl performed the mission given her and risked her life to produce

Amar before you." Afrasiyab conferred a precious robe of honor on Sarsar and said, "Open the bundle."

The bundle was not yet opened when a magic claw brought the letter from King Suleiman Amber-Hair in which he had given an account of sorceress Hasina's death and sought Afrasiyab's aid at Laqa's behest.

Afrasiyab read Suleiman Amber-Hair's note and wrote to Laqa in reply:

> "Your humble slave has captured Amar Ayyar, the deadly enemy of Your Lordship. I request you to send your devil designate, Bakhtiarak, to kill him with his own hand. On his return journey, I will accompany him with an army of sorcerers that will destroy Hamza's forces."

Afrasiyab handed the message to sorceress Princess Khumar to take immediately to Laqa.

Sorceress Khumar

Bearing the emperor's reply, Princess Khumar flew away by magic and speedily arrived at the fortress of Mount Agate. In deference to Laqa, she decided to announce her arrival at the gates of the court.

It so happened that the trickster Chalak had come to Mount Agate to spy on Laqa and his court in a macebearer's disguise. Sorceress Khumar saw him standing at the gates and said to him, "O macebearer, announce in the court that Emperor Afrasiyab's messenger sorceress Khumar has arrived from Hoshruba with a letter from the emperor." The false macebearer replied, "Wait here, I will go and announce your arrival." He stepped inside, waited a few moments, then came out and said to Khumar, "Come with me, O Princess, and receive your instructions."

Khumar followed Chalak, who brought her to a deserted corner and gave her a fruit, saying, "Lord Laqa has sent this fruit for you to eat before you appear in his presence. It will make your body glow with our lord's divine light."

Khumar prostrated herself and said, "O lucky me! His Lordship shows such munificence, even toward his insignificant creatures. No sooner have I arrived than I receive a gift from his bounty!" After expressing her gratitude, Princess Khumar ate the fruit. The effects of that drugged fruit became manifest to Khumar immediately upon eating it. Her head went down and her feet went up and she fell unconscious.

Chalak saw his chance. He took out his razor and shaved Khumar's head clean. Then he took out Afrasiyab's message from her bag and replaced it with one of his own composition. Afterwards, Chalak headed for Laqa's court to await Khumar's arrival.

After some hours, Khumar regained consciousness. She got to her feet and said to herself, *I must have lost consciousness from eating the fruit Lord Laqa sent. Indeed, such must be one of its properties. Surely, when the pollution and contamination of the former self are purged and the soul is renewed, a person would lose consciousness. Clearly, I am as clean and pure today as the moment I came out of my mother's womb.* Engrossed in these thoughts, Khumar headed for Laqa's court. Every now and then she inspected her limbs to see if they had started glowing with divine light. It never occurred to her that her hair had been shaved off.

Khumar entered the court and prostrated herself when she saw Laqa on the throne. The courtiers started laughing at the sight of the shaven-headed sorceress. Laqa said to Khumar, "Raise your head, O being of my creation! I bestow my mercy upon you." Khumar finally raised her head and Laqa offered her a chair beside his throne. As she took her seat, Bakhtiarak addressed the court, reciting,

> *"Neither her beauty altered nor my passion showed variance*
> *Even with her locks shaved I remain as miserable as before."*

Khumar did not understand the import of what Bakhtiarak said. She produced the envelope from her bag and offered it to Laqa. At a sign from Laqa, his court secretary took the envelope from Khumar, opened it and took out the letter. Seeing that it was full of invectives and insults, he humbly said to Laqa, "I am unable to read this letter as it seems to be written in a talismanic hand."

Bakhtiarak said, "Let me read it." When the court secretary gave him the letter and Bakhtiarak read it, he laughed uproariously and said, "Listen to the words of this missive, O Lord! It reads:

> 'Hear, O disgraced bastard, clown, ass, idiot, pimp, inane bear of the dark path, who is monkey-like, swine-natured, hideous of face, ill-born, astray, foolish-faced, dark of complexion and darker of disposition – to wit, Zamarrud Shah, alias Laqa – who is eternally cursed in the court of heavens and blighted by God. Hear this, O accursed creature after thousands upon thousands of curses, and may God make you a burning log in hell! You turned thousands of creatures away from the True

> Faith. You are ordered to present yourself forthwith in the dignified court of Amir Hamza the Lord of the Auspicious Planetary Conjunction to convert to the True Faith and renounce your false claim of divinity, otherwise my forces will march against you and I will depute an army of sorcerers to bring you to the door of ruin and destruction; the eyes of regret will shed tears at your terrible end and none will remain who will even remember your name. Consider this short message a memorandum of ample warning. End of Letter. Thousands of curses upon your head!'"

Laqa growled angrily like thunder and shouted, "That bastard Afrasiyab has courted a terrible calamity. I will now destroy him with an inauspicious fate and dispatch him hellward."

Witnessing Laqa in a rage, sorceress Khumar shook like an aspen leaf and said, "My Lord, this was indeed not the message sent by the Emperor of Hoshruba. It appears that along the way someone replaced the original. After Amar was captured and brought before Emperor Afrasiyab, he told his court secretary to write you to request sending your devil designate Bakhtiarak to kill Amar with his own hands and return leading an army of sorcerers to Mount Agate. Instead, I heard abuses written in this letter. It confounds me to think of an explanation for this marvel. But you are the Lord Almighty! To your eye all mysteries must be manifest and clear."

When he heard this speech, Bakhtiarak said, "Now I know how the letter was changed. Indeed, it is impossible to capture Amar. I know that he must have disguised another in his likeness and had him arrested. Amar must have accompanied you here secretly and found his chance to make you unconscious and replace the letter."

Bakhtiarak then asked Khumar, "O Princess, is it a fashion in Hoshruba for the women to shave their heads?"

Khumar thought that Bakhtiarak spoke in jest. She replied, "O devil designate of Lord Laqa, it is indeed your function to make light of everyone. But I am too insignificant a creature and a mere devotee of our Lord to be a worthy target of your quips. Why do you imagine the women of Hoshruba would shave their heads when it is reputed that their ringlets are the fetters for lovers' hearts and those bitten by the dark snakes of their captivating locks do not draw another breath?" Bakhtiarak said, "In that case, did you make a vow that you would shave your head before your audience with Lord Laqa? Feel your head;

you will know whether or not you have any hair left on it or if I spoke in jest."

Khumar felt her head and realized that Bakhtiarak spoke true. Her head was shaved clean; not so much as a bristle was left standing. She broke into tears and cried, "O Bakhtiarak, you spoke true when you said that Amar must have accompanied me here. Indeed, I felt a heavy burden on my shoulders. I am sure he rode me all the way. Today I was given fruit to eat by a macebearer that made me unconscious. That man must have been Amar. He had shaved my head once before."

Bakhtiarak cried loudly, "Blessings upon Muhammad and his progeny! Curses upon Laqa! Regard, O Khumar, what a favored creature Amar is of Lord Laqa that he showed you this day! You will presently see him make an appearance."

Be it known that Bakhtiarak said these words only to check whether or not Amar Ayyar was present in Laqa's court, for he knew well that Amar revealed himself whenever he was praised. Next, Bakhtiarak said, addressing Amar, "O True Master, pray show us your face if Your Honor has arrived here!"

Chalak, who was present in Laqa's court, had witnessed all these proceedings. He said to himself, *I should appear before them in Amar Ayyar's disguise. When Khumar sees him in Laqa's court she will be satisfied and tell Afrasiyab that she saw Amar at Mount Agate. Afrasiyab will become doubtful and think that the one he captured was not Amar. He will release the real Amar and everyone would praise my trickery, which secured Amar Ayyar's release from hundreds of miles away.*

Chalak went out of the court to assume the disguise. Bakhtiarak had not finished eulogizing about Amar when Chalak jumped over the pavilion and landed in the center of the court in Amar Ayyar's disguise. To make sure that Bakhtiarak was satisfied with his identity, he conspicuously displayed a false mole on the white of his left eye and cried, "O Khumar! You barely escaped my hands! I had every intention of killing you!"

When Khumar saw Amar she rushed at him, shouting, "O wretch deserving of beheading, you have invited your death by shaving my head a second time and disgracing me in the tilism and the court of Lord Laqa." As she neared him, the false Amar Ayyar hit her in the face with an egg of oblivion. Khumar fell unconscious upon impact and the false Amar leapt away and escaped. Laqa's attendants were well accustomed to the tricksters' ways and knew better than to waste their time by giving them chase. None of them stirred from their place.

Bakhtiarak restored Khumar to consciousness and said to her, "O Princess, now you should go back and show your shaved head to

Afrasiyab, describe to him what passed with you, and take the reply to his missive."

Bakhtiarak dictated a reply to Afrasiyab's letter from Laqa, which read:

> "I bestow my mercies on the Emperor of Hoshruba, Afrasiyab, who is a favorite among my favored creatures. Be it known to him that he is an unmindful king, easily tricked by his servants. His trickster girl brought him someone in the disguise of Amar Ayyar and he never felt the least suspicion. Amar Ayyar followed his messenger to our court. It would be little wonder if one day Amar killed him too, taking advantage of his lax guard. It is unworthy of our devil designate to visit the court of such a negligent and unaware person. He will pay the Emperor of Hoshruba a visit when he arrests the real Amar Ayyar. Now it is incumbent upon the emperor to send an army of sorcerers to the aid of His Lord or else His Lordship will visit his divine wrath on his tilism and go away in anger."

The court secretary wrote the letter, stamped it with Laqa's seal, and handed it to sorceress Khumar. After receiving the letter, she prostrated herself before Laqa and said, "O Lord! Make my hair grow back." Laqa replied, "Come to me on the day of Nowruz.[119] I will grant you such beauty and charm that even the houris of my heaven will envy you and you will receive eternal youth."

Laqa sent her off after offering her such words of comfort and hope.

Sorceress Khumar flew away with Laqa's letter. She soon arrived in the court of Afrasiyab, where he awaited Laqa's reply. Khumar presented it, along with the letter trickster Chalak had written, showed the emperor her shaved head, and narrated all that had passed.

Afrasiyab trembled with fright upon learning that abuses were addressed to Laqa in his name. He was also deeply grieved that his beloved Khumar's hair had been shaved off. Afrasiyab became convinced that Sarsar had produced someone in Amar's disguise to impress him with her resourcefulness. He ordered that Amar, who had been tied to a column in the Apple Garden, be brought before him.

Amar had already heard Khumar's entire account. He said to himself, *One of my disciples must have shaved this whore's head and created a ruse for my release.*

The sorcerers untied Amar and put spells on him so that he could not escape and presented him before Afrasiyab. When the emperor asked him who he was, Amar replied, "Your Excellency, Sarsar told me that she would present me before you in Amar's disguise, that I would be imprisoned, and when it was night, she would set me free and give me five thousand rupees. In return, I had to state before you that I was Amar when, in fact, I am a prostitute from the region of Zahir."

Afrasiyab said to the sorcerers, "Remove your spells from Amar." Then he said to him, "You are free to go where you please." He also rewarded Amar five thousand rupees for revealing the truth of the matter. Amar saluted Afrasiyab, collected his reward, and left the Apple Garden. Thinking that a calamity might soon follow upon the discovery of the truth and that he would be recognized and recaptured, Amar wrapped himself in his cape of invisibility.

In the Apple Garden, Afrasiyab called out, "Send for that whore and sham trickster girl Sarsar!"

The sorcerers conveyed the message to Sarsar, who rested in another part of the vast Apple Garden. When she heard the emperor's unexpected summons she arrived shaking and trembling with fear. Afrasiyab ordered, "Tie her up!" The sorcerers tied Sarsar to a column and gave her a thrashing at Afrasiyab's orders. Sarsar cried out, "What is my crime?" Afrasiyab replied, "O evil bitch, this is your reward for disgracing me before Lord Laqa! Read this message from him! You brought me a prostitute disguised as Amar Ayyar. Tell me the truth now or I will have your nose cut off from the root."

Sarsar replied, "That is not true. I satisfied myself that the man was Amar." Sorceress Khumar said, "See for yourself! Amar shaved off my hair. Why would I shave my own head just to show you to be a liar?" Sarsar addressed Afrasiyab, "Your Excellency should not believe me or anybody else but consult the *Book of Sameri*. If I have lied you should put me to death. But I would not have my name sullied for anyone who had her head shaved to bring disgrace on others." Khumar was incensed and said, "O whore! Do not cast aspersions on me! You have some cheek covering your crime by accusing others!" Sarsar retorted, "You are a whore yourself! Except for my lord emperor's, I won't listen to anyone's abuse!"

Feeling angry at them, Afrasiyab said, "Such altercations are unseemly in my presence." Then he looked into the *Book of Sameri* and learned that Khumar's head had been shaved by Chalak, that Sarsar spoke the truth, and that he had made an error in releasing Amar. Afrasiyab now set Sarsar free, conferred a robe of honor on her and said, "Amar will not be able to cross over the River of Flowing Blood. Hasten and arrest him and bring him to me."

Sarsar departed in Amar's pursuit and Afrasiyab adjourned the court. His ministers, commanders, and courtiers returned to their homes.

Sorceress Khumar nursed malice in her heart toward Sarsar for what had happened in the court that day. The trickster girl felt the same toward Khumar. We will hear more about it in the following pages.

Now hear of Amar Ayyar. He had put on the cape of invisibility as he came out of the Apple Garden. When he had traveled far enough away, he took it off and disguised himself as an Aghori fakir.[120] He tied on a waistcloth, covered himself with a rag and, carrying a carafe of wine in one hand and holding a human skull under his other arm, he headed onwards, shouting inanities. It was his plan to find and kill a sorcerer in whose disguise he could cross the River of Flowing Blood.

Amar was engrossed in these thoughts when he was sighted by the trickster girl Sarsar, who had pursued him. She recognized Amar in the fakir's disguise and challenged him by blocking his path and drawing her short sword. Amar had no choice but to fight.

As the two tricksters fought together, a sorcerer who lived in that wilderness happened on the scene.

When Amar saw him coming, he shouted, "Look who is behind you!" Amar got closer and hit Sarsar with an egg of oblivion as she turned. He caught Sarsar in his arms as she sank unconscious to the ground and put her into the zambil. He tried to run away but the sorcerer was already on his head and recited a spell that made Amar's feet stick to the ground.

The sorcerer said, "O Aghori, why did you fight with the woman? And what did you do with her when I approached? How did you make her disappear all of a sudden?" Amar replied, "That woman was my wife. As I was hungry, I ate her up." The sorcerer marvelled when he heard this and said, "I always sought but never found a way to gain admission to the court. Now I have found a wonderful one; there would be no sorcerer at the emperor's court who could swallow a person whole in one bite." The sorcerer caught Amar with a magic claw, recited a spell, and flew away with him.

It so happened that after Afrasiyab's court adjourned, his first minister, Baghban Magic-Gardener, retired to his garden where he sat drinking wine with his wife, sorceress Gulchin.

As the sorcerer carrying Amar flew past, sorceress Gulchin saw him carrying a man and said to her husband, "Send for him. Let's find out who they are." Baghban recited a spell to stop the sorcerer. He was an ordinary sorcerer and could not fly after Baghban's spell was cast. He descended and saluted the emperor's minister. Baghban asked, "Who did you take captive?" He replied, "I saw him fighting with his wife. Then all of a sudden he ate her up. I was surprised by that and decided to take him before the emperor."

Baghban also marvelled when he heard that account and scrutinized Amar with his magic gaze. As Baghban was a mighty sorcerer, the power and heat of his gaze made Amar's makeup evaporate and fly in sparks from his body. Baghban removed his magic gaze from Amar's body and said to the sorcerer, "This is Amar Ayyar, not an Aghori fakir." He asked Amar, "Who was the woman you ate up?" Amar replied, "I don't let my wife come out before strangers nor leave her alone at home, I keep her with me in my zambil. She is a matchless trickster girl herself. When I took her out from my zambil in the wilderness she started fighting. Then this sorcerer arrived. As he was a stranger, I put her back into my zambil. I did not eat her."

When sorceress Gulchin heard this she said to Amar, "I wish to see your wife. Take her out of the zambil." Amar answered, "I will not take her out before strangers. Dismiss the men and give me some money. Then I will show her to you." Gulchin dismissed the men from the garden. Baghban, however, kept sitting there. He said, "O Amar, bring out your wife before me. I will liberally reward you." Amar said, "There would be no harm done if you showed me the money first." Baghban and his wife sent for much gold and riches and offered it to Amar, who stowed it away. Amar then retired to a corner of their garden, pulled out Sarsar's head and changed her appearance with trickster's makeup. Then he returned, pulled Sarsar out of his zambil and put her before them.

Gulchin saw a comely girl of breathtaking beauty and said, "O Amar, your wife is indeed very pretty. Now restore her to consciousness." Amar replied, "She will run away if I do so." Gulchin said, "She would not dare run away from my presence." Amar said, "If she is unable to escape she will tell you all kinds of lies. She will say that she is the trickster girl Sarsar. Then you will turn against me." Both Baghban and Gulchin swore that they would not believe a word she said. Amar tied Sarsar to a tree and gave her a restorative.

When Sarsar came to, she saw Baghban and Gulchin sitting before her. She said, "O emperor's minister, why have you tied me to this tree? Don't believe a word this cameleer's son Amar tells you. Give him to me so I can take him before the emperor, who awaits his capture." Amar said, "O whore, why would you wish to take me before your lover, the emperor? Today I will cut off your nose." Sarsar cursed Amar.

Both Baghban and Gulchin took it for a marital feud. Gulchin said to Amar, "Your wife has a sharp tongue, indeed." Amar slapped Sarsar roundly and said, "O whore, will you ever wag your tongue again in my presence?" Baghban and Gulchin laughed at this spectacle. Sarsar said to them, "Ridiculing me will not bode well with you. I'll tell the emperor that his minister has joined hands with Amar." Baghban asked, "How would you gain entrance to the emperor's court?" Sarsar answered, "I am the trickster girl Sarsar. I have a seat at the emperor's court." Amar interjected, "Didn't I tell you that she would claim to be Sarsar? She is a sly one, surely." Amar slapped Sarsar some more.

Sarsar related to Baghban all that had passed in the court, including Afrasiyab's intentions before Amar's arrest and the counsels held in the court, and said, "If I were not Sarsar, how would I know these details?" Baghban became apprehensive and plucked a fruit from a tree; he recited and blew a spell over it whereupon the fruit opened and a bird of beautiful plumage emerged and warbled melodiously, "*The woman who is tied up is Sarsar!*" After making this utterance the bird flew away.

Baghban apologized to Sarsar and set her free. While Baghban and Gulchin were occupied with Sarsar, Amar found the opportunity to put on his cape of invisibility and disappear. When Sarsar was released, she shouted, "Where did that wretch of a trickster go?" Amar replied, "I am here." Baghban felt frightened as he could hear Amar's voice but not see him. Sarsar said to them, "I must leave now." Amar called out, "I will also accompany you."

Sarsar exited the garden but Amar stayed behind to think of some way to rob the place and murder the sorcerers. After Sarsar was gone, Gulchin said to Baghban, "Because of Sarsar's threats, Amar also went away. I have heard of his many talents. If he were here I would have liked him to display them for us." Amar answered, "I am here but invisible to you because you are sorcerers; you would arrest me and take me before Afrasiyab."

When Gulchin heard his voice, she said, "I swear by Lord Sameri that we would not deceive you." Amar said, "Very well. Arrange for some money so that I may reveal myself." When Gulchin put out an offering for Amar he took off his cape of invisibility and appeared.

Gulchin greeted Amar with respect and seated him. Then she said, "We are very anxious to hear you sing. Please regale us by singing a little for us." Amar produced a pipe and tied ankle-bells to his feet. He sang and danced and sent the audience into raptures of joy. The birds in the garden forgot their songs and listened, entranced, to Amar's voice. The flowers in that garden lent their ears to his melodious strains and the leaves rustled in applause of his honeyed notes. The tress swayed, the flower buds sat tight-lipped on branches, and the hearts of love-struck nightingales filled to bursting with fervor.

He sang the tappa[121] *with such mastery*
That every strain set the soul aflutter
The strains, they rose with a power that
Made restive every accompanying beat
His gatkari[122] *was a string of light drops*
Like a sparkler it continuously sparkled
The narcissi looked up at its sound
The flowers lent it their fragrant ears
The trees swayed with an enchanted fervor
And the cypress stood riveted and straight
The birds fell down from the trees entranced
The doors and walls became wonderstruck
The stones in the lake bed turned to water
The fountains, they broke into sprays
The odes of love the ringdoves sang
The nightingales flooded the garden with their tears
The strange power that the ragas have
Their talent to melt to water stones
Such an air and ambience in the garden it created
All hearts became of tenderness full
A scene of such marvel was painted there
Even the breeze issued dancing from the trees

Amar received jewels worth hundreds of thousands of rupees in reward and won over the assembly with his talent.

In the meanwhile, Afrasiyab returned to his court and consulted the *Book of Sameri* to learn what had passed with Sarsar after she left to capture Amar. He learned of her misadventures and discovered that Baghban sat listening to Amar Ayyar's song.

Enraged, Afrasiyab said to himself, *It is a great shame that my first minister should embrace my enemy; a travesty that one of the most celebrated officers of the empire joins hands with the foe.* He shut the book in anger and clapped.

A magic slave popped up from the ground. Afrasiyab commanded him, "Amar is singing in Baghban's garden. Go and bring both Amar and Baghban to me." After receiving his orders the magic slave departed.

In Baghban's garden, Amar took a pause during singing and heard a whirring sound. When he looked up he saw a magic slave swooping down. Amar quickly put on the cape of invisibility and disappeared. When the magic slave came down with a blinding flash, it did not find Amar. It caught Baghban by his waist, shouted, "*I came from Emperor Afrasiyab!*" and carried away the minister. A terrified Gulchin realized that calamity would now strike them.

The magic slave brought Baghban to Afrasiyab. At the sight of him the Emperor rose with a whip in his hand, gave Baghban a few lashes and said, "O traitor! How dare you socialize with and entertain my enemy in your house?" Baghban truthfully related to the emperor all that had passed from the time the sorcerer brought Amar, to Sarsar's feuding with Amar Ayyar. Then Baghban entreated Afrasiyab, saying, "This meek subject,

'Being a humble slave of your Majesty
Beholden as always to the salt of your vassalage,

would never ever dream of treason. Now the just emperor should release me so that I may produce that sly trickster in your excellent presence."

Afrasiyab detected the redolence of truth in his minister's words. He released Baghban, who departed in a fury to arrest Amar.

Now hear of Amar Ayyar. After the magic slave carried off Baghban and the threat moved away, Amar removed his cape of invisibility and said to Gulchin, "I have thought of a way to ward off Afrasiyab's anger. I would share it with you if you accompany me to the summerhouse."

Gulchin rose and followed Amar. When they entered the summerhouse Amar made her unconscious with an egg of oblivion, wrapped her in a rug and hid her in a corner of the summerhouse. Then Amar took out his trickster's paints and lotions and disguised himself as Gulchin. He attired himself in her clothes and returned to take her seat in the garden. The slave girls asked, "Where did Amar Ayyar go?" The false Gulchin answered, "He possesses the power of invisibility. God knows where he disappeared." The slave girls believed her and did not ask further questions.

In the meanwhile, Baghban returned and made the same query of the false Gulchin. She replied, "Amar disappeared even as the magic slave swooped down." Baghban said, "I'm going in search of that wretch; the emperor humiliated me before everyone on account of him. I'll arrest him because he won't be able to cross the river, and take him before the emperor." Baghban then recited a spell and flew away.

Amar said to himself, *When Baghban is unable to locate me after a close search, he will use magic to discover where I'm hiding. He will learn that I am in his garden in Gulchin's guise and speedily arrest me.* The false Gulchin sent for Baghban's daughters, sorceresses Nihal and Samar, who arrived at their mother's summons. After expressing tokens of maternal love and affection for the girls, the false Gulchin said, "Your father has gone in search of Amar, who is a veritable monster. Let us depart and track Amar too, lest he should inflict any harm on your father, or we attract the emperor's anger in case your father is unsuccessful in catching him." Sorceress Nihal said, "Very well, mother, let us go."

The false Gulchin asked her to send for a flying throne. Nihal hit a magic citron on the ground. The earth cleft and smoke issued out in a column rising up to the heavens. After a moment, a flying throne approached and descended near them. The false Gulchin left sorceress Samar behind to safeguard the house and sat on the throne with Nihal, to whom she said, "Let us see whether you know enough magic to make this throne fly, or if you've been wasting your time in idle play." Nihal recited a spell and the throne became airborne. As they flew near the banks of the River of Flowing Blood, the false Gulchin began to mumble, pretending to recite a spell. A moment later, she said to Nihal, "My magic has alerted me that Amar has crossed the river into Zahir. However, he has not yet emerged from the wilderness. If we hurry, we can apprehend him yet."

Nihal hastened the throne onwards. They flew over the River of Flowing Blood and crossed into Zahir.

Now hear of Baghban Magic-Gardener. He searched for Amar in all directions but failed to find any trace of him. Baghban finally untied a statue from his wrist, recited a spell and said, "O image of Sameri, I ask you in Lord Sameri's name to give me Amar's whereabouts." The statue spoke, "*Amar has landed across the river disguised as your wife. He is accompanied by your daughter, whom he is about to kill and then make his escape.*"

Upon hearing this, Baghban tied the statue to his wrist again and speedily flew toward Zahir. He soon arrived where Amar had landed.

As Amar was about to make Nihal unconscious with an egg of oblivion, Baghban shouted, "Beware, O wretch! I have arrived! You won't escape from me now!"

When sorceress Nihal heard her father's voice, she looked in all directions, wondering whom he challenged. Amar then cuffed Nihal, put on the cape of invisibility, and jumped from the throne shouting to Baghban, "Beware, O bastard! I am the Sun of the Sky of Trickery,

'I am Amar who stole headgears from emperors' heads
I am the one who drains Bakhtak's face of all blood
In the assembly of kings if I am a cupbearer appointed
Swords and shields, ewers and goblets I would embezzle.

"You escaped my hand, O Baghban, otherwise I would have dispatched you and your whole family hellward." Amar escaped after uttering this threat.

Baghban approached Nihal and said, "You made a terrible mistake conducting Amar across the river into Zahir." Nihal excused herself by professing her ignorance about the matter.

Finally, Baghban and his daughter returned home. Baghban searched for Gulchin and found her lying unconscious in the summerhouse. He restored her to her senses and gave her the entire account of what had occurred. Baghban said, "I will now go and arrest Amar from Mahrukh's court, where he is certain to make an appearance after taking off his cape of invisibility." Gulchin threw herself at Baghban's feet and said, "O Baghban, I beg you in the name of lords Sameri and Jamshed not to interfere in the tricksters' affairs. Since the tricksters cause even the emperor such grief, imagine how ill we would fare against them. You must desist from pursuing them lest the tricksters kill you in their exasperation. You saw how Amar traveled from Batin to Zahir in a trice, and the emperor was unable to do anything about it."

At Gulchin's advice, Baghban finally desisted from his plan. He went before Afrasiyab and gave him the details of how Amar escaped. Afrasiyab remained silent out of consideration of the fact that if he censured Baghban further, he might also join Mahrukh's side.

In the meanwhile, Amar Ayyar arrived in his camp. His presence caused great joy among his commanders and he joined the court.

Now hear of the trickster girl Sarsar. After she left Baghban's garden, she realized that Amar would be unable to cross the River of Flowing

Blood, Qiran would be in his abode in the wilderness and the remaining tricksters would be occupied with their own errands. She considered breaking into Amar's unprotected camp to capture someone eminent, like Queen Mahrukh or Bahar, so she could humiliate Amar in the same way he had disgraced her.

Sarsar crossed the river and entered Mahrukh's camp in disguise. She rested and waited all day long for an opportunity. When the Trekker of the Desert of Heavens[123] disappeared in its westerly pavilion and Night's Beloved[124] showed its moon-like face in the mirror of sky, the bride of heaven filled up her parting with stars.

Mahrukh adjourned her court and all her commanders returned to their pavilions.

It has been recounted that Queen Mahrukh's son, sorcerer Shakeel, was enamored of Heyrat's daughter, Princess Khubsurat. As Afrasiyab did not approve of the union, Khubsurat was put under magic incarceration in Batin. Every night upon returning to his pavilion, Shakeel remained engrossed in the memory of his beloved's locks; separation from her tormented him relentlessly. He recited these verses constantly,

"Entangled in her enticing locks
I myself made my heart her captive."

That night too, as was his wont, Shakeel returned to his pavilion with a heavy heart and restive soul and cried copiously like a cloud of spring quarter. In his grief, he rent his robe from collar to hem. Although it was a moonlit night, it was the same to him as utter darkness without the light of his beloved's beautiful, luminous aspect. Shakeel called out, "The old man of heavens has become my enemy. It's not the moon but a torch lit in the heavens to burn me! What glares at me from amidst stars is a ball of pitch!"

He recited,

"O Tyrant, on torment bent
Pardon all this sinner's sins
Given that beloveds are by nature cruel
Known to break their word and oaths
Yet be not so despotic that your subjects should die
Be not so excessive that your lovers breathe their last
If you truly wish to keep
Your lover from your presence away
I ask you – as a sacrifice for your charming locks,

May your coldness, cruelty and harshness flourish!
I ask you – in the name of your indifference,
May your airs of vanity and conceit endure!
Draw your relentless dagger, O lovely executioner
And slaughter me once, for all time
Then your lover would receive what he covets
All his griefs and sorrows would come to an end."

In this way, Shakeel made a hundred plaints
Without finding redress or eliciting a single reply
His passion grew stronger with every moment
He recited fervently these verses in love

"My eyes were made a vessel that overflows with tears
Their charity has not yet ceased
That you and I are irreconcilably apart
Makes life for me a worthless exercise
Who sleeps? Sleep seeks not my eyes
I am sought alone by tears and nights of separation
You disgraced my love first, then of my plight made light
None so disgraced as I could hope for last rites
She who never counted me among her favored ones
Finally counts the breaths that now remain to me
When alive I was driven away from her assembly, from her presence
In death none would expel me; I dance in her alley now as dust."

As he sat grieving, it occurred to Shakeel that he should lighten his heart by a jaunt in the desert and, Majnun-like, while away the night in the memory of his beloved. Shakeel's hands spoke to him, saying, "Let us reach again for the collar." His feet longed to roam the desert.

Shakeel told himself that he would return to his camp in the morning and no one would notice his absence. His laden heart would be lightened and grief would lift its dark shadow from his soul. Driven by these thoughts, crying and weeping, Shakeel headed into the wilderness, at every step shedding ears from his unrequited heart. He recited the verses:

"How to recount what became of my heart
It counts its beats in my beloved's alley, my heart
Neither I nor my heart wish to witness the other's despair
My heart avoids me and I avoid my heart

Now beside me now beside my beloved
Regard how omnipresent is my heart
Do not put it under the lodestone of separation
The frailest of all frail creatures is my heart
How can I call anyone my friend
When my own breast has borne an enemy – my heart
The caravan of past lovers has left in its wake the dust
In its cloud it dances particle like, my heart."

As Shakeel proceeded alone on his way, he was sighted by Sarsar, who awaited an opportunity. The trickster girl stealthily pursued him.

Once he entered the desert, Shakeel sat down under a hill on a stone slab and engrossed himself in the scenery to soothe his heart.

Sarsar was well aware of Shakeel's unhappy love for Khubsurat. Seeing Shakeel in a pensive mood, she disguised herself as Princess Khubsurat's attendant, approached and saluted the prince. Sarsar said, "Do you recognize me, O prince?" Shakeel replied, "I don't know who you are; I no longer even know who I am.

"Although I appear to be of this world
I don't know who I am, where I am."

Sarsar answered, "I am the attendant of your beloved, Princess Khubsurat. I have lived in this desert ever since she was exiled and imprisoned." When Shakeel heard that she was his beloved's attendant, he broke into tears all over again. The false attendant said, "Just as you are infatuated with the beauty of your beloved, she too, suffered pangs of separation from you. Such was her condition that,

"Each other's friends and familiars, you two
Became prisoners of longing and grief before long
While her love in your heart resided
Your love was kneaded into her very essence
Like Majnun you desert-wards headed
Crying, 'Ah! O beloved!' Crying, 'Ah! O longing and pain!'
And that picture of excellence, the princess
Dressed herself like the night in black
Candle like she melted away
But did not her secret suffering reveal
She ate neither a morsel nor drank a drop
The only thing that passed her lips, your name
Her story is a tale ripe with sorrow

This account is a fable most tragic
She is kept imprisoned in great pain and suffering
Her legs clasped in fetters, iron chokers round her neck
No longer of her past circumstances, no longer her former self
Like all tales of love hers too, in endless woe ends."

When Shakeel heard this account of his beloved, he embraced the false attendant and cried without cease.

He said, "O tyrannical heavens,

"Now to this miserable state I am reduced
Unable to seek union with my beloved, Khubsurat
In this life I will pine away in separation
My soul too, would remain unrequited in afterlife
This longing for union with my beloved will cause
My last breaths to leave with difficulty my breast
With the writhing and turmoil of my restless heart
I would raze my house, the tomb, once interred
I did not leave happy this life in love
Unfulfilled and unsated in love I left this world."

Seeing him in such agony, the false attendant took out a small box from her belt and placed it before the disconsolate lover. She said, "O sojourner on the path of commitment! O wanderer in the alleys of love! At the time of her imprisonment the princess touched her delicate lips to some green cardamoms and betel nuts and put them in this box. She asked me to bring these to her lover wherever I might find him, and to narrate to him her tragic state."

Shakeel ate the drugged cardamoms from the box and fell unconscious. Sarsar tied him into a bundle and headed for Heyrat's court.

In the meanwhile, the eastern lover with his bleeding heart emerged into the field of sky searching for his beloved,[125] and the dark old woman night disappeared behind the screen of light.

Pass me the ewer of wine, O cupbearer
For I while away the night in shedding tears
The sun of troubles dawns on me again
And the morning of sorrows begins anew

Sarsar arrived in Heyrat's court carrying the bundle containing sorcerer Shakeel, saluted the empress and put the bundle before her.

Heyrat asked, "Whom have you brought?" Sarsar replied, "I brought you Mahrukh's son and Princess Khubsurat's lover, Shakeel."

Heyrat put an incarceration spell on Shakeel and ordered that he be restored to his senses. When Shakeel opened his eyes he found himself a prisoner in Heyrat's court. He called out,

"If you look with kind eyes toward the sufferers of ill repute
Throw one glance at me, for you yourself took my repute away
I do not want the Tooba tree's[126] *shadow when I die*
I wish that cypress beloved's shadow to fall on my grave one day
If out of desiring you I have hundreds of troubles
I will never expel this desire out of my heart.

"O Empress, I am already imprisoned in the depths of grief. The locks on my beloved's forehead keep me chained. What purpose would it serve to imprison me further? I will die shortly on my own, even without any hardships you may inflict." After speaking these words Shakeel cried bitter tears of love.

Heyrat took pity on his condition and said, "O Shakeel, you are no stranger to me. You are the son of Mahrukh and the uncle of Afrasiyab's daughter Mahjabeen. If you submit allegiance to me and do not side with your mother, I will marry you to Khubsurat." Shakeel answered, "I wish neither to take sides with my mother nor you. I abhor the world. All I know is that I am helplessly in love with Princess Khubsurat. Set me any task you wish and I will fulfill it to attain my beloved. Order me and I will even go and fight my mother."

Heyrat removed the incarceration spell from Shakeel and conferred a robe of honor on him. She asked one of her attendants, sorceress Taus, to release Princess Khubsurat from her magic prison, bring her to the Pleasure Garden and bathe and dress her so that she could be restored to times of happiness and joy before meeting Shakeel.

As ordered by Empress Heyrat, sorceress Taus removed the spell from the magic Ferris wheel where Princess Khubsurat sat and brought her to the Pleasure Garden.

The arrival of the rosy-cheeked Khubsurat augmented the beauty of the garden. The princess, whose narrow mouth resembled a rosebud, adorned and decorated herself when she heard the news that she would soon meet her lover.

Meanwhile, in Mahrukh's camp the news circulated that Prince Shakeel had been captured. A little while later, news arrived that Shakeel had reverted to the faith of Sameri and joined Heyrat's camp. Mahrukh was devastated to hear this. Amar Ayyar, who was present in the court, said to Mahrukh, "O Queen, once the tilism is conquered, thousands of children will return to their homes. If some don't, there will be others to take their place. You should consider this event a blessing for your son; in our camp, he would have melted away and died for love of Khubsurat. There he will have reason to live. Thus, God created an excuse to save his life. You should be mindful of the bigger interests of your son and not let yourself be disillusioned by these day-to-day events. See my own example: Prince Asad was captured but I did not mourn. My brow did not become clouded in the least."

In the end, Queen Mahrukh dispelled grief from her heart and resolved to be patient and show perseverance.

Prince Shakeel asked Empress Heyrat if he could have her permission to visit Princess Khubsurat. Heyrat gave her consent, saying, "You may go and spend one night in the Pleasure Garden to soothe your eyes with the beauty of the one you seek."

At the same time, Empress Heyrat also secretly sent for sorceress Taus and said to her, "Furtively keep an eye on the two and ensure that they do not give in to their desire and commit the ultimate act." After receiving these instructions sorceress Taus left.

Now hear of Prince Shakeel. As the poet has said,

When the time of union approached
The fire of desire more fiercely blazed

Prince Shakeel bathed and decked himself out in a fine costume.

When he entered the bathhouse
His youthful body with perspiration beaded
After washing and laving that flower of youth stepped out
Like the bright moon emerges from within dark clouds
The prince, his bath complete
In a robe of honor was royally dressed

He was adorned with inestimable jewels
Until his body a sea of jewels became
Bands of pearls, ear decorations, a nau-ratan necklace, an aigrette
Each item of jewelry became him more than the last
Its folds like swelling sea waves
His golden headgear shone bright like sun's flower
The lovely bands he wore and bracelets of pearls
A sight to solace the heart, comfort the soul
Its every component a veritable Mount Tur
So brilliantly did the jewelry on his body shine
Thus adorned he proceeded out
Like a cypress sapling in full bloom
When he came out and mounted his steed
Salvers of pearls as his sacrifice were offered

When Princess Khubsurat heard of his approach, she too, adorned herself, decorated the garden, and arranged a musical assembly.

Quick O cupbearer, pass the glass of wine
Sound the notes O singers from your rebecks and lutes
Opened now is the door of revels and pleasure
Far from the heart is the familiar pain
The lover will have today the union long sought
As the assembly of revels its peak attains
Today I am released from constant longing
Today luck smiles even on the ill-starred
In the sky plays his tambourine the sun
In the heavens dances the lovely Venus
That delicate beauty, the garden's soul
Rose from her place and bedecked her house entire
She put a golden throne in the center
And placed chairs beside it in neat rows
Then she adorned herself and sat waiting
Her beauty that day a vision to behold
The very sight of her pretty face
For lovers' hearts was a thunderbolt
Her tender beauty of fourteen years
Was like the apex of the moon on the fourteenth day[127]
While she waited, the beautiful Shakeel
Arrived happy and joyous at her garden's gate
He called out to her from the entrance

"Your lover – your sacrifice – is at your door."
Hearing her lover's pining voice
That houri-like beauty rushed to the garden gate
Accompanied by her lover, that moon-like beloved
Returned to the assembly smiling happily
Seven circles of sacrifice around him she made[128]
Then said, "Ah, my sleeping fortunes did awake!
All praise to the Almighty, All Powerful Lord!
All my sorrows have turned to joy today.
The eye of my heart with light is filled,
Now that I am in my lover's embrace.
This was indeed my only wish,
This indeed my desire of old,
That I get sight of my dear beloved.
I prostrate myself to offer a thousand thanks."
Seeing this degree of devotion from his beloved
The lover was beside himself with joy
Himself used to the hardships of love
His cup of joy overflowed, he lost consciousness
That moon-like beauty rushed to fetch
The rose essence from the niche where it lay
She sprinkled his face with that fragrant water
That presently restored to consciousness that youth
He regarded the fickle heavens with unbelieving eyes
He doubted now his circumstances, now his luck
He washed with tears of unbelief his face
From the joy of union he copiously cried
He said continuously under his breath,
'Wondrous indeed are the ways of the Lord!
That I find myself in my lover's arms,
I wonder whether I am in a dream or awake.
I fear my heart from joy might burst,
I wonder if this joy my last would be."
Thus speaking, he rose from the throne where he sat
And prostrated himself on the floor of dust
Bowing his head before Almighty God
He made prostrations in thanks a hundred times
Then he cried and his heart melted and flowed out with his tears
So abundantly he wept that the dust to loam turned
Then that fairy like beloved raised him by his hand
And he rose and near that beautiful beloved sat

The assembly of revels anew now began
But the two hearts in love became restless, longed for more
Now that their earnest wish was granted them,
Now that they were happily together gathered,
They forgot their past suffering and sorrows, all
Their prayers answered, joyful were their hearts
A desire for union now overwhelmed the prince
From modesty and reserve the princess became quiet
To that moon-like beauty said the restless youth, the prince
"Come, let us depart for my mother's camp
We'll proceed there and get ourselves married,
To save our faith from destruction by the hand of lust."
"I am but your slave girl," the princess said,
"All you wish a command it is for me."
Hearing her reply, her devoted lover
Summoned with magic spells a flying throne
Then looking in all directions with caution's eye
He sat Khubsurat on the throne, and away
Toward Mahrukh's camp happily they flew
So that their longings may be soon fulfilled
Upon witnessing this scene sorceress Taus
Rushed forward to stop them from escaping

As instructed by Empress Heyrat, sorceress Taus had clandestinely kept an eye on Prince Shakeel and Princess Khubsurat to ensure they did not abandon themselves to their passion. When she saw them depart on the throne, she rushed after them. As Shakeel and Khubsurat flew out of the garden and approached a mountain, Taus caught up with the couple and challenged them.

Taus and Shakeel fought with magic spells and hurled magic citrons and magic limes at each other. Then sorceress Taus recited a spell on a magic coconut and hit it against the ground. Immediately, Shakeel sank into the ground up to his waist. Taus caught Shakeel, but before she could fly away with him, the trickster Zargham, who had arrived on the scene and witnessed the whole fight, loaded an egg of oblivion in his sling and fired at Taus. She immediately fell unconscious. Zargham pierced her tongue with a needle, tied her to a tree and afterwards restored her to consciousness.

Zargham now said to Taus, "If you do not submit your allegiance to Queen Mahrukh I'll put you to a painful death with my relentless dagger." Zargham then recited the praise of the Creator of Both Worlds with such eloquence that infidelity's rust fell away from the mirror of sorceress Taus's heart.[129] As her tongue was pierced, she gestured to Zargham that she was willing to submit her allegiance.

Zargham released Taus, who removed the spell from Shakeel and he emerged from the ground. All four of them now headed for Mahrukh's camp and soon arrived there.

Zargham brought the news to Queen Mahrukh, who came out with the nobles of her court to welcome her son and daughter-in-law and conduct them to the royal pavilion. Everyone embraced Shakeel. Sorceress Taus was given the robe of a commander, celebrations began, and an assembly of revels was held that would have been the envy of the court of Jamshed.[130]

After two days the news reached Empress Heyrat. It immediately ignited a blaze of rage in the chaffing dish of her breast. She decided to prepare her army to assault Mahrukh's camp and kill them one and all. But the trickster girls, Sarsar and Saba Raftar, who were present there, kept her from executing her plans, saying, "Put off your plans momentarily. We will go and capture the leader of their camp, Mahrukh. You may execute her instead of Shakeel." The two trickster girls then left on their mission.

Sarsar entered Mahrukh's court disguised as an attendant while Saba Raftar waited outside. A dance recital was underway at the court, with Amar Ayyar in attendance. He noticed an attendant standing in a corner, looking furtively in all directions. Amar realized that it was a trickster girl in disguise, taking stock of the situation. He rose with the aim of catching her by deceit but Sarsar realized Amar's intent. She ran clear past the screens, jumped out of the pavilion, and escaped after shouting her war cry, "I am Sarsar Swordfighter!"

The trickster girl Saba Raftar, standing outside the pavilion, was sighted by Qiran the Ethiope, who came from the direction of the wilderness. He stealthily crept up on her and picked her up in his arms. Saba Raftar struggled and tried to break loose but could not release herself from Qiran's hold. Sarsar, who witnessed this scene from afar, approached Qiran disguised as Amar and said, "O Qiran, since she is your beloved, you should let me chastise her. It is improper for you to say harsh things to her and hand out her punishment." Qiran surrendered Saba Raftar thinking it was Amar who spoke to him.

Sarsar cried, "I am Sarsar Swordfighter!" and ran away with Saba Raftar. At that moment the real Amar also came out of the court and both he and Qiran gave chase to the trickster girls, but they escaped with lightning speed, running like the wind.

The tricksters returned to their camp and Sarsar returned to Mahrukh's court in the disguise of another attendant, and came upon the pavilion of Mahrukh's mother, sorceress Mah. Because of her advanced age, sorceress Mah mostly remained confined to her pavilion and seldom went to the court.

Sarsar put on Amar Ayyar's disguise and entered Mah's pavilion. Mah greeted the false Amar and offered him a seat beside her. She placed wine before the false Amar who filled up a cup after drugging it and offered it to Mah. She said, "Please, have this yourself." The false Amar answered, "The devotees of life's pleasure do not stand on ceremony. I will have a cup too, but do have this one yourself." Mah took the cup from him and drank it up in one gulp. The false Amar dismissed Mah's attendants, saying he had some private business to discuss with her. When Mah fell unconscious after drinking the wine, Sarsar removed her to a corner and disguised herself as Mah.

In the meanwhile, the traveler on the path of sky[131] removed his golden headgear in the assembly of west and dark old lady night lodged in the house of time, and lit up the torch of the moon.

Disguised as sorceress Mah, Sarsar headed out to see Queen Mahrukh in her private pavilion. Mahrukh had adjourned the court and now took rest. Seeing her mother enter, she got up and offered the false Mah the seat of honor with great respect. The false Mah said, "My child, the trickster girls circulate outdoors. I will sleep beside you tonight and keep you under my protection so that no one may harm you." Mahrukh ordered that a jewel-enchased bed be set for her mother beside hers, and saw to all her comforts. The false Mah lay down on the bed.

When Mahrukh fell asleep the false Mah drugged Mahrukh unconscious, tied her into a bundle and escaped by slitting open the pavilion panels. The vigil squad making rounds of the camp sighted her and barred her way. Sarsar drew her dagger and injured a few soldiers. The noise of the skirmish was heard in the camp and Amar rushed out of his pavilion to pursue Sarsar, who fought her way out of the cordon and into the wilderness carrying the bundled up Mahrukh. There she ran into Qiran, who challenged her. They began to fight and before long, Amar also arrived on the scene and the two tricksters attacked Sarsar from two sides.

In the meanwhile, the cold forest air restored Mahrukh to consciousness. When she opened her eyes she found herself all bundled up. She recited a spell that ripped the trickster girl's bundle and the knots of the snare rope that tied her limbs fell open. Mahrukh broke out of the bundle and captured Sarsar with a spell.

Sarsar said, "Any sorcerer can capture a trickster with a spell. I am a match for tricksters, not sorcerers." Qiran said to Mahrukh, "She speaks true. You may release her. God willing, we will overpower her with tricksters' devices."

Mahrukh removed her spell from Sarsar. She and Amar stood aside to watch Qiran and Sarsar fight. The two tricksters fought with daggers, now deploying eggs of oblivion, now trying to entangle their opponent with their snare ropes.

The combat between them attracted a sorcerer named Nisar, who was one of Afrasiyab's devoted servants. When Nisar arrived on the scene to investigate the matter, Amar, Qiran and Sarsar all ran away to avoid involving the sorcerer in their feud.

Nisar recognized Mahrukh. He respectfully greeted her and asked, "What brought Your Honor to these parts?" Mahrukh explained how Sarsar had captured and brought her there.

Sorcerer Nisar said, "I wish to submit my allegiance to Your Honor and join your fellowship. If Your Excellency would condescend to visit her servant's house of sorrows and make it a palace of joy by supping with me, I will afterwards follow your lofty procession with my whole family and all my goods and chattels." Mahrukh granted his wish and accompanied him to his house.

Sorcerer Nisar brought the queen to a hill atop which stood a majestic palace that was his residence. Mahrukh saw that the palace was tastefully adorned and decorated with glass lights. The sorcerer seated her on a throne and presented a wine service and salvers of fruits. Nisar offered Mahrukh drugged wine, even as he expressed his devotion to her cause. After Mahrukh had a few cups, she fell unconscious and Nisar locked her up in a chest. He decided to take her before Afrasiyab and Heyrat the next morning.

When Amar Ayyar and Qiran the Ethiope returned to their camp they discovered that Mahrukh had not returned. They reckoned that Sarsar had planned to capture Mahrukh and must have caught her after they had left the scene. Amar set out again in search of Mahrukh.

He entered Heyrat's camp in a sorcerer's disguise and approached Sarsar, who stood outside the empress's court after returning from the wilderness. Amar said to her, "You accomplished a great deed today, O Sarsar, by capturing Mahrukh!" Sarsar looked hard at the false sorcerer and recognized Amar. She answered, "I didn't take anyone prisoner today." Amar said, "Do not try your tricks on me." When Sarsar swore that she had not captured Mahrukh, Amar headed out of the camp to search for Mahrukh elsewhere.

On the way, Amar met Burq the Frank and explained the whole situation to him. Burq also joined Amar in his search. The two of them searched for Mahrukh all night long. When the sun rose from its bed of sleep and started on its journey in the desert of sky, and the darkness of night retreated from the banks of the world, Amar and Burq arrived near sorcerer Nisar's abode. When they noticed the luxurious palace atop the hill they thought that perhaps Mahrukh was imprisoned there. Amar and Burq now parted company. Burq disguised himself as a sorcerer and arrived at the palace gates where one of sorcerer Nisar's sorceress attendants stood guard.

In his sorcerer's disguise, Burq smiled at her and said, "It has been so long since I've seen you. How have you been?" The attendant took Burq for an old acquaintance. She replied, "I am well, thank you. I pray for your well being. How have you been?" The false sorcerer replied, "Lord Sameri be praised, I am well! Tell me, why do you stand guard here by yourself?" She answered, "My master has captured Mahrukh and I am keeping watch on her."

As they talked some more in this vein, the false sorcerer approached the attendant, whose name was Nau Ratan, and said, "I wonder what kind of grass grows on this mountain. It has a bad odour. My hands started smelling after breaking one of its blades. See if you recognize the smell." The false sorcerer extended his hand toward Nau Ratan, who smelled it and immediately fell unconscious because Burq's hand was coated with a drug. He carried Nau Ratan to a deserted corner where he took off her clothes, disguised himself as her, and returned to the house.

The other servants said to the false Nau Ratan, "O Nau Ratan, you left your post without waiting for a replacement?" She replied, "I was on guard duty all night long and nobody came to relieve me even for a moment. Now send someone else. I am not the only guard here." At this terse reply the other servants fell silent.

The false Nau Ratan saw that sorcerer Nisar was awake and sat drinking on his throne. She stood behind Nisar fanning him with a kerchief.

Now hear of Amar Ayyar. He disguised himself as a musician and started playing a pipe. The enchanting notes reached the ears of sorcerer

Nisar, who ordered his servants to send for the musician. The servants conducted the false musician before Nisar, who saw a poverty-stricken, ragged old man before him. Nisar said to himself, *A man of such talent and in so ravaged a state! Wondrous indeed are the ways of Lord Sameri.* Nisar asked the false musician to play his pipe for him. The false musician made a humble bow and began.

Nisar was greatly pleased by his music. He rewarded him liberally and said, "O musician, I will listen to your music all day long and take Mahrukh to the Emperor of Hoshruba tomorrow."

The false musician asked, "Where do you keep Mahrukh imprisoned?" Nisar said, "In the chest that lies before you." After blurting this out, Nisar realized the musician must be a trickster, which was why he had wished to learn Mahrukh's whereabouts. Nisar laughed and said, "O trickster, I recognize you!" Then sorcerer Nisar recited a spell and captured Amar.

Burq the Frank, who stood behind sorcerer Nisar in the attendant's disguise, now struck from the back with his dagger. He lopped Nisar's head, which flew off his shoulders. The noises of his magic spirits began to fill the air and it started darkening. Nisar's attendants ran to investigate. Burq, who had already learned that Mahrukh was shut inside the chest, moved forward and opened its lid. Mahrukh had already been restored to consciousness at the moment of Nisar's death. She got out of the chest and killed all of Nisar's servants.

In the meanwhile, Amar swept the house clean with the Net of Ilyas. After the killing and pillaging they headed back to their camp.

Sorceress Sharara Blazing-Flame

On the way to their camp, Amar, Burq and Mahrukh crossed paths with a sorcerer in Empress Heyrat's employ, who recognized them and said, "Enjoy life's pleasures today, for tomorrow all of you will die." Mahrukh said, "Nobody except the Almighty God can kill us." The sorcerer replied, "I said all of you will die tomorrow because I was present in Empress Heyrat's court today when the emperor's missive arrived with the news that he would send sorceress Sharara Blazing-Flame to put all the rebels to death." The enemy sorcerer then went his way.

Mahrukh became terror-stricken and the blood drained from her face upon hearing the name of Sharara Blazing-Flame. Amar Ayyar again opened his lips to comfort Mahrukh, saying, "O Queen, don't become dejected at this news! The Almighty God is all-powerful. I leave now on my mission with the promise that Sharara won't reach her destination. I will intercept her before she even enters Heyrat's camp." With these words, Amar left. Burq the Frank headed in another direction.

Mahrukh returned to her camp and was received by all her nobles and resumed her seat on the throne.

Now hear of what passed with Burq the Frank. He stationed himself in the region of Zahir in the forest bordering the River of Flowing Blood. Like Amar, Burq too, planned to kill Sharara as she entered the region.

Upon arrival in the forest, Burq witnessed three women of dazzling beauty wearing jeweled garlands; they sat in swings hanging from the trees. Burq said to himself, *They must be sorceresses. I must avoid them and take another path lest they arrest me.* Burq changed direction and headed for another part of the forest. The women called out to him, "O Burq, give us one push before you go!" Burq did not answer and ran some miles away from them. When he came to a stop he saw the same women swinging from the very same trees. Burq now ran in a new direction but when he stopped after several miles he encountered the same women. He ran now in a fourth direction but this time too, after several miles he again beheld the familiar scene. The women said to him, "O fool, come give us a push! Why do you go running like mad all over the place?"

Unable to escape, Burq approached them and said, "It would not bode well for you to bother me as I am a trickster. Now you have been warned and may do as you please." Burq's threats had no effect on the sorceresses. They captured him and led him toward Afrasiyab's court.

Now we resume Amar Ayyar's account. Planning to kill Sharara Blazing-Flame, he arrived in a place in Zahir where a verdant forest enclosed by mountains abounded in flowers and aromatic herbs. Wherever he turned his eye he saw lush and refreshing sights. The birds on tree branches sang melodious notes. Flowers of many colors were in bloom.

Amar said to himself, *I should decorate this place and station myself here. This is a beautiful and enchanting part of Zahir. It would be little wonder if Sharara chose this place as her camping ground.* From his zambil, Amar took out carafes of rose and *keora* water mixed with drugs with which he doused all the tress in his vicinity. He made garlands of false flowers with drugs and hung them from the tree branches. The whole forest was now redolent with the perfume drug. Amar disguised himself as a hump-backed, ninety-year-old woman and came out from a mountain pass walking with the help of a cane, and hid himself in a nook.

From far away, Amar saw three women taking Burq away a prisoner. Crying and soliciting help, Amar approached the women. The sorceresses asked the false old woman why she cried. She answered, "Empress Heyrat appointed me a guard of this forest. This thief, deserving of beheading, stole my betel box. This is the third time he has done so. I want you to get him to return my stolen goods. I will die without having my tobacco!"

The sorceresses asked Burq, "O wretch, what did you do with her betel box?" Burq realized from the old woman's speech that it was Amar Ayyar come to rescue him. He replied, "If I return her betel box will you set me free?" The sorceresses began buffeting and slapping him. Burq took the opportunity to put plugs of antidotes in his nose and said, "Don't be angry with me. I'll tell you – I put this old woman's betel boxes in a cave near her house." The sorceress asked the false old woman, "How far away do you live?" She replied, "My house is on the other side of the mountain, past the forest."

The sorceresses and Burq accompanied the false old woman, who led them toward her house. When they arrived in that lush garden decorated by Amar, the sorceresses fell unconscious from inhaling the perfume drug. Amar and Burq immediately cut off their heads.

God's Mercy! Such a tumult rose as was never heard before. Fire and stones rained from the sky and the whole forest was destroyed. The guards of the River of Flowing Blood rushed to investigate the matter. Amar and Burq escaped after robbing the sorceresses of their jewels and clothes. The guards carried their bodies before Emperor Afrasiyab in the Apple Garden and narrated how the tricksters had killed the keepers of the tilism forest.

Afrasiyab was livid with rage. After giving instructions for the sorceresses' last rites to be performed, he ordered thunderously, "O Sharara Blazing-Flame, present yourself at once!" No sooner were the words spoken than flames lit up in the air and came together in the form of one giant flame, which approached the emperor. A woman of resplendent face, as beautiful as a fairy, draped from head to toe in ruby jewelry, stepped out of the flame and bowed before Afrasiyab.

The Emperor of Hoshruba ordered, "Depart immediately to Empress Heyrat's aid with the one-hundred-thousand-strong army at your command and destroy the enemy camp. Do not leave a single soul alive. Then you may await rich rewards from my bounty. You will be raised in station and honor and receive lands and fortune besides."

After receiving the emperor's commands, Sharara returned to her abode and arranged and readied her army. She concealed herself in the flame as before and advanced with great majesty toward Heyrat's camp.

She and her army speedily crossed over the River of Flowing Blood without making any stops and reached their destination.

Heyrat sent a welcoming party upon receiving the news of her arrival. Sharara entered the empress's court, made an offering, and received a robe of honor. Her army bivouacked and Sharara's pavilion was set up. A dance recital was ordered in Sharara's honor and cups of wine were passed around. After having a few cups and her humors charged with inebriation, she wrote a letter to Mahrukh, which read:

> "I am Sharara Blazing-Flame. My magic is known and familiar to all and sundry. There is no one who can counter me. O Mahrukh, it is incumbent upon you to present yourself to me upon receipt of this letter. I will have the emperor pardon your misdemeanours but in the event of your refusal, I will punish you severely."

Sharara sent this message with a magic slave, who brought it to Mahrukh in her court. After reading it, Mahrukh wrote a reply. It read:

> "Learn that I recognize neither Afrasiyab nor that whore Heyrat. I am a slave girl of Amar Ayyar, whom I consider my emperor. O Sharara, do all that you can in your power, and show me not the least mercy. My Lord is Mightier still."

Mahrukh gave her reply to the magic slave who took it to Sharara. Upon reading it, Sharara was enraged but bided her time as a few hours remained to the close of day. Before long, the world-illuminating star hid away in the fire temple of the west, and the lustrous moon of the sky ascended the throne of the Zanzibarian dark night and issued its coin of light.[132]

When the day departed and the night came
When the dark in the sky spread
The sound of war drums rose to the skies
From the camp of Sharara Blazing-Flame

The magic birds brought this news to Mahrukh, who ordered the magic fife to answer in reply from her camp. The tricksters hid away in the wilderness. The valiant and brave prepared for battle. The doors of the armory were flung open for the warriors. Sorcerers prepared their spells.

Mahrukh proclaimed:

"The criers and heralds should make ready
To proclaim aloud in our camp the news
Quicker than quick the troopers and foot soldiers
Put on their weapons, their armaments and arms
Throw open the doors of the armory wide
Lay before the warriors their weapons of choice
Prepare all night for the battle we must
Our name and honor in the morning to defend."

Everyone their arms and armor secured
Some made keener the point of their spear
Suddenly in the vault of the sky was glimpsed
The resplendent standard of the bright sun
In its preparations for the impending battle
The King of Stars appeared to the view
It did not ascend its azure throne
But rode instead the sky's steed
His lance of rays in his hand he wielded
The field of battle lay open before him
He sported not on his back a shield
His aspect itself a blinding shield became
The moon that made plans to battle Emperor Sun
With its entire starry horde was ensnared

In her bed of dreams Sharara the unclean
Opened her eyes and with her head of conceit rose
Ordered she, "My army should stand at ready,
Their vicious gaze to the battlefield turned!"
She sent for all her battle gear
All the trappings of her magic and sorcery procured
Prepared to head for the battlefield
The vile sorceress a magic dragon rode
Then her warriors also saddled their steeds
Readied themselves, on viciousness bent
Leading that vast, billowing army
From her encampment the blighted sorceress emerged
In her wake rose a dust cloud in such abundance
The sands of time it used up entire

Mahrukh too, her commanders ready for battle
Made due preparations on her side
The steel helmets on their heads sported
Their bodies in cuirasses and armor dressed
In their belts wearing lightning bolt-like swords
That were for the palace of life death's flood
When they unsheathed their blades in anger
The meaning of "To all creatures there is death" they revealed
They sat astride quick steeds whose hooves
Raised a dust so blessed it could serve to embellish the eyes
In valor the equal of lions were they
Swift in their charge like the commands of God
With such preparations Mahrukh the sanguinary
Departed now for the field of battle
Her glory like a crier proclaimed,
'The death of the foe approaches! Give way!'

When Queen Mahrukh entered the arena
The criers and heralds battle arrays made
The evil incarnate Sharara Blazing-Flame
Swiftly emerged from within her ranks
The magic dragon Sharara galloped
Entered the arena rutting elephant-like
She took her position in the field
And from her opponents sought combat
In Mahrukh's camp all were terror-stricken
All lost their senses at Sharara's sight
Mahrukh's commanders both celebrated and renowned
Became silent and still, portrait-like
Astride the magic dragon, Sharara recited battle chants
While her foe's trepidation and dread continuously increased

Now the audience may lend their ear
To hear the story of the wise Shakeel
He decided to answer Sharara's challenge
But before long a thought bothered his mind
The consideration that it may cause new trouble
For his lovely beloved Khubsurat the Beauty
Who did not magic or sorcery know
Someone might imprison her finding her alone
It would put Shakeel under immense pain
He would spend the rest of his life in remorse

Led by this consideration Shakeel summoned
Mehran, one of Princess Bahar's attendants
And commanded her when she presented herself
To remove Khubsurat from potential harm
The dutiful Mehran swiftly arranged
A magic peacock for Khubsurat the Beauty
The princess seated beside her, Mehran departed at once
And brought Khubsurat to a mountain pass
Now Prince Shakeel approached his mother
And asked with an untroubled mind
"Order me, O my noble mother,
To tear limb from limb the enemy!"
Mahrukh said, "My son, refrain from this terrible thought
You haven't seen wars, in silence watch
The sight of you covered in gore and dust surely would
Bring your mother to the door of her grave."
In short, Mahrukh did not give her son combat leave
Sorcerer Raad came forward to confront Sharara instead
Left and right he struck on the ground both feet
And by magic presently into the earth sank he
To emerge beside Sharara Blazing-Flame
And make his powerful, terrible scream.
Its impact felled Sharara from her magic dragon in a faint
But she recovered just as quickly, invoked her magic and made,
Sorcerer Raad a prisoner of her spell
Then she made ready to strike and put out his life.

But before Sharara could kill Raad, his mother, sorceress Mehshar Lightning-Bolt, came forward and fell at Sharara's feet, exclaiming, "O Sharara, consider me your slave girl and spare my son's life!" At these words, Sharara took pity on Raad and released him.

Sharara now grew magic wings, soared to the sky and stopped at a high point above the arena. From there she hurled a magic coconut at Mahrukh's camp. It broke open near the warriors and thousands of black serpents emerged from it, showering sparks from their mouths. They circulated in Mahrukh's army and the sparks they spewed became flames that leapt on Mahrukh's soldiers and wrapped themselves around their limbs. Mahrukh's commanders recited counterspells to ward off the snakes and rained magic showers to extinguish the flames.

In the meanwhile, Sharara hurled a magic citron and called out, "O my commanders, attack these rebels!" Sharara Blazing-Flame's army, wielding their tridents, pentadents, shining swords and such like weapons of sorcery fell upon Mahrukh's force.

At the same time, Empress Heyrat, who had accompanied Sharara to witness the fight, also attacked Mahrukh's camp. Mahrukh now advanced, her sorcerers casting their spells. The two armies exchanged magic citrons and magic limes, and magic swords struck like lightning bolts. As the two armies merged, a pitched battle was soon being fought with swords and magic.

The valiant warriors now advanced
Together the force took a forward step
Everyone drew from their sheaths their swords
Big and small, everyone now joined the fight
The sky its revolutions forgot, and the Earth
From the impact of fierce combat convulsed
The maces sang as they rained constant blows,
"Where is mighty Sohrab and where the great Rustam?"
The saddle-axes cleared saddles of their occupants
From head to navel the troopers it cleaved
Covered in blood, the stone-hearted swordsmen
Appeared like Yemenite rubies to the eye

With their spells, Princesses Bahar and Nafarman and Queen Mahrukh slew thousands and caused hundreds of others to lose their minds.

In the meanwhile, from the sky Sharara hurled another magic citron on the arena. The moment it crashed against the ground sheets of fire rose and fell on Mahrukh's forces. Before their eyes the sheets came together into a cloud of fire that descended on them and began to envelop Mahrukh's army. Queen Mahrukh, Prince Shakeel, Bahar and other celebrated commanders retreated at the sight. Unable to counter Sharara's magic, Mahrukh's army was dealt a resounding defeat. Both Sharara and Empress Heyrat gave chase and slew Mahrukh's retreating forces for many miles.

Queen Mahrukh, her commanders and her surviving army arrived near Mount Lapis Lazuli and took refuge in its passes. Many of their companions met their end, covered in gore and writhing in agony.

Toward evening, Sharara stopped the carnage of Mahrukh's retreating forces and turned back. She dispatched spies to find news of where the rebels were headed and where they had taken refuge. Then Sharara sat on the throne in her pavilion and recited a spell that created a blaze that covered and hid her from everyone's view. Her voice ordered revels to start and dance recital and music assembly to begin. In compliance with her orders, the festivities were soon underway.

The tricksters had witnessed how their army had been defeated. When they saw Sharara occupied with revels they set out to perform their trickeries.

Before long, Qiran the Ethiope arrived at Sharara's pavilion in an attendant's disguise. He was searching for some way to gain entrance when suddenly a voice exclaimed, "*Beware! Qiran comes!*" Qiran made a leap and escaped. Everyone in the court asked Sharara Blazing-Flame, "Whose voice was that?" She replied, "I deputed a magic slave at the pavilion entrance to call out the name of anyone who approaches."

Like Qiran, the other tricksters who came near the pavilion were also identified by the magic slave. All of them escaped and went to report to Mahrukh Magic-Eye. They arrived at her refuge and said to her, "O Queen, we are unable to perform our trickeries as we cannot even go near Sharara. It seems to us that our end is near."

A hue and cry rose from the camp at these words. During this time, Amar Ayyar arrived. He shed tears at the miserable state of his companions and offered words of consolation. In the meanwhile, the tricksters left again on their mission.

As Sharara watched the dance recital, she received Afrasiyab's missive, which read:

> "I consulted the *Book of Sameri* and learned that all the rebels are hiding in the passes of Mount Lapis Lazuli. Advance with your army and arrest all of them."

Upon receiving this message, Sharara ordered that the magic fife should sound in her camp to alert the warriors to march. Before long her army was ready. Sharara advanced speedily and surrounded Mount Lapis Lazuli. Queen Mahrukh and her camp were taken unawares; none of them could escape.

Amar said to Mahrukh, "It would be expedient for all of us to throw ourselves at the feet of this wretch Sharara and ask her to have our trespasses forgiven by Afrasiyab. Then she will spare us. Afterwards, I will deal with her in my own way."

Mahrukh found Amar's advice to her liking and took salvers of gold and jewels with her as offerings and left for Sharara's camp accompanied by all her nobles.

Sharara's army had encircled the mountain and her pavilion was set up nearby. When she heard the news of Mahrukh's arrival she came out.

Witnessing Mahrukh, Bahar and other commanders coming toward her with their hands tied with handkerchiefs in a gesture of submission, she stopped her soldiers from barring their way and stepped forward.

Mahrukh rushed forward to fall at Sharara's feet and repeated the words Amar had instructed her to say. Sharara embraced Mahrukh and all her commanders and was most pleased that, because of her, a great nuisance would be eradicated from the tilism. She conducted all of them inside her pavilion and offered them lofty stations.

Then Amar Ayyar entered Sharara's pavilion and said, "I also wish to enter the service of the Emperor of the Tilism." Sharara received Amar with respect and offered him a seat of honor. Afterwards, Sharara hid herself in the blaze and ordered musicians, singers and dancer to perform. A musical assembly began and cupbearers as beautiful as the moon passed around goblets of roseate wine.

Amar Ayyar said to Sharara, "Your Honor should also join the assembly." Sharara answered from within the blaze, "O Amar, it is for fear of you that I remain hidden in the fire." Amar said, "I had better leave if you still nurse doubts about me." Sharara replied, "Do not take offense at what I say. I will come out now." With these words, she leapt out of the blaze as a flame and took her seat on her throne, reverting to her real form. All those present saw a beautiful woman seated on the throne. Amar now said, "If Your Honor grants me permission I will display my refinements in the cupbearer's art." Sharara laughed and said, "Why don't you plainly say that you wish to make me unconscious with drugged wine?" Amar replied, "Heaven's mercy! I will never again utter a word about the cupbearer's art before you!"

While they conversed together, Afrasiyab again consulted the *Book of Sameri* and learned that Amar had presented himself before Sharara on false pretences and awaited a chance to overpower and kill her. Afrasiyab wrote a message and handed it to a magic slave to take to Sharara. It arrived before Sharara and delivered the emperor's message. She opened the message which read:

> "Do not believe a word Amar says for he has come to trick you. All the rebels are in your power at this moment. Arrest them and march toward Empress Heyrat's camp. I will soon arrive there myself and have them executed in my presence."

Sharara immediately cast a spell that caused a wall of fire to engulf Amar, Mahrukh and their companions. Fetters of flames encircled their arms and legs. All of them cried, "Your Honor, what is our crime?" Sharara replied, "You are all deceivers! The emperor alerted me about your duplicity and sent me this message."

Sharara imprisoned them and after loading them onto carts and curricles, headed for Heyrat's camp. Mahrukh had left behind some of her companions in the mountain pass to look after her remaining army and her goods and riches. When they witnessed these happenings, they shed tears and became convinced that all of them would die. They decided to fall upon Sharara's army and give up their lives with honor in combat. Qiran arrived there in the interim and, after hearing their resolve, dissuaded them from following that course of action. He said, "All of you should raise your hands in prayer in the court of the Almighty, All Powerful, Invincible God. I will now go and kill that harridan Sharara but I would like one sorcerer from among you to accompany me."

Qiran and a sorcerer from Mahrukh's camp proceeded onwards while their remaining companions beseeched the Almighty God with these words:

> *"Might and grandeur are for Almighty God alone*
> *And His dominion and property are they*
> *All governments, regardless of their kind are His alone*
> *And from His blessing and conferring exist*
> *In the name of those God-fearing souls*
> *Who gave their lives in His path*
> *You alone have power over life, O Merciful One!*
> *You are the One who is the Reviver of the Dead*
> *Give us refuge from the enemy's grasp*
> *And from their power keep us safe."*

While they busied themselves praying, Qiran brought the sorcerer into the mountain pass and asked him to create a magic peacock. After the sorcerer created one from wax, Qiran put a jewel-studded saddle on it, reined its beak with a pearl-strung cord, and adorned its neck with beautiful jewels. Then Qiran disguised himself in Afrasiyab's likeness and sat astride the magic peacock. He said to the sorcerer, "Begin reciting a spell that makes the magic peacock fly. Make whirlwinds rise and showers of fire and stone fall along the way so that the portents of a distinguished sorcerer's arrival appear before Sharara as I approach her." At Qiran's orders, the sorcerer changed into an attendant's dress, held Qiran's stirrups, and recited a spell that caused whirlwinds to rise and fire and stones to shower down from the sky. The magic peacock rose into the air with Qiran in the saddle and the sorcerer alongside.

Sharara was on her way to Heyrat's camp when the signs of a mighty sorcerer's approach manifested themselves. She stopped and looked up as the fire showers fell to await his arrival. Before long, the false Afrasiyab, sporting a jewel-studded crown and wearing a sumptuous dress, appeared in her view astride a magic peacock. Seeing the emperor approach, Sharara stepped out of the blaze and came forward to pay her respects.

The false Afrasiyab stayed his peacock and said, "Well done, O Princess! There are no words to describe the amazing speed with which you clinched victory over the rebels." With these words, he jumped down from the magic peacock. The sorcerer who accompanied him put an end to the spells that caused the whirlwinds and the rain of fire and stones. Sharara presented salvers laden with rich offerings, spread a gold brocade carpet in honor of the false Afrasiyab and ordered her attendants to set up her pavilion in that place.

While Sharara's attendants got busy carrying out her commands, the false Afrasiyab said to her, "I made a pilgrimage to the Dome of Sameri and learned a spell that can reveal the events that will take place from now up to twelve years into the future. If you sit down with closed eyes and recite "O Sameri!" thrice, I will teach the spell to you."

Sharara felt greatly honored by the false emperor's attentions and kindnesses. She sat down with eyes closed in a pure and clean spot in that wilderness and chanted the refrain, "O Sameri!" Qiran, who stood beside her, hefted his cleaver in his hand and struck out with all the leisure in the world, smashing Sharara's skull and making her brains fly out. Qiran then made his war cry and escaped. Sorceress Sharara Blazing-Flame thrashed about on the ground and was dispatched hellward. Her magic spirits cried out and her attendants ran to her aid. In the meanwhile, the wall of fire that enclosed Mahrukh, Bahar, Nafarman and others disappeared and a voice called out, "*I was killed! Sharara Blazing-Flame was my name!*"

When Amar heard this, he said to Mahrukh, "There, O Mahrukh, that ill-begotten sorceress was killed! Do not let her army escape alive now." Mahrukh and all her companions took their magic coconuts and magic citrons, grew magic wings and fell on Sharara's camp, which was already in upheaval at the proclamation of her death.

Thousands were killed and rolled in gore and dust in the very first charge of Mahrukh's warriors. Surkh Mu Wonder-Mane let her hair loose and thousands upon thousands of stars rained down shattering the skulls and bones of Sharara's men like a shower of meteors. Then Princess Bahar threw her magic bouquet at them. Spring manifested itself and a cold, refreshing breeze, which was like the breath of the Messiah, began to blow. The flower buds bloomed at once into flowers and vast gardens full of flowers and aromatic herbs appeared. Sharara's sorcerers fell under her spell. Then magic swords fell on them from the air,

The enemy skulls with arrows were riddled
Like a rose-filled garden all paths in red were bathed
Every severed head was like a fresh cut flower
That forest their bouquet became
Covered all in blood every sorcerer
The envy of the rose garden became
The springtide was a sword for their rose garden
That was harvested in springtime
Wherever one looked one saw harvesting in progress
The dead lay drowning in blood
The destroyer of the garden of life
The flower of cruelty and tyranny bloomed
Well acquainted with the garden of the world, I
Never saw in autumn's midst such a spring

The surviving sorcerers from Sharara's army escaped weeping and wailing toward Afrasiyab's court.

Earlier, when Empress Heyrat had heard of the arrest of Mahrukh, Amar and others, she headed for Sharara's camp. She was on her way when her sorceress-aide Yaqut presented herself and said, "I received news that Sharara has been killed and Mahrukh has returned victorious and triumphant." Heyrat returned to her camp after receiving this inauspicious news.

After Mahrukh returned from the battlefield, she gathered her dispersed army. Her companions, who prayed for her in the mountains, began to arrive after receiving news of her success. Kettledrums sounded notes of triumph and victory.

Mahrukh stayed in those environs for one day to organize her army anew. The following day the marching drums were beaten and the army advanced with great majesty and ceremony and reached its old campsite within view of Heyrat's camp. Mahrukh's triumph-incarnate army set up their tents. The pavilions of the nobles and commanders were raised and the camp came alive with the bustle of old.

Queen Mahrukh resumed her seat on the throne and said to Bahar, "One of your attendants removed Princess Khubsurat the Beauty from the battlefield and took her into the safety of the mountains; send for her now. Since we have as many friends as we do enemies, the princess must be brought back to the camp before any trouble finds her." In deference to Mahrukh, who had personally ordered her, Bahar departed to bring back Khubsurat the Beauty herself.

Sorcerer Naag the Serpent

Now hear of what passed with Princess Khubsurat. Bahar's attendant, Mehran, brought her to the banks of a river near the mountainside to enjoy the sights. It so happened that one of Afrasiyab's subjects, a sorcerer named Naag the Serpent, lived in those parts. He recognized Princess Khubsurat and approached Mehran and said, "O Mehran, there is no pleasure in killing you for you are a mere attendant, but Khubsurat is the daughter of Empress Heyrat and I will certainly take her back to the court."

Naag the Serpent recited a spell whereupon a black snake came out of the ground and coiled around Mehran. It was so venomous a snake that merely from its coiling around her skin Mehran fell unconscious. Naag the Serpent then caught Khubsurat and headed on his way.

In the meanwhile, the trickster girl Sarsar also arrived on the scene and witnessed Naag capturing Princess Khubsurat. She said to herself, *God knows what sorcerer Naag intends to do with the princess. I should snatch her from him lest he should dishonor her in any way.* Sarsar approached Naag and hit him in the face with an egg of oblivion. As soon as Naag fell unconscious Sarsar cut off his head. His magic spirits clamoured and cried out, "*I was killed! Naag the Serpent was my name!*"

Mehran regained consciousness at the death of Naag and headed in search of Khubsurat. In the meanwhile, Sarsar made Princess Khubsurat unconscious, made her into a bundle, and brought her to her pavilion. She said to her companions Saba Raftar and Shamima, "Keep watch to make sure nobody takes away this bundle." Then she went to Heyrat's court and said to the empress, "I can bring Princess Khubsurat the Beauty before you as a captive if you give me your word that you will not kill her." Heyrat said, "I would never harm her for she is my own daughter. Quickly capture her and bring her to me." After receiving the empress's assurance, Sarsar returned to her pavilion, picked up the bundled up Khubsurat and headed out.

Qiran, who was present in Heyrat's camp in disguise, saw Sarsar carrying a bundle and reckoned that it must be one of his own commanders. He called out, "O mistress, you would surely die if you took another step." Sarsar drew her short sword and fell upon Qiran. A great commotion rose in the camp as the fight broke out.

In the meanwhile, Princess Bahar arrived at the mountainside in search of Khubsurat and came upon the corpse of Naag the Serpent. Bahar saw no one around and realized that Khubsurat had fallen into trouble. She decided to search for her in Heyrat's camp and upon arrival beheld Sarsar with a bundle over her shoulders, fighting Qiran. Bahar recited a spell that made Sarsar's feet stick to the ground. Princess Bahar flew away with Khubsurat and also took Sarsar along with a magic claw.

In the meanwhile, Qiran decided that it would not do to stay in Heyrat's camp any longer and escaped from there.

Sorcerer Allama the Wise

When Bahar arrived in the wilderness with Khubsurat and Sarsar, she came across one of Emperor Afrasiyab's attendants, sorcerer Allama, who was on his way to Heyrat's camp to deliver the emperor's message. On an impulse, he challenged Bahar but when she turned to face him, he realized that he would not be able to fight her. Sorcerer Allama had with him a little soil from Jamshed's grave, which he threw on Bahar, making her fall unconscious. Allama carried Bahar, Sarsar and Princess Khubsurat in a bundle to Heyrat's court.

Burq the Frank, who was present in the wilderness, saw all this from afar and ran to Mahrukh's camp where he gave the whole account to sorcerer Shakeel. Hearing of his beloved's capture, in a frenzied state Shakeel rushed to aid her with tears in his eyes. His mother, Queen Mahrukh, could not bear to see him leave in such a distressed state. Overcome by maternal love, she followed him.

In the meanwhile, the trickster girls had departed in search of their leader, Sarsar. Seeing Mahrukh coming, Saba Raftar disguised herself as trickster Zargham.

She approached Queen Mahrukh in Zargham's disguise and made her unconscious with an egg of oblivion. Saba Raftar now bundled up Mahrukh but, as she headed for her camp, she ran into Qiran, who had come from there. He recognized Saba Raftar in Zargham's disguise and rushed at her, cleaver in hand. Saba Raftar dropped Mahrukh and escaped. Qiran restored Mahrukh to consciousness and the two of them headed onwards.

In the meanwhile, sorcerer Shakeel had intercepted sorcerer Allama, who was carrying away Princess Khubsurat. The two sorcerers invoked their magic and recited spells and charms against each other. Now, one sank into the earth by reciting a magic spell; now, the other flew heavenwards by magic. The smoke from the magic fires rose; the waves of the magic sea roared.

Sarsar, who witnessed their magic combat, found a chance to make Shakeel unconscious with an egg of oblivion. Sorcerer Allama now put Shakeel under magic incarceration and carried him toward Heyrat's camp. But Sarsar arrived first in Heyrat's camp and the empress received news that sorcerer Allama was bringing her daughter along with her lover and Princess Bahar. Heyrat immediately came out and proceeded on her conveyance to receive Allama.

In the meanwhile, it occurred to sorcerer Allama that, rather than take his prisoners to Heyrat's court alive, he should behead them, lest some misfortune should intercept him on the way and the prisoners be set free. Allama stopped near a mountain to carry out his plan.

When Shakeel had departed from camp to rescue Khubsurat from Allama, Amar Ayyar had also left after him. He arrived at the same mountain where Allama had stopped, appeared before him in a sorcerer's disguise and accosted him, saying, "O shameless wretch, why have you caught these women who embody someone's honor? You seem a most consummate rascal!" Sorcerer Allama asked him, "Who are you?" Amar answered, "The emperor has made me the custodian of this place. I am its master." Allama answered, "Don't be so cross. I only have the emperor's fugitives Shakeel, Bahar and Khubsurat in my custody." Amar said with a laugh, "I did not recognize you earlier. In fact, your wife is my sister-in-law by relation. You must share a meal with me at my house before proceeding onwards."

Allama made excuses and said with great politeness, "O brother, let us kill these fugitives first." Amar said, "Let me see a glimpse of Shakeel's face. I want to see for myself the comely face that made Princess Khubsurat renounce her own family." Allama had cast a spell to make his prisoners invisible to the human eye for fear of Mahrukh's sorcerers intercepting him. He removed it, cast many spells on Shakeel to render him completely powerless, and then showed his face to Amar.

When Amar saw his face he said to Allama, "Give him to me so that I may cut off his head." He then led Shakeel by his hand to a secluded corner and said to him, "I am the father of four and have been born from fifteen wombs. Make me an offering so that I may spare your life." Shakeel marvelled at this speech and wondered how the sorcerer could have been born from fifteen wombs since everyone is born from just one. Then he realized it might be Amar. Overjoyed, Shakeel replied, "I will pay you five thousand rupees if you release me." Amar made him take a pledge then returned to Allama and said, "I feel pity for him; he is already dying in separation from his beloved. Must you kill him?" Allama replied, "I will spare him only if he submits his allegiance to Emperor Afrasiyab." Amar said, "Let me go and persuade him." He returned to Shakeel and said, "It is entirely likely that after your release you may not pay me the sum you promised. I would then have no recourse to force you to pay. Therefore, I would prefer that you give me Khubsurat's bracelet." Shakeel now became certain that it was Amar and realized that he would be presently released. He was most pleased and said, "What of her bracelet? I am your slave and my beloved is your slave girl. You are free to take all her jewelry."

At these words, Amar also realized that Shakeel had finally recognized him. He returned to Allama and said, "You were right. These rebels are very headstrong and would not consent to submitting to the emperor. Bring me some large stones from the bottom of the mountain and let us smash their heads and make them die a most painful death." Allama said, "Keep guard on them while I fetch the stones." He went down the mountain and fetched some stones.

As he was on his way up, Amar took out a stone from his zambil and rolled it down toward Allama. The sorcerer's head broke into a hundred pieces when the stone hit him. Stones and fire showered from the sky and the noises of his magic spirits rose at his dying.

All the prisoners were released and Shakeel started for the camp with his beloved.

Sorcerer Zalim Kohi the Cruel

It so happened that a sorcerer named Zalim Kohi the Cruel lived on the mountain where Amar killed sorcerer Allama the Wise. Upon hearing the noises resulting from Allama's death, he rushed to the scene and captured Amar with a spell. At that moment, Princess Bahar hurled a steel magic ball at him and shattered Zalim's spine. His magic spirits made hellish noises as he died. A whirlwind rose from the ground and carried the corpses of both sorcerers Allama and Zalim toward Afrasiyab.

Princess Bahar turned to go back to her camp but Heyrat, accompanied by a few distinguished sorcerers, appeared on the scene and barred her way. She and Bahar began exchanging magic blows and then Mahrukh, with the trickster Qiran, arrived and joined the fight.

Bahar broke a garland from around her neck and threw it at the enemy. Suddenly, a cold breeze blew and a refreshing and bracing garden crowded with roses and jasmine appeared. The redolence of the flowers overpowered the senses of all of Heyrat's companions. The scenery became more lush and verdant every moment.

In that very pasture a garden appeared
Which seemed of Paradise borne
Although it was in appearance a garden
It was in reality a tilism
Like the hand of the bountiful philanthropist
No branch was empty of flower or fruit
Colorful was the expanse with its myriad-colored flowers
And the fruit varieties that from branches hung
Beyond count or number in that garden grew
Both seasonal and out of season fruit

Empress Heyrat too, fell under the spell. She swayed drunkenly and stepped into the garden singing the praises of flowers. She plucked a rose and was about to inhale its fragrance when a ringdove came flying and with her claws took the rose out of Heyrat's hand. The ringdove raised its head and spoke to Heyrat, saying, "*O Sovereign of the World! you are the Empress of the Tilism. Do not allow yourself to fall under Bahar's spell. Beware! Consider every flower in this garden worse than a thorn or you will come to terrible harm from the adverse seasons of the world, and the branch of inauspicious accidents will sprout a new calamity.*"

These words of warning from the ringdove brought Heyrat to her senses. She realized she would have lived to rue the day had she smelled the rose. The empress invoked her magic to come out of the tilism and confronted Bahar.

Suddenly, Afrasiyab felt the need to consult Heyrat over some matter and dispatched a magic claw to fetch her. Bahar and Heyrat had exchanged a few magic blows when the magic claw swooped down and carried Heyrat away to Afrasiyab. She saluted the emperor and gave him a detailed account of all that had passed.

In the meanwhile, Mahrukh, Bahar and others routed the companions of Heyrat, and killed many by targeting them with their magic citrons and magic limes. When nobody remained to challenge them, Mahrukh and others returned to the camp with Qiran.

The throne was decorated for Mahrukh and she ordered a music assembly to begin. The revels began and cups of wine made the rounds.

Sorcerer Shakl Kush Image-Cutter

Meanwhile, Afrasiyab said to Heyrat, "I sent for you to consult you because I plan to inform the grandson of Lord Sameri, sorcerer Daud, about the commotion that has destroyed the peace of the tilism. If things worsen tomorrow, sorcerer Daud will accost us asking why we did not inform him of the events sooner. Therefore, I wish to send him the news. I am certain even from far away he could cause the destruction of the rebels."

Heyrat replied, "O Emperor, it would not do to solicit the help of the grandson of Lord Sameri in such a casual manner. If you wish to seek his help you must go yourself and take thousands of rupees and living things in offerings and sacrifices. You must go for an extended period and meet him at leisure. He will lend his ear to your pleas for aid after awhile. If you sent someone in your place, it is all too likely that even an audience with him would be denied. Therefore, I suggest you write and send for sorcerer Musavvir the Magic-Painter instead. He is sorcerer Daud's half brother, born of his father's slave girl. Like sorcerer Daud, he too is an immortal sorcerer of Hoshruba. He would capture all the tricksters as well."

In the end, Afrasiyab sent a letter to sorcerer Musavvir the Magic-Painter. It contained all the news about the inauspicious events that had taken place in the tilism, including Mahrukh's rebellion and the trouble created by the tricksters, and expressed a desire that he come to their aid. Along with the letter, Afrasiyab also sent many gifts and offerings.

When Afrasiyab's message arrived before sorcerer Musavvir, he expressed concern at the hardships of the Emperor of the Tilism and ordered his armies to be ready so that he could depart to aid him.

As Musavvir gave the orders to his army, his son, sorcerer Shakl Kush Image-Cutter said to him, "I would that you assign this campaign to me. I would return triumphant and have an opportunity as well to practise my magic to my heart's content. It does not become the dignity of Your Honor to advance against an insignificant horde of rebels."

At first, Musavvir refused to grant Shakl Kush's wish. However, at long last he gave way and sent his son with a vast army of sanguinary sorcerers. Musavvir then wrote a message to Afrasiyab, which read:

> "I am sending my son to your aid. He will first destroy the army of the rebels then present himself in your court."

After sending the message to Afrasiyab, Musavvir said to Shakl Kush, "You must first head toward Empress Heyrat's camp to fight with Mahrukh. Only after you have destroyed or captured all the rebels should you present yourself before Afrasiyab." Musavvir then instructed his son in the strategies and pitfalls of war, gave him injunctions on the preparation of magic works, and sent him off.

He sent an army with him and said,
"You who are unmatched warriors, twins of glory
Save my life from Mahrukh and her companions
Advance and free me from all sorrows
And make sure to hang Amar Ayyar alive
To make my enemies' eyes full of thorns
If you bring me the head of that lion warrior
You will put on my head a golden tiara of obligation
I will make you the commanders of brave hearts
Only lions with lions deserve to fight."

At his command, a man-destroying magic dragon
Emerged all saddled, like a dragon from Mount Qaf
None could match its stature or from it hide
Under the azure sky, none matched that towering giant's height
The army started moving, the ground started shaking
And with darkness, the sky became overcast

As Shakl Kush's army headed on its mission, Musavvir's message arrived in Afrasiyab's presence. He sent Heyrat back to her camp with instructions to receive Shakl Kush with deference and accompany him onto the battlefield. Upon return to her camp Heyrat awaited Shakl Kush's arrival.

Before long, Musavvir's son, Shakl Kush, completed his trek and arrived near Heyrat's army. Heyrat welcomed him and brought him into her court. She arranged for Shakl Kush's army to bivouac and held a feast in his honor.

When the magic birds brought the news of Shakl Kush's arrival to Queen Mahrukh, she said, "We would have had good reason to fear if Musavvir himself had been sent on the campaign against us. There is no fearing this mere boy. God Almighty is all-powerful." With these words, Mahrukh busied herself in preparation for the battle.

In Heyrat's camp, the feast continued and everyone lavished attention on Shakl Kush and carried out his every wish. When the

Painter of Nature studded the empty expanse of the Nine Heavens with the planetary fixtures, and the bright face of the sun disappeared from the world's album,

The darkness of the night approached
In the eyes of champions, the world in darkness drowned
The blue sky wore a black garb
The warriors wished their enemy ill and became on mischief bent

The drums of war were beaten in both camps and warriors on both sides readied their arms and armor. Queen Mahrukh and Bahar made a magic pen and drew their own and their army commanders' portraits to counter Shakl Kush's magic; he would prepare their portraits and cut them with magic scissors on the battlefield.

Be it known that when Shakl Kush's magic scissors cut a part from the portrait's body, it severed the same body part of the person whose portrait it was. Mahrukh and Bahar drew their portraits with a magic pen and entrusted these portraits to their magic spirits so that they and their commanders would remain unharmed by Shakl Kush's magic.

While Mahrukh and Bahar busied themselves in making these arrangements, their camp prepared for battle. The arms and armor were readied and burnished.

Shakl Kush meanwhile, prepared magic scissors and drew the portraits of Mahrukh's army commanders. He put oblations of lard into the bonfires to prepare spells and finished his praying and worship rituals. His warriors likewise remained occupied all night long in their preparations.

Finally, it was time when the scissors of the world's revolutions cut up the curtains of night. They slashed the collar of dawn and attired the sun in a luminous dress.

The Emperor of the East emerged
And the signs of victory appeared with him
The True Believers, young and old alike
Stepped forward now lion-like to fight
They arrayed out in left and right flanks
The rings of obedience in their ears they wore
At that moment the blackguard Shakl Kush arrived
With blood-thirsty eyes he regarded his opponents
Whose blood he would soon start to shed

For he was matchless in making mischief
Mahrukh Magic-Eye realizing his intent
Led her army to attack and bring him down
The world exclaimed, 'Doomsday comes!'
Like a vessel of mercury trembled the sun

The warriors' war cries caused a blast like the Day of Judgment. The display of magic works by sorcerers caused such a din that it deafened even the ear of the heavens. After the two sides had made battle arrays and the arena had been cleared and cleaned, the criers came forward from both sides and stirred their champions by eulogizing past warriors, who had won glory on the battlefield. Like bright swords, their tongues sparkled in singing praises of the great battles of yore. They filled the heads of their champions with the desire to perform similar brave deeds.

Finally, it was time to do battle. Shakl Kush rode into the arena on his magic dragon, displayed his magic works and feats of sorcery and called out in challenge, "O tribe of ingrates, you will shortly witness your death and destruction at my hands. You will see how you roll in dust and gore."

Mahrukh rode into the arena on her flying throne and said, "Watch what you say O insignificant boy of trivial talent! In no time you will depart this world, full of unmet desires and unrequited hopes."

Mahrukh's words enraged Shakl Kush. He took out a magic effigy in Mahrukh's likeness from his sorcerer's bag and threw it into the arena with the command, "O Shamama,[133] in the name of Sameri go and bring me Mahrukh a prisoner!" The magic effigy started toward Mahrukh.

Queen Mahrukh leapt down from her throne, recited a spell on the magic effigy and picked it up in her hand, saying, "It's a pity that this magic effigy's limbs and shape are exactly like Shakl Kush's but it does not have his head. I will now give it the head of Shakl Kush as well." At these words, the face of the magic effigy became like Shakl Kush's and it turned upon Shakl Kush with hostile intent.

Shakl Kush recited a counterspell and put it back in his sorcerer's bag. Now Mahrukh began reciting spells and attacking Shakl Kush. But he countered all her attacks and continued making a portrait of Mahrukh with a magic pen. He reckoned, in his inexperience, that only after he had captured or killed Mahrukh would other sorcerers come out to challenge him. Catching him unawares, sorcerer Raad Thunder-Clap stomped both his feet on the ground and sank into earth. His mother sorceress Mehshar Lightning-Bolt witnessed this and flew up into the sky in anticipation.

Shakl Kush was engaged in magic warfare with Mahrukh when sorcerer Raad emerged from the ground beside him and screamed, causing Shakl Kush to fall unconscious from his magic dragon. As his army commanders ran to carry him away, sorceress Mehshar Lightning-Bolt flashed and struck, cleaving Shakl Kush in two and sank into the ground. Heaven's mercy! Shakl Kush was dispatched hellward and the heavens and Earth reverberated with thunderous and blood-curdling voices that exclaimed, "*I was killed! Shakl Kush Image-Cutter was my name!*"

Now Mahrukh found her chance and advanced, a steel magic ball in hand. Seeing their commander lying dead, Shakl Kush's warriors tore off their collars in grief and charged in avenging rage from the other side.

The two sides deployed their magic. Some recited spells that made their opponents vomit blood and die. Others invoked magic that killed their opponents with great agony. Summoned by spells, black serpents came out of the ground and bit the sorcerers targeted by the spell. Poisonous scorpions were unleashed by the spells of other sorcerers. Clouds of many colors flew above the battlefield, simultaneously showering fire and water. Heads flew off necks and rained on the ground; corpses floated in a river of blood.

A fierce battle was underway and in every corner, steel clashed with steel. When magic and sorcery were ineffective, the sorcerers struck their foes with their tridents and pentadents. Swordfights broke out and severed heads lined the ground like a freshly harvested crop.

Blood flowed from the swords
Like water from mountain veins
Glory to the renowned sword fighters
From blood the Earth looked a Yemenite agate
No sooner than a rider fell from his steed
Than the speeding steed's hooves made him dust

Shakl Kush's army secured his corpse with great difficulty and took the path of retreat from the battlefield. Heyrat, who had witnessed the combat with her army, thought of launching an attack on Mahrukh's camp but realized that with Shakl Kush's army in full retreat, the tide of the battle was now irreversibly turned. She struck the drums to announce the cessation of hostilities and returned to her camp.

Mahrukh entered her camp covered in glory and triumph. She took her bath and gave audience in the court, which filled up with her noble commanders. A dance recital began and a festive mood prevailed in the camp.

Shakl Kush's defeated army returned to Afrasiyab's court and placed Shakl Kush's corpse before him. Afrasiyab became very anxious and said, "Alas! He was sorcerer Musavvir's only son and fell in the battle for my cause. How will I be able to show my face to Musavvir now?"

Afrasiyab ordered that Shakl Kush's corpse be burned, and made a magic effigy of the sorcerer. He implanted a magic spirit within it, which made Shakl Kush's effigy come alive. Afrasiyab sent it to Musavvir with great ceremony, accompanied by Shakl Kush's surviving army. The Emperor of Hoshruba also sent a note to Musavvir, which read:

> "O Sameri's grandson, your son performed great deeds of valor before dying and passing into Lord Sameri's service. I have sent you his magic effigy. It will live for forty days. You may shower it with all the affection and love in your heart to give yourself solace."

After Shakl Kush's army left with his magic effigy, Afrasiyab thought of capturing the one responsible for Shakl Kush's death and sending him to Musavvir as well so that he might avenge his son's blood. Afrasiyab sent for the trickster girl Sarsar and said to her, "Bring me sorcerer Raad Thunder-Clap a captive!" Sarsar replied, "I shall present him in no time."

Sarsar prepared all her trickster's devices and set out. She entered Mahrukh's camp in disguise and awaited an opportunity. Witnessing an attendant come out of the court, she followed her and when she reached a secluded corner, Sarsar made her unconscious with an egg of oblivion. Sarsar now made herself up in the attendant's likeness and returned to the court and began moving the fly-whisk above Raad.

Amar Ayyar, who was present there, looked up and recognized Sarsar in the attendant's disguise. He rose from his place and came toward her to catch her unawares. But Sarsar read Amar's intent. She leapt and ran away. Amar called out, "Where do you go, O slave girl?" Sarsar replied, "Come to your senses, O slave born. Did even your father ever dream of having a slave girl?" Amar ran after Sarsar but she escaped.

Mahrukh asked, "Who was that ill-mannered slave girl who addressed such rude remarks to Amar Ayyar?" He replied, "Sarsar has come to kidnap Raad. She will take him away if she sees us drop our guard. We must remain on the alert." The alarm was sounded throughout the camp and everyone took precautions.

After Mahrukh adjourned her court all the commanders returned to their pavilions but both Mahrukh and Bahar remained awake for fear of the trickster girls.

In the meanwhile, Sarsar found an opportunity to disguise herself as sorceress Mehshar Lightning-Bolt. She went to Raad's pavilion and said to the guards, "All of you lack alertness. I shall guard my son myself."

The false sorceress entered the pavilion and made Raad unconscious in his sleep. But as she did not have the time to bundle him up, Sarsar decided to carry away the unconscious Raad over her shoulders. When the guards sighted her they raised the alarm and the whole camp rang with the cries of "Catch her! Don't let her escape!" Amar also rushed out when he heard the cries of alarm. Reckoning that Sarsar would head for the wilderness, he ran in that direction to intercept her. When Sarsar witnessed all the commotion she realized she should wait there while others headed for the wilderness in search of her. She took cover behind a tent.

When Sarsar found the field clear she finally made Raad into a bundle and went on her way. But when she entered the wilderness she ran into Amar Ayyar, who challenged her. Sarsar blew her whistle. Sarsar's vizier girl Saba Raftar the Quick rushed to the scene to offer her assistance. Amar hit Saba Raftar with an egg of oblivion and made her unconscious. In the meanwhile, Burq the Frank arrived on the scene and helped Amar corner Sarsar. However, Sarsar made Burq unconscious with an egg of oblivion and kept slowly retreating while continuing to fight Amar. Once she saw an opening, she turned and ran at full speed.

It so happened that Qiran the Ethiope was coming from the direction taken by Sarsar. Seeing her carrying away a bundle, he charged her, cleaver in hand. As he was about to deal her a blow, Amar, who was pursuing Sarsar, shouted, "Now, now! What are you doing? She is my beloved! Did you forget she is your master's darling?" Qiran stayed his hand but Sarsar realized that she was now under attack from the tricksters and, if she did not give up Raad, she would be captured herself. She threw down the bundle and escaped with her life. Qiran restored Raad to consciousness. Burq the Frank and Saba Raftar also came to and went their separate ways.

Amar and Qiran returned to their camp with Raad and said to him, "Now you should be doubly cautious." Then everybody retired to rest.

But Sarsar once again entered Mahrukh's camp disguised as a wine seller. A *tika* adorned her forehead, her eyes were lined with kohl, and her lips were painted with betel juice and *missi*. She sported a nose-ring and tinkling toe-rings. She wore a brocade-lined waistcloth and her mantle was knotted in front, bracing her shoulders. Carrying a small ewer on her hips and a bottle in her hand, she walked with a hundred coquetries.

The locks of that beloved rose in waves
For her ruddy cheeks were bright as flames
A girl born under auspicious stars
The sun of the sky of love she was

Thus, with such charm and allure, when she arrived near Raad's pavilion the guards and their commanders called out to her, "O wine seller, give us a little wine!" Sarsar placed the ewer before them, allowing them a glimpse of her breathtaking, fairy-like beauty. All of them fell head over heels in love with her and said, "You should give us a cup from your own hand. The pleasure of wine increases when one receives it from a charming cupbearer's hand."

Sarsar offered them a cup of wine each and, because it was drugged, all of them soon fell unconscious. Sarsar slit open the panels of Raad's pavilion and threw inside a handful of moths cast of a drug. They fell on the waxen candles and their smoke filled the nostrils of Raad's attendants within, who also fell unconscious. After a moment, Sarsar peeped in and, finding them lying unconscious, rolled inside. She sat near Raad's bed, filled a tube with a drug, blew it into his nostrils and made him unconscious as well. Afterwards, she made a bundle of him and headed out. As all the guards and attendants within and without lay unconscious, no one raised the alarm. Sarsar comfortably found her way out of the camp.

When Sarsar brought Raad to Afrasiyab's court he ordered her to take him before sorcerer Musavvir in that very state. Carrying Raad's bundle, Sarsar headed toward the City of Portraits.

Sorceress Surat Nigar Face-Maker

Now hear of what passed when sorcerer Musavvir received Afrasiyab's message and the magic effigy made in Shakl Kush's likeness arrived in his presence. When Musavvir learned that his son had been killed, he made loud lamentations and wept inconsolably. All his nobles dressed themselves in mourning.

Shakl Kush's mother, Queen Surat Nigar, fell unconscious from receiving the shocking news of her son's death. When she regained consciousness, she rent her collar and cried out, "O my son, you hid yourself from my eyes!

'When I think of you
My heart becomes restive
Where did death take you?
What evil eye felled you?"

Such plaints she continuously made
Her collar she continuously rent
And like clouds of the spring quarter
All her family and relatives shed tears

After crying much and shedding copious tears, Surat Nigar kissed the magic effigy of Shakl Kush, sat him in her lap, embraced him and showed him all the tokens of maternal affection. Then she wrote a note to Afrasiyab, which read:

> "We have cooled our eyes with the sight of our son in the magic effigy. Now we send him back into your keeping. We will muster our armies and arrive soon to avenge our son's death and destroy the enemy."

Surat Nigar Face-Maker dispatched this message to Afrasiyab's court with the magic effigy. Afterwards she ordered her attendants to make preparations for departure. After a day's preparations the tents and pavilions of her army were packed and loaded and, with an army of several hundred thousand ferocious sorcerers, Surat Nigar departed toward Empress Heyrat's camp.

One of Surat Nigar's daughters, Almas Fairy-Face, learned of her mother's departure on the campaign and insisted on accompanying her to kill her brother's murderer and avenge his death. Surat Nigar tried to dissuade her, saying, "My child, you do not know magic. You are still in your teens. Stay at home and occupy yourself with play and games. Do not insist on accompanying me for war awaits us where I am headed." Almas Fairy-Face, however, would not be deterred. Surat Nigar could not hold her back in the end and took her along and the army advanced with great majesty.

After his wife departed, sorcerer Musavvir organized his own army and, leaving one of his advisors in charge of his court's affairs, departed to aid Heyrat.

Surat Nigar Face-Maker arrived near Heyrat's camp first and ordered her army to pitch their tents and pavilions when they were a day's journey from Heyrat's camp. She ordered her royal pavilion to be set up and said to her commanders, "Tomorrow we will march from here to Heyrat's camp!"

The army bivouacked in the stretches of the forest and the acclivity of the mountains. Cauldrons were put on fire and food was prepared for the warriors. A dance recital began in Surat Nigar's royal pavilion and everyone occupied themselves with revels.

In the meanwhile, the trickster girl Sarsar Swordfighter, carrying sorcerer Raad's bundle, arrived in that forest. Upon regarding the large army camped there and sighting the royal pavilion, she asked one of the campers whose army it was and who was its commander. He replied, "It belongs to Shakl Kush's mother, sorceress Surat Nigar, who has come to fight Mahrukh." Sarsar was most pleased to hear the news. She told herself she would not have to journey all the way to the City of Portraits and could hand over Raad to Surat Nigar and turn back. Thus decided, Sarsar headed for the royal pavilion.

The attendants stopped her and asked her the purpose of her visit. She told them it was to inform Surat Nigar that Sarsar Swordfighter had arrived. When the attendants informed Surat Nigar, she sent for the trickster girl. Sarsar entered and witnessed a music assembly underway. Surat Nigar sat on the throne surrounded by thousands of sorcerers and sorceresses on seats and stations.

Sarsar saluted Surat Nigar, placed the bundle before her, and said, "I have brought sorcerer Raad Thunder-Clap, your son's murderer, to present before you!" Surat Nigar was delighted by the news. She conferred a rich robe of honor on Sarsar, offered her a high rank in her court, and sent her away after offering her the best of her hospitality.

Then Surat Nigar said to her attendants, "Send for Princess Almas Fairy-Face so that she may kill her brother's murderer with her own hand since she came expressly for this purpose." The attendants left to carry out her orders.

Princess Almas was strolling in the forest, enjoying the lush green expanse in the company of nine hundred attendants, slave girls and sorceresses when she received her mother's summons and arrived before her in all her allure.

Witnessing the resplendent beauty of her daughter, Surat Nigar glanced at her heel[134] to ward off the evil eye from Almas. She seated

Almas beside her and, after putting Raad under magic incarceration, had him restored to his senses and ordered him to be brought into her presence. Then she targeted Raad with her rebukes and imprecations.

Almas Fairy-Face beheld a beautiful young man in his early twenties standing before her, wearing magic chains and fetters. His face shone like the moon. She saw his thick eyebrows, his muscular arms and shoulders, and the signs of bravery, serenity, courage and fortitude on his face.

Was it his stature or a cypress in the garden
In his perfection he was peerless and beyond belief
His height was one the calamity of doomsday would acquire
A ringdove would fall in love with that cypress beloved
His knitted brows were a calamity for loving hearts
The mole on his gold-like face the touchstone
His locks were the snares for lovers' lives
His mole a bait for the birds of souls
His eyebrows from humility were not bent
But were a mosque's arches, where lovers prostrate
Lit up with kohl from the Mount Tur[135]
His eyes were the source of divine light
The pink hue on the whites of his eyes
Were red clouds over the moon in the sky
Everyone who glimpsed his eyelashes praised
Those lattices on the entrance of a friend's house
How could one describe the beauty of his cheeks
How can one encounter two moons at one glance
His thin and shapely, beautiful lips
Were two goblets brimful with pure wine
His smile was the lofty smile of beauty
His lips, the confidants of his beauty's secret
Shaped like an ewer's, a rarity was his neck
More lofty than the lofty heavens his neck
His wrist, his arms, his hands, his feet
Truly matchless were in the world entire
In short, from head to toe, he was
Doubtless the envy and pride of desire

Seeing his lovely face, Princess Almas fell head over heels in love with him. Entangled in the snare rope of his locks, she felt restive, bit her lips, and regarded his face with longing. Her heart became restless and she began to lose her self possession. From her burning desire she became frenzied and shed tears.

When Princess Almas Fairy-Face thought of the fruitlessness of such a passion, and realized that the difference in her situation and the circumstances of Raad would make a union between them impossible, she was overpowered by her emotions and broke into tears.

Her mother embraced her and reckoned that when she saw her brother's murderer before her eyes she cried from grief remembering her dead sibling. Surat Nigar said to Almas, "My child, your tears will not bring your brother back from the dead, they will only make your heart melt in blood."

Witnessing the princess overwhelmed by emotion, everyone attended to her. Some offered her words of comfort. Some offered to take all her calamities on their heads.[136] Others offered themselves in sacrifice to the princess to protect her against any calamities. A hubbub rose in the court.

Hearing the noises, Raad Thunder-Clap, who stood passively with his eyes lowered and his head bowed, looked up. His eyes beheld that destroyer of life and faith, to wit, Princess Almas Fairy-Face, and the same moment his love was claimed by the hawk of her glance. He saw her marvellous, world-adorning beauty. Her dark locks seemed to be the envy of the dark of the night; the midday sun offered itself as the sacrifice to her refulgent cheeks; her delicate lips robbed the delicate jasmine petals of their pride; the redness of her lips made the heart of the Badakhshan ruby melt into blood with jealousy. Dressed in mourning for her brother, she seemed like the Fount of Life in the Land of Darkness. The worlds of coquetry, airs and dalliance all sacrificed themselves at her least movement. The most alluring beauties of the world submitted her their allegiance for her superior beauty.

Moon-like, moon-faced and wearing pearls in her ears
The owner of beauty, in gold clad
Full of brightness her luminous face
Even a mirror could not reflect such blinding light
Her high nose was such
That it taught her conceit
Her eyebrows delicately bent
Were the life of the world entire
If her eyes were narcissus-like, her ears were like roses
On one side the proud rose on the other the self loving narcissus
From the redness of her lips, the bright sheen of her teeth

The oyster and the pearls to the depths of sea sink
When in a smile her teeth were displayed
Pearls offered themselves as their sacrifice
How to define the dimples on her cheeks
They were golden citrons made by nature's hand
The light of morn her bright neck was
The mole on her bright face the morning star
Who could match the matchless hand
That would such a neck embrace
The color of henna on her hands the blood of lovers
Her fingers the envy of coral branches
How could one describe the clarity of her torso
Like a mirror her stomach shone bright
Like two citrons were her two breasts
Or two apples from Rizwan's paradise
Her body was clad all in black
She was grieving, was most sorrowful
Clad in her black apparel she was
The mecca of lovers' hearts draped in black
Beholding her beautiful existence
Raad became like an arrow-pierced prey
Before, young and old were engrossed by his beauty
Now, portrait-like, Raad became engrossed by hers
Overwhelmed by that image of beauty
With her Raad became besotted
Seeing her luminous aspect
Like a mirror he stared wonderstruck
He said to himself, If fortune should favor me,
And would confer a beloved like her on me
If I could have with her but a single tryst
With my heart and soul my dedication I would show.
He had this conversation in his heart
Then became all quiet, helpless as he was

Sorceress Surat Nigar sent for the executioner to put that poor youth to death. At that moment, God Almighty willed it so that a message arrived for her from sorcerer Musavvir. It read:

> "My princess, I hear that Raad has been brought to you a prisoner. Do not kill him where you are stationed. Instead, you should take him to Empress Heyrat's camp, which is close by. I will also arrive there. Then

> we will hang him in full view of the rebels, and also chastise any who come to his aid from the rebels' camp."

After reading the letter, Surat Nigar stopped the executioner from putting Raad to death. She ordered one of her attendants, sorcerer Faulad Iron-Puller, to keep Raad in custody for the day.

Faulad took Raad into a mountain pass and put magic chains and fetters on him. Afterwards, Faulad recited a spell and a wall of fire encircled the mountain pass. Smoke rose from the fire in such abundance that it completely covered the place where Raad was imprisoned. Sorcerer Faulad set up his own tent at some distance from the wall of fire and rested there with his companions and attendants.

After Raad was taken away from Surat Nigar's pavilion, the absence of her beloved made Princess Almas Fairy-Face inconsolable. A few moments later, she said to her mother, "Now I will go to my pavilion and take some rest." Her mother granted her leave and Almas sent for her conveyance. A palanquin with latticed doors arrived and the princess's procession made ready. She mounted her palanquin and the group proceeded. A eunuch named Ishrat accompanied it on horseback, supervising the arrangements of the procession.

While these events were underway, Raad's attendants returned to their senses in Mahrukh's camp. When they found their master absent they went to Mahrukh and reported that someone had kidnapped Raad. His mother, sorceress Mehshar Lightning-Bolt, became disconcerted. She cried with grief and gave in to ecstasies of anxiety. Amar comforted her and said, "Trickster girl Sarsar was in wait of an opportunity and she must have kidnapped him. Do not grieve. I will go and secure his release." Then Amar left on his mission.

On the way, Amar met Burq the Frank and gave him the news. Burq also headed to look for Raad and, in his search, chanced upon Surat Nigar's camp. He infiltrated the camp in disguise and witnessed Raad being taken by sorcerer Faulad Iron-Puller to the mountain pass and imprisoned there.

Burq tried to think of some trickery to secure Raad's release. He was engrossed in these thoughts when the procession of Princess Almas passed and he accompanied it. After making queries, Burq determined that it was the procession of sorcerer Musavvir's daughter. Burq continued onward with her procession, waiting for an opportunity to kidnap her.

In the meanwhile, he saw a servant of the eunuch Ishrat stop to prepare his hookah. Burq approached him and said, "Look here for a moment!" When the servant looked up, Burq made him unconscious with an egg of oblivion. He hid him in the nearby bushes and brought the hookah to the eunuch.

As he handed it to Ishrat, Burq said, "I would like you to stay behind a moment and let others carry on along their way. I heard terrible news about your employment and wish to inform you of it." The eunuch became full of anxiety. He stayed behind with the false attendant while the procession moved on. Burq waited until the procession had moved well ahead. Then, with the egg of oblivion, he made Ishrat unconscious too, causing him to fall from his horse. Burq disguised himself as Ishrat and followed the procession of the princess on horseback, joining it before long.

In the meanwhile, Princess Almas arrived at her camp. It was set up far away from Surat Nigar's camp to allow the Princess a chance to enjoy the scenery and amuse herself with revels. The princess sent all her attendants, confidantes and slave girls away. She ordered the panels of her pavilion overlooking the forest to be raised.

She sat looking at the expanse and remembering her beloved. Sometimes she cried, sometimes she complained of the fickle heavens. Sometimes she made frenzied utterances. At other times, she addressed the passing breeze. Thinking of her beloved, she recited:

"More beautiful than flower orchards is each flower
in your garden face
Desire for them grows in my heart like a thorn
If I behold a rose garden that is not your face
May its flowers become in my eyes as thorns
You are as beautiful now as you were in the past
All beauties have this claim, but none your match
Your renown fills the marketplace
Your house is the Egypt of delicate beauty,
You are like Yusuf of Canaan.
The news of your sale excites the bazaar
I am ready to lose my head in your purchase
As I lost my life in your desire
For you I humbled myself many times
In this act I proved myself the worthiest
Every moment I look for you; I am always in your quest
I wish to die time and time again before your eyes

The cypress in embarrassment hides
As you with your lovely stature step toward the garden
Every moment I pluck at my breast like a lute with my nails
Hundreds of cries and lamentations rise vibrating from my veins
Drink wine in the garden and watch the cypress and jasmine
And I will attain my happiness to have you before my sight
O knower of my secrets, do not blame me for what I do
For I have shunned all honor in my beloved's quest."

While the princess sat engrossed in her beloved's remembrance, Burq the Frank arrived in the eunuch Ishrat's guise and noticed her sitting by herself, looking grief-stricken. The false Ishrat concealed himself to hear the princess's heart-rending lamentations and the tale of grief she narrated.

The princess sighed and said, "O Raad, you bought my soul for a glimpse of your face. I will now depart this world with the hope of our union unmet." When the false Ishrat heard this, he realized that the princess had fallen in love with Raad. He came out of his hiding place and approached the princess. Noticing him, she stopped crying, dried her tears, and turned an annoyed face toward him.

The false Ishrat leaned forward and whispered in the princess's ear, "O Princess, I know that you are in love. You conceal it from me for no reason. I am your family's slave. If ordered I would even pluck the stars from the sky for you. Tell me your secret and I give you my word that none will ever hear it from my tongue. And I would do all in my power to unite you with your beloved besides."

When Princess Almas found him to be kindly disposed, she narrated her entire plight. The false Ishrat said, "O Princess of the world, let us go to the place where your lover is imprisoned. You should tell the prison guard that you have a question for your brother's killer. He will let you in and then I will secure Raad's release, for I am in reality the trickster Burq the Frank come in disguise to secure his release."

Princess Almas's rosebud-like lips blossomed into the flower of laughter upon hearing these auspicious words. She joyously called out,

"If I give up my life from happiness it would be proper
For these happy tidings have made my soul fully content."

She ordered her palanquin and rode in it to Raad's prison. Burq accompanied her in Ishrat's guise. When they arrived at Faulad Iron-Puller's camp, he came out and bowed before Princess Almas. She told him that which Burq had instructed. Faulad removed the fiery cordon from Raad's prison and she went in and found solace in her beloved's sight.

The false Ishrat stayed outside with sorcerer Faulad Iron-Puller, who offered him wine and meat. At first the false Ishrat coyly refused but, when Faulad insisted, he filled a goblet with red wine and secretly drugged it. He offered it to Faulad saying, "You must have a cup first, only then will I drink." Faulad took the wine and drank it. The false Ishrat then offered drugged wine and drugged sweets to all of Faulad's attendants too, saying, "Have a taste. These sweets are from the princess's own table." All of them ate the sweets and drank the wine and fell unconscious.

Burq the Frank immediately cut off their heads. The moment they died, darkness enveloped the place. A great hue and cry rose and Raad was released.

As Princess Almas felt frightened by the growing commotion, Raad said to her, "O Princess, you witnessed how easily Faulad was killed while you watched." The princess too, marvelled at the alacrity of the trickster. While they still stood in shock, Burq came in and said to them, "O pair of lovers, we must now hurriedly depart lest Queen Surat Nigar hears these tidings and sends some calamity your way. She is camped only a few miles from this place."

Princess Almas said, "O Burq, there's a forest near my royal pavilion that no one frequents. Let both Raad and me proceed there to pack my belongings and rest. Then we will depart for Queen Mahrukh's camp." Burq said, "You will be provided all you need, but now's not the time for that. It's not safe to stay around any longer." But Princess Almas insisted still, and Burq had no option but to give in to her wishes.

Princess Almas Fairy-Face brought Raad to her camp and seated him on a luxurious seat. She sent for all the paraphernalia of revel making. The wine service and salvers of kebabs for accompaniment were provided and the two began drinking.

The two of them to the pleasure chamber retired
Where a carpet of gold thread and bed awaited them
In that place, finally alone, they
Began kissing and fondling each other
While Raad made a thousand plaints
The princess his every request denied
While Raad's desire and passion grew
She at once offered and denied herself to him

That fairy like beauty told her lover
"In your camp we will fulfill our desires."
Dejected and unsuccessful, Raad finally said this,
"Bring me some wine then from the niche."
With a hundred coquetries that beauty rose
And stretched her hand toward the niche
She took down the bottle of wine with one hand
And with the other a goblet picked
The two drank the wine and inebriated became
Intoxicated already from the ecstasy of love
One's arms became the other's pillow
One's lips became the other's solace
They drank and then drank some more
To all joys and sorrows indifferent,
They became oblivious of themselves
They became their own cupbearers and their drinkers
To his fairy-like beloved, Raad made love
Every too often they kissed and embraced
Now he took her in his arms to sleep
Now with his lips he fondled hers
Occupied while they were in these endearments
A sleeping menace became awake

That cruel woman, that tyrannical sorceress
To wit Surat Nigar Face-Maker, deceitful and sly
Came to learn that Raad was released from prison
And his guards and keepers all beheaded were
And that the cause of these terrible events
Was none other than her own daughter Almas
Who went to the prison without informing others
And dispatched to hell the prison keeper and guards
Hearing this report of her daughter's doings
An enraged Surat Nigar burned like a blaze
She departed at once with fury filled
And arrived at the entrance of the princess's pavilion

All the attendants and slaves of Princess Almas ran away in fear at the sight of Surat Nigar and she barged into the pavilion. Finding Almas lying in Raad's embrace, she was overtaken by ecstasies of rage.

Surat Nigar recited a spell and struck her hands. The piece of ground on which the princess's bed lay rose from the earth into the air. Surat

Nigar also flew by invoking magic. Burq, who stood under the pavilion watching this calamity unfold, tearfully followed the flying piece of ground carrying Raad and the princess.

In the meanwhile, both Raad and Princess Almas awoke from their dream of oblivion. Raad tried to recite a spell and fly away with Princess Almas but Surat Nigar's spell kept him from remembering any. He said to the princess, "It appears we have become captives of magic." The princess started crying and washing her face with tears of remorse, saying, "O unfaithful, unloving heavens, you could not bear even a short happy union between two lovers. You robbed us of it in no time." She complained about their tyrannical fate at times and, at other times, they cried in each other's embrace.

She would cry,

"What a hand, O Fate, you dealt me
My lover you took from me
Before whom should I make my complaint
That you left me unhappy and forlorn?
That you put to sword my desire's house
Ah my comely lover, alas! Alas!"

While the princess made these laments, sorceress Surat Nigar recited another spell and the flying piece of ground broke into two pieces, separating Raad and Princess Almas, and the two pieces went flying in different directions.

The heart of the princess became cleft with grief and laden with a thousand sorrows. The two lovers were in a state of shock and grief that cannot be described. Even the pen that composes this breaks into dark tears.

When the two of them separated in that manner, Burq the Frank, who followed them on the ground, could not decide whether to follow Raad or Princess Almas. In the end, he ran back to his camp and gave the news to sorceress Mehshar Lightning-Bolt.

Unnerved by the terrible news about her son, she speedily flew by magic and reached the piece of ground that carried Princess Almas.

Sorceress Mehshar thunderously flashed and swooped down, catching Princess Almas in her magic claw. But Surat Nigar quickly reached her side and cast a spell at which thousands of magic slaves flew up and caught Mehshar. She tried to break free by reciting spells; she thrashed about and fluttered her wings, but to no avail. Surat Nigar put a magic incarceration spell on Mehshar and took her and Princess Almas to a horrible, dreadful wilderness.

Sorcerer Zalim Black-Face

Once she landed in the wilderness, Surat Nigar recited a spell and directed it skywards. The piece of ground carrying Raad came flying down and descended beside her.

Surat Nigar wrote a spell and gave it to a magic slave. It disappeared and, after a few moments, the earth cleft and a sorcerer emerged from it. He bowed respectfully to Surat Nigar and stood awaiting orders. Surat Nigar said to him, "O sorcerer Zalim Black-Face, I have summoned you so that you may keep these three as your prisoners. It would not have been wise to keep them prisoner in the camp since my daughter is among them and everyone high and low would come to learn that sorcerer Musavvir's daughter was kept in captivity because of her love. Moreover, the tricksters would infiltrate the camp and secure the release of their commanders and companions. Therefore, I brought them here to put them in your custody."

After that, sorceress Surat Nigar flew away toward her camp. Sorcerer Zalim Black-Face made a magic tower and imprisoned Raad, Princess Almas and sorceress Mehshar inside. We will hear more of them before long.

ᘓᘐᘖ

Now we return to give an account of sorceress Surat Nigar. After returning to her camp, she ordered her army to prepare to march. Packing and loading their tents and pavilions, she and her defeat-incarnate army headed for Empress Heyrat's camp.

The magic birds conveyed the news to Heyrat that sorceress Surat Nigar and her army were approaching to present themselves in her service. Upon hearing this, Heyrat took her nobles and ministers along and went out to welcome the sorceress. The empress ordered that carpets inlaid with jewels be spread in the path of Surat Nigar. Heyrat received her warmly and brought her to the court with great esteem and honor. Surat Nigar's army was camped beside Heyrat's own and the empress gave commands that all comforts be provided to Surat Nigar's commanders and men. And in this manner, her army set up camp in great comfort.

Surat Nigar said to Heyrat, "I have returned after imprisoning Princess Almas Fairy-Face and Raad. Your daughter Khubsurat the Beauty is enamored of Mahrukh's son Shakeel, and mine of Mehshar's son Raad. The same adverse fate has marked both of us. O Heyrat, I wish you to strike the drums of war so that tomorrow I may wipe out the rebels and avenge the blood of my son."

Heyrat feted and regaled Surat Nigar all day. When the revolutions of heaven brought about a change and the face of the bride of the sky became darkened with the blackness of the night, the sound of war drums rose from Heyrat's camp as per sorceress Surat Nigar's wishes.

The spies took this intelligence to Queen Mahrukh and conveyed it to her after singing her adulations and praises. The clarions of war answered the call to war from Mahrukh's camp as well. Both camps prepared magic weapons and readied their arms and armor.

Be it known to the readers that thousands of battles take place in this story. Therefore, the humble narrator has given their description with an eye to brevity. Lengthening a narrative unnecessarily is an idle exercise. Thus only those battles that are entertaining and take place between renowned, illustrious sorcerers will be described in detail. The rest will be mentioned in passing so that neither the audience nor the readers of this tale become weary and disinterested.

Now we return to our story.

All night long the two camps bustled with the preparations for battle. When the sun, flying its golden standard in Earth's every corner, appeared and showed its majestic sight to the world, Surat Nigar and Empress Heyrat led their armies into the battlefield with great stateliness.

Queen Mahrukh Magic-Eye and Princess Bahar arrived from the other side with the champions of the world and decorated the battlefield with their presence. They settled the dust clouds with magic rain. The battle arrays were formed. The criers made their calls and withdrew, and the proclaimers made their proclamations and retreated. Surat Nigar rode out on a magic dragon and challenged her opponents.

Princess Bahar came out to answer her challenge. Surat Nigar hurled a magic coconut that exploded and released thousands of portraits. These portraits crept like shadows and wrapped themselves around Bahar.

In answer to Surat Nigar's spell, Bahar took off her bracelet and threw it toward the sky. Immediately, everyone saw a pearl-strung cord appear that hung down from the heavens to the Earth. Bahar climbed it and reached high into the air from where she invoked her magic. A flame shot down like a sunburst and burned up all the shadows wrapped around her body.

When Surat Nigar witnessed this, she drew a portrait and threw it at the pearl-strung cord. The portrait fell to the ground and came alive, releasing flames from its mouth that burned up the pearl-strung cord. Bahar dropped to the ground but, with her magic, she survived the fall.

She plucked a few hairs from her head and threw them at the portrait. Those hairs ensnared the portrait like a snare rope and dragged it before Bahar, who cut it up with scissors.

Then Bahar took out a bouquet of flowers and hurled it at Surat Nigar. Gold and silver flowers rained down on Surat Nigar and her companions, all of whom fell under their spell. They swayed in ecstasy and sang praises to Bahar.

At that moment, the earth cleft and magic slave girls emerged. They gleaned the flowers from Bahar's bouquet and called out, "*O Queen Surat Nigar, to fall under the spell of a chit of a girl like Bahar ill becomes the wife of Sorcerer Musavvir. Beware!*"

At these words, Surat Nigar came to her senses. She drew her magic sword and attacked Bahar. The two sorceresses engaged in magic swordplay. In the meanwhile, Empress Heyrat ordered her army commanders to attack and sorcerers charged from all sides. Queen Mahrukh too, advanced with her warriors and the two armies merged and a pitched battle was fought. Clouds that made magic showers rose by the sorcerers' spells from both sides. Tempests blew with great violence; fire and stones rained. The cries of "O Sameri! O Jamshed!" rose from the battleground. Corpse piled over corpse, and the dead lay in heaps. The sorcerers on both sides targeted each other with steel magic balls and the floor of the forest became red with blood as a powerful turmoil unfurled into wholesale carnage.

When the golden-robed emperor[137] moved to its westerly court and the King of Stars[138] – the adornment of heavens – with its starry hordes, ascended the seat of the sky, the armies disengaged themselves from their opponents and returned to their resting places in their respective camps.

Surat Nigar said to Heyrat, "I will now make portraits of Mahrukh's commanders because today I suffered great ignominy at the hands of that inconsequential girl Bahar. None of them will escape my wrath." Heyrat answered, "You may take all the steps you deem appropriate."

While they conversed, the ground cleft and a magic slave appeared and handed a letter to Heyrat. It was from Emperor Afrasiyab, who had written:

> "O Empress, I need to consult you on a matter of importance. Come to the Dome of Light and ask Surat Nigar to postpone the battle for the present."

When Heyrat read the message she said to the magic slave, "Inform the emperor that his command will be carried out." Heyrat asked Surat Nigar to postpone the battle until her return then she sent away the magic slave and dressed and adorned herself for the journey to the Dome of Light.

Heyrat gave injunctions to Sarsar, saying "You are a trickster girl. Make sure that no tricksters attack and cause the least grief to Queen Surat Nigar with their deceptions." Sarsar answered, "Rest assured, no trickster would dare show his face here." After making all these arrangements, Heyrat finally departed and Sarsar remained in the camp to keep watch.

After the armies returned from the battlefield, the tricksters set out on their mission, resolved to attack and kill sorceress Surat Nigar at the first opportunity. Each infiltrated her camp in a different disguise.

Amar entered Surat Nigar's court disguised as a carpet-keeper and started trimming the wicks of the candles. He put drugs on the burning candles and the rising fumes spread, rendering many people unconscious.

Sarsar recognized Amar and said to Surat Nigar, "There is Amar, disguised as the keeper of carpets, trimming the candlewicks." Surat Nigar recited a spell. Two magic slaves emerged from the ground and caught Amar. When they brought him before Surat Nigar, she asked, "Who are you?" Amar answered, "I am the Angel of Death, who extracts sorcerers' souls." Surat Nigar asked, "Didn't you feel the least bit afraid you would forfeit your life by breaking into my camp?" Amar replied, "No one can kill me but God Almighty."

Enraged at these words, Surat Nigar decided to put Amar to death. At that moment, Sarsar said, "Put him in my custody. I will take this trickster before Empress Heyrat." Surat Nigar replied, "Very well, take him."

Meanwhile, cries of "Amar is caught!" had risen from Surat Nigar's camp when Amar was captured by the sorceress. All the tricksters present there in disguise heard this.

Burq the Frank quickly changed his disguise to the trickster girl Saba Raftar and headed for Surat Nigar's pavilion. He saw Sarsar bring Amar from the other side. The false Saba Raftar greeted Sarsar and said, "Where do you take this wretch?" She answered, "To the Dome of Light." The false Saba Raftar said, "You can stay behind and keep watch on the camp. Put him in my custody. I'll take him there." Sarsar was fooled and handed Amar to the false Saba Raftar. Burq led Amar away and after they had gone some distance he cut off Amar's handcuffs and fetters and said, "Master, it's me, your own Burq the Frank."

Amar was greatly pleased at Burq's cunning. Then Burq returned to guard Mahrukh's camp. Now, Amar disguised himself as Saba Raftar and returned to Heyrat's camp, where he ran into Sarsar again. She asked, "O Saba Raftar, how did you return so quickly?" The false Saba Raftar answered, "I was on my way to the Dome of Light when a magic claw came down and carried Amar Ayyar away, crying, 'I was sent by Emperor Afrasiyab!'"

At this explanation, Sarsar did not ask further questions.

The false Saba Raftar said, "I have a headache. I should get some sleep." She then lay down to rest.

ꙮ

Now hear of the real Saba Raftar. She disguised herself as the trickster Zargham and headed for Queen Mahrukh's camp to arrest Burq the Frank. She saw Burq standing outside his camp and called out to him. But Burq recognized Saba Raftar in Zargham's disguise and rushed at her, dagger drawn. Saba Raftar shot an arrow at Burq, who jumped into the air to dodge it, but the arrow struck and injured his big toe. Yet, Burq continued chasing Saba Raftar. She ran toward her camp, removing Zargham's disguise as she ran, lest her camp mistake her for the enemy trickster, and sought refuge in Surat Nigar's pavilion.

Surat Nigar and Sarsar had recently seen Amar in Saba Raftar's disguise. When they saw another Saba Raftar enter the pavilion they arrested her. When Saba Raftar told Sarsar the secret codes with which the trickster girls recognized each other, Sarsar realized that she was the real Saba Raftar.

Amar Ayyar, who lay close by disguised as Saba Raftar, heard this conversation and ran to escape. As the trickster girls Sarsar and Saba Raftar gave him chase, he threw drug bombs at them. The two trickster girls jumped back to evade them but the drug-filled smoke had already spread all around. Before they had gone any distance, one of them fell unconscious by a lakeside and another at the foot of a mountain.

Instead of following them, Amar now changed into Sarsar's disguise and returned to Surat Nigar's pavilion and said to her, "O Queen, I will show you a marvel if you would accompany me." Surat Nigar accompanied Amar, taking him for the trickster girl. Amar brought her to the edge of the camp and then hit her in the face with an egg of oblivion, bundled her up, and carried her away.

In the meanwhile, the real Sarsar and Saba Raftar regained consciousness. They returned to their camp and heard cries that someone had kidnapped Surat Nigar. The two of them ran to pursue the culprit.

Amar, in the meanwhile, resolved to kill Surat Nigar but the moment he attempted to do so, the Earth shook and horrible cries rose. Amar realized that Surat Nigar was a powerful sorceress and he would not be able to kill her by himself. He decided to take her to his camp and headed there, planning to kill her with the help of other sorcerers and sorceresses.

The trickster girl Sarsar did not follow Amar but headed for Queen Mahrukh's court instead. She entered there in the disguise of Burq the Frank and said to the queen, "Please come with me to the border of the camp. Amar wishes to see you there." As Mahrukh never denied her tricksters' requests, she accompanied the false Burq. When they reached a deserted corner Sarsar hit Mahrukh in the face with an egg of oblivion, made her unconscious and hid her in a nook in the wilderness. Then she returned to Mahrukh's camp in the queen's disguise and said to the attendants, "I am resting in the front courtyard. Should Amar Ayyar come and ask for me, send him there." Then the false Mahrukh lay down in the courtyard and pretended to be asleep.

In the meanwhile, Amar arrived at his camp carrying the bundle of Surat Nigar. When he asked for Mahrukh, the attendants guided him to the courtyard. Amar woke up the false Mahrukh and laid the bundle before her, saying, "O Queen, I have brought you Surat Nigar a prisoner."

The false Mahrukh said, "She will not die easily. In my bedchamber lies my sorcerer's bag in which I keep the magic devices of Sameri. If you bring me the magic steel ball from that bag I will be able to kill her."

While Amar went to Mahrukh's bedchamber to bring the magic steel ball, Sarsar lifted Surat Nigar's bundle onto her shoulders, slit the pavilion panels with her dagger and escaped. Once she had put a safe distance between herself and Mahrukh's camp, she called out, "Sarsar Swordfighter is my name! Regard, O Amar, how trickeries are performed and how I fool people by throwing dust into their eyes!"

The camp guards and sorcerers ran to catch her and a commotion arose. Amar also rushed out when he heard that Sarsar had carried away the bundle in Mahrukh's disguise. His heart sank when he thought that Sarsar may have killed Mahrukh, which was why she had been resting so comfortably in the camp in her disguise. Amar ran after Sarsar with great trepidation.

Meanwhile, the sorcerers chasing Sarsar began reciting spells to catch her by magic. In anticipation, Sarsar restored Surat Nigar to consciousness. When she came to her senses she saw Mahrukh's sorcerers and Amar Ayyar running toward her. She picked up a handful of soil from the ground and began reciting a spell to ward them off. Seeing this, Amar called out to his men, "Run for your lives. She is a powerful sorceress and will kill all of you."

Some of Mahrukh's sorcerers flew into the sky by invoking magic, others sank into the ground. Amar ran away but kept shouting, "O Sarsar, I swear by my fidelity to Hamza that I will kill you if you have harmed Mahrukh."

Sarsar made no reply.

Amar ran toward Surat Nigar's camp, entered it in an attendant's disguise, and awaited Surat Nigar in her pavilion. Before long, the sorceress arrived there with Sarsar. Once she settled down she asked Sarsar, "What did you do to Mahrukh?" Sarsar answered, "I left her unconscious in the wilderness." Surat Nigar said, "Go and bring her to me." When Sarsar left, Amar followed her. As Sarsar came out of the camp, Amar called out, "Where do you go?" Sarsar ran in terror upon hearing Amar Ayyar's voice because Amar had sworn to kill her.

Amar threw his snare rope at Sarsar, who jumped to escape its coils but her head bumped into tree branches and she fell down. Amar tied her up and drew his dagger to slit her throat. Sarsar looked into Amar's eyes and said meekly, "Yes, O Amar, indeed you have every right to kill me." As Amar was besotted with her, his eyes welled up with tears at her words and he asked, "Tell me, O Sarsar, what happened to Mahrukh?"

Before Sarsar could answer, one of Afrasiyab's subjects, a sorcerer named Naqus the Trumpeter appeared on the scene from the nearby mountain pass. Seeing Amar, he recited a spell, arrested him, and released Sarsar, whom he recognized as the emperor's trickster girl. Sarsar escaped and ran for two miles in fear for her life. When she stopped to rest she heard someone call, "There's nowhere you can run from me." When Sarsar turned to look she saw Qiran the Ethiope coming after her, wielding his cleaver. Sarsar again ran. But Qiran stopped in his tracks and did not follow her when he saw sorcerer Naqus the Trumpeter arrive there, leading Amar a prisoner.

Qiran quickly disguised himself as a sorcerer and called out to him, "Who are you? Why have you entered this land, which is under my writ?" Naqus the Trumpeter said, "Do not become upset my brother. I am taking the emperor's fugitive, Amar Ayyar, a prisoner to his court." The false sorcerer approached Naqus and said, "That may be, but who is that other sorcerer behind you?" As Naqus turned to look, Qiran struck with his cleaver, shattering Naqus's skull to pieces. His magic spirits cried and made a tumult and Amar was released.

As Amar made his way back through the wilderness, he saw Burq the Frank exchanging sword blows with Saba Raftar while Mahrukh Magic-Eye lay tied in a bundle on the ground.

It so happened that Saba Raftar passed the place in the wilderness where Mahrukh lay unconscious. Saba Raftar tied her up in a bundle and headed for her camp. In the meanwhile, Burq arrived there and challenged her. Now, seeing Amar arrive, Saba Raftar became unnerved. As her attention was diverted toward Amar, Burq found a chance to make her unconscious with an egg of oblivion. She fell down and Burq made her into a bundle. He then restored Mahrukh to consciousness and said, "You may now safely return to the camp but do not be duped in this manner in future."

After Mahrukh Magic-Eye returned to her camp, the tricksters disguised themselves – Amar as Saba Raftar and Burq the Frank as Mahrukh. The false Saba Raftar made a bundle of the false Mahrukh and, carrying her across his shoulders, entered Surat Nigar's pavilion and put the bundle before the sorceress, saying, "I present Mahrukh Magic-Eye before you as a prisoner." Surat Nigar was delighted to hear this. She richly rewarded the false Saba Raftar. When Surat Nigar ordered that Mahrukh be restored to consciousness, Amar signalled to Burq to become conscious.

In the meanwhile, Surat Nigar stepped out to attend the call of nature. To her pavilion's right was a staircase where seven magic slave girls made by Empress Heyrat were deputed. They came down from the staircase. One of them said, "Surat Nigar seems very happy today." Another said, "She is happy because Saba Raftar brought her Mahrukh a prisoner." The third said, "It is not something to be happy about." The fourth magic slave girl said, "Shall I reveal the secret?" The fifth said, "I will tell you the whole story." The sixth one said, "What would you tell?" The seventh magic slave girl said, "Stop talking nonsense, o wretches. What was destined to happen came to pass. It is neither Saba Raftar nor is it Mahrukh. It is Amar Ayyar disguised as Saba Raftar who brought Burq the Frank disguised as Mahrukh." When Surat Nigar heard this she quickly attended to the call of nature and returned to her pavilion.

Now, Amar too, had been listening to the conversation of the magic slave girls. He quickly disguised himself as Sarsar. As Surat Nigar entered the pavilion, Amar signalled to Burq to get up and run out. The false Sarsar called out, "O Queen, I am Sarsar. When I arrived

Amar ran away at the sight of me. Now Burq too escapes. Catch him!" Surat Nigar ran after Burq and Amar followed her disguised as Sarsar. When Surat Nigar was far from her camp Amar made her unconscious with an egg of oblivion, quickly bundled her up and brought her into Mahrukh's court.

Mahrukh ordered all her sorcerer commanders to gather and kill Surat Nigar with a hail of magic arrows. The commanders began gathering at her orders.

In the meanwhile, Sarsar entered Surat Nigar's pavilion and learned that someone had kidnapped the sorceress. Sarsar immediately set out and entered Mahrukh's camp in an attendant's disguise. While Mahrukh's commanders made preparations to kill Surat Nigar, Sarsar approached the sorceress, who lay bundled up, and hit her in the face with an egg of awareness.

Surat Nigar came to her senses and, reciting a spell on a magic ball, hurled it at Mahrukh. Then Surat Nigar flashed like lightning and struck Mahrukh's throne. Mahrukh dove into the ground to foil her attack and her son, sorcerer Shakeel, hit Surat Nigar with a magic citron. It injured Surat Nigar's foot but she still managed to fly away carrying Sarsar in her magic claw.

As Surat Nigar entered her pavilion, she found Empress Heyrat had recently returned from the Dome of Light. Surat Nigar said to her, "Since you left, the tricksters have shown no let up in attacks. If Sarsar hadn't risked her life to save me, I would have died." Heyrat conferred a resplendent robe of honor on Sarsar and listened to the account of the tricksters.

Sorcerer Baran the Rain-Master

At that moment, a magic slave arrived and handed Heyrat a message that informed her that the Emperor of Hoshruba was approaching. The empress made preparations and went out to greet him.

After a moment, Afrasiyab's conveyance arrived with great pomp and majesty. Everyone present paid him their respects. Afrasiyab entered the pavilion and sat on the throne. After he heard a complete account of the tricksters' attacks, he said to Surat Nigar, "You put yourself to all this trouble for no reason. Now you may rest and watch."

Afrasiyab recited a spell and struck his hands. Immediately, a sorcerer emerged from the earth and bowed before Afrasiyab, who said to him, "O sorcerer Baran the Rain-Master, go and destroy Mahrukh's camp, but take Princess Khubsurat to the magic Ferris wheel beside the banks of the River of Salt and incarcerate her there." After giving these orders Afrasiyab remained there a little while longer, then mounted his conveyance and departed for the Apple Garden.

In the meanwhile, a separate pavilion was provided for sorcerer Baran, who mustered his army. After he made his preparations, he barged into the court of Mahrukh Magic-Eye and occupied a vacant seat. He addressed the court thus: "O group of ingrates, I have come to punish you for you rebelled against the emperor's authority."

When Amar heard these words he threw his snare rope at Baran. But the sorcerer took the form of a cloud and escaped out of the loops of Amar's snare rope. Then he thundered and struck, carrying away Princess Khubsurat the Beauty.

Mahrukh's sorcerers threw magic citrons and magic coconuts but they could not stop Baran. He flew away with Khubsurat to the banks of the River of Salt and put the princess on the magic Ferris wheel, imprisoning her there as before.

Prince Shakeel was beside himself with grief at Khubsurat's capture. He made plaints, cried, wept, and recited love verses. Amar comforted him and asked Mahrukh, "What is the special magic of Baran the Rain-Master?" She replied, "He causes showers. Anyone on whom even a single drop of his rain falls turns into a tree. Baran was once under the authority of sorcerer Raad Thunder-Clap and his mother, sorceress Mehshar Lightning-Bolt. They were his commanders. Had they not been imprisoned, Baran wouldn't have dared to show his face here." Amar said, "I will now go to free Raad and Mehshar. If possible, I will also secure Khubsurat's release."

With these words, Amar left. Once out of the camp, he blew his trickster's whistle and all the tricksters presented themselves. Amar enjoined all of them to search for Raad Thunder-Clap and sorceress Mehshar, and the tricksters left in search of them.

Sorcerer Baran the Rain-Master returned to his pavilion from the River of Salt and began preparations for battle. When Sun's spring flowed into the River of the West and the luminous brook of the Milky Way began coursing through the sky, the blast of Turkic flutes and war bugles rose from sorcerer Baran's camp. The noise reached the august ears of Queen Mahrukh Magic-Eye, who ordered that the call to war be answered from her camp. The timbales of war now rumbled in both camps. The warriors burnished their weapons; sorcerers invoked spells, made sacrifices to magic spirits, and lit the worship fires. For four watches of the night the two camps remained gripped by similar commotion.

When the Hindu of the Skies performed its worship and left the dome of heavens, and the Idol Worshipper of the East, carrying its golden disk, entered the idol house of the skies,[139]

The sky put on the bright veil of the sun
The bride of the sky revealed its brightest jewel
The umbrella of the night folded up
And dawn conquered the night

In the morning, the two sanguinary, blood-thirsty armies filed into the arena with great majesty and grandeur. Queen Mahrukh and sorcerer Baran positioned themselves in the center of their respective armies. The battle drums beat constantly. After the battle arrays were formed, a sorcerer came out from sorcerer Baran's ranks and sought combat.

Sorceress Surkh Mu Wonder-Mane emerged from the other side to answer his challenge and hurled a steel magic ball that shot through the enemy sorcerer's chest. Before long, Mahrukh's sorcerers and sorceresses had killed several of Baran's army commanders.

Baran the Rain-Master became enraged at the slaughter of his commanders. He rode into the arena, recited a spell and blew it skywards. Suddenly, dark clouds rose from the mountainside and rain clouds flew in from all corners and covered Mahrukh's army. Then it started raining on Mahrukh's camp. Everyone on whom a drop of rain fell turned into a tree and sprouted leaves. Renowned sorcerers of Mahrukh's camp recited counterspells but they proved ineffectual.

At that moment, Princess Bahar came forward carrying a bouquet of flowers. Baran realized that if he allowed Bahar an opportunity to invoke her magic she would make him frenzied with her spells. He flew toward Bahar and sprinkled her with some soil from the grave of Jamshed that he carried with him. Princess Bahar fell unconscious.

Now Baran recited a spell and struck his hands and the rain came down more heavily. Mahrukh's warriors began turning into trees in greater numbers. A stampede began and a great majority of them retreated to save themselves from such a fate.

In the meanwhile, Baran led his army back to its camp to the notes of triumph and victory. As Baran was certain that the tricksters would attack him in his camp before long, he did not stay there. He headed for a spot near the region of Batin where he made a magic pond and hid himself at the bottom.

When the tricksters saw the plight of their camp they decided that instead of going in search of Raad and sorceress Mehshar, they should first find and kill Baran the Rain-Master. They immediately set out on their mission.

Previously, it has been mentioned that Burq and Amar left Saba Raftar unconscious and tied up in a bundle in the wilderness to arrest Surat Nigar in her disguise. When she regained consciousness, she called out to passersby to release her and told them that thieves had left her tied up there. Finally, a man released Saba Raftar and she headed back to the camp. On the way, she encountered the group of tricksters going on their mission to kill Baran.

The tricksters were preoccupied and avoided her but Burq the Frank threw his snare rope at Saba Raftar and she fell down entangled. However, even as she fell, Saba Raftar hit Burq with an egg of oblivion and he became unconscious. After some time Burq regained consciousness and noticed that the loops of his snare rope had become knotted around Saba Raftar's neck. Afraid that she might die of strangulation, Burq began untying them out of consideration that Saba Raftar was Qiran's beloved. After he had untied the knots, Saba Raftar cried, "Ah my arm is broken!" In panic, Burq released her and Saba Raftar took one leap and escaped.

Now Burq too, headed out to kill Baran. But the first to reach the place where Baran was hiding was Zargham. Seeing the trickster arrive, Baran began reciting a spell. When Zargham saw this he ran to escape but Baran caught him by magic and brought him to the pond to kill him. Before he could carry out his plans, however, a magic slave arrived to give him Afrasiyab's message. It read:

> "O Baran, bring the people you have arrested, including Mahrukh and the others, to the banks of the River of Flowing Blood. Amar Ayyar will come there in an attempt to release them and I will arrest him as well. I will then send for the devil designate of Lord Laqa, Bakhtiarak, to come to the tilism and kill Amar with his own hands. I had invited Lord Laqa's devil designate once before but suffered great embarrassment. Now I want satisfaction for that occasion."

When Baran read the letter, he got out of the pond and returned to his camp with Zargham. He ordered his camp to march and loaded Mahrukh's soldiers, who had been transformed into trees, onto carts and brought them along under strict guard.

When Baran arrived at the banks of the River of Flowing Blood he set up his pavilion by the riverside and ordered the prisoners be unloaded and placed within sight of his pavilion. He threw Zargham too, among the prisoners. Then Baran sat down in his pavilion in great comfort and luxury.

The other tricksters tracking Baran followed his army and arrived at his camp. Jansoz entered his pavilion in a sorcerer's disguise but the moment he entered Baran recognized him and put him under the same magic incarceration as Zargham. Then Baran wrote a message to Afrasiyab, which read:

> "As ordered by My Lord and Master, this humble servant has arrived at the banks of the River of Flowing Blood with the emperor's prisoners."

When Afrasiyab received the message he said to sorceress Khumar, "O Princess, all the rebels have been arrested by the grace of Lord Sameri. Only Amar Ayyar and a couple of tricksters are still at large. You already know Amar from the time he shaved your head. Find him and bring him a prisoner by any means possible. You suffered great humiliation on account of him when you went to Lord Laqa's court to bring the devil designate, Bakhtiarak, here. Now, if you can capture Amar, our shame will be washed away." Khumar answered, "Very well, I now go in search of him and will bring him to you a prisoner." Afrasiyab now turned toward Khumar's sister, Makhmur Crimson-Eye, and said to her, "You too, should go along to help your sister."

It was previously reported that both sisters were Afrasiyab's beloveds, but the fear of Empress Heyrat had kept them from giving in to his advances. The sorceresses left after receiving their orders and went in different directions to look for Amar.

Sorceress Khumar crossed over the Bridge of Magic Fairies and arrived near Baran's camp. She found Amar in the wilderness disguised as a wizard and called out to him, "O wizard, stop awhile and tell me how you fare." When Amar saw Khumar and heard her words, he realized she had recognized him. He immediately put on the cape of invisibility and disappeared. Sorceress Khumar looked all around for him but could not find him.

Finally, she headed for sorcerer Baran's pavilion. He welcomed Khumar and offered her a seat of honor with great deference. Then he asked the reason for her visit. Khumar told him she had come in search of Amar and said, "Now I will invoke my magic and no matter where

Amar is hiding, by its power, he will arrive here by himself. But do send a sandalwood seat for me on which I can sit and prepare the spell." Baran ordered his servants to provide Khumar with a sandalwood seat. Khumar occupied herself with her preparations and with washing and bathing herself.

Amar Ayyar, who had disappeared from Khumar's sight by putting on the cape of invisibility, finally removed it after he saw the sorceress discontinue her search.

He saw a macebearer come out of Baran's camp. Amar approached him in a sorcerer's disguise and said, "Where are you headed, my dear friend?" The macebearer said, "I was deputed at the entrance of sorcerer Baran's pavilion. My shift is now over. I am going home." Amar took out a fruit from his pocket and offered it to the macebearer, saying, "This fruit is hanging from the trees in the forest in the thousands; have a bite. You will never have eaten a better tasting fruit." When the macebearer heard such praise of the fruit, he accepted, ate it, and fell unconscious. Amar hid him in a cave, removed the macebearer's clothes, dressed himself in them, and put on his disguise.

Then Amar went and stood at the entrance of Baran's pavilion. At that very moment a sorcerer came out. The false macebearer asked, "Are there any orders for me?" The sorcerer replied, "Our master requires a sandalwood seat for sorceress Khumar. She will sit on it and invoke her magic." The false macebearer looked on as two sorcerers brought a sandalwood seat. When the sorcerer sent by Baran took the chair inside, Amar put on the cape of invisibility and followed.

Sorceress Khumar finished bathing, put on a waistcloth and sat down on the sandalwood seat with all the apparatus for making spells lying before her: swallow wort, thorn apples, sweet marjoram leaves, balsam, fumigation agents, mustard seeds, cotton seeds, black kite, and a fork-tailed shrike. She made a worship fire and, after making offerings of wine and swine, began reciting spells.

Amar sat on the sandalwood seat behind her wearing the cape of invisibility. As Khumar's spell was meant to summon Amar and he was already there and invisible, those gathered to witness the power of Khumar's spells saw they showed no results. Khumar learned nothing about Amar with her magic. Because she could not see Amar she thought her magic had failed her when it told her that he was there. In the end, Khumar said to Baran with great frustration, "I can't find any trace of Amar Ayyar." He answered, "He is no ordinary mortal who can be summoned by your spells. He is consummate in his art. Even Lord Sameri praised him in the *Book of Sameri*."

While they were having this conversation, the macebearer whom Amar had drugged unconscious regained his senses. He recalled that before losing consciousness he had felt a tingling sensation as if his soul were departing his body. He reckoned that he had died and had now been resurrected as people believed, but that it was his dead body, not he who lay there.

He tried to move his limbs and, seeing he could exercise them, he stepped out of the cave in great anxiety – and completely naked because Amar had taken away his clothes. The macebearer headed in the direction of the camp, looking all around him with eyes of wonder. But then it occurred to him that dead men do not walk and he quickly lay down on the ground.

After some time, he reasoned with himself that, now that he had control over his senses, he must not keep lying on the ground. He started again. When he arrived near Baran's camp he came across one of his friends, who asked, "Brother, why are you walking around naked?" The macebearer only then realized that he was naked and appeared thus to other people, but he remembered being fully dressed when he lost consciousness. He said to himself, *Indeed, I have died. And certain it is that I was not buried in a winding-sheet but thrown naked into a hole.*

Because he considered himself dead, he did not answer his friend, thinking that the dead did not speak. As he tried to turn away, his friend held him by his wrist and said, "Why do you walk away without answering?" The macebearer asked, "Do you see me?" His friend replied, "Very clearly. You stand before me completely naked. Do you take me for a blind man?" The macebearer said, "My brother, I am dead. You are my friend and I do not wish to hurt you, otherwise I would have killed you by now."

When his friend heard these words he ran away in terror, realizing that thousands of people had been killed in the tilism and there was a good chance the macebearer had become a ghost. Seeing his friend run in terror, the macebearer became fully convinced that he was the ghost of a dead man.

From there he headed for sorcerer Baran's pavilion. The sorcerer was incensed to see him barge naked into his pavilion. The sorceresses present there also screamed and rose to avoid the embarrassing scene. Baran shouted, "O insolent clown, what is the meaning of this?" The macebearer asked, "First, tell me whether I am alive or dead." Baran laughed when he heard him say that. The sorcerer's companions too, rolled about in ecstasies of mirth and made even more fun of the macebearer.

Baran the Rain-Master said to them, "He appears to be suffering the results of exercising his powers of imagination to the limits. The doctors have said that imagination is a creative faculty and engenders nightmares. Gradually, one begins to lose consciousness and can start biting. Sometimes this is the result of an imagined grief or excessive joy and happiness. Sometimes it is engendered by the passion of love and overwhelming desire that suffers the heart to become heated. In this case, it appears it was grief that caused his symptoms."

Baran asked the macebearer to approach. He offered him words of consolation and comfort, and asked, "Tell me, how do you pass your days? Did you recently meet with some accident?" The macebearer replied, "I met a man along the way who offered me some fruit and I died after eating it."

Baran turned to Khumar and said, "Witness this, O Khumar. Amar Ayyar only made him unconscious but it was his doubt that made him believe he was dead. But it is a wonder that Amar was close by and did not come when you cast spells and summoned him by your magic. It must be ineffectual magic that you deployed."

Khumar was greatly embarrassed at these words from Baran.

Baran diagnosed the macebearer's imagination to be suffering from some setback. In order to dispel the thought from the macebearer's mind and cast away his anxiety, he ordered that the macebearer be executed.

When the executioner arrived with his shining blade, the macebearer said to himself, *Had I been dead I would have disappeared from the eyes of people. They could not have ordered me killed. Therefore, I must be alive. I will lose my life for nothing now; I should plead for mercy.* He immediately began importuning Baran for mercy.

Baran said to all assembled there, "Regard that when exposed to danger his intellectual faculty overcame his imaginative powers and he became well again." Baran's companions praised him highly. Baran gave some money to the macebearer and told him that he had been drugged by a trickster. When he heard these words the macebearer became fully recovered and left.

Amar also left, wearing his cape of invisibility and went into the wilderness.

A humiliated Khumar now invoked a spell that caused a cloud of magic smoke to appear. Khumar said to it, "O magic smoke, bring me Amar Ayyar wherever you find him!" The magic smoke departed at her orders.

Because Amar had taken off the cape of invisibility upon entering the wilderness, the magic smoke found him. It wrapped itself around Amar and took him away twisting like a whirlwind and brought him before sorceress Khumar in Baran's pavilion. She said to him, "O Amar, you have killed thousands of sorcerers and have shaved my head as well. Now tell me yourself, what should be your reward?"

Amar answered, "My work is indeed what you just described, and the person who pays my price will have my utmost fidelity. My current master, Hamza, sent me into the tilism to cause death and destruction among its inhabitants. If you hire me instead, I will perform the same services for you with equal vigor." Khumar said, "O sly thief, don't imagine that you can fool me with these words. Now I will take you to Afrasiyab, who will invite Lord Laqa's devil designate to behead you."

Amar was unnerved upon hearing this but he steeled his heart and said, "Jabber all you like, O whore! For all I know, Afrasiyab's death is near since you are taking me to see him. Last time I only shaved your head. This time I will slice your nose, too." Enraged, Khumar hurled a stone at Amar and he fell down unconscious. Khumar bundled him up in a sheet, took her leave of sorcerer Baran, and headed for Afrasiyab's court.

The tricksters in Baran's camp had heard the news of Amar's capture from the soldiers. When they saw the sorceress carrying away a bundle, Burq the Frank and Qiran the Ethiope followed her from different paths.

Burq was challenged by the trickster girls Sarsar, Saba Raftar and Tez Nigah, who surrounded him. He fought with them but he was outnumbered. Sarsar hit him in the face with an egg of oblivion and tied him up. Suddenly, a magic claw came down like lightning and carried away the trickster girls along with Burq.

The next moment, the trickster girls found themselves in sorceress Surat Nigar's pavilion. They saluted her and asked, "Why did you send for us?" She replied, "O Sarsar, ever since you secured my release from the tricksters by risking your life, I commissioned a magic claw to accompany you and carry you away whenever you are challenged by Amar and his tricksters."

Sarsar replied, "There is no denying the great kindness the queen of the world has shown with her consideration. But we are tricksters. You do not know of our plans and strategies. If the magic claw were to carry us away in this manner we would be unable to perform our duties. We request you keep the magic claw from doing so or else we must excuse ourselves from your service."

Surat Nigar was embarrassed to hear Sarsar's words and stopped the magic claw from accompanying the trickster girls. Then she rebuked and lambasted Burq the Frank. Afterwards, she recited a spell whereupon sorcerer Zalim Black-Face approached flying. Surat Nigar said to him, "O Zalim Black-Face, take this trickster into your custody and imprison him, along with sorceress Mehshar and Raad."

Sorcerer Zalim flew away carrying Burq and passed over Baran's camp where trickster Qiran saw him and followed him clandestinely. After traveling some distance, he saw the trickster girls coming. Qiran said to himself, *I must not accost them on this occasion lest I am also captured as I am the only trickster left free.* He changed his direction and followed sorcerer Zalim Black-Face from another path. Sarsar saw him and said to her companions, "Qiran never avoided us until this day. It is best that we leave him to his own devices." They continued on their way.

Qiran kept following Zalim, who arrived in a desolate and terrible wilderness in which a palatial dome stood. The sorcerer recited a spell and struck his hands. A window appeared in the dome, Zalim went inside carrying Burq and the window closed behind him.

Left standing outside, Qiran soon thought of some trickery. He tied a waistcloth, smeared himself in dust and, eating a clod of earth, arrived before the dome and started shouting like a madman. "A pigeon sits on the dome. A deer swallows it. A camel is in the deer's tail. The horse eats the elephant. The eagle carries it away. A donkey sits on my head. Here! Take this! This pearl! Look here now! Bravo, O wretch! Look at you dance! The whole house inside the ear! Eat the bed on the head! The season of the wind fills up! Death gives a litter! The night lays an egg! The morning couples with the lizard!"

Perplexed at hearing someone shout such nonsense, sorcerer Zalim came out to investigate and saw a raggedly dressed man in a frenzied state standing there. Zalim approached Qiran and said, "What are you shouting? You scream to no purpose." Qiran replied, "If you were not blind you would see why I shout. Eat this clod of earth and your eyes will open up."

Zalim reckoned that the man must be one of the Lord's favored ones and he must not refuse what is offered. Zalim took a bite from the clod of earth, which Qiran had mixed with a sweet drug. Discovering the sweet taste of the clod, Zalim became convinced that the madman was indeed one of his Lord's favored creatures. Zalim Black-Face ate up the entire thing and soon fell unconscious.

Qiran immediately beheaded him. The dome crashed into pieces and disappeared. Qiran saw Raad Thunder-Clap, sorceress Mehshar Lightning-Bolt, Princess Almas Fairy-Face and Burq the Frank lying unconscious on the ground. He sprinkled their faces with water and they regained consciousness. All of them asked Qiran how he had secured their release. Qiran told them about his killing sorcerer Zalim Black-Face and also gave them the news of their camp. He told them that sorcerer Baran had arrested all of their companions and the whole camp lay destroyed and ruined.

Sorceress Mehshar said furiously, "How cunning of Afrasiyab to send Baran to attack after we were captured. And that wretch Baran also styles himself a great sorcerer now! He gives himself a lot of airs. But now he has asked for his death. He exists because of us and from our strength. Now I shall encounter him and see what that bastard can do. If I do not kill him instantly I will renounce my name." Thus speaking, Mehshar Lightning-Bolt left with Raad.

Qiran drugged Almas Fairy-Face unconscious and made her into a bundle. Then he and Burq went toward Baran's camp.

In the meanwhile, Afrasiyab wrote to Baran asking him to bring all the prisoners across the River of Flowing Blood into the region of Batin so that they may be killed. Baran the Rain-Master prepared boats and ordered his sorcerers to load the belongings of the camp and the captives for the passage across.

As Baran stood at the River of Flowing Blood giving orders to his men, sorceress Mehshar Lightning-Bolt and Raad Thunder-Clap arrived overhead. Baran the Rain-Master ran in terror when he saw Mehshar approach, flashing, and Raad come rumbling. Raad immediately sunk into the ground and the next instant rose beside Baran and screamed. Baran fell unconscious to the ground and sorceress Mehshar struck him, cleaving him in two, as she sank into the ground. A doomsday-like clamor rose. Thunderous noises and darkness spread far and wide at his dying.

Mahrukh, Bahar and other commanders of their camp who had turned into trees returned to human form and regained their senses. All of them were already armed with their magic devices and sorcerer's bags as they had all fallen under Baran's spell on the battlefield. They immediately attacked Baran's camp.

Bahar threw a bouquet of flowers causing a spring spell. The trees in the wilderness bloomed and flowered. Vast gardens full of redolent herbs and plants and dark red tulips appeared on all sides. Flocks of birds crowded the tree branches. The captivating songs of the songbirds filled the air. Spring manifested itself, prancing and preening like a peacock, and everywhere myriad-colored flowers bloomed.

The sorcerers in Baran's army fell under Bahar's spell and forgot all about fighting and counterspells. They were showered with magic citrons, magic coconuts and magic limes by Mahrukh's camp. Princess

Nafarman targeted them with hails of arrows. Mahrukh hurled steel magic balls at them. In no time, another river of blood began flowing beside the River of Flowing Blood.

Bodies fell over each other. Corpses piled up. The magic swords struck and snuffed out lives and bathed their victims in gore and dust. A terrible calamity was unfolding for sorcerer Baran's camp and death did not allow any one of them to escape.

In writing these lines here
My heart became clear of sorrow's dust
Mahrukh set out like a flame
Galloping on her steed made from the wind
Like the hungry lion goes toward sheep
The army of tyrants their self-possession lost
With blood so full was her blade
It looked like a crescent on a gory night
In any which direction she galloped her steed
Ranks of champions she cut down in swathes
The eagle of death above her foe hovered
And souls out of bodies like birds flew
From the barrage of arrows that flew across the sky
The stars became wounded and bled
The earth became a swelling sea of blood
In which swords like raging waves flashed
One could not see the ground for blood
Unbloodied was left not a patch of ground

None was left alive in Baran's camp. But as they were at the banks of the River of Flowing Blood and within easy reach of Afrasiyab's renowned sorcerers on the other side of the river, Queen Mahrukh did not stay there long after the carnage and turned back to her encampment. Except for Amar, who was captured by sorceress Khumar, all other tricksters were freed and accompanied Mahrukh.

Sorcerer Guhar Bar the Pearl-Rainer and Sorceress Sadaf the Oyster

It was already night by the time they began their march. The luminous moon with its army of stars descended into the arena of the heavens and the great star hid its face from fear. After marching for some twenty miles, Mahrukh's army realized they had lost their way. Mahrukh said, "It appears from the sights we see around us that we are in the region of Batin. Let us take another direction lest we are captured. It will be very difficult to escape if we are lost here." Bahar answered, "You speak true. Let us hurry and leave."

They changed direction and headed to their right. After they had marched another twenty miles, they saw a majestic palace that was lavishly appointed. It was draped with curtains of green, red and yellow Kashan velvet.[140] Its doors were carved of sandalwood, and it had canopies of gold brocade and screens of pearl strings. Dew-catchers covered its roof while jewel-encrusted gold and silver water basins were installed outside. Many-colored glass lights, chandeliers, glass shades, lustres and crystal shades made in the shape of lotus flowers illuminated the palace. For miles on end, the expanse was decorated with colored crystal bowls potted with blossoming roses, tulips, narcissi, jasmines and poppies. Peacocks and pheasants preened themselves at the acclivity of the mountains that surrounded the place. Watercourses crisscrossed that most captivating and blossoming expanse and waterfalls cascaded down from the mountains in sheets.

A wondrous palace whose doors
With gold brocade canopies were equipped
It was adorned with gold-threaded screens and curtains
And outdoors, spring humbly stood
The silver strings stretched through the palace
Like moonbeams across the sky
The screens like the eyelashes
Enmeshed and hindered the vision
The feet of desire were tempted
By the velvet carpet spread indoors
Where the redolent unguents burned
Perfuming night and day the mind
With a gold thread carpet the ground was covered
From the Earth to the sky it shone
Earth's surface and the face of the sky
Like the gold and silver foils it made
All white were the doors and roofs
Every arch appeared the morn of hope
Both Earth and sky were made of light
Wherever one turned one's gaze there was light

All of them stopped in that captivating and blooming expanse to revive their spirits with such pleasant sights. Suddenly, a voice called out, "*O Sorceress, watch where you trespass. this is one of the palaces used by the*

Emperor of Hoshruba for his excursions. You must retreat into a nook if you wish to rest here for the night."

Mahrukh said to sorceress Mehshar Lightning-Bolt, "God knows what place this is and whose voice warned us. I never saw this palace in all my life. We are lost and must do all in our power to escape."

Queen Mahrukh and others invoked their magic and rose into the air. They flew left for another twenty miles but no matter which direction they took they saw the same sights and mountains and tulip beds. Before long they had traversed a distance of three days march and yet they found themselves in the same expanse. Finally, they descended and Princess Bahar said to Mahrukh, "God's will be done. We must spend the night here. In the morning we will find our way out. We should not fear anyone because we are no easy prey."

While they conversed, a sorcerer appeared and said, "O Princesses, I recognize you and your friends. You are the ones who rebelled against Afrasiyab. But I have no enmity against you. You may rest here for the night and depart in the morning." Mahrukh asked, "Can we get something to eat?" He answered, "Yes, everything will be provided." After saying that, he left and returned momentarily with platters of food and wine. A carpet was spread on the floor at Mahrukh and Bahar's orders and they sat down to eat and drink.

They asked the sorcerer, "What is your name and the name of this place?" He replied, "My name is Guhar Bar the Pearl-Rainer and I live in the environs. This is Mount Quartz – one of the areas where the Emperor of Hoshruba, Afrasiyab, comes for his excursions. For hundreds of miles the area between the regions of Zahir and Batin are similarly adorned. The River of Flowing Blood flows out of a pass in Mount Quartz. Where you have set camp is within the bounds of the Zahir region."

The sorcerer Guhar Bar stayed with them until it grew late. Then he took his leave and went home and narrated the whole account of Mahrukh's arrival to his mother, sorceress Sadaf the Oyster. She said to him, "My son, you must not allow them to rest here lest Afrasiyab should hear that we offered refuge to his enemies and makes us the target of his approbation." Guhar Bar replied, "They will leave on their own accord in the morning. We have no issue with them and there is no witness to report anything to Afrasiyab." His mother fell silent but later sent a message in secret to Empress Heyrat with a magic slave, containing an entire account of the events that had taken place.

Heyrat came to learn of them and said to her sorceress-aide, Zamarrud, "It appears that sorcerer Baran was killed. But all praise to the glory of Emperor Afrasiyab, we know that Mahrukh and his other enemies are now camped at Mount Quartz. There is nowhere they can run from there." Both her sorceress-aides, Zamarrud and Yaqut answered, "May the calamities that mark you strike us instead. The Emperor of Hoshruba must have ordered his magic to encircle them."

Heyrat mounted her magic peacock and departed for Afrasiyab's court carrying sorceress Sadaf the Oyster's letter. Upon arrival, she sat beside Afrasiyab and gave him sorceress Sadaf's message. Afrasiyab read it and said, "I was also informed by the magic slaves that Baran had been killed and the prisoners set free. Now I have learned that they are camped at Mount Quartz. I will have them captured at once."

Sorcerer Kamil

Afrasiyab recited a spell and struck his hands. A pitch-black, ungainly and ill-fated sorcerer presented himself. Afrasiyab ordered him, saying, "O sorcerer Kamil, the rebels are camped at Mount Quartz. Bring me all of them captive." The sorcerer departed at Afrasiyab's orders. Then Afrasiyab said to another sorcerer, "Go and tell the trickster girls to depart for Mount Quartz and safeguard sorcerer Kamil."

The sorcerer dispatched by Afrasiyab with the message to the trickster girls conveyed the emperor's orders to them and they left on their mission.

Now Afrasiyab said to Heyrat, "I will hold a fair at the Emerald Well in celebration of the rebels' capture and destroy all of them. You should return to your camp and await my orders." The empress departed and arrived at her camp.

Meanwhile, sorcerer Kamil arrived beside Mount Quartz and cried, "Hear O ingrates, there is nowhere you can run now!" He recited a spell on a magic coconut and threw it toward Mahrukh's camp. It burst and released forty magic slaves. They shouted, "*O rebels, your death brought you here!*"

Bahar recited a spell and answered, "Who do you call a rebel? We are the believers of Sameri, Zardhasht and Jamshed, and the loyal subjects of Emperor Afrasiyab." Kamil replied, "You are liars, you ingrates. Were you loyal, this calamity would not have struck you." With these words, he signalled to the magic slaves, who surrounded Mahrukh and her army.

Sorcerer Kamil then threw a second magic coconut and it caused both Mahrukh and Bahar to sink up to their waists into the ground. They recited counterspells but to no avail. The magic slaves chained all of them with one chain and led them onward.

Sorceress Mehshar Lightning-Bolt and Raad, who had slept by the banks of a spring far from Mahrukh and her companions, escaped being imprisoned. When they woke up and returned to where Mahrukh and others had camped they found no one there. They flew in search of them and saw a sorcerer leading them away as prisoners tied with one chain. Seeing this, Raad sank into the ground and emerged beside sorcerer Kamil, who was taken unawares. When Raad screamed, Kamil fell unconscious from the deafening blast. Immediately, sorceress Mehshar struck from the heavens, cleaving Kamil in two, and sinking into the ground.

A terrible roar arose: "*I was Killed, Sorcerer Kamil was my name!*" All forty magic slaves created by Kamil's magic were destroyed at his death. The links of the magic chain fell open and all the prisoners were released.

In the meanwhile, the collar of the morning was rent to reveal the world-illuminating sun. Mahrukh and her companions saw the path back to their camp. They headed toward it in a procession but the tricksters separated and took a separate path so that they might help them in time of need.

Sorceress Chashmak Zan Lightning-Bolt

While Mahrukh and her warriors departed for their camp, Afrasiyab's magic slave girls alerted him that sorcerer Kamil had been killed. He immediately sent for sorceress Chashmak Zan Lightning-Bolt and said to her, "Go and kill every single rebel. Bring me their heads. If you fail or do otherwise, I will punish you severely." In a raging fury Sorceress Chashmak Zan immediately flew away on her mission.

But the trickster girls, who had departed earlier to safeguard Kamil, arrived there first and saw Mahrukh and her army on the way to their camp. They quickly disguised themselves as the tricksters and mingled among the commanders. While they made small talk with Princess Bahar and others, they kept blowing drug powder into the air. Mahrukh's commanders inhaled it, sneezed and fell unconscious.

The trickster girls spread out their trickster mantles and tied up as many as they could carry. Then they hid the others in the bushes to come back for them later, and headed toward Heyrat's court. Sorceress Chashmak Zan arrived there only after they were gone and did not find Mahrukh and her companions. Chashmak Zan's rage and fury against the rebels only increased. She struck a mountain in anger and burned it to its core.

Now Burq the Frank was in the vicinity of that mountain. He saw a sorceress with gold and silver locks hit a mountain with a lightning bolt. Burq decided to kill her and disguised himself as a sorcerer. He tied idols from elbow to shoulder, hung a sorcerer's bag around his neck and wrapped a snake made of pasteboard around his waist. In that guise he went before sorceress Chashmak Zan and said, "O Princess, is anything the matter? Why do you show such anger?"

Taking Burq for a sorcerer, Chashmak Zan narrated the whole account to him and said, "I feel totally powerless. I will now return and tell the emperor that Mahrukh and the others escaped. If he orders me, I will capture them from their own camp." Burq answered, "Indeed, you are as powerful as you describe, but as you have come from afar, do take some rest first. I have some dry fruit that I can offer you should you wish." The sorceress thought a moment then said, "There's no harm in that. We are both as one. There are no formalities between sorcerers." Burq took out drug-laced almonds, raisins and pistachios from his sorcerer's bag and put them before the sorceress.

When the sorceress looked at the dry fruit with her magic gaze, it informed her that she must not eat them because they were drugged. Upon learning this, she angrily caught Burq in her magic claw and flew away and took him to Afrasiyab in the Apple Garden. Chashmak Zan said, "I could find no other, except this trickster."

Afrasiyab reckoned that Chashmak Zan considered herself too delicate and precious and therefore did not search for the rebels, since there was no possibility that she had been unable to find them. He knew they were on their way to their camp. How could they have arrived at their camp before Chashmak Zan could reach them? Afrasiyab waxed wroth with her and said, "O whore, I did not order you to bring me one trickster and not search for your tribe. Get out of my sight and take this trickster to Empress Heyrat!"

Chashmak Zan was petrified by Afrasiyab's censure and took Burq before Heyrat. The empress greeted her, gave her a seat in her court and asked her the reason for her visit. Before Chashmak Zan could answer, a sorcerer presented himself and said, "The trickster girls have arrived carrying bundles." Heyrat asked her sorceress-aide Zamarrud to go to Sarsar's pavilion and inquire who they had brought.

Zamarrud went and returned with the news that the trickster girls had captured Mahrukh and her commanders. When sorceress Chashmak Zan heard this she said to Heyrat, "The emperor is angry with me for not arresting the rebels. If you could ask Sarsar to give them into my custody I will take them before the emperor, receive forgiveness and kill all of the rebels in the emperor's presence." Heyrat said, "You may take them into your custody. I see no harm in that."

From there, Chashmak Zan went to Sarsar and said to her, "Give the prisoners into my custody so that I can take them before the Emperor of the Tilism." Sarsar replied, "You are an example of the crow that eats the fruits of the ringdove's labors.[141] There is no question of your taking the rebels before the emperor. We will take them because we caught them."

The sorceress was angered by Sarsar's reply and began cursing and abusing her. Sarsar signalled to Saba Raftar, who hit Chashmak Zan with an egg of oblivion and she crashed unconscious to the ground.

Sarsar bundled her up and took her before Heyrat and stated the facts. Heyrat became furious with Sarsar and said, "How dare you insult a princess of the tilism? Restore her to consciousness this instant!" Sarsar brought Chashmak Zan to consciousness.

The moment Chashmak Zan regained consciousness she shouted, "O Sarsar, I will flash and strike you momentarily and cut you in two." Heyrat angrily censured, "Yes, kill the trickster girls who risk their lives night and day to protect yours and mine!" Chashmak Zan said, "O Heyrat, ever since you ascended the throne, blinds have fallen over your eyes. You have forgotten your humble days. I have no desire to stay a moment longer in this court."

Sorceress Chashmak Zan quietly removed her spell from Burq the Frank and said to Sarsar before flying away, "I will report your deed to the emperor. Wait till he hears of it."

Hearing these words, Sarsar became frightened and fell at Heyrat's feet to seek her protection. She raised Sarsar and embraced her, saying, "Have no worries. Our heads will fall together."

Now, Heyrat turned toward Burq the Frank and said to him, "Tell me now, what should be your reward?" Burq felt that his body did not feel oppressed but light and realized he was no longer under the magic spell. He answered, "O Empress, since I was brought here it means a few of you must die." Heyrat shouted, "What nonsense you do talk, O wretch." Burq replied, "I speak the very truth. Wherever we tricksters go we are not satisfied until we have plundered many and severed scores of heads."

A furious Heyrat reached for a magic citron with which to hit Burq but he leapt, whacked Sarsar and ran away. The trickster girl ran in pursuit and immediately a hue and cry rose from the camp.

As Burq ran he kept shouting, "Run my friends, the enemy army has attacked." Upon hearing that, Heyrat's whole camp was thrown into turmoil. The sellers began packing their goods. The goldsmiths shouted, "They will have to kill us before they touch our money," and lay down on top of their gold and coins. The women embraced their men, screaming, "For Lord's sake, do not step out of the tent." The men answered, "We will fight if anyone attacks us here. There's no use going out." In short, a great commotion held Heyrat's camp in its grip.

Burq ran into the wilderness where he was finally cornered by Sarsar and they exchanged sword blows. Burq hit Sarsar's wrist with the flat of his sword so as not to sever her arm. The rings on Sarsar's fingers fell off from the expert blow. As Sarsar bent down to pick them up, she got entangled in the snare rope that Burq threw. But at that very moment, Heyrat arrived and, seeing Sarsar caught in the snare rope, flashed and swooped down in the form of a magic claw to save the trickster girl. As Heyrat was out of sorts herself, she did not follow Burq as he ran to escape but instead carried away Sarsar across the River of Flowing Blood into the region of Batin.

Burq returned and picked up Sarsar's rings. He disguised himself as a sorcerer and followed Heyrat across the river. When he arrived at the Bridge of Magic Fairies, the path opened up because of Sarsar's special ring but a guardian of the river ran after Burq shouting, "*O trickster, hand me the ring the emperor has given Sarsar or I will surely kill you.*" Burq took off the ring whose jewel was engraved with Afrasiyab's name and threw it away. But when he took a step forward flames began rising from the river, horrible noises filled the air, and he found his path blocked. Helpless, Burq turned back. He decided that he should help secure the release of his commanders now as he had already heard that Sarsar had brought them captive to Heyrat's camp.

Burq changed his disguise to Sarsar's and entered the trickster girls' pavilion where Saba Raftar sat guarding the bundles made of Mahrukh and her commanders. Saba Raftar witnessed the false Sarsar enter, panting and sweating in a state of great disarray. Her short sword was badly serrated from combat and the bosses on the shield were broken. Seeing her in that condition, Saba Raftar asked, "What happened to you?" The false Sarsar answered, "Did you not hear? I had a fierce sword combat with Burq. Give me the bundles now so that I can take them before Heyrat." With these words, the false Sarsar quickly moved to open the bundles and gave restoratives to Mahrukh, Bahar and others.

When Saba Raftar saw the sorceresses regain consciousness she ran to escape. Mahrukh and a handful of her sorcerers attacked Heyrat's camp with magic citrons and magic limes. In the meanwhile, those of Mahrukh's companions whom the trickster girls had left lying unconscious, regained their senses and arrived in the vicinity as well. Seeing Mahrukh and her companions battling Heyrat's camp, they too charged, wielding their tridents, pentadents and magic devices. Heyrat's camp had already been unnerved by Burq's false rumors earlier. Now, when they found the battle upon them, they fled in utter panic. But the courageous ones among Heyrat's warriors, and Afrasiyab's illustrious sorcerers, fought back bravely.

In fierce skirmishes, swords flashed like lightning. A river of blood flowed in which torsos writhed and heads floated away like bubbles. A rain of fire fell. The magic spirits screeched. Raad Thunder-Clap rose from the earth to shatter the enemy warriors' skulls with his screams. Mehshar Lightning-Bolt flashed and struck, wreaking havoc. A great calamity unfurled itself in Heyrat's camp as noisily as doomsday. The fire of sword blows scorched alive both young and old. In the pitched battle, all distinctions were erased.

On their steeds the fierce lions of battle emerged
Holding aloft their victory-incarnate standards
From the tolling of bells and the beating of drums
The breath was knotted in the world's breast
Like the wind stirs the water surface
The hatred of the foe stirred the warriors' ranks
Like screaming thunder, the relentless army
Killed the foe with its lightning blades
Finished with the carnage in the arena
The braves looted and pillaged the foe
The champions trussed up the booty
And with gold and silver rich became

Mahrukh's remaining army, which lay dispersed in the mountain passes and hills, also joined the fight when the commotion of battle reached their ears.

Finally, Heyrat's camp was defeated and they started to retreat. Mahrukh and her army took possession of the tents and pavilions they had lost in the earlier fight with sorcerer Baran the Rain-Master, and which were now in Heyrat's possession. Afterwards, they returned to their campsite. The queen's lofty pavilion rose as of old, the bazaar was established, shops opened up, the vigils made their rounds and the administrators of the camp took charge.

Mahrukh's noble commanders entered her pavilion. The queen ascended her throne with great majesty and glory. The court had returned to its usual bustle and revels were planned. Fairy-faced dancers presented themselves and began performing. Houri-cheeked cupbearers carrying cups of rose wine circulated among the drinkers to regale and intoxicate them. The tricksters presented themselves and received robes of honor from Queen Mahrukh. Then everyone raised their hands and prayed for Amar Ayyar's release from the clutches of sorceress Khumar.

At that moment, Burq said, "I wished to go across the Bridge of Magic Fairies but I returned to help secure your release. Now I shall resume my mission to secure Amar's." Saying that, Burq departed and the other tricksters also left.

Once Empress Heyrat arrived in Batin carrying Sarsar she stopped and said to the trickster girl, "O Sarsar, I was so bewildered that instead of taking Burq captive I brought you here. Now I am headed for the emperor's court to forestall sorceress Chashmak Zan from igniting his anger after the altercation with you. You should return to the camp."

Sarsar did as she was ordered and Heyrat headed for the Apple Garden.

When the empress arrived, she looked around for Chashmak Zan Lightning-Bolt but did not find her there and reckoned that she must have returned to her land. Heyrat then narrated the entire account of Sarsar and Chashmak Zan's dispute to Afrasiyab.

The emperor said, "I already knew all the details of this incident by magic. O Heyrat, infighting is the first sign of the downfall of an empire. It happens when reason becomes corrupted. What harm was there if Sarsar had given over the captives to Chashmak Zan when she asked for them? How would you like to hear that once you arrived here Burq the Frank restored the sorcerers of his camp to consciousness? Those rebels plundered your camp and now sit in great comfort as they did in theirs before. Not only did we lose our captives, we also have an irate Chashmak Zan on our hands, and the dead to mourn in your camp. All this happened because our dear Sarsar decided to show off her influence and authority. But why did you, being the administrator, allow it to happen and let a trickster girl persuade you against our greater interests? If our subjects were loyal to us they would have realized it was the same whether they or someone else conducted the captives to the court. The purpose of the whole exercise is to kill the enemy by any means possible, but nobody among you cares about that. Return now to your camp and gather together the dispersed army. I await sorceresses Khumar and Makhmur, who have gone to arrest Amar. Once they return with Amar I will send for the devil designate of Lord Laqa's court to kill him because Amar is the hardiest, most recalcitrant rebel of the entire lot. Then I will take care of the others too."

Heyrat was greatly embarrassed by Afrasiyab's censure. Hearing of the destruction of her camp, she hurriedly returned and reassembled the dispersed army.

Heyrat's pavilion was established on the same scale as before. The bazaars opened up and, to hide away the shame of her defeat, the empress ordered a musical assembly at her court. A dance recital began in her camp too.

Now hear of Sarsar. She knew that since Burq the Frank had been released, he would have freed his companions. She crossed the river engrossed in thoughts of returning to Mahrukh's camp to perform some trickery. She made herself up in Amar's likeness and carried on toward Mahrukh's camp. But before she had gone far, she ran into a group of sorcerers. Seeing her in disguise, they reckoned that it must be one of the enemy tricksters and caught her by magic after reciting a spell. Sarsar protested that she was the trickster girl Sarsar and a servant of the Emperor of the Tilism but they did not believe her; one of them took her aside to behead her.

Burq the Frank, who had departed in search of Amar, happened upon that place and saw the sorcerer about to kill a trickster. When he approached he saw Amar's face but upon looking closely he recognized Sarsar.

Burq said to himself, *I should help her get released. She is, after all, my master's beloved.* He quickly disguised himself as a sorcerer and called out to the one holding Sarsar, "Well done, my friend! You performed a great deed by catching this sly thief. Quickly cut off his head." Sarsar looked around perplexed to see which new enemy had arrived on the scene.

Burq approached and said to the sorcerer, "I will cut him into pieces and eat his flesh. He has killed thousands of sorcerers. To kill him and make a magic spirit of such a one would be wonderfully useful."

As Burq came closer, he said softly to Sarsar, "My lady, if you wish I can save you. I am Burq the Frank." Sarsar answered, "Who do you call your lady, O wretch? And what great favor do you wish to do me? I just have to utter the words, 'He is a trickster like me,' and you will instantly be killed too."

Burq was unnerved when he heard this and cursed Sarsar for her ingratitude and threats. But since she was Amar's beloved he felt duty bound to secure her release. He approached the sorcerer and engaged him in conversation. Then, finding an opportunity, he hit him in the face with an egg of oblivion and cut off his head. Immediately, a great noise rose as his magic spirits cried out and proclaimed his death.

Sarsar was released and ran to escape. Burq called out, "Either have your forehead engraved or your nose tip cut off so that people can differentiate between tricksters and trickster girls."

Sarsar answered, "O wretch deserving of beheading, you also dare to make fun of me. It is your ill fate that makes you say that."

Burq said, "My lady, do not be angry now, and forgive me. But do tell me who captured and took away my master." Sarsar answered, "It was sorceress Khumar who captured Amar and took him to the region of Batin. For Amar to be released from there is all but impossible."

Burq answered, "God the True Master is all powerful."

With these words the trickster girl Sarsar and the trickster Burq the Frank parted and went their separate ways.

END OF BOOK 1

Notes

1. *Most Great Name*: according to Muslim tradition God has ninety-nine known names. Besides these God has a name which is revealed only to prophets and saints. It is the Most Great Name of God. A holy guide named Khizr taught God's Most Great Name to Amir Hamza. With its power Amir Hamza can counter and revoke magic but he cannot conquer a tilism with it, nor use it to free someone imprisoned within a tilism.
2. The combination of occult sciences used to create a tilism is called *himia*. Different sources offer different definitions of *himia*. It is generally described as the science of conquering planetary forces and enslaving jinns, and is a combination of at least four occult sciences *simia, kimia*, *limia* and *rimia*. The science of creating illusions and transferring spirits between bodies is *simia*. It manipulates the imagination and presents non-existent and imaginary things to the human eye; the science of the transmutation of physical properties of elements and bringing them to the highest pinnacle of their essence is called *kimia*; the science of runes – letters or words – that cause super-natural effects through interaction with the function of heavenly bodies is called *limia*; and *rimia* is the science of configuring and exploiting the inherent physical forces of the Earth to create extraordinary marvels.
3. Heavens' Hunter: an allusion to the sun.
4. The species of lentil described here is *maash* which is used in Indian magic as a vehicle for producing spells and enchantments.
5. Painter of Creation: an allusion to God.
6. Tasveer: the literal translation of the word *tasveer* is "picture", "portrait" or "image".
7. Omnipotent Causer of Causes: an allusion to God. Note that while the princess herself believes in Laqa, the narrator is a True Believer, and for him only the One God is Omnipotent. He describes the ultimate authority in the universe as such in his narrative. This characteristic sometimes also enters first person speech.

8. *Her heart was marked by the prince's love like the tulip;...all delicate and fragile like the spikenard*: in the Urdu poetic tradition the tulip symbolizes a lover's heart which is marked by love, the narcissus a lover's eye that looks his beloved's way, and the spikenard the locks and ringlets of the beloved.
9. Seven Climes: an approach used by the classical Islamic geographers to divide the Earth into the Greek system of seven zones or climes.
10. King of Stars: an allusion to the moon.
11. Heavens' Prisoner: an allusion to the sun.
12. Calmuck Tartar: Turkic and Mongol peoples of the Mongol Empire were generically referred to as "Tartars", i.e. Tatars.
13. *...conversing together like the rose and the nightingale*: in the Urdu poetic tradition the nightingale is portrayed as the lover of the rose.
14. Virgin of the Heavens: an allusion to the Virgo.
15. Kaaba: the holy shrine in Mecca toward which all Muslims turn when saying their prayers.
16. Hoopoe Throne: the name of Amar Ayyar's official seat in Amir Hamza's camp.
17. *gugal*: a fragrant gum-resin obtained from the *saal* tree or the *Balsamodendron mukul.*
18. *maulsari*: the tree *Mimusops elengi.*
19. ... *moon of the sky of excellence...like Greek-partridges*: in the Urdu poetic tradition, the Greek-partridge or *chakor* is alluded to as the lover of the moon.
20. *old man heavens*: an allusion to the sky.
21. Light of Tur: according to Islamic folk belief Mount Tur was burned from God's dazzling glimpse when he revealed it to Musa (Moses). This verse alludes to that divine light.
22. *nau-ratan* bracelet: a bracelet consisting of nine jewels: pearl, ruby, topaz, diamond, emerald, lapis lazuli, coral, sapphire, and *go-meda.* These nine pearls are supposed to represent the nine planets known to ancient astronomers.
23. "*May what the Scribe of Fortune...Writer of Destiny has engraved on our brows come to pass.*": Scribe of Fortune and Writer of Destiny are both allusions to God; the following phrase is an allusion to a folk belief according to which a person's destiny is written or engraved on his forehead.
24. Eagle of the Heavens: a northern constellation named Eagle.

25. Bull of the Earth: according to legend the celestial bull on whose horns the Earth is balanced. According to another tradition it is the allegorical name of the energy implanted in the heart of the Earth by its creator.
26. Emperor of the Russet Throne of the East: an allusion to the sun.
27. Help O Ali!: the traditional call for help in the name of Ali, the fourth Caliph of Islam, who was known for his strength and valor.
28. *naad-e Ali*: a prayer beginning with the words *naad-e Ali,* which is in the praise of Ali, Prophet Muhammad's son-in-law and the fourth Caliph of Islam. It is recited for luck and good fortune.
29. *Made the layers of Earth six, and eight the skies*: according to folk belief there are seven layers of the Earth and seven layers of the heavens. This couplet describes how one layer of the Earth rose to the skies with the billowing dust and became the sky's eighth layer, leaving the Earth with six layers.
30. Rampart of Sikander: according to legend, this was the great wall built by the prince Sikander the Bicornous to keep Yajuj and Majuj (Gog and Magog) from raiding population centers.
31. *sarod*: a stringed musical instrument similar to the lute.
32. Goblet of demon Ifrit's skull: Ifrit was the leader of the demons who rebelled against Emperor Shahpal of Mount Qaf. He was killed and beheaded by Amir Hamza. A goblet made from his skull was kept by Amir Hamza as a souvenir.
33. True Master of Both Worlds: an allusion to God.
34. "Two of Lord Laqa's own daughters had eloped with Hamza's sons": a reference to earlier encounters between Laqa and Amir Hamza.
35. See *Of the Tilism called Hoshruba and the Master of the Tilism, Emperor Afrasiyab*.
36. Imam Zamin: a coin pledged in the name of Ali Raza bin Musa al-Kazim (148–203 A.H.) whose alias was "Imam Zamin." The coin is tied to a traveller's arm by his relatives for safe journey. It is given away to a person of the Syed caste upon the traveller safely reaching the destination.
37. Westbound Traveller: an allusion to the sun.
38. *Verily We have conferred clear victory upon you:* a verse from *The Quran* (48:1)

39. *khurdnok* shoes: a shoe with a slightly upturned toe from Lucknow, India, made with velvet, red kid-leather, and leather obtained from the back of the wildass or the belly of a horse or ass.
40. *keora*-water: the essence of the *keora* flower.
41. Aloe-wood: Aloe is a tree that yields a rich perfume. It has been used in various religious rituals since ancient times.
42. *koriyala*: a black flower with white spots.
43. Virgin of the Ethereal Sphere: an allusion to the Virgo.
44. *tilak*: the ornamental or ceremonial mark Hindus make on the forehead with colored eye-earths, sandalwood or unguents.
45. *cowries, coins, dirhams and dinars*: cowry shells were used as the smallest unit of currency in the Indian subcontinent until the early twentieth century. Dinar and dirham were coins.
46. Moon of Canaan: an allusion to Yusuf (Joseph).
47. Valley of Ayman: the name of the valley of Mount Tur. According to Islamic folk belief Mount Tur was burned from God's dazzling glimpse when he revealed it to Musa (Moses).
48. *The ringdove sang…plaints for its beloved rose*: in the Urdu poetic tradition, the ringdove is considered a lover of the cypress tree and the nightingale of the rose. The connection between the dove and the box tree is uncertain.
49. heavens' Gold-Feathered Bird: an allusion to the sun.
50. Mirror of Sikander: an allusion to the folk belief that the mirror was first invented by Sikander (Alexander).
51. So luminous was her leg…reached its proximity: this alludes to the mystical level of devotion the lover (seeker) and the beautiful leg (sought).
52. *Surely the narcissus…one who died in love!*: in the Urdu poetic tradition the narcissus represents the eye of the beloved. A narcissus flower growing on the grave represents eternal wait and longing.
53. lac dye: a dye obtained from the lac insect.
54. *lahgam*: a kind of cloth.
55. *tika*: an ornament worn by women along the parting of their hair.
56. Azad fakir: a caste of fakirs distinguished by a mark from the top of the nose to the forehead.
57. Traveller of Heavens: an allusion to the sun.
58. Trekker of the Desert of Space: an allusion to the moon.
59. Sorcerer of the East: an allusion to the sun.

60. Brahmin: a Hindu priest.
61. *"Four paisas per ser"*: a paisa is the smallest coin; *ser* is a measure of weight equal to approximately two pounds.
62. All praise is due only to God and His Prophet: The narrator, Muhammad Husain Jah, has made a note here which is reproduced in full: "*Be it known that this tale is from before Prophet Muhammad's times but since every prophet had announced the coming of the last prophet Muhammad, Amar Ayyar and his companions also believed in him.*"
63. Shining Executioner of the Heavens: an allusion to the sun.
64. *missi*: a powder, chiefly composed of yellow myrobalan, gall nut, iron filings, vitriol, and other ingredients, used by women for coloring their teeth.
65. Emperor of the Armies of Stars: an allusion to the moon.
66. King of Planets: an allusion to the sun.
67. *king crows and kites*: the blood sacrifices of carrion eaters are employed in Indian magic to power spells.
68. Chapter of Light: this refers to the twenty-fourth chapter of *The Quran*.
69. *Smell the flower of the shield and partake of the fruit of the sword:* the embossed designs made on the Mughal era shield were called flowers. The word *phal* means both "fruit" and "sword blade" allowing the use of the double entendre.
70. King of the Stars: an allusion to the moon.
71. King of Noon: an allusion to the sun.
72. Emperor of Planets: an allusion to the sun.
73. Holi: the spring festival observed by the Hindus. The faith of the sorcerers and their magic devices are a mix of many different faiths practised in India.
74. *Its dark mole the dark mark on the heart*: this is probably an allusion to the legend that the dark mark on the heart represents Aadam's (Adam's) first act of disobedience against God. Here the mole on the ear refers to the inviting beauty of her ear that creates mischievous desire in a lover's heart.
75. The Angel Jibrail (Gabriel) had declared Amar Ayyar his protégé. He had fed Amar Ayyar three grapes. The first grape gifted him with a melodious voice. The second gave him the power to change into seventy two different forms, and acquire the shape of anyone he chose. The third grape gave him the ability to converse with all creatures and understand their language.
76. *ghazal*: a genre traditionally used for composing love sonnets

77. Dancing Girl of the Heavens: an allusion to the sky.
78. King of the Stars: an allusion to the moon.
79. Bright-Faced Turk of the Sky: an allusion to the moon.
80. Beloved of the Sky: an allusion to the sun.
81. *Beloved of the Sky...the World-Illuminating Lamp*: these are both allusions to the sun.
82. Wise like Mercury: an allusion to the ancient belief that the planet Mercury presides over knowledge and intelligence.
83. The inauspicious Saturn: astrologers traditionally attributed death, destruction and other evils to the planet Saturn.
84. *Every sword became a mirror...reflected the face of death's bride*: an allusion to the South Asian Muslim ritual of *aarsi mushaf* in which a mirror is put between the newly-weds and the bridegroom sees the bride's face for the first time in the mirror's reflection.
85. *The sorcerers who submitted allegiance...thoughts of God to solicit His aid.*: the sorcerers and sorceresses fighting on the side of the True Believers have not yet converted to the True Faith because once a sorcerer or sorceress converts they can no longer exercise magic as it is proscribed in the True Faith. Stripped of their magical powers they would be unable to help the cause of the True Believers. The sorcerers and sorceresses have pledged allegiance to it and, by the same token, also to God.
86. Beautifier of the World: an allusion to God.
87. *Held up the mirror of sun...the beloved morn*: an allusion to the South Asian Muslim ritual of *aarsi mushaf* in which a mirror is put between the newly-weds and the bridegroom sees the bride's face for the first time in her mirror reflection.
88. Red bird: the red bird described here is *lal*, the male of the species *Frangilla amandava.*
89. under-cap (*araq chin*): a cap worn under a turban to absorb sweat.
90. Daughters of the Corpse: the constellations Ursa Major and Ursa Minor which consist of seven stars, four of which are thought in Muslim folk tradition to resemble a corpse and the other three to be the daughters walking in front of it.
91. The Afrasiyab mentioned in this instance is an ancient King of Persia. Not to be confused with Afrasiyab the Emperor of Hoshruba.
92. Night's Watchman: an allusion to the moon.

93. Emperor of the Fourth Heaven: an allusion to the sun.
94. Darling of the Night: an allusion to the sun.
95. *gilauri*: a large preparation of the areca nut seasoned with spices and chunam and enveloped in leaves of the betel palm.
96. Turk of the Heavens: an allusion to the sun.
97. Luminous Bird: an allusion to the sun.
98. Ninth Heaven: the Ninth Heaven is deemed the seat of God.
99. *You see spears and lances even in a carafe of urine*: a metaphor for finding improbable things where they cannot possibly exist. Refers to the old medical practice of visually inspecting urine samples to diagnose illness.
100. Prince of Darkness: an allusion to the sky.
101. Sultan of the Golden-Headgear: an allusion to the sun.
102. World Conquering Emperor: an allusion to the sun.
103. Badakhshan is a region in north Afghanistan that was famed for its rubies.
104. Emperor of Afternoon: an allusion to the sun.
105. Lord of the Day: an allusion to the sun.
106. World's Hall of Audience: an allusion to the sky.
107. *lalit, bherveen, and bhibhas*: names of three Indian classical *ragas*.
108. *tulip or the* calamus draco: the tulip is the symbol of the slain or martyred. The berries of *calamus draco* yields *resina draconis* or Dragon's Blood—a red resinous substance used in medicines and varnishes.
109. World-Illuminating Wanderer: an allusion to the sun.
110. Lord of Darkness: an allusion to the night.
111. Great star: an allusion to the sun.
112. The lesser star: an allusion to the moon.
113. The dinar coin was minted in many denominations but they were usually silver, hence the association with the moon. A gold dinar was called a *surkh* (red) dinar.
114. *Pheni*-eating: *pheni* is an Indian vermicular sweetmeat that is served soaked in milk. Here the term is used in a derogatory sense. By calling Landhoor a *pheni*-eater Prince Alam Shah is suggesting Landhoor is less powerful than the meat-eating prince.
115. Tutor of Angels: according to Islamic folk belief, Azazil (Satan) was a jinn who lived on earth and on account of his piety he was invited to teach the angels and received the title

of *Muallim al-Malakoot* (Tutor of Angels) until he was driven away from the Heavens for refusing to prostrate himself before Adam.

116. Lord! Lord: the original words are *sat! sat!* which can be interpreted variously. It could also mean "Right is Right!" but since Princess Hilal plans to burn herself and become one with her Lord the above interpretation was chosen by the translator.
117. *Sati*: a Hindu woman who burns herself alive in her husband's funeral pyre. However, Princess Hilal Magic-Wringer is not Hindu because her gods are Sameri and Jamshed.
118. *the bright and luminous star…of the Night Sky's Beauty*: an allusion to the unrequited love between the sun and the moon who must forever remain separated in day and night.
119. Nowruz: the first day of the Persian New Year. Laqa and his religion are an amalgam of many faiths of which Hinduism and Zoroastrianism are only two. Here he describes Nowruz as his day for granting requests and prayers.
120. Aghori fakir: a caste of Hindu fakirs who worship the god Shiva (*Aghor* is a title of the god Shiva). The Aghori fakirs are known for their unclean habits and a reputation for eating human carcasses.
121. Tappa: a style of Indian classical singing developed and refined by the musician Mian Shora associated with the court of Asaf-ul Dawla in Avadh, India.
122. *gatkari*: the throatal, resonating sound produced by Indian classical singers
123. Trekker of the Desert of Heavens: an allusion to the sun.
124. Night's Beloved: an allusion to the moon.
125. *Eastern lover…his beloved*: an allusion to the sun searching for the moon.
126. Tooba tree: the name of a tree in heaven.
127. *apex of the moon on the fourteenth day*: a full moon usually falls on the fourteenth day of the lunar month.
128. Making seven revolutions around someone is a sacrificial ritual by which a sacrifice is pledged.
129. *…infidelity's rust fell away from the mirror of sorceress Taus's heart*: in the poetic and mystical traditions, the heart is described as a steel mirror that may become clouded with impurities or rust and, once they are removed, returns to its pristine clarity.
130. Court of Jamshed: not to be confused with the sorcerer god Jamshed of Hoshruba. The Jamshed referred to here is an

ancient king of Persia. This name is often attributed in legend to Prophet Suleiman and Sikander. It is invoked in this book in connection with Queen Mahrukh's court to convey the grandeur of her court.

131. Traveler on the path of sky: an allusion to the sun.
132. The act of issuing a coin meant that the person (entity in this case) was now the ruler or king because the coins carried a ruler's image on one side.
133. Shamama: the sorcerer Shakl Kush is addressing the magic effigy by this name.
134. Looked at her heel: a common superstition among Indian women who glance at their heel after looking at their children's beauty to ward off the evil eye.
135. Kohl from the Mount Tur: the kohl (black eye liner) made from the burned stone of Mount Tur. See also note 21.
136. *Take all her calamities on their head*: a ritual by which someone pledges to sacrifice himself or herself to keep a loved one from coming to harm.
137. Golden-Robed Emperor: an allusion to the sun.
138. King of the Stars: an allusion to the moon.
139. *the Hindu of the Skies performed its worship and left the dome of heavens and the Idol Worshipper of the East carrying its golden disk*: an allusion to the planet Saturn and the sun.
140. Kashan: the name of a city in the province of Isfahan, Iran, famed for its velvet.
141. According to a folk belief, the crow eats the ringdove's eggs and replaces them with its own for the ringdove to hatch them.

Amir Hamza's Powers, Holy Gifts, Weapons and Occult Contraptions

Amir Hamza, the Lord of the Auspicious Planetary Conjunction was taught archery, wrestling, and the language of all creatures, including the Jinni language of the jinns, by the angel Jibrail (Gabriel). During his adventures he also received the following powers, holy gifts, weapons and occult contraptions.

THE MOST GREAT NAME: According to Muslim tradition God has ninety-nine known names. Besides these God has a name which is revealed only to prophets and saints. It is the Most Great Name of God. A holy guide named Khizr taught God's Most Great Name to Amir Hamza. With its power Amir Hamza can counter and revoke magic but he cannot conquer a tilism with it, nor use it to free someone imprisoned within a tilism.

WAR CRY: A gift of Aadam. It is heard up to a distance of one hundred and twenty-eight miles.

AADAM'S ARMLET: An armlet whose power helps Hamza triumph against his enemies and his arm is never lowered by his foe in battle. It also helps Hamza's sword surmount his foe, even if he should be a thousand-yard-tall.

DRAGON-SHAPED STANDARD: Buzurjmehr had made this standard for Amir Hamza with dragon-skin. It is shaped like a dragon's head and has thirty-six holes. When the wind fills them, they exude the fragrance of musk and ambergris, and resound with the rumble of "*O Sahibqiran!*" that strike fear in the hearts of Amir Hamza's enemies, and raises the spirits of his men.

MUSIC BAND OF SULEIMAN: A gift from Prophet Khizr. It plays when Amir Hamza's armies are on the march.

TIMBAL OF SIKANDER: A gift from holy Khizr. When struck, its sound reaches for one hundred and twenty-eight miles. It is beaten when Amir Hamza's camp issues the call for war. Amar Ayyar has the exclusive privilege to strike the Timbal of Sikander in Amir Hamza's camp. In his absence either his sons or the masters of the kettle-drums strike the timbal.

TIMBAL OF HASHSHAM: The timbal of the the warrior Hashsham.

ROVING PRAYER TENT: A portable mosque made of cotton stuff belonging to Hamza. It is moveable and can be easily set up.

PAVILION OF DANIYAL: A gift from Buzurjmehr. Constructed of paper it can miraculously shrink or expand according to the number of its occupants. (Not to be confused with DANIYAL'S TENT which was a gift given by Prophet Daniyal to Amar Ayyar).

PAVILION OF SULEIMAN: A wedding gift that Aasman Peri gave to Amir Hamza. It exists simultaneously in two realms – Earth and Mount Qaf. If a sorcerer were to set foot in it he would be combusted. No weapon can cut through its walls and no trickster can dig his way underneath it: The pavilion's walls keep sinking into the ground no matter how deep one digs underneath. No one can leap over its walls because the wall rises higher than anyone can jump, by itself.

PAVILION OF HASHSHAM: Amir Hamza took it after killing the raider Hashsham. Amir Hamza confronts and punishes sorcerers in this pavilion because Pavilion of Suleiman burns them and they cannot set foot inside it.

AMIR HAMZA'S HORSES

ASHQAR DEMON-BORN: A horse from Mount Qaf whose father Arnais was a demon and whose mother Laneesa was a *peri.*

SIYAH QITAS THE BLACK: A horse. A gift from the Angel Jibrail (Gabriel).

Amir Hamza's Arms and Armor

Samsam: A sword. A gift from Angel Jibrail (Gabriel).

Qumqam: A sword. A gift from Angel Jibrail (Gabriel).

Aqrab-e Suleimani: A sword acquired by Amir Hamza in Mount Qaf. It becomes a scorpion when anyone else picks it up.

Vest of Ismail: A gift from Angel Jibrail (Gabriel).

Helmet of Hud: A gift from Angel Jibrail (Gabriel).

Chain Mail of Daud: A gift from Angel Jibrail (Gabriel).

Arm Guard of Yusuf: A gift from Angel Jibrail (Gabriel).

Ankle Guards of Saleh: A gift from Angel Jibrail (Gabriel).

Cummerbund of Rustam: A gift from Angel Jibrail (Gabriel).

Dagger of Rustam: A gift from Angel Jibrail (Gabriel).

Shield of Garshasp: A gift from Angel Jibrail (Gabriel).

Mace of Sam Bin Nariman: A gift from Angel Jibrail (Gabriel).

Scimitar of Sohrab: A gift from Angel Jibrail (Gabriel).

Lance of Nuh: A gift from Angel Jibrail (Gabriel).

Thigh Guards of Yunus: A holy gift.

Bow of Ishaq: A holy gift.

Bow of Daud: A gift from the shrine of Prophet Saleh.

Amar Ayyar's Powers, Holy Gifts and Occult Contraptions

Amar Ayyar is Amir Hamza's childhood companion. The Angel Jibrail (Gabriel) had declared Amar Ayyar his protégé. Angel Jibrail had fed Amar Ayyar three grapes. The first grape gifted him with a melodious voice. The second gave him the power to change into seventy-two different forms, and acquire the shape of anyone he chose. The third grape gave him the ability to converse with all creatures and understand their language. Amar Ayyar also received the following powers and gifts. Amir Hamza had forbidden Amar Ayyar from using his holy gifts to kill anyone, including his enemies.

Net of Ilyas: A net that makes large and heavy objects light to carry in it.

Daniyal's Tent: A gift from Prophet Daniyal. Magic has no effect on it and no sorcerer can enter it. It can increase in size at Amar's command. (Not to be confused with the Pavilion of Daniyal that was a gift given to Amir Hamza by Buzurjmehr).

Do-tara: A stringed instrument that was a gift from Prophet Daud. The audience were enraptured whenever Amar Ayyar played this instrument.

Singing: A gift from Prophet Daud (David). When Amar Ayyar sang he captivated his audience and they became enamored of his singing.

Speed: A gift from Prophet Saleh which made Amar Ayyar run faster than the wind without becoming tired.

Power to ward off Death: A gift from Prophet Muhammad to Amar Ayyar that he would not die until he asked for his death three times himself.

The Most Great Name: A gift from Prophet Ishaq.

Dev-jama: A lionskin which kept Amar Ayyar safe from demons and malignant jinns.

Zambil: A bag that could contain the entire world in it. Nothing that entered the zambil or was consigned to it came out without Amar's consent. Amar Ayyar could placc his hand on the zambil and acquire any shape he desired. The zambil disappeared whenever he was arrested or searched.

Cape of Invisibility: A cape which allowed Amar Ayyar to become invisible upon wearing it.

Snare-rope: A gift from Mount Qaf. It was sent for Amar Ayyar by the mother of holy guide Khizr, Asifa Ba-Safa.

Bread-cake: An everlasting breadcake that was a gift from the holy Khizr.

Water Flask: A flask which never ran out of water. A gift from the holy Khizr.

Conch Shell: A gift from angel Gabriel. When blown its sound reached to far away places.

Goblet of Ishaq: A goblet which always remains filled with water from heaven.

Egg of Oblivion: Oval balls filled with an intoxicating drug liquid that explode upon impact. The victim falls unconscious as he inhaled the drug. Amar Ayyar and his band of tricksters also used other means for administering intoxicating drugs to their enemies. They burnt drugs in fire to fumigate the air, mixed drugs in food or drinks, and blew the drug powder directly into the nostrils of their enemies with the help of pipes.

List of Characters, Historic Figures, Deities and Mythical Beings

Aadam: Adam. In the dastan tradition, Aadam is mentioned as a prophet

Aadi: The master of Amir Hamza's camp. An extremely fat man and a voracious eater.

Aafat: Sorcerer in Afrasiyab's service. Husband of Princess Hilal Magic-Destroyer.

Aala Gurd: Warrior in Amir Hamza's service

Aamir Rodbari: Warrior in Amir Hamza's service

Aasman Peri: Amir Hamza's peri wife and the queen of Mount Qaf

Abul Adan the Warrior: Warrior in Amir Hamza's service

Abyssinian: Native of Ethiopia

Abriq Mount-splitter: Afrasiyab's fourth-ranking minister

Abu Tahir the Blood-spiller: Messenger and spy in Amir Hamza's service

Abul Fatah: Trickster in Amir Hamza's service

Afrasiyab (Emperor of Hoshruba): Sorcerer. Master of the Tilism. Husband of Heyrat.

Afrasiyab (Historic figure): Ancient King of Persia. Not to be confused with the Emperor of Hoshruba Afrasiyab.

Aghori: A caste of fakirs

Alam Shah: Amir Hamza's son

Ali: Fourth Caliph of Islam who was known for his strength and valor. Husband of Prophet Muhammad's daughter Fatima. He was titled "Lion of God".

ALLAMA THE WISE: Sorcerer in Afrasiyab's service

ALMAS FAIRY-FACE: Daughter of Musavvir the Magic-Painter and Surat-Nigar the Face-Maker

AMAR AYYAR: Also Amar. Amir Hamza's chief trickster

AMIR HAMZA: Also Hamza. The Lord of the Auspicious Planetary Conjunction. The commander-in-chief and figurative head of the True Believers.

ARZHANG OF THE STONE FIGURINE: Sorcerer in Afrasiyab's service

ASAD BIN KARIB: Amir Hamza's maternal grandson. The designated Conqueror of the Tilism.

ASHQAR DEMON-BORN: Amir Hamza's horse. Born from the union between a demon and a *peri*.

ASIFA BA-SAFA: A pious woman. In the *dastan* tradition she is the mother of Khizr and Ilyas. She sent Amar Ayyar his miraculous snare-rope as a gift.

AZAAB: Sorcerer in Afrasiyab's service

AZAD: A caste of fakirs

AZAR OF THE PORTRAIT TABLET: Sorcerer in Afrasiyab's service

AZHDAR DRAGON-MOUTH: Sorcerer in Afrasiyab's service

BADIUZ ZAMAN: Amir Hamza's son

BAGHBAN MAGIC-GARDENER: Afrasiyab's third-ranking minister

BAHAR OF SPRING-QUARTER: Also Bahar. Sorceress Princess of the City of Mount Solace. Heyrat's sister.

BAHMAN: Persian folk champion

BAHRAM: Warrior in Amir Hamza's service

BAKHTAK: Emperor Naushervan's vizier. Father of Bakhtiarak.

BAKHTIARAK: The devil-designate of Laqa's court. Son of Bakhtak.

BANAFSHA: A false name made up by trickster Jansoz to fool sorcerer Azar

BRAHMIN: A person of a priestly caste of the Hindu religion

BARAN: Sorceress. Raad Thunder-Clap's beloved.

BARAN THE RAIN-MASTER: Sorcerer in Afrasiyab's service

BUBRAN LION-RIDER: Sorcerer in Afrasiyab's service. Heyrat's nephew.

BURQ THE FRANK: European trickster in Amir Hamza's service

BUZURG UMMID: Diviner. Buzurjmehr's son.

BUZURJMEHR: Emperor Naushervan's vizier. Father of Buzurg Ummid.

CALMUCK: A Tartar. See Tartar.

CHALAK: Trickster in Amir Hamza's service. Amar Ayyar's son.

CHAMPA: Mother of Sharara Flame-Spirit's gardener

CHASHMAK ZAN LIGHTNING-BOLT: One of seven sorceresses in Afrasiyab's service who exist in the form of lightning and strike as lightning bolts. They also appear in human form as beautiful, golden-skinned women.

DANIYAL (PROPHET): Daniel

DARA: King Darius the Third of Persia

DARAB THE WORLD-CONQUEROR: Amir Hamza's son

DARYADIL: Diviner. Buzurjmehr's son.

DAUD (PROPHET): David

DAUD (SORCERER): An immortal sorcerer of Hoshruba

DIL AARAM: Sorceress. Princess Mahjabeen Diamond-Robe's aide.

DUKHAN THE STEAM: Sorcerer in Afrasiyab's service

FARAMURZ: Emperor Naushervan's son

FARAZ AAD MAGHREBI: Warrior in Amir Hamza's service

FARIDUN: Ancient King of Persia

FATIMA: Prophet Muhammad's daughter. Wife of Ali "Lion of God".

FATTAH KISHORI: Trickster in the service of Prince Darab the World-Conqueror

FAULAD: Sorcerer in Afrasiyab's service

FAULAD DRUG-GLUTTON: Sorcerer in Afrasiyab's service

FAULAD IRON-PULLER: Sorcerer in Afrasiyab's service

GARDIYA BANO: Badiuz Zaman's mother. Amir Hamza's wife.

GUHAR BAR THE PEARL-RAINER: Sorcerer in Afrasiyab's service

GULCHIN: Sorceress. Wife of Baghban Magic-Gardener.

GULRANG: A name made up by Amar Ayyar as his mother's name

GULSHAN: Empress Heyrat's female attendant

HAMNASHEEN: Old sorcerer in Afrasiyab's service

HAMZA: See Amir Hamza.

HASHIM SWORDFIGHTER: Amir Hamza's son

HASHSHAM: A warrior from the city of Khaibar

HASINA MAGIC-BEAUTY: Sorceress in Afrasiyab's service

HEYRAT: Sorceress. Empress of Hoshruba. Afrasiyab's wife.

HILAL MAGIC-WRINGER: Sorceress. Aafat's wife.

HOSHIAR THE CUNNING: Sorcerer in Afrasiyab's service

HOURI: The beautiful female companion in heaven

HUD: Heber

IBRAHIM: Abraham

IJLAL: Sorcerer in Afrasiyab's service

ILYAS: Elias. In the dastan tradition he is Khizr's brother.

INDRA: King of the gods in Indian mythology. His court is synonymous with a place of pleasure.

INTIZAM THE ARRANGER: Sorcerer. Ijlal's companion.

IRAJ BIN QASIM: Amir Hamza's grandson

ISFANDIAR: An ancient Persian king

ISFANDIAR SHAH GILANI: Amir Hamza's son

ISHAQ: Isaac

ISHRAT: Eunuch in Princess Almas Fairy-Face's service

JAMHUR WORLD-CONFLAGRER: Warrior in Amir Hamza's service

JAMOSH: Sorcerer in Afrasiyab's service

JAMSHED (GOD OF SORCERERS): Celebrated sorcerer and one of the gods worshipped in Hoshruba

JAMSHED (KING OF PERSIA): Not the sorcerer god Jamshed of Hoshruba. The Jamshed referred to here is an ancient king of Persia. This name is often attributed in legend to Prophet Suleiman and Sikander. It is invoked in this book in connection with Queen Mahrukh's court to convey the grandeur of her court.

JAN NISAR THE LIFE-SACRIFICING: Sorcerer in Afrasiyab's service

JANSOZ: Trickster in Amir Hamza's service. Qiran's son.

JIBRAIL: Gabriel

KAIKAUS: Ancient king of Persia whose name is invoked to describe the majesty of his person and court

KAIKHUSRU: King Cyrus whose name is invoked to describe the majesty of his person and court

KALVA: Dark-faced spirit summoned by sorcerers to help invoke magic

KAMIL: Sorcerer in Afrasiyab's service

KARIB THE COURAGEOUS: Warrior in Amir Hamza's service

KARIT SHIELD-WHIRLER: Warrior in Amir Hamza's service

KAPI ARZAL: Warrior in Amir Hamza's service

KAPI ZALZAL: Warrior in Amir Hamza's service

KAYUMARS: Name of an ancient king

KHATIF LIGHTNING-BOLT: One of seven sorceresses in Afrasiyab's service who exist in the form of lightning and strike as lightning bolts. They also appear in human form as beautiful, golden-skinned women.

KHIZR: A holy person of Islamic legend who led Sikander the Bicornous to the Fount of Life. He guides the lost travellers.

KHUBSURAT THE BEAUTY: Heyrat's daughter. Sorcerer Shakeel's beloved.

KHUMAR: Sorceress in Afrasiyab's service. Makhmur Crimson-Eye's sister.

KHURSHID BIN HASHIM: Amir Hamza's grandson

KOHAN: Sorcerer in Afrasiyab's service

LACHIN: The real emperor of Hoshruba deposed by Afrasiyab. One of the immortal sorcerers of Hoshruba.

LALAN RED-ROBE: Supreme Commander of King Suleiman Amber-Hair's armies

LAMAE LIGHTNING-BOLT: One of seven sorceresses in Afrasiyab's service who exist in the form of lightning and strike as lightning bolts. They also appear in human form as beautiful, golden-skinned women.

LANDHOOR: Amir Hamza's deputy. Emperor of India.

LAQA: Giant who claims to be a god and is worshipped by sorcerers

MAH: Sorceress. Mahrukh Magic-Eye's mother.

MAHJABEEN DIAMOND-ROBE: Afrasiyab's niece

MAHRUKH MAGIC-EYE: Sorceress Princess of the City of Manycolors. Shakeel's mother.

MAHTAB MOON-MAKER: Sorcerer in Afrasiyab's service

MAJNUN: Literally, "the frenzied one". Hero of the romance *Laila and Majnun*.

MAKHMUR CRIMSON-EYE: Sorceress in Afrasiyab's service. Khumar's sister.

MAKKAR THE CUNNING: Trickster Chalak in disguise

MALA GURD: Warrior in Amir Hamza's service

MALIK AZHDAR: Warrior in Amir Hamza's service

MALIK QASIM: Amir Hamza's grandson

MANDVAIL ISFAHANI: Warrior in Amir Hamza's service

MANI: Persian painter. Founder of the Mannichean sect. The beauty of his house is proverbial.

MANZUR CROW-EYE: King Suleiman Amber-Hair's nephew

MARZUQ: An ancient king of Persia

MAUT THE DEATH: Trickster Amar Ayyar in disguise

MAYKHAR RHINO-HEAD: Commander of Princess Bahar's army

MEHRAN: Sorceress. Princess Bahar's female attendant

MEHR NIGAR: Amir Hamza's wife. Naushervan's daughter. Grandmother of Saad.

MEHSHAR LIGHTNING-BOLT: One of seven sorceresses in Afrasiyab's service who exist in the form of lightning and strike as lightning bolts. They also appear in human form as beautiful, golden-skinned women.

MUGHEELA: Sorceress. Mother of Sorcerer Hoshiar the Cunning.

MUHAFIZ: Sorcerer in Sharara Flame-Spirit's service

MUHLEEL JANG IRAQI: Warrior in Amir Hamza's service

MUNSARIM THE ORGANIZER: Sorcerer. Ijlal's companion.

MUQARNAS SILVER-BODY: Sorcerer in Afrasiyab's service

MUQBIL VAFADAR: Also Muqbil. Amir Hamza's personal attendant and a gifted archer.

MUSA: Moses

MUSAVVIR THE MAGIC-PAINTER: One of Hoshruba's immortal sorcerers. Husband of Surat-Nigar.

NAFARMAN: Sorceress Princess of the City of Purple Poppy

NAAG THE SERPENT: Sorcerer in Afrasiyab's service

NAGAN: Sorceress. Sarmast's mother.

NAIRANG: Princess Tasveer's aide

NAMIAN KHAIBARI: Messenger and spy in Amir Hamza's service

NAMRUD: Sorcerer in Afrasiyab's service

NAQUS THE TRUMPETER: Sorcerer in Afrasiyab's service

NARIMAN: Legendary Persian warrior. Father of Sam.

NASREEN AMBER-HAIR: Daughter of King Suleiman Amber-Hair. Beloved of Ijlal.

NAU RATAN: Sorcerer Nisar's female attendant

NAUSHERVAN: Emperor of Persia. Amir Hamza's father-in-law.

NAY NAVAZ THE FLUTIST: Sorcerer in Afrasiyab's service

NAZIR CROW-EYE: Nephew of King Suleiman Amber-Hair

NIHAL: Daughter of Baghban Magic-Gardener and Gulchin

NISAR: Sorcerer in Afrasiyab's service

NOMAN BIN MUNZIR SHAH YEMENI: Warrior in Amir Hamza's service

PERI: Female fairy

PHARAOH: The ruler of Egypt in the time of Musa (Moses)

QAHHAR: Sorcerer in Afrasiyab's service

QIRAN THE ETHIOPE: Trickster in Amir Hamza's service. Amar Ayyar's deputy.

RAAD THUNDER-CLAP: Sorcerer. His scream sounds like a thunder clap. Mehshar Lightning-Bolt's son.

RAHDAR: Sorcerer in Afrasiyab's service

RIZWAN: Keeper of Heaven

RUTAS: Sorcerer in Afrasiyab's service

RUSTAM: Legendary Persian warrior. Father of Sohrab.

RUSTAM ELEPHANT-BODY: Title of the Persian hero Rustam

SAAD: King of True Believers. Amir Hamza's grandson.

SAM: Legendary Persian warrior. Son of Nariman.

SABA RAFTAR THE QUICK: Trickster-girl. Minister of Sarsar the Swordfighter. Beloved of Qiran the Ethiope.

SADAF THE OYSTER: Sorceress. Mother of Guhar-Bar the Pearl-Rainer.

SAIF THE AMBIDEXTROUS: Warrior in Amir Hamza's service

SAIQA BAR LIGHTNING-BOLT: One of seven sorceresses in Afrasiyab's service who exist in the form of lightning and strike as lightning bolts. They also appear in human form as beautiful, golden-skinned women.

SALEH: Prophet sent to the people of Samud. Sometimes he is associated with the biblical Shelah.

SAMAK: Trickster in Amir Hamza's service

SAMAN-AZAR: Sorceress. Attendant of Sharara Flame-Spirit.

SAMAR: Daughter of Baghban Magic-Gardener and Gulchin

SAMERI: Renowned sorcerer worshipped as a god in Hoshruba

SANAT MAGIC-MAKER: Sorceress. Afrasiyab's first-ranking minister.

SANDAL: Sorceress. Mahjabeen Diamond-Robe's aunt.

SARHANG MAKKI: Messenger and spy in Amir Hamza's service

SARMA ICE-HURLER: Sorcerer. Afrasiyab's second-ranking minister.

SARMAST: Sorcerer in Afrasiyab's service

SARSAR SWORDFIGHTER: Leader of the trickster-girls in Afrasiyab's service. Governor of the City of Portraits.

SATIAL NUR LIGHTNING-BOLT: One of seven sorceresses in Afrasiyab's service who exist in the form of lightning and strike as lightning bolts. They also appear in human form as beautiful, golden-skinned women.

SAYYAH: Sorcerer in Afrasiyab's service

SHADDAD: Cruel monarch who claimed divine powers and made a garden to rival Paradise

SHADEED: Sorcerer in Afrasiyab's service

SHAGUFA: Princess Tasveer's attendant

SHAHBAZ: Sorcerer in Afrasiyab's service

SHAHPAL: Emperor of Mount Qaf. Father of Aasman Peri.

SHAKEEL: Sorcerer. Mahrukh Magic-Eye's son.

SHAKL KUSH IMAGE-CUTTER: Sorcerer. Son of Musavvir Magic-Painter and Surat-Nigar the Face-Maker.

SHAMAMA: Name given to a magic effigy by sorcerer Shakl Kush Image-Cutter

SHAMIMA TUNNELER: Trickster-girl. Companion of Sarsar Swordfighter.

Beloved of trickster Burq the Frank.

SHAMSHAD ELEPHANT-BODY: Sorcerer. Commander of Surkh-Mu Wonder-Mane's army.

SHARARA FLAME-SPIRIT: Sorceress. Princess Tasveer's aunt.

SHARARA BLAZING-FLAME: Sorceress. Exists in the form of a flame.

SHOLA RUKHSAR FLAME-CHEEK: Sorceress. Attendant of Sharara Flame-Spirit.

SHOLA THE BLAZE: Sorcerer in Afrasiyab's service

SHOLA BAR LIGHTNING-BOLT: One of seven sorceresses in Afrasiyab's service who exist in the form of lightning and strike as lightning bolts. They also appear in human form as beautiful, golden-skinned women.

SIKANDER: Name used for both Alexander of Macedon and the prince Sikander Zulqarnain (Alexander the Bicornous)

SIMURGH: A giant mythical bird

SIYAH QITAS THE BLACK: King Saad's horse

SIYAVUSH: Diviner. Buzurjmehr's son.

SOHRAB: Legendary Persian warrior. Son of Rustam.

SULEIMAN: King Solomon

SULEIMAN AMBER-HAIR: King of Mount Agate

SUNUBAR SNARE-ROPER: Trickster-girl. Companion of Sarsar Swordfighter. Beloved of trickster Jansoz.

SURAT NIGAR FACE-MAKER: Sorceress. Musavvir Magic-Painter's wife. Shakl Kush Image-Cutter's mother.

SURKH MU WONDER-MANE: Sorceress. Governor of the City of Scarlet Locks.

TADBIR: Sorcerer in Afrasiyab's service

TAMTARAQ: Sorcerer in Princess Bahar's service

TARAR THE SPEEDSTER: Trickster in the service of Bakhtiarak

TARTAR: Turkic and Mongol peoples of the Mongol Empire who were generically referred to as "Tartars", i.e. Tatars.

TARTUS HATCHET-THROWER: Warrior in Amir Hamza's service

TASEER: Sorcerer. An inhabitant of Hoshruba.

TASVEER: Empress Heyrat's daughter

TAUQ BIN HEYRAN: Warrior in Amir Hamza's service

TAUS: Sorceress in Heyrat's service

TEZ NIGAH DAGGER-FIGHTER: Trickster-girl. Companion of Sarsar Swordfighter. Beloved of trickster Zargham.

TOMIAN KHAIBARI: Messenger and spy in Amir Hamza's service

UMAYYA BIN AMAR: Trickster in Prince Badiuz Zaman's service

WAQWAQ: Sorcerer. Brother of Tamtaraq.

YAQUT: Sorceress. Empress Heyrat's aide.

YUSUF: Joseph

ZAAFRAN: Sorceress in Afrasiyab's service

ZALIM BLACK-FACE: Sorcerer in Surat Nigar Face-Maker's service

ZALIM KOHI THE CRUEL: Sorcerer in Afrasiyab's service

ZAMARRUD: Sorceress. Empress Heyrat's aide.

ZANZIBARIAN: Native of the Zanzibar island in Africa

ZARDAM: Sorcerer. Sorcerer Sarmast's retainer.

ZARDHASHT: An ancient sorcerer

ZARGHAM THE LION-HEARTED: Trickster in Amir Hamza's service

ZUBAIDA SHER: Amir Hamza's daughter

ZULAIKHA: Potiphar's wife

ZULMAT PITCH-FACE: Sorcerer in Afrasiyab's service

ZUNNAR: Sorcerer in Afrasiyab's service

ORIGINAL PREFACE TO *TILISM-E HOSHRUBA* BY MUHAMMAD HUSAIN JAH

IN THE NAME OF ALLAH THE COMPASSIONATE AND MERCIFUL

A hundred thousand praises and a million laudations befit [God] the Cupbearer of Eternity, whose euphoric call of *Let There Be* caparisoned the desolate expanse of the world. Everyone who sips from perception's glass must needs likewise eulogize and glorify [Prophet Muhammad] who, deep in his cup of Original Covenant, cured all quaffing the dredges of impiety and perdition with the restorative goblet of his Advent (May God bless him, his illustrious family and worthy companions).

After that homage, I, Syed Muhammad Husain Jah, ask your indulgence to look upon myself as a gleaner of the gardens of men of learning and wisdom, and those erudite in the subtle and the sublime; and as one who is as the dust under their shoes. I petition the attentive ear of those who are tolerant of a mortal's errors and steeped and versed in letters, that *The Adventures of Amir Hamza* is a tale both excellent and enchanting, a favorite of the seeker and the sought, a veritable pearl from the sea of eloquence, and a dazzling sun of the noon of rhetoric such as humbles the tongue singing its praise, and overawes the narrative describing its glory.

This epic contains a most astonishing tale, *Tilism-e Hoshruba*, which is the choicest of its choice books. Thus, I set my heart on transcribing this wonder, which is the soul of adornment and epitome of grace in the realm of the written word, employing proper idiom and chaste expression of the Urdu language to convert devotees of beloved lore to its marvellous charms with the grace and boon of my Lord, and His guidance and succor.

Broadcast by the Transcriber for the Worthy Readers of this History

Let it be known that *The Adventures of Amir Hamza* comprises seven books and it is a difficult proposition to understand the history of personages such as Amir Hamza, Amar Ayyar, Zamarrud Shah alias Laqa, Bakhtiarak, sorcerer Afrasiyab, et. al. without perusing the said books. Keeping that in mind, I introduce Amir Hamza, who is the son of Syed Khvaja Abdul Muttalib, the chieftain of Kaaba; Amar, who is Amir Hamza's trickster; and Saad bin Qubad, Hamza's grandson, appointed by him as the king of his camp. Amir Hamza is the commander-in-chief of the armies. All of Hamza's sons pay allegiance to Saad bin Qubad, who is also their king. Besides, many other potentates from the face of the world are also attached to his camp with their armies and will be duly mentioned in the pages of this history.

Amir Hamza is warring with King Zamarrud Shah Bakhtari or Laqa, an illustrious king who has proclaimed himself God; to make him renounce his false claim. Several times, Laqa has escaped Amir Hamza's hands into lands whose sovereigns and laity pay allegiance to him as their God, and do battle with Hamza at his behest. Accompanying Laqa is Faramurz, the son of Emperor Naushervan of Persia, who has thrown his lot with Laqa and battled Amir in the past. Bakhtiarak, son of Bakhtak, the vizier of Faramurz, is the devil-designate of the court of His Holiness Laqa – for the seat of deity needs a fiend to make it complete. Previously, Laqa had sought refuge in the Tilism of Hazar Shakal, and upon its destruction at Amir Hamza's hands, he headed for the mountainous lands of Kohistan. The tale of the Tilism of Hazar Shakl precedes the history of Hoshruba. But your humble narrator abandoned it in the favour of the latter to avoid gratuitously prolonging the narrative.

Hoshruba: Authors, Narrators and Contributors

Muhammad Husain Jah
(Born: ? – Died: 1891–93?)

Muhammad Husain (pen name Jah) was Urdu's greatest prose stylist and an accomplished poet. His father, Syed Ghulam Husain, was a *rammal* or diviner. Hardly any information exists about Jah's life before he published his first composition, *Tilism-e Fasahat,* in 1874 through the Naval Kishore Press, Lucknow. He was of the Shia faith and trained in narrating the episodes of Husain's martyrdom at Karbala. After Jah's success with *Tilism-e Fasahat,* Naval Kishore Press hired him to compose the *Tilism-e Hoshruba.* A first volume was published in 1883. According to Jah's own account, he compiled the legend of *Tilism-e Hoshruba* using traditions from the three written accounts of Mir Ahmad Ali Rampuri/ Amba Prasad Rasa, Muhammad Amir Khan, and Ghulam Raza. He also used traditions from Shaikh Tasadduq Husain, a fellow *dastan* narrator and *dastan* writer. The second volume of *Tilism-e Hoshruba* came out in 1884. But there was a delay of four years before the third volume was published in 1888–89. Considering the popularity of *Tilism-e Hoshruba*, the Press demanded that Jah finish the subsequent volumes speedily. It appears Jah could not meet those demands.

Jah was also devastated by the deaths of his young son and daughter, which occurred while he wrote the third volume. For awhile he even stopped writing and only resumed it at the encouragement of publisher Munshi Naval Kishore. After the printing of the fourth volume of *Tilism-e Hoshruba* in 1890, the Naval Kishore Press replaced Jah with another Lucknow *dastan* narrator, Ahmed Husain Qamar.

We know that Jah's work on *Tilism-e Hoshruba* was close to his heart and he continued with it even after his disassociation with the Naval Kishore Press. In December of the same year, he started his own press, named Husaini Press, and privately published the first part of *Tilism-e*

Hoshruba's fifth volume. Only one copy of this book is known to exist, which was recently discovered by the Urdu researcher Rifaqat Ali Shahid. Its first four pages, in which Jah may have explained his reasons for leaving the Naval Kishore Press, are missing. Nothing could be said with certainty at this time about the exact circumstances in which Jah separated from the Naval Kishore Press and what happened to his other works, if there were any. In a notice printed in the fifth volume of Hoshruba, published by the Naval Kishore Press, Ahmed Husain Qamar mentions that "some chance accidents" brought about the end of Jah's association with the publisher.

Other notices at the back of the various editions of *Tilism-e Hoshruba* reveal that Jah's death occurred between December, 1890, and October, 1893. According to Urdu scholar Shamsur Rahman Faruqi, the time recorded for the death of Jah's young children and a comparison of his contemporaries' ages reveals that Jah died at a relatively young age.

Meanwhile, Ahmed Husain Qamar continued his work on the remaining volumes of the *Tilism-e Hoshruba*. He proved extremely prolific, perhaps in competition with Jah's Husaini Press, or in reaction to public demand. The fifth volume was published in two parts in 1891. The publication of the sixth volume in 1892 was quickly followed by the seventh and last volume in 1893.

Only fragmentary information is available about the professional relationship between Jah and Qamar. Jah duly credited all his sources. In his first published work, *Tilism-e Fasahat*, he mentions Ahmed Husain Qamar as his instructor. But according to Faruqi, the uncharacteristic exaggeration and hyperbole he uses to credit Qamar suggests that Jah did so ironically. Qamar himself never made any claims to be Jah's teacher, although he did make many false and contrary claims to appropriate the credit for the authorship of the *Tilism-e Hoshruba* from Jah and past authors and narrators of the legend.

From documentary evidence, three people are known to have taught Jah. None of them were *dastan* narrators and may not have influenced his *dastan* narration. They were Mir Fida Ali Fida, a *nisar* or prose narrator; Mushi Ashraf Ali Ashraf, a calligrapher employed at the Naval Kishore Press; and a poet who used the pen name Sehr. The poet Mirza Jafar Husain Qamar Lakhnavi is mentioned as Jah's pupil.

The *Tilism-e Hoshruba* became a bestseller and remains the best known legend of fantasy literature in the Urdu language. Eight editions were published from 1883 to 1930 from Lucknow alone.

Mir Ahmed Ali
(Lived 1850s)

Mir Ahmed Ali Rampuri was a *dastan* narrator of Lucknow. He later migrated to the princely state of Rampur to join the court as a *dastan* narrator in the reign of Navab Muhammad Saeed Khan (1840–55). According to Jah's statement, it was he who invented the *Hoshruba* legend that was transcribed by his student, Amba Prasad Rasa, who was also a *dastan* narrator. This was one of the versions Jah used as his source to create the legend of *Tilism-e Hoshruba.* No further details are available about his version of the *Hoshruba* legend except that Muhammad Husain Jah had obtained a copy after a long search.

Mir Ahmed Ali has two unpublished manuscripts to his credit. The first book was in Persian and was co-authored with another Lucknow *dastan* narrator, Mir Qasim Ali. It was the *Qissa-e Amir Hamza* and contained the *Naushervan Nama*, *Kochak Bakhtar*, *Bala Bakhtar*, and *Iraj Nama.* Composed in 1853–54, it had 1,052 manuscript pages and was calligraphed by Navab Ali Khan's secretary, Ratan Lal. Mir Ahmed Ali's second book was the Urdu language *Tilism-e Tahmuras Deoband.* It contained 398 pages, was edited by Amba Prasad Rasa and calligraphed by Ghulam Raza. Mir Ahmed Ali taught *dastan* narration to Amba Prasad Rasa and Hakim Syed Asghar Ali Khan.

Amba Prasad Rasa
(Born: c.1790 – Died: 1886)

Amba Prasad (pen name Rasa) was a famous *dastan* narrator of Lucknow. His father was Chandi Prasad Kayasth. Rasa was the student of Mir Ahmed Ali Rampuri in *dastan* narration and followed his teacher to the Rampur court in the reign of Navab Muhammad Saeed Khan (1840–55). Rasa converted to Islam in later life and assumed the name of Abdur Rahman. He died in his nineties in 1886. Rasa compiled the two volumes of *Kochak Bakhtar* in 1853 and the sixth volume of *Naushervan-Nama,* which he finished late in life. Until recently, it was assumed that, like his teacher Ahmed Ali Rampuri, Rasa did not compose any version of the *Hoshruba* legend himself. In Jah's privately published fifth volume, we learn that he did, indeed, transcribe a version of the *Hoshruba* legend from the notes of Mir Ahmed Ali Rampuri. Jah obtained it after a long search and used it as one of his sources. No other record of this version exists. Rasa's son, Ghulam Raza, was his student in *dastan* narration.

Ghulam Raza Raza
(Lived 1850–1880 or 1888)

Ghulam Raza (pen name Raza) was the son of Amba Prasad Rasa. He wrote the *Hoshruba* legend in the Urdu language in fourteen volumes. The manuscripts of his unpublished works, *Tilism-e-Hoshruba-e Batin* (4 volumes, 1858–59) and *Tilism-e-Batin Hoshruba* (10 volumes, 1876–80), are preserved at the Rampur Raza Library. Muhammad Husain Jah had a copy of his version of the *Hoshruba* legend, which he used as one of his sources for composing his work.

Muhammad Amir Khan
(Lived 1850–1880s)

Muhammad Amir Khan was a Lucknow *dastan* narrator and a contemporary of Muhammad Ḥusain Jah and Ahmed Husain Qamar. According to one account, Khan specialized in writing the episodes about tricksters. He wrote a version of the *Hoshruba* legend of which the second volume is preserved at the Rampur Raza Library. The total number of volumes he composed is not known. Muhammad Husain Jah had a copy of his version of the *Hoshruba* legend, which he used as one of his sources for composing his work.

Sheikh Tasadduq Husain
(Born: ? – Died: 1911–17?)

Sheikh Tasadduq Husain was a *dastan* narrator of Lucknow. He was also a narrator of the Karbala tragedy in the prose and *marsia* forms. He mentions Mir Azam Ali as his teacher. Muhammad Husain Jah credits him for a segment he borrowed from his version of the *Hoshruba* legend. Sheikh Tasadduq Husain compiled and co-authored several *dastans* of the 46-volume Amir Hamza cycle, published by the Naval Kishore Press.

Ahmed Husain Qamar
(Born: 1845? – Died: February–March, 1901)

Ahmed Husain (pen name Qamar) was a famous *dastan* narrator of Lucknow and *nisar* or prose narrator of the Karbala tragedy. He was commissioned by the Naval Kishore Press to finish the remaining volumes of *Tilism-e Hoshruba* after Muhammad Husain Jah separated from the project. Qamar wrote volumes five (in two parts), six and seven between 1890 and 1893. According to Ahmed Husain Qamar's own account, his family participated in the 1857 Mutiny against the East India Company forces. Two of his brothers died in the fighting. Qamar survived and was released from the charge of mutiny but as he was not yet of age, he could not lay claim to his estate, which was confiscated by the government. He studied law and became an agent at one of the local courts but when he appeared for his confirmation exam, the old charge of participating in the Mutiny was dug up and cited as a reason for his disqualification. He became interested in *dastan* narration and took it up as a profession. He was of the Shia faith and continued to narrate the events of the Karbala tragedy as well.

Ahmed Husain Qamar had a son, Ishtiaq Husain, who was a poet (pen name Suhail) and a daughter. While the name of Qamar's daughter is not known, his son-in-law, Nadir Mirza, wished to pursue a career as a professional *dastan* narrator but had to give it up because he developed elephantitis.

Besides the three volumes of *Tilism-e Hoshruba*, Qamar compiled other *dastans* of the Amir Hamza cycle published by the Naval Kishore Press. He claimed to have written many more *dastans* as well, but there is no known record.

Hoshruba and the Amir Hamza Cycle of Tales

The *Dastan-e Amir Hamza* exists in Urdu in three separate, single-volume versions and one 46-volume version. The three single-volume versions are:

a. *Dastan-e Amir Hamza* by Khalil Ali Khan Ashk (Calcutta, Fort William College, 1801)

b. *Tarjuma-e Dastan-e Sahibqiran Giti-sitan Aal-e Paighambar-e Aakhiruz Zaman Amir Hamza bin Abdul-Muttalib bin Hashim bin Abdul Munaf* by Mirza Aman Ali Khan Bahadur Ghalib Lakhnavi (Calcutta: Hakim Sahib Press, 1855)

c. *Dastan-e Amir Hamza Sahibqiran* by Mirza Aman Ali Khan Bahadur Ghalib Lakhnavi and Abdullah Husain Bilgrami. (Lucknow: Naval Kishore Press, 1871)

The *Hoshruba* tale does not exist in any of the above versions. It was a part of the 46-volume Amir Hamza cycle published from the Naval Kishore Press.

The following catalogue that lists their sequence and the corresponding year of publication has been prepared with the help of Shamsur Rahman Faruqi's dastan study, *Sahiri, Shahi, Sahibqirani.*

Book One (4 vols.)

Naushervan Nama. Vol 1 (1893), Vol 2 (1898–99) By Syed Tasadduq Husain

Hurmuz Nama. (1900) By Syed Tasaduq Husain

Homan Nama. (1900) By Ahmed Husain Qamar

Book Two (1 vol.)

Kochak Bakhtar. (1892?) By Syed Tasaduq Husain

Book Three (1 vol.)

Bala Bakhtar. (1899) By Syed Tasaduq Husain

Book Four (2 vols.)

Iraj Nama. Vol 1 (1893), Vol 2 (1893?) By Syed Tasaduq Husain

Book Five (7 vols. in 8)

Tilism-e Hoshruba. Vol 1 (1883), Vol 2 (1884), Vol 3 (1888–89), Vol 4 (1890) By Muhammad Husain Jah; Vol 5 Part I (1891), Vol 5 Part II (1891), Vol 6 (1892), Vol 7 (1893) By Ahmed Husain Qamar.

Book Six (1 vol.)

Sandli Nama (1895) By Muhammad Ismail Asar

Book Seven (2 vols.)

Turaj Nama. Vol 1 (1896) By Syed Tasadduq Husain and Pyare Mirza, Vol 2 (1897?) by Syed Tasadduq Husain and Muhammad Ismail Asar

Book Eight (26 vols. in 27)

La'l Nama. Vol 1 (1896) Vol 2 (1896?) By Syed Tasadduq Husain

Aftab-e Shujaat. Vol 1 (1903?), Vol 2 (1903), Vol 3 (1904), Vol 4 (1905), Vol 5 Part I (1908), Vol 5 Part II (1908) By Syed Tasadduq Husain

Gulistan-e Bakhtar. Vol 1 (1909), Vol 2 (1909), Vol 3 (1917) By Syed Tasadduq Husain and Muhammad Ismail Asar

Tilism-e Fitna-e Nur Afshan. Vol 1 (1896?), Vol 2 (1896), Vol 3 (1896?) By Ahmed Husain Qamar

Baqiya-e Tilism-e Hoshruba. Vol 1 (1897), Vol 2 (1897) By Ahmed Husain Qamar

Tilism-e Haft Paikar. Vol 1 (1897), Vol 2 (1897), Vol 3 (1897) By Ahmed Husain Qamar

Tilism-e Khiyal-e Sikanderi. Vol 1 (1897?), Vol 2 (1897?), Vol 3 (1897?) By Ahmed Husain Qamar

Tilism-e Naukhez-e Jamshedi. Vol 1 (1901), Vol 2 (1902), Vol 3 (1903) By Ahmed Husain Qamar

Tilism-e Zafaranzar-e Suleimani. Vol 1 (1905?), Vol 2 (1905) By Ahmed Husain Qamar and Syed Tasaduq Husain, edited by Muhammad Ismail Asar

Selected Sources

English

Fallon, S.W. *English–Urdu Dictionary* (Rpt., Lahore: Urdu Science Board, 1993).

Ghalib Laknavi, Abdullah Husain Bilgrami, and Musharraf Ali Farooqi, *The Adventures of Amir Hamza: Lord of the Auspicious Planetary Conjunction* (New York: Modern Library, 2007).

Ibn-e Khaldun, and Franz Rosenthal. *The Muqaddimah: An Introduction to History.* Bollingen series, 43. (New York: Pantheon Books, 1958).

Platts, John T. *A Dictionary of Urdu, Classical Hindi and English (*Rpt., Lahore: Sang-e Meel, 1994).

Pritchett, Frances W. *The Romance Tradition in Urdu: Adventures from the Dastan of Amir Hamzah* (New York: Columbia University Press, 1991).

Seyller, John. The Adventures of Hamza: Painting and Story-Telling in Mughal India *(Washington, D.C., and London: Freer Gallery of Art; Arthur M Sackler Gallery, Smithsonian Institution, in association with Azimuth Editions, 2002).*

Steingass, F. *A Comprehensive Persian–English Dictionary* (New York: Routledge & Kegan Paul, in association with Iran University Press, 1995).

Urdu

Abdul Haleem Sharar, and Habibulah Khan Ghazanfar, ed. *Mashriqi Tamaddun Ka Aakhri Namoona Yani Guzishta-e Lakhnow* (Karachi: Ghazanfar Academy, n.d.).

Alimuddin, Mirza. *Tilism-e-Batin-e-Hoshruba.* Vol I (MS, 1913–16, Rampur Raza Library), Vols II–III (MS, 1916, Rampur Raza Library), Vol IV

(MS, 1916, Rampur Raza Library), Vol V–VII (MS, 1917, Rampur Raza Library), Vol VIII (MS, 1917–18, Rampur Raza Library), *Zamima Tilism-e-Batin-e-Hushruba Mausum Ba Dastan-e-Zalzal*. Vol I (MS, 1918, Rampur Raza Library), Vol II (MS, 1918-19, Rampur Raza Library), Vol III–IV (MS, 1919, Rampur Raza Library). *Tilism-e Lalazar* (MS, 1923-25, Rampur Raza Library), *Tilism-e Chah-e Zamarrud* (MS, 1925–26, Rampur Raza Library).

Ashk, Khalil Ali Khan. *Dastan-e Amir Hamza* (Calcutta, Fort William College, 1801; rpt., Lahore: Adamji Abdullah Publishers, n.d.).

Askari, Muhammad Hasan, ed. *Intikhab-e Tilism-e Hoshruba* (Lahore: Maktaba-e Jadid, 1953).

Bazm, Syed Ashiq Husain. *Tilism-e Ajaib* (MS).

Bilgrami, Abdullah Husain. *Dastan-e Amir Hamza Sahibqiran* (Lucknow: Naval Kishore Press, 1871; Microfilm, British Library. Reference Number: 306.24.B.21).

Buhar Library, *Qissa-e Hakim Failsuf* (MS, Kolkata: National Library, India).

Dehlvi, Syed Ahmed. *Farhang-e Asifya*. Vols I–II (Rpt., Lahore: Urdu Science Board, 1995).

Faridi, Qmrulhuda. *Tilism-e Hoshruba: Tanqid wa Talkhis* (Aligarh: Qamrulhuda Faridi, 1999).

Faruqi, Shamsur Rahman. *Sahiri, Shahi, Sahibqirani: Dastan-e Amir Hamza ka Mutalaa,* Vol I, *Nazari Mubahis* (New Delhi: National Council for the Promotion of Urdu Language, 1999). Vol II, *Amali Mubahis* (New Delhi: National Council for the Promotion of Urdu Language, 2006). Vol III, *Jahan-e Hamza* (New Delhi: National Council for the Promotion of Urdu Language, 2006).

Ghalib Lakhnavi, Mirza Aman Ali Khan Bahadur. *Tarjuma-e Dastan-e Sahibqiran Giti-sitan Aal-e Paighambar-e Aakhiruz Zaman Amir Hamza bin Abdul-Muttalib bin Hashim bin Abdul Munaf* (Calcutta: Hakim Sahib Press, 1855; microfiche, Library of Congress. Control Number: 85908676, Call Number: Microfiche 85/61479 [P] So. Asia).

Ibn-e Khaldun, and Raghib Rahmani. *Muqaddimah-e Tarikh-e Ibn-e Khaldun*, 11th ed. (Karachi: Nafees Academy, 2001).

Jafri, Raees Ahmed, ed. *Tilism-e Hoshruba*. (Lahore: Shaikh Ghulam Ali and Sons, 1959). Abridged.

Jah, Muhammad Husain. *Tilism-e Hoshruba*. Vols I–IV (Lucknow: Naval Kishore Press, 1883–90; rpt., Lahore: Sang-e Meel Publications, n.d.). *Tilism-e Hoshruba*. Vols I–IV (Rpt., Patna: Khuda Bakhsh Oriental Pablic

Library, 1988). *Tilism-e Hoshruba.* Vol V Part I (Lucknow: Husaini Press, 1890; rpt., Patna: Khuda Bakhsh Library, 2000).

Jain, Gyan Chand. *Urdu ki Nasri Dastanen* (Lucknow: Uttar Pradesh Urdu Academy, 1987).

Kakorvi, Noor-ul Hasan Nayyar. *Noor-ul Lughat.* 2 vols. (Rpt., Lahore: Sang-e Meel Publications, 1983).

Khan, Muhammad Amir. *Tilism-e Hoshruba.* Vol I (MS, Whereabouts unknown), Vol II (MS, Rampur Raza Library).

Khan, Hakim Syed Asghar Ali. *Dastan-e Darya-e Neel wa Neelam Jadu wa Loh giriftan az-o muta'aliqa Hoshruba zakheem.* (MS, c. 1860. Rampur Raza Library?).

Majeed, Khvaja Abdul. *Jama-ul Lughat.* Vols I–II (Rpt., Lahore: Urdu Science Board, 1999).

Khuda Bakhsh Oriental Public Library. *Muqaddama-e Tilism-e Hoshruba* (Patna, India: Khuda Bakhsh Oriental Pablic Library, 1988).

Qamar, Ahmed Husain. *Tilism-e Hoshruba.* Vols V–VII (Lucknow: Naval Kishore Press, 1890–93) (Rpt., Lahore: Sang-e Meel Publications, n.d.); *Tilism-e Hoshruba.* Vols V–VII. (Rpt., Patna: Khuda Bakhsh Oriental Pablic Library, 1988); *Baqiya Tilism-e Hoshruba.* 2 vols. (Rpt., Patna: Khuda Bakhsh Oriental Pablic Library, 1993).

Qazwini, Imaduddin Zikriya bin Muhammad bin Mahmud Alkamuni. *Ajaib al-Makhlooqat.* Fifth ed. (Lucknow: Naval Kishore Press, 1916; rpt., Lahore: Dost Associates Publishers, 1998).

Quraishi, Akbar Husain. *Farhang-e Tilism-e Hoshruba* (Islamabad: Muqtadira Qaumi Zuban, 1995).

Raza, Ghulam Raza. *Tilism-e Hoshruba-e Batin.* 4 vols. (MS, 1858-59, Rampur Raza Library). *Tilism-e Batin Hoshruba.* Vols I–II (MS, 1876, Rampur Raza Library), Vols III–IV (MS, 1877, Rampur Raza Library), Vols V–VII (MS, 1878, Rampur Raza Library), Vols VIII–IX (MS, 1879, Rampur Raza Library), Vol X (MS, 1880, Rampur Raza Library).

Raza, Rahi Masum. *Tilism-e Hoshruba: Aik Mutala'a* (Bombay: Khayaban Publications, 1979).

Subuhi Dehlvi, Ashraf. *Dilli Ki Chand Ajib Hastiyan* (Delhi: Anjuman-e Taraqi-e Urdu, 1943).

Syed Tasadduq Husain, and Syed Abid Husain. *Lughat-e Kishori* (Lucknow: Tej Kumar Press, 1952; rpt., Karachi: Mir Muhammad Kutub Khana, n.d.).

Persian

Abu Tahir Tarsusi, and Husain Ismaili. *Abu Muslim Nama*. 4 vols. (Rpt., Tehran: Intisharat-e Mueen, 2001).

Ali, Wajid. *Matla-ul Uloom wa Majma-ul Funoon* (Lucknow: Naval Kishore Press, 1902; rpt., Quetta: Maktaba al-Quds, n.d.).

British Library, *Shah-e Mardan Ali*. (MS, British Library).

Ghiyasuddin Muhammad, Sirajuddin Ali Khan, and Mansur Sarwat. *Farhang-e Ghiyas al-Lughat wa Farhang-e Chiragh-e Hidayat*. (Tehran: Intisharat-e Amir Kabir, 1944).

Hamdani, Haji Qissa-Khvan. *Zubdatur Rumuz*. (MS, c. 1613–14. Khuda Bakhsh Library, Patna).

Kitab-e Rumuz-e Hamza (Tehran: AH 1274-76 [1857–59]; British Museum Library).

Mirza Muhammad Khan 'Malik-ul Kuttab'. *Kitab-e Dastan-e Amir Hamza Sahibqiran*. (Bombay: Matba-e Sapehr-e Matla, AH 1327 [1909]).

Muhammad Badshah Shad, and Muhammad Dabir Siyaqi. *Farhang Anand Raj*. 7 vols. (Tehran: Kutubkhana-e Khayyam, 1917).

Shiar, Jafar, ed. *Qissa-e Hamza*. 2 vols. (Tehran : University of Tehran Press, AH 1347 [1968–69]).

Acknowledgments

I have benefited immensely from *dastan* scholar Shamsur Rahman Faruqi's work, *Sahiri, Shahi, Sahibqirani* – a voluminous study of the poetics of the Urdu *dastan*. It will remain the starting point for all future *dastan* criticism.

I also relied on Gyan Chand Jain's encyclopaedic study, *Urdu Ki Nasri Dastanen*. He performed a great service to Urdu literature by compiling this record of Urdu *dastans*, *qissas* and other classical literature dispersed in private and public libraries.

I am indebted to Professor C. M. Naim for his guidance in translating some difficult passages and verses, and for his encouragement of my translation work.

The guidance and encouragement of my friend, Professor Muhammad Umar Memon, has helped me discover and explore many facets of our literary culture. His friendship has always been a great support in my work. He was the first to publish an excerpt from my translation of *The Adventures of Amir Hamza*, and the first to publish an excerpt from *Hoshruba* in the *Annual of Urdu Studies.*

My friend and editor Bob Wyatt, with his natural sense for stories, has been one of my most trusted guides in literature. If a novel fell on Earth from a distant planet, I am sure he would be able to read and make sense of it, and send it back marked with his edits. As my fiction editor, his first instinct is to keep me focussed on my original writing. But knowing that my translation work also informs my original writing, he has decided to let me simultaneously ride my two wobbly boats, and also to lend a hand with the rowing.

My friend Elham Eshraghi helped in translating the Persian verses and phrases, looked up many references to the Hamza legend in Iranian libraries, and found dictionaries and reference books. She has an abiding interest in promoting the joint cultural heritage of the region through her 7Zones project and has always been supportive of my work.

Dastan enthusiast Syed Mujtaba Abbas sponsored the editing of this book. He is also in the process of publishing in Urdu a new edition of the complete 46-volume set of the Amir Hamza *dastan* cycle.

One of the pleasures of working on this project was to make the acquaintance of this book's copy editor, Rick Johnson (www.finalcopy.ca) whose professional care and attention kept the publication on schedule.

In the completion of this work, I owe the single greatest debt to my friend Haleema Jazmin Quill. As a child, she listened to the adventures of the trickster Amar Ayyar from her father, Marghoob Ahmed Quraishi, who retold them – in the best tradition of storytellers – with his own embellishments. She was the first reader of this translation and her enthusiasm for this tale kept me working on the translation even on days when I felt lazy, or slow, or both. She painstakingly edited the manuscript; the hundreds of queries she sent me about various aspects of the story helped make this translation more coherent and fluid. I was extremely lucky and privileged to have her support.

During this ongoing translation adventure, the sufferer-in-chief has been (and will be) my wife Michelle. She read the different drafts, gave her feedback, and made drawings of trickster girls, sorcerers and giants that made me imagine this story in a new light. She also took care of my share of housework when I acted the martyr, hiding behind and using my translation work as excuse.

About the Translator

MUSHARRAF ALI FAROOQI is an author, novelist and translator. He was born in 1968 in Hyderabad, Pakistan. His critically acclaimed translation of *The Adventures of Amir Hamza* by Ghalib Lakhnavi and Abdullah Bilgrami was published in 2008. His children's picture book *The Cobbler's Holiday Or Why Ants Don't Wear Shoes* was published in 2008; and his novel *The Story of a Widow* was published in India in 2009. A translation of contemporary Urdu poet Afzal Ahmed Syed *Rococo and Other Worlds* is forthcoming in 2010. Farooqi is currently collaborating on the graphic novel *Rabbit Rap* illustrated by Michelle Farooqi.

www.mafarooqi.com

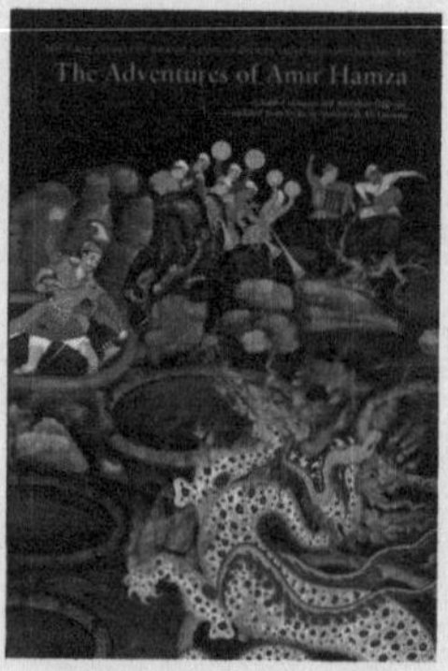

The Adventures of Amir Hamza

Musharraf Ali Farooqi's definitive English translation of *The Adventures of Amir Hamza* (2008) presents the spellbinding story Amir Hamza, adventurer and uncle of prophet Muhammed, who travels to exotic lands, defeats countless enemies, and encounters along the way warriors and kings, tricksters and fairies, courtesans and magical creatures.

"Non-Urdu-speaking readers can at least appreciate an epic 'on par with anything in the Western canon.'…the classical pantheon populated by the indomitable Achilles, cunning Odysseus and righteous King Arthur will now be joined by a new, beloved hero: mercurial, mighty Amir Hamza, astride his winged demon steed, soaring to the heavens." —*Time*

"Extraordinary. Farooqi has translated into English what most of us thought was untranslatable. *The Adventures of Amir Hamza* have beguiled readers in many languages for centuries." —C.M. Naim, Professor Emeritus of Urdu Studies, University of Chicago

Coming Soon

The Prisoner of Batin

Book 2 of *Tilism-e Hoshruba*

The Master of the Tilism, Emperor Afrasiyab, seals the region of Batin the Hidden, making the trickster Amar Ayyar a virtual prisoner in the tilism. Unable to escape, Amar Ayyar avenges himself on the sorcerer emperor, causing death and destruction in Batin.

Read more about Hoshruba at
www.hoshruba.com